Praise for "Thou~

"I loved it :) Historically c~ ~ women and they're small t~own as the ~ ~ ~ Vis~ LaPres, what an outstanding debut! ~ou ~ ~ ~ead it. I promise you won't be disappointed."

"I totally enjoyed the writing of this first time author. It was clear, concise and factually accurate to the era. I would not hesitate to read another of her works!!"

"I love historical fiction and I felt that this book was well written and factual. I can't wait for the sequels to come out. Nice job for a first time author."

"I had trouble putting the book down. Couldn't wait to find out what was going to happen next. I look forward to reading more about the other characters."

"Well written and factual. Couldn't put it down. Looking forward to the next book."

"This is an awesome book to read. It got me so involved it was hard to put down. I can't wait to read the next one. I highly recommend this book."

"I just finished the book and thoroughly enjoyed it. You included so many elements in your book that are often overlooked with the "strategy" of war. Through the relationship of 4 amazing women (and one antagonist), you were able to discuss the personal relationships of friends, husbands, and families. You presented the struggles of these women and the prejudiced that existed besides that of color. And you added the struggle of faith as well."

"Read your book. It was AWESOME! And I really mean it. Interesting characters, great plot, even had tears in my eyes a couple of times!"

Other Books by Marie LaPres

Be Strong and Steadfast: A Fredericksburg Story

The Turner Daughters: Book 2

Marie LaPres

Cover Photo: Chatham Manor on Stafford Heights by Susan Emelander

To the reader...

This is a fictional novel based in Fredericksburg, Virginia during the American Civil War. The story is centered on four women and their wartime experiences. Throughout the novel, the main characters have flashbacks to earlier years. Flashback sections are written in italics. This novel also contains letters written by the characters to each other. Letters are written in bolded italics.

Since this is a historic fiction novel, some characters are individuals that I have created. Others are based on actual historic figures that lived in Fredericksburg or were in Fredericksburg at some point during the war. Be sure to read my Author's Note at the end of the book to learn more about these individuals. I have also included images in the back of the book of some of the individuals and places that are noted in this book and existed in real life.

This novel is dedicated to my family. I have been very blessed with two sisters and a brother who are my best friends, as well as incredibly supportive parents, wonderful siblings-in-law, and the most amazing nieces and nephews. You make my life so rich and full and I don't know what I would do without you all!

Fredericksburg–The town and surrounding areas

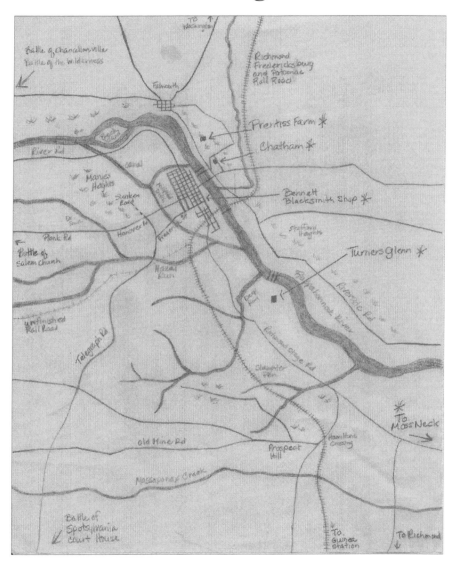

Family Trees

Turner Family

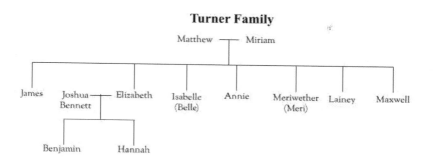

Matthew — Miriam

James   Joshua Bennett — Elizabeth   Isabelle (Belle)   Annie   Meriwether (Meri)   Lainey   Maxwell

Benjamin   Hannah

Corbin Family (Moss Neck Manor)

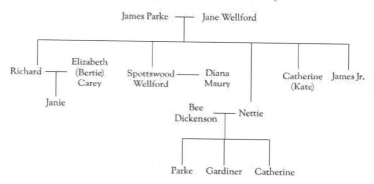

James Parke — Jane Wellford

Richard — Elizabeth (Bertie) Carey   Spottswood Wellford — Diana Maury   Catherine (Kate)   James Jr.

Janie

Bee Dickenson — Nettie

Parke   Gardiner   Catherine

Prentiss Family

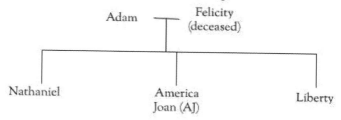

Adam — Felicity (deceased)

Nathaniel   America Joan (AJ)   Liberty

I command you: be strong and steadfast! Do not fear nor be dismayed, for the Lord, your God, is with you wherever you go.

Joshua 1:9

Prologue:
1860

Friday, December 21, 1860
Bennett Blacksmith and Farrier: Fredericksburg, Virginia

James McCann Turner ran a hand through his neatly trimmed black hair as he knocked on the door of the small home connected to one of Fredericksburg's blacksmith and farrier shops.

"I'm sure they already know what's happened, James." James looked at his sister, who patted her perfectly coiffed, midnight black hair.

"I know they do, Belle, but I would still like to see Joshua."

The door opened, and James and Belle were greeted by the smiling face of their sister.

"James! Belle! What brings you into town?" Elizabeth Turner-Bennett's blue eyes sparkled.

"We missed you at dinner on Sunday," James said as Elizabeth opened the door wide to let them in.

"Uncle James!" Benjamin's excited voice rang through the small, three-bedroom house, followed by the pattering of feet. The four-year-old threw himself at James, who bent to catch the boy in his arms.

"Benjamin!" James gave his nephew a big hug. Dark-haired and blue-eyed Benjamin was the spitting image of his father. He looked over at Belle and reached for her.

"Aunt Belle!" Belle stepped closer to her brother and took Benjamin in her arms, squeezing him tightly.

"Benjamin Matthew, you need to keep quiet. Your sister just fell asleep, and we don't want to wake her up." Elizabeth wiped her hands on her white apron.

"Sorry, Mama. Does that mean it's my quiet rest time?"

"Yes, sir, you know it is." His mother smiled at him, then addressed her siblings. "Joshua should be in shortly for a late lunch. He got caught up with a project. I assume you two have eaten?" Benjamin slid out of Belle's arms.

"Yes." James nodded.

"Alright. I will be right back." She nudged Benjamin toward the back of the house where the bedrooms were.

"But Mama, I didn't get a chance to see Papa yet." He protested.

"You'll see him when you get up." She told him. The boy headed toward his room with no further argument, Elizabeth following behind him.

Just as Elizabeth closed the bedroom door, the side door that led to the blacksmith's shop opened and Joshua Bennett entered. Joshua was not only Elizabeth's husband, he was also James's best friend.

"James, Belle, it's good to see you." Joshua stopped at the indoor pump to clean himself up. "I hope you'll excuse me if I eat while we visit." He wiped his hands and face, then opened the oven to take out the plate that Elizabeth had saved for him.

"Not at all," James said. The difference in social status between him and Joshua was constantly in James's mind. It had never affected their friendship. James had no job and very few responsibilities, living off of his family, while Joshua had to work almost every day since his father passed away five years ago.

Elizabeth came back into the room that served as both a kitchen and dining room. "James, Belle, can I get either of you something to drink?"

"No thank you," James said and Belle waved her hand in agreement. Elizabeth joined them at the table.

"I suppose you two have heard the big news," Joshua said after a bite of his fried chicken.

"We have. It's hard to not have heard about it." James replied.

"South Carolina has seceded." Elizabeth wrapped her hands around her cup of coffee and hung her head.

"That's about all we've heard. What is the word around town? What are the details?" James asked.

"It happened yesterday and was expected, after the election of Lincoln." Joshua frowned. "What I didn't expect was the fact that it was unanimous"

"Agreed," James said. "What have your customers been saying about the possibilities of war?"

"It seems as though other states will follow South Carolina. I'm not sure about Virginia, though. From what people are saying, the southern states don't really want war but if the North wants to try and stop the South from being its own country, the South will defend itself. It sounds as though South Carolina will demand the Federal army vacate all the forts in the state."

"And if they don't?" Belle asked. This was not the kind of conversation she usually participated in, and the topic of current events and politics bored her, but she felt that she needed to know some of the information. Her future depended on it.

"If they don't, I'm sure that South Carolina will force them as best as they can," James said.

"Those would be the first shots of a war, I imagine." Elizabeth glanced somberly at her husband.

"Most likely." Joshua nodded, pulling Elizabeth's hand into his.

"If Virginia does secede and goes to war, what do you plan on doing, James?" Elizabeth asked.

"Do you mean will I go and fight?" He glanced out the window. "It depends on certain issues, I suppose."

"He means it depends on Nicole Austin," Belle interjected. "His going off to war might help him grow up and become a more suitable match for Nicole. You know how his lawyership, Mr. Theodosius Austin is."

"Belle…" James looked at his sister, slightly annoyed.

"Well, its true, James. That's exactly what is going on. Nicole loves you and you love her and you are both in the upper crust of Fredericksburg society. It's not like the daughter of a planter marrying a common laborer. I mean no offense, Elizabeth, Joshua."

Elizabeth glanced at Joshua, who squeezed her hand and gave her a brief smile over the glass of water he was drinking. They were both used to Belle's inability to think before she spoke when in the company of her family and close friends, as well as her tendency to be condescending regarding the relationship between Joshua and Elizabeth.

Belle continued, "For some reason, even though you are the heir to the Turner Plantation, well, James, the problem is you just don't want to grow up and take on responsibility. I think you believe that joining the southern army will prove that you are mature and you can be brave, therefore making you good enough to marry Mr. Austin's precious daughter."

"Belle, I told you to let that be. My reasons for joining the army, if I do, are none of your concern."

"They might be if you're killed," Elizabeth spoke softly. Joshua entwined his fingers with hers.

"You don't know that I would be killed. Even if there is a war, most believe it won't last long."

"We can still hold on to the hope that Virginia won't secede, and shots will never be fired," Joshua added.

"God willing." Elizabeth nodded.

"As much as I would like to stay and talk some more, I have a lot of work to finish up." Joshua grinned at his friend as he stood. "James, you are always welcome to join me out there."

"Not today." James stood. "I'm actually leaving Belle here for a bit while I visit Nicole." He looked at Elizabeth. "I hope that's not an imposition."

"Not at all, James. You know that family is always welcome here."

"Wonderful." He grabbed his hat, shook Joshua's hand, and headed out the door. Joshua leaned down to give Elizabeth a brief kiss, then smiled at Belle. "You ladies have a wonderful visit." Elizabeth's eyes followed him as he headed back to his shop. After he closed the door, she glanced at Belle, only to catch her rolling her eyes.

"What?"

"I've said it before, I will say it again. You two are seriously nauseating sometimes."

"I can't help that I found my perfect match, have two wonderful children and love the life that God has given me. If only certain politicians didn't want to tear our country in two, my life would be close to ideal."

"Will Joshua fight? He has always been more the peaceful type, and it's quite apparent that he doesn't like the idea of secession and he's never cared for slavery. Why...he even claims Daniel as a friend." Daniel was a slave, the carriage driver for the Turner family.

Elizabeth took Joshua's plate to the water basin. "Those won't be the only reasons that men go and fight for the South. Joshua hasn't come right out and said anything, but I know he will enlist." She quickly washed the dish, dried it, and sat back down. "The circumstances...it's just...I don't want him to go but I know his loyalty to his home and his friends. He'll feel as though he needs to protect his family." She paused and looked toward the blacksmith shop. "I love his morals and his loyalty but I fear those things that I love about him will take him away from me." She smiled and looked briefly at Belle, who immediately noticed the start of tears in her sister's eyes. "But enough about me. I saw Lucy Beale at the store yesterday and she asked if the rumors are true about you and Samuel Gray. People are saying he is preparing to ask for Father's permission to marry you."

"Is that so?" Belle smiled smugly. "Well, I can't say I'm surprised. We've been courting for almost a year and we were dancing around a courtship for years before that. I'm still not sure why we took so long to make it official. He's twenty-five now and gaining good experience helping his father run their plantation. I'm becoming an old spinster, already twenty-one. I'm not sure why we aren't already married."

"You're positive he's the one for you?" Elizabeth asked cautiously. She often worried about her sister's idea of a good husband.

"Of course! What's not to like about Samuel? He's good-looking, tall, muscular, he has a good disposition, is attentive to me. He's not argumentative at all."

"Yes, he is extremely mild-mannered and rarely has a thought of his own," Elizabeth muttered.

"Elizabeth, that is not true. He will make a wonderful planter and a wonderful husband. Honestly, Elizabeth, if the rumors are true and Samuel is going to ask, well...I just might say yes."

"Belle, marriage is not something to be so casual about. If Samuel is the man for you, that is wonderful, but if you're not sure, you should wait."

"For whom, Elizabeth? Fredericksburg is not very big and while we have traveled a bit, I haven't met anyone who would suit me better than Samuel."

"What about Nathaniel Prentiss? You two would do well together and he has more... he has more of a..." Elizabeth tried to think of something to say other than "personality", but couldn't. Nathaniel was the brother of America Joan Prentiss, a good friend of both Belle and Elizabeth. He and his family farmed a plot of land across the Rappahannock River on Stafford Heights.

"Elizabeth, just because you were able to leave your life of privilege and marry someone who, not only has to work for a living, but also causes you to have to work every day...Elizabeth, that is not the life for me. Even after five years, I come and visit and see you cooking and doing dishes and I can't believe you gave up wealth and prestige for love. There were many wealthy men in the area who would have courted you."

"I know, and I loved life at Turner's Glenn. I loved living in the country with my family and spending every day with you all. It was nice having others cook and clean for me. I liked dressing in the latest fashion and spending my days visiting with friends and waiting for the next social engagement, but Belle," she glanced toward the blacksmith shop, then in the direction of her children's' rooms. "Belle, the life I have, the love I share with Joshua, having Benjamin and Hannah in my life...I wouldn't trade it for anything in the world."

"Well, Elizabeth, I am happy for you. I just know that I could never do that. In regards to Nathaniel, the Prentiss's are good people. AJ is almost as close to me as any of my sisters, I dearly enjoy Liberty's antics and Mr. Prentiss has always been very kind. I like Nathaniel, he is a good friend and would no doubt take care of me as best he could but it would never be enough. I could never live as you do."

"I'm sorry to hear that," Elizabeth said. She decided to change the subject. "Do you really believe James will join the southern army just to prove his worth to the Austin family?"

"I'm not sure if it's more to prove himself to the Austins or if it's more to prove his bravery to himself," Belle replied.

"Is Father still putting pressure on him?"

"He is, but it's the same as usual. You know James. This relationship he has with Nicole is the first time he has ever taken anything seriously. Father feels James will never be a hard worker. He will do an adequate job running the plantation eventually but Father will not be stepping down for many years."

"By that time, God willing, Max will be able to help James run things." Elizabeth smiled. "In all honesty, though, I believe James will do a fine job once he settles down. Nicole will be good for him."

"I believe she already has been. He has been different since he's gotten more serious about her. It is as if he wants to prove that he is settled enough to ask for her hand."

"Perhaps she is all he needs to act mature and be the man he needs to become," Elizabeth concluded.

Part 1:
1861

Saturday, February 9, 1861
Bennett Home

"The southern states who seceded have taken the next steps," Joshua said, coming into the kitchen.

"What do you mean?" Elizabeth dumped some cut up potatoes into the beef stew that she was making for the midday meal.

Joshua tossed a newspaper onto the table. "The Confederate States of America has been formed. They've elected a Mississippian named Jefferson Davis as their president."

"Jefferson Davis. I feel like I've heard his name before." Elizabeth picked up the paper and scanned the article. "That's it! He has a home near Vicksburg." She continued reading the article. "This says they expect to force the Union army out of Southern forts, to use violence if necessary." She slid into a chair at the table. Joshua sat next to her, pulling his own chair as close to hers as possible.

"I can't see the Union army just giving up those forts. When they don't, the South will feel the need to take action to force them out. This will quickly snowball into an armed conflict, Elizabeth." He reached for her hand.

"What will you do, Joshua? What will you do if Virginia joins the Confederacy?"

He sighed and ran his other hand through his hair.

"I really don't know, Elizabeth. I don't want to fight. I don't want to leave you, leave the children. There is a part of me that feels I should go if Virginia calls for troops to fight against the Union. If the men in this town enlist, especially James, I feel like I would have to join them. I won't have you married to a man who is considered too cowardly to fight."

"Joshua, you know that's not what would happen. You're well-respected in this town, and even if people would say things against you, I wouldn't care. I know that it isn't true. You are anything but a coward. In fact, I believe it would take more courage to stay behind."

"I'm not sure about that, but I love that you believe that about me," Joshua said.

"I know you, Joshua. I have seen you lose both of your parents, take over your father's blacksmith shop, marry me, and become a father to two children. You are anything but a coward."

"Thank you for saying that, Elizabeth. I appreciate it." He paused. "So what is your opinion of Miss Nicole Austin? Your brother is very smitten with her."

"She's nice enough," Elizabeth replied. "She's quiet. I don't really know much about her. She obviously cares for my brother and has captured his attention. I've always known James to be a good judge of character, no matter his other faults. It is a bit disappointing that she won't stand up to her family about her true feelings."

"Well, not all women will stand up against the expectations of others and marry someone who is considered lower than her."

"Not everyone has an understanding family and a father who just wants his daughter to be happy," Elizabeth replied.

"So if your family wasn't so understanding, you wouldn't have married me?" Joshua said with a smile.

"Oh, I still would have. I would have eloped to be with you, Joshua. I can be very stubborn when I want to be." She smiled back at him.

"I know that to be true. Luckily, you don't usually have to be with me." He brushed a strand of hair back from her forehead.

"No, you are a perfect match for me, Joshua. My father and mother knew it."

"You still don't regret marrying me?" Joshua asked. No matter how many years they had been together, no matter how many times she reassured him of her feelings, he was still unsure if his marrying her had been in her best interest.

"Joshua." Elizabeth took both of his hands into hers and looked into his blue eyes. "I love you more than anything on this earth, with the exception of the two children we have together. I don't regret for one moment choosing you to be my husband. How many times must I tell you that?"

"I just want to make sure you're happy." He said.

"Well, I am. Very." She smiled and hugged him tightly.

Monday, April 15, 1861
Turner's Glenn Plantation~Outside Fredericksburg

"Papa! Mama!" Maxwell Turner ran into the plantation house towards the formal dining room, his clothes soiled from running and playing. His father, mother, brother, and four of his sisters sat around the dinner table, waiting. The only family members not in attendance were his oldest sister, Elizabeth and her family.

"You're late for dinner, Max. We have been waiting on you." Miriam Turner said.

"Sorry, Mama." The six-year-old sat down, a huge smile on his face. "Grayson was out at his Grandfather's and his servant was bringing him

16

home. You will never guess the news he told me!" Grayson Gray was Max's friend and the nephew of Samuel Gray. He lived in town.

"What did he tell you?" Matthew suspected he knew the answer to his son's question. Firebrands in South Carolina had announced secession a while ago, but the Federals had yet to leave the garrison at Fort Sumter in the Charleston Harbor.

"The other night, the South Carolina militia bombed Fort Sumter! The Yankees were forced to leave! The fort is now ours!"

"How many men died?" Nineteen-year-old Annie asked somberly.

"Grayson wasn't really sure, but he said we're officially at war!"

Miriam looked down at her plate, then at her husband. At 51 years of age, he still looked young, even though he hadn't had the easiest of lives. When Matthew was only seventeen, his father died, leaving him to run the plantation and raise his three younger brothers. Samuel, was a soldier in the Federal army. Hiram, owned a farm in Pennsylvania. Charles was a lawyer in Mississippi. Miriam sighed. She had serious concerns about the nation being at war and the Turner family being divided in two.

Matthew looked at Miriam's worried face. Samuel, the officer in the US army, had once said that if a war between the states ever broke out, he would stay in the Union army and fight for the North, even if it meant fighting against his brothers. Samuel Turner disliked slavery and couldn't stand Southern politicians. Matthew looked at his younger son.

"Max, do you realize what a war means?"

"Yeah, it means we're gonna kick those Yankees right back to where they came from and show them they can't boss us around."

"Max, war means killing. Taking another person's life. That cannot and will not be an easy experience to live through." Matthew explained.

"I know that Pa, but the Yankees have it coming to them."

"What about your Uncle Samuel?" Matthew asked.

"Pa, Uncle Sam isn't a real Yankee. He'll fight for our side." Max insisted.

"Will he fight for the South, Father?" 13-year-old Meri asked.

"I don't think so, Meri. He told me once that he would always stay loyal to the Union."

Max looked up from his meal in surprise. "Uncle Sam wouldn't. He couldn't."

"Yes, he would," Matthew said.

"What about Uncle Hiram?" Annie asked.

"Honestly, I am not sure about his loyalties, but if he does sign up to fight, I would imagine he would fight for the Union, with a Pennsylvania unit."

"That will leave Charlotte alone on their farm," Belle commented with a toss of her dark hair. "I can't imagine Uncle Hiram doing that to his daughter."

"There will be many fathers leaving their families, Belle," Matthew replied.

"Papa, will you fight?" Ten-year-old Lainey piped up.

"I hope not, Lainey, but if I am called to serve, if Virginia secedes and needs men, I will go." He looked at Miriam, whose eyes were watering. "I will go to protect my family and home."

"I'm going to sign up as soon as possible." James, the oldest in the family, looked down at his roast beef, not meeting his father's eyes.

"I wish you would change your mind, James," Matthew said.

"I'm sorry," James said, stone-faced. "The decision is made."

"What would you do in the army? You have no experience soldiering." Belle pointed out.

"Neither will a lot of the Southerners who enlist, but we will no doubt have excellent military leaders who will train us. We will defeat the Yankees within a few months." James replied.

"I'm not sure that will be the case, James," Matthew said. "I believe this war will be longer and more difficult than anyone is thinking."

"So what are you gonna do for Confederacy?" Max asked. "Infantry? Cavalry? Artillery?"

"I haven't quite thought that through yet," James said. "Most likely the infantry. It will likely be the easiest to learn."

"Imagine that, James taking the easiest route," Belle muttered to Annie. James shook his head and stood.

"It will not do you any good to try to talk me out of this. I have made my decision. I leave as soon as possible." He then strode out of the dining room, leaving the rest of the family stunned.

Saturday, April 20, 1861
Bennett House

Elizabeth pushed the pan of cinnamon chicken into the oven. It was one of Joshua's favorite dishes.

"Elizabeth?" The front door opened in conjunction with the sound of knocking. AJ Prentiss poked her head into the kitchen. "Are you in here?"

"Yes, AJ. How are you?"

"I'm doing well. I had to come into town for some supplies and wanted to stop by and see you. Joshua told me you were in here." AJ sat down at the table, pushed a lock of her blonde hair behind her ear and smiled. The blue dress she was wearing made her blue eyes shine.

"Yes, I was just putting dinner in the oven. How are things across the river?"

"Good. Nathaniel has informed us that he is going to join the Confederate army now that Virginia has left the Union." AJ took a deep breath. "I suppose many Fredericksburg men will leave now."

"James said that he is going to enlist. I know that once he does, Joshua will be right behind him. My husband will not let his best friend go without him."

"Joshua is a good man," AJ remarked. "You're lucky to have him."

"You will be blessed with a good husband someday, AJ."

"I surely hope so," AJ replied, unsure if she would ever find a good man like Joshua. "Anyway, have you heard the news? Shots were exchanged yesterday in Baltimore."

"Oh my goodness, no. I haven't heard this yet. What happened?"

"There were pro-Confederates in the city who ambushed Union troops from the state of Massachusetts. From what I understand, the Union soldiers were switching from one train to another when a mob of civilians attacked them and blocked the route. Since the route was blocked, the soldiers got out of their wagons to march and the mob followed them. They even damaged property in their efforts to stop the soldiers. Then they attacked the soldiers with bricks and pistols. A giant brawl broke out when the soldiers fired into the mob. The regiment was finally able to get on the train. They left much of their equipment behind."

"Was anyone killed or injured?" Elizabeth asked.

"Four soldiers and twelve civilians died," AJ replied. "They also say that over thirty soldiers were wounded and left behind."

"Oh, Lord, be with their families," Elizabeth said a short prayer.

"Yes. They are calling these deaths the first casualties of war. I was thinking, this event really reminds me of the Boston Massacre. Many similarities."

"I just cannot believe that Americans are so ready and willing to kill one another," Elizabeth said. "I can only hope and pray that it will be short-lived."

AJ nodded. "That's actually one of the reasons that Nathaniel decided to join. He was quite offended and disappointed that the newly elected President of the United States would ask for so many volunteers to invade and attack their countrymen."

Elizabeth sighed and rubbed her forehead. "I just cannot believe we've come to this. How did we even...how?" Elizabeth was at a complete loss for words.

"It seems as though it has been a long time coming. Nathaniel and I were discussing it the other night and Father joined our conversation. He

19

said that this conflict has been brewing since our country wrote the Constitution."

"So it has been brewing since the very beginning of our nation. Seems hard to believe." Elizabeth said with a sigh. "I wish slavery had never been brought to this land. It seems to be the main reason for much of this conflict."

"Don't say that too loudly," AJ warned. "We may not be in the Deep South, but Virginia will go to war to protect the right to keep slaves."

"And it may prove to be our undoing," Elizabeth replied.

Wednesday, April 24, 1861
St. George's Episcopal Church

Elizabeth entered the church and smiled at the number of women who had gathered for the first meeting of the newly formed "Mutual Aid and Soldier's Relief Society". Women from the city's most powerful families wanted to discuss how they could help the war effort on the home front. Elizabeth waved at Kate Corbin and Belle, who had already found seats. It was good to see Belle in a church, even if it was just for a meeting.

"Ladies, how are you all doing?" Elizabeth sat down next to them.

"Quite well," Kate said. "Bertie heard about the gathering of this new society and we decided we just had to come. My brother is seriously considering joining the Southern army." Kate was one of Belle and Elizabeth's good friends. She lived with her siblings, James Parke Jr., Wellford, Nettie, Richard, and Richard's wife Bertie, at Moss Neck Manor, a beautiful home outside of Fredericksburg. Her father lived nearby at Belle Hill, another manor home that the family owned, with his second wife. Kate's mother had died when she was sixteen. The Corbins had been an influential family in Virginia for many years.

"James and Samuel are considering joining as well," Belle said.

"It seems like so many men are excited about fighting," Elizabeth said. "I spoke with Lucy Beale the other day and she said that her brothers John and Charles will enlist at the first chance they get." Lucy was another young woman who lived in Fredericksburg. She worked with her mother, who taught some of the children in town.

"And what about Joshua?" Kate asked Elizabeth.

"I believe he will fight for the Confederacy," Elizabeth replied. "We've spoken about it a few times. He may not completely agree with what the South is fighting for, but he wants to be able to defend his family." Elizabeth could feel the excitement coursing through the room. It was the same excitement that was going through the entire town.

Elizabeth was unenthused. It was times like this when she felt as though she was alone in her thoughts.

"Well, it sounds as though the men will have a very good leader to fight under." Elizabeth glanced up to see AJ slide next to her.

"AJ! I am so glad you could make it." Elizabeth smiled. Since AJ lived on the other side of the river, it wasn't always easy for her to make it into town.

"Of course. I wouldn't miss such an important meeting!" AJ also seemed excited at the prospect of war. Elizabeth frowned. She had hoped that the usually level-headed woman would have been less enthusiastic. AJ was the kind of friend who followed current events and Elizabeth knew that her friend longed to make a difference in the world. She had once been pudgy and believed she would never catch a man with her looks so she decided to develop her mind and other skills. In the past few years, however, she had been able to lose some of her excess weight.

"Who are you talking about, AJ?" Kate asked, leaning forward to see her friend.

"Rumor has it that yesterday, Robert E. Lee became the commander of land and naval forces for our fair state of Virginia," AJ replied. "It likely won't be long until the government leaders see how talented he is and promote him to an even higher position."

"Robert E. Lee? That's wonderful." Belle said. "James was worried that the Union would offer him a major position in their army."

"They did," AJ said. "He turned it down. He said that he didn't agree with all Southern arguments, but he couldn't turn his back on his Virginia home."

"Bravo," Kate said.

"Even better that he was able to turn the Yankees down," Belle said with a smug smirk. Elizabeth tried not to show her irritation. Would anyone else in the town be thinking about this war rationally? She was getting more and more worried that no one would. It was almost as if they wanted the fight to come. She looked up to see Betty Herndon Maury stand and call the meeting to order. Betty was the daughter of Matthew Fontaine Maury, a well-respected Fredericksburg man who was high in the Confederate Navy. She and her husband had been living in Washington, D.C. before the outbreak of the war, but she had moved home and quickly embedded herself back into Fredericksburg society.

Virginia just seceded, and from the way the women were talking, that measure was not opposed by the people of Fredericksburg. Elizabeth's mind wandered, trying to remember when all of this chaos had started. What event had caused this severe division between the North and the South? She remembered discussing it with Joshua before they were married when he had been teaching her about God's

21

forgiveness and the Bible. They had been discussing the division of God's people into Judea and Israel, the Northern and Southern Kingdoms…

Sunday, May 25, 1856
The Banks of the Rappahannock River

Seventeen-year-old Elizabeth sat on a quilt, leaning against a tree. Joshua, age twenty-one, sat opposite her. They both had Bibles open to the First Book of Kings. They didn't usually study the historical books of the Bible, but Joshua had suggested it. She was always willing to follow his suggestions. As they talked, Elizabeth couldn't help but see the parallels between ancient Israel and their own nation.

"Why do people always feel the need to take sides and fight?" She asked, exasperated.

Joshua looked at her, understanding exactly what she meant. They always seemed to know what the other was thinking. It had been that way for a while, especially since they had begun meeting to study and discuss the Bible three years ago.

"I don't know, Elizabeth. I wish I could tell you."

She looked across the river. "Joshua, do you believe what people are saying? That violence will erupt between the northern and southern states of our country?"

"It already has," Joshua replied. "Just last week in Lawrence, Kansas. Did you not hear?"

"No," Elizabeth answered. "What happened?"

Joshua scooted closer. "Lawrence is a town that was founded by anti-slavery settlers a few years ago. They wanted to help make sure that Kansas would become a free state after the Kansas-Nebraska Act of 1854 decreed that states' voters would determine the legality of slavery in that state."

"I knew that act would cause issues," Elizabeth said. "It seems like a good idea, but…oh, I just knew."

"I know." Joshua reached over and took Elizabeth's hand. Her heart gave a little jump. As close as they had gotten over the last few years, he usually refrained from physical contact. "Anyway, Lawrence was attacked and ransacked by pro-slavery settlers, who obviously wanted to scare the townspeople, among other things."

"Oh my goodness!" Elizabeth exclaimed. "Were there any serious injuries or deaths?"

"One wounded abolitionist and one dead attacker. It seems as though the pro-slavery men wanted to scare the abolitionists and destroy the presses of an anti-slavery newspaper in the town."

"Why? What was the reasoning?"

22

"Senator Sumner is an abolitionist from Massachusetts who gave a speech a couple of days earlier. He verbally attacked slaveholders, including a relative of Congressman Brooks. Brooks' Southern pride got the best of him and caused him to retaliate."

"I don't know how I didn't hear about either of these events," Elizabeth said. "Did Senator Sumner survive?"

"Barely," Joshua said. "It's also going to make the tensions between the North and the South even more strained."

"Do you believe we'll eventually go to war?" Elizabeth asked, her voice quiet.

"I'm not sure, if we do, it may not be for a few years yet. Hopefully, things will get sorted out before it comes to that."

"Would you fight?" Elizabeth's blue eyes met Joshua's soft green ones. He looked down, then glanced at her.

"I don't know, Elizabeth. What would you do if I said yes?"

"I would tell you that I wouldn't want you to go. That I would miss you dearly. But that I trust you to make the best decision for you. I know that you would pray about your decision and that no matter what, God would look after you."

Joshua smiled. "He would." Almost hesitantly, Joshua leaned forward and brushed his lips over hers.

"Elizabeth, I..." Please don't say you're sorry. Elizabeth thought.

"Elizabeth, I have to tell you. You are one of the best friends that I have ever had. I feel like I can talk to you about anything, even more than with your brother. I've...I've fallen in love with you." Elizabeth smiled as he continued talking. "I know I have nothing to offer you. I'm just a blacksmith and will never have the means to care for you in the way that you are accustomed. But would you welcome...if I were to ask your father's permission to court you, would you be in favor of that?"

"Joshua. I would be in favor of you asking my father's permission to marry me. I love you. I have for a while."

"You don't care that you won't have slaves to care for you? Even if I could afford them, I wouldn't ever consider owning slaves. You would have to...learn to work, do you realize that?"

"You're not trying to talk me out of marrying you, are you?" Elizabeth said with a smile.

"No, I'm not." He replied. "I'm just making sure that you realize what you're getting into."

"Yes, I do. I would enter into marriage with a kind, strong, hardworking, wonderful man who loves the Lord and encourages others to do so as well. Oh, Joshua, I know very well what I'm getting myself into."

"And you're okay with that?"

23

"Yes. As long as you're okay with a wife who is willing to work, but very inexperienced."

"Well, I know you're a fast learner, and as long as you can get Ruthie to teach you to cook. I do enjoy her meals."

"Our cook does have a special talent." Elizabeth smiled.

"So are we really doing this?" Joshua asked. "Are you really ready to be a married woman? You are only seventeen."

"Oh, I am more than ready to be your wife, Joshua. She smiled. "Mrs. Elizabeth Bennett. I like the sound of that."

1861

Elizabeth smiled at the memory. Just a short while ago, they had been young and full of hope that things would work out between the North and the South, that the heated issues between the two sections would cool down. Now, her own friends and sisters seemed to be asking for a fight. She could not understand it.

"So, ladies, are we in agreement?" Betty asked. "We agree not to purchase any article or gown that was imported into a Southern state from the North and that ornamentation should be withheld, if necessary, to support the South." All of the women nodded.

"Wonderful," Betty said. "We can now adjourn."

Elizabeth, Belle, Kate and AJ walked out of the church.

"Isn't it exciting?" AJ asked. "Our men will go off, fight our oppressors, and come home heroes."

"Yes, it is only a matter of time," Belle said. "I only hope this war doesn't interfere with my courtship with Samuel Gray."

"I'm shocked that he finally made your courtship official." Elizabeth muttered.

"Oh, Elizabeth, just because you married at seventeen and Joshua was only 21 doesn't mean that everyone wants to be tied down that early. Samuel said that he's always intended to court me, but he needed a little freedom first. I can understand that."

Elizabeth shook her head. Samuel Gray was a good-looking young man, with a good disposition, an air of politeness, and was usually quite attentive to Belle. He could also be shallow, and from Elizabeth's perspective, boring. He never seemed to have a thought of his own, and usually just followed the lead of his friend, Richard Evans. Elizabeth believed that was another reason Belle preferred him. She could totally control him.

"I'm just not sure if he is the best choice for you," Elizabeth said.

"Oh, come now, Elizabeth. I have never understood why you object to Samuel. He has more prospects than Joshua could ever dream of."

AJ and Kate both looked from Belle to Elizabeth. They were used to these kinds of disagreements. Elizabeth would try to get Belle to consider things the way that Elizabeth did, and Belle would make small, cutting remarks about Elizabeth, usually about her marriage and husband. Elizabeth, with her patience, kindness and aversion to arguing, would drop the conversation. It happened again today.

"If that's what you believe, Belle. It's your decision, who you marry. I don't have to agree with your choice any more than you have to agree with mine."

"Good, because you know that even though I adore Benjamin and Hannah I will never understand why you married a common laborer."

Elizabeth took a deep breath to calm herself, something she did often while around her sister. She wished she had the courage to tell Belle just how wrong she was. Belle was stubborn and Elizabeth knew it was impossible to win any argument with her.

"Well, I don't see him as just a common laborer but let's stop arguing about this when we know our opinions will not change. It's bad enough the country is headed to war."

"Of course, Elizabeth," Belle said with a smug smile.

"Well, ladies, I must find Nathaniel so we can head back home," AJ said. "It was wonderful visiting with you."

The women said their goodbyes and started off in different directions. Belle saw the Turner's carriage driver, Daniel, drive toward her and Elizabeth.

"Well, here's my ride. Give the children my love," Belle said.

Elizabeth nodded. "We should be at Sunday dinner after church."

"Until then." Belle waved.

That night at dinner, Elizabeth's thoughts drifted. She desperately wanted to get through to Belle on so many topics but was thwarted every time she tried. Joshua knew that something was bothering her and the children also sensed something was wrong.

"Mama's not eating her dinner." Benjamin pointed out.

"Nope, she isn't. I'm wondering if she has finally realized how difficult her food is to eat." Joshua flashed a teasing smile at his wife, trying to coax a smile from her. Instead, she glared at him.

"Mama is a good cook," Benjamin said, sticking up for her as all good sons did.

"I don't know, Benjamin, ever since your mother had Hannah start eating her own food, your mother's cooking has gone downhill. I mean, look at these biscuits." He gestured to them, then joked, "They're so hard that I could use them to pound iron in the shop."

Elizabeth ground her teeth, then took one of the biscuits and flung it at Joshua. He ducked and laughed.

"Mama threw food!" Benjamin shouted, disbelief in his voice. "If Hannah or I did that, we would get a spanking!"

Joshua grinned. "You're right, Benjamin. Maybe your mother needs a spanking." He stood and took two steps toward her before she stood and held up a hand.

"You wouldn't dare." She backed away from him, knowing that he would never hurt her.

"Come over here for your punishment, Mrs. Bennett. You know better than to throw food." Joshua walked toward her, slowly and stealthily. Elizabeth pulled the chair she had been sitting in between her and Joshua as he continued creeping forward, looking over at his children and winking at them. Hannah giggled and Benjamin watched them with amusement.

"Joshua..." Elizabeth hesitated, then bolted toward the back door, not really thinking about what she would do if she made it out. Joshua darted after her, quick, despite his size. He wrapped his arms around her waist and pulled her to him. She laughed briefly and saw a smile on his face as he looked at Benjamin.

"I don't know, Benjamin. Your mother does work hard. Maybe I should let her off with a warning."

"Yeah. I think that's okay." Benjamin said. Hannah just grinned. Joshua gave Elizabeth a quick kiss on the cheek. "No more throwing food."

She smiled back. "Yes, sir."

Elizabeth cleaned the kitchen as Joshua got the children ready for bed and tucked them in. She was just putting the dishes away when she felt Joshua's hands circle her waist and pull her tightly against him.

"I love you." He murmured, then took the washrag from her and started wiping down the dinner table. She looked at him, overjoyed at the man God had given her. So thoughtful and kind and funny.

"That's what Belle needs to see." Elizabeth murmured.

"Excuse me?" Joshua looked at his wife.

"Oh, Belle was saying things again about our marriage and you. Negative things. She says she just doesn't understand us. I wish she could have witnessed this evening, see what I see in you. Then, maybe she would understand."

"I don't know about that. Your sister places a lot of importance on material things. I know you love her, but you do know that about her, don't you?"

26

"Of course I do. It just frustrates me that she is always so negative about our life together."

"I know it does, but your mother and father approve of the match and understand us. James has supported our friendship since it began, and your other sisters have no problem with us."

"Meri has made a comment or two," Elizabeth said.

"Because she's proud to be like Belle." Joshua placed his hands on her shoulders. "I'm surprised you're concerned with the opinions of a thirteen-year-old."

"I'm not." She sighed. "You're right. It shouldn't matter."

"But it does to you. I understand. You are a kind, caring person. It's who you are. I love that about you." Joshua led her to a chair near the fireplace. He sat down and pulled her into his lap.

"Sometimes I wish I didn't care so much," Elizabeth said, laying her head on his shoulder.

Joshua kissed her gently on the forehead. "You never said how the ladies' meeting went today. I must say that everyone at the dinner table knew something was bothering you."

"It's just so frustrating to me, Joshua. Everyone is so excited about the war with the north and that includes AJ, who I can usually count on to be calm and level-headed. This war fever seems to be taking over the entire town."

"You're right about that. Almost everyone who's come into the shop since Lincoln's election has been talking about it, even though that happened months ago. Unfortunately, it seems as though this war has been a long time coming."

"I just wonder if there is anything that anyone could have done to stop it," Elizabeth commented.

"I don't know," Joshua replied. "I feel like this situation has been spiraling out of control since the first slave was brought over from Africa."

"You may be right, and now I fear that there is nothing we can do to stop it." Elizabeth sighed.

Friday, May 24, 1861
Turner's Glenn

Belle checked her reflection in the mirror. She smiled at what she saw. Midnight black hair, perfectly pinned back in a chignon with gentle curls cascading down her neck, a pale, clear complexion, and green eyes many would describe as "flashing". She smoothed her linen, cream-colored day dress lined with maroon piping, and turned to her personal slave, Zipporah.

"Zipporah, I honestly do not know what I would do without you. I look absolutely perfect, thank you. Please have Daniel prepare the carriage. I would like to visit with the Corbins."

"Yes, Miss Isabelle." Zipporah bowed her head and left. As she exited, Miriam entered.

"Good morning, Mother," Belle said, standing.

"Good day, Belle. What are your plans for today?"

"I just sent Zipporah to have Daniel prepare the carriage. It's been too long since I have been out to Moss Neck Manor to see Kate and Bertie."

"That's a wonderful idea. You should bring Zipporah and stop at Elizabeth's on your way. Elizabeth could go with you while Zipporah watched Benjamin and Hannah."

"I'm sure Elizabeth has many chores to attend to. She's always too busy to simply go visiting. Besides, going into town is quite out of the way." Belle tried not to let her resentment to that fact show.

"I wish you would talk to Elizabeth more. You two used to be so close."

"Yes, well, she's the one who went off and got married. Joshua and the children are her life now."

"As it should be. You'll know that feeling someday Belle, but that is no reason to snub your sister."

"Perhaps, but I assure you, I will not feel that way about a common workingman. That could never make me happy."

"Maybe." Miriam wished her two oldest daughters were closer like they used to be. All she could do was encourage them to talk more. "I came to tell you some news. Daniel should be aware as well."

"What's happened, Mother?"

"Virginia will now be part of the Confederate States of America," Miriam said, not wanting to believe it herself.

"Well, that's not a surprise, mother. All of the men said that would happen."

"Yes, well, just be aware. I am your mother and still worry about you. I have no doubt that Daniel will take good care of you."

"Is that all?" Belle asked. "I must be on my way. I'd like to be back in time for dinner."

Samuel Gray adjusted his maroon cotton frock coat and knocked on the front door of the Turner plantation home. Tiberius, the doorman, opened the door and invited him in. Samuel took off his pecan-colored top hat and greeted the servant.

"Would you like me to send for Miss Isabelle, Mr. Gray?"

"Actually, I would like to see Mr. Turner first."

28

"Yes, sir." Tiberius left to inform Mr. Turner of the visitor. Samuel turned and looked in the mirror at himself. He had dressed to impress more than usual tonight. His coat lay overtop a white wing-tipped shirt, brown Arlington vest, and a brown puffed cravat. He ran his hands down his black trousers with a thin gold stripe, then brushed a hand through his dark blond hair.

Tiberius soon returned and ushered Samuel into an office. Matthew Turner was seated at his large mahogany desk. Miriam Turner was also present, seated in a chair near a window.

"Good evening, sir." Samuel offered his hand as Matthew stood and shook it.

"Samuel. Good evening. What can I do for you?"

"Well, sir, I'm here to ask you a question." Samuel adjusted his cravat.

"Go ahead, Samuel."

"I would like to ask your permission for Isabelle's hand in marriage. We have known each other almost all our lives. I've decided to enlist in the Confederate Army. That may make an engagement difficult but I am confident that the South will quickly take care of the Federal Army. We will be our own nation in just a short time."

"Well, Samuel, you should know that I have no basic objection. You are a fine young man with a promising future. I do have concerns about the fact that you will be away at war. I can and will grant you permission to speak with Belle. I would never give her hand away without her opinion being taken into consideration. Again, I am concerned about the uncertain future. I would feel better if the two of you were to wait until after the war is over. When that happens and I pray that it will be soon, I will be more than happy to give the two of you my blessing."

Samuel smiled. "Thank you, sir. Could I have your permission to take Belle for a stroll and speak with her? I would like to say goodbye, as I am leaving for Richmond in the morning."

"Of course." Matthew stood and walked Samuel to the door of the office. "Good luck, Samuel. Take care of yourself. Know that you will be in all of our thoughts and prayers."

"Thank you, sir." Samuel headed back to the entryway to wait for Belle.

Almost half an hour later, Belle glided down the stairs, looking as radiant as ever. Her dress was a hunter green, trimmed with a slightly lighter green silk trim and black velvet ribbon above gold fringe.

"Isabelle. You look lovely, as always."

"Why thank you, Mr. Gray." Isabelle held her hand out for Samuel, who took it and kissed it.

"Would you give me the privilege of escorting you through the back gardens?"

"Of course," Belle replied, taking Samuel's arm. The evening was perfect and there would be just enough light left for a leisurely stroll and good conversation. Samuel led her out the back door and turned. He could barely keep his eyes off her beautiful face.

The sun was casting brilliant colors across the nearby Rappahannock River as the two walked through the well-manicured gardens. When they reached the far side of the formal garden, Samuel stopped at an elegant bench. He turned toward her, confident in the way the conversation would go.

"Belle, I might be acting a little forward in asking you this but I am compelled to. I care for you more than anyone else in this world. I would like to marry you and make you the happiest of wives. Will you..." He paused. "Will you wait for me and marry me when I come home from the war? It shouldn't be long."

Belle smiled confidently. She had expected Samuel to propose to her tonight when she heard that he was speaking with her father. He would make the perfect husband for her. Wealthy, handsome, and completely devoted to her. She knew he would eventually propose.

"Samuel, you know how much I care for you. I have been waiting for you to ask for such a long time."

"I must add that I would marry you tomorrow before I leave for Richmond, but your father insists that we wait," Samuel said.

"As much as it pains me, that is likely the best course," Belle said. "Besides, it will likely take me longer to plan our wedding than it will for our Southern boys to defeat the Yankees."

"Then I will look forward to the day," Samuel said.

Monday, May 27, 1861
Prentiss Farm, near Stafford Heights, Virginia

Adam Prentiss smiled to himself and headed into the house. He saw his middle child, America Joan, affectionately known as AJ, at the stove fixing dinner. It smelled like baked chicken, one of his favorites. He could almost imagine it was his wife standing at the stove. No matter how many years passed, he felt Felicity's absence with the heaviest of hearts. He loved his children and thanked God every day that he had them in his life as a reminder of his beloved wife. AJ turned.

"Father! You're back. Perfect timing. Dinner will be ready in just a few minutes." Even though she was twenty-one, she had been taking care of the family since Felicity died ten years ago.

"Very good." Adam nodded. As soon as A.J. placed the vegetables on the kitchen table, Nathaniel and Liberty came in from outside, where they had been working, repairing fences around the farm. AJ quickly made up two plates and placed them in the oven to keep warm for Andre and Gage, the two slaves the family owned, then the family sat down and Adam blessed the meal. Thirteen-year-old Liberty, always blunt, didn't even take one bite before she asked her father what he had been doing in town.

"You all act like I never take a trip into town," Adam said. All three of his children were focused on him, waiting on his response.

"You do, that's true, but usually not in the middle of the week, unless we need supplies." Twenty-three-year-old Nathaniel commented.

"You're never so secretive about your activities, Father," AJ added.

"I see." Adam put down his fork and folded his hands in front of him. "Well, I went into town today because I have been struggling with a decision as of late and I finally made up my mind. Today, I enlisted in the Confederate Army."

Liberty dropped her fork. AJ closed her eyes and slowly lowered her hands into her lap, tears forming in her eyes.

"You're serious?" Liberty asked, a bit concerned. "You've really enlisted?"

"I did," Adam said. "I realize this will be difficult for you to understand but it is something I need to do. I will be part of the Virginia Artillery."

"Artillery?" Nathaniel looked at his father. "How are you qualified to fight in the artillery?"

"Before I moved to Virginia and met your mother, I had a history with the military in the British army."

"I never knew that. Why have you never told us?" Nathaniel asked, stunned. He would never have guessed that his mild-mannered father had once fought in the powerful British army.

"It was in a previous life. Not one that I am always proud of. I came here to Virginia, was blessed enough to meet your mother and settled in Fredericksburg. Felicity changed the entire course of my life." He smiled sadly, thinking of his departed wife.

"Well, as much as we all miss Mother, we still have each other," Liberty said.

"That is very true, my dear," Adam said. "Very true indeed.

Saturday, June 1, 1861
Bennett Home

Elizabeth pushed a lock of dark curly hair from her face as she stoked the fire. Joshua had asked to tuck Hannah and Benjamin in bed as he was leaving the next day. She could hardly believe it, didn't want to believe it. The door to the children's room latched shut and her husband's tall, muscular form entered the main room of their small, comfortable home.

"Are they asleep?" She asked.

"Yes. Tucked in and sleeping soundly." He sat down in a chair facing the empty fireplace and ran a hand through his black hair. "I keep telling myself to be positive and that I will have another opportunity to tuck them in again but there is a part of me...I fear that I won't."

Elizabeth felt tears well up in her eyes. She stood and crossed the room, heading for the pantry. As she passed by him, Joshua caught her arm.

"Elizabeth." He knew she was upset. He wasn't happy either. He didn't care for secession or for the war. He had never wanted either unlike so many of his neighbors and friends.

"I was just going to get that bottle of wine mother gave us for our anniversary last month. I'd like to drink enough of it so I don't have to think about you leaving tomorrow." She tried to grin, but it was halfhearted. "I know what you have decided and I know why you are leaving. Deep down, I do understand, but I don't like it. I just don't want to think about you being gone, especially because of where you are going."

Joshua pulled her into his lap and circled her waist with his arms, hugging her tight and putting his chin on her shoulder. "I know. I hate to put you through this, Elizabeth, you know I do but I don't feel as though I have any other options."

"I don't want to think about saying goodbye tomorrow and trying to be strong for the children, trying not to cry. I just want tonight to last forever and to stay here, just like this."

"I agree the morning will come way too soon for my liking." He kissed her temple. "I don't know how I'm going to say goodbye. To you, to Hannah or Benjamin. You are my life."

She nestled herself in his strong arms, the wine forgotten. Being a blacksmith had kept him strong and muscular. He had been that way for as long as she had known him, which seemed like forever. He reached up and pulled her hair loose, dropping the pins on the floor. She lifted her head to gaze into his eyes,

"I will write you every day. You may not get all of the letters I write but be assured, I will be thinking of you every moment."

"I will write often as well but I am unsure of how much time I will have to do so." He shrugged. "Besides, writing is something that I have never been great at."

"No, that may not be one of your strong suits but that has never mattered to me. You are a wonderful and devoted father. You are a kind and loyal friend. You are a hard worker and good blacksmith, and as a husband..." she kissed him. "I couldn't have asked for a better one." He smiled and pulled her close.

"Not even Richard Evans?" Joshua asked, half joking. Richard was considered the best catch in Fredericksburg and had shown interest in Elizabeth years before.

"Lord, no. Richard is handsome, I will agree, but unless he changes drastically, I fear he will make some poor girl a terrible husband."

Joshua was silent for a moment.

"What's on your mind now?" Elizabeth asked.

"You mentioned I was a loyal friend. You know, sometimes I wish that I wasn't. One of the main reasons I feel I have to join the Confederacy is to keep an eye on James. He can be far too reckless as it is, and I feel like I need..."

"You feel like you need to convert him before something happens to him."

Joshua nodded.

"Well, if anyone can convince my stubborn brother to accept God's love and saving grace, it's you. I personally don't believe it will be as difficult as you think. He has a good faith foundation. He just needs a little bit more encouragement." She smiled and kissed him again. "Just like you gave me all those years ago."

May 1853
Outside Fredericksburg

Fourteen-year-old Elizabeth made her way along the Rappahannock River, humming the new Stephen Foster tune, My Old Kentucky Home, My Love, hoping that she wouldn't be late for dinner again. Mother and Father were usually lenient with her but she was getting older and needed to be more responsible. She was so preoccupied that she didn't even see Joshua Bennett until she was right on top of him.

"Joshua!" Her brother's best friend smiled at her and stood, bracing his hand on the tree he had been leaning against.

"Elizabeth, I am sorry. I didn't mean to startle you." He closed the book he had been reading and smiled at her apologetically. Elizabeth smiled back.

"Don't you worry about it. What are you doing all the way out here?" She always felt at ease with Joshua. Since he was her brother's best friend, it felt like he was really a member of the family even if he was only the son of a blacksmith and her father owned one of the most successful plantations along the river.

"My father gave me a rare afternoon off. This is one of my favorite places to come and relax. Read." His blue eyes shone bright, helped, no doubt, by the bright blue shirt he wore. He usually didn't wear such

formal clothing, as his work as a blacksmith obviously caused his clothes to get dirty fast. Elizabeth couldn't help but notice that the shirt was a little tight. At eighteen years of age, Joshua was taking over and doing work for his ailing father and it showed in his physique.

"Yes, it really is very relaxing," Elizabeth replied. "We have a lot of good places to read around here, although my favorite place is in the East barn. It is quite close to the river so you can hear the water rush by and if you climb into the hayloft and lay there you can smell the horses." She stopped, realizing how strange that may sound to Joshua. Elizabeth's sister Belle thought her love of the outdoors was unladylike. Her mother and father didn't seem to mind that she spent most of her time out of doors. What would Joshua think? And why did it now matter what he thought?

"I bet that's a wonderful place to read as well." Joshua smiled. "What do you enjoy reading the most?"

"Nothing too important." Elizabeth slowly began walking, her hands clasped in front of her. Joshua fell into step next to her. "I like any romance novel I can get my hands on. I really like this author, Jane Austin. She's British and I really enjoy her stories. I've read three of her six novels so far and I can't decide which one is my favorite. I am hoping to get another of her novels for my birthday next month."

"Your birthday is next month already? You'll be fifteen if I'm not mistaken." Joshua gently took her arm and helped her step over a muddy spot on the path.

"You are correct." Elizabeth gave him a smile of thanks for his assistance. "What were you reading? You must have been very focused if you didn't hear me coming."

"I was focused. I was reading from the book of Joshua." He held up his book.

"Oh, the Bible." Elizabeth nodded. "James mentioned you like to read that. I didn't realize people read the Bible for pleasure. I thought it was just for church or to learn history. Are you named after this Biblical Joshua?" Elizabeth knew the basics of the Bible and Christianity and her family went to services once in a while but she really didn't practice her faith.

"I am named after Joshua, the leader of the Israelites after Moses died. I haven't read this particular book in a while. The book of Joshua has one of my favorite passages but I forgot how good it was."

"Good? The Bible?" As soon as the words escaped her, she realized how harsh they sounded. "Sorry, that came out wrong. It's just...I never thought the Bible really had anything interesting. The information about Jesus is good, but..."

34

"But you prefer Mr. Darcy?" Joshua asked with a half grin. Elizabeth looked at him, surprised that he knew the name of the Pride and Prejudice character. "My mother also enjoys Jane Austin." He explained.

Elizabeth giggled. "Darcy is okay, but I prefer Captain Wentworth from Persuasion."

"I don't know that Mother has read that one," Joshua said. "Listen, I know what most people think about the Bible. It's probably the same view that your brother has. I've tried on occasion to explain to him what religion and the Bible mean to me but he's just not interested yet."

"That doesn't surprise me," Elizabeth said.

"I know he thinks it's boring and irrelevant, but to me, well, it's like God is speaking right to me. I mean, look here." Joshua pulled on Elizabeth gently, stopping her and turning her to face him. He opened the book to the page that he had been studying when she had come across him. "In this chapter, the first of the Book of Joshua, God is talking to Joshua, who has just taken over as leader of the Israelites. Joshua is scared because he has to conquer the Canaan city of Jericho. The problem is, he has very few resources, and his spies were almost captured, but they were saved by a woman named Rahab. God tells Joshua to 'be strong and steadfast, do not fear or be dismayed, for the Lord your God is with you wherever you go." Joshua closed the book. "You see, God is not just talking to the biblical Joshua, he's talking to us too. I have been so worried about some of the problems at home, like my father's failing health and my having to take over his shop. Here God is, telling me not to fear. It's just what I needed to hear."

"Joshua, it sounds to me like you should be a preacher, not a blacksmith. I have never heard you so passionate about anything."

Joshua shook his head. "Some preacher I would make. I can't even convince my best friend that he needs to do more than just go to church once in a while to be a Christian."

"Well, you have my attention," Elizabeth said. It was the truth. She loved to read and learn. The way Joshua spoke of the stories had her very interested in the Bible. "What else do you need to do? You know, to be a good Christian."

"You need to have a personal relationship with God. Talk to him, listen to him..." He looked at her. "You're really interested? You're not just trying to be nice to me?"

"No, I'm really interested. So what happens to Joshua? Does he ever take over Jericho?"

Josh smiled and handed her the book. "Read it yourself and find out." She took the book and flipped through it. She noticed that passages were underlined and notes were written in pencil.

"You trust me with this?"

"Of course I do. I would love to have someone more my age to talk about religion with."

"Oh, so I don't just get to read it, we have to talk about it?" She teased him.

"If you want." Joshua looked at her, she felt as if his eyes were looking right into her soul. "I would love to talk more with you and spend more time with you."

1861

"You were so easy to talk to," Joshua said, running his hand up and down her back. "So eager to learn. So happy when you found out there were some pretty good love stories in the Bible."

"Ruth and Boaz for one. Not to mention my appreciation for the book of Songs, especially after I fell in love with you." She kissed his forehead, his cheek, and then his lips. "Shakespeare's sonnets can't even be compared to King Solomon's poem." She rested her forehead on his. *"I have found him whom my soul loves. I held him and would not let him go..."* She trailed off, fresh tears filling her eyes. "I don't want to let you go, Joshua." She buried her face on his shoulder.

"Nor I you." Joshua pulled her back so he could look in her eyes. He cupped her cheek and kissed her gently. "Just always remember that first bible verse we discussed. Be strong. Don't fear. The Lord will be with you, and He will be with me."

Tuesday, June 4, 1861
Trinity Episcopal Church

Elizabeth entered the church, ready to do her part for the war effort, even though she didn't fully support the war. Joshua, James and the rest of the young Fredericksburg men had already left for camp. Some of the older men had enlisted as well, including Elizabeth's own father. He had joined the infantry, along with Joshua and James. It was hard to believe that so many men were willing to fight.

"Elizabeth! You made it!" AJ came to her, a big smile on her face. "Who is watching Benjamin and Hannah?"

"My mother came into town to do so, allowing me to come. Annie is keeping an eye on things at Turner's Glenn."

"I see. Your mother didn't want to come?" AJ took Elizabeth's arm and led her to where some of the other younger women had gathered.

"She would have, but it's been awhile since she has gotten some quality time with her grandchildren, and she wanted me to get out of the house. I think she doesn't want me to sulk around too much and she's afraid that if I stay home, I will do just that."

"Well, you did just send the love of your life to war." AJ pointed out.

"Yes, but many other women did too, including her," Elizabeth argued. "But I'm glad, really. It is nice to get out and see everyone."

"Elizabeth! Welcome." Betty Herndon Maury greeted her. The woman stood from her place, where she was sitting with her sister Molly and her aunt Mary.

"Betty! It's so good to see you." Elizabeth stopped to speak to her friend. "When did you return to Fredericksburg?"

"We came in from Washington just yesterday. Let me tell you, it is already something to see. Soldiers everywhere Elizabeth, from both sides. We weren't even going to make it out of that horrid city but Major Robert E. Lee himself made sure that William, Nannie Belle and myself received passes. It still was not an easy trip. At one point, we missed a boat and I had to leave so much behind, including a trunk of my clothes, our house in Washington, furniture, oh Elizabeth, I left so much undone."

"But you're here, safe now, and if all goes well this war won't last but a few battles, so you will be able to return if that's what you wish."

"Indeed." Betty smiled. "And you're right, it should be a quick victory for our boys."

Saturday, June 15, 1861
Fredericksburg

Kate sat behind the driver of the Moss Neck carriage and looked around the town. Fredericksburg was slightly busier as of late. She saw Elizabeth walking on the sidewalk and she called out for her driver to stop. She then climbed down with his assistance and joined her friend.

"Elizabeth! How are you doing?"

"Good afternoon, Kate. I'm doing well. What brings you into town?" Elizabeth adjusted the basket of goods on her arm. She had stopped by the post office and Mr. Hugh Scott's mercantile and was now heading home.

"Oh, I just wanted to stop at the milliner's to see about a new hat, then stop at Mr. Noteware's confectionary for some chocolate. I'm glad that I caught up with you, though."

"Why?" Elizabeth smiled. "Do you need something forged in the shop?"

"No, although I hear that young Mr. Dawson is doing a nice job taking over for Joshua. He must have been trained well."

"Yes, he was. Joshua is an excellent blacksmith and an even better teacher." Elizabeth's smile faded a little, thinking of her husband. Kate noticed and placed a comforting hand on her arm.

"I have wanted to come and see you, to catch up with you. I was able to see Belle and your mother the other day. They informed me of a lot of the family news, but it's not like actually seeing you." Kate looked around. "It is so strange having the men gone."

"Yes, it is." Elizabeth agreed. "We're just now getting into a routine. I'm lucky that Eric is so good with my children and reliable. He's watching them right now."

Eric Dawson was a young man who was working and learning the blacksmith trade from Joshua. He and his mother had moved to Fredericksburg two years ago from Britain. Elizabeth wasn't sure what had happened to Eric's father. The fourteen-year-old never spoke of him. He was quite stoic and never talked much unless it was necessary.

"How is Mrs. Dawson doing?" Kate asked, brushing a strand of dark blonde hair back from her face.

"Not well. The doctor doesn't think she'll last to the new year. She's just too weak. Eric does his best but there is nothing anyone can do,"

"That's too bad," Kate said. "Are you staying busy enough for the shop to survive?"

"So far, yes. There are still horses to be shoed and plows to be fixed. Eric needs the job and we try to help him care for his mother as much as we can."

"The benefits of close neighbors," Kate remarked. "A benefit I've never really had."

"That was something to adjust to a little bit," Elizabeth said with a smile. "But you're right, it does have its benefits."

"Yes." Kate agreed. "So, what is the news around town? Is there any word on when any fighting will happen?"

"There already has been. There was an engagement in Virginia already. Big Bethel, they're calling it, over near Newport News."

"My goodness. That's not too far from here. Were there any casualties?"

"Around twenty killed from the Union but only one Confederate killed. More were wounded, of course, but not too many."

"One is enough if he's dear to you." Kate pointed out.

"Absolutely. Well said, Kate. If Joshua was the only casualty in a battle, it would be too difficult to bear. There were rumors of a battle near Newport News, but I'm not sure if that's supposed to be the same one as Big Bethel. If we have a lot of these smaller battles, it may be difficult to keep everything straight."

"That's true," Kate said. "I hadn't even considered that." She shook her head as they neared Bennett's Blacksmith Shop and Elizabeth's home.

"Would you like to come in? I have some coffee ready to be put on."

"I would like to, yes, but unfortunately, I cannot. I have a schedule to keep or Bertie will get upset with me."

"I see," Elizabeth said. "Well, it was good to talk with you. Take care!"

"Same to you!" Kate waved and was assisted back into the carriage that had been following alongside them and drove off.

Sunday, June 16, 1861
Bennett Home

"Aunt Meri, will you please read me a story?" Hannah asked, pulling at her aunt's shirt. Meri had come into town with Belle and Annie and had immediately been approached by her niece. Meri looked at Elizabeth.

"Go right ahead." She said. "It's either that or come work on more socks for the soldiers."

Thirteen-year-old Meri made a face. She detested knitting. "I would love to read to you, Hannah-Bear." She said, as she took Hannah by the hand and pulled her towards the small, fenced-in backyard. All of the Bennetts loved to read so Joshua had created a reading nook out back years ago. It was Hannah's favorite spot. Benjamin was playing with some of the neighborhood boys so it left just the women to go into the house.

"I don't like knitting any more than Meri does," Annie said, only half-serious.

"You can look around my pantry and start preparing dinner," Elizabeth said, knowing how much Annie loved cooking.

"Really?" Annie asked in genuine excitement. She rarely got the opportunity to do so, as Ruthie, a servant at Turner's Glenn, did all of the cooking.

"Yes. I was actually hoping that you would want to." Elizabeth smiled. Cooking was a chore that Elizabeth didn't particularly like to do so she was happy to have her sister help.

"Great! I will see what you have." In her exuberance, Annie almost knocked over AJ and Kate, who had just arrived. "Sorry." She said. Elizabeth laughed.

"Let Annie into your pantry and kitchen and she turns into an excited little girl," Elizabeth said. "Welcome." She addressed AJ and Kate as they entered the home. They sat down and pulled out their knitting to begin work. "So has everyone heard the news?" AJ asked.

"Do you mean about the fight that was supposedly at Newport News but was actually somewhere between Hampton and York?" Belle asked. "If that is the case, yes, we have,"

"No, not that. Something bigger. Harper's Ferry was evacuated by the Yankees. It's said that our troops are somewhere between there and Winchester."

"Oh my goodness," Belle exclaimed. "Those poor people! I can't imagine what it would be like to be driven from your home."

"Nor I." Elizabeth agreed. Kate nodded.

"I have found though, that in the short time since we've been involved in the conflict how bad and inaccurate the rumors of these fights are," Belle stated. "It might not be true at all."

"Agreed, but it must be difficult to obtain accurate information," AJ said.

"Yes, but it would be nice for them to at least let us know the facts and where the danger might be," Belle said. "Everyone wants to believe in their side."

"I'm not sure if that's something anyone can predict." Elizabeth pointed out. "I don't know exactly how battles start or work but it seems likely they happen in random and unexpected places, depending on when the armies meet."

"Yes." AJ agreed. "Hopefully, we will never need to worry about that."

"I pray every night that this war will end soon and stay far away from us," Elizabeth said. "Although I fear since we are so close to Washington, we may be more likely to be in the midst of some of the fighting."

"Perhaps," Belle said. "I have complete confidence that our Confederate soldiers will make sure we're protected."

"They say the North has so many more men than we do," Kate said.

"Our men are better, smarter, stronger and more handsome," Belle argued.

"While that may be true, and I would agree that Southern boys will take to soldiering more easily than Northern ones, Kate has a point," Elizabeth said. "In the long run, their numbers may become a problem for us."

"Well, we know our men will just take care of them sooner rather than later," Belle said. "That way, we won't have to worry about the Yankee's numbers."

"I do hope you're right," Kate said, then turned to AJ. "How are things on the farm with just you and Liberty?" She asked. "Will you be able to run it successfully with your father and brother away at war?

"Quite well so far," AJ answered. "We still have our two field hands and that's been quite helpful. Liberty is probably the biggest help. She is having no problem filling in. I was lucky today to get away though. It's not easy for me with so much added work. I do think we will be planting a lot less if the war continues for more than a year. We'll try to maintain our current crop but if it gets too difficult..." She shrugged her shoulders. "I'm not sure what we will decide to do."

"Well, while Mother has taken on some additional responsibilities, I am happy to say that life at Turner's Glenn hasn't changed overmuch," Belle said. "It is a little more boring with less company visiting and I dearly miss Father and James and Samuel. Our old overseer, Mr. Jarvis still runs the plantation quite smoothly and our people are content as ever."

"Will Mr. Jarvis enlist?" Kate asked.

"I don't believe so," Belle said. "He could surprise us all and leave."

Elizabeth's thoughts went to Belle's comment about the people at Turner's Glenn being 'as content as ever'. She wondered if the slaves were content at all. She withheld a sigh. She wanted to speak the words aloud but knew that starting an argument would be futile.

"And how are things here, Elizabeth?" AJ asked.

Elizabeth shrugged off her thoughts. "Horses need to be shod and machinery needs to be fixed. Eric is doing a wonderful job. He's having to work extra but I have been trying to help out with his mother more so he worries less about her. My sweet Benjamin has been a little man and has taken on more chores."

"To think that one of my nephews has...chores." Belle gave an over-exaggerated shudder.

"It's perfectly fine for a child to have chores, Belle." Elizabeth pointed out.

"Yes, yes. Of course. If you can't afford any other options, I suppose."

"Belle, I really hope you never have to work," AJ said lightly. "I'm not quite sure you could handle any type of physical labor, much less housework."

"I could if I really needed to but why should I?" Belle responded. "I would bet that Kate feels the same way, don't you?"

Kate looked at Belle. "I do. I'm quite glad I don't have to do menial labor and have Negroes to take care of all my needs."

Belle gave Elizabeth a look that clearly said: See, I'm not the only one. Elizabeth tried not to roll her eyes. Why did Belle always try to act better than her?

"I'm glad things haven't changed too much for anyone," AJ said. "I fear that will not be the case for long."

"As long as we all make sure we are there for each other, we will make it through," Kate replied.

Wednesday, June 26, 1861
Gibs and Alexander Tobacco Factory

Elizabeth entered the factory and immediately felt a coldness wash over her. She had never been inside before, but earlier in the month, it had been established as a hospital for sick Confederate soldiers. There had been reports of the ill soldiers suffering because of a lack of proper medical attention and good nursing. The women of Fredericksburg had decided to take action. Elizabeth didn't have as much time as some of the other women to help but she still wanted to do her part.

Elizabeth looked around with despair in her heart. She had heard rumors of the conditions of the soldiers but seeing them made it even worse. Men lay on the floor moaning in pain. Elizabeth quickly made her way to the nearest one. Sweat drenched his face and she took out a handkerchief to wipe away the grime. His lips were dry and cracked. He was so parched and weak that he could not move.

"Bless you, thank you, ma'am." He choked out. "Ain't nobody been to see me since I was brought in."

"How long ago was that?" Elizabeth asked, hoping that she was hiding the disgust in her voice.

"I don't really know, maybe yesterday?" The man could barely hold his eyes open he was so fatigued. "I'm just...ma'am, would you...the man next to me. Could you check on him? He was tossing and turning when I came in but I haven't heard nothing from him in quite some time."

Elizabeth slowly stood and looked over to the second man. Her stomach turned and she felt appalled at what she saw. She felt the soldier's white forehead. It was eerily cold to the touch. A tear slipped down her cheek and she choked back a sob. She didn't need to listen for a breath to know that the man had died. It was obvious in his lifeless eyes.

"Ma'am?" The first soldier called. He reached a hand out to her and she grasped it. "He's gone, isn't he? It's okay, Ma'am. It must have been his time to go." Elizabeth gave his hand a squeeze.

"You're right but that doesn't make it easier." She wiped the tears from her eyes trying not to be sick. "I'll be right back." She told him. "I'll go and get you some water and try to find someone to take care of this brave young man."

Elizabeth strode off. How could humans allow each other to be treated like this? As she walked through the building, she was horrified to see even more neglect. Many of the soldiers were on the floor, lying on thin pallets or just on blankets. She became quickly frustrated when she couldn't find anyone who looked like they were working, someone who could point her in the direction of a person in charge. Someone who could do something about the pitiful conditions around her. Finally, she came upon two men arguing. They appeared to be doctors.

"We can't just let them go, McClanahan. If we let the patients go to private homes, there is no way we'll be able to keep track of them."

"We'll be keeping track of corpses if we don't, Mason." The other said. "We need their assistance. They're willing to help. The whole town has an interest in what we're doing here. One of the men even went to General Holmes about what's going on. We're losing too many men."

"Excuse me." Elizabeth took another step toward the two men. "I'm Mrs. Joshua Bennett. I came in today to offer my assistance, as many of the women in town have. I hate to inform you that you have lost another patient. He's been lying dead in there for so long that he's cold to the touch." She tried to temper her anger. "Gentlemen, I didn't mean to overhear your conversation but I would like to say that I know the people of this town would help in any way that they could. We're already coming here to help but we have no direction. We're sewing for the soldiers as well."

"Ma'am, with all due respect." The doctor who had been speaking when Elizabeth had approached them spoke again. "We began using this factory because we don't want to take over your churches, your homes, stores, hotels, public buildings...we don't want to inconvenience you."

"With all due respect to you, sir, you may be bent on politeness but as the mother of two and the wife of a soldier in the 30th Virginia...I have to tell you that if my husband was the one who was sick or injured, I would hope that those around him would do whatever it took to make sure he was comfortable. To be able to have the food and water that he needed to get better. I can only offer to do the same for these men to the best of my ability and in any space that I have available."

The first man, Dr. Mason clenched his teeth while the other man nodded.

"It's just as I was saying, Mason. If we don't let them go, we may have a sort of mutiny on our hands." He leaned close and spoke softly but Elizabeth could still hear. "None of us need reports of suffering and neglect on our records."

Dr. Mason shook his head. "Do they want a hospital or do they want their homes invaded? No. I must protest. I do not approve of this."

Dr. McClanahan threw his hands up. "All right. Let it be noted that you, Dr. Mason protested this action. I am going to take the steps necessary to get these men the help they need." He turned to Elizabeth as Dr. Mason stalked away. "Ma'am, we would be grateful to you and your family if you would be willing to take in a few of our sick men."

"Of course." She nodded quickly forming a plan in her mind. "I could take two comfortably, one or two more if really necessary." She would send Benjamin and Hannah to stay at Turner's Glenn for the duration. It would be safer for them and would free up some space in their home. She could probably convince Annie to come and help her as well. "I live adjacent to Bennett Blacksmith and Farrier in town."

"Of course. I know your husband, Mrs. Bennett. He is a good man." Dr. McClanahan looked toward the door. "How about you head home and get everything in order. We'll move some men to your home and hopefully other homes in the area by dinnertime. Would that give you enough time to get situated?"

"It would. I will expect you then." Elizabeth turned and headed back to the first man she had encountered to give him some water and kind words. Then proceeded to her home to begin preparations.

Monday, July 8, 1861
Moss Neck Manor

"Daniel, you should probably stay here," Belle said, descending from the carriage. "I'm not sure how long I'll be, but it won't be more than a few hours." She then headed up to the Corbin's front door. She was immediately ushered into the parlor, where Kate joined her within a few moments.

"It's so nice to see you!" Kate said. "I'm glad you made the trip out here."

"I decided it was a good time. I was getting bored. There's only so much I can do around Turner's Glenn even with Benjamin and Hannah staying with us."

"Why are Benjamin and Hannah at Turner's Glenn?" Kate asked, adjusting the skirt of her pink and black checkered day dress.

"You know Elizabeth, the savior of all. She is one of the townspeople who has taken in sick soldiers. The talk around town was that they were being neglected when they were at the hospital that used to be the A & G Tobacco Factory. Elizabeth witnessed it herself. There were many reasons why the townspeople were upset, so they took action. When civilians started taking the soldiers into their homes, she had to be one of them. She didn't want Hannah and Benjamin around the sickness, so she sent them to stay with us. Mother is ecstatic to have them around all day. Annie went to stay with Elizabeth so she wouldn't be alone caring for the men and to help her with their care."

"It's good that she and the others are caring for the men. It doesn't sound as though anyone else will." Kate said. Rumors of the horrid

44

conditions of that hospital had reached Moss Neck. "Tell me, did you find it difficult coming out here? With all the soldiers around, that is."

Confederate soldiers from all across the South had been passing through town and the surrounding area. Some were passing through on their way to the front lines in Northern Virginia. Others were there to stay and garrison the town, as well as to protect the industrial businesses and river crossings nearby. "They're our troops, Kate," Belle said. "Why would I be concerned? They're Southern gentlemen, as expected. So in answer to your question, no, it wasn't difficult at all."

"I am glad to hear that. Is there any other news from town?" Kate asked.

"I haven't heard all that much. Yesterday, I briefly talked to Lucy Beale and stopped to see Elizabeth and Annie. Daniel brought me, with Benjamin and Hannah so that Elizabeth could see the children and take them to church services. I did hear that there was an attempt to blow up a Yankee ship. The Pawnee, I believe it was named. Apparently, the real issue wasn't that the plan was a failure, but the plan was discovered by the Yanks before we could execute it. However, it is very difficult to know what to believe nowadays. There are so many half-truths and exaggerations. It seems like every time I go into town there is exciting news about all these big battles when in reality, there haven't been any battles, nor does it really sound like there will be one soon."

"I agree with what you say about the rumors. It is quite bothersome." Kate said. "But you must be excited with so many soldiers in town. Why, just think what that will mean for our social amusements."

"Yes, that's true. One of the military companies, the 'Flying Artillery' gave some of the young ladies in town a picnic and held a dance a few nights back. Annie was invited and I would think that it would be a great opportunity to go out and socialize, but she decided not to go. You know she has never been very outgoing."

"That is true about Annie. It does seem like she prefers more of the domestic life."

"Yes." Belle agreed. "It's odd. I feel as though she will become like Elizabeth. Get married, have children and rarely visit with others."

"Well, not everyone can be as socially adept as we are." Kate paused. I must ask, you mentioned a 'Flying Artillery.' What is that?"

"It is a light artillery that will give fire support for our Army," Belle explained.

Kate nodded and changed the subject. "We've briefly spoken, but always have others around us. How did you and Samuel leave things when he left to go fight?"

45

"We have an understanding, I'm sure you realize that," Belle said. "But honestly, just between you and me, and if you ever tell Elizabeth I will be extremely distressed. Sometimes, I'm not sure if Samuel is really as good a match for me as I think. He proposed to me before he left to enlist and I accepted. I discovered, however, while he did ask Father's permission to marry me, and my Father said yes, Father told Samuel that he would have to speak with me. Father actually had some reservations about the engagement. When Samuel asked me, he made it sound like we had Father's complete and total blessing."

"Oh, dear," Kate said.

"I never had the chance to discuss this with Samuel because I found out after he left. It just unsettled me and I'm not sure why."

"I can see where that might be a bit upsetting. I would want complete honesty in the relationships. If that is your only objection to Samuel, I believe you'll be okay. I did wonder why you didn't get married before he left, and why you wouldn't want Elizabeth to know."

Belle shrugged. "It would have been too rushed. You know me. I've always had plans for the biggest wedding celebration. Trying to get my perfect wedding arranged in such a short time would have been too difficult. I want all of my friends and family to be here. Especially my cousins Charlotte, Victoria, Mary, and Bekah. No, it would have been too much to organize in such a short time,"

"I'm not sure if that's how I would be," Kate said. "I have no objection to wartime marriages. Who knows how long the war will last? If you postpone the wedding until after, we may all become old unmarriageable spinsters. Look at the Revolution of the 1770's. It took eight long years for us to win our independence then. It may take that long or longer for us to win independence a second time."

"You approve of wartime marriages? Says the woman who all but spurned Stockton Heth." Belle pointed out.

"I did nothing of the sort," Kate said. "Mr. Heth and I never had an understanding." Stockton Heth was a young man who many felt would win Kate's, heart. While she dearly enjoyed his company, she never felt as though he was the one she was meant to marry.

"Well, that's what makes my choice different from yours," Belle said. "I won't be a spinster. Samuel and I are engaged, and that's as good as an actual marriage, according to him. We'll be married as soon as he's back."

"So, according to him, you're as good as married..." Kate paused, unsure of how to tactfully ask the question that she wanted to ask. "Belle, he didn't...you didn't..."

"No, of course not." Belle waved her hand. "Who do you think I am, Margaret Buckley?" Margaret Buckley was a young woman from town who had a reputation of allowing men certain liberties. Belle didn't intend to sound so harsh, but rumors about Samuel and Margaret had made her a little defensive on the subjects. "There are certain situations that will not be happening until his name legally becomes mine. Between you and I, he did try to persuade me for more than just a kiss, as always, once I told him no, he relented. He's good about giving me what I want."

Kate shook her head in amusement. "Like every other man you've ever spoken with."

"It's not my fault I have all the charm," Belle said flippantly.

"Heaven help us if you ever meet a man who doesn't fawn all over you," Kate said.

"I'm not sure I would have time for a man like that," Belle spoke in a light, almost teasing tone, but Kate knew that she was partly serious. "The war will end soon, though, and Samuel will be back and then we can be married."

"Until then, you can continue planning your dream wedding."

Wednesday, July 17, 1861
Turner's Glenn

"Mama, I miss you." Hannah held Elizabeth's face. "I wanna come home."

"I miss you too, Hannah-Bear," Elizabeth said. "Those sick men still need your Aunt Annie and me to take care of them, so you and Benjamin need to stay here for a little while longer. It's for the best."

"Like Papa fighting the Yankees. It's for the best." Benjamin said from his place on Elizabeth's lap. "Remember what Grandmother said, Hannah? Sometimes, we hafta make sacrifices."

"That's very true. Your grandmother is very smart." Elizabeth smiled and kissed the top of his head. She well knew the sacrifices that had to be made and couldn't wait until her children could come home.

"How long are you going to stay today Mama?" Hannah asked.

"At least until dinner," Elizabeth replied. Annie had persuaded Elizabeth to go to Turner's Glenn for a visit. It was the same day that Belle had invited AJ, Liberty, and Kate to the plantation. They planned on sewing and knitting some items to send to the men in the 30th Virginia Regiment. Letters from camp to families at home had described some of their needs, and the women of Fredericksburg were ready to help.

"Not any longer than that?" Benjamin asked.

"No, I don't want to leave your Aunt Annie alone at home for too long."

47

"Oh, all right," Benjamin said with an exaggerated sigh that only a four-year-old could give. Hannah followed with a small sigh of her own. Elizabeth couldn't help but smile as she pulled both her children into a tight hug.

Belle entered the parlor, followed by AJ and Kate.

"Look who's here, children!" Belle said. Hannah and Benjamin jumped out of Elizabeth's lap and ran to hug both women.

"Is Liberty here?" Benjamin asked excitedly.

"Yes, she and Meri went to the back porch to do some work and talk on their own," AJ said. "I know Liberty is excited to see you two as well." The two children ran off.

"Those two love your sister," Belle said, sitting down.

"The feeling is definitely mutual," AJ replied. "Liberty is always finding ways to see them." AJ and Kate sat as well. One of the Turner house servants, Delia, served the women sweet tea.

"So, Elizabeth, you are the only one here who is living in town. What's the news?" Kate asked, picking up her stitching. "Actual news? Or gossip?" Elizabeth gave a quick glance to Belle, who usually preferred the latter.

"News," Belle said. "It would be wonderful if we had any news. Maybe about a battle where we are victorious and trounced the Yankees."

"No Belle, that hasn't happened yet," Elizabeth said. "There is some discontentment throughout the town and probably the whole state."

"Are you talking about Lincoln's call for troops and money?" AJ asked. "I heard about that. 40,000 men and $400,000 to help their war effort."

"That happened about a week or so ago," Elizabeth said. "It's making people think Lincoln is preparing for a longer conflict. The news that is causing so much turmoil, though, is the fact that Governor Letcher ordered our militia from all the counties in Virginia to assemble north of the James River. They are preparing for a potential fight."

"What's so bad about that?" Belle asked. "We are at war."

"I can see the problem with that," AJ said. "Why is our militia being called out first? We've already been sending a larger percentage of our men off to fight. The cotton states should be called out first."

"That's what people are saying." Elizabeth continued. "Also, there was a rumor circulating Monday night that Confederate General Wise's Legion in Western Virginia was defeated and around 100 of our men were killed or taken prisoner."

"The problem is, we really have no idea if that information is the truth, a lie, or an exaggeration." Kate pointed out.

"Yes, I agree," Elizabeth said. "Unfortunately, it sounds like Virginians are divided and there are a group of counties in Western Virginia who want to secede from our state and they've sent several members to Congress in Washington, not Richmond. They've also elected their own governor."

"Traitors, if you ask me," Belle said.

For what? Elizabeth wanted to ask. *What they did is exactly what we did.* Elizabeth didn't want to start an argument with Belle. She focused on the sewing she was working on; a new shirt that she wanted to send to Joshua.

"It's safe to say there is a lot going on, and here we sit, sewing and knitting and watching over things while the men go off and make a real difference in this war," AJ said.

"We are doing something important, AJ. Once the fighting really starts, the men will need what we provide, especially if the war continues into the winter months." Belle gestured to what was in their hands. "The socks and the shirts will be greatly needed, and your farm products could provide food to the troops, as well as other supplies they need. We will be of great assistance to the cause."

"I suppose," AJ said. "I just...I wish I could do more, and let me tell you if the opportunity arises for me to do more, I will."

"Well, I suppose we'll just have to start calling you Molly Pitcher," Belle said.

"If I could support our men like she supported hers...well, I would be proud to do so," AJ replied.

"Molly Pitcher..." Kate racked her brain. The name sounded familiar but she couldn't recall who it was.

"It's the nickname given to Mary Hays," AJ said. "During the Battle of Monmouth in our Revolution against the British. She carried pitchers of water to soldiers. Then, after her husband collapsed during the battle, she took over the operation of his cannon. I would be proud to do what she did."

"I don't know that your heroism will even be needed," Belle said. "The war will be over soon, in one big battle. That is all we will need."

"Men will still die in that one battle, Belle," Elizabeth said, worry for Joshua apparent in her voice. "Men already have died." She thought back yet again to the young soldier who had died at the hospital.

"Those men will die heroes," Belle said.

Friday, July 19, 1861
Fredericksburg

"Good afternoon, Mr. Thom," Kate said, stepping up to the Post Office counter and smiling at the 78-year-old postmaster. Reuben

Triplett Thom had been the postmaster of Fredericksburg since 1840. Many people had feared he would lose this position when Lincoln was elected, as Thom was an outspoken secessionist, but it had become a moot point when Virginia had seceded.

"Miss Corbin. How are things out at Moss Neck these days?"

"Oh fine, just fine," Kate replied. "With Richard and Bee away fighting, I have been splitting my time between Moss Neck with Bertie and Janie and alternately living with Nettie and her boys over at Echo Dell."

"That's right. I recall your sister married Bee Dickenson and they live out in King George County."

"Yes. I have been trying to keep up the morale of both Nettie and Bertie. I wouldn't be surprised, though, if Nettie and her boys eventually move back to Moss Neck."

"That would make things a bit easier for you."

"I love my nephews and Janie. I really do enjoy spending time with them, but you are right. It would be much more convenient if they moved to Moss Neck."

"Well, that's all good." He smiled. "Tell me, what can I do for you today, Miss Corbin?"

"I'm here to check and see if we have any mail or packages," Kate said. "I would also like to send this." She handed him a letter addressed to her friend, Sallie Munford, who lived in Richmond. "I'll actually take any mail for my family if that is all right. I will make sure they get it."

"I will see what I can do with this." He held up the letter. "I don't have much mail for anyone. No trains from Richmond are coming in. All of the cars have been put on the Central Road to carry troops over to Manassas Junction. Word is they'll be some fighting up there soon. Troops from both sides are gathering thereabouts."

"Manassas Junction? That's not too far from here, is it?" Kate asked.

"Only about 40 miles." Mr. Thom replied.

"My goodness. I knew the war may come close to us but haven't really thought about what that would mean."

"Well, I'm not figuring it will ever get close, but I am sure it will probably mean more than just trains not coming in. I remember back in 1812 when we were fighting against the British. Just because the battles weren't nearby didn't mean we did not feel the effects." He placed a hand on the counter. "Ships had a lot of trouble on the seas, which made it difficult for traveling and getting raw and finished products to the ports."

"I suppose," Kate said.

"Well, let me take a look in the back and see if I have anything for you." Mr. Thom turned and shuffled toward the back room, but came back empty-handed. "Sorry, Miss Corbin, no mail for anyone in your family."

"It's all right. I will have someone stop by in a few days. Maybe the war will be over if this battle near Manassas Junction comes to fruition, and the trains will start coming through like normal."

"I do hope so." Mr. Thom agreed. Kate said her goodbyes and headed out to her waiting carriage.

Friday, July 26, 1861
Bennett Home

"My dearest Elizabeth,

We have just received word of the first major battle of the war. It was near a city called Manassas. The Confederacy was victorious. Our regiment was not a part of this fight, but we are training and very well may be a part of the next big battle. The talk around camp is very positive. We not only won the battle but we chased the Federals off the field. It was quite an embarrassment to them.

Many of the men are saying that our victory is a sign that God is with us and that we are His chosen people and the Lord will not allow the South to be defeated. I am not sure about any of that kind of talk. However, as unprepared as the Union was during the battle, I believe they will regroup. I also have a bad feeling that this war will not be a quick conflict like many people believed it would be. The North has so many more men, as well as factories. I fear the Confederate Army may grow overconfident after Manassas and perhaps make some mistakes.

I am doing well. Many of the men have come down with a disease, and some have already died without ever setting foot on a battlefield. I have spent a lot of time praying with some of the sick and dying men. As a result, some of the other men have taken to calling me "Preacher". I don't mind the nickname at all. It is better than a lot of other nicknames I could have received.

I miss you and the children dearly. Please give them an extra hug for me. I love you all. Before I stop writing, I leave you with these words from the 3rd Psalm.

"I lie down and I fall asleep, and I will wake up, for the Lord sustains me. I do not fear, then, thousands of people arrayed against me on every side."

Joshua"

Elizabeth opened the door to find AJ on the other side. Elizabeth and Annie had taken in two more ill soldiers, bringing their total number of patients to four. They remained busy with caring for them, managing the blacksmith shop and running the household. The children remained at Turner's Glenn. Elizabeth missed them dreadfully and while she didn't want to turn away sick men, she couldn't wait to bring her family home.

"AJ! It is so nice to see you in town." Elizabeth smiled.

"I brought in some extra vegetables to Mr. Bradley's store." James H. Bradley was a grocery merchant in town and a deacon in the Baptist church. "He needs fresh produce to sell and I can provide it. We have an abundance of grain, vegetables, and even some extra fruit. We are having a fine growing season this year." The two sat at the kitchen table and Elizabeth poured some apple cider. "Liberty and I were actually thinking that it may be profitable to grow more vegetables than anything. Depending on how this war goes. If it lasts into the next year, I'm not sure tobacco will be practical to sell."

"You're probably right about that," Elizabeth said. "I'm really glad you stopped by. Did you hear any news around town? We've been a little isolated in here with the sick men."

"There's lots of talk about our victory earlier this week. It sounds like the more we hear about it, the greater the victory seems to be."

"Ah, yes. Our overwhelming Confederate victory in Manassas." Elizabeth nodded.

"We took 54 cannons, 400 wagons filled with provisions, and several thousand firearms. Supplies we can really use. The Northern army was quite well-equipped with traveling blacksmith shops and medicine wagons. From what it sounds like, the North believed they couldn't possibly be defeated."

"I heard the other day that there were civilians who came down from Washington to watch the fight. Has that proven to be true?"

"From what I understand, yes. Our soldiers found tables set at Fairfax Court House and Centerville, set and ready for their Yankee victory. The arrogance!"

"Were any of the civilians killed?"

"Not that I've heard. The one civilian casualty that I heard about was an elderly woman who couldn't leave her bed."

"Oh, how very sad!" Elizabeth said with dismay.

"Yes. Many people are talking about how Lincoln is conducting the war and it is a bit disgraceful if you ask me."

"What do you mean?"

"Well, he says that he wants to conduct the war on humane and merciful principles but that is just not what is happening. He declared that the Army will confiscate all medicines and surgical instruments as contraband of war."

"Even if it's personal property?" Elizabeth asked.

"Yes, even then," AJ said. "This could take away our ability to attend to our own sick and wounded. Even worse is the Yankees just left all of their wounded soldiers from Manassas on the field. They didn't recover their wounded or bury their dead. They just left them for the people of Virginia to take care of."

"Well, they were chased off the field, running for their lives. I'm sure that burying the dead as they left was not a priority."

"They could have come back under a flag of truce." AJ pointed out. "I feel as though most of the news I have received is fairly accurate. It's from Nathaniel. He stopped by yesterday. He's doing some scouting for the Confederacy and was passing through town. He told me our soldiers buried the Yanks in trenches, fifty to sixty men in one grave."

"That's horrible! Barbaric! Not even individual graves? How will their loved ones know where to find them?"

"I don't think they ever will, Elizabeth," AJ said. "I don't know how the armies on either side are even keeping track of fallen soldiers. I'm not sure how the armies will notify families when their loved ones die if they don't even know."

"Unfortunately, I fear we will find that out. The idea that the Union will give up so easily is clearly not the case."

"Most likely, not, I agree," AJ said. "I think our men now realize it might be a bit longer than anticipated. Something else that Nathaniel said is quite sad. He saw some of our soldiers taking the shoes off the dead bodies. They felt they had to, for the leather. They can use it in many different ways."

"Oh, that just seems wrong," Elizabeth said.

"Yes, maybe, but just think of how the soldiers see it. Why bury shoes or coats or guns or any other useful products that a soldier can use again. That would be a waste."

"I see your point. I would argue that all those lives lost are a bigger waste." Elizabeth replied, thinking of Joshua. She then led the conversation in a different direction. "I was thinking, next spring, of expanding my own small vegetable garden. If the war does continue and Fredericksburg remains as busy, we may be able to make some extra income, as you said."

"That wouldn't be a bad idea," AJ replied. "Soldiers will need fresh food and we'll likely continue to have them passing through on their way north."

"Yes, that's what I was thinking." Elizabeth agreed. At that moment, Annie poked her head out from the soldiers' room.

"Elizabeth, I'm sorry to interrupt, but can I get your help? Private James needs to use the privy." Since Annie was still a maiden, they both agreed to keep with propriety and have Elizabeth take care of the more delicate matters with their patients.

"All right, I will be right there," Elizabeth said, standing. AJ pulled out her chatelaine and watch.

"I should be going anyway. I would stay to help you, but I need to make sure that Liberty and our field hands have their dinner."

"I understand," Elizabeth said. "I'm glad you stopped by though. It's always so good to talk with you."

"And you," AJ said, hugging Elizabeth goodbye.

Sunday, July 28, 1861
Bennett House

AJ knocked three times on the Bennett door, then let herself in. Elizabeth sat at the kitchen table, needle and cloth in hand.

"AJ!" She exclaimed, a smile on her face. "What brings you back so soon?"

AJ pulled out a chair and joined her friend. "I wanted to stop by after Mass and see how things were going with you and your family. The area is still crawling with soldiers coming and going. Men trying to get to Richmond to join up and men protecting the town. Fredericksburg appears to be quite well-protected by our Southern soldiers."

"We do feel quite safe." Elizabeth agreed. Annie walked out of the children's room.

"Good afternoon, AJ." She smiled as she brought two empty bowls into the room. "Our patients drank the broth right down." She told Elizabeth.

"How are the soldiers doing?" AJ asked.

"Better than they would be at the Tobacco Hospital. I still cannot believe how those men were being neglected. It's said the poor soldiers are begging to be taken away."

"I'm glad you're helping," AJ said. "I wish we were able to help, but we are too far away from the town. The quicker we can get them healthy, the quicker we'll be able to get them back with their regiments."

"And end this conflict so our loved ones can come home," Elizabeth said quietly.

"Yes, that too," AJ said.

"Is there any news as you came through town?" Elizabeth asked.

"Yes, actually, there is. I can't believe you haven't heard any of the commotions. Didn't you go to church this morning?"

"No, I didn't get the chance. Annie was helping to tend to the soldiers here and I need to bring some food over to Eric's and check on his mother. I'm trying to finish up some shirts that I told Betty I would make. She's getting some packages made for a family friend and his fellow travelers from Maryland. They're going to be joining up."

"I see," AJ said. "After Mass, we heard a whistle, like from a steamship, even though there is no packet boat expected for a week. Everyone in town headed down to the wharf. It was a Yankee steamer that had been captured by our Confederates. It was called the St. Nicholas. Word is, we took some prisoners as well."

"Well, that's good," Annie said as she finished washing the two dishes.

"Yes. I'm sure there will be more to this story later on." AJ said.

"Have you heard that the Confederacy is moving its capital to Richmond?" Annie asked. "Fredericksburg is now directly in the middle of our capital and Washington."

"Why did they move it from Montgomery?" Elizabeth asked.

"They wanted it to be closer to where all of the action will be. It sounds like they believe it will be more strategic."

"I really hope that doesn't mean a plethora of soldiers marching through all the time," Elizabeth said. "I just don't want to think about how that would affect the town and the surrounding farmland."

"That may be a concern if the war lasted for a few years, but like I've been saying, I doubt that will be the case. We'll probably have another battle within the month, trounce the Yankees like we did before, and our men will be home, back on their land before we know it." AJ replied.

"The fact remains that many men will die in those battles." Elizabeth reminded her. Her thoughts flew, as they often did, to the young man she had found at the hospital. Pale. Cold. Lifeless. She had discovered later that his name was Obadiah Parkinson. Elizabeth still had nightmares of finding him dead. In her most horrible of nightmares, the cold, lifeless body belonged to Joshua. She had woken up in a cold sweat almost every night since then. It didn't help that she wasn't spending much time with her children the past few weeks. She knew it was necessary, but knowing that didn't make it any easier.

Annie glanced at her sister and knew what she was thinking by the look on her face. "Elizabeth found a soldier who had died on the floor of the Tobacco Hospital. He had been lying there for so long with no one helping him that he was already cold and stiff. She's been having nightmares ever since."

"I'm sorry I've been waking you up," Elizabeth said quietly.

"Elizabeth, I'm not concerned about that, I'm concerned about you," Annie said. "I know you're trying not to be, but you've been quite despondent ever since Joshua left." Annie came to sit at the table. "I know you're trying to be positive and you're going out of your way to stay busy by helping the cause, but you're not yourself right now. Even Belle made a comment about the change in you."

"I'm sure she did." Elizabeth sighed. "You're right. I am trying but it is so difficult without Joshua here. These last few weeks, not seeing the children, it's just been hard."

"Joshua's only been gone two months." AJ pointed out. "The transition will be difficult. Elizabeth, I have to ask...how many times have you missed church services since Joshua left?"

"We went the first Sunday that he was gone, but AJ, it's difficult. There's so much to take care of with Joshua being gone."

"Elizabeth, I'm telling you this as a friend. You know that is just an excuse. You know Joshua would expect you to take the children. The Elizabeth he fell in love with and married would make every effort to go because she wanted to. Because she needed to go for herself." AJ said.

A tear slipped down Elizabeth's face. "It may sound silly, but it's too hard being there, without him sitting next to me. Going to church was something that we always did together. My family didn't go very often when I was growing up. Maybe to an Easter or Christmas service, but not like when I went with Joshua. I just feel a huge void, knowing Joshua is not with me." She blew out a breath. "But you're right. When I say it out loud, it does sound like a flimsy excuse."

Annie reached over and touched Elizabeth's wrist. "I know I'm a poor replacement for Joshua, even if I don't take up as much space in the bed." Elizabeth smiled and Annie continued. "But if you want, I will start going with you. If it's that important to you, I'll go with you and the children. To be honest, it's something I've been wanting to do for a while."

"Thank you, Annie. I appreciate the offer." Elizabeth smiled.

"You know that if you ever want to get a different viewpoint, you are more than welcome to join me at St. Mary's," AJ added.

"I still can't believe you come over to this side of the river every week for Mass," Annie said.

"It's not too far," AJ said. "If something is important to you, you can make it happen."

"I suppose that is true," Annie said. "Church is a great place to pray."

"I just hope God answers them soon," Elizabeth said.

Saturday, August 17, 1861
Bennett Home

Elizabeth looked outside her front window. Soldiers had been passing through town on their way to Brooks Station for days. It seemed as though thousands of men had passed through already. She sighed.

Why did she have this bad feeling that the constant stream of soldiers wouldn't be gone? She saw Annie push through a crowd, having finished running her errands. Elizabeth went to the door and opened it for her sister.

"How did things go?" Elizabeth asked.

"Busy," Annie replied, setting down her basket. She blushed. "So many soldiers. Lots of young men."

"I see." Elizabeth smiled at her sister. "How many proposals did you get today?" Ever since the men started coming into town, Annie received a great deal of attention from the soldiers, as had many of the other young women in town. Annie shook her head, embarrassed.

"Only two." She spoke softly, then reached into her basket. "I brought some peppermint sticks from Mr. Noteware's. I thought it would be a nice treat for the wounded men in our care and..." She smiled and pulled out an envelope. "A letter from Joshua."

Elizabeth smiled as she took the letter, slid it open and began to read. Annie started putting some things away. "What does Joshua have to say?"

"He says that the soldiers of the 79th New York staged a mutiny near Washington DC. The men felt as though they were tricked when the three-month volunteers in their regiment were allowed to return home, while they, who had signed on for three years, could not. The mutineers claimed that they had performed their duties equally well, so they should be able to return home to New York as well. It sounds as though they had some other grievances as well, but Joshua doesn't go into detail."

"If they signed on for three years, they should expect to stay for three years," Annie said.

"I suppose," Elizabeth said. "Although it makes you wonder what the other complaints were." She continued reading. "He says that the mutiny has actually been an energizing story for the Confederate soldiers." She read to herself and a huge smile lit up her face. "And here is some more wonderful news! He said that he will spare me the details for now, but James has been more open to religion. James has even been attending Sunday Bible meetings."

"Well, that is good. It can only help James." Annie said, pulling some vegetables out of the pantry. "It should help him in battle and to finally settle down and do something productive with his life after the war."

"I agree. I'm getting you to church more often, and Joshua is getting to James. I feel that Mother and Meri would go more often if they could, which would mean Laine and Max would go. If only I could get through to Belle."

"I don't hold out much hope for that, Elizabeth. She may prove to be ten times harder than James ever was. I am glad you've been bringing me along, though."

"Well, I'm glad to hear that," Elizabeth replied, tucking the letter in her apron pocket. "We're going to need as many prayers as we can to get us through this mess."

Tuesday, August 20, 1861
Christ Episcopal Church

Elizabeth made her way to another Ladies Meeting, this one held at the request of Betty Maury's father, Matthew Fontaine Maury. She walked in, found Lucy Beale and sat down next to her.

"Elizabeth! It's so good to see you." Lucy greeted her.

"Good afternoon Lucy. It's good to see you as well." Elizabeth enjoyed Lucy's company greatly.

"I heard you took in some soldiers from the hospital," Lucy stated.

"You heard correctly. Annie is staying with me and the children are with Mama out at Turner's Glenn."

"That must be difficult, sending your children away, especially since Joshua enlisted and is gone too."

"It's almost unbearable," Elizabeth replied softly. "But I am comforted in the fact that I am doing good for others. It's what Joshua would want me to do as well." She shrugged. "Enough about that. How are things with you?"

"My brothers write often." She replied. "You know that John has enlisted as well. He's actually heading further west to train and fight from what I can understand. Maybe Tennessee."

"It is hard to get much information, such as the whereabouts and locations of regiments from Joshua in his letters." Elizabeth agreed. "Nothing specific at all in regards to that, but I'd rather hear vague happenings than not to hear from him at all."

"Very true," Lucy said, then turned to the front of the church as Betty began talking.

"Good evening ladies. I am so pleased you all could make it." Betty smiled. "As many of you know, I am calling this meeting at the request of my father. He would like us to send a petition to Congress for a new flag. I rather agree with him. He suggests a flag with a blue background with a cross of eleven stars near the staff. I believe this to be both simple and suitable. We claim to be a people under God's special protection and providence, and that fact should be reflected in our flag. We can call it the Southern Cross." Betty gestured to her cousin, Ellen Mercer Herndon, and Mrs. Hart, who both stood and held up a model of the flag. Elizabeth liked the overall look of the model but was unsure about her feelings in regards to the meaning of the flag. Supporting Southern rights, which supported slavery and this war wasn't what she wanted.

"Now, I personally believe the blue background is rather dark. I am more inclined to a white flag with red stars, but I would like to hear what you all think."

"I like it," Lucy said. "It's a good idea as well."

"I agree with Lucy." Mrs. Jane Beale, Lucy's mother, added. "Because we all know the good Lord is behind us."

Elizabeth kept her jaw clenched, desperately wanting to speak up against slavery and the fact that God was not behind the South if it meant some of His people were still being held in bondage, but she knew this was not the time or the place. No matter how hard she tried, she couldn't convince the people of Fredericksburg of that fact.

"I believe you should be made President in charge of this endeavor." Sarah Alsop said, speaking to Betty.

"I second that!" Fanny Bernard called out.

"All in favor?"

"Aye!" Elizabeth also gave her vote to Betty, who would do the job well.

"Any opposed?" No one spoke up.

"Wonderful." Betty smiled. "I would like to nominate Mrs. Hart as secretary, as she has been taking notes for us and doing quite a wonderful job."

"I accept." Mrs. Hart said.

"Well, then, it is all settled. We will start work on all this straightaway."

Monday, August 26, 1861
Fredericksburg

"My Dear Elizabeth,

I received your last letter. It was wonderful to hear from you. I have found that receiving letters from home is the best thing for a soldier. I am quite proud of Benjamin for writing me a short note and as silly as it sounds, I cherish what Hannah 'wrote' me. Though someone else may see it as simply scribbles, it makes me smile and miss you all so much.

Everything is going as expected. We spend most of our time drilling and training. It can get quite boring, but it will come in handy once we see a battle.

There is still talk of the New York mutiny. We heard that the mutineers were both sullen and drunk when they rebelled but quickly submitted when faced by troops that were sent to take care of them. Thirty-five men were singled out as mutineers, and more than a dozen

59

were incarcerated for it. As I said before, they had several grievances, such as being denied a trip home and the right to select their commander per militia custom. It is said, however, that the soldiers ultimately regretted the mutiny. I still believe the idea of our enemy fighting amongst themselves is a good sign. If there is so much discontent within their ranks, it gives me hope that there will be a quicker end to this conflict. I pray that is the case.

As always, I miss you and the children terribly. I cannot wait to be home and hold you all in my arms again. I wish I could have more time to write, but I want to get this posted and sent by tonight, and I have picket duty this afternoon.

With all of the love I possess,
Joshua

"It is so good to hear from him." Elizabeth turned to Lucy Beale. "Thank you for bringing this by. Joshua has been gone for three months, but it feels like it has been three years."

"I can understand that." Lucy agreed. "There has been so much loss of life in that short time."

"The Battle of Manassas was a rude awakening." Elizabeth placed the letter in her pocket, the same pocket that she kept her tintype image of Joshua in. "I'm so glad that your brothers made it through unharmed."

Lucy nodded. "We all pray for Charles and Will every night. I don't know what else we can do for them."

"I know. There isn't much else. We just have to pray and live our lives the best we can."

"Yes." Lucy sipped the tea that Elizabeth had brewed. "How are you getting along without Joshua financially?"

"Before he left, Joshua was training Eric Dawson, kind of like an apprentice. Eric greatly admires Joshua, so when Joshua left, he made Eric promise to stay and run things here as best as he could. The boy is doing a good job, especially since he is only fourteen. Also, Daniel, you know the carriage driver at Turner's Glenn, he was very close to Joshua. He stops by almost every day to help Eric take care of things here. He oftentimes will bring food from the plantation and I've been keeping a garden in the backyard as well."

"That's good. It doesn't surprise me that Joshua has such loyal servants."

"I agree. He is such a good man, but he considers them his friends, not servants. Eric is almost like a younger brother or even a son to Joshua." Elizabeth looked over at the mantle where the photograph of her and Joshua on their wedding day sat. She took a deep breath and smiled. She wasn't the only woman who had a husband fighting in the war. "How is John?"

"Good, as far as I know."

"And your mother?" Elizabeth asked.

"She is doing well also. Preparing for the fall term. She looks forward to having your sister Lainey in class again. The girl is a very quick learner."

"She is." Elizabeth smiled fondly, thinking of her sister. "I only wish that I could see my siblings more often."

"I understand that sentiment," Lucy said. "Family is very important."

"Indeed," Elizabeth said, looking towards the back yard area where Benjamin and Hannah played. They had returned home a few days ago after the last sick soldier had left the home. She was so happy to have them back in her life every day. Her family was indeed of the utmost importance in these difficult times.

Thursday, August 29, 1861
Prentiss Farm

Liberty let out an audible breath and glanced outside.

"Will this rain ever lighten up?" She asked, annoyed. "I hate being cooped up inside. You know that."

AJ smiled, not looking up from her knitting. "You could go out to the barn and do some cleaning."

"I could," Liberty replied. "I suppose I could do some extra work with the horses too, even if we are stuck inside the barn."

"You could pick up a needle and thread and do some sewing. I'm darning socks for Father now, but I wanted to repair one of Nathaniel's old shirts and send it to him. You could work on either one."

"You know that I'm not good at sewing," Liberty replied.

"Because you never practice." AJ pointed out.

Liberty shrugged. "Maybe later."

"That's what you always say," AJ said. "You just let me know when you would like to start." AJ glanced up from her work to look at her sister. "You never said, but did you hear anything interesting when you were in town yesterday?"

"Actually yes. A couple of things." Liberty said, perking up a little bit. "Some of the men outside the tavern were talking about Northern oppression. They were saying that free speech and press were denied to some Northerners. Papers in New York and Pennsylvania were shut down by the government because they've been pushing for peace. A mayor was even arrested because he didn't take the oath of allegiance to Lincoln."

"That goes to show just how much of a tyrant Lincoln and his government are," AJ said bitterly.

"Yes, that's true," Liberty replied. "They were also saying that a...oh, what were their names? Oh, yes, a Mrs. Eugenia Phillips, a Mrs. Goodwin, and a Mrs. Rose Greenhow were arrested. They're all from Washington and were arrested for being spies. Can you imagine? Female spies. They say Mrs. Greenhow and Mrs. Phillips have guards placed in their homes to keep an eye on them."

"In their own homes? How intrusive! That's horrible."

"Yes, but at least they weren't thrown into prison like most spies, or even executed." Liberty pointed out. "I found it funny that a lot of the men I overheard were doubting if the rumors of women spies could even be true."

"What do you mean?" AJ asked, puzzled.

"Oh, you know how men can be," Liberty said. "They're doubting the rumors because they don't believe a woman could be so devious or smart enough to pass on intelligence, you know, actually do something for the war effort other than just stay home, take care of the children, and knit and sew and cook."

"That is frustrating. Women would actually be the perfect spies simply because most men would never suspect them." AJ paused. "I wish I could do something more for the war effort. To be able to do something other than just sewing clothes for them. I could gather intelligence..."

"Yes, because Union secrets are abundant here," Liberty replied. "Don't misunderstand me, that would be something I would like to do if there were Yankees around, but they are not and probably never will be. Would you be okay with the chance that you may be arrested? I mean, being a spy would be terribly exciting, but..."

"I'm not sure. I would like to think that I would be fearless and daring. I think that I could be. It's tough to really know for sure until you're actually in that situation."

"Well, apparently, the female spies got their information from being flirtatious with the officers who could give them the information. They were saying that some even used seduction. No offense meant, AJ, but you're not the best when it comes to charming the members of the opposite sex."

"No offense taken," AJ replied, knowing that it was a very true statement. She wasn't sure why, but she had such difficulty speaking to men. The more attractive they were, the harder it was for her. She could banter with her brother with no problem. She had short, successful conversations with Joshua Bennett and James Turner but only after they made their intentions known to Elizabeth and Nicole Austin, respectively. Once it was clear to her they could only be just friends, she was more at ease. With the other young men in town, well, she hoped one day she could overcome her social awkwardness.

"Well, who knows what the next few months have in store for us," Liberty said. "Hopefully the opportunity to help more will come."

"I sure hope so," AJ replied. "I do hope so."

Wednesday, September 11, 1861
Turner's Glenn

Elizabeth took a deep breath as Turner's Glenn came into view. She didn't want to be the bearer of bad news, especially where her sister was concerned. She touched her pocket, where a letter from Joshua was. She usually enjoyed receiving any letter from him in the few months that he had been gone. This last letter...she just wasn't sure how she was going to give the news to Belle.

Daniel was coming out of the stable and greeted her.

"Afternoon, Miss Elizabeth." He said, giving her his hand to help her down.

"Good afternoon, Daniel." She mustered up a smile. "Do you happen to know where Belle is?"

"Well, Miss Kate Corbin came by for a visit from Moss Neck Manor. I 'spect they out in the flower garden today, see'in as how it's such a fine day."

"Yes, Belle does enjoy the flowers," Elizabeth said. "Thank you, Daniel."

The driver gave her a nod and tied up the horse while Elizabeth headed toward the side of the house.

"Elizabeth!" Belle stood from a stone bench. Kate did as well. "What are you doing out here, not caring for your home and perfect family?" Only Elizabeth could detect the slight cutting tone in her sister's voice.

"Belle, I came out because I received a letter from Joshua today."

"Well, bully for you," Belle replied. "Was there anything in the post for me? I haven't heard from Cousin Bekah nor Samuel in weeks."

Elizabeth took a deep breath. "No, there were no other letters for anyone, Belle, but..." Elizabeth glanced over and saw Zipporah standing at the edge of the garden. She was always waiting to do whatever struck Belle's fancy. "Zipporah, would you please go and ask my mother to come out here?" The woman nodded and headed into the house.

"Elizabeth, what is this? Why do you need Mother?" Belle put her hands on her hips, an annoyed look on her face.

"Belle, you may want to sit down," Elizabeth said, wishing she could avoid this conversation, but Joshua had asked her...

63

Belle sat down with a heavy, exasperated sigh.

"Belle...in Joshua's letter, he...he had a message for you. It seems as though...well...you know that we've had reports that many men have died from sickness, right?"

"Yes." Belle looked at her sister warily.

"Well, it pains me to tell you this, but...well..." Elizabeth looked at the house, wondering what was taking her mother so long. "Belle, Samuel Gray is dead. He came down with dysentery and he died."

Belle's face turned whiter than Elizabeth had ever seen it.

"Dead?" She asked, unbelieving. "Where? When?"

"In a hospital near Richmond a few weeks ago," Elizabeth said.

Kate sat next to Belle and put an arm around her friend. "Belle, I am so sorry."

"Are you sure that Joshua wasn't mistaken?" Belle asked.

"No, he's not mistaken, Belle." Elizabeth knelt in front of her sister and took Belle's hands in hers. Belle was trying to hold back tears, but her eyes began to water. She pulled a hand out of Elizabeth's and wiped a tear from her cheek. "I just can't believe it. He and I were going to be married."

Elizabeth glanced up and saw her mother walking towards them.

"Belle, what's happened?"

"It's Samuel, Mama. Joshua wrote to tell us that Samuel was overcome with dysentery and he...he didn't make it." Elizabeth explained. Belle stood and began pacing.

"I just can't believe it. Samuel was going to be a war hero. He was going to come home and we were going to be married. We would make the perfect couple. He's...he's everything I could have asked for in a husband. He just...he can't be dead. Not like this. Not from some senseless illness. If he was going to die, why couldn't he have been killed in a battle? That would have been worthwhile, but not this way.

Miriam pulled her daughter into an embrace. "Belle, dear. I don't know what to say."

"There's nothing to say," Belle said. "My life...my future...it's ruined!" She pulled away from her mother and walked into the house as quickly as she could.

Belle sobbed into her pillow. How could this have happened? Samuel was one of the best catches in all of Spotsylvania and Stafford Counties, and he had proposed to *her*. They could have had a wonderful future together. If only they had been married before the war, at least then, she would have the distinction of being a war widow. Why did he have to die of an illness? It was so senseless. He should have died doing something daring and dashing.

"God, why? Why did you allow this to happen? Why would the doctors not care for him? Aren't they supposed to heal the soldiers? Sure, they will care for the wounded in battle but not those who get sick from all the poor living conditions."

A man killed in battle was an honor, but dying just because he got sick? That could happen to others, but not her Samuel. She laid on her bed and cried until she fell asleep.

Monday, September 16, 1861
Turner's Glenn

Elizabeth pulled the horse to a stop and turned to her children. "You two remember to be good. I need to talk to your Aunt Belle."

"Can I play with Max?" Benjamin asked.

"Of course, but make sure you give your regards to your grandmother first."

Elizabeth hopped down from the seat of the wagon and helped her children down.

"I hope Lainey reads to me," Hannah said with a hopeful look on her face.

Daniel came out of the stable, followed closely by Timothy.

"Afternoon, Miss Elizabeth," Daniel said, taking the horse's reins.

"Good afternoon, Daniel. Do you know how Belle is doing?"

"Not right sure 'bout that, Miss Elizabeth. I haven't seen her outside at all since you come by last time."

"Hmm, that's not good." Elizabeth turned and looked at the house. Benjamin was already leading Hannah to the front door.

"I'll go and see if she'll talk to me. Thank you, Daniel." Elizabeth went into the house and found her mother, Meri, and Annie in the parlor.

"Elizabeth dear, what brings you out here?" Miriam put down her knitting and stood to hug her daughter.

"Good afternoon, Mama. I came to get away from the city for a while and to check on all of you but especially to see Belle. I am not sure if you have heard the news, but many people in town are afraid right now because of an outbreak of Scarlet Fever."

"Yes, we've heard about that. Has anyone succumbed to the disease?" Miriam asked.

"Not yet, not that I have heard of, at least," Elizabeth answered. "Mama, I would like to leave the children here again, if that is all right. I would feel safer having them out here, away from the sickness."

"Of course. Miriam said. "They are always welcome. You are as well."

"Thank you, Mama," Elizabeth said.

"Are there still a lot of soldiers out and about town?" Meri asked.

"Yes, there are," Elizabeth replied. "Tell me, how is Belle doing?"

"She hasn't left her room since you told her about Samuel," Annie answered, looking up from her sewing.

"Hmm, that is not what I wanted to hear," Elizabeth said. She looked around. "Did Hannah and Benjamin already come through here?"

"They did," Miriam said with a smile. "You have done a very good job raising them. They were very polite. They came in and gave us all hugs, then skedaddled."

"Thank you for the compliment, mother, but they are good children. They make it so easy." Elizabeth smiled.

"I can't wait until you have another," Meri said with a smile. "I love being an aunt."

"Well, I'm afraid you will have to wait," Annie said, grinning. "She needs Joshua to be home for that."

Meri's cheeks reddened. "Of course I know that."

Elizabeth tried to smile, but a sense of longing came over her. She missed Joshua so much it made her ache deep inside. "So, where did my children go?"

"Benjamin ran off to find Max. Hannah pulled Lainey off to the library." Annie replied.

"Hannah-Bear does like getting read to." Elizabeth gave her mother and sisters a genuine smile. "All right. I am going upstairs to try and talk to Belle."

"Try to see if you can get her to come down, or at least get her to eat something of substance," Miriam said.

"I will," Elizabeth said, not liking at all what she was hearing about Belle. Although she really couldn't blame her sister. If Joshua died, she wasn't sure how she would be able to go on. She had cried herself to sleep the night she had told Belle about Samuel. She was lucky that her children had been able to get some sleep.

Elizabeth knocked twice on Belle's bedroom door, then let herself in. The room was dark and stuffy, the curtains closed. Belle was sitting in a chair in the corner, staring at nothing. She at least looked her usual impeccable self, her hair perfectly coiffed, her mourning gown freshly pressed. Elizabeth was glad to see that Belle had taken care with her appearance, otherwise she would have been extremely worried.

"Belle, you're looking beautiful as always. How are you feeling?" Elizabeth walked in.

"Elizabeth. Good to see you." Belle's voice was flat and emotionless. Elizabeth walked over to the window and began to pull the curtain back.

"What are you doing? Close those curtains. I don't want them open."

"You don't want to see the beautiful sunny day?" Elizabeth asked.

"No, I don't."

"Belle, it has been almost a week since you have heard the news about Samuel. I know what you are going through is rough. I cannot even begin to truly understand. Whenever I think of something happening to Joshua, I...I just don't know."

"Well, something didn't happen to Joshua, it happened to Samuel. If something did happen to Joshua, you at least would have been married. You would at least have the status of being a widow. You have two children by him." Belle paused. "Joshua probably never would die because of a disease. He would probably die a hero's death."

Elizabeth sat on the bed, facing her sister. "Is that one of your issues? Not that he died, but how he died?" Elizabeth couldn't believe it. She knew that Belle could be shallow, but this was extreme, even for her.

"No, but it doesn't make it easier. If I could say that he died valiantly, it might make his death worthwhile. He was my perfect match, my future husband. We would have been the most charming of couples."

Elizabeth considered her sister's words. "Belle, do you realize, that in all of our discussions we have ever had about you and Samuel...you've never mentioned love."

"Love? Of course I loved Samuel. Would I consider marriage to him if I didn't?" Belle's voice got a little more emotional.

"People marry for reasons other than love all of the time. For money, power, position, prestige, but that's not the way it should be. Love is important in a marriage, so important. Did you really love Samuel?"

Belle sighed and looked out the window. "I would like to say yes, I did, but I don't know if I honestly can." She looked back at Elizabeth. "You don't know how much I hate to admit that, especially to you. Please do not take offense."

"None was taken." Elizabeth smiled. "I'm actually glad that you feel as though you can open up to me." Even if only a little bit. You usually don't confide in me at all.

Belle looked back out the window. "Elizabeth, do you think I'll ever have someone? Someone just for me? Like Joshua is for you. I mean, I will never understand your relationship, truly. I don't understand why he makes you so happy, but he does. I can see that he does."

67

Friday, September 20, 1861
Turner's Glenn

Elizabeth stepped into the parlor at Turner's Glenn and was immediately swarmed with hugs from her son and daughter. She held them tightly, tears forming in her eyes. Things hadn't been going well in town. Elizabeth missed her children. She had looked forward to having them home the moment she and Annie had sent the sick soldiers home or back to their regiments. Benjamin exclaimed. "Can Hannah and I come home with you today? Are people feeling better?"

Elizabeth smiled sadly. Benjamin immediately sobered. "We can't come home yet, can we?"

"Not yet, Benjamin. I wish I could take you home this minute, but no, not yet."

"Why not?" He asked, disappointment obvious in his voice. Elizabeth wiped a tear from her cheek.

"Benjamin, you know some of the children in town have gotten sick. I don't want you and Hannah at home where it will be easier for you to get sick too." She brushed back his smooth, dark hair. She wasn't quite sure how to tell her son that eight-year-old Wilmer Hudson had died on Sunday from scarlet fever. The disease continued to spread through town, quickly becoming an epidemic. Unfortunately, Wilmer probably would not be the only child to perish from the disease before it ran its course. She didn't want her children anywhere near the town where they could potentially catch the disease.

"Is everyone going to be okay?" Benjamin asked, concern in his voice.

"I'm not sure, Benjamin, but I assure you, the second I can bring you and Hannah home, I will."

"Yes, ma'am." Benjamin hugged his mother and ran off. Elizabeth watched him, then saw her sister standing in the doorway.

"Belle, how are you doing?" Elizabeth wiped her eyes again.

"At the moment? Better than you, it seems." Belle entered the parlor and sat down. "What is wrong?"

"Wilmer Hudson died of the Scarlet Fever. The first child to succumb."

"I see, that is so sad," Belle said. "Did you tell Benjamin?"

"No, I just couldn't find the right words. He's not really friends with Wilmer, as the boy was several years older than Benjamin, but he knew who he was. Not to mention there are several other children who have come down with the disease. One of them is little Joey Mason, who is one of Benjamin's favorite playmates." Elizabeth shook her head. "It's hard for me to understand why all of this is happening. It's as if the war hasn't been enough for us to handle, God feels the need to challenge us with this epidemic."

"Well, I understand very little on why God does what He does," Belle said. "So I am definitely not the person you should talk to about that."

"I suppose," Elizabeth said. "You didn't really answer my earlier question, Belle. How are you doing?"

Belle shrugged. "I'm getting by." She said flippantly, then changed the subject. "Other than the fever, is there any war news?"

"Well, something is going on in the Fredericksburg area. If you're outside and listen closely, you can actually hear the gunfire. I am not sure exactly what is going on, though."

"Really? I suppose that can be considered exciting news."

"I suppose. Although it was a little unnerving coming out here, I needed to see my children. The idea that the war is so close-close enough that we can hear it? It frightens me,"

"Any idea where the fighting actually is?" Belle asked.

"I heard a rumor that it's over in Arlington Heights, near Washington City, but they're also saying that the Yankees are planning a secret expedition around the Rappahannock. It is interesting that it's supposed to be a secret and yet everyone in Fredericksburg is talking about it."

"That is rather amusing. Those Yankees sure are bad at keeping secrets. Must be why they haven't been able to beat us, and they won't."

"Well, I'm still not sure about that," Elizabeth replied. She looked out the window in the direction of Washington City. "I'm not sure about a lot of things."

Wednesday, October 23, 1861
Turner's Glenn Plantation

"Mother!" Belle called. "Are we going to be picking up Elizabeth on the way to the wedding?" Belle ran her hands down the emerald green evening gown. She, Elizabeth, Annie and their mother had been invited to the wedding of Nannie Herndon. Belle had been excited about the event since the moment she heard about it. AJ, Kate, Kate's sister, Nettie, and Kate's sister-in-law, Bertie were all supposed to be there. Bettie Maury and Lucy Beale-Brent had also been invited.

"Yes, we are," Miriam said. "We should leave soon. Zipporah is watching over the children."

""I'm so glad we were invited. So many influential people will be there." Belle said as she and her mother descended the stairs. "It feels like before this ridiculous war began. We can socialize, as we should be able to. It's almost as though there is no war to worry about."

Miriam smiled sadly. She didn't want to correct Belle's statement for a few reasons. First, her immediate reaction was that Matthew and James and Joshua were gone. Also, Miriam wasn't sure how fragile Belle was in regards to losing Samuel. At first, her daughter had acted like her world was at an end, but after a few days and a conversation with Elizabeth, Belle was acting the exact opposite. It seemed as though Samuel had never existed to her. Neither of these reactions was good for her daughter. Now, today, apparently, Belle was no longer in mourning for Samuel, as her dress was nowhere close to mourning garb. Miriam hesitated to bring any of this up. It had been six weeks, and she knew that Belle should mourn longer, but she wanted Belle to enjoy life again. Unfortunately, many families were in mourning, not for soldiers killed in battle but for loved ones who had died from illness. The town had already lost so many children to the scarlet fever epidemic that still raged through Fredericksburg.

Miriam and Belle met Annie at the landing and proceeded out. Daniel assisted them all into the carriage, and the three women talked about mundane topics as they were driven into town. Belle began the conversation with news of a different wedding that was supposed to be but hadn't happened.

"When Elizabeth was over yesterday, she commented that Richard Herndon and Sue Crutchfield were to be married yesterday. He was finding it difficult to obtain leave for his own wedding, can you imagine?"

"I would imagine it is very difficult for poor Sue not to know when or whether she will be a bride or not," Annie said. "Did Elizabeth say what happened?"

"She did not," Belle answered. "She did say that her cousin, Mrs. Hart, was inviting family over for oysters and ice cream, whether Richard would be there or not. It would just be a family party if he didn't show."

"Betty Maury and her family sure are busy," Annie commented as Daniel pulled the carriage up to the Bennett home. The servant hopped down and went to the front door to let Elizabeth know they had arrived.

"I know, but it's so nice to see life moving on, even though we are in the midst of a war," Belle said, patting her hair.

"As well as we can, at least," Miriam added as Elizabeth was assisted into the carriage.

"So, is Susan Crutchfield now a Herndon?" Belle asked as Elizabeth sat in her seat. "Was Richard able to get leave?"

"No, I hope to speak to Betty about it today and get some details." Elizabeth said. "Not that I want to take anything away from Nannie's day, of course. I just feel so bad for Sue."

"Yes, it would be horrible, having your wedding put on hold and your day ruined because of this war. At least she has the hope that someday soon, Richard will receive his furlough and come to her." Belle tried to sound flippant when in reality, she just wanted to break down and cry, but she couldn't do that. She couldn't show that she really felt sad and empty inside. Her real feelings were what she had almost shared with Elizabeth a few weeks ago. She felt sad and empty because she wasn't as upset about losing Samuel as she probably should have been. She was ashamed that she was more upset about losing her perfect future.

The wedding of Nannie Herndon was a simple affair, held at the home of the bride. George Anderson Mercer looked dapper in his Confederate uniform and neatly trimmed hair and beard. He was from Georgia and had been stationed in Savannah. He had been promoted to lieutenant not long ago.

"Nannie! You make such a beautiful bride!" Elizabeth said, giving the woman a hug. Annie and Belle followed suit, and Kate and AJ were right behind.

"Thank you, ladies. I'm just so happy that George was able to get a full month's furlough. Cousin Richard wasn't so lucky."

"We did hear about Richard and Sue's unfortunate news," Belle said. "That is so sad."

"It is. I don't blame her at all for not wanting to be here today. I would be just as distressed if George couldn't have made it, especially if something had happened to him before we got married."

AJ, Kate, Elizabeth, and Annie tried to inconspicuously read Belle's reaction. Her courtship with Samuel hadn't been a secret, but they had seldom gone on outings as a couple. Only a few people knew that Samuel had even proposed to her. It was clear that Nannie didn't know about Belle's relationship with the recently deceased Samuel, but Belle's expression did not show any reaction from the conversation. The group moved along, stopping to greet the groom, then continued on to get some refreshments. They were immediately greeted by Betty Maury. After the initial pleasantries had been exchanged, Belle asked the question everyone was wondering.

"Betty, life seems to be going extremely chaotic for your family right now. We heard that your brother couldn't get leave for his own wedding."

"You heard correctly. Poor Susan." Betty replied. "It was always questionable if he would be able to get the leave. I don't know how anyone even has the heart to prepare a party or wedding entertainment in these war times. I am impressed and happy that today's celebration came to fruition."

Kate said, "It's difficult to look even one day into the future. Everything in front of us looks dark, gloomy and unpredictable."

"Indeed." Betty agreed. "Even this very night, our dear ones may be engaged in a great and terrible battle. That is the main reason Richard and Susan had to make the postponement. We received a telegram from him Friday night saying he would not be able to make it. I still held out hope, but when I visited Sue on Monday, she read us a letter she had received from my brother. He said that even if he was given the leave, he just couldn't abandon his regiment, as an important battle is expected any day. It's interesting how the condition of this country changes everything."

"What do you mean?" AJ asked.

"Well, six months ago, if a gentleman failed to keep an engagement like his wedding, he would be forever disgraced. Now, it is scarcely a matter of comment." Betty explained.

"Or people applaud him for his dedication to his fellow soldiers and his commitment to the cause," AJ added.

"Exactly," Betty said.

"Well, that still probably doesn't make Sue feel any better about the situation." Elizabeth pointed out. "How is she handling it?"

"As well as can be expected," Betty said with a glance at Belle. "She knows they will have another opportunity. Which reminds me, Belle, I am very glad that you decided to come out of mourning. A wedding can't be an easy event for you to attend. I know that Samuel was officially courting you shortly before he left for the war. My condolences to you for your loss."

"Thank you," Belle said. "It was a cruel blow, but I feel better knowing that he left with every honorable intention of defending his home, family, and friends."

"Unfortunately, the Gray family has another illness to deal with. Samuel's nephew, Greyson is one of the children currently ill with scarlet fever." Elizabeth said.

"Indeed? How horrible." Kate said.

"I fear for my daughter Nannie Belle every day," Betty said. "Lewis, one of my Uncle Charles's twin sons, died last week Sunday. I'm not sure if it was the fever or not. I went there that evening to offer to sit with him, but they told me that I wasn't needed. I didn't think of it at the time, but it could have been bad if he did have the fever. I wouldn't want to bring it home to Nannie Belle."

"That is a good point," Kate said, thinking how hard it would be if any of the children in her family caught the disease.

"Ladies and gentlemen." George Mercer called to the guests, his new wife holding his arm and grinning broadly. "Mrs. Mercer and I would like to invite you in for dinner." The women followed the crowd and found a place at the table near one another. Just as they were about to sit, a young man approached them. "Pardon me, ma'am." He said, speaking more to Annie than any of the others. "My name is Jonathan Diggle. I am a cousin of the groom." The young man was handsome, with light brown hair that lay in curls on his head, soft brown eyes, and a charming smile. "I was hoping that I could persuade you to sit next to me at dinner, and perhaps save a dance for me later on."

Annie blushed. She wasn't usually the type of girl that handsome young men paid attention to. She glanced at Elizabeth, who smiled kindly and nodded encouragingly.

"It would be my pleasure, Mr. Diggle." Annie took his arm and sat with him at a table where she could still be watched by her sisters.

"Well, that doesn't happen often," Belle said, her tone sounding slightly offended that the young man, who was probably only eighteen or nineteen, hadn't asked for her company.

"I think it's nice," Elizabeth said. "Annie is a lovely girl and I am happy that she is finally getting some attention." She took AJ's arm and gave it a squeeze. "Some men just don't know how to look at a woman for who she is, not just what she looks like."

AJ smiled in gratitude for her friend. It was very difficult for AJ to get a man's attention as well. It didn't help that she had only recently thinned out, but was still stouter than most other women in town. It was difficult when men only noticed outer beauty at first glance. It also didn't help that AJ had no skill in the art of flirting, unlike Belle and Kate. It was true that, although pretty, Kate wasn't a great beauty, yet she possessed a friendly and flirtatious personality that was able to attract many men.

"What a wonderful setting!" Belle said, spreading some jam on a biscuit and taking a bite. "This jam is amazing!"

"This is the first bit of jam I have had since we left Washington City!" Betty said. "I heard that ice cream is being served later as well."

"Ice cream! Heavens, I cannot wait." Kate said.

AJ looked at the jam. "I wonder if putting the strawberry jam on the ice cream as a topping would taste good." She mused.

"That is such a great idea!" Elizabeth said. "We should try it."

The conversation continued, and it wasn't long before the talk turned to the war.

"Betty, you must hear a great deal of news with your father in such a high position with the Navy," Belle stated.

"Yes, I do, although it's still not always reliable information. The communication in this war leaves much to be desired."

"I believe we can all agree to those words." Belle added.

"Yes. Not long ago, a rumor revolved around a man, a Yankee, that I have been acquainted with." Betty stated.

"Do tell. That sounds interesting." Kate said.

"Yes, a General Burnside is commanding the forces that were expected to come up the Rappahannock. This general was here years ago to stand up as a groomsman for Cousin Dabney. We all went up the river on a pleasure party. I was not yet sixteen at the time. It was my first time as a bridesmaid and my first time at a grown-up party. Obviously, it made a vivid impression on my mind, even to this day. I wonder if he also recalls these interactions."

"He might," Elizabeth said. "That's another interesting aspect of this war. Many Southerners have quite strong ties to Northerners. You may recall that Belle and I have family on both sides."

"Yes, that's true," Belle said. "While I understand why my cousin Charlotte sympathizes with the Yankees, I really do wonder what Cousins Jason, Gregory, Jacob, and Jonah are doing."

"Jason and Gregory are our Cousin Victoria's brothers from Vicksburg. I am fairly certain they are both siding with the Confederacy." Elizabeth explained. "Jacob and Jonah may prove to be more complicated. They're Cousin Bekah's brothers. Their father is an officer in the United States Army. Father heard that he is on a list of high-ranking Federal officers now."

"Who knows where their loyalties are," Belle added. "Jonah definitely had his father's opinions, but Jacob, I would think likely sided with the South, and if I know Bekah, her sympathies lie with the Yankees."

"Jonah was a soldier in the US army before the war broke out, as well as his father. If either brother will fight for the Union, it will be Jonah."

"These are the Petersburg Turners, correct?" AJ clarified.

"Yes," Belle answered.

"Why do they live in Petersburg if their father is a Yankee from Fredericksburg? Why not live here or up North somewhere? Betty asked.

"Well, Aunt Suzanna's family is from Petersburg. They've always used that city as a 'home base' if you will." Belle explained. "Although I would love to have Bekah live close. Other than her Yankee opinions, I quite enjoy her company." Belle smiled at the memory of the last time she had been able to visit with Bekah.

May, 1860
Petersburg, Virginia

"Charlotte and Uncle Hiram are due tomorrow and Victoria and her family should be here on the evening train." Bekah Turner said. "But not Mary. She gave birth to a daughter two weeks ago and is in no condition to travel. Aunt Rachel is staying with her." She smiled and hugged Belle again. "I am so happy to see you! I can't wait to show you around."

"We're glad to be here," Belle answered genuinely. "We are so excited to attend Jonah's wedding and meet his future wife."

"You will love Bethany. She is a sweetheart. She will fit nicely into our family." The women sat down in the parlor. "It has been wonderful having Jonah on leave and at home again. With all of this talk of our country's problems and divisions, I really fear for our whole family."

"What do you mean?" Belle asked. "Charlotte and Uncle Hiram may end up in a separate nation if the South secedes, but the rest of the family would support the Southern cause."

"I'm not so sure," Bekah said softly. "While it is good to have Jonah home like I said, it hasn't been the most peaceful of visits." She sighed. "Jonah and Jacob have been arguing a lot, almost every time they are in the same room."

"Really? That doesn't sound like either one of them." Elizabeth said. Bekah shrugged.

"It's happening all over the country. This will not be an easy time, with all of the talk of secession, and state's rights. Even if secession doesn't erupt into a war, there will be big changes." She replied.

"He wants to preserve the Union." A loud voice said from out in the hallway. "Why can't you see that?" The girls looked up to see a tall, young man walk by the doorway. He was dressed in a white, button-up shirt with blue, army-issue suspenders and white Army-issue pants.

"No, Jonah, Lincoln will tear this country apart if he wins the election." A second young man grabbed the soldier's arm and pulled him around. "Yes, he'll allow slavery in the states where it already exists, that's true, but he has said time and time again that he will not allow slavery to expand into the new territories and states. It's an immense threat to our economy and our way of life." The second man was dressed impeccably, in dark brown pants and a matching jacket covering a red and green tartan patterned waistcoat and white shirt. The only piece of his outfit that was out of place was his slightly askew brown cravat.

Jonah turned to his brother and flung Jacob's hand off his arm. "Yes, Jacob, I've heard that argument time and again, but I have yet to see any proof that will be the case, and quite honestly, having slavery

75

abolished in this country would be a good thing and you know it. That's what you were raised to believe."

"It's not about the morality of slavery, Jonah, it's about rights. The citizens of each state should be able to decide how they will live, what laws should be passed and they should be able to protect their own way of life."

"By tearing the nation in two? If the government allows the south to have their way now, then when will it stop? It seems like each time there's an issue, the North has to give in. Every compromise for the past 30 years has been in favor of the South. You know that. Why are you so blind to all of this?"

"Actually, Jonah, you need to stop following and believing everything Father says just because he says it and you need to start thinking for yourself," Jacob replied.

"What, are you saying? That I'm less of a man just because I agree with our father?"

"No, I'm saying that you need to start thinking for yourself and not believe everything Father tells you is the Gospel truth. You'd better hope you don't get separated from him when the South decides to fight back. Upon further reflection, maybe you should bring him with you on your wedding trip. You may need help knowing how to be a husband."

Jonah shoved Jacob. "What kind of statement is that?"

Jacob returned the shove. "A true one. Have you ever done anything without Father's approval? I'm shocked you were able to romance Bethany at all without him telling you exactly what to do."

"Enough!" Jonah lowered his shoulder and drove it into Jacob's chest, tackling him through the doorway and into the parlor. Belle, Elizabeth, and Bekah all stood and quickly got out of the way as the two continued fighting, Jacob rolling on top of Jonah.

"Jonah, Jacob, stop it this instant!" Bekah said, moving to grab Jacob's shoulders and trying to pull him up.

Matthew and Samuel Turner, who had heard the commotion, burst into the parlor from the adjacent men's sitting room and quickly moved to pull the brothers apart.

"What's wrong with you two?" Their father, Samuel asked. "This is beyond unacceptable. You both should be ashamed of yourselves. Jonah, I am especially disappointed in you."

"I'm sorry Father, but Jacob said..."

"Do not give me excuses. A good soldier will rise up above any taunts that are thrown at him." Samuel said.

"Yes, Sir." Jonah wiped at his split lip.

"And Jacob..." Samuel said. "What are you thinking? It's three days before Jonah's wedding. Why would you try to goad him into a fight?"

"Sorry, Father," Jacob said with sarcasm evident in his voice. "I should have known better than to speak my mind in your house, especially when you're home." He quickly turned to the women. "Excuse me, ladies." Adjusting his jacket, Jacob stormed out of the room. Jonah nodded in acknowledgment to his sister and cousins, then exited as well. Samuel and Matthew shook their heads and started talking in low voices as they went back into the other room. The girls sat back down, slightly flustered about the whole incident.

"Do you see what I mean now? I am so sorry you had to witness that. I cannot believe Jacob would act like that, especially in front of guests. I wish he would stop listening to the other secessionists around here. They are so vocal about states' rights. Secession would be wrong for our country."

"Amen," Elizabeth said.

"I would have to disagree with you there, Bekah. I'm on Jacob's side. The South needs slaves to survive, and we need to make sure that the government knows how we feel. It's all about our rights."

"No, I would always believe first and foremost that the Union should remain one entity. Our ancestors fought for freedom for all of the United States. The South wants to destroy all of the work our ancestors have done to try and make life here good for everyone."

"Well, if the people of the country don't like what's going on, shouldn't they have the right to leave and do things their own way?" Belle argued.

"Not when we agreed to be a united country," Bekah responded. "We all signed a contract, the Constitution."

"We joined a group, we should be able to leave that group whenever we desire to do so," Belle argued. "Besides, WE didn't sign it. Our ancestors did, and they are no longer alive."

"No..." Bekah started a retort, but Elizabeth placed a hand on her arm.

"Don't even bother trying to argue with her, Bekah. You won't win, it's not worth it."

Belle smiled smugly, glad to win yet another argument. Bekah looked like she wanted to say something more, but reconsidered.

1861

Belle refocused on the conversation at the dinner table. Betty was speaking.

"Mother wasn't able to make it, as she was feeling under the weather, so Will and I are going to have to bring Mother a plate of food. This has truly been a wonderful meal." Betty referenced her husband."

"Indeed it has," Belle said, then glanced at the rest of the wedding guests. "I do hope there are enough gentlemen here to dance with. From what I see in this room, it looks as though they will be scarce."

"Oh, I'm sure there will be enough," AJ replied, looking around. She had also noticed the lack of men and had resigned herself to the fact that she may not be dancing at all. When eligible ladies like Belle and Kate were around, AJ felt overlooked. She was used to it. Besides, she would rather be overlooked than mocked and teased, which had happened to her in the past.

The musicians began warming up their instruments. The band was a much smaller group than in years past. The guests finished their meals and, one by one, left the tables to begin mingling more with each other. Mr. Diggle was still paying very close attention to Annie. As Elizabeth observed the couple, Annie introduced Mr. Diggle to their mother. The man was polite-looking and nice. Annie glowed under his attentions. The music started in full and Nannie and George Mercer took the dance floor. Other couples were quick to join them. Belle was immediately asked to dance by a handsome, unknown soldier, and she accepted without hesitation. Elizabeth watched as Mr. Diggle escorted Annie onto the dance floor. It wasn't long before Kate and even AJ had been asked to dance. AJ's partner was George's young cousin who appeared to be around fourteen years old, but AJ looked as though she was enjoying herself.

"Why are you not out on the dance floor, Mrs. Bennett?" Elizabeth quickly turned at the familiar voice, not believing her ears.

"Joshua, what are you doing here?" She threw her arms around his neck and held him tightly. He turned his head and kissed her chin.

"I was able to get a weeklong leave. We're still doing a lot of training, but honestly, it's not looking as though we will be a part of any engagements in the near future."

He pulled back and they each looked at each other. Joshua brushed the side of her face with his fingertips and she covered his hand with hers. He looked different but still as handsome as ever. His hair was longer than she had ever seen it, as it brushed his collar. He had a scruffy, but well-trimmed beard, something that she also rarely saw. His warm, kind eyes and loving smile remained the same.

"What is this?" She touched the hair on his face.

"Well, I could tell you that I'm being smart and growing it long to protect myself. Many men are leaving their beards long, not only to be fashionable, but because they offer some protection for our necks, and they will keep us warm once the colder weather hits."

"Well, that is clever," Elizabeth said.

"It is." Joshua smiled. "But in all honesty, I just haven't bothered to shave or get a haircut. I would prefer to have you take care of that if you don't mind."

"Of course I don't mind," Elizabeth said.

"Joshua!" AJ hurried over to the couple. "It's so good to see you!"

"It's wonderful to see you," Joshua said. "I noticed your dancing partner. I must say I approve, although the age gap causes me some concern."

"Yes, Henry is sweet." AJ smiled. "He would be a good choice for me if he were at least four years older." She shrugged. "How did you get leave? We've been hearing about an impending battle and even Richard Maury couldn't get a furlough to go to his own wedding."

"That is too bad," Joshua said. "I am not sure about Richard. I know that I applied for leave and it was granted. Perhaps different regiments have different rules. I believe he is in the 24th Virginia, while I am in the 30th." Joshua grinned again as Annie hurried over to him and gave him a hug.

"Joshua! You're home! For how long?" Annie had always loved Joshua like another older brother.

"I'll be able to stay for a few days." He replied.

"And what of James? And Father? Were they able to come and visit?"

"They did not get leave just yet," Joshua replied. "However, they may be able to visit soon as well."

Annie nodded, then glanced over at Belle, who was chatting with a handsome soldier as he led her to the dance floor. Miriam looked over and the moment she recognized Joshua, she also hastened over, but Belle continued to dance with her partner, even though Annie was sure she had noticed Joshua's appearance.

"Mrs. Turner, it is wonderful to see you." Joshua hugged his mother-in-law.

"The children are at Turner's Glenn right now, Joshua," Elizabeth explained. "Would you like to head out there immediately, or stay here. I leave the decision to you."

"Well, they're likely already asleep, and I do enjoy dancing with my wife." He took her hand and kissed it. "We can go see them first thing in the morning."

"All right." Elizabeth glanced at Belle. "I'm so glad Belle came right over to greet her brother-in-law." She said, annoyed.

79

"Elizabeth, dear, put yourself in her shoes," Joshua said. "I'm home, but her beloved Samuel will never be coming home. Seeing men on leave has to be difficult for her." He squeezed her hand.

"Well said, Joshua." Miriam agreed. "I believe I will be heading back to Turner's Glenn now. I would like to see Max, Meri, and Lainey before they go to bed and write letters to your father and James. You wouldn't mind taking some packages back to camp with you, would you, Joshua?" She asked.

"Of course not," Joshua assured her. Miriam smiled, then turned toward Annie.

"Tell Belle that I will send Daniel back for the two of you. Stay as long as you would like."

"Yes, Mother," Annie said, as she left Elizabeth and Joshua alone together.

Sunday, October 27, 1861
Fredericksburg

Elizabeth squeezed her husband's arm as they walked toward the church. It was so nice having him home for the past few days. She didn't even want to think about how hard it was going to be when he left again. Benjamin walked proudly next to his father and Joshua held Hannah in his other arm.

The family had stayed in town last night so that it would be easier to go to services in the morning. Citizens, especially children, around the city were still falling ill with scarlet fever. The disease had also been spreading to a few of the farms and homes surrounding the town. Elizabeth decided to no longer keep her children at Turner's Glenn. The latest child to fall ill was Betty Maury's daughter, Nannie Belle. Betty had told Elizabeth that it was the measles and not Scarlet Fever but Elizabeth knew that the measles could also be deadly.

Before they entered the church, the Bennett family stood outside and conversed with other churchgoers. It was a warm and sunny day, nice for late October. Many of the men wanted to speak with Joshua about his time as a soldier.

Just as the congregation was about to head into the church, the sound of hundreds of horses pounding their hooves on the ground could be heard. They instantly knew it was a military unit. The crowd gathered at the side of the road, straining to see if these soldiers were Union or Confederate. Joshua, who was wearing his army-issue uniform, tensed.

"They're our men." He finally breathed a sigh of relief when the riders came closer. "A cavalry unit."

"What's a cav-il-ry, Papa?" Benjamin asked.

"A cavalry is a unit made up of the soldiers who ride horses when they fight," Joshua explained. "They also do a lot of scouting, trying to find out where the Federals are and telling our generals what they discover on their travels."

"Can I be a cavalry when I grow up?" Benjamin asked. Like his Aunt Laine, Benjamin loved anything that had to do with horses. "That's what I want to do when I'm old enough." Elizabeth gave Joshua a concerned look.

"Well, Benjamin, that is a possibility, but hopefully the war will be done long before you're old enough to join."

"Yeah, I guess," Benjamin answered, then watched with wide eyes as the men rode through town.

"Where are you boys all from?" Called out a spectator.

"North Carolina." One of the soldiers replied.

"Well, good luck to ya'all." The man said with a wave.

Elizabeth saw Mr. Randolph, the pastor, gesturing to the congregation. "It looks as though Mr. Randolph wants to get the service started." She noted.

"With all the excitement out here, he may have better luck trying to herd a dozen cats into the church than to get the rest of the congregation inside."

Elizabeth grinned at the image that had popped into her head.

"Well, I suppose we can at least set a good example and start heading in ourselves," Joshua said as he led his family into the church.

"It's so empty in here," Elizabeth said as she looked around. They were the only people in the church except for two elderly couples. The Bennetts slipped into a pew and Joshua pulled out his Bible and checked his pocket watch.

"Yes, it is. I'm guessing the service will be delayed a bit longer, at least until everyone settles down."

"Well, I'm okay with that," Elizabeth said as she laid her head on Joshua's shoulders.

Sunday, November 3, 1861
Bennett Home

"Whereas, with grateful thanks we recognize His hand and acknowledge that not unto us, but unto Him, belongeth the victory, and in humble dependence upon His almighty strength, and trusting in the justness of our purpose, we appeal to Him that He may set at naught the efforts of our enemies, and humble them to confusion and shame."

Elizabeth tried not to roll her eyes at the words that AJ read. President Jefferson Davis had issued a proclamation to the Confederate States of America and it had been printed in most Confederate

81

newspapers. AJ continued reading, and Elizabeth tried listening, but she lost focus on what AJ was reading.

AJ smiled when she finished. "I can support a day of prayer to support our troops and Southern Rights."

Elizabeth couldn't refrain from sighing and unfortunately, AJ heard it and set down the paper. "What was that for, Elizabeth?"

"I'm sorry. I know how you feel about slavery and states' rights, I just can't agree with you, though. I simply cannot understand how you can be such a good Christian and believe that it is okay to keep slaves. It doesn't make sense to me. I just don't know how you can justify slavery." Elizabeth was frustrated. Even in church that morning, Mr. Randolph had mentioned Mr. Davis's decree. It was all Elizabeth could do not to get up and walk out. But she hadn't wanted to make a scene.

AJ shook her head. "Elizabeth, slavery is even discussed in the Bible. St. Paul's letter to the Ephesians tells slaves to obey their masters." She said.

"Anyone can take many of the verses in the Bible and give them a different interpretation. If slavery is so approved by God and the Bible, then why did Moses bring the Israelites out of slavery in the Book of Exodus?"

"I'm not sure about many of God's plans, Elizabeth, and you're right, people twist the words of the Bible all the time. The Good Book clearly says 'Thou Shalt Not Kill', but that didn't stop John Brown from plotting to murder slaveholders in Kansas a few years ago. 'In the name of God', he said." AJ spoke in a harsh tone that Elizabeth seldom heard from her.

"I'm not saying that John Brown and his sons and other followers were justified in killing anyone," Elizabeth said. "I would agree that what they did was murder. There has been violence on both sides. And you can't tell me that there are not Christians on the Northern side who are praying for a victory also. Which side will be victorious, AJ? Whose prayer will God answer?"

"The right side. Our side. Your own husband is fighting for our side. How can that not be the side you want to support?"

Elizabeth squeezed her eyes shut, trying to stop the tears from falling down her face. "Don't you think I know that, AJ? But Joshua is fighting to keep his family safe, not to support slavery." Elizabeth rubbed her temples. "Oh, I don't even know why we are discussing this, AJ. We both know this is something that we may never agree on."

"We'll just have to agree to disagree." AJ put a hand on Elizabeth's shoulder. "We're too good of friends to argue on this subject. So many families and friendships have been torn apart by this war already. At least we're on the same side when it comes to supporting our armies. You love Joshua too much to really want the Yankees to win."

"I just want this war to be over, AJ. I want my family back together." Elizabeth didn't want to admit that she felt as though her real loyalty was to the North.

"We can surely agree on that fact, and if the Confederacy is just left alone, well, that's all I really want. Elizabeth," AJ put a hand on Elizabeth's arm and added in a quiet tone. "Elizabeth, you're my friend and I care about you, so I have to tell you. Please be careful with whom you share your opinions on slavery with. I don't want you hurt. People in this town can be vicious. Look at poor Mr. Hunnicutt. He just might be the most hated man in Fredericksburg because of his Unionist views."

James Hunnicutt was a minister and editor of the local paper, *The Christian Banner*. The paper had been popular with the citizens until Hunnicutt began speaking and writing against secession. With his unapologetic views, the townspeople seemed less willing to support him or the newspaper. Others who dared to speak out against slavery or the Confederacy were also being ostracized. There hadn't been any physical violence yet, but AJ feared that it would only be a matter of time.

"I know that. I can't do or say anything that would put my children at risk. I have to think of them first, and Joshua's reputation, of course."

"And you." AJ stood and hugged her friend. "This world would not be nearly as sweet without you in it."

"Thank you, AJ. I feel the same about you and I'm sure I would not feel safe enough to have this conversation with anyone else."

"Well, that is exactly what friends are for," AJ replied with a smile.

Friday, November 8, 1861
Turner's Glenn

Kate smiled as one of the house slaves led her into the parlor, then left to notify Belle of her guest. She wouldn't be a bit surprised if her friend was still abed, even though it was almost the noon hour. After just a minute, Kate was pleased and surprised to see Elizabeth walk through the parlor door and smile.

"Kate! Welcome. How are you doing?"

"I'm doing well, Elizabeth. I had no idea you were here or I would have asked for you to come down for a visit as well."

"I have been staying here occasionally. I still don't want Hannah and Benjamin in town any more than they have to be, what with scarlet fever still coursing through town. I hope being out here will keep them safer."

"I agree with you. If my niece or nephews lived in town, I would certainly encourage my sisters to move out to Moss Neck to lessen the chance of them getting ill. I am happy to say that Bertie and I may have convinced Nettie to move in with us. It will be nice for several reasons, but the best part for me would be having the boys, especially Gardiner, around."

"That would be wonderful, and it would surely help you," Elizabeth said, sitting down. "Are you still splitting time between the two homes?"

"Yes," Kate replied. "I am moving from Bertie at Moss Neck to Nettie at Echo Dell every week or so. I much prefer to stay at Moss Neck. I have to keep their spirits up and assist wherever I can, and I dearly love the children." Kate smiled. "I must confess that Gardiner is especially dear to me." She sobered. "This epidemic is so frightening. I heard the news that Betty's Nannie Belle has the fever. I am praying for her and all of the patients to get well soon. I have lost count of the number of children who have died of this dreadful outbreak."

"Too many," Elizabeth replied. "Although one child lost is too many."

"Very true," Kate said. "They say that the epidemic is spreading more. There have been reports of Scarlet Fever as far away as Richmond." Kate glanced up as Belle entered the parlor. "Belle, I wasn't sure you would even be up this early."

Belle gave her friend a sweet smile. "Of course I'm awake, my dear friend. I knew you were coming." Belle sat. "So what's the news, Miss Corbin? Soldiers still fill the land between my home and yours, correct?"

"They are, and all our boys are ready to defend us from an attack if needed," Kate replied. "I did hear that the Union navy was heavily damaged on Friday night when we had that terrible storm. Of course, the Confederacy is saying that it was divine providence and proof that God is on our side."

Belle looked at Elizabeth, almost daring her to say something. Instead, Elizabeth stood. "Kate, I am sorry that we cannot talk more, but I want to spend time with my children since I will be heading home after dinner today. I need to make Eric and his mother dinner as well. I fear Mrs. Dawson is getting worse."

"It was good seeing you, Elizabeth. We should get together in town soon. Once the sickness passes." Kate said.

"Yes, I would enjoy that. We could work on some clothing to send to the men." Elizabeth smiled, then left.

"Can't you ever just be nice to your sister?" Kate asked Belle.

"Whatever do you mean?" Belle asked innocently.

"I saw the look you gave her earlier. We both know her feelings about the war. I probably shouldn't have even said what I did, but it was almost as if you wanted her to leave."

"Well, that's just not true, and I am nice to her. Really. Elizabeth is the one who always acts as if her family is the only thing that matters. She has the perfect husband, the perfect children, and she acts so perfect and noble that she can not only keep her house, but she can now take care of old Mrs. Dawson and Eric."

Kate sat back in her chair. "If I didn't know better, I would say that you're jealous of Elizabeth."

"Hardly." Belle laughed. "I may envy the fact that she was able to marry a man who dotes on her, but that is it. As you well know, Kate, with Samuel's untimely death, my future was taken from me before it was even started."

"Yes, and that was horrible, but you didn't seem too broken up about it at Nannie Herndon's wedding. Did you even acknowledge that your brother-in-law was there? Or were you too busy dancing with every eligible man there?"

"A few who were not eligible." Belle smiled. "No, Kate. I had to keep company with those men at the risk of being left alone. Elizabeth had Joshua, you were spending time with Mr. Heth, and Annie had Mr. Diggle. Even AJ was having fun and talking with a variety of other guests."

Kate shook her head. "Belle, I feel as though those are excuses. You could have gone over and at least acknowledged him."

"I did. Eventually." Belle said. She stood and walked over to the window, looking toward the direction of Richmond. "Kate, everyone thinks I'm made of stone. I know that. I try hard not to show my emotions, but I do have them. Knowing that Joshua was home on leave and knowing that my betrothed would never be coming home again? It hurt. A great deal. I just felt that there was too much...I don't know how to describe it. Was I happy for my sister? Yes, I was, but is it so wrong for me to want to be happy too?"

"You can be happy again, Belle. This war has changed many things for us, but we have to have faith that God will see us through."

"You sound like my sister." Belle scoffed. "Or AJ."

"Well, maybe it is because they're right."

"Perhaps. I'm just not sure about the whole 'God cares about us' idea. Obviously, some higher being created our world and made it work. I just don't feel it in my life." She shrugged. "I don't know."

"Well, I hope, for your sake, that someday, you will feel it."

Sunday, December 15, 1861
Turner's Glenn

"I absolutely love the Christmas season!" AJ said, entering the Turner house. It felt warm inside. Her breath had been visible in the crisp air outside. She loved that feeling. The family had done their best to decorate for the holidays especially since the Bennett family would be staying. The scarlet fever epidemic continued and the death toll continued to rise.

Benjamin ran up to AJ and gave her a hug.

"Is Liberty here too?" He asked, excitedly.

"She is," AJ replied. She's with Meri right now. They're putting some finishing touches on the garland out on the porch railing."

"Yay!" Benjamin shouted and ran out the door.

"Benjamin, your coat!" Elizabeth called out, coming into the entryway with a crate of decorations. She shook her head. "I'm doing all I can to keep him healthy, and then he runs out into the cold without any warm clothing."

"It's not that cold," AJ said, taking her cloak off and hanging it on a peg. "He'll be fine. Besides, I've heard that the epidemic is waning."

"Waning, but not over." Elizabeth pointed out, setting the crate down.

"True," AJ replied. "I thought we were going to bake some cinnamon and molasses cookies today. It looks like you are all too busy decorating for the holidays."

"We're doing both," Elizabeth said. "Meri and Liberty will help Mother with the children in decorating. Mother loves that part of Christmas. Max and Eric are out getting a tree right now. You, and I, along with Belle, Annie, and Kate, when she gets here, will work on the cookies. Mother told all of the slaves they could have part of the day off, so that means Annie is in charge of the kitchen."

"Just as she always wanted to be," AJ said with a smile as Kate walked in, followed by Janie, Kate's niece, and Gardiner, and Parke, Kate's nephews.

"Good afternoon. I hope it's okay that I brought the children." Kate said, knowing that Miriam Turner loved being surrounded by young ones.

"Of course!" Mrs. Turner said, entering the room with Hannah. "More hands will make the work much more enjoyable."

Kate smiled and turned to follow Elizabeth and AJ down into the kitchen.

"Belle will be down soon, and Annie is already starting to prepare the kitchen for baking," Elizabeth said. "Although she'll also be working on dinner. As I said, Mother was very insistent about the servants having the rest of the day off, especially Ruthie."

"That's good of your mother to do," AJ said. I would like to do that with Andre and Gage, but there is so much work to do with Father and

Nathaniel gone. It is good to know that I can leave them and trust them to do the work when I go out and am not around."

"That is benevolent," Kate said, then looked up and smiled as Belle entered the room.

"Good afternoon everyone!" She said with a smile. "I am so glad that we could get together again this year. This may be one of my favorite holiday traditions."

"Mine too." Elizabeth agreed. Getting together to bake and decorate was something the four of them did annually, probably for the past five years. They all immediately started to work on their individual tasks.

"It's a good thing the fighting has been far enough away," AJ said. "We are still able to get all of the ingredients we need. I would bet that some areas where the armies are wintering will be busy keeping the men fed and clothed."

"I'm just glad we haven't had a disaster like the fire down in Charleston, South Carolina last Wednesday," Elizabeth said. "Mr. Randolph brought it up in church this morning. They say the fire burned for three days and left more than a quarter of the city in ruins."

"Fr. Schmitz talked about it as well," AJ said. "Two large hotels, the theater, St. Andrew's Hall and the Cathedral were destroyed, along with about 600 homes. They say General Lee and some of his staff witnessed the fire. Luckily, no one was reported as being killed."

"I find that hard to believe," Belle said. "All that damage? It's incredible that no one died."

"It's a miracle, to be honest." Kate murmured.

"Do they know how it started?" Belle asked.

"The rumor is some slave refugees had a fire going and they let it get out of control," AJ said.

Of course, they would blame it on the Negroes. Elizabeth thought but was unwilling to bring up her thoughts or create an argument.

"We'll be taking a special collection next week to benefit the people of Charleston," Elizabeth said.

"Same at St. Mary's," AJ said. "President Davis sent a special message to Congress, telling them that the Confederate States need to help South Carolina immediately. We owe them a debt that should be paid at once. They are the ones that took the first steps in gaining Southern independence for all of us."

"I understand that," Belle said. "We should help. I'm sure they would do the same for us."

"Most likely." AJ agreed. The savory smell of cinnamon and other spices mixed with the fresh smell of wood smoke brought a smile to Elizabeth's face. She loved the holiday season. She couldn't wait until the magic of Christmas Eve.

The women continued working and making small talk. It wasn't long before Belle, AJ, and Elizabeth noticed something wrong with Kate. Belle brought it up first.

"Kate, you're rather quiet today. Have you heard from Stockton Heth as of late?"

Kate glanced up from mixing the gingerbread. "No, not any more than usual." At the looks on her friends' faces, she explained more. "He is a good friend, and I can, at times, see a future with him. Other times, however, I'm not as sure. I feel like marriage is something you should be absolutely sure of." She shook her head. "No, I am quiet because I am upset. While in town earlier, I heard that another boy succumbed to the fever. This time, it was Greyson Gray."

"Greyson? Not Samuel's nephew?" Belle exclaimed. "How will the Grays be able to handle another death?"

"I agree, it is so hard," Kate said. "I just keep thinking about how horrible it all is."

Elizabeth glanced toward the stairs that led from the kitchen to the main level of the house. "Greyson...are you sure? Greyson is one of Max's best friend. How...how have we not heard about this yet?"

"It sounds like it just happened. Maybe last night, maybe early this morning. I'm not sure." Kate said. "It's just so hard to understand. Every time I hear of a child that has died, I imagine how I would feel if I lost Janie, Parke or Gardiner. I just don't know that I would be able to handle it. And they're not even my children. I can't imagine loving my own children more than I love those three. I know that someday, God-willing, I will have children of my own, but even then, I just could not bear to lose them."

"That is how I feel every day," Elizabeth said. "My children are the most precious things on earth to me. It has been very difficult having them stay here since the outbreak began. I would rather have them safe here and struggle to be apart from them than to have them be in town and be exposed to the disease."

"I still don't understand why you don't just stay here all the time," Belle said. "It would make things easier for everyone."

"Yes, but I still want to be able to take care of Eric and his mother. I would like to bring her out here, for the holidays, but she is refusing. Some things we just have to do, whether it's convenient or not."

"I feel like we'll have a lot more than just inconveniences in the next year or so," AJ said. "We will just have to do our best to get through."

Wednesday, December 25, 1861
Turner's Glenn Plantation

"I want to sit by Liberty!" Benjamin said. The Bennetts and Turners had invited the Prentiss sisters to Christmas dinner. Benjamin and Hannah had been very excited about seeing Liberty, as always.

"I want to sit next to her!" Hannah said.

"Oh, you two. Liberty has two sides. You can both sit by her." Elizabeth said, smiling at her two children. Last night and this morning had been almost perfect. The only thing that would have made it better was if Joshua, Matthew, and James were home. She knew she should be thankful that she had been able to spend time with Joshua a few months ago, and that he was still alive and healthy. Many families would never have their loved ones home again, like her own sister.

"Do you think Papa got the present that we sent him?" Benjamin asked. They had mailed a new shirt, new gloves and hat, as well as some hand-drawn cards from the children.

"I'm sure that he did," Elizabeth replied, her words more confident than her thoughts. She hadn't received a letter from him since they had sent the package, but she knew he would write whenever he could. The mail was unpredictable, yet she had been pleasantly surprised by how often she had heard from him. However, she still felt a void in her life. Nothing could take away from his actual presence.

Belle came down into the parlor and immediately noticed her brother. Max was sitting in one of the window seats, staring at the light blanket of snow.

"Hey, Max." She placed her hand on his shoulder. "How are you doing?" He turned and tried to hide the tears in his eyes.

"I just keep thinking of Greyson. I want to have fun and enjoy Christmas and my presents and do things with Benjamin and Hannah, but just when I start having fun, I remember him, and I feel bad because I'm here having fun and he's...he's...dead. Can he even have fun anymore?"

Belle took a deep breath. She was probably not the best person to be talking about this with Max, but she felt that she could help him in some ways.

"I know what you mean." She sat next to him and pulled him onto her lap. "I feel the same way about Samuel. I know I might not act like it, but I really do miss him and what I could have had with him. He was a good friend to me."

"Yeah, but you still have good friends. Miss Kate and Miss AJ and Elizabeth are your best friends. Greyson was mine."

"I know." Belle pulled him closer. "I am so sorry that you lost him, but you know what?" Max looked at her. "Greyson is in heaven now, and you can be sure that he'll be watching out for you up there, and

89

having fun while doing so. Which means you can have fun down here. I don't think Greyson will mind."

"Thanks, Belle." Max hugged her tightly. "I'm glad you know how I feel. Not that I'm happy that Samuel died, just glad that there's someone I can talk to."

"I know what you mean, Max. I feel the same way and I'm glad that I can help you."

Max released her, then stood. "I'm gonna go play with Benjamin and Hannah." He jogged out the door, almost running over his mother. Miriam, who had been standing in the doorway, smiled at Belle.

"That was very kind of you. Max needed that."

"Well, I'm glad that my loss can help someone," Belle replied. "I'm glad that my pain can be good for something."

"The way that you've been acting lately, it's hard to believe that you are still hurting. Your attitude has had a complete reversal from just after Samuel's death. It's like you're completely back to your old self. I am not sure that is a good thing."

"I'm fine, Mama, and I am not sure why or what happened to make me feel so normal again?" Belle felt her mother was the one person that she could really open up to, provided her mother had time for an individual conversation. "I thought I loved Samuel. He was a good man. I know he slightly misled me about Father giving his permission to marry me, but I believe that Samuel really just wanted to marry me before he went off to fight." Belle paused. "Mama, sometimes I just don't know what's wrong with me. I'm 22 years old. Most women my age are married. Elizabeth had both of her children by the time she was my age, and Samuel is the only man who has ever shown serious interest in me. Is there something wrong with me?"

"There's nothing wrong with you. I believe that you intimidate certain men with your beauty and charm, with your strong personality, but I also believe the men of Fredericksburg have known for a while that Samuel had his eye on you. Have there been any other men that you've fancied?"

Belle's mind flashed to Nathaniel Prentiss. The common farmer would never be up to her standards, no matter how much she enjoyed his company. He would never be able to care for her in the way that she was accustomed. She could be friends with him and of course, his sisters, AJ and Liberty, but to marry into the family? She shook her head. "No, Mama. Not really."

"Well, it's probably not the best time for you to begin a new romance anyways," Miriam said. "With the war going on and all. I know they say that it won't last long, but when it does end, you can get a new start with another young man. You deserve only the best."

"Thank you, Mama, and thank you for talking with me. I really do appreciate it."

"Anytime, my dear." Miriam rubbed Belle's arm. "It's probably about time for our guests to arrive. Shall we finish our preparations for them?"

"Of course," Belle said, and the two made their way to the dining room.

Dinner was simple but still enjoyable. Daniel had shot a turkey, and Ruthie had outdone herself yet again in the kitchen. Elizabeth tried to enjoy herself, but it was difficult not to think of Joshua. He loved Christmas. Going to church last night had been difficult. She couldn't help but think of her husband and his love of that particular service. She prayed that he was safe and that he had been able to worship somewhere. Maybe he had even been able to bring James with him.

"AJ, Liberty, did you enjoy your Christmas service today?" Miriam asked between bites.

"It was very nice, as always. Thank you for asking and thank you again, so much for inviting us to your wonderful family dinner. It was so kind of you."

"The more, the merrier," Miriam replied. "Besides, you girls and your brother and father have been like family for quite some time, especially since your dear mother's passing. I will not lie to you, AJ, before James was so involved with Nicole Austin, I had hopes that you would become an official member of the Turner family."

AJ smiled politely. She too had entertained thoughts of marrying James Turner once upon a time.

"Well, it is still possible," Liberty said. "James isn't married yet, and there is another way our families could be joined. Nathaniel could marry Belle, or Annie, or even Meri."

"Don't you think of trying to get me to marry your brother," Meri said. "I will admit that he is quite handsome, but he's way too old for me."

"Ten years isn't that much older." Liberty turned towards Belle and added. "Anyways, if Nathaniel were to marry any of the Turner women, it would be you, Belle."

"Would it, now?" Belle asked. She always had a soft spot in her heart for Nathaniel, as she had been reminded of when she was talking to her mother. Could she possibly lower her standards and her aspirations to marry a man who would never be more than a farmer? She suspected that Nathaniel had fancied her at one time. It was something she might have to consider.

"We were in town last night for services," Elizabeth said, changing the subject. "There didn't seem to be any news. Was there anything this morning?"

"Not really," AJ replied. "We did pray for all of the families who are suffering through the epidemic, especially the new family from Germany. David Heller and his wife Mary lost both of their daughters last night."

"Heller, the new grocer?" Miriam asked. "Both daughters? On the same night and Christmas Eve at that? How horrible. It's unimaginable."

"How old were they?" Elizabeth asked, her voice choking as tears welled in her eyes.

"They said Mary was eight and Katherine was seven," AJ replied. "I am sorry to deliver such sad news."

"On Christmas Eve. That's heartbreaking." Miriam shook her head. The group was silent for a moment, almost like everyone was saying a silent prayer. Finally, Liberty looked over at Benjamin.

"So, Benjamin. What did Santa bring you?"

Benjamin smiled broadly. "A set of dominos! Max has a set here and I love playing him. Now, I have a set of my own. I can't wait for Papa to come home again so I can play him."

Liberty smiled, then turned to Hannah. "What about you, Hannah-Bear?"

"A new doll!" She smiled. "She is wearing a pink dress!"

"A pink dress? Well, that's just perfect." Liberty looked across the table. "And what did Max the gentleman get?"

"I got a new ball with a leather cover. What I really wanted was a drum and drumsticks. I want one in case I'm ever able to go and be a drummer in the army. I need to practice."

"Santa obviously didn't agree with that request," Miriam said.

"I guess," Max said, dejected. "But I'd still like to be a drummer."

"I wanna be a drummer boy too," Benjamin said.

"Well, God-willing, the war will be long over by the time you two are old enough," Elizabeth said. She couldn't ever imagine sending her son to war. Letting Joshua enlist was hard enough, but her son? Elizabeth glanced at her own mother. How did she manage to send both James, her son and Matthew, her husband to war? It had to be the most difficult thing she could think of, short of losing either one of them. She withheld a sigh. Oh, why was this war even happening? And would their lives ever get back to normal?

Friday, December 27, 1861
Bennett Home

"My Dearest Elizabeth,

It is hard to believe that Christmas has come and gone while we are separated. As always, I miss you and the children every day.

Our Savior's birthday was a quiet affair here. Nothing much was done but we tried to make it special. I wish that I could send you and the children something, but, unfortunately, I have nothing to give and even if I did, there would be no way of knowing that the package would make it to you.

I can't tell you where we are stationed for the winter, but it is not far. We are encamped pretty tightly together. I do enjoy the fact that we have a more permanent camp. It is nice to get to know my fellow soldiers a little bit more, and it is nice to sleep in a hut rather than just a tent. Luckily, my talent with metalwork is helping me assist others in making more solid huts in camp.

Winter camps are set up much like small villages. We have streets, sutlers' shops, and of course, churches. Some men even have their slaves or families with them. I miss you, terribly but I am glad you are far away from the war and camp life, as this is no place for a family in my opinion. I do wonder if some of the winter's sickness comes from these closed-in quarters.

The worst part for me and everyone is boredom. We continue drilling, we keep the camp in order, we have religious services, tell stories, and your brother and I even had a snowball fight with some of the other men the other day. James's favorite pastime has become card playing. I know that it is something he partook in back home before the war, but with all of the free time, I fear he may become addicted. Some of the games are harmless, and I have sat in on a game or two, but it is something that slightly worries me. At least he hasn't fallen into the vice of drunkenness that many have.

Give the children a hug and a kiss from me. I love you all and miss you desperately. I long for the day when I can hold you in my arms.

Elizabeth sighed and withheld tears. It didn't appear as though Joshua had received the Christmas package that she and the children had sent. It was, perhaps, still in transit, but she doubted it. The mail was completely unreliable. She was, in fact, surprised that this letter she had just read had gotten to her so soon. Unfortunately, the shirt, hat, and gloves she had sent would be coveted items for a lot of men, and she had a feeling they had been either confiscated or intercepted and stolen. The cards were only sentimental to him. She should have sent them separately.

93

"Mrs. Bennett! A letter from your Joshua, I hope." Elizabeth turned to see Betty Maury approach her.

"Yes, it is," Elizabeth said, forcing a smile on her face. "And how was your holiday?"

"Overall, it was quite nice. Although the Trent affair did not have quite the result I and many others were hoping for."

"I'm sorry, I am unfamiliar with that," Elizabeth said, pulling her cloak closer. "What is the Trent affair?" If Elizabeth were to guess, she would believe it had something to do with naval affairs. Betty often had that information because her father was an officer in the Navy.

"Ah, you have some catching up to do," Betty said. "No matter, I know all of the details. The Yankee Navy illegally captured two Confederate diplomats from a British ship coming from Havana, Cuba. This was back in November. The British steamer's name was Trent and our two diplomats that were taken, Misters Mason and Slidell, were carried to Fortress Monroe and held there. Britain was not happy about this because they are not formally involved with either side in this war. Father and I were hoping that this would cause Great Britain to declare war on the United States, or that they would at least come in on our side of this war."

"That would definitely help end this conflict more quickly," Elizabeth said.

"Large meetings were held in London and Liverpool. They felt as though their country had been insulted by the Yankees. Queen Victoria even got involved and held a cabinet meeting and she demanded the return of Mason, Slidell, and the other Secretaries that had been captured."

"My goodness," Elizabeth said. "I cannot believe this is the first I have heard of this."

"Yes, well, it came down to the Yankees having to choose between public disgrace and a war with England. From the tone of their papers, it sounded like they would choose the latter. The end was in sight!"

"Clearly, that didn't happen," Elizabeth said, disappointed.

"No. On Christmas Eve, we heard that the Yankee Government had decided to return our two men and the others. So now, we will have to fight this out by ourselves, as England will remain neutral for the time being."

"That's too bad. We could have used the help of the British." Elizabeth said.

"Well, it is still possible. I believe one of the main issues is the fact that they do not want to support a nation that depends on slavery as much as we do. I believe that they will eventually come to our side. I mean, the war is being fought for Southern Rights. Slavery may be a part of that, but this war is about so much more."

"Yes, that's true," Elizabeth said. Would Joshua have enlisted if the Confederate cause was strictly for keeping slaves? She didn't know. "How is everything with your family?"

"Everything is going well. Nannie Belle had me worried over Christmas again. She had taken cold on Christmas Eve but is much improved, and you? Are your children still staying at Turner's Glenn?"

"Yes. People may not believe me, but I truly believe that it is safer for them out there. I am sad to say that Mrs. Dawson is not going to live much longer. Taking care of her is the main reason I am staying in town. I need to watch out for Eric. He may be mature for his age, but he is still just a boy."

"Indeed, you have been so kind to help them. I must confess, I don't recall how your families even became close.

"I met Mrs. Dawson at church. It was quite easy to see that she and her son needed help. Joshua gave Eric work doing chores in the blacksmith shop and they haven't stopped working together since."

"Ah, yes, that makes sense," Betty said. "What will happen to him once his mother passes?"

"Eric knows that he will always have a home with us. Joshua and I have both made that clear to him. I believe that he will stay here and help Joshua with the blacksmith shop, even when the war is over."

"When the war is over," Betty said. "Hopefully, that day comes sooner rather than later."

Part 2:
1862

Saturday, January 19, 1862
Prentiss Farm

Belle knocked twice before opening the door to the Prentiss home.

"AJ, are you home?" She walked into the front room, then crossed into the kitchen. AJ sat at the kitchen table, sewing buttons onto a shirtwaist.

"I'm here, Belle." She greeted her friend with a smile. "It's nice to see you on my side of the river for a change."

"I come over here once in a while. I definitely enjoy seeing Chatham as I pass by. I have some good memories of wonderful parties there. Speaking of Chatham, how is your cousin, Betty doing?" AJ's relatives owned the impressive Georgian-style home that perched on Stafford Heights overlooking the Rappahannock River. From the house, a person had a wonderful view of the entire city of Fredericksburg.

"As far as I know, they are well. J. Horace is aide-de-camp to General Daniel Ruggles and Betty and the children have moved to southwest Virginia to stay with another family. They fear the war will come to the area, what with us being between Washington City and Richmond."

"I'm not sure that will actually happen, AJ. Our men simply will not allow it."

"Well, I hope you're right." AJ poked her finger with the needle. "Ouch! I hate buttons." She set the shirtwaist down and stuck her finger in her mouth. When she removed her finger, she asked: "Any news from town as you passed by?"

"Not much. The accused spy, Rose O'Neill Greenhow is in the news again. She has been transferred from house arrest to Old Capitol Prison in Washington."

"Sent to prison? My goodness." AJ commented.

"They say she helped our side win the Battle of Manassas."

"Incredible," AJ said. "How amazing would it be to say that you were able to help our army win a battle? Or do something so important you could help win the war or change the course of the war?"

"Do you have aspirations of war glory?" Belle asked. "You're the wrong sex for that, my friend."

"Being a female never stopped Joan of Arc or this Miss Greenhow." AJ pointed out. "Anyways, I don't want glory or fame. I would just like to find some way to help the Southern cause. I wouldn't need any recognition for it."

"Unlike some of the men," Belle said, thinking of Samuel and James and their desire to make a name for themselves.

"Well, not all men are like that," AJ said. "Some of them just want to do what they know is right, and if I get the chance, I won't throw away an opportunity to do that myself."

"Even if it means social disgrace and Federal prison?" Belle asked.

"Even then," AJ said. "I will do my part and do what it takes to help us defeat the Yankees. We are in the right here."

Tuesday, February 12, 1862
Turner Home

"Disaster and defeat from all sides," Belle said, tossing a newspaper onto Elizabeth's kitchen table as she sat down.

"These past few days have been miserable and anxious. I wish I would hear from Joshua. As far as I know, the 30th hasn't been sent into battle and they're still in winter camp. Oh, I miss him so much!"

"I didn't think there would even be any fighting during the winter months, but we've lost Roanoke Island, which, according to this article, is a vital, strategic point. It puts many North Carolinians in danger."

"I'm afraid the Federals will continue gaining ground in the South, and that cannot be good. It will only cause a strain on the citizens that live there."

"Agreed." Belle turned the paper and read a bit more. "More bad news for the Confederacy out west. The Yankees have pushed into North Alabama as far as Florence. It says here the Yankee's plan for winning is to surround the Southern coastline and crush the Confederacy like a "giant anaconda" would its prey." She shook her head. "That will never happen, too bad for the North. Our soldiers will be able to overcome this strategy. I have complete confidence in victory. With you and your praying and the ability of our soldiers, we should have no problems defeating the enemy."

"They could be your prayers too," Elizabeth said, taking the opportunity to bring this up to her sister.

"I don't know, Elizabeth." Belle sounded slightly exasperated. "You always bring this up. I'll be honest with you. There are times when I want to have more faith that God is right here, helping me with everything, but I'm not sure that I can fully...accept the idea."

"Well, you know I am here if you ever want to talk about it." Elizabeth reminded her.

"I do know that," Belle replied thoughtfully. "Perhaps someday."

"Perhaps when the men come home, you and James and the whole family can make going to church a weekly habit."

"I wouldn't be opposed to that." Belle's smile was uncharacteristically vulnerable. "Not really." She thought a moment, her demeanor changed. "Do you believe Samuel is...in heaven?"

"According to Joshua, Samuel did believe in God and had attended services with him every week prior to getting sick. I would have to say yes. Samuel is in heaven. He's probably spending some fun time with his nephew."

"I suppose that could be so," Belle replied. "I hope so."

Wednesday, February 19, 1862
Turner's Glenn

"Fort Donelson is lost," Elizabeth said, sitting in the parlor of Turner's Glenn. Her mother, Belle, and Annie looked at her, disappointment evident in their face.

"I thought we had the victory," Annie said. "When I came into town Sunday to go to church with you, they were saying we won."

"They were mistaken again," Elizabeth said. She held Hannah close to her, leaning back in her chair. "The Federals took all our men, arms, and equipment. It fell Monday. It's been reported that 15,000 men were captured, including three of our generals."

"My goodness. So many disasters, especially out west." Miriam commented.

"Where is Fort Donelson again?" Belle asked. It was hard to remember all of the geographical details.

"Tennessee," Elizabeth replied. "The Federals have some bulldog of a general named Grant who is doing a lot of the damage.

"Bulldog?" Belle asked, amusement in her voice.

"That's what they're calling him. A general who will accept nothing less than unconditional surrender from the enemy."

"I see," Belle said, even though she still thought the nickname silly. "Well, at least the Army of Virginia is taking care of things here at home."

"True. Overall, I believe we are faring well." Miriam said. "I'm just happy that the 30th hasn't had to fight yet. I'm sure this town needs no more tragedies, what with the epidemic taking our children, the soldiers sick here and dying and simply worrying about our family members here and in the army."

"Yes," Elizabeth said. "It appears as though the epidemic is winding down though. Hopefully, I can bring my children home soon. I can't tell you enough how much I appreciate you watching over them, Mama, and keeping them safe." Elizabeth rubbed her daughter's back. Hannah had begun to breathe evenly and Elizabeth was sure the child had fallen asleep.

"You know we adore having them here, and you also know that you are more than welcome to stay here whenever you want to." Miriam smiled at her daughter. "I know you feel the need to watch over your home, but you can always come back here whenever you need to."

"I know," Elizabeth said, trying to hold back the tears that threatened. Why was she so emotional as of late?

"Is there any other news from town?" Belle asked her sister.

"Nothing much about our army here. I did get a letter from Joshua, and he said there is a rumor that the Union General McClellan is waiting to advance from the Potomac until May."

"But our men...their enlistment is up in May." Annie pointed out. "If they all come home, the Yankees won't have anyone to stop them. Even if they do, the men will be new recruits who have little or no training."

"According to Joshua, they believe that's the Federal Army's plan. Unfortunately, the letter also said that most of the men say they'll reenlist. They know the risk of going home at a time like this. At least three-quarters of the men will stay."

"Did Joshua say anything about our family members reenlisting?" Belle asked.

"He did." Elizabeth laid her head on her daughter's. "He said he's going to reenlist, for the same reasons that he enlisted in the first place."

"That means James is staying too," Miriam said, trying not to get too emotional.

"Yes," Elizabeth said. "Father likely will also. I'm sure they will both be writing soon."

"I do hope so, even if they don't give me the news I want to hear," Miriam replied.

"Well, I'm sure everything will work out fine," Annie said, a positive attitude as usual.

"We can only hope and pray for that," Elizabeth said as she held her daughter close.

Sunday, March 16, 1862
Fredericksburg

Elizabeth stopped walking and looked down at the grocery list she had made that morning. She had finally brought her son and daughter home, as no children had died of the fever since five-year-old Thomas Wolfe had succumbed a few weeks ago. No new cases had been reported since then. It seemed as though the threat was over, but not before claiming almost 100 children living in and around Fredericksburg. Elizabeth thanked God every night that her children had been spared, but still mourned for all the little lost lives and their families.

As she looked up, a Confederate soldier brushed her shoulder, making her stumble. He continued on his way without an apology. She sighed. Fredericksburg had dealt with the scarlet fever epidemic, but now was facing another threat. She could hear soldiers and townspeople alike discussing the news.

"Grant does it again."

"Nashville is now in Yankee hands."

"Lincoln relieves McClellan as General-in-chief of the Federal armies."

"Our boys have evacuated Leesburg and Winchester."

"Enemy pickets are at Manassas and a Union flag flies over Evansport."

"We won a battle down in Arkansas."

Elizabeth was as confused as everyone else. It seemed as though no one knew for sure how far the Confederate forces had fallen back or would fall back in the near future. There were reports of enemy soldiers advancing into the state, but no one could confirm the information.

"Elizabeth!" Lucy Beale Page wove through some civilians and soldiers and approached. "Can you believe all of this commotion?"

"It is genuine chaos. There must be tens of thousands of soldiers in and around the town. I'm just hoping to find groceries at Doggetts and then I need to stop at Buckley's. I need buttons and fabric for some new pants for Benjamin. The boy grows out of his clothing almost as quickly as I can make them."

"I was going to stop at Buckley's," Lucy said. "Shall we shop together?"

Elizabeth nodded and the two made their way to the dry good store. It was busy in there as well, women looking around and talking. The men doing the same.

"I don't see Mr. Buckley," Elizabeth commented, looking around. The sight of many empty shelves and containers worried her. There didn't appear to be much left to buy.

"Margaret!" Elizabeth noticed the grocer's stepdaughter and called out to her. Margaret Buckley was a year younger than Belle and was always kind when Elizabeth came into the store, but Margaret did not have the best of reputations in town. It was alluded to, that she was overly friendly with some of the men. Belle wouldn't speak to Margaret at all, based on rumors that Samuel Gray had a questionable relationship with her. Elizabeth continued treating Margaret as a friendly acquaintance, despite Belle's request for her to do otherwise.

"Mrs. Bennett." Margaret gave Elizabeth a small smile. "How can I help you?"

"How long have you been this busy?" Lucy asked. "There is so little on the shelves."

"Ever since the troops came through. They're buying up a lot of our goods."

"Can we get some cloth? Benjamin grew out of another pair of pants. I will also need some buttons."

"Of course. What can I get you, Mrs. Page?" Lucy gave Margaret her list and the young woman hastened to fill the two orders as best she could, she then turned to lead the women to the counter. After Elizabeth and Lucy paid for their items, Margaret glanced over at her stepfather, who was watching her. "If there's nothing else you need, I should go and help other customers."

"Of course," Elizabeth said. "Thank you so much for your help." Elizabeth and Lucy walked out of the store. "I wonder if Fredericksburg will ever return to the quiet 'finished' town it was before the war," Lucy said.

"I wonder that as well," Elizabeth said. "At the beginning of the war, it was said we would be a city that would potentially see a lot of military presence. Looking around, unfortunately, they were right."

"It doesn't seem as though the war will be over as quickly as we initially thought either," Lucy said. "It's a bit daunting, with John fighting out west in Tennessee and all of the engagements there going the North's way. I hope to hear from him every day, but there is nothing. I worry so about him."

"I know how you feel. It's almost been a year since Joshua left. I thought things would get easier, but I miss him more every day." Elizabeth said. The women began walking towards the grocery.

"Yes, but at least we have the hope that our husbands will come back. There are so many women and families whose loved ones will never make it home."

"I know. I pray for them as much as I pray for Joshua and James and my father's safety as well as for sanity to return to our country's leaders to end this war so all the men who are fighting can return home." Elizabeth looked at the many men in uniform. "I look at Belle and how she lost Samuel, a man that she was only promised to. I can't imagine how I would handle life and running my home if I lost Joshua."

"I believe you would get through it. You have a strong faith, Elizabeth Bennett, and you have the support of friends and family to help you get through whatever comes your way."

"You're right," Elizabeth said with a smile. "I do. I had a momentary feeling of melancholy. Forgive me." The two finally arrived at Doggett's grocery. "I'm so glad I ran into you today, Lucy. It has been wonderful catching up with you again."

"I agree with you," Lucy said. "Until next time, Elizabeth."

Elizabeth headed into the store and Lucy went on her way.

The grocery store was even busier than the dry goods store. Sarah Doggett, the wife of the proprietor, smiled and came over to Elizabeth. "Mrs. Bennett! How are you doing today?"

"I am well. How are you? Do you hear often from your husband?"

Sarah's husband, Hugh Doggett was one of the first men to volunteer for service, and because of his years of experience in the Fredericksburg militia, he was elected second lieutenant. He had been very active in the town's affairs before volunteering, being a city councilman, a magistrate, and even a director of the Bank of Virginia. He not only ran the grocery store, but he was also a cabinetmaker.

Mrs. Doggett smiled. "I received a letter from him not long ago. He seems to be doing well. I hope it is the same for your family?"

"It is." Elizabeth nodded and looked around the busy store. "Are we able to get some groceries? I'm looking for flour, eggs, meat, butter, and sugar."

"The sugar and flour we have." Mrs. Doggett said, leading her over to the items. "But we are currently out of our best meat selections and we are out of eggs. I might be able to get some butter from the crock for you."

"Goodness. When will you get more stock?" Elizabeth asked, taking the items from Mrs. Doggett and placing them in her basket.

"I have no idea. All the soldiers are buying up everything before it even gets into town. It is making my life difficult."

"I suppose I will take whatever I can get then, thank you," Elizabeth said.

Mrs. Doggett nodded and wrote down Elizabeth's order, then added it to Elizabeth's account. Elizabeth then thanked the woman and headed home.

Saturday, March 22, 1862
Bennett Home

Belle looked out the window of Elizabeth's home. "I hope Kate gets here soon. I would hate for her to miss seeing our president."

AJ smiled at her friend's impatience. "He and General Johnston will be here for most of the day, they say."

"Well, this could be a once in a lifetime opportunity, AJ," Belle responded. President Jefferson Davis and other men highly placed in the Confederate government would be visiting the Fredericksburg area that day. Belle was anxious to see the president, and since she, Kate, Elizabeth, and AJ had already made plans to get together it didn't take

Belle much time to convince the others how exciting it would be, so they decided to meet at Elizabeth's home.

"Patience, Belle," Miriam said from the table where she was playing checkers with Benjamin. "You'll be able to see President Davis." She had come along to watch the children.

"I hope so," Belle said. Elizabeth came back into the room.

"Hannah is down for her nap." She said. "Benjamin shouldn't need one today, right?" Elizabeth kissed the top of her son's head.

"Right! I'm not tired at all." Benjamin smiled.

"Make sure you are well-behaved for your grandmother," Elizabeth told him. "Thanks again, Mama, for watching them."

"You know I love spending time with them. I miss them being at my home." Miriam replied. "Besides, it's good for you to go out with your friends, Elizabeth."

"I see Kate!" Belle said. She turned to AJ and Elizabeth. "Are we all ready to go?"

"Yes, let's go," AJ said. They met Kate outside.

"I am so sorry I'm late," Kate said. "Bertie had received a letter from my brother, so I wanted to see how he was doing. We are excited to report that he is now a Lieutenant in our Navy."

"How wonderful. Congratulations." Belle said. "That is exciting news." They continued to walk toward the bridge that led across the Rappahannock.

"This is so exciting," AJ said. "Imagine, a man like Jefferson Davis, here in our own town."

"I'll be honest, it kind of frightens me," Elizabeth said. "The highest man in the Confederate government and some of his highest ranking generals paying us a visit? I would be willing to bet that it will not bode well for our town."

"They will be meeting with General Holmes," AJ said. "They'll be looking around to make some strategic plans."

Belle started asking familiar townspeople she was acquainted with if anyone knew when the president would be passing by, but no one seemed to know for sure.

"I do hope we didn't miss him," Belle said.

"Me too," AJ replied. "Did either of you meet the president on your trips to Vicksburg? I understand that he has ties to the city."

"We may have, but I don't recall for sure," Elizabeth said. "His main residence, Brierfield Plantation, is just south of the town, but the last time we visited that branch of the Turner family, Mr. Davis would have been a congressman."

"I recognized his name immediately when it was announced he had been named as our Confederate president." Belle said. "I'm sure Cousin Victoria or Cousin Mary has mentioned him at some point."

AJ and Kate nodded. Just then, the crowd became restless as a small group of men on horses approached.

"That must be them!" AJ said. Everyone strained to look. Belle was ecstatic to see that it was, indeed, President Davis. He sat atop his horse, a hat resting on his graying hair. He looked intelligent and distinguished, as a president should look, not like the gaunt man in the Federal office. The entourage continued riding through the crowded street, then across the bridge toward Stafford Heights.

"They're off to your side of the river, AJ," Kate commented.

"Well, if you want to protect Fredericksburg, you need to control Stafford Heights," AJ said. "If the Yankees gain that position, well, they could just rain cannon and all sorts of ammunition down on the town. Chatham Manor has a great view of the city, which means it is a perfect vantage point for the enemy. We definitely need to keep control of my side of the river."

"That is true," Kate said. "The Yankees having control of the Heights would be horrible for the town, but I wonder if they really believe the war will come this close to us."

"I suppose it depends on how you look at it," Belle said. "With the hundreds of troops here in town and Davis visiting, you could say that the war has already come to our sleepy town."

Sunday, April 6, 1862
Bennett Home

Elizabeth jumped as Belle burst into her home and slammed the door.

"A pass! I needed a pass to come into town today! To come and see my own sister. This is ridiculous, absolutely insane." Belle sat down in an uncharacteristically distressed huff.

"It is strange," Elizabeth said. "We are truly a city under military rule."

"At least it is our own men using Fredericksburg as an outpost," Belle said. "I can't imagine how the Yankees would be treating us if they were the ones that had control of the town.

"I pray every night that we don't have to find out what that would be like," Elizabeth said. "I really hope AJ can make it over today. I heard that last Thursday, the Yankees drove our pickets back and had taken over the Stafford Court House, but that's not confirmed."

"Only a marauding party," AJ said. She had quietly entered the house and heard the tail end of Elizabeth's statement.

"That's certainly good to hear," Elizabeth said, relieved. Everyone in town was on edge. The Confederate forces had fallen back to the Fredericksburg side of the Rappahannock and the civilians were constantly subject to alarms about the approach of the enemy.

"Were you searched and made to get a pass to come into town?" Belle asked, clearly still put out. AJ made a face.

"Yes. I actually brought some butter and vegetables, but they were confiscated. 'For the soldiers fighting for my safety.' they told me. I was happy to help our soldiers, but I had wanted to bring them to you, Elizabeth. I am sorry."

"We have been without butter for a few days," Elizabeth stated. "That would have been nice. It seems impossible to get much of anything at the grocery stores. The last time I bought butter, it was a dollar a pound."

"Incredible," AJ said. "I probably could make a pretty penny trying to sell some extra."

"If you could even get it into town to sell," Belle said. She looked up as Kate came through the door. "Kate, glad to see you made it."

"I almost didn't get a pass to come in." She replied. "The soldiers are taking their job quite seriously." She took a seat next to Belle. "It's unbelievable how much this town has changed in the past month or so. It even looks as if many of the stores are closed."

"There's really no goods to be bought. We were just discussing that." Elizabeth said. "Last time I was in the millinery shop, you couldn't find ten-cent calico cloth for less than fifty cents." She held up her spool of cotton thread. "When I went to buy this it was thirty-seven-and-a-half cents. I gave Mr. Wellford half a dollar and my change? Two five-cent stamps and a row of pins. These are hard times for everyone."

"At Mass this morning, Fr. Schmitz announced we would be giving our Church bell to the Confederacy to make cannons. Many other churches are doing the same."

"I received a letter from Sallie Munford," Kate spoke up. "She said that the ladies of Richmond are actually building an iron-clad gunboat to be presented to the government for the protection of the city. I find it amazing that the women are doing manual labor and they are taking an interest in winning the war."

"That is good," Elizabeth said, then changed the subject to happenings closer to home. "We see the militia in town every day. With them here, I have noticed that the mail service is reliable."

"Wonderful. I'm glad that you hear from Joshua, at least occasionally." AJ said. "We rarely hear from Nathaniel. I'm not even sure exactly what he's been doing. I would assume he's learning to fight and train for battle, but I honestly am not sure."

"Interesting," Belle said, then thought. Was Nathaniel moving up in the ranks, making a name for himself in the army? If he could find a way to elevate himself past the status of a common farmer....

"Yes. Although I imagine he misses being home and working the farm. You all know that he's always wanted to be a farmer. I am sure that hasn't changed."

Belle wondered if AJ had been reading her mind and had wanted to remind Belle of that fact. AJ had informed her multiple times that she thought Belle and Nathaniel would be a good match. If only Belle could get past some of her selfish desires. She needed wealth and prestige and to be a member of high society. She knew that she could have Nathaniel if she wanted him; he could never say no to her. If only she could determine her own feelings for him.

Tuesday, April 8, 1862
Bennett Home

"Mama, how many soldiers are there?" Benjamin asked. He was at the window, watching the continual stream of soldiers marching through town. Elizabeth had gone outside earlier to offer some of the men what comfort she could with fresh drinking water and bread that she had. The soldiers were on their way to Yorktown. She felt bad for them, as it had been raining earlier and they were still soaked to the skin. She grabbed a basket of freshly made bread, covered it with a napkin, and draped a shawl across her shoulders and over her head.

"Benjamin, I'm going back out to give them some food. Please make sure your sister stays away from the stove."

"Yes, ma'am."

As Elizabeth went outside, many of the men tipped their hats to her.

"Goodbye, ladies!" They called out to her and the other women bringing out food and water. Elizabeth began handing out her bread. In spite of the miserable weather, the men looked bright and cheerful.

"Thank you so much, ma'am." One of the men said. "This bread sure is good. Reminds me of how my Mama makes it back home." The soldier was young, with a smooth, unshaven face and blonde hair. Elizabeth guessed his age to be only sixteen or seventeen. Soldiers were supposed to be over eighteen, but many young men had found ways to join up.

"I'm glad you like it," Elizabeth said with a smile at the young man. She quietly sighed, thinking of Eric. His mother likely wouldn't survive the year. Would Eric decide to enlist when she was gone, in spite of his promise to Joshua? The young soldier touched his hat and continued on his way. Elizabeth quickly handed out the rest of her bread, thankful she had put some more bread in the oven before she had come out. The line of soldiers looked endless. She wished she could give them all a hot dinner and a dry place to sleep.

"Elizabeth!" A slightly familiar voice from the line of soldiers called out. She looked at the man and saw a scraggly bearded soldier heading her way. She barely recognized her cousin.

"Jacob!" She smiled and threw her arms around him. He had filled out since the last time she had seen him, but he still had the same smile. He picked her up and gave her a turn.

"I am so glad I saw you. I was hoping I would see a familiar face in Fredericksburg. How is everyone in the family?"

"Fine, just fine." Elizabeth tucked a damp strand of hair behind her ear. "Joshua, Father, and James are in the 30th Virginia. The rest of the family is doing well and staying out at Turner's Glenn. How about your family?

"My family is not as harmonious, I'm afraid." He replied, rubbing at his chin. "Father and Jonah are fighting with the Yankees, as I expected. Mother, Bekah, and Bethany are still at our Petersburg home, though. I haven't heard from Father or Jonah, nor do I expect to. I hear from Mother and Bekah, but neither of them mentions Father or Jonah. At this point, I'm not even sure they hear any news from them, and frankly, I don't care."

"Jacob. They're your family." Elizabeth placed a hand on his arm.

"Yes, well, I'm not sure I want to admit that anymore." Jacob looked toward the direction of the marching soldiers. "I have always felt like an outsider in my family. I feel more of a kinship with your brother and our Cousins Jason and Gregory than I do with my own brother and father. Even Bekah. I don't know why the lot of them just never moved north."

Elizabeth pulled her cousin into a hug. "We care about you, Jacob, and your family does too. This war is hard on all of us. I'm sure your father and brother want you to be safe, and I know your mother and Bekah do too. They all care about you." She pulled back and looked at him. "I pray that you'll survive this war and be able to make amends with your family."

"I'm not sure about that, Elizabeth, but I appreciate any prayers that you can send my way." He looked again at the marching column of soldiers. "It was wonderful to see you, but I must rejoin my company." He hugged her again, then ran to join the men. Elizabeth pushed another wet strand of hair from her forehead. It had started to rain again.

"God, please help all of the men survive the coming conflict." Elizabeth prayed. "And please end this war soon, but, as always, thy will be done and not mine."

Wednesday, April 16, 1862
Prentiss Home

Liberty calmly walked into the Prentiss home, but AJ could tell right away that her sister was distressed.

"What is it, Liberty?" She asked, wiping her wet hands on a dishrag. Liberty immediately moved to the window.

"Some of our men came across the river. I overheard some of them say that they were headed toward Falmouth."

"That's not far away at all." AJ joined her sister at the window.

"No, it's not," Liberty said. "One of the men told me it would be wise for me to stay inside. I felt it was best to listen."

"I agree," AJ replied. "We haven't had any fighting this close yet."

"No. The enemy hasn't made it this far south." Liberty said, then turned to AJ. "What's for dinner? Is there any food we can give to the soldiers?"

"They seem to be moving pretty quickly with deliberation. I'm not sure it would be the best thing to do right now. I wouldn't want to distract them either."

"Those are all good points," Liberty said, then moved to the stove. "I just hope that, whatever happens, it will be good for us and our cause and not the Yanks."

Later that evening, AJ sat in front of the fire knitting as Liberty paged through a book. They had been hearing sporadic gunfire for most of the evening. AJ felt anxious. She didn't know what tomorrow or even that night would hold. The fighting seemed so close. At any moment, the engagement could shift and end up in their own fields.

"Do you think the Yankees will take control of this side of the river, AJ?" Liberty asked, uncharacteristic worry in her voice.

"I'm not sure," AJ replied. "On Sunday, I heard that all of our forces were moving out of Fredericksburg. Folks are worried about the Federals being so close. They're also worried about having their slaves run off or worse, having the Yankees free them."

"People are saying that Fort Pulaski near Savannah fell to the Yankees." Liberty rambled. "We haven't heard from Father or Nathaniel in so long. I guess I'm just a little nervous."

"I know how you feel." AJ placed her knitting into the basket, then stood and stretched. "I'm not sure how much sleep I'll be getting tonight, but I'm going to try. You should too." She gave her sister two quick pats on the shoulder. "Come on. Things will hopefully look better in the morning."

Thursday, April 17, 1862
Prentiss Home

AJ pulled on her plain yellow work dress and quickly buttoned it.

"AJ!" Liberty called from the main floor. "Come down! Quick."

AJ hastened down the stairs and followed Liberty out the front door onto the porch. AJ could see columns of smoke rising from the river. From the direction of Falmouth, Yankee soldiers marched toward the bridges. It appeared that the Confederate soldiers had retreated to the Fredericksburg side of the river. All three of the bridges were on fire, all in a bright blaze from one end to the other.

"Oh, no! Who set the bridges on fire? How will we get to the city?" AJ asked softly.

"I think it was our soldiers. They probably wanted to stop the Yankee advance." Liberty replied. They heard the boom as beams and timber splashed into the water.

"Dear God, help us," AJ said.

"Should we leave too?" Liberty asked, gesturing to the many rafts on the river. The rafts navigated between a dozen vessels that were also wrapped in flames, even in the middle of the river. The rafts carried families heading toward Fredericksburg, loaded with slaves, supplies and even some horses.

"I think we'll be okay here," AJ said. "At least, I hope so. Either way, we can't abandon our farm and home."

"I suppose you're right." Liberty sat on the step, cupped her chin in her hands, and stared at the burning bridges. "I didn't realize it would come to this." She said quietly. AJ sat next to her.

"What do you mean?"

"The war. I understood that men like Father and Nathaniel would leave. I understood that they may not come back, like Samuel Gray, but I didn't think about the fact that the battles may be fought nearby, that the armies would destroy property, that even those of us staying here could be injured or even killed." Liberty took a breath. "It almost broke my heart when I heard about that elderly woman who died at Manassas. She couldn't leave her home, so she died and her home was destroyed. It makes me sad, even now."

"I know what you mean, Liberty," AJ said. "I think there were very few people who actually realized exactly what might happen, just those men who had fought in previous wars or had studied war in detail." AJ wrapped a comforting arm around Liberty's shoulder. "It could prove to be a great test for us, especially with the Yankees now on our side of the river."

"Do you think it will get even worse?" Liberty asked.

"Honestly, if I were to guess, I would say we will likely see more of the conflict. Hopefully, not actual fighting, but I would say that we will see more of the Yankee army marching around."

"They could destroy our fields if they do so," Liberty commented.

"They could. We'll just have to survive the best we can if that happens." AJ said. "In the meantime, we can pray for those whose lives have been destroyed so far and for those who will be harmed in the future."

Fredericksburg

Elizabeth clutched Hannah to her chest and gripped Benjamin's hand. She had just wanted to go to the grocery store but was regretting her decision when she saw how chaotic the streets were. The Confederate soldiers quickly made their way through town, quietly telling citizens goodbye. The streets were filled with wagons, and many men and women in carriages and buggies heading out of town.

"Mama, why is everyone leaving?" Benjamin asked. "Are we going to have to go to Turner's Glenn again?"

"I'm not sure, Benjamin." She replied. Smoke rose from the direction of the river. "But I think we'll stay in town for now."

"Elizabeth!" Betty Maury called out. Elizabeth turned towards her friend.

"Betty! What is going on?" Elizabeth asked.

"Oh, so much. The Yankees have taken over Falmouth. Some say the enemy are 10,000 strong, but it could be less, no one is sure. The town council has met and they decided to send over a flag of truce asking the enemy to come quietly and not shell the town, as there will soon be no Confederate forces here. They are deserting us. We will allow the Yankees to take possession of the town whenever they wish."

"How will they get across the river?" Elizabeth asked. "It looks like the bridges have been burned."

"They will likely wade across the river above Falmouth or cross on rafts." Betty replied.

"We're just going to let them come into our town?" Elizabeth said, her voice just above a whisper.

"Yes. We expect them at any hour." Betty replied. "It's all we can do. We don't want them to destroy any homes."

"I suppose." Elizabeth looked around. The roads were starting to empty out. She thought maybe she could bring herself and the children out to Turner's Glenn, but she wondered if that would be any safer than staying in town.

"You may want to get over to the Commissary stores," Betty said. "It's actually where I was headed. The supplies that have been left by the army are to be given to the citizens at one o'clock. They don't want the Yankees to benefit from their departure."

"That's generous of them," Elizabeth said.

"I agree," Betty replied. "It will be good to have some supplies. There's no telling what this occupation may bring. I told my husband I would be willing to follow him anywhere. He is leaving to join the army and is determined to leave me here."

"I'm sure he only wants what's best for you," Elizabeth stated.

"I suppose," Betty said. "I suspect we will all see what unfolds within the next few days."

Saturday, April 19, 1862
Bennett Home and Blacksmith Shop

"Elizabeth! I am so happy to see you safe." Elizabeth looked up from working in her small vegetable garden. She smiled at Kate.

"Good afternoon!" Elizabeth stood as Kate opened the gate to the front yard. "It is so wonderful to see you. Do you have time to come in for a cup of tea? I would love to have a conversation with you."

"I do have a little time. The Lord only knows how much longer we'll be able to move freely around town."

"I have the same worry," Elizabeth said, then called out to Benjamin and Hannah, letting them know she was going inside for a spell and they were to watch out for one another.

"I can't believe the town has raised three white flags to the Yankees and they still haven't come in to take the town," Kate said. "It's been three days since our Confederate troops retreated."

"I know. I heard we sent quite a spirited letter to the Yankees, telling them that our army has retired, and we have been forced to surrender. It said we want to submit quietly, although we did make sure the Federals knew that the townspeople were good and loyal citizens of the State of Virginia and the Confederate States of America."

"And so we are," Kate said emphatically.

"I do hope AJ and Liberty are okay over there. I am so worried about them. I was hoping they would cross the river with the others and stay here, either with me or at Turner's Glenn. The enemy is right at their doorstep, some even staying on their land, I'd bet." Elizabeth said. "I wouldn't be surprised if their slaves have left them and found refuge with the Yanks."

"I heard no trains will be able to come in or leave," Kate said. "But I'm glad that the citizens can come and go for now."

"As am I," Elizabeth said.

"Mama!" Benjamin burst into the house. "Soldiers! Riding into town."

"Can you tell if they're Union or Confederate?" Elizabeth asked.

"I think it's our side," Benjamin said. "I thought they were Yankees at first, but then they started taking letters from townspeople. They say they'll bring them back to camp and make sure they get sent out."

"Really?" Elizabeth stood and hastened to the small desk and grabbed a letter. "Excuse me just a moment, Kate." She took the letter and quickly walked out the door. She was back within a few moments.

"They are our pickets," Elizabeth said. "It's nice of them to gather the letters. They'll likely have a better chance of getting delivered through the army than the local postal system."

"So are you writing to anyone in particular?" Elizabeth asked.

"My brothers, of course, and I write most often to my friend Sally Munford in Richmond. She and I became dear friends at Mrs. Powell's school for girls."

"Yes, I've heard you mention her a time or two," Elizabeth said. "Is there anyone else special?"

"I know what you're grasping at, Elizabeth. And yes, I am writing to a gentleman."

"Stockton Heth?" Elizabeth asked with a smile.

"Yes, Mr. Heth," Kate said. "But not with any regularity on my part. I know many a person in Fredericksburg has us already engaged, but it is not true."

"Well, who knows what the future will hold," Elizabeth said.

"Indeed," Kate said, looking across the river.

Sunday, April 20, 1862
Turner's Glenn

"Elizabeth, we are so glad you're here, I just wish it wasn't for a visit," Miriam said, sitting in the parlor and pulling out some sewing.

"Sorry, Mama," Elizabeth said. "I'm glad that we are having Sunday dinner out here, like old times. Mother, you know that you and the children can always join Annie and me for Sunday services in town, don't you?"

"I have been thinking more on that." She replied. "It might be a good idea to start going to church more often. Heaven knows we need the prayers."

"Elizabeth, how are things in town?" Belle asked. "It doesn't sound like the Yankees have moved in yet?"

"They haven't," Elizabeth said. "Some Confederate scouts came in yesterday and offered to carry letters to Richmond. It's good to know they are still close by. We can see the Federal soldiers and their tents across the river. They even have cannon situated on Stafford Heights. I worry so about AJ and Liberty, right in the middle of all that commotion.

113

Many families have come over to this side of the river to stay with others here in town. I brought it up to AJ earlier, she said she and Liberty would be fine at their place."

"Where did you see her?" Meri asked.

"I passed her in town today. She was attending her church this morning."

"How did they even get over here?" Belle asked. "The bridges were destroyed."

"Rafts," Elizabeth answered. "You all should know that it would take a lot more than burned bridges to keep AJ from getting to a weekly Mass."

"That's certainly true," Belle said sarcastically. Religion was one thing Belle did not understand about her friend.

"From what people are saying in town the Federals received a reinforcement of ten thousand more soldiers last night."

"It's so strange that the enemy is at our back door," Annie said. "We are technically under their control."

"The town is so quiet," Elizabeth said. "Stores have been closed for the past three days. Streets are deserted, with the exception of some negroes."

"What are the darkies doing out on the streets?" Belle asked, a trace of disdain in her voice.

"They come in groups of fifteen or so. They're going to the commissary depots to get the provisions they're handing out. The other day I saw some with slabs of bacon and small barrels of flour."

"And the commissary is just giving them food?" Meri asked, shocked.

"They are," Elizabeth said. "But I am sure they would give the provisions to anyone who needed them."

"Well I don't think they should do that. It seems strange. Why don't they save it for their army?" Meri said.

"I agree. I am not sure about a lot of what is going on." Annie said. "However, it doesn't matter. It is out of our hands."

"Annie is right," Miriam said. "When you think about it, we've actually been quite blessed. The Yankees could have done a lot worse after our soldiers pulled out of town. There are not a lot of them here yet, but they will likely move in for good soon."

"True," Elizabeth said. "It's strange, though. Last night, we could hear the Yankee soldiers. They must have had a full brass band out there playing. We heard tunes like 'Yankee Doodle', and 'The Star-Spangled Banner'. It just...it really made me realize that they're our enemy and invaders, yet the music brought feelings of nostalgia. To be honest, it was almost painful. These Yankees aren't just our enemy, they are

114

humans too. They have family at home that worries about them just as we worry about our loved ones."

"It is strange," Annie said. "Especially since we have family fighting on both sides."

The mention of family reminded Elizabeth of seeing her cousin.

"Oh goodness, I forgot to mention it earlier, but the other day when the Confederates were passing through, I saw Jacob."

"Cousin Jacob?" Belle exclaimed. "Why are you just telling us now? How is he, and the rest of the Petersburg Turners?"

"I must admit, I just forgot to tell you all," Elizabeth said sheepishly. "He said that he hasn't heard from Uncle Samuel or Jonah. Unfortunately, he said that he didn't care if he did, as they both stayed with the Union Army. He said he hears from Aunt Susannah and Bekah regularly, and they are both fine. He said Bethany is staying with them too."

"A son and husband fighting for the Union and a son fighting for the Confederacy. That is so distressing to hear." Miriam said. "I cannot imagine how Susannah must feel. She must be so despondent."

Elizabeth brought the conversation back to what was happening in Fredericksburg. "It's difficult to know what to expect next. Will the Federals just sit on the other side of the Rappahannock, or will they come and take possession of the town? What will happen to AJ and Liberty?" She sighed. "There is just so much that will forever alter our lives."

"We just keep living our lives and keep praying," Annie said.

"Amen," Belle said quietly.

Prentiss Farm

Nathaniel quietly opened the door, hoping to give his sister a nice surprise. AJ stood at the stove, checking the biscuits in the oven. He quickly slipped behind her and put his hands on her shoulders, startling her. She whirled around to see his smiling face and broke into a grin.

"Nathaniel! What are you doing here?" She glanced outside, her expression sobering a bit. "Do you not realize there are Union forces camped out all around here? They've taken over this side of the river. If you're caught..."

"I know this land too well, AJ. I doubt they could ever catch me." Nathaniel sat down at the table. "Where's Liberty?"

"She's over at Chatham checking in at the Union camp there. She wants to see if any of the men there need laundry done."

"So you're aiding the enemy?"

"We're trying to make ends meet, Nathaniel. We have to make a living. You have probably noticed the state of the fields. It was hard enough right after you and Pa left, but with the troops constantly moving in and scavenging, it's just been impossible to produce a decent crop. We're going to try planting mostly vegetables in the near field. We plan on selling any extras we may have, as well as eggs, to the soldiers so we can get money to take care of repairs and upkeep until you and Father come home. We need any income we can find."

"I'm not judging you or Liberty, AJ. I understand." Nathaniel thought for a moment. "To be honest, I just thought of an idea." He leaned forward. "Do you ever overhear any of the Yankees talking?"

AJ gave him a puzzled look. "I suppose. I don't really pay that much attention, but if I did, I could probably hear what they're saying. Why?"

Nathaniel folded his hands in front of him on the table. "If you and Liberty did start to really listen and pay attention...well, do you think you two could write some things down and maybe get the message to me somehow? If you could do that, then I'll get it to some of my commanders who will know what to do with the information."

"You want me to spy?"

"I wouldn't call it that, AJ. Just see what you can find out and let me know. There could be a major battle here. With the Yankees here, halfway between their capital and ours, you could probably learn a lot. We can use as much information as we can get. Even if you don't think the information is important, we may be able to use it. You're smart, AJ. My commander was just saying how having intelligence from the Yankees would greatly help the cause."

"But aren't we winning almost every battle?" AJ asked.

"Yes, we are whipping them, but with more information from the Yankees, we could finish this conflict quicker."

"I could actually play a role in supporting our new government." AJ liked the sound of that. Bringing her brother and father home sooner. She was definitely in favor of that. "All right. I'll do it. I only wish that I was more like Belle. She would be able to charm any information out of those Yanks."

"You are perfectly charming in your own way, AJ." Nathaniel paused. "How is she doing? All of the Turners, actually."

"Samuel's death affected Belle. She was distraught and despondent for weeks. It was a rough time."

"That's too bad. Samuel wasn't the brightest man in the town, but he was a good man." He looked down at his hands. "We've lost a few good Fredericksburg men, and we'll probably lose more before all this is finished."

"You could go visit Belle. She would love to see you and it would probably boost her spirits."

"I would enjoy seeing her as well, but I will not have time. I was only given enough leave to check in here. I was lucky to get that." He glanced at the clock. "In fact, I should probably be heading back now."

"Nathaniel, what happened between you and Belle? You used to be close. I actually believed that you two might end up courting and getting married. Now you barely want to talk about her."

"She made the choice, AJ. She chose Samuel Gray." Nathaniel stood. "It's all right, really. I learned long ago that, while we make wonderful friends, it could never be more. It's okay. I can live with that. It's just...it's too soon right now. Besides, I..." He trailed off and looked in the distance toward Turner's Glenn. "I suppose there's just some other plan for my future that doesn't include Belle Turner."

"All right, Nathaniel." AJ stood and walked him to the door. "If I am able to get information from the Yanks, how am I to get the report to you?"

Nathaniel thought for a moment. "How about if, in one week's time, we meet at our private fishing spot, you know that secluded spot on the Rappahannock."

"The one near Ficklin's home?"

"Yes, just South of Belmont," Nathaniel confirmed. "If I can't make it, I'll make sure it's someone that you know."

"Why can't I just leave it in an empty tree hole or under a rock or something?" AJ asked.

"I feel that would be too risky. Someone else may find it, or it could blow away or something like that. I feel meeting the person would be best."

"You would know that better than I." AJ nodded. "Okay, I can do this, and if I don't have any information, I can just report that."

"Yes, but I'm sure you can come up with something."

"I will do my best. Please take care of yourself." AJ gave Nathaniel a hug.

"And you." Nathaniel tapped his hat in a short salute and then was out the door.

Wednesday, April 23, 1862
Bennett Home

"Thank you so much, AJ. I can't tell you how much we need these supplies." Elizabeth put the milk and butter aside. She would properly put it away later. "I am so glad you were able to keep some of your livestock, especially with the Federal Army camped so close to you. The way people are talking, the army is confiscating a lot of crops and livestock."

"I'm sure they would have taken more, but Liberty and I decided to be proactive about things. I made a deal with the commander. We keep our animals, they can get fresh eggs, milk, and butter from us at a very fair rate. We are also doing laundry for them, and I have agreed to cook a homemade dinner for the commander once a week. Soldiers love their home cooked meals."

"That was smart," Elizabeth replied. "Although you'd better be careful. Many of the townspeople might not understand your friendly relations with the enemy. Even though I understand, some people can be persnickety."

"Yes, well, the monetary benefits are helpful. I'm glad that we have a way to get some income, no matter how small." AJ glanced toward the door that led to the blacksmith's shop. "It is also about gaining the trust of the Yankees." She spoke quietly.

"Why would that matter?" Elizabeth asked.

"Elizabeth, I need to tell someone, just in case something happens to me." AJ quickly told her friend what Nathaniel had asked her to do. "So making deliveries to the camp has proven to be very helpful."

"The Federals haven't suspected anything?" Elizabeth asked. "I'm worried about that. I'm worried about you and Liberty. You know how she speaks without thinking."

"Of course I do. Liberty knows very little and will not know anything more than she absolutely needs to know. Don't worry about us."

"I worry about everyone these days. Father, James, Joshua, everyone over at Turner's Glenn, all of my cousins from around the former United States." She sighed. "I am so worried for our country, AJ. Who could have imagined that this conflict would still be raging on after a year?"

"I agree," AJ replied. "That's one of the reasons I felt the need to do what Nathaniel asked, to bring information to the Confederate troops. Hopefully, we can win this war more quickly."

"It needs to end soon if we're going to win," Elizabeth commented. "The North has so much more in terms of provisions, railways, and soldiers."

"But we're smarter and have better men." AJ pointed out.

"True," Elizabeth said. "The battles we've fought have proven that."

"Yes. I'm not so sure that's true out west near the Mississippi River." AJ commented.

"I have heard that too. The Battle of Pittsburg Landing over in Tennessee was a tragedy for us." Elizabeth stood and crossed to a side table in the living area. She picked up a newspaper from the week before. "An estimated 11,000 killed, wounded, captured or missing for

Johnson and Beauregard's Army of Mississippi, including Johnson himself."

"A huge loss to the Confederacy," AJ said. "Johnson was trying to lead a charge against the Yankees. I briefly spoke with Nathaniel about the battle. He said that a bullet from a Confederate gun is probably what injured Johnson. No Union soldiers were ever behind Johnson and he was shot in the back of the leg."

"What a shame," Elizabeth said. "Can you imagine how smoky and confusing those battlefields can get? James and Joshua took me hunting once and just the smoke from their guns made visibility difficult. The smoke from hundreds of guns must be blinding."

"And cannon," AJ added, thinking of her father in the artillery.

"And the noise." Elizabeth shuddered. "It frightens me, how close the war has already come to us here. That big battle at Manassas Junction was only 40 miles away, and now the Federals are occupying the Heights right across the river."

"We will be fine," AJ said. "The occupation will hopefully end soon and prove to be only an annoyance."

"As well as an opportunity for you to gather some intelligence," Elizabeth added.

Monday, April 28, 1862
Fredericksburg Cemetery

Elizabeth raised her face toward the sun to catch the full warmth of its rays. It was a beautiful day. Flowers were beginning to bloom, the sun was shining warmly and it felt like a perfect day. She looked around the cemetery. About fifty children from the town and its outskirts had come together, bringing flowers to decorate the graves of their siblings and friends who had died the previous winter from the scarlet fever epidemic. Max, Hannah, and Benjamin were among them.

"I still cannot believe we lost over 100 children to that dreadful disease," Belle commented. She had brought Max into town, as he had really wanted to pay his respects to Grayson.

"I know." Elizabeth agreed. "I hope and pray every night that we never have to deal with a catastrophe like this again."

"With this ridiculous war going on, who knows what will happen next," Belle said, almost sounding frustrated. "We began so well with the victory at Manassas Junction and subsequent smaller battles, but the latest news is that New Orleans has fallen to the Yankees. To make matters worse, both in town and on the nearby plantations, with the Yankee occupation, many Negroes feel as though they can just up and leave. The nerve!"

"I know you'll probably disagree with me, but can you blame them?" Elizabeth asked. "They finally have the opportunity for freedom."

"Poppycock! What do they need freedom for? We give them food and shelter and work to do. They have no concerns to worry themselves over. Why would they want to leave that security for uncertainty?"

"They'll be able to have a life of their own choosing, so they won't have to worry about their families being torn apart when a harsh owner sells a wife or child with no thought to how that will impact any other person," Elizabeth argued.

"Oh, for heaven's sake, Elizabeth." Belle interrupted. "That doesn't happen. I have never known Father or anyone else to do that."

"Just because you don't see it doesn't mean it never happens. How can you continue to turn a blind eye to the horrors of slavery?"

"My goodness, Elizabeth. Since when are you such a fanatic? Not to mention so dramatic?"

Elizabeth sighed. If her sister couldn't come up with a good argument, she resorted to avoidance and changing the subject.

"Belle, someday, you won't be able to manipulate your way out of an argument. Someday, I hope and pray that you will be able to see the immorality of slavery."

Belle shrugged nonchalantly. "The children are being quite well-behaved. Very quiet and respectful.

"Yes, they are." Elizabeth rubbed her temple. So typical of Belle, changing the subject when the conversation was not to her liking.

"Do Confederate soldiers still come into town?" Belle asked. "It would be nice to see some local boys. We don't see any soldiers out at Turner's Glenn."

"I see. Do you have one, in particular, you would like to see?" A new one picked out? She wanted to say. "Maybe Richard Evans?"

Belle shook her head. "No, he's handsome and all, but I have heard that he and his father had a rather large falling out when Richard enlisted with the Virginia Cavalry. Apparently, his father forbade him to go, and when Richard joined anyway, Mr. Evans disowned him."

"I can't believe that," Elizabeth said, slightly impressed. It was hard to believe Richard had gone against his father's wishes, especially when that meant that he lost the wealth and privilege that he had grown up with.

"Believe it," Belle responded. "AJ has even confirmed it. You know she never gossips or spreads rumors. She always seems to know everything that has to do with Richard, for whatever reason."

Elizabeth knew the reason but kept it to herself. "He's not good enough for AJ anyways," Elizabeth spoke more to herself than Belle, but her sister still heard the comment.

"AJ and Richard?" Belle scoffed. "The idea of a relationship between those two is laughable. She is not his type at all and besides, she would never even consider courting someone like him."

Elizabeth really wanted to tell Belle what she knew, but she would never break a confidence. She clearly remembered the party that had been held at Chatham Manor, what seemed like so many years ago. Elizabeth had been pregnant with Hannah, and Cousin Charlotte had been visiting. Elizabeth had encountered a crying AJ, racing out the door. All her friend had said was that she couldn't be 'around him' ever again. It was cryptic and Elizabeth knew there was more to the story, but AJ wasn't ready to discuss it. The next day, Elizabeth had sought out her friend.

1859

Elizabeth knocked twice on the door of the Prentiss home, then let herself in. She found AJ at the stove, working on the dinner meal.

"Back at work so soon after the big day?" Elizabeth asked.

"Elizabeth! Good afternoon. It's good to see you." She wiped her hands on her apron. "Have a seat." She smiled. "And yes, I was able to play the fairy tale princess last night, but its back to the kitchen today. Just call me Cinderella." The two women sat at the kitchen table.

"I saw you run out of the ball last night like Cinderella, but I'm not sure you were running from your prince. What happened?"

"It had to be you that I ran past last night. Belle, Kate, or the others wouldn't have even really noticed. It had to be you."

"Yes, it did," Elizabeth replied. "Do you want to talk about it?"

"I don't know. I was just so excited about the ball. I've been working hard on my figure. I felt so grand in my beautiful dress and I have such wonderful friends. I shouldn't have let one person ruin the whole evening."

"Probably not," Elizabeth said. "Who was it?"

"Richard Evans." AJ sighed. "I don't know why I...why I care so much about what he thinks of me, but I do. It's been that way since we were children. I thought we had a special friendship at one point, years ago. It must have been me just imagining things. I thought now, at this party, I could attract his attention, but then I heard him at the party. He told Samuel, well...that I was the last person he would ever consider dancing with, and I...I'm not sure if I can explain it. I can barely even get it to make sense in my own head."

"Do you love him?" Elizabeth asked.

"No, I don't, at least, I don't think so. That's the odd thing about this. I still want his approval. I'm not sure why Elizabeth. Really, I

121

don't. I don't understand these feelings." She shook her head. *"Any suggestions?"*

"I wish I had advice for you. I'm afraid I don't."

AJ sighed. "Well, I appreciate you listening to me, at any rate."

1861

"Elizabeth!" Belle said, giving her sister a gentle shake. "Are you not paying attention?"

"I'm sorry, Belle, my mind was elsewhere," Elizabeth replied.

"It's all right," Belle said. "I'm going to get Max and start heading home anyway. The children look like they're finishing up."

"Yes, so it appears," Elizabeth said. "It was good seeing you, Belle. Please give Mama my love. Take care." She then found her own children and headed home.

Wednesday, April 30, 1862
Fredericksburg

"I'm so glad you could run errands with me," AJ said, smiling at Elizabeth. The streets were empty, in part because of the Yankee threat, but also because of a drizzly, cool rain that was falling.

"I'm glad you had the foresight to bring Liberty along. Benjamin and Hannah absolutely love her, and it gives me a chance to get out for a while without prevailing upon Eric to watch them."

"Liberty loves your children," AJ said. "It's refreshing to see my sister enjoy some womanly pursuits. I can never get her to enjoy anything domestic."

"Her poor future husband," Elizabeth said with a smile as they turned the corner towards the milliners, one of the few shops that were still open. "It will take a special man to tame her."

"It will, but that man will be quite lucky," AJ said. "I believe she's getting more interested in the idea of marriage and young men. She's been paying more attention to her appearance. She doesn't want to make a big deal about it because she's always making such a fuss about Meri and Marion Beale's flirtatious ways, she doesn't want to appear like them."

"I see," Elizabeth said with another grin. "Meri does enjoy flirting with men. She's so like Belle in that way."

"Indeed," AJ replied, then smiled as Lucy Beale Page came into view. "Lucy! How are you? It has been so long."

"I'm doing well, AJ. How are you? And you, Elizabeth?"

"I'm well," AJ said.

"As well as can be expected," Elizabeth said. "We were actually just talking about our sisters, Meri, Liberty, and Marian. How is your sister doing?"

"The same as usual. Mother just received a letter from her. She's still at Mr. Sterling's school in Greensborough, North Carolina."

"That's good, isn't it?" AJ said. "But it must be hard for your mother, having your sister so far away, especially in these troubling times."

"It is. My sister seems quite distressed at the idea of being cut off from home and everyone dear to her."

"I can't imagine being far away from home," Elizabeth said. "How is everyone else in your family?"

"Mostly doing well," Lucy said. "We've heard from my brothers William and Charles. They're near Yorktown preparing for a possible battle. My Aunt Helen, you remember, my mother's sister, she is quite afraid. She left her home here in town in a hurry to avoid the possible capture of her husband with the Yankees so close. As you know, my uncle is a naval officer and may be taken, prisoner. The Yankees seem to be on the lookout for any men who have taken any active part in what they call 'the rebellion'."

"That is a lot for your family to be dealing with," AJ said. I surely hope your uncle stays safe."

"Thank you. I feel he will be." Lucy smiled. "AJ, I am surprised to see you on this side of the river. How did you cross over?"

"Liberty and I have been using a raft. Other families are doing the same." AJ answered. "The Yankees are building a bridge across the river, using canal boats. Their boats are placed close together, side by side."

"I wonder if they'll let civilians use the bridge." Elizabeth wondered.

"I don't think it's likely," AJ replied. "I did see the soldiers building the bridge yesterday shouting and talking to the colored men and women. They may let them use it." AJ's words sounded hostile.

"I heard Yankee generals asked the town for tools to build their bridge," Elizabeth said.

"That's true," Lucy answered. "Mayor Slaughter told them that since our authorities had thought it best to destroy the bridges, we couldn't help them build one."

"I think that was the perfect response," AJ said.

"Except if we helped them build it, they may have been more likely to allow us to use it." Elizabeth pointed out.

"I doubt that," AJ stated. "They'll do whatever they can to make our lives miserable, just you wait."

Thursday, May 1, 1862
The Banks of the Rappahannock River, Near Falmouth

AJ glanced around cautiously, her mission heightening her senses. She grabbed her father's pistol from the saddlebag and peeked out the door, wary of Union patrols. The barn she had been hiding in smelled of old straw, but she could also smell fresh horse. This was the first time she had ventured out so far. Nathaniel had told her that a Confederate officer would be meeting her. Nathaniel had spoken with a Major Ebenezer Daniels, who was an intelligence officer in the army, and he would be AJ's contact if she ever needed help and Nathaniel wasn't available. Nathaniel had given her all of the information she would need to meet the officer tonight. She had her contact code words memorized. She was ready, but her nerves were not.

Dark shadows in the distance soon formed into four riders, all wearing Confederate colors that she could see in their flickering lanterns. They came to a stop at the front door of the house. Two of the soldiers dismounted and strode up the front steps. A third soldier turned his horse toward the rear of the house, likely making sure there was no danger. The fourth soldier approached the barn. AJ's heart raced. It was too early to meet her contact. These soldiers were on her side, but not all Confederate soldiers were proper Southern gentlemen. These men could be deserters. If they found her...

AJ quickly ducked into the shadows, hiding in the last stall, praying the soldier wouldn't give a thorough check. She heard the creak of leather as the soldier dismounted and his footsteps crunched the hay as he entered the barn. She dared to peek around the stall. The soldier was tall and broad-shouldered. He wore his uniform neat and tidy. As he raised the lantern to look around, glints of the light caught his face. She couldn't stop herself from gasping in surprise and recognition. The strong jawline, the clean-shaven face, the impeccably barbered, dark blonde hair. The cocky, arrogant expression. Richard Evans. He swung the lantern in her direction and drew his pistol from the holster. She ducked into the stall and pressed her back against the wood. Running into any Confederates could be troublesome and with her history with Richard, she suspected that running into him would definitely be a problem.

"Who's there?" Richard said, his lazy drawl the same as ever. He cocked his pistol and crept closer. "I know someone's in here. Just come on out and we won't have any trouble." He quickly turned to look into the last stall and pointed his Colt 1851 Navy Revolver at the human form pressed against the side of the stall. He quickly noted that it was a female form.

"Get that gun pointed away from me Richard Evans." A shaky voice spoke.

Richard frowned. He couldn't place the voice. He raised the lantern and saw the familiar, bright blue eyes of the young, full-figured girl he used to tease endlessly as a child, and then ignored when he was a young man. The voice and eyes were all he recognized of America Joan Prentiss.

"Miss Prentiss?" He moved the lantern so he could take in the rest of her. "It can't be you."

"Why do you say that?" She tried to speak with authority, but her voice was quiet. Richard Evans could always make her feel utterly unattractive. She had always wanted him to admire her for who she was, but he never had.

"You have changed." He took a long look at her. She had lost weight and now had a pleasant, womanly figure. "How did you manage to transform yourself?"

"Transform myself? You are just as condescending as ever." AJ sounded stronger, more confident, and unaffected by his mean-spirited words. In reality, her heart was pounding. Though Richard had a spoiled, selfish disposition with roguish ways, she still wanted him to approve of her. She knew he would never consider her a prospect for marriage, or even as a friend. Every eligible young lady in Spotsylvania County wanted this handsome man to take notice of her. AJ would never have a chance.

"Condescending? Me?" Richard gave a short laugh. "Never." He looked her up and down. "Your...physical appearance is not all that has changed about you."

"What do you mean by that?" She pulled her shawl tighter against her to block out the chill and his gaze.

"I think I have heard you speak more in these last few minutes than I ever did growing up."

So you have forgotten some of our interactions. That should surprise me but doesn't. She thought.

"Thank you for reminding me of my faults, Mr. Evans. Is there more you would like to make a judgment on?" AJ couldn't believe the ease of the words coming from her mouth. Richard was right in that sense. Usually, in the presence of men, she could barely string two coherent words together.

"I'm not quite sure yet, ma'am." He uncocked his revolver and slid it back into the holster. "I do have to ask you what you are doing here. We are quite a long distance from Fredericksburg."

"I'm not sure I can trust you, Mr. Evans." With my secrets, or being alone with you. She thought.

125

"It's Captain Evans, actually." He said pompously.

"Well, as I said. I am not sure I can trust you. Perhaps I can trust the soldiers you rode in with, but I know from personal experience and trustworthy sources that you are not to be trusted. Especially not alone and in the dark." She picked up her saddlebag and pushed past him. The other soldiers couldn't possibly be worse than Richard Evans.

"Miss Prentiss, you have never been in any danger from me, especially not the kind you are implying." His flippant answer crushed her yet again.

"Lucky me." She said, trying not to let him hear the tears in her voice. She continued walking toward the barn door, but as she reached it, he caught her, grabbing her arm.

"I must insist you tell me what you are doing here, Miss Prentiss. It is not a request, it's an order." He gently spun her around to face him. She was tall, almost as tall as he was, so she found herself looking straight into his blue eyes. "If you don't tell me now, I will assume the worst, that you're a Union spy."

AJ smacked his hand off her arm. "I would never...how dare you imply...I am not...I would never in any way support the Union, Mr. Evans, I assure you. I am more loyal to the Confederacy than you could even imagine."

"Then why are you here?" Richard asked.

"Captain Evans, what..." a second soldier entered. When he saw AJ, he stopped and removed his hat which revealed his white-blonde hair. "Pardon me, miss." He looked at Richard. "Captain, what's going on?" The soldier was tall and large, with arms as thick as tree trunks. AJ wondered how his horse was able to carry him. He looked young, probably only a year or so older than she was.

"Lt. Robinson, may I present Miss America Joan Prentiss. I know her from Fredericksburg. I found her hiding in the barn and she was just about to tell me what she is doing here."

AJ looked at Richard, then took a deep breath.

"If you must know, I am helping a Major Daniels of the Confederate Army."

Richard gave her a surprised look. "You? You're our informant?" His gaze traveled from her head to her toes. "I never would have guessed that."

"Well, you never really took the time to know me, so I don't know why anything I do would surprise you." Nice response. AJ mentally cheered herself on. She could actually handle some verbal sparring with Richard Evans. She really could.

"I suppose you have a point, Miss Prentiss." He said with a small shrug. "So, what information do you have for the Major?"

"I'm sorry, Mr. Evans, but that information is strictly for the Major, or, rather, his officer. I mean, my contact." AJ's brain and mouth felt detached. She knew what she wanted to say, but the words wouldn't come out right.

"Yes, Miss Prentiss. The thing is, I am the contact you are looking for. Believe it or not, Major Daniels and I know each other from way back."

"You're the contact? You're the soldier I'm supposed to meet up with?" This cannot be happening. AJ thought to herself.

"We are, yes. Daniels didn't give me a name. He didn't even give a description of you just some code words so I would know for sure you were the person I was looking for."

"Really?" *Like I was ever the person you were looking for.* She shook her head. "The code words are Major Ebenezer Daniels' favorite bible verse. I should ask you what it is."

"John 3:16. 'For God so loved the world that he gave his one and only Son, that whoever believes in him shall not perish but have eternal life.'"

"Well, I never thought I would hear Richard Evans quote scripture," AJ said. Lieutenant Robinson tried to hide a chuckle.

"I do what I need to do to get the job done," Richard said. "Besides, I did attend church as a boy, the same one you did if I recall correctly. Not much sunk in, but I do recall bits and pieces." He smiled his charming smile. Why did he have to be so handsome?

"All right, that is his favorite. You have proven to be my contact, but why you? Is there something wrong with Nathaniel? Why didn't he come?" AJ asked.

"I don't know. Your brother runs many errands for the army. He is quite good at evading the enemy and getting the job done. Quite impressive for being just a farmer."

"Just a farmer, really?" AJ said. "Well that's just...you can thank a farmer every time you eat."

Richard looked at her, amused. "Miss Prentiss, you are actually quite funny when you decide to talk."

AJ looked at him, a bit hurt. Did he really not remember the friendship they had once had? "Yes, Mr. Evans. You've actually told me that before."

"Really?" Richard asked with a glance at his fellow soldier. "I'm not sure I recall..."

"Captain Evans." Another soldier entered the barn, lantern in hand. "I see some horses and lights coming down the road. They're likely Yankees. We should get moving." The young man looked at AJ and pulled his hat off in a gentlemanly gesture. "Ma'am." This soldier was

127

young, probably a year older than Liberty, tall and skinny with unruly black hair that looked like a little boys'. She smiled and nodded at him.

"All right, Private Alexander. Good work." Richard turned to AJ. "What do you have for Daniels?"

AJ handed him the small packet, which contained some information she had overheard while selling fresh bread. "Here. There's also a letter in there for my father. Lt. Daniels usually finds him and delivers it for me."

"I'll give everything to Daniels." He looked at her, and she could have sworn that she saw a brief flicker of concern in his eyes. "Do you need any help getting home?" He gently laid a hand on her arm.

"I'll be fine, but please go. I wouldn't want a letter to my father to be found with stolen information." AJ gave Richard a quick nudge, then quickly slipped out the barn door herself and quietly headed into the woods toward her home.

Friday, May 2, 1862
Bennett Home

"I'm so glad that we could all get together today," Belle said. "It's been ever so long."

"It has been," Elizabeth said, setting a teapot and cups on the kitchen table. "I only hope the shirts I'm working on for Joshua will actually get to him. The Federals are almost done with their bridge and they could ride through town any day now. When they get here, they may confiscate any and all goods they want."

"That would be unfortunate," Kate said. "On a positive note, perhaps AJ can come over the bridge instead of that rickety old raft."

Two knocks on the door sounded and AJ walked in.

"AJ, you made it!" Belle exclaimed.

"I did, and I was lucky to do so. The Yankees have finished that makeshift bridge. I would expect them to be coming down the street at any time."

"They're here? In Fredericksburg? Oh, heaven help us." Kate said. The women all stood and followed AJ outside. Benjamin and Hannah were right behind them. Belle scooped up Hannah while AJ took Benjamin into her arms. The small group stood outside Elizabeth's door, grim looks on their faces. Federal officers and accompanying horsemen rode through, triumphant looks on their smug faces. Other townspeople had gathered on the street as well; some shouted insults at the soldiers.

"Well, I suppose we truly are a city overtaken now," Elizabeth said.

"I cannot believe our soldiers have allowed this," Belle added. "Will the Federals take over our private homes and farms as they did in Falmouth?"

"Probably, just like Chatham has been overtaken," AJ said. "Their officers are using the house as some sort of headquarters and their men have set up camp all around the grounds." She quickly glanced at Elizabeth, the only one who knew her secret. Elizabeth caught her eye, then looked back towards the men.

"At least our pickets have been able to retrieve the supplies they left here, slowly but surely," Belle said. "I would hate to see the Yankees get their hands on our soldiers' supplies."

"Amen." AJ agreed. "And may God be with us during this invasion."

Monday, May 5, 1862
Maury Home, Fredericksburg

"Elizabeth! As always, it is so good to see you." Betty Maury led Elizabeth into the small parlor. "I'm glad you brought Benjamin and Hannah to play with Nannie Belle."

"I'm glad the thought occurred to me," Elizabeth said, taking the seat that was offered her. "I feel our young ones don't get as much of an opportunity to be just children anymore."

"I agree," Betty said. "Especially with all of our Negroes running off. Life is so different now that our city is under control of the Federals."

"Indeed," Elizabeth said. "It was interesting how some Federal soldiers attended some of the Fredericksburg Church services yesterday."

"Yes, I know," Betty said. "I'm not sure if you recognized him, but General Van Rensselaer attended our church. He had the audacity to sit in the mayor's pew."

"I did see that, but couldn't find where Mayor Slaughter sat," Elizabeth said.

"As far away as he could," Betty replied. "In the gallery."

"I heard this General Van Rensselaer is distantly related to Alexander Hamilton," Elizabeth stated.

"Not by blood." Betty scoffed. "My father said that General Van Rensselaer's father's first wife was Miss Peggy Schuyler, the sister of Elizabeth Schuyler, who was the wife of Alexander Hamilton."

"That is quite a distant connection," Elizabeth commented. "What did you think of how Mr. Randolph handled the Yankees in his congregation?"

"Omitting the prayer for President Davis and the success of the Confederate cause?" She clarified. "I thought it was cowardly."

"Perhaps, but I can understand his reluctance," Elizabeth said. "Yet, you would think that we should be consistent with our prayers. We need as many as we can get."

A knock sounded at the parlor door before Betty could respond to Elizabeth's statement. A servant who had chosen not to leave came in and told Betty she was needed posthaste at the front door.

Betty stood and Elizabeth followed her. Betty found three Union soldiers in the entryway. The one who appeared to be in charge spoke, appearing apologetic. He removed his hat, but Elizabeth noticed that he didn't introduce himself.

"Ma'am. We have been informed that guns are concealed here." He said, his voice commanding. The other two soldiers hadn't bothered to take off their hats, as a gentleman was to do for a lady. That inadvertent act slightly rankled Elizabeth. The soldier in charge continued to speak. "We need to search the home and retrieve them. I do apologize for the inconvenience, but we have our orders."

"There are several swords here, but no firearms," Betty said. If Elizabeth didn't know Betty as well as she did, she would have missed the slight tremor in her friend's voice. "Come to the parlor and retrieve them. They have been put there to prevent my home from being searched." She led them to the parlor, Elizabeth following. Betty pointed to five old swords. "Here they are." The soldiers gathered them. "Do you now intend to go upstairs and raid the rest of my home?" Elizabeth looked at the soldiers as Betty spoke. Both women knew that the soldiers could do whatever they wanted and there was nothing the women could do to stop them. The soldier paused. Elizabeth took a step closer to Betty, hoping to show her friend some support. Finally, the leader spoke.

"No, Ma'am. Your word is sufficient that these are all the weapons you have." He replaced his hat and put a gloved hand to the brim of it. "My apologies for the intrusion. Good afternoon, ladies." The soldiers left as quickly as they had arrived.

"Betty, how would the Yankees know that you had weapons here?" Elizabeth asked.

"It had to be one of our servants, I just know it." Betty sounded agitated, almost angry. "They are getting very insolent and almost unbearable." Betty marched back into the parlor and sat down in a huff.

"Were the swords valuable?" Elizabeth asked, taking her seat.

"No, not really, no sentimental value at least," Betty admitted. "But it is quite humiliating to have to give them up."

"At least the man in charge was fully apologetic." Elizabeth pointed out.

"That matters not to me," Betty said. "They're Yankee apologies and I will pay no heed to them. If he were truly sorry, he wouldn't have come here at all."

Elizabeth refrained from replying. She wanted to point out that he was just following orders, as he had said, but she didn't want to start an argument. Instead, she changed the subject. "Have you heard any news about our army? Your father is usually very much informed."

"He is. There is actually quite a bit going on right now. As you probably know, New Orleans is in possession of the enemy, as the forts below the city have surrendered. It sounds as if the Yankee leader down there is being horrid to the people, an absolute beast. Confederate forces in Baton Rouge burned all of the cotton in the city so that the Yankees couldn't use it. Our people are loyal, so noble. They would rather destroy their own property than to allow the Federals to prosper. I'm sure you've heard that our forces have fallen back from Yorktown?"

"I have," Elizabeth answered.

"Father was overseeing some gunboats being built on the Pamunkey River. He had to break them up and abandon the project."

"Why would he do that?" Elizabeth asked.

"He had to. The enemy has left him no water to build upon with all of their blockades." She sighed. "If only our Congress had allowed him to start building sooner. He would have had the gunboats done. Their service to the Confederacy would have been invaluable."

"They would have. It seems like our navy is beaten at every turn."

"I blame Congress," Betty said. "They are so slow to approve what we need to be victorious in some cases."

"And so the war drags on," Elizabeth replied glumly.

Friday, May 9, 1862~Evening
Prentiss Home

"AJ, could you come outside?" Liberty called into the house. AJ grabbed a shawl and followed her sister. She loved gathering intelligence but had been on edge ever since she had started doing so, and the encounter with Richard Evans last week had increased her anxiety. Why did she let him get to her? AJ needed to find time to go into Fredericksburg and discuss the last encounter with Elizabeth. Maybe she should go to Moss Neck or Turner's Glenn and open up to Kate or Belle. They always seemed to know what to do when it came to men, although that would require her to explain what she was doing, and the fewer people that knew, the better.

AJ pulled the shawl on as she joined her sister.

"What's going on?" AJ asked. It was a cool night, and darkness had fallen about an hour ago. A flash of light from across the river caught AJ's eyes. She focused in that direction, specifically near the courthouse tower.

"It's the Yankees," Liberty explained. "It looks like they're using light to signal each other across the river, back and forth."

"They actually look beautiful," AJ said as she watched the responding light flash from the hills on the other side.

"And kind of mysterious," Liberty added.

"You are right," AJ said. "It would be nice if I could figure out what the flashes meant."

"So you could pass the information on to Nathaniel and the others?" Liberty asked. "When will you be meeting with a contact again?"

"Don't you worry about that, Liberty. In case something ever happens, the less you know about the details, the better."

"I still wish you would let me help more. I could really be an asset to you." Liberty buttoned up the jacket she had on.

"Perhaps." AJ placed her hands on the porch railing and leaned slightly forward. "I don't want you doing anything that might get you into trouble. No argument."

"Yes, Mother," Liberty said jokingly. As they continued to watch the lights, Liberty commented. "You never went into detail about what happened at the last rendezvous. You just said that you didn't see Nathaniel."

"Which is all that you're going to know. I'm serious, Liberty. Leave it alone."

"You are such a killjoy," Liberty said with a sigh. Then she perked up. "What if I asked you about the contact's looks? His age, color of his hair, his eyes. Was he handsome?"

Too handsome. "What does that have to do with anything? Why would that make me more likely to talk about my meeting?" AJ asked, confused.

"Well, you know me, I'm not much for 'romantic' talk. If you and I are actually talking about handsome gentlemen or men in general, maybe you will accidentally slip and give me details about what really happened."

"You are being a very persistent pain, dear sister," AJ said. "Are you sure there isn't a particular young gentleman that you would like to be talking about?"

"No." AJ couldn't be sure in the darkness, but she thought she detected a hint of a blush on Liberty's face. "The only men I see nowadays are Yankees and I'd rather die an old spinster than consider a Yankee in that way."

"Famous last words," AJ said with a smirk.

Sunday, May 11, 1862
Bennett Home

"I'm glad you two decided to spend the night here," Elizabeth said to her sisters. "It will be nice for the three of us, like old times."

Annie smiled and added some herbs to the venison stew she was cooking. "I'm just glad that we were able to get into town, especially with the food and supplies that we brought."

"It is quite ridiculous, how the Yankees have taken over. What right do they have to dictate what I bring into town?" Belle said.

"They certainly didn't get any resistance from our soldiers when they came in," Elizabeth said.

"I am sure that our boys in gray will be back soon and make those darn Yankees get right on out of here. They are a dangerous nuisance." Belle said, annoyance apparent in her voice.

"That's not necessarily true, Belle. Betty Maury and I were just discussing how much more disciplined the Federal soldiers are compared to our soldiers. I haven't seen a drunken man since they've been here. Unfortunately, that wasn't always the case when the Confederate soldiers were here."

"The Yankees seem healthier as well," Annie commented. "Not coughing constantly during drills like our Dixie boys used to do."

"Well, aren't you two being critical of our soldiers," Belle said. "You shouldn't be so hard on the men who are protecting us and our way of life. If you don't show proper respect, why, I'm not sure what others in town may think."

Elizabeth glanced at Annie, who gave a small shrug and threw some chives into the stew. Belle glanced outside. "They should show some more respect on the Sabbath, with their drumming and trumpeting all day."

"Since when do you care about keeping holy the Sabbath, Belle?" Annie asked.

"Since it gave her an opportunity to complain more about the Federals," Elizabeth said.

"That's not true," Belle said. "I have actually been considering going to services." She spoke hesitantly as if she wasn't sure if she wanted to admit that fact.

"Belle, you know we would love to have you join us, and the children would love to see you there as well." Elizabeth's voice softened.

"Yes, I know. I won't lie, the idea has been instilled in me because of a letter James wrote. He said some things that made me think. According to him, Elizabeth, your husband is just as good a preacher as he is a blacksmith."

133

Elizabeth was shocked. It almost sounded as though Belle had given Joshua a complement. "I agree. He is rather good at a lot of things. Sharing his faith is one of them."

Belle looked at Annie "Is dinner almost ready? It smells incredible."

Annie checked the oven. "The biscuits are golden brown on top, which means we're ready." She used a towel to pull the biscuits out.

"Has Joshua been sharing anything in his letters about the actual war? James's last one didn't really do so." Belle asked. "Did anyone at your church service have any new information?" The music continued to play loudly outside. "Such as why the Yankees are so boisterous this evening?"

"I'm not sure, actually. They shouldn't be celebrating. The rumors this morning were that we claimed victories in Williamsburg and around West Point." Elizabeth leaned outside to call Hannah and Benjamin in for dinner. "They say we fought under great disadvantages, with our army in retreat."

"I've heard that also," Belle said as Annie placed dinner on the table and Benjamin and Hannah sat down. "It makes me wonder about our leaders and generals. Why are we always fighting under such disadvantages? Is it a lack of preparation and planning?"

"Now who's being critical about our troops?" Annie commented.

"I said nothing truly negative. It's quite impressive with all of those disadvantages that our soldiers keep winning." Belle replied. Annie and Elizabeth sat down. Belle was reaching for a biscuit when Benjamin whispered to her. "Aunt Belle, we didn't pray yet."

"Of course," Belle said with a genuine smile at her nephew. They all joined hands while Benjamin said grace.

The family had barely started eating when they heard cheers and yelling from outside.

"Mama, what's going on?" Benjamin asked, worry apparent in his voice.

"I'll go look. You stay put, young man." Elizabeth said, rising.

"I'll come with you," Belle stated.

Elizabeth turned to Annie. "Would you mind staying in here with the children?"

"Of course not," Annie said. Belle and Elizabeth quickly made their way towards the commotion. A crowd had gathered down the road.

"Can you see what is going on?" Elizabeth asked, but when the sisters finally arrived at the crowd, they quickly realized what was happening.

"Are those..." Belle began to say.

"Confederate prisoners." Elizabeth finished.

"Oh, my goodness." Belle watched in horror as Union soldiers marched the small group of Confederates down the street. The Federals were cheering at the prisoners, but it was taunting in nature. Elizabeth listened and she overheard the Union soldiers talking loudly.

"Rebels evacuated Norfolk and Portsmouth."

"...destroyed the Navy Yard as they left..."

"We now have possession there..."

Belle turned to her sister. "Now we know what the Yankees were cheering about all day long."

"They will likely continue to celebrate. So much for the news we heard earlier." Elizabeth said. "I was happy before, that you and Annie were going to spend the night, but with all of this excitement, I am now deeply grateful that you will be here." Belle put a comforting arm around her sister.

"I'm glad that I can ease your mind for a change."

Wednesday, May 14, 1862
Fredericksburg

Elizabeth hurried through town in the direction of the Beale home. She had learned late last night about the death of Charles Beale and she wanted to comfort Lucy. She knew that Charles had a temper and was strong-willed, but according to Lucy, her brother had been changing his ways.

Elizabeth opened the gate that led into the Beale yard and hurried up the walkway to the white, two-story home. Even though food was scarce, she carried a pot of chicken and potato stew, hoping that it would help the family.

Lucy opened the door, eyes red as if she had been crying. Elizabeth set the food down and immediately wrapped her arms around her friend. Lucy held onto Elizabeth tightly.

"I don't want to believe it, Elizabeth. I simply cannot believe it." Lucy said between sobs.

"I can't imagine the pain you're going through right now, Lucy." Elizabeth patted Lucy's back, tears trailing down her own cheeks.

"He's just...he's gone. I will never see him again. He was becoming such a better person, more considerate, caring, living a more Christian life. He was a better son and brother..." Lucy trailed off as she and Elizabeth ended the embrace and walked into the house, arm-in-arm. As they turned toward the parlor, Elizabeth noticed a slave pick up the pot of chicken and potato stew and walk toward the kitchen.

"Thank you for coming and thank you for the food," Lucy said. We've had several visitors, both last night and today. They have been bringing kind messages..."

"I would have come sooner, Lucy, but I didn't find out until late yesterday and with the children…"

"Elizabeth, I understand. I do. I wouldn't expect you to drop all of your responsibilities to come visit."

"Lucy, you're my friend. When you hurt, I hurt. My deepest sympathies are with you and your family." The two entered the parlor, where Mrs. Beale sat with Reverend Lacy. The two stood, and Elizabeth immediately embraced Mrs. Beale.

"I am so sorry for your loss, Mrs. Beale." She said. "I know it's a small consolation, but if there is anything I can do, don't hesitate to ask."

"Thank you, dear." Jane Beale replied. "Small comfort that it is, I know that my Charles is in heaven."

"Yes, I am sure he is," Elizabeth replied.

"Elizabeth brought us some food, Mama," Lucy said.

"I know it's not much, but I felt as though it would help a bit," Elizabeth explained.

"The thought is definitely appreciated, dear." Mrs. Beale replied.

"Elizabeth," Lucy turned to her friend. "Do you have time for a short visit? I would like to sit on the porch."

"Absolutely," Elizabeth replied, and they headed back to the front of the house to sit and converse.

"I keep thinking that if I go to sleep, I will wake up, and realize that this is all a dream," Lucy admitted, sitting in one of the two rocking chairs. Elizabeth took the other seat.

"I understand, Lucy," Elizabeth replied.

"How did you find out?" Lucy asked, slightly choking on her words.

"It's all over town," Elizabeth said. "Some folks are still talking about how those Confederate soldiers blew up the CSS Virginia, but the talk has definitely turned to Charles. Neither is a happy topic."

"I had heard about the CSS Virginia, but I didn't know that we blew it up ourselves. Why would we do that?"

"The ship was cornered and had no place else to go, so the Captain decided that it was better to blow it up than to let the Union army take it," Elizabeth explained.

"I suppose that makes sense," Lucy said. "It seems like such a waste, though."

"Yes." Elizabeth hesitated before she asked her next question, not wanting to upset Lucy, but wanting to know. "How did you all find out?"

Lucy sighed. "Mama actually read about it in the paper. It was very upsetting. It wasn't the best of ways to find out."

"No, I should say not," Elizabeth said. "There is never a good way. A letter from a fellow soldier or doctor or nurse? Perhaps. The army

136

allowing a soldier in their company to come and tell the family in person? That would be almost impossible." She looked out across the yard in the direction of where the armies had last been reported. She missed Joshua. She couldn't imagine losing him. The very thought...she couldn't bear thinking about it.

"You're right about that." Lucy agreed. "It's just...there really should be a better way."

Friday, May 16, 1862
Charity School-Caroline Street, Fredericksburg

Belle sat down next to Elizabeth and Betty Maury. "I just learned that we are here at the school because the Yankee general wouldn't allow us to meet at the Church." She sat down in an over exaggerated huff.

"At least we can meet here," Elizabeth said. "It was kind of Elizabeth and Mary to allow us in." Elizabeth and Mary Vass were the teachers of the Female Charity School of Fredericksburg. Many children in town went to private schools, mostly in the home of the teacher, such as Jane Beale. The Female Charity School, however, had been created by St. George's Episcopal Church of Fredericksburg, and it was supported by the citizens of Fredericksburg.

"Where are all of the students?" Belle asked.

"They evacuated the school when the Federal troops began to enter the town. The girls were taken to a plantation house south of town. I'm not sure when they'll move back." Elizabeth explained.

"Tell me, Elizabeth, how are Lucy and her family?" Betty asked.

"I haven't visited since Wednesday, but at the time, she was as well as can be expected," Elizabeth replied. "I'm planning on stopping for a visit after we are done here. I know the news has been difficult for them."

"Indeed," Betty said. "I could not handle losing someone dear to me." Betty's words escaped her mouth before she had a chance to think about them. "Oh, Belle. I'm sorry. Forgive me, I forgot..."

"Don't distress yourself, Betty," Belle said. Elizabeth took a good look at her sister. Belle had been slightly different as of late, a little kinder, and a little softer. Elizabeth reached out and gave a comforting touch to Belle's shoulder.

"Matters are getting worse and worse every day in regards to the negroes." Betty changed the subject quickly. "They are leaving their homes by the hundreds. Those who are staying are starting to demand wages."

"The nerve of them," Belle answered. "I declare, the next thing they're going to want is to be able to join the army and fight and then vote in elections. It upsets me so. Is that why there are so many of them loitering around town?"

"Yes. The citizens are refusing to hire their own slaves or their neighbors' slaves." Betty said.

"Well, it's good to hear the townspeople are showing their solidarity," Belle commented.

"I agree," Betty said.

Elizabeth kept her thoughts to herself. She didn't think it was at all unreasonable that the black men and women earn a wage. It was a perfectly acceptable request. The Negroes she knew well were intelligent and resourceful. Ruthie was extremely smart in the ways of cooking and knowing how best to manage a kitchen. Zipporah was very knowledgeable about how to make a woman look her best. Solomon was a born leader and knew how to encourage people to be their best. Daniel, even though he was uneducated, was the most intelligent man she had ever met, white or black.

Elizabeth sighed. She missed Joshua for a myriad of reasons, but one of the biggest ones was being able to discuss topics like this with him. He just might be the only person in town who thought the same as she did when it came to slavery and secession and state's rights. She was wary about writing her thoughts in a letter because she wouldn't want anyone to read it and judge Joshua. Perhaps she should start keeping a diary. Record all of her thoughts and feelings and then have Joshua read them when they were reunited.

"Elizabeth, what do you think?" Betty asked, pulling Elizabeth from her daydream.

"Forgive me. My mind was drifting. What were you saying?"

"We were discussing how important the naval engagements have been," Belle replied. "These ironclad ships are changing warfare quite a bit."

"Yes," Betty said. "We were discussing the Battle of Hampton Roads that occurred back in March. The engagement is receiving worldwide attention. My father said that Great Britain and France have now stopped producing wood-hulled ships."

"My goodness. I must confess, I don't know that much about naval warfare. Most of my knowledge comes from you, Betty. I suppose it is an important part of the war, and it should gain more attention."

"Yes, it is said that Union Admiral Farragut wants to take control of the Mississippi, which would cut our Confederate nation in two." Betty said.

"That would be a disaster," Elizabeth said.

Monday, May 19, 1862
Bennett Home

Elizabeth was measuring some flour into a bowl, preparing some bread dough for dinner when there was a knock at the door.

"It's open!" She called, wiping her white powdered hands on her apron. The door opened and Daniel came in, two skinned rabbits held in his hands.

"Miss Elizabeth, I've some fresh meat for you and your young-uns."

"Daniel! Thank you so much. I declare I don't know what we would do without your hunting and trapping skills."

"Happy to do it, Miss Elizabeth. I been able to take young Mr. Turner with me and teach him about trapping and setting snares, and he be pickin' things up right quick. I keep meaning to take your boy, Eric out and teach him how to hunt, but I'm not sure, with the Union army all around us"

"Well, he will have a fine teacher to learn from when the time comes." She smiled and accepted the meat. "How are things over at Turner's Glenn?"

"Life be good. There be lots more work to do soon, some da people are talking of up and leaving now that them Federal soldiers come in and taking over."

"Yes, the soldiers occupying our town have caused quite a stir. In fact, I should have asked, was it difficult for you to come into town? Were you able to obtain a pass?"

"Aww, those Union soldiers don't pay no attention to no colored man like me. I just' explained what I was about doin' and they just let me on through."

"That's good." Elizabeth brought the rabbit's meat over to the sink and began giving it a thorough cleaning. "What do you think, Daniel? Will all our people leave?"

"I think most of them will. 'Cept maybe a few of us."

"What about you, Daniel?" Elizabeth asked. "Why are you not leaving? I can actually see you joining the Union Army and making a fine soldier."

"I promised Mr. Joshua that I would watch out for you an' Mr. Benjamin an' Miss Hannah. Even though he an' me had a bit of a disagreement 'fore he left, thet don' mean I'm gonna break my promise."

"Daniel. It's very kind of you to keep your promise, and I appreciate it, but you know that there would be no hard feelings if you were to take this opportunity. I know…"

"Miss Elizabeth, I 'preciate what you say. I knows you and Mr. Joshua are no friends to slavery, even if he is fightin' for the Confed'racy, but ma'am, I made a promise and I aim to keep that

139

promise. You an' your sisters need my help and I aim to do what I can to get ya'all through this war."

Elizabeth rinsed her hands, dried them on her apron, then crossed the room and placed a hand on Daniel's shoulder.

"You are a good man, Daniel. I want you to know that I will do whatever it takes to set you free when Joshua comes home, no matter what the outcome of the war is."

Daniel gave Elizabeth a small smile. "Thank you, Miss Elizabeth. I do appreciate your words."

"Will you be able to stay for supper?" She asked. "I was just preparing some fresh bread and these rabbits will cook up pretty quickly. We would love to have you eat with us."

"Naw, Miss Elizabeth. I appreciate the offer, but I'd best get back to Turner's Glenn. With so many people leavin', Solomon and I been takin' care of the fields, along wit' young Timothy. I thanks you for askin' just the same."

"All right, Daniel. You take care. Thank you again, so much for the dinner."

Thursday, May 22, 1862
Fredericksburg

"Mama, look at those soldiers. What's that around their necks?" Elizabeth was driving her children out to Turner's Glenn for a visit. She looked to where Benjamin was pointing. Two soldiers were tied back to back to a tree in front of the courthouse. They each had a board hanging around their necks that read: 'For entering private houses without orders.'

"They broke the rules," Elizabeth answered. "That must be their punishment."

"I'm sure glad that's not how you punish me," Benjamin said. Hannah nodded in agreement.

Elizabeth looked around. There was no escaping the fact that Fredericksburg was an occupied town. Federal flags flew everywhere, from the foundry to the bank, to all of the local stores. Many Northern civilians had made their way into Fredericksburg as well, most likely trying to make money. Federal soldiers had even taken over Mr. Scott's foundry and were working it every day to produce their own materials.

Benjamin looked up as the wagon passed underneath a line of Union flags that was stretched across the street.

"Mama, how many flags do the Yankees even have? They're everywhere." He pointed. "Look, there's even one on that oxen."

Elizabeth followed his finger. Sure enough, a flag was tied to the horns of a Federal ox. Flags were tacked onto trees and even stuck to the guns of the soldiers. Elizabeth pressed her fingertips to her temples. Oh, why couldn't things just return to normal?

They neared the post office and Elizabeth stopped the wagon and hopped down. She wanted to see if there were letters for her or Turner's Glenn.

"You two stay here. I'll be right back."

Elizabeth entered the building and smiled at Mr. Thom, the postmaster. "Good morning." She said. "How are you doing on this lovely day?"

"Quite well, Mrs. Bennett. Are you holding up all right with all of this madness?"

"As well as can be expected." She smiled. "I know it's not likely, but are there any letters for myself or anyone at Turner's Glenn? I'm on my way out there now."

"No, Ma'am. We've been scarce on letters ever since the Yankee occupation. We'll get a few on occasion, but I do not have one for you or your family. I am sorry."

"It's hardly your fault, Mr. Thom. Thank you for checking. Enjoy the rest of your day." Elizabeth smiled a bit sadly and walked back out to the wagon. She looked toward her children and she felt her heart clench. A Union soldier was holding the reins of the horses and an officer was talking to her children. She rushed over as quickly as she could.

"Can I help you, gentlemen?" She asked. The men didn't look threatening, but she still didn't want to take any chances. The officer talking to the children looked at her. He was of average size, with dark blonde hair and brown eyes.

"No, ma'am." The man took a step away from the wagon. "It's just that I have two children of my own back home about the same age as yours. I was just talking to them and asked if they wanted some candy that I just bought at the confectionary. My young'uns like taffy, but your boy was telling me that they weren't interested."

"No, they're not. My apologies." Heart pounding, Elizabeth took her seat in the wagon. "We'd like to be on our way if you would be so kind as to release our horses."

The soldier holding the reins looked to the other, who gave him a quick nod, then he released the reins.

"You have a nice day, ma'am." The soldier who had been talking to her children gave Elizabeth a short tip of his hat and joined the other soldier with a dejected look on his face.

"Mama, we didn't want to talk to him," Benjamin said. "He just came up and started talking to us."

Elizabeth's voice shook.

141

"You two did the right thing. We need to be careful of strangers." She picked up the reins and gave them a snap. "You need to be careful of anyone that you don't know. Do you understand?"

"Yes, Mama," Hannah said. Benjamin nodded. Elizabeth took a deep breath. She must keep a closer eye on her children from now on. Their peaceful town was not as safe as it used to be.

Friday, May 23, 1862
Bennett Home

"I wonder what all the commotion is," AJ said, looking out Elizabeth's window.

"I can't imagine," Elizabeth said, joining her. "The streets are full of more wagons and soldiers than usual."

"It was quite difficult navigating the streets on my way here, and it is getting worse," AJ said. "There's definitely something going on." She bit her lip. "I'm sorry, but I must go out and see if I can get any information. If it's relevant, I can get a message through to Lieutenant Daniels."

"Who's Lieutenant Daniels?" Belle asked. AJ had told Belle and Kate about her missions after much deliberation. She had decided that it was safe to do so. Belle, Elizabeth, and Kate were her closest friends, and they not only deserved to know, it would give AJ other confidantes.

"He's the man that decides what to do with the supplies and intelligence I bring in," AJ replied. "Nathaniel introduced him to me. He's very smart and is so detailed. Also, unlike a lot of men in society today, he understands how much a woman can do to assist the war effort. In fact, he told me that women make the best informants because most men don't suspect them."

"Sounds like a smart man to me," Elizabeth replied.

"Is he a married man?" Belle asked.

AJ blushed and replied. "That would be the first question you would ask. It is always your main concern." She rolled her eyes. "As a matter of fact, he is. His family is from the Alexandria area and that's where his wife and daughter are staying."

"I see," Belle said. "That's too bad. I was thinking that you could find a husband during this war."

AJ's thoughts quickly flashed to Richard Evans. "No, Belle. I seriously doubt as though that will happen. I'm not doing this to find a beau."

"We thank you for your contribution to the war effort, AJ," Elizabeth said. "Though I do wish you weren't risking so much."

"Well, someone has to." Something outside caught AJ's eye. "Is that? It can't be..." She rushed out the door. Belle, Elizabeth and Kate exchanged a look, then dashed out the door behind her.

"AJ, what..." Elizabeth stopped as she realized what had pulled AJ out the door. "Is that Abraham Lincoln?" Elizabeth looked at the tall, lanky president as he walked with a man she recognized as General Irvin McDowell.

"Yes. I believe it is. No other man can possibly look like that gangly being." Belle said. "What do you suppose he is doing here of all places?"

"I don't know," AJ said, standing at the picket fence with her three friends. "But I definitely need to find out." She began moving closer to the two men as they walked. The crowd was not quiet, but no one cheered as the president of the United States passed by. The women did, however, hear many grumblings and complaints about the hated president.

Elizabeth, Kate, and Belle watched as AJ made her way through the crowd.

"I don't like what AJ is doing at all," Elizabeth told her sister quietly. "It's so very dangerous."

"For once we agree on something," Belle whispered back.

AJ got within twenty feet of President Lincoln and General McDowell. She couldn't get any closer without being conspicuous. She followed for a block or so, then headed back to Elizabeth and Belle.

"I can't hear exactly what they're saying, but it sounds like they're discussing military housing or something along those lines." She reported. "With thousands of loyal Confederates in the streets, I doubt they would say anything too important."

"Military housing here in town?" Elizabeth asked, a bit of anxiety in her voice.

"No, I don't believe so," AJ assured her. "I am sorry I can't stay to visit. I should go. I have some chores that I haven't finished, some laundry to do."

"Laundry?" Belle looked confused. "I thought we were going to do some sewing together. Come now, AJ, it has been so long since we've actually had time to sit for a visit."

"Yes, I'm sorry. I have to finish the chores if I am to ride out to deliver my information." AJ replied. "I'll pick up my things. Elizabeth, would you mind if I sent Liberty over here, just in case this takes me longer than anticipated? I don't want her staying at home alone overnight."

"Overnight? AJ, you're crazier than..." Belle tried to reason with her friend, but AJ shook her head.

"Belle, I have to do this. Elizabeth, would that be okay?"

Elizabeth nodded, and the three solemnly walked into the Bennett home as AJ disappeared down the street.

May 25, 1862, Evening
Confederate Camp in Virginia

AJ sat outside a tent by the campfire, arms wrapped around herself trying to keep the chill out. The night air was heavy and damp. As soon as she felt safe enough to leave, she had ridden out to the location Nathaniel had told her to use if she ever had immediate information. She had given her information to Lieutenant Daniels, but by that time, it was almost dark, so he had brought her to Captain William Marshall of the Virginia Cavalry. Captain Marshall, a true gentleman had given her a tent of her own for the night and had given direct orders that she was to be left undisturbed. She looked up at the sound of footsteps and saw none other than Richard Evans.

"What are you doing all the way out here?" He asked, his voice smooth, but slightly accusatory. "The same thing you were doing when we met up a few months ago? What happened to you going home and staying safe?" He added a piece of wood to the fire and sat down on a rickety camp chair. AJ pushed a strand of hair from her face and tried to find the right words to say.

"You...I...Captain Marshall...I thought the Captain made it clear that you...all of you...were to leave me be." As usual, she stumbled over her words. In the flickering firelight, Richard looked even more handsome than usual. He hadn't had the chance to shave in what looked like a few days, so he had a scruffy beard that made him look ruggedly handsome.

"I did hear mention of that, but you and I? We're old family friends." He adjusted his left leg, placing the ankle on his right knee and leaned forward. "Seriously, America. I thought you were going to stay at home where you belong."

AJ didn't speak for a moment. "Mr. Evans. Clearly, that's not true."

"Clearly not." He said. "You're going to get hurt out here. Someone is going to shoot you, capture you or mistake you for someone you may not be."

AJ's cheeks reddened. "I just want to help the Confederate cause." She finally gathered her thoughts. "This was the best way I could find to do so. Just because I am a woman doesn't mean I can't do my part."

"So you decided to gather intelligence. May I ask how you obtain the information you give to my commander? You know, a lot of women spies..."

AJ pushed to her feet. "I offer to cook and do laundry." She cut off his words. "The Union troops are stationed at Chatham Manor, just

144

down the road from my own farm. The men sometimes let down their guard when I bring them fresh, flaky Southern biscuits, and you would be surprised what I can learn while doing laundry, or just by walking through the camps."

"I probably would be." Richard leaned back and looked at her as if trying to figure something out.

"Is there anything else you need to know, Mr. Evans?"

"Mr. Evans?" He smiled. "Surely we know each other well enough for first names, America."

"I'm not sure that we do." It was the second time he had used her given name and she was concerned by how comfortable it made her feel. She turned to go into her tent. Richard stood and blocked her path.

"What now?" She snapped, her heart beating fast.

"I just wanted to make sure you made it to your tent all right." Richard lowered his head and kissed her. It took AJ a second to register what he did before she pushed him away.

"What was that for?" She asked. Richard shrugged as if the kiss meant nothing.

"It felt like the right thing to do. Besides, I know you've fancied me in the past."

"What?" AJ's cheeks burned with embarrassment. Out of all the questions she wanted to ask, she stuttered: "I...who told you that...that I fancied you?"

"Margaret." He answered nonchalantly. "Margaret Buckley. Quite honestly, it would surprise me if you didn't fancy me. I know all the girls do."

AJ wanted to slap Richard, she wanted the earth to open up beneath her and swallow her up. She turned and ducked into her tent, tying the flap closed from the inside so that Richard wouldn't be able to follow. She heard him chuckle to himself and move away. AJ threw herself on the cot that had been provided for her.

"Could I have been any sillier?" She muttered to herself. "There are so many things I could have said, that should have been said. He probably thinks I am an absolute blithering idiot. No wonder he thinks I am an unfit person to be gathering intelligence. I'm never intelligent when he's around." She sighed and wrapped herself in the blanket and tried to fall asleep.

Sunday, June 1, 1862
Prentiss Farm

AJ and Liberty returned home from church to an unusually quiet home.

"Where are Gage and Andre?" Liberty wondered aloud. "They're usually out here, playing a game of checkers."

"It is their day off, Liberty. Maybe they went fishing." AJ said. Ever since she could remember, her father had allowed the farm hands every Sunday off. Once he had gone to war, AJ and Liberty had continued the practice.

"I suppose, maybe they did," Liberty said. She looked around as she entered the house. "What can I do to help with dinner?'

"Oh, good." A male voice came from the kitchen. "I was hoping to get some dinner during my visit today." Nathaniel stood from a chair at the table, a big smile on his face.

"Nathaniel!" Liberty ran and threw her arms around her brother. "I can't believe you're here."

"Neither can I." AJ walked to her brother. "George Washington Nathaniel Hale Prentiss. What are you thinking?" She smacked him on the arm. "There are Yankees all over. More so than the last time you snuck in here. Fredericksburg is under Federal control. This is dangerous. Your uniform is like a bullseye to them."

"AJ, they would have to see me first," Nathaniel replied. "Do you have some information?"

"Yes, but that also means that I meet a contact down by the river. It doesn't mean that you risk your life by coming to the house."

"AJ. Settle down. I got here perfectly fine and I will leave just as easily."

She shook her head. "If you get killed or captured while trying to leave here, I will never forgive you." She gave him a quick hug. "I am so glad to see you, though." She made her way to the stove. "Do you have any requests for dinner?" She asked.

"Chicken and dumplings?" Nathaniel asked hopefully.

"I think that can be arranged if you have the time." AJ began gathering the needed ingredients. "How have things been with you? I wish I had more information for you today, but I don't. I have, however obtained some quinine from Chatham and a cartridge box full of bullets. You won't be leaving empty-handed."

"Good work. The items you have will definitely be put to good use."

"Good." AJ continued working on dinner while Liberty and Nathaniel sat down at the kitchen table.

"Any news from camp?" Liberty asked.

"Bits and pieces," Nathaniel said, grabbing a biscuit from the bowl on the table. "Jackson won a huge victory for us in a city called Winchester. The Yankees were also driven out of Martinsburg and Harper's Ferry, back across the Potomac. Our informants up North say there's quite the panic in Washington."

"Good," Liberty said. "There should be."

"Yes." Nathaniel smiled at his sister. "They've called up the militia to defend the capital. Militia from all different states."

"Even better. I would think our regular army will do well against their militia any day." Liberty said.

"I'm sure that's what King George said in 1774, Liberty." AJ pointed out.

"Yes, I know, but that was the British army against our militia. Our regulars are so much tougher and smarter and won't underestimate their enemy. Right, Nathaniel?"

"You are right, Liberty," Nathaniel said. "The Yankees have shown us they can hold their own out West, but we have them licked in the East. We have the better generals and the better soldiers."

AJ put the chicken and dumplings into the oven, then joined her siblings at the table.

"Have you had the chance to see Father at all?" AJ asked.

"Once in a while, yes. He is doing well. In the grand scheme of a battle, the artillery is fairly safe. You shouldn't worry about him too much."

It's not just the battles, it's all of the diseases I have been hearing about. AJ wanted to bring that up but didn't want to worry Liberty. "Are you still scouting mostly, Nathaniel?" Liberty asked.

"I am doing whatever is asked of me," Nathaniel said. "Scouting, carrying messages, meeting informants, skirmishing. Whatever I am needed to do, I'll do."

"Good for you," Liberty said with a smile.

"Just make sure you..."AJ's words were interrupted by a knock at the door. Her heart skipped a beat.

Nathaniel jumped up. "Were you expecting anyone?" His voice was quiet and calm.

"No," AJ said.

"It could be Gage or Andre," Liberty suggested.

"I don't think so," AJ said. She looked at her brother. "Should I answer?"

"You have to. Go ahead." Nathaniel grabbed the package that had the morphine and cartridges AJ had put on the table and pulled out his pistol. "I'll take care of myself." Whoever was at the door pounded again? "You just keep them busy for as long as you can. Go on now."

"Be careful," AJ said, then made her way to the front door. She took a deep breath and pulled it open. A Yankee officer stood on the other side. She recognized him from the camp but didn't remember his name.

"What can I do for you, sir?" She asked, hoping her voice sounded normal.

"Well, ma'am, we've had a report that there's a Confederate soldier here. We need to search the house and the grounds."

"A soldier? I should say not. Who made such a report?" AJ asked. She could see other Yankees in the yard and one went into the barn.

"A couple of Negroes. They said they used to work here."

"What?" AJ's stomach dropped. Gage and Andre had betrayed Nathaniel? What if they had noticed her extra activities? Had they been spying on her for the Yankees?

"Yes, Ma'am. So that's why we need to search the place. If you will allow us."

AJ took a deep breath and stepped aside. She had to believe that Nathaniel had escaped because she could not lose the trust she had built with the Yankees in camp. "Go ahead. If there is a Confederate soldier here, I would like to know as well."

The soldiers entered the house. Liberty joined AJ in the entryway and said one word. "Faith." She then gave her sister a smile.

The Yankees were in the house for what felt like hours, when in reality, it was only about ten to fifteen minutes. AJ kept waiting for a commotion to start, knowing that Nathaniel wouldn't go down without a fight.

Finally, the Yankees began to file out of the house. The officer who had initially knocked on the door was the last one and he stopped in the entryway.

"You didn't find anyone?" AJ said, hoping the fear in her voice would be attributed to the thought of a potential stranger in her home.

"No, Ma'am. No one, but we'll have some men patrol the area, just in case. We wouldn't want a Reb straggler or deserter to be creeping around your property."

"Thank you, sir." AJ forced a smile onto her face. The soldier tipped his hat and quietly shut the door behind him. AJ and Liberty both let out the breaths they had been holding in.

"Did he get out or did he hide?" AJ asked quietly.

"He headed upstairs when you went to open the door. I think he was going to try and get out. He must have been successful or we would have heard a commotion."

AJ rubbed her temple. "Oh, I pray that he stays safe."

"He's smart. He'll be fine." Liberty said.

"I hope you're right," AJ replied. "I desperately hope you're right."

Wednesday, June 4, 1862
Turner's Glenn Plantation

Elizabeth looked around, noting an unusual silence around the plantation. She pulled the wagon up to the front steps.

"Mama, where is everybody?" Benjamin asked.

"I'm not sure, Benjamin. We'll find out." Elizabeth climbed down from the wagon and helped Hannah down. Benjamin jumped to the ground. Elizabeth was concerned that Daniel hadn't come out to take care of the horses. The family went up the steps and walked into the house.

"Good afternoon," Elizabeth called out. "Where is everyone?"

Lainey came down the stairs first. "Elizabeth! Goodness, you came on a bad day."

"Why do you say that?" Elizabeth asked. "Why does it feel like no one is here?"

"Because it's the truth. Everybody left last evening."

"What do you mean everybody left? Who left?" Elizabeth was astounded.

"All of the servants. They just up and left. We couldn't do anything to stop them, especially with the Yankees so close."

"No one stayed?" Elizabeth couldn't believe it. She had just spoken on this topic with Daniel, and he would never have left without saying goodbye.

"Ruthie stayed, Timothy is still here too. So is Daniel. Zipporah stayed too, so that means Solomon stayed, on account of him wanting to marry her."

"Everyone else left?" Benjamin asked, shock evident on his face. Elizabeth was shocked as well. Turner's Glenn was an average-sized tobacco and wheat plantation. Before the war, she knew the family had around twenty slaves. Now they were down to four.

"Yes," Lainey replied. "I don't know what we're going to do without servants."

"Where is Mother? The rest of the family?"

"Mama and Annie went out to the fields with Solomon and Daniel. Belle and Meri are in the garden. Max and Timothy ran off somewhere, I don't quite know where, and I'm here, I was just running some errands and helping Mama."

Beth smiled at her sister. "Well, I am glad that you were here to explain everything to me. I'm going to talk to Belle and Meri. Would you mind taking Benjamin and Hannah down to the creek? They would like to go wading."

149

"Sure. Maybe we can even catch some tadpoles!" The three ran off and Elizabeth made her way to the back patio.

"Belle? Meri?" Elizabeth found her sisters. "What is going on?"

"Oh, you mean how all except our most loyal of servants have deserted us to go God only knows where?" Sarcasm laced with anger was evident in Belle's words.

"You have no idea where any of them even went?" Elizabeth sat on the stone bench across from Belle and Meri.

"I heard one of the darkies mention Richmond, others are just heading north," Meri replied. "I'm not sure what they expect to do there."

"I can't believe Mother just let them go," Elizabeth said.

"Well, what was she supposed to do?" Belle asked. "All of the men around here are Yankees, and once our people heard through the grapevine, it was only a matter of time before they betrayed us and left."

"I don't see why you would call that a betrayal, Belle. They only want what they believe is best for their families."

"Oh, will you desist with the abolitionist nonsense, Elizabeth. How can you even think to bring that up at a time like this?"

"Belle, I didn't mean to. I am just trying to understand…"

"I do not want to hear it. I just don't. Once again, my world is turned upside down. Thank goodness Zipporah and Ruthie are loyal, and poor Solomon, Timothy, and Daniel will have their work cut out for them."

"I don't mean to sound harsh, but you do realize you all may have to do some of the labor around here," Elizabeth asked.

"What do you mean? Work in the fields side by side with slaves?" Meri asked.

"That will never happen," Belle argued. "Mama won't make us."

"Belle, if you only have five slaves on this plantation, it will not be run efficiently as it has in the past. It's just not possible. You really need to consider the fact that life here will be changing and you will have to help Mother out. Besides, you can hardly call them slaves now, since they are here of their own free will."

"What am I supposed to do? Go out and work the fields? Hardly." Belle shook her head. "That will never happen."

"So you're going to make everyone else do all the work? Someone is going to have to work the fields, Belle." Elizabeth was more frustrated with her sister than she ever had been before. How could she be so selfish?

"Why don't you just come back here where you belong and help us? You already know all about hard, menial labor. You'd be a bigger asset than both Meri and me combined."

"There's no reason to bring Meri into this conversation. I'm sure, if asked, Meri would pull her own weight and help out, wouldn't you?" Elizabeth turned toward Meri, who looked down and gave a small shrug. Elizabeth then looked at Belle again. "Belle, you're not the only one suffering because of this war. We all are, and we will likely suffer more. Things are changing, all over this country."

"Well, forgive me for wishing that my world could remain the same, for not wanting to work like a common servant. I suppose I'm not as good or as perfect as you are." Belle then turned and walked away in a huff. Elizabeth watched her leave, wanting to go after her. Meri stopped her with a hand on her arm.

"Just let her go, Elizabeth. She'll get over it soon enough. It's just been a hard week for everyone."

"What else has happened?" Elizabeth asked. "Father and James are all right, aren't they?"

"We have heard from both of them. I think Belle feels a little betrayed by James."

"Betrayed? Why?" Elizabeth was puzzled. Belle and James were closer than any of her siblings.

"He made a comment about attending church services with Joshua, and he thought Belle should do the same."

"How in the world is that a betrayal?" Elizabeth asked. She was glad that James was going to church, but couldn't understand Belle's reaction.

"You know how prideful and stubborn Belle is. James has always been her ally when it comes to churchgoing. Now she feels he's joined your side." Meri explained.

"Why must it be my side or her side?" Elizabeth asked.

"I don't know why, but it's how she feels. I think she's afraid of going to church and discovering that she enjoys it."

"Except that her life would be so much better if she just embraced it."

"Probably," Meri said. "I think you need to just give her some time."

"You're right." Elizabeth sat down on the stone bench, then looked at her younger sister. "When did you become so intuitive?"

"I have always noticed different attributes about members of this family. My older siblings just haven't always been willing to listen to what I have to say."

"Meri, I..."

"Don't worry about it, Elizabeth, really. I know many people believe that I am just a 'miniature' of Belle, but I do have my own thoughts and opinions."

"I know you do, Meri. I'm sorry if I've ever made you feel as though you're not your own person."

"It's okay. Really. Don't worry yourself about it."

Elizabeth smiled. "Perhaps some of these changes we're experiencing will end up being for the best."

After checking on Benjamin, Hannah and Lainey, who were having quite a bit of fun, Elizabeth walked toward the field where her mother was supposed to be. She found her, wearing one of her plain dresses and holding a parasol, talking with Daniel and Solomon. Solomon was one of the field slaves Matthew Turner trusted the most. He and Zipporah, whose main charge was caring for Belle and Annie, as well as most of the housework, had been sweet on each other for quite some time. As Lainey had said, that was most likely the reason he had decided to stay on at Turner's Glenn.

"Mama!" Elizabeth gave her mother a hug. "I heard what happened." She turned to Solomon and Daniel. "Thank you two, so much for your loyalty to my family. If my mother hasn't already told you, it is deeply appreciated.

"Yes, Miss 'liza," Solomon said, not meeting her eye.

"Thank you for saying so," Daniel said with a nod.

"Meri said you received letters from Father and James…" Elizabeth asked.

"Yes, and we have a letter for you as well. From Joshua." Miriam smiled, knowing the letter would make her daughter's day

"Really?" Elizabeth exclaimed. Her heart skipped a beat. She hadn't heard from her husband in what felt like ages. "How did you come upon it?"

"It was in a package we received from your father. He had a friend bring it by on his way home from Richmond." Miriam turned to Daniel and Solomon. "Thank you, boys. We can talk more tomorrow."

Elizabeth and her mother walked back toward the plantation house.

"Mama, what do you plan on doing now that the slaves are gone?" Elizabeth asked. "What can I do to help?"

"We'll manage somehow. We plan to harvest as much as we can come fall and just plant something more manageable for next season. Even if we win the war, we'll likely not be getting all our people back." Miriam sighed. "It truly will be a change in our lifestyle."

"Indeed," Elizabeth said. "Please let me know if I can help at any time. I can bring Eric over as well."

"Once harvest time comes, that would be very helpful," Miriam said. "This is such a…I don't even know, Elizabeth. I am just so thankful that Daniel, Solomon, Ruthie and Zipporah stayed, and Timothy, of course.

He will be a big help as well. I don't know what we would do without them. If any of them do eventually leave…"

"I can't see that happening, Mama. Ruthie loves taking care of all of us too much, and Zipporah and Belle are quite close. I believe Belle confides in her more than anyone else. Solomon won't go anywhere without Zipporah, and Daniel promised Joshua he would watch out for us. He's had other opportunities to leave this past year but didn't. I don't believe he'll change his mind anytime soon."

"That's all quite comforting," Miriam said as they walked up the steps of the front porch.

"What does Father have to say in his letter?" Elizabeth asked.

"Much of the same. They haven't 'seen the elephant' yet, as the soldiers say." Miriam replied.

"See the elephant?" Elizabeth was puzzled.

"Apparently, it means experiencing battle," Miriam said with a smile. "Which makes me feel better, although it seems James is really anxious to be involved in a battle himself. The big news is that Robert E. Lee has taken command of the Army of Northern Virginia. Your father has nothing but praise for Lee and his leadership ability."

"Yes, that is the news in town also," Elizabeth said. "It sounds like most Virginian soldiers would follow Lee to the ends of the earth."

"That's exactly what your father said." Miriam handed Elizabeth her letter.

"Thank you so much, Mama." Elizabeth smiled, excited to read her husband's letter. "Oh, I wish this war would end so the men could come home. I know that life will never be the same, too many things have already been severely altered, like you were saying earlier, about the slaves being gone." Elizabeth sighed. "I just…sometimes I don't know what's going to happen next and it frightens me." Tears were threatening and Elizabeth tried to hold them back. Her mother wrapped her arms around her and hugged her tightly.

"My dear Elizabeth. Where is that faith you're always talking about?" Miriam led Elizabeth into the parlor and sat down, her arm still around her daughter.

"I'm sorry, Mama. I'm trying so hard to keep the faith. I really am. I know it will all turn out for the best." She wiped a tear from her cheek. "Honestly, I shouldn't complain. Nothing bad has happened to me yet, which is what scares me. If I'm having a difficult time dealing with small things, how will I handle, God forbid, something…" Elizabeth couldn't stop the tears from sliding down her cheek.

Miriam hugged Elizabeth again. "Oh, Elizabeth, all will be fine. I will always be here for you. I will help you through whatever happens." She handed Elizabeth a handkerchief.

153

"Thank you, Mama. I don't know what I would do without you." Elizabeth wiped her cheek and took a deep breath. "We will get through this. You're right. We'll get through this together."

Thursday, June 12, 1862
Moss Neck Manor

Elizabeth pulled her wagon up to the beautiful Corbin home.

"I can't wait to see Gardiner and Parke!" Benjamin said. "Is Liberty coming?"

"I don't know, Benjamin. She may come over with AJ." Elizabeth replied.

"I hope so." He said, then hopped out of the wagon.

Elizabeth helped Hannah down, then followed Benjamin into the house. Kate had come to the door to welcome them in.

"The children are all out back." She informed Elizabeth. "We have servants out there to watch over them, that way we adults can really focus on our work."

"That will be nice," Elizabeth replied. Many women of her acquaintance didn't spend much time with their children. The slaves or servants would act as nannies and raise the children. Elizabeth never understood the practice. She loved having her children around, and wouldn't want anyone else raising them. Her own mother had altered the practice somewhat, and Elizabeth was glad of it.

"Your sister is already here and we hope AJ will make it as well. The bridges have been restored, which should make it easier to cross the river."

"It's just nice to be together again," Elizabeth said. "I'm glad that we meet like this every so often."

"Agreed," Kate replied. "With the Yankees controlling the town, it may get more difficult."

"Indeed. It's sad to see how much life has changed since the occupation."

"At least the Yankees aren't destroying public property. They could make life extremely difficult for those of us in and around the town, but luckily nothing terrible has happened."

"Well, that all depends on who you listen to," Elizabeth said. "With so many slaves leaving, many people feel like their whole world has been turned upside down."

"If you're in reference to me, Elizabeth, it's true. My whole world is turned upside down, and if you would stay out at Turner's Glenn, you would understand more how we feel."

"Of course, Belle." Elizabeth did not want the day to be ruined by an argument with Belle but still said. "Things are difficult for everyone. I know it's hard at the plantation."

"I know what your family is going through," Kate said. "At least you have some loyal slaves that stayed, as we do."

"That's true." Belle agreed. "I would be truly distressed if Zipporah left. She truly is a perfect companion. No offense to either of you."

"None was taken." Elizabeth said.

"I completely understand," Kate said. "We all have slaves that are more than just servants to us. They're part of the family."

The three sat down in the parlor. Each had brought their own sewing projects to work on. Kate had planned for tea to be served.

"I wish I had more than tea to offer," Kate said. "Things have been difficult, money-wise, according to Father. There's not much to be bought, even in the stores that remain open."

"Yes," AJ answered from the doorway. "The Yankees have no problem taking the food we farmers have worked hard to raise."

Kate, Elizabeth, and Belle greeted their friend.

"Have you really had food taken from the farm?" Belle asked.

"Yes," AJ said. "Liberty and I wanted to bring some vegetables into town to sell, but they were taken by the soldiers standing guard at the bridge. 'Confiscated' they said. Like there's even a difference."

"That's so sad," Elizabeth said. "I am sorry, AJ."

"What is the news on this side of the river?" AJ asked. "All the information I hear is from the Yankees and their newspapers. They give a rather subdued and almost confusing account of the news."

"How so?" Kate asked.

"They report by saying: 'They were outnumbered five to one and had to retreat' when really, they were simply whipped by our boys. It sounds like General Thomas Jackson has been very successful, though. Even the Yanks respect him."

"Stonewall Jackson?" Belle asked.

"Yes, the very same dashing Virginian who will be forever remembered by his actions at Manassas," AJ said. "It sounds like he defeated three Yankee generals on three successive days. He's now somewhere between Winchester and Staunton. The Yanks are miffed."

"There seems to be a contrast in the tone of the papers, depending on which side is doing the reporting," Elizabeth added. "I read a newspaper not long ago from Richmond, giving accounts of a battle fought at the end of May. We were victorious, of course, but the writers were raising some questions about our generals and their decisions. Our papers have no boasting or exaggerations, but are still critical, quite unlike the Northern papers in that way."

"But we're winning. That's all that matters." Belle said.

"In Virginia, we are," Elizabeth said. "It doesn't sound like we are successful in many other places. Memphis is in the hands of the enemy and it is said that Charleston and Savannah are as well. I'm not sure exactly how true that is."

"There should be a better way to report on activities and deliver correct information and news," Kate said. "And the mail system can definitely be improved."

"Yes, the mail!" Elizabeth said. "A huge bundle must have gotten through. We were quite lucky to receive some letters yesterday. Most were from Joshua, but I also got one from my father, one from James, and one from my cousin, Victoria. It was so nice to hear from everyone and to hear that everyone is okay. I treasure every letter I receive."

"Agreed," Belle stated. She turned to AJ. "Do you hear from Nathaniel and your father?"

"They are safe, as far as I know." She briefly told them what had happened a few weeks ago, when her brother had visited but had nearly been caught. "We learned later that he escaped by climbing out the window in Father's room to the tree next to the house. I just can't believe Gage and Andre would betray us like that. I truly believed they were more...we treated them like family, for them to just abandon me and Liberty..." She shook her head, still in disbelief.

"I can't even think of how life would be if Zipporah left," Belle said.

"We're having to make sacrifices at every turn, it seems," Kate said.

"But we'll survive," AJ said confidently. "We just need to keep praying and supporting each other."

Wednesday, June 25, 1862
Union Army Camp~Stafford Heights

AJ walked through the Union camp, a basket of fresh eggs on her arm. She knew it wouldn't take long for her to sell all of them.

"Miss Prentiss!" a voice called from the side of her. "Miss America Joan Prentiss?" AJ turned. She noticed a young soldier heading her way. He was tall, with broad shoulders and dark hair stuck out from underneath his hat. He looked familiar, but she couldn't place where she knew him from.

"I'm sorry, sir, you have the advantage on me," AJ replied with what she hoped was a charming smile.

"Of course. It has been a couple of years since we were acquainted." He smiled. "I went to school in Michigan with Nathaniel. I actually met you when I came down here for a visit, I believe it was in '59."

"Yes! Of course, Mr. Spencer." AJ smiled. "From the Michigan Agricultural College. It is so good to see you again."

"And I, you." He said. "Do you hear much from your brother?"

"Not as often as I would like to." She replied.

"I haven't had time to stop at your farm. I had heard that he is fighting for the Confederacy."

"You are correct. He is with the 30th Virginia. My father is also serving in the artillery." She paused but knew she could share this information with him. James Spencer was a gentleman. "Unfortunately, our servants all left the moment your troops arrived in town."

"So that leaves you and Liberty alone on the farm?"

"Yes, Mr. Spencer, all across our country, women are being left alone at their homes. Why, I have a friend across the river, Belle Turner, you may recall her from your visit here. Her father and brother are fighting as well, so the plantation was left in the hands of women and little seven-year-old Max. You may also remember her cousin, Charlotte from your visit. Her father left her all alone on their farm on the outskirts of Gettysburg in Pennsylvania. So you see, women on both sides of this terrible conflict have been left to take on greater responsibilities in the absence of the men."

"I have no doubt that you, Miss Belle, Miss Charlotte...I have no doubt that all of you will handle your responsibilities admirably."

"Yes. Liberty and I are making the best of this trial. I am quite lucky to have her, actually. She has always taken a great interest in farming, so she is quite adept at running the farm and I run the household. Though I cannot say I actually enjoy having you Yankees here, being able to sell eggs, vegetables, milk and taking in laundry has really helped us manage."

"Well, I'm glad you feel that way," James said. "I know there are very few who appreciate our presence here."

"We consider you an invading army, Mr. Spencer. Whyever would we appreciate your presence?"

"You have a valid point, Miss Prentiss," James replied. "I will admit, it's strange, this feeling of being in hostile territory in the very place I was welcomed not three years ago."

"A lot has changed since then. I know I was preoccupied when you visited, but I know you and my brother had an intense argument at one point."

"We did." Captain Spencer grimaced as if he was remembering the day. "He is one of the closest friends I have ever had, we just realized we couldn't talk about certain issues if we wished to remain friends. There was no way either one of us was going to change our minds."

"Well, that's how this whole war started, Mr. Spencer. Two sides that firmly believe they are in the right." AJ said.

"That is true, Miss Prentiss. I know that Nathaniel and I are not the only friends on opposite sides of this war. I know many families are split as well."

"I know some as well. Belle's family, for instance."

"Ahh, yes, the Turners. Tell me…" James smiled. "Is there more than a friendship between Nathaniel and Miss Belle Turner yet? The way he spoke of her always made me wonder."

"Not that I'm aware of," AJ admitted. "I could always see they had strong feelings for one another, but Belle, even though I love her dearly, she is very much into appearances. I don't believe she would ever allow herself to have a courtship, much less a marriage with him, as he is not in her class. She loves flirting with him, she loves flirting with any man, and they are friends. I can see them being a good match, but I believe her need for prestige would outweigh any of her personal feelings."

"That's too bad for Nathaniel."

"No, I believe he has always known that about her, so he has never really expected anything more from their relationship, though I could be wrong."

"I see."

"She was engaged just prior to the war and Nathaniel was not happy about it. Her fiancé, Samuel Gray, died from dysentery only a few months after he left."

"A common situation on our side as well. I am sorry to hear that."

"Really? You're sorry to hear that? Mr. Spencer, Samuel was a Confederate soldier. Now that he's dead, that's one less Rebel to fight." AJ tried to keep her voice neutral.

"Yes, Miss Prentiss. I am sorry. I honestly wish this war would be over. In fact, I wish that it had never even started. In spite of my being a soldier, I do not like the killing or death, but I don't agree with secession and I have definite doubts about the morality of slavery."

"Well, I suppose that's something." AJ sighed, then looked up at Chatham Manor. She decided to change the topic to a happier time.

"Do you remember this place, Mr. Spencer?" She asked. "The ball at Chatham Manor? There was so much going on that evening."

"There was indeed." He replied. "It was all for you if I remember correctly."

"Yes, and although it was nice in many ways, I must admit to you that, unlike Belle, I did not like being the center of attention."

"I do recall that, and it's understandable. Not everyone enjoys the attention as much as Miss Belle does." James commented. "Even I could see that."

"Yes that is true, Belle was named quite appropriately. She thrives on being the 'Belle of the Ball'." AJ laughed.

"Yes, she does." James took a good look around. "These grounds sure have changed. What happened to the family that lived here? They were your relatives, correct? I believe the Lacy's."

"Yes, Mrs. Lacy is a cousin to my mother. James Horace, the father, enlisted. He is a staff officer to...someone, I don't recall whom. I probably shouldn't tell you anyway." She smiled at him. "Cousin Betty and the children stayed here until your army rode in the first time and confiscated her property. They live across the river now with some other relatives.

"I see." James closely observed the house. Chatham Manor was a Georgian-style home, built of brick, two stories, flanked by two brick wings and fireplaces. "It really is a beautiful place, and has an amazing view of the town." From where the two stood, James and AJ could see almost all of the buildings in the city, most notably the tower of Grace Episcopal Church.

"Indeed," AJ said. "I am sure that is why you Yankees have decided to occupy this very spot. It does have a wonderful vantage point from a military perspective I would think."

"That is one of the benefits." He agreed. "Some of the men say that George Washington once visited here."

"They would be correct. Chatham does have quite an interesting history. It was built around 1770. William Fitzhugh, a friend of George Washington, owned Chatham for a time, which is why Washington was a regular visitor. The Fitzhugh family farm, from when Washington was a boy, is actually right down the river. Washington's mother, Mary, had a home over in Fredericksburg." She paused, then continued. "You might be interested to know that there was also a slave rebellion here at Chatham. In the early 1800's. An awful business, no whites were hurt, but three slaves were killed and two others were deported. Our General, Robert E. Lee, has ties to Chatham as well. I don't remember the exact connection, but it has to do with his wife, Mary Anna Custis, who, as you may know, is a descendant of many important Southern families, including George Washington Parke Custis, the step-grandson and adopted son of George Washington."

"Amazing." James looked at AJ, admiration in his wide eyes. "That's quite a bit of history for a beautiful home. I am impressed that you remember it all."

AJ smiled. "I enjoy history. Besides, you forget, down here, family connections are quite important."

"I suppose that's true no matter where you live." James rubbed his jaw.

"How have you been?" AJ changed the subject once again. "Farming in Michigan? I believe my brother mentioned that you are married now and manage the family farm."

"Was." His voice was quiet. "My wife Helena died in childbirth a year ago, last April."

"Oh, Mr. Spencer. I am so sorry. Truly I am."

"Thank you. It has been hard, but I trust that God has a better plan."

"Thy will be done." AJ murmured.

"Thy will be done?" James asked. "Yes, I agree. Miss Prentiss, if you need anything…"

James trailed off as a drum sounded. "Miss Prentiss, that's role call for me. It was truly wonderful to see you, and if you need anything, anything at all, please, don't hesitate to find me."

"Thank you, Mr. Spencer."

"Take care of yourself, and give my regards to Liberty. Your father and brother too, the next time you see them."

"I will. God be with you, Mr. Spencer." And she meant it.

Saturday, June 28, 1862
Bennett Home

My Dearest Joshua,

I wish you could come back for a visit, but I would also not wish for you to put yourself in danger. I miss you dearly. I know you would find our town much changed.

Runaway Negroes come in from the country every day. It is such a pitiful sight, as they come in with packs on their backs that likely contain all the meager possessions they own. They look anxious and unhappy, even though they know they are free. We have heard that most of them will head north, but since there is so much need and suffering, the rumor is that many Negroes will be shipped to the Caribbean island of Haiti.

Our town, as you may know, is now held by the Federals. It looks and feels as though it has always been this way. The stores in town have opened back up under Northern citizens. One of them has even built a house in town.

There are also issues of different currencies. I went to buy Benjamin a new pair of shoes, but the cost was a certain amount in coins, another price in Yankee paper and still another in Confederate notes. It is all very confusing.

The children are doing well, but they miss you. They are growing up so fast. I hope that you still recognize them when you return! We hear little from you, but every letter we do get is greatly treasured. We understand that the mail delivery is poor, and I often wonder how many of my letters reach you.

Take care of yourself, Joshua. We love and miss you dearly.
Elizabeth

Elizabeth folded the letter she had written to Joshua and placed it into an envelope. She wanted to get it to AJ, who could hand it off to her contact and pass it on through the Confederate mail carriers. It was a much better way of making sure the letters got to him.

"Benjamin, Hannah, we're going to leave now," Elizabeth called. Her children came into the room.

"I can't wait to see Liberty!" Benjamin said. The three of them got into the wagon that Eric had readied and started the trip. The Federals had finally rebuilt a bridge, and AJ had invited the Bennetts, Turners, and Corbins over for a mid-week coffee and luncheon. It would be nice to visit and forget all of the problems and uncertainty in their lives. For perhaps the thousandth time, Elizabeth just wished the war would end and Joshua would come home. As they neared the bridge, Elizabeth noticed two Federal soldiers standing guard. When the wagon was close enough, one of them grabbed the reins of her horse.

"Excuse me, sir. I'd like to pass over the bridge, please. I have business on the other side."

"What business would that be, ma'am." The second soldier asked. He looked younger than Eric but had a distinct air of authority.

"I'm heading over to Stafford Heights to visit a friend." Her heart beat quickly. "I trust that is okay with you."

"Who are you visiting?" He shifted his rifle from one shoulder to the other.

"Miss America Joan Prentiss and her sister, Liberty. They live on a farm east of Falmouth."

"How long will you be over there?"

"Just for lunch. We'll be coming back before evening." Elizabeth gripped the reins, her palms starting to perspire.

"Are you bringing anything over?"

"Just sewing materials, sir," Elizabeth said, gesturing to the basket at her feet.

"I need to look through that, ma'am. It is our procedure."

"Of course." Before the soldier could reach for the basket, she handed it to him. The only thing she was worried about him finding was the letter to Joshua, for that would only lead to questions about how she was planning on mailing it. She didn't want to bring any suspicion onto AJ. Luckily, she had tucked the letter in her bodice, hoping it would be safe there. The soldier took the basket and looked through it. He didn't find anything but the sewing supplies. He handed the basket back to Elizabeth.

"All right then, ma'am, you can pass. Just make sure you come back into town with exactly what you left with. He stepped back and she noticed he didn't tip his hat to her, as a gentleman would. She lifted the reins and gave them a snap.

"I am so glad you all made it safely," AJ said, placing a plate of biscuits in front of Belle, Elizabeth, and Kate. "I hope the Yankees didn't give any of you too much trouble while crossing the river. I hesitated in inviting you all here due to the occupation. We are used to crossing the river and the soldiers know Liberty and me by now, but I wondered if you would have difficulty."

"Not too much," Kate said. "They're just men and luckily, I know how to handle them."

"As do I," Belle said. "It was a difficult decision to make. You know, should I flirt with the men who are our enemy and destroying our lives just to get what I wanted, or should I remain cool and distant show them my anger." She shrugged. "I decided to get what I wanted."

"It must be nice to get what you want simply by batting your eyelashes," AJ said. "I have never had that gift. I likely never will, but we all do what we must." She sat down and picked up her sewing.

"AJ, you will find someone special. We all will." Kate said.

"Yes, and when are you and Mr. Heth going to announce an engagement?" Elizabeth asked with a small smile.

"Oh, Elizabeth, stop your jesting. It could happen in the future, perhaps, but not quite yet. His feelings for me are ever so much stronger than mine at this point, but he is a rather dashing man."

"He is that," Belle said, then changed the subject. "While passing through town, I was pleased to hear that General Thomas Jackson gained another victory for the Confederacy. They say that Fredericksburg will be relieved of our occupation by this wonderful general within the week. We would have our town back to normal."

"Really? I hadn't heard that. How wonderful." Elizabeth said. "A step towards getting our way of life back in order." She completed a row of stitches in the skirt she was working on. "That would be unbelievably wonderful.

Friday, June 27, 1862
Bennett Home
Lainey poked her head into the front room. "Good afternoon, Elizabeth."

"Good afternoon to you as well, little sister. How was your last day of school for the year and what brings you here? I would have expected you to go straight home."

"No, Daniel wasn't able to come and get me this afternoon, so Mama told me to come and ask if Eric could escort me home. I told her I could just walk, but she really didn't want me to, on account of the soldiers guarding the roads and all."

"I agree with Mama. We definitely don't want you walking by yourself." Elizabeth smiled as Lainey sat down at the table. "How was the last day of school? You never answered me."

"It was all right. Mrs. Beale received a lot of gifts from her students. I gave her an embroidered handkerchief that I'd been working on. I think she liked it. She said she really enjoyed all of the gifts because they were given with love. She even got some cologne bottles and cream pitchers, but Elizabeth, guess what?"

"What?" She asked.

"Mrs. Conway is back from her visit to Boston. She came in to see Mrs. Beale just as we were leaving. When we were walking home, some of the girls were saying that she's a Yankee sympathizer."

"Just because her son is living in Massachusetts?" Elizabeth asked.

"That's part of it. He's also an abolitionist." Lainey whispered the word as if she thought she would get in trouble for speaking it. Elizabeth frowned.

"Lainey, we must take care not to gossip." She reminded her.

"Oh, Elizabeth, I know, but who's to know whether they're rumors or the truth? I also heard that France and Belgium have, oh, what's that word... acknowledged our Southern Independence, but Mrs. Beale said that has happened before."

"About twenty times now, I believe," Elizabeth said, placing a plate of biscuits on the table.

"Yes, that is what Mrs. Beale said too, and she said that General Johnson and General Smith had an attack of paralysis and are unable to lead their armies." She explained proudly.

"My goodness, you are a fountain of information. Did you learn anything other than war rumors in school today?" Elizabeth asked. "Do you even know what paralysis is?"

"Paralysis is not being able to move. We usually don't talk so much about the war, but since it was the last day of school, we got to talk a little more about what we wanted to talk about."

"I see." Elizabeth smiled. "Mrs. Beale is doing a splendid job with your education."

163

"Yep, I mean, yes. I like Miss Lucy as a teacher best." Lainey said. "It's still so very sad about Mr. Charles. I don't know what I would do if my brother died."

"I know what you mean, Lainey," Elizabeth said. Eric opened the door that connected the blacksmith shop and Bennett home.

"Good afternoon, Mrs. Bennett. Miss Lainey." He smiled.

"Good day, Mr. Eric!" Lainey replied.

"Eric, I was just about to come out and see you," Elizabeth said. "Would you mind driving Lainey home to Turner's Glenn?"

"Not at all, ma'am." He grabbed a biscuit, then gently tugged Lainey's braid. "I'll see that no harm comes to her. Might Benjamin want to ride along?"

"I believe he would," Elizabeth said, then poked her head outside to speak with him. He quickly bounded inside.

"I am always ready to go for a drive with you, Eric! I will ride shotgun for you any day."

"Benjamin, how do you even know what that means?" Elizabeth asked, amused.

"Mama, everyone knows that a shotgun rider sits next to the driver, shotgun in hand, making sure that no harm comes to the wagon." He held out his hands, his expression serious. "I will need Papa's shotgun, Mama."

Eric and Lainey couldn't contain their laughter, but Elizabeth tried to hide her amusement.

"I don't know, Benjamin," Eric said. "The shotgun is taller than you are. I think we'll be okay for today. There are Yankee soldiers crawling all over these parts, but if we don't bother them, I doubt they'll bother us."

"Well, all right, Eric. If you say so." Benjamin crossed his arms on his chest, a mannerism he had to have picked up from his father. "I trust you." Benjamin looked so much like Joshua in that moment, Elizabeth wanted to laugh and cry at the same time.

"All right, Benjamin, Miss Lainey, let's head out." Eric grabbed his floppy felt hat from the peg and the three of them left.

Sunday, June 29, 1862
Bennett Household

Elizabeth looked out the window. "The rain is letting up." She said to AJ, who had come by after Mass. "I was hoping it wouldn't rain at all today. I felt maybe Mother and Belle would bring the rest of the family into church with Annie."

Annie came into the dining area from the kitchen.

"I think they would have, but the combination of poor weather and having to get through Yankee guards was a little too daunting." Annie shrugged. "I am glad that I was able to come." She sat down.

"How are things at Turner's Glenn, Annie?" AJ asked. "Has it been difficult with most of your servants gone?"

"Mama is taking on a lot. I am afraid that once the harvest is ready, we'll all have to put on our worst gowns and go to work in the fields ourselves. There is no one else around. Hopefully, the Yankees won't confiscate it."

"How do Belle and Meri feel about that?" AJ asked.

"I don't think it has really sunk in that they'll have to do work of that nature," Annie answered.

"You know Eric, the children and I will be there when the time comes," Elizabeth said.

"Liberty and I can also help if we have the time available," AJ said. "It might be difficult for us as well, though. We have different crops, so maybe we can all help each other." She sighed. "It feels like Sundays at Mass and the occasional visit here or at Moss Neck and Turner's Glenn are the only times that I have to myself. What with working the farm, as well as doing the extra baking and laundry jobs for the Yankees, I don't have any spare time to read or relax or even sew. I am very thankful for days like today."

"I have to agree with you, AJ," Elizabeth said. "But..." Cheering from outside interrupted her. "What in the world?"

The three women rose and quickly went outside. They could see celebrating up and down the street and it was the civilians cheering. Federal soldiers were nowhere to be found.

"Mama, what is all the yelling for?" Benjamin and Hannah, who had been taking a rest, came out of their bedroom.

"I am not sure," Elizabeth said. "Excuse me. Sir!" She called out to a man passing by. "What has happened?" She braced herself for the answer. Could the war actually be over? She wanted it to be true more than anything.

"McClellan is retreating." The man said, excitement in his voice. "Our army is pursuing them and taking guns and munitions as they go. They say that we've taken entire batteries. The Yankees are having to destroy their own stores as they go because they don't want us to get our hands on them. The Yankees are leaving our own town so quickly, we couldn't tell them goodbye if we wanted to."

"That's right." Another man came up and clapped the first man on the back. "This could be the beginning of the end. Won't be long before the Yankees accept us as a separate country and our own soldiers will be coming home!"

165

Tears of happiness rose in Elizabeth's eyes. If only that would prove to be true!

Thursday, July 3, 1862
Bennett Home

AJ yanked the door of the Bennett home open.

"Elizabeth! I have a letter for you. A contact of mine asked that I deliver it to you. I was told that it's urgent."

Elizabeth's heart was pounding as she tore the envelope open.

My Dearest Elizabeth,

I received your last letter, dated June 20. It is so difficult to comprehend just how much has happened since then. I am not sure if your father's letter has already reached your mother, but if not, I placed this letter in certain hands to make sure this one got to you.

James has been wounded. He was wounded during the battle of Glendale, or as some are calling it, 'The Seven Days Battle." He was hit in the leg with a Minié ball. I have tried to visit every day, but the timing has never worked in my favor. Your father was briefly able to see him before he was moved from a field hospital to a hospital in Richmond. That means he is likely closer to you now than he is to us. I hope and pray that the wound will not be life-threatening or that he will not lose a limb.

I hope this letter finds you and the children well and safe and the town back to its former self while unoccupied. I can't believe I missed Benjamin's fifth birthday party and that Hannah is turning three already. I dearly hope that I will not miss any other holidays or special events. We are doing well in many battles, and the Federal Army of the Rappahannock has lost two-thousand men to disease and desertion alone since the occupation of Fredericksburg. Hopefully, things will continue looking good for us.

As I'm sure you know. I miss you dearly. All I can think about is fighting hard so that I can make it back to you and the children as soon as possible.

I love you more than life,
Joshua

"There is no other information on James?" AJ asked, looking over Elizabeth's shoulder.

"No. He's in Richmond. I must go out and see Mother. Will you watch the children for me? Benjamin is doing a lesson and Hannah fell asleep during her afternoon rest."

"Of course! I will stay as long as you need me. Liberty has things taken care of across the river."

"Thank you so much." Elizabeth tucked the letter deep in her bodice, then hurried to saddle the horse and head out to Turner's Glenn.

"A hospital in Richmond?" Miriam said, letting the letter fall into her lap. "I must go down there immediately."

"Mother, you cannot!" Belle exclaimed. "You cannot leave us with...with just the four servants. You just can't!"

Miriam stood, almost as if she hadn't heard Belle's protest. "I must pack and find a way to Richmond. Perhaps Eric or Daniel can drive me down there. If we leave early tomorrow morning, we could get there by the end of the day. Perhaps we can find a train station on the way that will allow a Southern lady to travel on it."

"Some of the trains are running out of Fredericksburg now, Mother," Elizabeth said. "We can check on that tomorrow morning. It would be safer, and you could still take Daniel or Eric."

"You are actually supporting this madness, Elizabeth? How can you?" Belle stood, anger apparent on her face. "Mother, how can you actually consider leaving us?"

"Belle, your brother has been wounded. Joshua doesn't even know how badly and I have heard nothing about this from your father. I need to go to James, Belle. I can only hope that you will find it in your heart to understand." Then, Miriam quickly walked out of the room.

"I cannot believe this!" Belle stood and strode over to the window. "I cannot believe she is just abandoning us. Who will take care of us?"

"Belle, you are twenty-one years old." Elizabeth tried keeping her temper. "Annie is just a year behind you, Meri not that much further. You will have Daniel, Solomon, Ruthie, and Zipporah here. What is there to take care of, Belle? You would rather have James sit in some Richmond hospital, wounded and alone? That is just selfish."

"Selfish? You're calling me selfish?" Belle turned to her sister.

"Yes, I am. Belle, things will be just fine for you here." Elizabeth stood and gently grabbed her sister's sleeve. "Mother will find James and likely bring him home. It's just temporary. It will be all right,"

"Yes, but once again, just as my life is returning to normal with the Yankees leaving, my world will get turned upside down, altered severely." Belle pulled her arm away. "While your perfect life will remain just the way it was."

Elizabeth's jaw dropped. "What? Belle, what has addled your brain?" She pulled her sister around to face her. "How can you say that my life hasn't been altered?" Belle avoided Elizabeth's eyes. "I go to an empty bed, every night, alone, crying after my nighttime prayers because Joshua isn't there next to me. Every time I see my children, I fear to have to one day tell them that their Papa has been killed in a battle and won't be coming home. I want to cry every time I look at Benjamin because he is the very image of his father and I fear that Joshua may never see his son grow. Belle, my life is far from perfect and you know it."

"You are completely missing my point," Belle said. "That doesn't surprise me. As always, everything in your life revolves around Joshua."

"Yes, Joshua and my children, my family is my world, as it should be," Elizabeth argued.

"No. Not your family. When is the last time you've come to Sunday dinner? I would be willing to bet that you can't recall."

"I can recall. It was Easter Sunday."

"Easter was months ago, Elizabeth!" Belle stormed across the room. Elizabeth thought for a moment. Unfortunately, Belle may have a point. Elizabeth took a deep breath.

"Belle. Belle, you're right. I haven't been here for Sunday dinner in a while, but circumstances haven't been the ideal of late. I do try to be a good wife and mother, and that may have had a negative effect on how good of a sister and daughter I have been. I...I may not have been the best of friend to you either."

Belle looked at Elizabeth, a little bit shocked, a little surprised. "I never expected you to say that."

"I do try to admit when I am wrong. Forgive me."

Belle eyed her sister. "Will you apologize for calling me selfish?" Elizabeth pulled Belle to the settee and sat, her hands clasping her sister's.

"Belle, I won't do that. I truly believe your reaction is unreasonable. Mother would do the same if any of us were in James's position."

Tears started to form in Belle's eyes. "I know that, but I can't help thinking that Mother won't come back and she won't bring James home either. I just have this horrid feeling that this injury of James's is worse than we all believe and that he'll never..."

"Belle, it's just an leg injury. I can't believe it's going to be life-threatening. We must think positively"

"But Elizabeth, Samuel...Samuel died from a disease that shouldn't have killed him. Who could imagine that so many soldiers would die from having a mild illness?"

Elizabeth pulled Belle into a hug. "You are right about that. We have lost so much in this war."

"Between you and me, I really worry that things may continue going badly for us. If Mother's going to be gone, I will be the one in charge. I'm not sure I am qualified for that."

"I believe you are," Elizabeth said. 'I believe you are very capable, and I will help you in whatever way I can."

"Thank you, Elizabeth." Belle looked down. "It may not always seem like it, but I do value your help and your opinion."

"And I greatly value you." Elizabeth smiled.

Monday, July 14, 1862
Turner's Glenn Plantation

AJ waved to Elizabeth, who had been out in the fields working with Daniel, Timothy, and Solomon. The tobacco and wheat crops would be slightly smaller than years past, but they would make it through to the next year. Elizabeth waved back and began walking towards the house. Liberty hopped down from the Prentiss wagon.

"I'm going to find Meri. She's probably with the children."

"All right. I'll wait for Elizabeth to come in."

It didn't take long for Elizabeth to join AJ, who had moved to the outdoor pump and had filled a dipper of cool water for her friend. She held it out and Elizabeth took it.

"Thank you so much," Elizabeth said. She drank the water down, then pumped some water into her hand and splashed it on her face.

"Do you need any more help out there?" AJ asked.

"No, I know you have your own share of work out on your farm. I can be done for the day."

"All right. We can enjoy a little bit of visiting time. Tea today?"

"Not unless you like acorn tea. It is so expensive to buy any luxury items in town. Tea, chocolate, any type of sweet, even articles like soap are difficult to come by," Elizabeth added.

"No chocolate or sweet? That's difficult to believe, especially in a town that is known for its many confectionaries." AJ and Elizabeth began walking towards the house. "Any other news that I may have missed?" AJ asked.

"Well, they had the funeral for Bob Anderson," Elizabeth said.

"I had heard about his passing," AJ said. "So sad. I was very much hoping that he would recover. Only 23 years old." AJ shook her head. Bob Anderson was a Confederate soldier who had been taken prisoner and later released. He had gotten ill after that, however, and had passed away at home.

"At least his family had time to spend with him before he died," Elizabeth said. "There is still such overwhelming despair for the Anderson family."

"Unfortunately, that is true," AJ replied. "Have you heard any news from your mother?"

"Not yet, and if I were you, I would not bring up that conversation with Belle. She is not at all happy about Mother leaving." Elizabeth led AJ into the house and the parlor.

"Well, that doesn't surprise me," AJ said

The two women sat down. "Belle will be in shortly, I'm sure," Elizabeth said. "I hope Kate will still be able to come. I never heard a definite reply from her."

"I am so glad we can still get together," AJ said. Elizabeth glanced toward the doorway.

"How are things going with your...extra missions?" She asked. The Federal soldiers had yet to leave the town of Fredericksburg, and they still controlled Stafford Heights, so AJ was still using that to her advantage.

"I have been quite successful," AJ replied quietly. "Nathaniel was right, the men don't always take care of their words when I'm around. I can get information on troop positions and the number of men the Yankees have stationed there."

"That's good. How is Nathaniel?"

"I actually haven't been meeting him. In fact, the last contact I met was...another Fredericksburg native."

"Really." Elizabeth's curiosity was piqued, not only by AJ's words but also by the slight blush that formed on her cheeks.

"Richard Evans," AJ said so quietly that Elizabeth could barely hear her.

"Richard? Do tell." Elizabeth sat up straighter. AJ's extra work was getting more and more interesting.

"Yes. Richard Evans. He's as arrogant and conceited as ever."

"Handsome?" Elizabeth asked, trying to stifle a smile. She wasn't sure why, but she favored a relationship between AJ and Richard and always had. She knew that Richard had many flaws, but also suspected that AJ could be the one woman who would be able to get Richard on the right path.

AJ blushed deeper at Elizabeth's comment. "Yes, if possible, Richard Evans is more handsome than I remembered."

"Where did you see Richard?" Belle's voice came from the doorway. Kate walked in behind her.

"I...he...we just ran into each other." AJ looked to Elizabeth for help, but Elizabeth didn't know what to say either.

"Really?" Kate said as she and Belle sat down. "You ran into a Confederate cavalryman in an area that is crawling with Yankee soldiers."

"I..." AJ thought about telling Kate where she had met Richard, and she had mentioned to them that she was taking things from the Yankee camp and giving them to Nathaniel, but she could not implicate Richard in any way.

"Are you secretly courting him?" Kate asked, her eyes widening.

170

"What? No, what would make you say that?" AJ's blush turned a deep pink.

"It is the only explanation that makes sense," Kate said. "Why else would you see him in the middle of this war?"

AJ again glanced towards Elizabeth. "I...he...he had some letters for me from Father and Nathaniel. He said he was secretly visiting his mother and when my father found out, he asked him to deliver letters to us, so he did." AJ knew the excuse was weak but hoped that it was good enough.

"Well, then why didn't you just say so?" Kate said. She looked as though she accepted the reasoning.

"Kate, we were afraid that you wouldn't be able to make it all the way over here," Elizabeth said, changing the subject for AJ.

"I wondered that as well. Father was against my traveling, but once I decide on something, it is difficult to change my mind." Kate said.

"With some things," Belle said with a smile. "With other things, such as a relationship with Stockton Heth, you are quite indecisive."

"Not so," Kate said. "I have decided to be indecisive when it comes to Mr. Heth."

Belle chuckled and AJ relaxed, glad that the conversation had moved on.

"Well, you should decide. If you're not careful, he may move on to someone else." Belle said.

"If he would be so flippant as to do such a thing then he is not the man for me," Kate responded.

"If you're still not sure after all this time, perhaps he is not the man for you," Elizabeth said.

"Oh, Elizabeth, not everyone knows from the age of thirteen who they want to marry," Belle said with a roll of her eyes.

"I suppose I was lucky." Elizabeth agreed. She wanted to add a remark about Belle's engagement and relationship with Samuel, but that would be in poor taste, so she restrained herself.

"I overheard some of the soldiers on my way here," AJ said. "They were saying that the western counties of our own state of Virginia were recognized by the US Senate as their own independent state, West Virginia. I must say this information distressed me."

"The nerve of them!" Belle exclaimed, clearly agitated. Elizabeth wanted to bring up the fact that West Virginia had done exactly what the Confederate States had done, but she knew that it would only create a more hostile environment and she didn't want that at all. Instead, she picked up her sewing and began working.

"I agree, the situation isn't ideal," AJ said. "You could, however, argue that those western counties are only doing what the southern states did." Elizabeth looked up, surprised, but pleased at what her friend said.

"But a Virginian's first loyalty should be to Virginia," Belle argued. "Virginia decided to fight for the South, so all Virginians should follow suit."

"A person should be able to choose what they're fighting for, Belle," AJ said. "If we're going to tell people what to do and who to fight for, we are no better than the Yankees and their telling us what to do."

"That is a good point, AJ," Elizabeth said.

"Well, I disagree," Belle said. "Loyalty to your state should mean more than self-interest. It's your home, your family. Even Joshua understood that." Belle said.

"I happen to agree with Belle on this one." Kate piped in. "If you can't be loyal to your home state, if you're not willing to fight for your home and family, then...you really have nothing."

"Hear, hear," Belle said.

"Must we argue politics?" Elizabeth asked, briefly looking up from her project. "There has to be another subject we can discuss that won't make us choose sides."

"Of course, Elizabeth." Belle picked up her embroidery. "Always the peacemaker." Elizabeth withheld a sigh.

Sunday, July 20, 1862
Fredericksburg

"I'm going to stop at the Dawson's to see Eric's mother first. I'll be back shortly." Liberty said to AJ.

"All right," AJ replied. She watched her sister walk down the road towards Eric's home. Eric and Liberty had been friends for many years. AJ often wondered if their friendship would ever bloom into romance as Elizabeth and Joshua's had. AJ knocked on the Bennett's door. Benjamin opened it, but his smile faded when he saw that AJ was alone.

"I thought Liberty was going to be with you." He said, disappointment clear in his voice.

"Benjamin, that was very inconsiderate." AJ heard Elizabeth's voice from the kitchen area. Benjamin opened the door wide to let AJ in.

"Sorry, Miss AJ." He said.

"You are forgiven, Benjamin," AJ said, entering the house. "Liberty wanted to check on Mrs. Dawson and Eric before coming over."

"She is coming? Yeah!" Benjamin exclaimed, then ran out the back door.

"Sorry about that. I do hope he didn't hurt your feelings." Elizabeth said.

172

"Oh, don't worry. I understand." AJ said. "How have you been this past week?"

"I can't complain too much," Elizabeth replied. "I am concerned for Mrs. Dawson, though. I don't believe she will live much longer. I have been over there every day this week, bringing food and reading to her. We just started a fairy tale written by a French man called *Beauty and the Beast*. I think I am enjoying it more than she is. The poor woman is just in so much pain."

"What exactly is wrong with her? Liberty doesn't seem to know."

"None of the doctors seem to know," Elizabeth replied. "She just gets weaker and weaker. It is as if something is attacking her from the inside."

"How is Eric dealing with it?"

"It's hard to understand how he's feeling. He loves his mother and is fiercely protective of her. He hates seeing her in pain. I overheard him tell Meri that he wants her to get healthy, but if she's not going to, he wants her to go to heaven soon so she is no longer in pain."

"That must be difficult for him to admit," AJ said.

"Yes," Elizabeth said. "He tries to act tough and uncaring most of the time, but the truth is, he cares so much for her."

"That is not a bad thing," AJ said. "Have you heard any news from your mother?"

"No, I am concerned about her and Zipporah traveling alone, but I am glad that Daniel, Solomon, and Eric all stayed here. We really need their help."

"Do you think Zipporah will come back once your mother finds James?" AJ asked. "I wanted to ask last week when we were out at Turner's Glenn, but I didn't want to needlessly upset Belle."

"Good choice." Elizabeth said "I believe Zipporah will return. She could have left when all of the other slaves left. She'll come back for Solomon, whom she loves dearly, and of course, she loves Belle."

"At least some of the Negroes stay loyal to their families," AJ said, thinking of Andre and Gage.

"I suppose," Elizabeth replied. "Did you hear any interesting news at St. Mary's today?"

"Most people are praising the women of Richmond. During the recent battles surrounding the town, they apparently waited calmly and quietly in their homes until they could actually get out and assist the wounded and suffering. There was no screaming or shrieking or running around in fear, despite being able to see the flashes of light and hearing the cannon the whole time."

"That was the talk at my church as well," Elizabeth said. "They just waited calmly until the wounded were brought to their homes. Many of

173

the women have established private hospitals and will take in soldiers." She sighed. "I don't know how Mother is going to locate James. The situation must be so chaotic. I wish Mama would go the extra distance to Petersburg and have Aunt Susannah and Rebekah assist her."

"That would be nice," AJ said, then thought again about the women of Richmond. "I would hope the women of Fredericksburg would do the same as the women of Richmond if we had some major fighting here."

"I believe we would," Elizabeth said. "We already have. You remember how we opened our homes to the ill soldiers at the beginning of the war."

"Yes, I had forgotten that, and like them, we've given food to hungry soldiers as they've passed through." AJ agreed. "It must be our Southern hospitality. The people of Richmond haven't done any more than what other Confederate cities would do, anything for our Confederate soldiers, of course." She didn't mention the lack of hospitality that was currently the rule in Fredericksburg. AJ felt as though a war of a more subtle sort was being waged between the townspeople and the occupying Federal soldiers.

"You have to admit, even though we don't want the Federals here and they make life more complicated, they are quite well-behaved." Elizabeth pointed out.

"I can agree with that. However, I wonder how genuine the behavior is." AJ replied. "On one of my visits to the Yankee camps, I overheard one soldier tell another about how 'kind indulgence and gentle words will soon have the Fredericksburg girls on the Union side.' As if we could be so easily swayed." AJ gave a short laugh. "I heard one of our women in town responded to all of the Union flags by taunting the soldiers with a black flag flying from her window. They responded by nailing flags to her front door and when she brought out a gun to protest, General Reynolds stripped all of the foliage from a tree in her front yard and hung a large flag from it. Then, he placed a guard in front of the home with orders to shoot anyone who tried to remove it."

"Unbelievable," Elizabeth said. "It amazes me how this war can change people."

"Indeed. I would never have thought to see Belle Turner doing any type of manual labor. I haven't actually witnessed it yet, is it true?"

"I'm not sure that pumping water and carrying it out to those who are actually working counts," Elizabeth said. "It is better than her doing nothing, I suppose."

"She does deserve a little credit."

"Yes," Elizabeth answered. "We will appreciate any work we can get from Belle."

Monday, July 21, 1862
Turner's Glenn

Elizabeth rode up on a horse to Turner's Glenn. Meri and Lainey sat on the front porch, patching some of Max's shirts.

"Where is everyone else? I have a letter from Mama." Elizabeth quickly dismounted and tethered her horse.

"Belle is out back," Lainey said. "Annie and Max are out in the fields. I'll go get them if you get Belle." She raced off towards the fields.

"No need to get me." Elizabeth turned and saw Belle come around the corner of the house. "I heard you ride up. What does the letter say?"

"She found him. James is in a hospital. He's alive..." Elizabeth handed Belle the letter and she began reading.

"Oh, dear Lord, no..."

"Belle, what is it?" Meri asked.

"He was wounded in the leg at a battle called Glendale. Mama says they had to amputate the wounded leg."

"What's amputate mean?" Max asked, running up to the group.

Belle glanced at Elizabeth. She had caught her breath, and her face was white.

"It means that his leg wasn't good anymore, so they had to...they had to cut it off so it wouldn't hurt the rest of the body," Elizabeth explained.

"You mean James only has one leg left?" Max asked, horror apparent in his face. "How will he do anything? How will he ride a horse and go hunting and...and..." the boy trailed off. His eyes shimmered with tears. Elizabeth bent and circled his shoulders with her arms. He pushed away from her, then ran off towards the river. Belle began following him, but Elizabeth pulled her back.

"Let him go. He needs some time alone."

Annie finally made it to the group with Lainey at her side.

"What's wrong with Max?" Annie asked. "Please tell me it's not James, that he's not..." Elizabeth quickly explained what her mother had said in the letter.

"Amputation?" Meri shook her head. "Why would they even do that?"

"I have heard that it is happening all the time with wounded men." Elizabeth said. "Doctors don't want the wounds to get infected, which can end up killing the patient. If they amputate, the person has a better chance of surviving."

"It's because doctors are butchers." Belle said venomously. She had tears forming in her eyes and looked angrier than Elizabeth had ever seen

175

her. "They don't want to take the time to care for the wound, so instead, they just chop off whatever limb is injured. It's easier for them."

"Belle…" Elizabeth tried to calm her sister down.

"No. The doctors in this war do not know what they are doing. They let Samuel and so many others die of a simple illness. They cut off James's leg with no thought as to how it will affect the rest of his life."

"Belle, I'm sure it was a last resort. It is unfortunate, but at least he is still alive." Meri said.

"For now." Belle wiped at her cheek. "I wouldn't be surprised if he also catches some dreadful disease from that hospital he is at and ends up coming home in a pine box."

With that, Belle turned and stormed away.

Wednesday, July 23, 1862
Bennett Home

"Where could Eric be?" Elizabeth wondered, looking at the clock. He was never this late. She poked her head out the door and finally saw him coming down the road at a quick pace.

"Eric, what's wrong? Is it your mother?"

"Mrs. Bennett, I am so sorry I'm late. It's not Ma, but it's not good news either. The Yankees have arrested some of our townsmen. Mr. Barton, Mr. Knox, Mr. Welford and Mr. Gill."

"What? Why?"

"No one knows for sure, but they're saying that Stanton and General Pope issued commands that won't give us any leniency. The Provost Marshall was charged for being too kind to us."

"Oh, dear, that's not good news." Elizabeth's heart beat wildly. Even with the occupation, their lives had been only mildly inconvenienced by the Federals. Would these new decrees alter their lives more?

"Yes, ma'am, and the stores, all the stores are closed so we can't get supplies of any kind." Eric was clearly distressed, more so than Elizabeth had ever seen him. She grabbed his arm, trying to calm him down. She fully realized how absurd they must look, as Eric was taller than she by almost a head, and she was the calm one.

"Eric, calm yourself. We will be fine."

"Mrs. Bennett, they'll start doing all they can to harass us and maybe even persecute us, but ma'am, that's not the worst part."

"Eric, tell me."

"They're sending wagons out to all the neighboring farms. The word is they're going to take hay and any supplies they can find." Eric looked truly worried. "Ma'am, Turner's Glenn…"

176

"Oh my goodness. Belle." Elizabeth could only imagine what would happen if Belle were to resist the Yankee soldiers.

Belle swept the long braid from her shoulder to her back as she looked down the road that led to Fredericksburg.

"What in the world?" She asked herself as she noticed a wagon flanked by a few Union soldiers on horseback. She wasn't far from the front porch, so she turned back to meet them. As she reached the front porch, Annie and Meri joined her.

"Yankees coming." Belle's heart pounded. What did they want? Lainey also joined them on the porch.

"What's going on?" Lainey asked.

"I'm not sure," Belle said. "Lainey, go quickly and get Daniel and Solomon. Hurry."

Lainey did as Belle asked without any question. The soldiers drew closer and one broke away from the group and approached the sisters.

"Good morning, ladies." He swept his hat off to reveal light brown curly hair. "We are here to requisition some supplies." He rubbed his beard. "Who's in charge of this plantation?"

"I am, sir," Belle said, deciding quickly to turn on the Southern charm she was known for. "Who do I have the absolute honor of addressing?"

"Ma'am, my name is Jeremiah Weber. I am with the Federal army, the first New York." He remained on his horse, not dismounting like a gentleman would. "The Federal army needs supplies for its troops. We need hay and any other goods that you have available. So if you would kindly just point us in the direction of your food stores, we'll load up and be on our way."

"Now, sir, what would you want to be doing that for? We really don't have all that much that would interest men like you."

"If you have any food or hay, then you do have something that we're interested in. Now, if you do not cooperate, we'll just have to search this farm and take what we need, by force if necessary. We may not be so careful about looking for the goods."

"Sir, I do appreciate your need for food, but I have my family and people to provide for. We have at least a dozen people on this plantation who depend upon me to supply them with what they need. You can't just take everything."

"We actually can, ma'am. We have whole armies to feed. My being able to feed my men is more important to me than you feeding your Reb family." He motioned to the men in the wagon. "Don't worry." He said with a smug grin. "We'll only take what we need."

177

No!" Belle cried, as the other men went into the barn. "You can't do this!" She hastened down the porch stairs.

"Ma'am, you are in no position to tell me what I can and cannot do."

"Sir!" Not thinking, Belle grabbed his horse by the reins. Annie gasped, unable to believe the uncharacteristic impulsive move.

"You had best watch your actions." The soldier jerked the reins from her hands. His horse shifted and bumped into Belle, almost knocking her over. Belle's heart pounded and her anger rose. She barely registered the sound of another horse riding up to her.

"How dare you!" Belle cried out. She looked on in frustration as the soldiers with the wagon drove towards the barn.

"If you don't stop right now, I just may be forced to arrest you." The soldier looked as though he might enjoy doing that. "We've had to arrest some fairly influential townspeople today. I'm sure my commander would understand if I took in a she-rebel like you."

"Belle!" Elizabeth, who had jumped off her horse, reached her sister and grabbed her arm. "Belle, stop." She pulled her sister close. "He's right, they can and will arrest you." She then gave Belle's arm a squeeze and addressed the soldier. "Sir, please. Please excuse my cousin." Elizabeth hoped that none of her sisters would let on to her lie. "She just lost her mother and her brother has been mortally wounded. She's not in her right mind, sir." The man looked at her and she took a deep breath, hoping she could make him believe the lie she was about to tell. "Please, sir. My name is Rebekah Turner. My father is an officer in your Union Army. This is his family. This was his childhood home. I don't think he would appreciate you ruining his home and allowing harm to come to his daughter and nieces." She prayed that none of her sisters would do something to cause this soldier to question her lie. The soldier clenched his jaw as if he were considering her words.

"What did you say your father's name was?" He asked.

"I don't know that I did, sir, but my father is Major-General Samuel Turner."

The soldier glanced at the wagon. She could tell that he recognized the name and that he may even know Jonah. She had to use whatever she could to make him believe her. "You may also know my brother, Major Jonah Turner."

"I have heard of the Turners." The soldier said, then rode over towards the men who were about to load the wagon.

"What are you doing?" Belle whispered.

"Trying anything and everything I can think of to save as much as we can," Elizabeth whispered back.

The Captain rode back towards the women just as Solomon and Daniel approached with Lainey.

"Miss Turner, we do need to take some provisions, as an officer's daughter, I am sure you understand that, but you being a loyal, Union daughter, we can leave you some goods." He turned to the two slaves. "You two, you know that you're free to leave whenever you wish. You are no longer slaves. You can even come and work for the Union Army if you wish."

Daniel spoke first. "We know that, sir. We've been free to leave for some time now."

"Yes, sir," Solomon added. "We're still here because we want to be. The Turners is good people."

"All right, then. If you change your mind, remember you are free." And with a motion to his men, they left in the direction of town.

Elizabeth quickly went to Daniel and Solomon, thanking them for their friendship. Annie and Meri both breathed a sigh of relief. Belle sank onto the porch steps, her heart still beating erratically.

"Belle, what were you thinking, arguing with a Federal soldier. He really could have had you arrested." Elizabeth strode over to her sister, a mixture of fear, frustration, anger, and relief coursing through her. Belle looked up at her. "What were you thinking?"

"I was trying to prevent the soldiers from taking all our food, what did it look like I was doing? You don't have to treat me like a child." Belle said, using the railing to pull herself back up. "You're not my mother and I am doing just fine out here without you. We don't need you here."

Elizabeth was taken back. It was true that she hadn't been coming out to the family home much, but she had been busy at her own home.

"Belle, I'm sorry if I offended you. Really, I am, but the Federals have already arrested four townspeople today. I don't want you to be another one."

"Forgive me for trying to actually do something to help around the plantation. Everyone around here thinks that all I can do is flirt and be a hostess, but when I do step up, you come into the picture on your great white horse to rescue us all."

"Belle, I only wanted to help," Elizabeth explained.

"Well, we don't need your help. We're doing just fine on our own. So go back to town and let us get back to our work here." With that, Belle turned and strode into the house. Meri followed her and Daniel and Solomon tipped their heads to Elizabeth and went back toward the fields. Lainey ran off to the barn. Annie quietly approached Elizabeth.

"Don't let her get to you. I believe she really is putting forth an effort to work around here, but is just unsure of how to do so. She just...does not have much of a knack for field work or house work."

179

"Well, it's unfortunate for her, and I'm glad that she is trying to help more, but she doesn't need to take her anger out on me."

"Is it just anger? I was detecting a lot of fear." Annie said.

"Again, you are right." Elizabeth sighed. "I should really go. I left the children with Eric in quite a rush." She gave Annie a small smile. "Thanks for everything you do for the family. I'll try to come by on Sunday. Maybe we could bring back Sunday dinners. We may not have much, but we can still spend time together as a family.

"That's true. Family is what we need during these tough times." Annie agreed. "Speaking of families, I do have to compliment you on your quick thinking; using Uncle Samuel was a stroke of genius."

"The idea came to me as I rode out here. I'm glad they believed me."

"Most of what you said is true. This is Major General Samuel Turner's childhood home, and we are his family." Annie said.

"I suppose." Elizabeth looked toward the house. "I wish Belle knew that I only wanted to help. I miss the days we trusted each other and talked with each other, now it seems we are always arguing. There is always tension between the two of us."

"I must agree, unfortunately," Annie replied. "I wish I could tell you what to do, but I honestly don't know. It will get better with time if the two of you work on it."

"I suppose." Elizabeth nodded. "I wish I could stay longer, I need to get dinner started. You take care, Annie."

"Same to you, Elizabeth," Annie said.

Tuesday, July 29, 1862
Prentiss Home

AJ walked into her home to find Elizabeth sitting at her kitchen table.

"Elizabeth! Good afternoon!"

"Good afternoon, AJ. Liberty let me in. She said you would be back soon."

"I hope you haven't been waiting long." AJ placed her bag on the table. "Can I get you something to eat or drink?"

"No, thank you. I haven't been waiting long. I wanted to show you this." Elizabeth tossed a newspaper onto the table.

"Belle Boyd has been captured?" AJ quickly scanned the article, then looked up. "This is interesting and unfortunate for her, but what does this have to do with me?"

"I think you should stop what you're doing. Stop taking ammunition from soldiers in camp, stop trying to get information from the officers, stop passing things to Nathaniel or Richard Evans or whomever. You have done enough, AJ. I appreciate and support anything that will bring this war to a swift conclusion, but I do not want you sacrificing yourself. It's not worth it. The men will likely be more suspicious of a smart Southern girl spending time in their camp. First Rose O'Neal Greenhow, now Belle Boyd. AJ, you need to stop smuggling.

"How would it look, Elizabeth, if all of the sudden I stop doing what I have been doing since they arrived? That would be suspicious."

"You can still bake for them and do laundry and earn the extra money. You can be kind to them so you are able to keep your livestock and provisions. Act like you did before Nathaniel talked you into this idea of stealing and spying."

"Elizabeth, I appreciate your concern, really, I do, but I am doing something to help the Confederate cause. I feel like I am actually making a difference. I could someday bring information that may help bring the war to a close or information to help our men in a future battle. Information that could save lives."

"But AJ..." Elizabeth tried to interject, but AJ raised a hand.

"No, Elizabeth. I need you to understand. The information I bring helps our troops. I also bring much-needed ammunition and sometimes medicine. Today, I was able to get my hands on quinine and morphine, something our doctors desperately need. Just think, this is medicine that could lessen James's pain and possibly help him recover sooner. I knew what I was getting into when I started this. I will see it through."

Elizabeth sighed and rubbed her temple. She had known AJ wouldn't be easy to convince, knew that it would take a miracle for her to stop smuggling. "I knew you wouldn't listen," She said with a small smile. "I knew, but you are one of my best friends. I had to try.

Wednesday, July 30, 1862
Bennett Home
My Dear Children:

It is with a heavy heart that I tell you that our beloved James has died. His amputation caused an infection and he passed away. I cannot convey the depth of my sorrow. My only solace is that I was with him until the end. I am not quite ready to come home, however. I have found that nurses are in great need. I now have experience in this, not much, but enough. I have decided that I am going to stay here and offer my services for the time being. I know that you, Elizabeth and Belle, can take care of the home in my stead. Solomon can manage the fields. I know this is not easy to hear. It is not easy to write and was not an easy decision. I wish I could be with you all, but sacrifices must be made. I trust you all will understand and make the needed sacrifices that you can as well.

My dear Elizabeth, you are a wonderful mother to Benjamin and Hannah. I know you will be the same for your siblings while I am gone. Belle, I know you will be a wonderful help to your sister and to Solomon. Annie and Meri, I expect you to help, especially with the younger children, as you are both wonderful with them. Lainey, you are becoming a young woman, no longer a girl. I expect you to help your sisters and work on your lessons. I know you will do well. My dear Maxwell, you are now the man of the house. You must be strong and brave and watch out for your sisters.

I love you all more than you can imagine. I will write as often as I can.

-Mother

Elizabeth's heart sank. Dead? James couldn't be dead. He had an amputation: those were supposed to make people get better. It was supposed to stop any illness. The letter slipped from Elizabeth's fingers.

"What does your mother have to say, Elizabeth?" Lucy asked. She had dropped by to deliver the letter to Elizabeth, confident that it held good news for her friend. "Is she bringing James home soon?"

"She's not coming home. She's staying in Richmond. James, he's...he didn't make it."

"What?" Lucy exclaimed. "No, I thought he was supposed to be all right." Lucy couldn't hold back her tears. She was still wearing black, in mourning for her own brother, Charles.

Elizabeth stood and walked over to the window, watching her two children playing in the backyard. How could she tell Benjamin that James, his hero, was dead? And Max? It had been hard on all of them when they found out James had been wounded. How would everyone react to the fact that James was never coming home? What about Nicolle, the woman whom James wanted to marry? Elizabeth choked out a sob and wiped tears from her eyes. Joshua. How was he dealing with the loss of his very best friend? She hugged herself but soon felt Lucy's arms encircle her. Elizabeth turned and held her friend tightly. It wasn't lost on her that not long ago, their roles had been reversed and it had been Elizabeth comforting Lucy after she lost her own brother.

"What can I do for you, Elizabeth? How can I help?"

"Ohhh, I must go to Turner's Glenn and tell my family, and I need to go tell Nicolle Austin. They had a relationship that James hoped to make permanent."

"I see." Lucy said. "I can stay with Benjamin and Hannah while you're gone."

"Thank you." Elizabeth replied. "I'll pack some clothes first, then go over to the Austin's home to talk with Nicolle. I will come back here and pick up the children and leave for Turner's Glenn. I'll need to stay there for a night or two." She took a deep breath and began pacing. "I'll need to talk to Eric as well, let him know what is going on."

"You do what you need to do, Elizabeth, and I will stay with the children. I do understand." She hugged Elizabeth again. "I remember all too well."

Elizabeth snapped the reins, urging Prince, the family horse, to go a little faster. She had spent more time at the Austin's home than she had anticipated. She wanted to get to Turner's Glenn before it got dark. Benjamin and Hannah sat in the back of the wagon, quiet and sullen.

Nicolle had taken the news as Elizabeth expected. She had at first denied it, unable to believe what had happened. Then she had cried, which made Elizabeth believe that the girl truly did care for James, something that she and her sisters had wondered. It wasn't long before Nicolle's mother had come into the parlor and Elizabeth was able to leave. She had quickly gone back to her house, and put her children in the wagon and headed out to the plantation. She had to stay busy, had to keep comforting others. If she thought too much about what had happened...well, she wasn't sure what she would do. Her big brother, James, her funny, easy-going brother, the man who was a favorite uncle to her children, the best friend of her husband and a wonderful friend to her. She sighed. The last thing she wanted to do right now was bring the news to the rest of her family. She had no idea how she would find the strength to do so.

"Mama?" Benjamin looked up at her from his place on the seat. "How long are we gonna stay at Grandma's?"

"I don't know, Benny. It depends on how the news is taken."

"Yes, ma'am." He looked ahead of them. Hannah clutched her doll. She had said very little when Elizabeth had told her and Benjamin about James. Elizabeth wondered how much she actually understood. She dearly hoped that Hannah would have some memories of her uncle.

"Mama?" Benjamin spoke up again.

"Yes, Benjamin?"

"Will I never get to see Uncle James again?"

"Not for a very long time, Benjamin, he's in heaven now." She spoke the words that she hoped and prayed were true.

"With Jesus?" Hannah piped up.

"Yes, Hannah, with Jesus." A tear slipped down Elizabeth's face and she quickly wiped it away.

"Is Daddy gonna go to heaven?" Hannah asked.

"I'm sure he will someday, Hannah-Bear, but I hope it's not for a long, long time." Her eyes continued to water and she wiped them again with the sleeve of her dress. She should have changed into a black dress, but she wanted to break the news to her siblings slowly and showing up in mourning would be obvious. She had brought her dress, though, and hoped her family had a dress for Hannah. She sighed and rubbed her forehead.

"Why did Uncle James have to go up to heaven now? He's just as old as Daddy." Benjamin pointed out.

"That's true, Benjamin, but sometimes age doesn't matter. God needed Uncle James in heaven, so he brought him up there. We don't know why, but God does."

"Because God knows everything," Hannah said proudly.

"That's right, Hannah-Bear." Elizabeth smiled and ran a hand down her daughter's braid.

"So God needed Greyson and Johnny Evans and Auburn and George?" Benjamin asked about some of the children who had died in the Scarlet Fever epidemic.

"Yes, He did," Elizabeth answered.

"Why?" Benjamin asked.

"I don't know. Sometimes we don't know why God lets things happen, but we just have to trust Him."

"We're lucky God loves us so much, aren't we, Mama?" Hannah asked.

"Yes, Bear. We are." God, give me the strength to get through all of this. Elizabeth prayed as the plantation house came into view.

At the sound of the wagon, Daniel stepped out of the stable and made his way toward the visitors.

"Miss Elizabeth. What brings you out here so late in the day?" The man asked. "Everything all right?"

"No, it's not." Elizabeth allowed Daniel to take her gloved hand and help her down, then he lifted Hannah and Benjamin down. "I'm afraid we have bad news about James."

"What's happened to James?" A voice from the porch spoke up.

Elizabeth glanced up to see Meri standing there, clutching the railing. She felt tears once again well up in her eyes. Meri slowly made her way toward her oldest sister. "Elizabeth, what happened?"

Elizabeth pulled out the letter. "Mama wrote, James, he…"

"He went to heaven to be with Jesus!" Benjamin said, a look of seriousness on his face. When did he get so mature? Elizabeth wondered. Meri shrieked and sank to the ground, sobbing.

"Miss Meriwether!" Daniel exclaimed. Elizabeth hurried over to her sister and knelt beside her.

"Meri?" Elizabeth put her arms around her sister and looked up at the porch where Annie and Max now stood.

184

"Elizabeth, what's happened?" Annie asked.

"James!" Meri called out. "No, not James."

"What happened to James?" Max asked. Elizabeth closed her eyes. Meri shook with sobs. This was not going at all like she wanted it to.

"I received a letter from Mama." She said. "It said...Mama said that James developed an infection and he...he didn't make it."

"James is dead?" Max asked.

"Yes, he is in heaven with Jesus," Benjamin told him.

"No! James." Meri called out again. Elizabeth hugged her tightly and looked around.

"Where's Belle?" She asked.

"She was in the back, in the garden cutting flowers for the house," Annie said. "Lainey is out riding."

"I'll go find Miss Isabelle," Daniel said. "You all should be gettin' into the house." He nodded at Elizabeth, then called into the barn for Ruthie's son: "Timmy!" Elizabeth helped Meri stand and they began to make their way into the house. The curly-haired black boy ran up to Daniel, who immediately instructed him to take care of the horse and wagon and to bring in the Bennetts' bags.

Elizabeth had to practically carry Meri up the stairs and into the parlor. Annie led Max, the boy visibly fighting hard not to break into tears. Benjamin took Hannah's hand and pulled her along.

Once they entered the parlor, Elizabeth saw that Belle had already come in and was arranging flowers in a vase.

"Why, Elizabeth! Whatever are you doing here?" She turned and her smile fell as she noticed the looks on her siblings' faces. "What happened?"

Elizabeth led Meri to the settee and helped her sit down, then turned to Belle. "We received a letter from Mother today. Lucy Beale brought it over. Belle..." Elizabeth couldn't say the words again, so she silently handed the letter to her sister. Belle took it and read it, her face turning more and more ashen with every line.

"No!" Belle cried out, much like Meri had. She looked up. "I don't believe it. I can't. He was getting better." She sank into a chair. "How could this have happened?"

"Infections happen, Belle. They just do." Elizabeth had no other explanation.

"The doctors let James, my brother, my best friend, die. I told you they would."

Elizabeth tried not to let the words hurt her. Before her marriage to Joshua, she had been Belle's best friend. "I'm sure they did all they could, Belle," Annie said from the other settee, where she sat with Hannah on her lap. Max and Benjamin sat on each side of her.

Belle looked at the letter again. "Mother staying in Richmond? She is going to abandon us?"

Annie stood. "You didn't tell us that, Elizabeth."

"I didn't get a chance to," Elizabeth explained.

"Mama's not coming back?" Meri looked as though she would collapse again.

Elizabeth crossed the room and sat next to Meri, placing an arm around her. "She'll come back, Meri," Elizabeth said. "She just wants to help the soldiers, and the doctors a bit longer."

"Yes, it is apparent those doctors need all of the help they can get." Belle scoffed. Annie walked towards the door.

"Annie, where are you going?" Elizabeth asked.

"I'm going to find Lainey." She replied. "She needs to know."

Elizabeth nodded. Belle stood and paced, first to a window, then across to some bookshelves.

"I just don't understand," Belle said. "I don't. Doctors are supposed to help people. Not let them die."

Tears streamed down Max's face. Meri was hunched over, still sniffling. Benjamin had started to cry and Hannah clutched her doll. Belle continued pacing, muttering under her breath. Elizabeth continued to rub Meri's back, trying to comfort her, then opened her arm and gestured to Max, silently inviting him to hug her. He stood, took a step toward her, then turned and sprinted out the door. Elizabeth sighed. How was she going to get her family through this?

Saturday, August 2, 1862
Turner's Glenn Plantation

The house felt empty, much like Belle's insides. She didn't want to think. She hadn't eaten since mother's letter had come three days ago, but she wasn't hungry. She wandered out to the front porch and sat on the swinging bench, tucking her legs underneath her. She leaned her head against the rope that held the swing and gazed out across the land. A light breeze blew through the grass. Max was in his room. He hadn't left since Elizabeth had come out with the news that James wouldn't be back. Lainey was in the barn, caring for the horses. Riding had always been her passion, a love that she had shared with James. Lainey hadn't spoken much. Belle wasn't quite sure where Elizabeth and Meri were. Annie was in the kitchen, helping Ruthie.

The sound of hooves pounding on gravel caused Belle to turn her head toward the road. A female rider on a brown bay was coming up quickly. Belle soon recognized AJ. She stood to greet her friend.

"Belle!" AJ threw herself from the horse and hurried up the stairs. "Oh, Belle, I am so sorry." AJ threw her arms around her friend and hugged her tight. "I came out as soon as I could. I cannot believe it." AJ pulled back and looked at her friend, blue eyes filling with tears. "I would ask how you are doing, but I can tell just by looking at you. When is the last time you have had anything to eat?"

"I don't know. What day is it?" Belle asked. "I haven't really eaten anything since we received Mother's letter. I haven't had an appetite. The letter told us that our brother was dead and that she was abandoning us."

"Belle, that's not true. I can promise you that." AJ sat down next to Belle on the swing. "I've just come from a meeting with Nathaniel. He saw your father just before he came to see me. Your mother is working at Chimborazo Hospital in Richmond. Your father agrees she should stay there for now and care for the other patients. He said that she is truly a wonderful, caring and talented nurse."

"But she's a mother first. We just lost James. We need her here. I want my mother here."

AJ was silent, not knowing what to say to her friend. Underneath her carefully prepared image, Belle looked awful. Her hair was perfectly coiffed, as always, her black mourning dress was beautifully tailored and fit her perfectly, even at this low point in her life, Belle looked beautiful, but underneath all that, AJ saw tired, haggard eyes and a vulnerability in Belle's manner that she rarely saw. Her usual confidence and arrogance weren't as apparent as they usually were.

"I hate that she's not here," Belle said.

"She will be back, Belle," AJ replied.

"You don't know that." Belle stood. "I've lost Samuel, I've lost James, and now, I have lost my mother."

Monday, August 11, 1862
Bennett Home

Eric knocked on the door and poked his head in. "Miss Elizabeth, I'm here."

"Thank you for letting me know. How was your walk over?"

"Busy. There's still talk of a battle about forty miles to the west, a place called Cedar Mountain, near Culpepper Court House. There's talk about General Pope's order from last week. Folks are still really upset about that."

On July 30, the Union General Pope had issued an order requiring all male citizens living within his lines to take an oath of allegiance to the Union or leave under penalty of being shot. They had also passed a confiscation bill, which seized the property of all who had refused to take the oath. Elizabeth wasn't sure how that would affect her, Turner's

187

Glenn or the Prentiss Farm, as the landowners were away fighting. She hadn't been able to talk to Kate about what her father was going to do.

"It is an upsetting situation." Elizabeth sighed and looked out the window. Over the past month or so, many people had poured into Fredericksburg. Some had come to speculate and make money. Others came in from the surrounding countryside to buy supplies. Still others had come into town to look for and recover their slaves. The roads were lined with carriages, wagons, and men on horseback.

"Now, the Yankees have announced a 9:00 curfew." Eric shook his head. "I hate what has happened to this town, Mrs. Bennett."

Elizabeth crossed the room and placed a hand on Eric's shoulder. "I know. It's difficult, but I need you to realize how much we need you here. Benjamin, Hannah and I need you. My family out at Turner's Glenn needs you too."

Eric gave Elizabeth a rare smile. "Don't worry, Mrs. Bennett. I made a promise to Mr. Bennett. I won't leave you to go and fight, besides, I still have my mother to care for and I would never abandon her." He spoke quieter. "Not like my father did."

Elizabeth pulled Eric into a hug. "You are a caring young man, Eric Dawson."

"Thank you, Ma'am." He pulled back and gave her a nod. "I'll be in the shop."

Elizabeth watched him leave, then moved back into the kitchen. She stared into her pantry, a sinking feeling in her stomach. She had no idea what she was going to do in a few days when she ran out of some necessary supplies. At least she had vegetables, but there was very little meat, and it was unlikely she would be able to get any soon. Federals covered all of the main roads and confiscated all goods that came through doing a thorough search of all people coming into and leaving town. Even if Eric and Daniel went out hunting, they wouldn't be able to bring any game home. They truly were a town overtaken by the enemy.

Elizabeth turned at the knock on the door. The door opened to a smiling, but damp AJ.

"America Joan, what has happened to you? It's not even raining. Why are you so wet?"

"Well, I had to get into town undetected somehow," AJ said. "Those Yankees are blocking every route into town making it impossible to get here. I didn't want them finding this." AJ placed a sack on Elizabeth's table.

"What did you bring?" Elizabeth grabbed the bag and looked inside.

"Just some things from the farm that I knew would be difficult for you to get here in town." AJ smiled. "Hard-boiled eggs, a chicken, cheese and some venison jerky. I figured you could use some meat most of all."

"AJ, thank you so much." Elizabeth hugged her friend tightly, tears of relief welling up in her eyes.

"Oh, Elizabeth, I did not mean to make you cry. What's wrong?" The two women sat down.

"I am just so relieved. It's been...difficult. I don't have any fresh meat, and it is so expensive to buy. We could get fresh meat if the Federals would just let Eric go out and hunt. We have some vegetables, but not much else. The supplies at the groceries are so expensive, more than I can justify paying or can even afford." She then changed the subject. "I want to go and visit my family and see how they are doing since our brother died." She wiped her eyes. "I'm sorry. I am just so emotional right now."

"It's all right, Elizabeth. I understand." AJ clutched her friend's hand. "Have you heard from Joshua lately?"

"No," Elizabeth replied. "I know the Federals are withholding the mail, and I am sure that he's fine, but his letters were always so uplifting to me." She sighed. "I'll just have to continue re-reading the letters I have."

AJ saw the absolute misery in her friend's eyes. "I'll see if there's any way I can use my contacts to get a message through to you from Joshua. In fact, I would be more than happy to wait until you write another letter to him. I'm fairly confident that it worked last time."

"I appreciate that, and your current offer, but I don't want to add to your danger."

"You're not, Elizabeth." I'm meeting up with a contact in two days anyways. I'll be there whether you give me a letter or not."

Elizabeth sighed, then stood. "There's no reason you need to wait for me to write one." She went over to the side table and picked up a letter. "I already have one that I was waiting to post." She handed it to AJ. "I appreciate you taking it for me." She sat back down. "How did you get into town anyways?"

AJ smiled. "I crossed the river way downstream, where it's shallower and the trees overhang over the river near the island. Then, I snuck into town using some back paths that the Yanks haven't found yet. I'll get back home the same way."

"I see, and you didn't run into any problems with the soldiers?"

"Not at all. I didn't even see any. I have gotten quite good at blending in."

Elizabeth shook her head. "You are one of the kindest women I know. Someday the right gentleman will see what we all see and he will become one of the luckiest men in the world. I don't know if you have noticed, but you seem to have blossomed this past year with all of your activity. You're quite beautiful."

"Thank you for saying that, Elizabeth. I am lucky to have you as a friend."

"And I you," Elizabeth said with a smile. "Did you hear any other news as you passed through town? Eric brings me the news, but you usually have a different perspective on things."

"Well, I'm not sure what he told you, but there are some ugly-looking attitudes showing in our town."

"What do you mean?" Elizabeth asked.

"Our Fredericksburg women are doing whatever they can to make sure the Yankees don't feel welcome here, as they have since the occupation started. They are refusing to walk under the Union flag, treating the soldiers with contempt. I also hear that we cannot even sing the songs we want to sing."

"What?" Elizabeth asked. "That doesn't make sense."

"No, it doesn't. I briefly spoke with Lucy the other day and she told me that any woman heard singing a Southern song could have their nearest male relative arrested. It's enough oppression to make a Unionist living here upset."

"This is madness!" Elizabeth sat back in her chair. "Just plain madness."

"I know, Elizabeth." AJ sighed. "I know."

Tuesday, August 12, 1862
The Banks of the Rappahannock River

"Miss Prentiss, so nice to see you again."

AJ stood from the large rock she had been sitting on. She had seen Richard Evans coming and had mentally prepared for meeting with him. She hoped.

"Mr. Evans." She handed him the package.

"Thank you." He replied. Her hand brushed the riding glove that he was wearing. She was thankful that it wasn't his skin.

"There are some letters in there, too. I'm hoping you can get them to the 30th." She didn't meet his eyes.

"Of course I can do that." He said, an air of total self-confidence about him.

"Thank you." She was about to leave when his words stopped her.

"How are things in town?"

AJ couldn't read his tone, but he seemed genuinely concerned.

"They're not good." She replied. "The Yankees have arrested several men, including Mayor Slaughter and sent them to Old Capitol Prison. You need a pass to get into or out of town, and it can be quite difficult to get the pass. Prices for goods are extremely high, and if a neighbor tries to bring food to either give or sell to friends, they're stopped and their goods confiscated. Most of our local store owners have left town, but very few other civilians have."

"Do you...do you happen to know if my parents are still there? My mother, especially." He looked down, almost as if he were embarrassed to be asking about his family. It touched her heart. There was kindness in this man as she had known all along.

"I haven't heard, although to be honest, I haven't really made a point to do so. I can stop by the next time I'm in town. Would you like me to deliver a letter?"

"Actually, I did bring one. If you wouldn't mind." He handed an envelope to her. "I would question your ability to get that into town undetected, but I have seen what you can do."

She smiled. "Yes, and you should never forget it."

Richard took a look around. The sun was falling in the sky, causing pink light to reflect off the slow-moving river. "This is such a beautiful spot." He commented. "I had almost forgotten." He leaned against a boulder and crossed one ankle over the other. "You know, once in awhile, I would sneak down here to fish." He looked longingly at the water.

"I know. I did too." AJ paused. "I'm not sure if you even remember, but we met up once down here."

"We did?" Richard looked surprised.

"Yes. I was probably eleven or twelve at the time. I remember being nervous at first because you were always so conceited, especially when you were with your friends. That afternoon, however, I saw some kindness in you." AJ wasn't sure what made her so bold to talk with him about the past. She leaned on the boulder next to him. She didn't mention that the kindness she had observed had been erased the next time she saw him when he had once again belittled her in front of his friends.

"I really don't remember ever seeing you here before, Miss Prentiss." He looked down at her. "I'm sorry."

AJ shrugged. "I don't know why you would."

"Why would you remember, then?" Richard's voice was soft. She looked up at him. His eyes were fixed on her, and she was closer to him than she had thought. Too close for her comfort. She looked away and took a deep breath.

"I don't know, Mr. Evans. Perhaps women tend to remember all social interactions with men while men look at women as conquests and easily forgotten."

"I suppose that's true," Richard said.

191

AJ looked at the sun, which had continued to drop in the sky. "I had better get home. It will be dark soon."

"Of course. I need to get back to camp too. I will see that these letters get to the 30th." He gave her a smile, so bright that it would light up a cotton barn.

"I will be sure to get your letter to your mother the next time I'm in town." She assured him.

"My mother, not my father," He clarified. "Thank you. I really do appreciate it. The whole Confederacy thanks you for what you're doing." He held up the package she had brought.

"You are welcome. Take care of yourself, Mr. Evans."

As AJ walked through the familiar woods back to her farm, she couldn't get the conversation with Richard out of her mind. She wished that she could find hope in the kindness he showed her today, but that hadn't happened last time.

Tuesday, April 5, 1853
Banks of the Rappahannock

"Catching anything?" Thirteen-year-old AJ turned to the voice behind her. Her breath caught. It was none other than Richard Evans, one of the best-looking young men in town. He was two years older than her, with a charming, bright smile, blonde hair, and sparkling blue eyes. Many a young woman in Fredericksburg fancied him. AJ was just starting to notice the opposite sex and definitely thought Richard the most handsome boy she had ever seen. He jumped down from a boulder to stand next to her. His hair was mussed, and he wore dark gray trousers with a light blue button-up shirt.

"Not much today, no." She said, wishing that she had taken a little more care with her appearance today. She was wearing one of her old dresses, as she didn't want to dirty a new one. She was heavier than most girls, and she strongly disliked that about herself. She knew she would never be a striking beauty like her friend Belle. Even Kate and Elizabeth had better figures than she did. AJ knew she would only have her skills as a cook and seamstress to catch a husband, but that was still a long way off.

"You're Nathaniel Prentiss's little sister, right?" He asked.

"Yes. America Joan, but most folks just call me AJ."

"That's right." Richard pulled out some bait from the bag he had slung over his shoulder.

"I thought your family lived in town. What are you doing on this side of the river?" AJ asked.

"The fish bite better over here." He said with a shrug, then cast his line into the river. AJ looked at him.

"That can't possibly be the only reason." She pointed out.

"Ah, so you're a perceptive girl." He glanced at her and smiled. "Well, between you and I, America, the main reason is that my father is less likely to find me over here."

"Why would your father care if you go fishing?" AJ asked. Her father was always glad when she, Nathaniel or Liberty could bring home some fresh fish or game.

"Fishing isn't a respectable pastime for gentlemen. According to my father, if it won't further my future, as in following in his footsteps, then it's not worthwhile."

"So having fun is out of the question." She asked, joking obvious in her voice.

"Absolutely." Richard smiled. "The more fun, the less he approves."

"You can at least attend parties and the like, correct?" She asked.

"Yes, as those could potentially advance my future career."

"Future career? You can't be much older than me. Why do you need to worry about that already?"

"My father's been preparing me to take over his business. I can't remember my life being any other way." Richard said. He reeled in his line, frowned when he saw it was empty, then cast it back out.

"Is that what you want to do?" AJ asked.

"I don't know. Maybe. It will probably be a long time before I ever have to take over completely, so I just don't worry about it." He shrugged. "I can still have fun when he doesn't know, and I plan to, starting this weekend. The Lacys are having people over for a barbecue."

"Yes, I know. They're family, so I will be attending as well. It should be a wonderful time."

The bells of St. Mary's Church rang four o'clock.

"Well, that's my warning bell. I need to get home to finish preparing supper for my family." AJ smiled. "Maybe I'll see you this weekend."

"Yes, it was good talking to you, America. I'll see you Saturday."

1862

"He talked to me all right," AJ said to herself, shaking her head at the memory. She had approached him while he was with his friends. He had ignored her and acted as if he didn't even know her. She had been heartbroken, devastated. Nathaniel had found her upset and tearful next to the horse barn and threatened to harm Richard, but she didn't want to create a scene and had begged him not to do anything. She had learned a valuable lesson that day, which was why she wouldn't get her hopes up, or expect anything from the amiable, pleasant conversation with Richard Evans. She wouldn't let her heart make the same mistake again.

Thursday, August 28, 1862
Bennett Home

"That was my easiest entry into town since the Yankees took over the city," Kate said with a smile as she dismounted from her horse, Flirt. "I didn't get stopped once. The Yankees seem preoccupied."

"They are," Elizabeth said with a smile. "I heard they are finally preparing to evacuate. Stonewall Jackson captured and plundered a Union supply depot at Manassas Junction. That's probably where they're headed.

"Another battle where our men can show those Yankees what this war is all about to us, our Southern independence." Kate said.

"Yes, let's hope we win again so this war can be over." Elizabeth said.

"I feel as though we should celebrate now," Kate said. "Get messages out to Turner's Glenn and AJ's farm and all of us gather together. Maybe have a feast." Kate smiled as a soldier passed them. "We should have it here at your house, just because we can."

"I wouldn't object to that," Elizabeth said. "Being able to travel wherever I wish, to go to the grocery and get whatever I need to feed my family, to get fresh meat from the woods. I will never take any of that for granted again."

"You're right. It has been strange, not being able to travel as freely as I wish. It will be a nice change."

"I believe it may take a week or so to get the town really back to normal. Well, pre-occupation normal, that is."

"Yes," Kate replied. "I hope all of our shopkeepers return soon to open their businesses."

"It hardly seems real. These past few months have felt like years. Is it possible for anyone to ever get used to being occupied by an enemy army."

"I surely couldn't. I honestly don't know how you all survived in town as well as you did."

"It is incredible to find out what one is truly capable of," Elizabeth said. "This whole war has been proof of that. If you were to ask me two years ago how long I could survive not being with Joshua, I would have said maybe a few days would be the maximum. It has been so much longer and I have survived." They had entered Elizabeth's house and sat down to continue their conversation. Elizabeth poured some watered down tea.

Kate took a sip. It was weak, but soon they would be able to get a better quality. "It must be nice, though, to have...someone you love that much. Someone who loves you so much he wants to get home to you."

"It is," Elizabeth answered. "I thought you and Stockton Heth were still courting."

"We are, and I do care for him. He is very attentive to me, but it sometimes seems as though he's trying to...win me. I'm not sure why I feel that way, but I do."

"I understand why that would make you hesitant."

Kate paused. It wasn't often that she spoke with her friends about her fears. She wanted to be married more than anything.

"Elizabeth, how did you know that Joshua was the right man for you?"

"I honestly don't know how to explain it," Elizabeth said. "One day, I looked at him and I just knew. We had been friends for years. We could just talk and talk for hours. One day I just looked at him and realized I couldn't live my life without him. I had always thought him handsome." She sighed. "It seemed so easy for me. I never doubted the relationship, even though some pointed out, quite frequently, I might add, the fact that he was of a lower class than me."

"I remember you and Belle arguing about that all the time," Kate said.

Elizabeth nodded. "I love my sister dearly, but there is a lot we disagree on. I won't lie, I never thought she and Samuel were a good match. I told her that many times."

"You would be in the minority with that view," Kate said.

"I am often in the minority with my views," Elizabeth admitted. "I have always believed there is someone out there who would be a better match for her. I'm not saying that I'm glad Samuel is dead. Not at all. He had his good qualities, but I am glad Belle didn't end up married to him."

"What was it that made you object to him, if you don't mind my asking?" Kate said.

"I don't mind you asking. I told Belle enough times." Elizabeth looked at her tea. "I never saw any love between the two. He was attentive and caring and she enjoyed being with him, but I didn't feel any love. I think her reaction to his death was also very telling. It's interesting, how you said that you feel as though Mr. Heth is only courting you as a prize to be won. That is how I felt Samuel and Belle's relationship was. He started pursuing her because she was desired by so many young men." She shrugged. "I don't know. I could be wrong, maybe they really did love each other. I just didn't see it."

195

"Perhaps it was different between them when no one else was around," Kate suggested.

"Perhaps," Elizabeth replied. "Going back to your original question, however. My advice would be that if you're asking yourself if he is really the right man for you. Well, if you're having any doubt, he's probably not the right choice."

Kate leaned back in her chair. "You've certainly given me some things to consider. Thank you."

Elizabeth nodded. "I may not be an expert, Kate, but I'm always willing to talk a situation over."

"I know. I feel lucky to call you a friend." She smiled.

Sunday, August 31, 1862
Turner's Glenn

"Oh, happy day!" Kate said, entering the parlor at Turner's Glenn. The four women had finally gotten together in celebration of the Federal withdrawal. They had decided to meet at Turner's Glenn, not the Bennett house because the town was still extremely busy. Elizabeth wanted to get out of town and Benjamin and Hannah wanted to get out into the country as well.

"Will AJ and Liberty be making it out here as well?" Kate asked. "I was going to bring my nephews and Janie, but my sisters were being difficult. I'm not sure why. It did make my travel a little easier. I was able to saddle up Flirt and enjoy a refreshing ride."

"Did you run into any Federals on the road on their way out?" Elizabeth asked.

"I saw a few, but they are still quite preoccupied with getting out of here as quickly as they can. Thank the good Lord."

"I let myself in, I hope you don't mind," AJ said, coming into the parlor.

"Of course we don't mind," Belle said. "We are just so glad you could make it. Is Liberty with you?"

"Yes, but of course she was pulled immediately away by all the children."

"Did we even have to ask?" Elizabeth said with a smile. "She is an angel to those little ones."

AJ sat down, unusually quiet. Her friends could tell right away that something was wrong.

"AJ, what is bothering you?" Belle asked. "You do not seem yourself today. Did something happen at church?"

"We didn't make it to church this morning," AJ said quietly.

Elizabeth, Kate, and Belle all exchanged a concerned look. AJ never missed church.

"What happened?" Elizabeth was almost afraid to ask.

"Liberty and I had to clean up around the farm. We almost didn't come today, but we really needed a break." She took a deep breath. "As they were leaving, the Yankees decided to take the most direct route to get wherever they were going, whether there was a road or not. The most direct route was right though our wheat field. They knocked over some of our fences and destroyed at least half the crop. It is just gone. Flattened." Tears glistened in her eyes. "I am so upset with the Yankees. Ruining a perfectly good crop with no thought or consideration to anyone else. Thankfully, we still have the vegetables, as those were planted closer to the house."

"You also have Liberty, who is a very good hunter," Belle added.

"You have us." Elizabeth reached out to grasp AJ's wrist. "We will do whatever we need to help you out."

AJ wiped at her eyes, brushing the tears from them. "I know, and God will provide."

"He will," Kate said. "We just have to support one another and keep the faith. All will turn out for the best."

Tuesday, September 2, 1862
Fredericksburg

Elizabeth picked up a small sack of flour and placed it in her basket, then made her way to the front of the store to settle her account. Mrs. Sarah Doggett smiled at her from behind the counter.

"Good afternoon, Mrs. Bennett. Have you heard from your mother lately?"

"Not in a while. She's still working as a nurse in Richmond. How is Mr. Doggett?"

"He is doing well." She smiled. "All of his experience in the Fredericksburg Greys is helping him immensely."

"How wonderful for him," Elizabeth replied. "Is there any news on the war?"

"Afraid so." The woman frowned. "Another fight at Manassas. The 30th was involved this time."

Elizabeth's face paled. "Did we...was anyone..." she couldn't say the words, her heart beat wildly.

"Oh, Mrs. Bennett, you have nothing to fear. I didn't see Joshua or your father on the casualty list. We did lose Jedidiah Buckley, though."

"Oh, goodness. Poor Margaret." Elizabeth placed a hand over her heart, glad that her family was safe. "I am so sad for Margaret. Now she is all alone in the world.

"That she is. Such a shame."

"Are you talking about Margaret Buckley?" Mrs. Jane Beale, Lucy's mother came to the counter, hands on her hips. "Poor Mr. Buckley, you mean. Saddled with that girl all those years, even after her mother passed, she was constantly a burden and then she brought so much shame on him."

Elizabeth stayed silent. She wanted to defend Margaret. She was a sweet, kind girl, even though it was rumored that she kept inappropriate company with men. Many women, Belle included, judged her harshly and shunned her.

"Seems to me a girl like that deserves everything she gets." Mrs. Beale continued. "I do wonder what she'll do now. No kind stepfather to care for her and no decent man will marry her with her disreputable reputation."

Elizabeth shrugged, wishing she had the courage to say something in defense of Margaret, but she didn't want to upset Mrs. Beale. Margaret Buckley did have a reputation, but Elizabeth had a very strong suspicion that the rumors were unfounded.

"No one deserves to lose someone they love." She said quietly. Mrs. Doggett heard her and nodded.

Mrs. Doggett finished adding up her groceries, and Elizabeth paid, thanked her, and left. As she exited the mercantile, she paused. Going left would bring her home to her family. Going in the opposite direction would bring her to the Buckley Millinery Shop. She quickly decided she had time to go and comfort Margaret. She had a feeling that not many people in town would do the same.

"Good afternoon, Mrs. Bennett." Reverend Dominic Wetherly smiled at Elizabeth as he approached her. The Reverend was a good friend of Joshua's. His father was also a preacher and Dominic aided him and would one day take over his father's position. "Running errands today?" He smiled, his brown eyes warm and inviting. Elizabeth was quickly reminded of how much she preferred Dominic's sermons of love and redemption to his father's passionate speeches of fire and brimstone. Dominic was a good man.

"I was at the Doggett's store and discovered that Margaret Buckley's stepfather was killed at the latest battle of Manassas. I was going to offer my condolences to her."

"Mr. Buckley is dead? This is tragic news." Dominic looked in the direction of Buckley's Millinery. "Would you mind if I went with you? Miss Buckley may be in need of my services."

"I wouldn't mind at all, Dominic." She replied. "In fact, I believe your company is just what Miss Buckley needs." Elizabeth wasn't usually a matchmaker, but it occurred to her that Dominic and Margaret would be good together. From the look of concern on Reverend Wetherly's face, he had some feelings for her.

Elizabeth and Dominic made their way to the shop that was also the Buckley home. The door was unlocked, so the two walked in. A red-eyed Margaret stood behind the counter. Elizabeth immediately set her basket down and went to hug her.

"Margaret, I heard what happened. I am so sorry for your loss."

Margaret hugged her back. "Thank you so much for coming by Mrs. Bennett. You are too kind." Margaret looked up and her heart skipped a beat as she saw Dominic Wetherly standing there. "Reverend." She nodded at him.

"Miss Buckley." He gave the slightest of bows. In spite of the circumstances, Elizabeth grinned to herself. The usually outgoing reverend looked unsure of himself in Margaret's presence. Was it because of her reputation, or did he truly have feelings for Margaret? She was a beautiful woman, with blonde hair, blue eyes, and a kind smile. She was quiet and some people called this behavior uppity, but Elizabeth felt her attitude had more to do with her reputation than her disposition.

"Margaret, I just wanted to let you know that if there is anything I can do, please let me know," Elizabeth said.

"I thank you again for your kindness," Margaret replied, tears forming in her eyes. "But I wouldn't want...I wouldn't want your reputation to be tarnished because of an association with me."

"Margaret, I thought..." Reverend Wetherly started to speak. "Margaret, please do not tell me that you are wasting your tears on him!"

Elizabeth turned toward Dominic, shocked. Anger was obvious on his usually friendly face and his fists were tightly clenched. Elizabeth had never witnessed such emotion from him and couldn't help but feel as though she was hearing a conversation that she shouldn't be.

"I'm...I'm not. It...it's worse than that, Dominic." She shook her head. "I mean, Reverend Wetherly." Margaret took a breath. "I'm crying because...because I'm actually relieved." Elizabeth took a step back from Margaret as Dominic came around the counter to take her into his arms.

"It's all right," Dominic said, rubbing her back gently. "He's gone and you're safe now."

Elizabeth stared at the two, confusion giving way to understanding as she pieced together the comments made by both Dominic and Margaret, along with observations she had made in the past. Margaret had started crying and Dominic continued to hold her. Elizabeth picked up her basket and quietly left, knowing she would visit Margaret again soon.

Wednesday, September 3, 1862
Banks of the Rappahannock River

"Nathaniel! I am so glad it's you!" AJ threw her arms around her brother. "How have you been?"

"I am fine, and Father is well too. We are actually quite happy, especially now that the Yankees have left Fredericksburg for good. I expect we won't let them back around these parts."

"I will hold you to that, Soldier," AJ said with a smile.

"You can count on it." Nathaniel grinned back. "Do you have anything of importance for me?"

"I have these." AJ handed him several packages that contained bullet cartridges, medication and even a bayonet that the retreating army had left. "As well as a note about some observations that I made while the Yankees were leaving." AJ didn't tell him about the destruction of their fields. She didn't want to worry him when there was nothing he could do about the situation. "Since the Yanks are gone, I won't have any new information. Even so, please tell Lt. Daniels that if he ever needs me for anything: missions, information gathering, anything like that, he just needs to contact me."

"I will let him know," Nathaniel said, pride evident in his voice. "Has everything been okay with your other contacts?"

AJ wasn't sure if he knew her only other contact was Richard Evans, but she wasn't going to be the one to tell him.

"Yes, everything has gone quite smoothly." She forced a smile. "Although it would be nice if it was always you. I miss you and father so much."

Nathaniel shrugged. "I'm sent on a lot of missions, mostly carrying messages. I've actually been over the mountains to the western states carrying messages a few times or meeting contacts halfway between here and the western theater. It has been an interesting experience."

"I am happy that you are able to stay away from the battles." AJ smiled. "How often do you get to see Papa?"

"Once in a while. Not as much as I would like to." Nathaniel replied. "How is Liberty?"

"She's fine. Hasn't changed much since you left. She's upset that I won't let her help with any of the spying or smuggling. I give her few details, as I don't want her involved."

"That's probably smart, she can be a little reckless at times." Nathaniel nodded, then looked down the river and rubbed his jaw. "I should be going, even with the Yankees gone, there may be some stragglers or deserters. I don't want to run into either one, and I definitely don't want you to."

"Oh, Nathaniel. You know I can take care of myself." She reached into her pocket and pulled out a derringer. "I can handle anyone who tries to harm me."

"I have no doubt." Nathaniel smiled as he looked at the small pistol in her hand. "I'm the one who taught you how to shoot, although that is a lot smaller than what we used. You still need to be careful."

"I know." AJ tucked the derringer back into her pocket. "I appreciate your concern." She hugged her brother again. "Take care of yourself, Nathaniel."

"Same to you, sister." He replied.

Thursday, September 4, 1862
Fredericksburg

"Mama, how many people do you think are here?" Benjamin asked, tugging at his collar. Elizabeth had dressed both of her children in their Sunday best, as many people were coming into town from the surrounding countryside. The Turners, Prentis women, and Corbins were all due soon. The town wanted to get together to celebrate the end of the occupation. Mail had finally been delivered and many citizens were hearing from their family members for the first time in months. There was much excitement.

"I'm not sure, Benjamin. It should be a lot, though."

"Best of all, no dirty Yanks." He said. Elizabeth sighed. She had hoped Benjamin wouldn't take on the judgmental attitude of the local citizens in their dislike of the Federals, but unfortunately, he had.

"Benjamin, Hannah!" The Bennett children turned to see their aunts. Lainey had been the one to call out to the children as she wove through the crowd.

"Lainey! We're free!" Hannah yelled and jumped into her aunt's arms.

"That we are, Hannah-Bear." Lainey smiled, then bent to hug Benjamin.

"We can come out and see you whenever we want and not have to worry about them Yankees stopping us!" Benjamin added to his sister's statement.

"That's right! We don't have to worry about getting passes or getting searched just to come for a visit." Lainey said. Max, Meri, Annie, and Belle joined the small gathering, smiles on everyone's faces.

"There sure are a lot of people in town today," Belle commented. "We just had Daniel drop us off and we walked the rest of the way. It's hard enough walking, let alone navigating a carriage through the town."

"People are excited," Elizabeth said. "And rightly so. It is wonderful not to constantly be worried about the soldiers."

"I'm sure this will be good for the whole Confederacy." Belle looked up the street and saw AJ and Liberty walking towards them.

"This is so exciting!" AJ said as she approached the group. She was smiling and her eyes sparkled.

"It is such a relief to travel into town with no hassle." Liberty added. "Hassle from the enemy, that is. The celebrating crowds are fine."

"How is the farm coming along, AJ?" Elizabeth asked.

AJ shrugged. "It's not as bad as we initially thought, just so much added work." She replied. "The crop loss is still quite concerning."

"I can imagine," Belle said. "Barbaric Yankees have no respect."

"You can't say that of all Northerners, Belle," Elizabeth said. "Some of them showed a lot of respect and restraint."

"If you say so," Belle replied. "Shall we move to Elizabeth's porch?"

"I'm going to go to Nannie Alsop's and visit if that's all right," Annie said. Nannie was a good friend of Annie's.

"Of course, Annie," Elizabeth replied.

"Meri and I were hoping to see Marion," Liberty said. Marion Beale was Lucy's sister and a friend of Liberty and Meri.

"Of course, go ahead," AJ said. "You all be careful."

Lainey looked at Max, Benjamin, and Hannah. "I suppose the four of us can play in the backyard. Send any Corbins back when they get here."

Elizabeth couldn't help but chuckle at her younger sister, always so matter-or-fact. As the children ran to the backyard, the women sat on the front porch.

"She is growing up quickly," AJ said of Lainey. "I hate to say it, but if this war lasts much longer, your father might not recognize her, or Max for that matter."

"Hannah and Benjamin either," Belle added flippantly. "Perhaps not even Turner's Glenn. There may be a lot of things that Father won't recognize."

"Some things won't change, Belle. Such as his love and commitment to your family." AJ assured her.

"I suppose," Belle said. "It's difficult to imagine what he'll think when he comes home."

"Hopefully it will be sooner than we all expect," AJ said.

Elizabeth nodded and gently rocked her chair. It wasn't long before Kate approached the house, with Janie, Parke, and Gardiner in tow. The women greeted Kate and the children were brought to the backyard. It wasn't long before the conversation turned to the news. There was so much to catch up on.

"Belle, I have been meaning to ask you," AJ said. "Does Annie still keep in contact with that young man she met at the Herndon-Maury wedding?"

"That cad? Jonathan Diggle?" Belle scoffed. "No, thank goodness. We are glad for it. She wrote him a few letters after he went home to Georgia, and he has never answered them."

"Annie is convinced that she was only temporary amusement for him," Elizabeth added. "Unfortunately, it appears as though she's right."

"That's too bad," AJ said. "I thought they made a good-looking couple."

"I don't agree," Belle said. "Annie can absolutely do so much better, so I personally have never thought that to be the case."

"Some man will be extremely lucky to marry her," Kate added.

"I agree with you for a change," Elizabeth said, then turned at the sound of the crowd shouting and hooves pounding the road. "It's the cavalry." She stood and walked the ten feet to the white picket fence to get a better look. Kate, AJ, and Belle joined her as the horse soldiers came into view and people cheered.

"Confederates!" Belle exclaimed, and pulled her handkerchief to wave at them. "Bless you, boys!" She called out. The children ran to the fence, and they all joined in the cheering and waving. AJ's eyes caught those of a familiar Confederate officer. Richard Evans. He smiled at her and tipped his hat in an arrogant manner, then rode over to them.

"Good evening, ladies!" He exclaimed, not dismounting.

"Why, Richard Evans, fancy seeing you around these parts." Belle gave him a flirtatious smile.

"Just here to protect our beautiful Virginia belles." He said. "You ladies are all looking splendid."

"As are you, sir."

AJ inwardly seethed. What was Belle doing, flirting with her dead fiance's best friend? Shouldn't she show more restraint, more respect? What she really couldn't figure out was why it bothered her so much. Deep down, AJ knew. She knew that, after all these years, she still wanted to be the one receiving the attentions of Mr. Richard Evans.

"Well, thank you, Miss Turner. I must say that being out and about our beautiful Virginia countryside has been agreeing with me over this past year or so."

"It certainly has," Belle responded.

"It is good seeing you all, but I must be off to visit some other acquaintances. Mrs. Bennett, Miss Corbin, Miss Turner." He tipped his hat to each of them, then focused his gaze on AJ. "Miss Prentiss. Always a pleasure." He then turned and rode off to the east.

"Belle, really," Kate said. "Flirting already, and with Samuel's best friend? Are you really ready to move on so soon?"

"With Richard Evans? Probably not." Belle said. "I can't see him settling down anytime soon. To be honest, he probably is on his way right now to visit Margaret Buckley, if you know what I mean."

AJ's heart sank. Belle was probably right. Why does it matter to me, whose company he keeps? Why do I care so much?

"Belle, that's not true. Be kind to Margaret." Elizabeth said. "You remember, her stepfather was recently killed at Manassas. She's all alone in the world."

"Yes, because all of the men she was friends with are fighting," Belle stated in a judgmental tone.

"All I'm saying is that we should always take care with what we say and how we act toward others," Elizabeth said. "Things may not always be what they seem." Elizabeth thought about Reverend Weatherly and his reaction to Mr. Buckley's death. If the Reverend was a friend of Margaret's, then perhaps there was more to the situation than what the rumors reflected.

"As usual, Elizabeth. You have your opinions, and I will have mine." Belle said. "Perhaps I won't take Richard Evans completely off my list of potential suitors. The war certainly has enhanced his looks, if that's even possible. Perhaps it will also help him settle down."

"You have mentioned that before." Elizabeth stifled a sigh, once again not understanding her sister.

The streets began to clear of soldiers as they dispersed to their destinations.

"Well, I should probably start dinner," Elizabeth suggested.

"That sounds like a plan," Kate said, and they all made their way inside the house.

Sunday, September 7, 1862
Episcopal Church

"That was a fine sermon today, Reverend," Elizabeth said, shaking Dominic's hand, Benjamin and Hannah both at her side. "Your father must be glad to know that he can take a week off and leave the congregation in such capable hands."

"Thank you, Mrs. Bennett." The Reverend replied with a slight smile. "I appreciate your kind words."

"I would like to invite you to dinner this afternoon. I can't offer you a five-course meal, but I can promise you something tasty. That is, if you don't already have plans."

"Thank you. I would be happy to accept." Dominic replied. "Mother went with Father to Richmond, so I would be cooking for myself, and I must admit I wasn't looking forward to that."

"Wonderful!" Elizabeth replied. "I will see you shortly, then."

After a simple, but filling meal of chicken and potatoes, Elizabeth offered the Reverend some weak coffee and put Benjamin and Hannah down for a midday rest.

"I must confess, Mrs. Bennett, I am glad you asked me to dinner today for more than one reason. I have been meaning to discuss something with you."

"Oh? What's that?" Elizabeth asked, hoping she would finally be told more about his relationship with Margaret Buckley.

"You recall last Tuesday, I am sure, when we heard of Jedidiah Buckley's death?"

"Of course," Elizabeth replied.

"Margaret and I realize you may have witnessed some...interaction between the two of us that may have been considered inappropriate."

"I did notice, but I would never say anything, believe me," Elizabeth said. "Well, perhaps to Joshua, but not in a letter and never to anyone else."

"We know that, Mrs. Bennett, and I must tell you that I appreciate the kindness you show to Margaret. Not everyone is quite as benevolent."

"Including my own sister," Elizabeth admitted.

"Yes, true." Dominic acknowledged. He folded his hands on the table in front of him. "What I am about to tell you...I know you will keep the information in the strictest of confidence, but I...well, I need someone to know. I will tell you my side of the story and hope Margaret will fill you in on her side."

Belle nodded and Dominic continued. "Margaret and I have been friends for quite some time, ever since we were children as a matter of fact. She has always been dear to me, always kind and considerate. It was quite difficult when her real father died."

"In a hunting accident, wasn't it?" Elizabeth asked in recollection.

"Yes." The Reverend nodded. "As you know, not a year later, when Margaret was thirteen and becoming a beautiful young woman, her mother remarried. She was struggling to keep their farm afloat, so was relieved when the respectable shop owner asked her to marry him." Dominic paused, gathering his thoughts.

"Yes, I remember all of that," Elizabeth said.

"Margaret and I continued to be friends, but about a year later, well, that's when I knew something was wrong. I eventually found out that Jedidiah was abusing her in the worst way. He also hurt her physically, then would say condescending, hurtful things to her, making her feel worthless. I told her that she needed to tell someone, anyone, but she wouldn't, and she made me promise never to tell a soul. She was so ashamed. She didn't want anyone to know and hated that she had even confided in me. She wouldn't even tell her mother and said that if I spoke a word of it to anyone, she would deny it. I feel as though her mother did know, however."

Elizabeth shook her head, tears in her eyes. "How could a man...how could he do that?"

"You would be surprised what some men can do, Mrs. Bennett," Dominic said. "Margaret and I had an argument. I wanted to confront the...excuse me, her stepfather. I am ashamed to admit that I stopped communicating with her. I hated having to keep her secret, hated having everyone in town look at Jed Buckley like he was a wonderful example of kindness and generosity. Everyone thought he was so wonderful because he gave Margaret and her mother a home and kept Margaret under his roof even after her mother died."

"Yes, when Margaret was what...fifteen? A horrible accident."

"To be honest, I'm not entirely certain that it was an accident, Mrs. Bennett. I have never believed that Margaret's mother really fell down those stairs."

Elizabeth gasped. "How horrible, do you mean...are you saying that he pushed her?"

"I have my suspicions. I believe she was trying to defend her daughter at the time. After her mother died, I tried to talk to Margaret. I tried to get her out from under that man's control. It didn't work. She was too scared about what he might do and was convinced that no one would believe her. With her mother gone, it was his word against hers. No one would believe an upstanding man like Jed Buckley was capable of doing what she proclaimed."

"That's a sad statement, but it is probably true," Elizabeth commented.

"Well, Margaret and I had another argument and I deserted her yet again. Not long after is when rumors started circulating about how she was spending time and keeping inappropriate company with men like Richard Evans and Samuel Gray."

"From what I could tell, they were all just rumors," Elizabeth suggested. "There was never any proof."

"I thought they were true at the time, but now I am not sure," Dominic replied. "I asked Margaret about the rumors and she just shrugged it off and acted like it was of no concern to her. I should have confronted Evans and Gray, but I didn't want them to confirm the rumors. I now realize Margaret acted like she did because she really

206

didn't care about herself or her reputation. I sometimes wonder if it was a subtle way of getting back at her stepfather. For whatever reason, she was ostracized by the people in this town after those rumors began. The citizens saw Jedidiah was now even more benevolent and tolerant. I turned my back on her yet again. I wish you had lived in town then. You could have been a better friend to her than I was."

"Dominic, you were angry, frustrated about something that you could not control. I can see both points of view, both yours and Margaret's."

"You've just proven my point." He said with a small smile. "You could have helped both of us, but that's water under the bridge, as they say." He sighed. "I must admit that I am in love with her. I always have been. I have tried to express my feelings to her, but she rejects me still. When she turned eighteen, I asked her to marry me. I wanted to get her away from her stepfather and into a good, caring, loving relationship, but she turned me down. I believe she is ashamed and sees herself as damaged goods."

"You could try again, Dominic, from what I witnessed on Tuesday, she accepted your comfort very naturally. I believe she has feelings for you."

"I did ask her again. She said 'no', again. Said that I deserved someone who could love me better than she ever could. I know her self-worth is very low, but nothing I say can convince her she is worthy of God's love, as well as mine."

"I am so sorry." Elizabeth put a comforting hand on his. "What can I do to help?"

"Unfortunately, I am leaving Fredericksburg, Mrs. Bennett. I feel the Lord is calling me to a new position. I am joining the army as a chaplain. I should have done it earlier, but I really felt I needed to watch over Margaret. With her stepfather out of her life, I feel comfortable leaving. The reason I have confided in you is that it would bring peace of mind to me if I knew...if I knew someone here was watching out for Margaret. You are one of the most understanding, kindest women in town. You taking the time to comfort her when that scum of a stepfather died reinforced my belief in that." He ran a hand through his hair. "I apologize for my loss of propriety. I should not have said that. I'm not asking you to be best friends with her, but..."

"Dominic," Elizabeth interjected, then smiled. "I have always tried to be kind to Margaret, that's true, but she seemed to always keep me at a distance. Now that I know more, there is nothing that will keep me from reaching out to her. You have my word on that."

"Thank you, Mrs. Bennett. I knew I could count on you. I have said it before, and I will say it again, Joshua is very lucky to have you."

"Well, I have always believed that it is the other way around, but thank you." She smiled and a feeling of longing coursed through her, as it always did whenever Joshua came to mind. "Dominic, I do ask something in return."

"Of course." He said. "What is it?"

"Prayer." She replied. "Prayer for our country and our families and my Joshua, but especially prayers for Margaret so that she is able to open up to me."

Dominic smiled. "I have already been doing that, but I will continue to do so."

Saturday, September 27, 1862

My Dearest, Elizabeth

I hope this letter finds you and the children well. I miss you dearly and pray every day and night that we will soon be reunited.

We were again involved in a battle, this one near the town of Sharpsburg, Maryland. It is possibly the bloodiest, most destructive battle of our continent's history. It still hurts me to think about how much life was lost on both sides.

When the fighting was over, we remained on the field for almost another day. Afterwords, we crossed to the southern side of the Potomac, but we are still not sure why we waited or crossed. We have lost much in the way of supplies during this engagement, and are in need of simple things like underclothes.

I am not sure who even claimed the victory, if either side can. So many men lost. Many of the Fredericksburg men survived, others were casualties, and still others, we do not know about, such as the fate of John Wesley Hilldrup. Hopefully, he has only been wounded and is in a hospital someplace.

Elizabeth, I look around at what has happened and at what is happening and I am more fearful than I have ever been. I don't wish to alarm you, but I find it difficult to understand why God is allowing this all to happen. My faith is being tested on all sides. I have been trying to look for hope in this war, and I must say I have seen some great acts of compassion, courage, and mercy.

I keep reading my Bible and find many passages reminding us to have courage and not to fear. So I will leave you with the passage from First Corinthians: "Therefore, be strong and steadfast, always fully devoted to the work of the Lord, knowing that in the Lord your labor is not in vain." We must remember this, Elizabeth. Be strong and steadfast.

Yours Forever,
Joshua

"It's starting to get very worrisome," AJ said after Elizabeth read parts of the letter aloud. "So many men are dead or wounded. Their lives and their families are forever changed." She sighed. "Did you hear what happened around Shepherdstown?"

Elizabeth shook her head 'no'.

"A division of Yankees crossed the river into the town. General Stonewall Jackson's Brigade captured or killed the whole lot of them." AJ looked down at her folded hands. "They say the Potomac was dammed up by their bodies. I'm not fond of the Yankees, you know that, but I cannot believe that men can kill each other this way. I know we are fighting for our freedom, but so many lives have been lost."

"I heard in town that, at Sharpsburg, two-hundred of the 30th Virginia were killed or wounded out of the three-hundred that were engaged, others were on guard duty or sick." Elizabeth said.

"I heard it said that only 236 of our men went into the battle and of those, around one-hundred and fifty were killed or wounded."

"Either way, it is too many." Elizabeth looked at her friend. "Do you really think that all this death is worth keeping slaves? Slaves that we may never get back anyways?"

"It's not about that anymore, Elizabeth. It's never really been about that. It's about our rights and now, it's about pride."

"Southern pride. Yes, I do hear quite a bit about that." Elizabeth said.

"So in answer to your question, unfortunately, yes. I believe the sacrifice is worth our freedom. We've come this far, fought this hard. We need to continue the fight until the end, until we win our victory."

"You're still willing to sacrifice your home, your father, Nathaniel and even your own life just because of Southern pride and Southern rights?

"Yes. If that's the price we need to pay." AJ's words sounded final.

Elizabeth sighed. This was what she was worried about. Most of the Southerners fighting were as passionate as AJ and would likely fight until the bitter end. It was a frightening thought, and even though the Confederate army was winning, Elizabeth had a strong feeling the worst was yet to come.

Thursday, September 18, 1862
Episcopal Church

"Kate!" Elizabeth made her way to her friend. "I'm glad you could make it." They quickly embraced.

"Of course. Bertie and Nettie are here as well. We are completely in support of President Jefferson Davis's proclamation."

"As am I. I very much agree with the idea," Elizabeth said.

A few days ago, the townspeople had received word about President Davis's proclamation for setting Thursday, September 18 as a day of prayer and thanksgiving for great mercies to our people. Southerners from all the Confederate States were meeting in their places of worship to give thanks and to pray for God to get the country through the perils that surrounded them and to appeal to God to allow them their freedom.

"Is anyone else from your family coming?" Kate asked.

"Actually, yes. The plan was for Belle and Annie to bring Meri, Lainey, and Max. We are then going back to have a family dinner at Turner's Glenn." Elizabeth smiled. "You and yours are welcome to join us. Daniel shot a rather large buck yesterday and Annie and Ruthie undoubtedly did a wonderful job preparing it. With the Federals gone and life back to the way it was before the occupation, it really is a day of thanking God for our blessings."

"We would love to join you, but our people have been preparing a large meal for tonight as well." The two began walking into the church to reserve seats. "We have even more reason to be thankful. Did you hear, on Monday, it's said that eight thousand of the enemy surrendered at Harper's Ferry. They say we have taken control of the city, along with all of their arms, ammunition, commissary, and ordnance that the stores accumulated there."

"What a great victory," Elizabeth said, then rose as she noticed her family enter the church and make their way down the aisle.

"Kate, it is so good to see you!" Belle said as she approached. She looked around. "My goodness, I can't remember the last time I was in this church, or any church, to be honest."

"You should come more often," Kate said. "I will be here on Sunday."

"As will I," Elizabeth added, putting an arm around Hannah and pulling her close.

"Me too, Aunt Belle." Benjamin piped up.

"I am planning on going as well," Annie said. "You know you are always welcome. If Meri, Lainey or Max don't want to come, then Ruthie or Zipporah can watch them."

"It would be nice, being all together every Sunday at church," Meri said. "We could start having Sunday family dinner again."

"That was a wonderful tradition," Belle said. "It will never be the same without James, or Mother and Father for that matter."

The service was nice. Belle felt at peace for the first time in years. Afterward, the family went back to Turner's Glenn for dinner. It was a very enjoyable day. That night, after the Bennetts had left, Belle sat on a bench in the flower garden, angled so that she could see the waters of the river. She truly did love Turner's Glenn. She couldn't count the number of times she had spent at this very spot with James or Elizabeth, before she was married. Belle heard someone approaching and turned to see Zipporah.

"Miss Isabelle, Miss Annie is wondering where you are." The woman approached cautiously. "I told her dat I would try and find you. I figured you might be here, sittin' in your favorite spot."

"Yes. You do seem to know me best, even back when Elizabeth was living here and you cared for both of us." Belle gestured for Zipporah to sit. The servant complied. "I always can count on you to talk to and I know you will listen. I do appreciate everything that you do for me, truly I do. I need you to know that."

"Of course, Miss Belle." Zipporah nodded but didn't meet Belle's eyes.

"Can I ask you something, Zipporah?" Belle asked. Zipporah nodded again.

"Why did you stay? When all of our people left, why did you choose to stay?" Belle clutched her hands in her lap. She wasn't quite sure why she asked the question. Usually, when she asked Zipporah something, it was an opinion that had to do with fashion. She knew Zipporah would always listen to her and help in any way that she could.

"Well, Ma'am, I jus' didn't want to abandon you. I knew that you would need my help and Solomon's too. Wit' my Mama and Papa passing away years ago, my Auntie Ruthie and Timothy are the only family that's I have, and ya'all, o' course."

"I have always felt as though we were close, almost family." Belle agreed.

"Yes, Ma'am," Zipporah said. "Anyways, I jus' thought stayin' here, where you all have always treated me well and where I know I'll have food and shelter was best. Those that left got so much uncertainty. They doan' even know where they were gonna go. I's much prefer the safety of Turner's Glenn. I'm not so fond of change."

"We appreciate you being here, especially with Mama gone and all. We all know that Solomon is staying because of you." Belle playfully nudged her servant with her shoulder. Zipporah smiled shyly but continued to keep her eyes down.

"Yes, ma'am. I believe he is. He a good man. Strong and kind and hard worker. Forgivin' too. Many a man would be quite angry at the lot he's been given in life, but he's not hateful or spiteful. He just keeps on doing what need be done."

"I can't imagine what we would do without him, and you." Belle looked out at the landscape. "It's so peaceful out here. Makes it hard to believe that the war is so close."

"Yes, ma'am." Zipporah said.

"With all hope, it will continue to stay away and end soon," Belle said, then changed the subject. "What did Annie want me for?"

"She wanted to know iffin you could help her in the kitchen today. Auntie Ruthie is feelin' poorly an so Miss Annie needs help."

"Good heavens. It seems like I can't get a moment to myself anymore." Belle sighed heavily. "All right, then. I suppose I can go and offer my help." She stood and headed into the house, Zipporah following her.

Saturday, October 4, 1862
Bennett Home

"Winchester can't be terribly far away," Belle said, drawing her needle in and out of the long johns she was sewing. "If the 30th is going to be encamped there, why can't they come here for a visit?"

"If all of the soldiers went on leave just because they were relatively close to home, the Confederacy would have a hard time keeping any soldiers in their ranks," AJ said. She, Kate and Belle had come into town and met at Elizabeth's house to visit while they made underclothes for the soldiers of the 30th Virginia. Joshua's latest letter, along with letters from other Fredericksburg soldiers, had reported that many of them had lost or damaged clothes at the Battle of Sharpsburg.

"I wish they could at least take turns visiting their families," Elizabeth said. "Just one or two soldiers at a time, so I could see Joshua, even for one day, even for one hour." She looked down at her sewing. "Just so I could see him and make sure that he's okay." She took a deep breath and looked at AJ. "I'm sorry AJ. How are things on your side of the river? Have you had any discussion lately with Nathaniel?"

"No. I haven't had anything substantial for the Confederacy since the Yankees moved out. I'm not going to put our men in danger if I have nothing of import to give them." AJ replied.

"That's a good idea," Belle said. "It's likely safer for you as well. I still can't believe you are smuggling goods. At least you aren't spying, that is a much more serious offense."

Elizabeth glanced at AJ, who avoided her friend's eyes. While Kate and Belle knew about the smuggling, they did not know about the passing of information. She wasn't sure why she wanted to keep that part a secret, from them, but she did.

"If another opportunity to help comes up, I will do what I can for our soldiers," AJ replied.

212

"I admire your dedication to the cause," Belle said. "Who knows the impact those supplies make for the Confederacy."

"I do hope I have made a contribution," AJ said.

"I'm sure you have," Kate said. "Even though I wish you wouldn't put yourself in danger, I am proud that I have a friend as courageous as you. I wish I could share what you do with the whole of Virginia, but I obviously won't."

"Thank you, Kate," AJ said. "To be honest, we are all doing our best to help the Confederacy. Whether it's the prayers we say or the letters we write or even what we're doing now." She held up the undergarment she was working on. "It may not seem like much, but even the smallest tasks we do can add up and really make a difference."

"You make a good point," Elizabeth said.

❦

Friday, October 10, 1862
Bennett Home

Joshua,

How difficult I feel it is for the both of us, being so close, and yet unable to see each other. My wish is that you can somehow find a way to perhaps be able to come home and visit. I wish to see you so badly.

As you are aware, our son turned six yesterday. His birthday wish was that you were home to celebrate with us. He was mildly disappointed that it didn't come true, but he understood. He just smiled and said that he 'had to at least try.'

You would be so proud of the children and how they are both growing and changing. Benjamin can now read many words and can sound out even more. He practices every day, even though he would rather be outside playing with his friends. Hannah can already say the alphabet and can write her name. She loves being read to, as always and is already looking forward to going to school, even though it is still a few years away. I believe she will be reading before we know it!

I have spoken to Daniel on numerous occasions about his leaving Fredericksburg. He refuses to do so, based on the promise he made to you at the onset of the war. He is a good and true friend. Eric is the same way. I have been watching him carefully as well, waiting for any signs that he is ready to go off and enlist, but he seems content to stay here and look after the shop for you.

I must tell you, Eric is doing very well in the blacksmith shop. He is working hard and starting to teach Benjamin some simple projects. You would be proud of him, he is a very special young man. I am not sure how much longer his mother will survive. I do plan on having him live with us once she does pass on. I know you would approve of that decision.

Things here are going as expected. It has been a shock to all of us to see a slight change in Belle. She has been attending church services with us and is not as condescending as she used to be. She can still put on airs, of course, and will still argue with anyone she disagrees with, but she is making strides to becoming a better person. Perhaps losing James, as unimaginable as it was, made her see the kind of person she was.

It's strange, about James. There are many times when I can imagine that he is still just away at war, with you and Father, and that he will come home when the war is over. If only that were true.

We have heard that President Davis has asked Virginia to draft 4,500 black men to complete fortifications at Richmond. I am hoping that doesn't mean Richmond is in danger from the Federals. What was the government thinking, moving our capital so close to the northern border? We can only pray the situation will come to a peaceful conclusion before much longer.

I pray that you stay safe and will soon be at home where you belong. I will remain strong and steadfast, as you asked, until that time.

With all of the love I possess,
Elizabeth

Elizabeth made her way to the Dawson home after posting the letter to Joshua. She held a basket with some soup and bread and clutched a book under her arm, a favorite of both hers and Hannah's. She had been reading the French novel to Eric's mother and she planned on finishing it today. Eric had reported that his mother was weakening, and Elizabeth had noticed the same at her last visit. Meri had come into town and she had been more than willing to watch her niece and nephew while Elizabeth went to visit the ill woman.

Elizabeth entered the small home and made her way to the only bedroom, where Mrs. Dawson lay.

"Good afternoon, Elmyra." Elizabeth greeted her. The pale woman looked up from the Bible she had been paging through. Though her vision was extremely weak, she insisted that the book brought her comfort.

"Mrs. Bennett. I am so glad you are here." Mrs. Dawson's voice and smile were feeble.

"It is good to see you." Elizabeth sat down. "I brought Madame de Villeneuve's Beauty and the Beast. I was thinking we could finish it today. I also brought some chicken soup. I could keep it warm over the stove for later or you can eat some now." Elizabeth gently placed a hand over one of Mrs. Dawson's.

"My dear, I am always glad to see you, but especially so today." The woman, who wasn't any older than Elizabeth's own mother, placed her other hand on top. "I have had a feeling all day that my time has come."

"Oh, Elmyra, you must just be feeling a bit run down." Elizabeth's stomach felt nauseous.

"I don't believe I will live to see tomorrow. It is my time. My only concern now is my Eric. I don't want him to come home to find me cold with my soul in a better place. It's not that I would rather have you find me, but I would rather it not be my son. To be honest, I would feel better if you could just stay with me."

"Of course. I understand." Elizabeth said, trying to hold back tears. "I will stay with you for as long as you need me to."

"Good," Elmyra said. "Now, I would like to hear what happens with Beauty and her beast. I find it strange that such a smart and kind girl cannot see that the beast is really the prince of her dreams." Elizabeth smiled and opened the book.

"...and they lived happily ever after." Elizabeth finished reading, smiled and closed the book.

"I do love happy endings." Mrs. Dawson said. Her voice was little more than a hoarse whisper, her eyes closed.

"Me too," Elizabeth said softly. "But we believe that in the Lord, we will all have happy endings, if not on earth, then in the next life."

"Amen. Well said, Mrs. Bennett." Mrs. Dawson took a shallow breath. "If you would, I would like to hear the 23rd Psalm."

"Of course," Elizabeth replied, taking the Bible and leafing through the pages.

"Make sure the bible goes to Eric." Mrs. Dawson said. "I know that we have spoken of this before, but will you please..." She drew in another shallow breath.

"You know Eric will always have a home with us, Elmyra. I can promise you that. He already is a member of our family." The tears that Elizabeth had been holding back began to softly fall down her cheeks.

"You are a wonderful woman and a marvelous mother. I couldn't ask for a better person to care for my son."

"Thank you." Elizabeth wiped her cheeks and finally found Psalm 23. "The Lord is my shepherd; I shall not want." As she finished the verse, Elizabeth looked up. She immediately noticed a stillness about Elmyra Dawson. "Mrs. Dawson?" Elizabeth gently shook the woman. When she didn't respond, Elizabeth checked to see if she was breathing but she was not. Tears began to fall steadily down her face. The woman was at peace. Eric had now lost both parents. She rose from the chair and began preparing Mrs. Dawson for the undertaker.

When Elizabeth returned home, it was much later than she had anticipated. She found Eric at the table with Benjamin, playing a card game. Hannah sat in front of the stove with Meri, paging through a book written for young children with many pictures in it, telling her aunt the story. They all looked up as Elizabeth closed the door.

"Meri, will you help Hannah and Benjamin, get ready for bed?" She asked softly. Meri nodded and followed the children. Eric's face was void of emotion. He slowly and methodically put the cards back in the box. Elizabeth sat down next to Eric.

"Eric, I have to tell you something…" She placed a hand on his arm.

"You don't have to say anything." Tears welled in his brown eyes and he ran a hand through his brown hair. "I know. I knew this morning, ma'am when I left home." He wiped a tear from his eye. "Did she…did she suffer much?"

"No, Eric. It was as if she simply fell asleep and didn't wake up. No pain. No suffering. Not anymore."

He nodded. "That's a small comfort, at least." He swallowed. "I suppose…I suppose I have to figure out what to do next."

"That is what took me so long, actually. I went to see the undertaker and the cemetery caretaker. Arrangements for the funeral are taken care of. I saw Reverend Lacy as well. You shouldn't have to do anything."

"What about the house?" He asked. "I mean, I can live there…"

"No, you can stay here. In fact, I insist upon it. We can make room."

"I don't want to impose." He protested.

"It is no imposition at all. For the time being, you can stay in the room with Benjamin. Hannah can sleep with me. You should go home now and gather some belongings. We can decide on what to do with the house later, I know Mr. James Corbin will help you if you would like to sell it or keep it to rent out. You will not go through this alone."

"No, ma'am. That I do know." Eric gave her a small smile. "I do know that. Thank you for everything you did for my mother and for me."

"Of course, Eric." Elizabeth said. "You are family, and we will take care of you."

Tuesday, October 28, 1862
Beale Home

"Have you heard from Joshua lately?" Lucy asked, sitting down.

"Not since a few weeks after Sharpsburg," Elizabeth replied. "Or Antietam, if you live in the North. It is so strange that every battle seems

216

to have two names depending on the Federal or Confederate viewpoint." She shook her head. "Anyways, he was well then, thank the Lord. We've recently sent some clothing over to the 30th after hearing it is what they need most. I do hope they receive it. There have been many times when our packages do not make it to the proper destination.

"A very unfortunate situation," Lucy said. "How is your young Mr. Dawson doing?"

"Better than I thought he would be," Elizabeth replied. "He knew it was a long time coming and was expected, but he now knows she is no longer in pain."

"Indeed. We all know that a kind soul like Elmyra Dawson has her eternal reward in heaven."

"No truer words have been spoken," Elizabeth said. "How is the new school year going?"

"Good, good. We have a full class and our time is occupied with the students. I'm glad I actually found time to meet with you. We do miss Lainey, though. We could find a place for her if your circumstances change."

"Thank you for saying so." Elizabeth, Annie, and Belle had decided to keep Lainey at Turner's Glenn for the time being. They needed her help on the plantation and couldn't spare Daniel to bring her into town every day as before. The only other option was to have her stay with Elizabeth, but that still left the family without her help. "Lainey does miss school. It is just too complicated right now."

"I understand," Lucy said. "As does Mother."

"How are other things, aside from school?" Elizabeth asked.

"Good. My Brother Willie arrived home on Saturday; he's on a furlough. We were all so excited to see him. He will hopefully stay for a while."

"What wonderful news." Elizabeth agreed. "Having family around in these times is so important."

"Very true," Lucy said. "Unfortunately, Cousin Minnie left this morning to return to school in North Carolina."

"So friends and relatives coming and going on a daily basis at the Beale's home." Elizabeth smiled. "That sounds normal to me."

"Yes. If only the one person I really wanted home would return." Lucy looked longingly toward the door.

"I definitely agree with you there," Elizabeth said. "Someday soon, this war will be over and all our loved ones will come home. I know they will."

Lucy gave a small nod. Both women stood at the knock that sounded on the parlor door as it quickly opened.

"Lucy." The man smiled beneath a trimmed, full beard.

"John!" Lucy flew into her husband's arms. Elizabeth smiled to herself.

"Oh, Lucy, I've missed you so much." John kissed her briefly on the forehead and turned toward Elizabeth. "Mrs. Bennett. It's good to see you. I trust that Mr. Bennett is doing well."

"Last time I heard from him, after Sharpsburg, he was well. I would assume he and the rest of the 30th Virginia are preparing camp for the winter." Lucy's husband, John Brent had enlisted in a different regiment and was fighting mostly in engagements further west.

"Perhaps," John said. Lucy laid her head against his shoulder.

"It is very good to see you home and healthy, Mr. Brent," Elizabeth said with a smile. "Lucy, I must be going, as you now have much better company. It is getting late anyway, and I should get home to tuck the children into bed." Elizabeth began to make her way to the door.

"Thank you for coming by, Elizabeth." Lucy released her husband for a brief moment to give Elizabeth a hug goodbye.

"I'm glad we had the opportunity, even if it wasn't long, Lucy." She smiled at John. "Take care of yourself, Mr. Brent." She gave him a quick pat on the arm. "You both stay here. I will find my way out." She said and left the couple to each other.

Sunday, November 9, 1862
Outside Grace Episcopal Church

The Turners, Bennetts, and Corbins walked out of the church into the crisp, November weather.

"Belle, I am so glad to see you coming to church on a weekly basis," Kate stated.

"I am glad as well." Belle patted her hair.

"And we…" Elizabeth's words were cut short by distant gunfire. "What in the world?"

"Get down!" Someone in the crowd yelled. Belle and Kate looked around as they crouched down. Max and Lainey dove to the ground and Meri ducked behind a fence post. Elizabeth carefully threw herself on top of Benjamin and Hannah.

"Yankees!" They heard someone yell. "There is fighting in the street!"

"Where is it coming from?"

"What is going on?"

People from all around began to slowly stand back up as they realized the shooting was a few blocks away. Not willing, however, to continue standing in the street or leave for home, the congregation headed back into the church for protection.

"How long will this last, Mama?" Hannah asked, quietly shaking.

218

"I'm not sure, Hannah-Bear. I'm not sure at all."

Not even an hour had passed when people started filtering out of the church. It had been a while since they had heard gunfire. Kate cautiously walked out, followed by the Turners and the Bennetts.

"Can we go and see what happened?" Max asked.

"No, we most certainly cannot," Belle said. "I do not need another brother getting shot."

"Mrs. Bennett!" The group looked up to see Eric making his way toward them.

"Eric!" Elizabeth gave him a quick hug. "Thank goodness you're all right." She pulled back to look at him. "Do you know anything? What happened?"

"It was a skirmish." He said excitedly. "The Federal cavalry crossed the river up at Falmouth and then came into town. Our cavalry was already here, so fighting broke out."

"Was anyone hurt?" Kate asked.

"Yes, ma'am. One man on each side was killed, and about twenty of our men were captured."

"Are they gone now, Mr. Dawson?" Meri asked.

"Yes, ma'am. As soon as our Captain Samson from the Home Guard gathered his forces on the outskirts of town, he attacked the Yankees and chased them away. Some citizens also joined in and threw stones at them."

"What good did that do?" Max asked.

"They actually knocked a Yankee off his horse and we were able to take him prisoner," Eric told them. "It's proof that civilians can make a difference."

"Indeed they can." Elizabeth agreed. "We just have to look for opportunities to help." She focused on Eric. "Do you know anything about our casualties? Where our captured men were taken? Who were the two that were killed?"

"I don't rightly know, Ma'am," Eric said. "We should find out soon."

Monday, November 17, 1862
Bennett Home

"I'm not sure I like seeing soldiers in our town again," AJ said, sitting at Elizabeth's table.

"I'm just glad it's our soldiers and not the enemy," Elizabeth answered.

"Very true, although when the Yanks were here, I could at least get some information to pass along and I felt like I was actually doing something." She looked out the window towards the river in the direction of Falmouth. "It seems as though something is going on near Falmouth. I'm not sure if it's Yankee or Confederate, but something is happening. I mean to go over there later to check it out."

"Oh, AJ, I wish you wouldn't. You have no idea what you may run into."

"Elizabeth, I will be careful. I'm sure I won't get into any trouble. I have gained the respect of the men, on both sides." She smiled.

"That wouldn't stop an errant bullet from hitting you or some Federal soldiers from accosting you."

"I can see your point. I promise I will be careful." She looked toward the door. "Where is the battery of Confederate soldiers stationed?"

"In the field beyond White Plains," Elizabeth answered. "A Colonel Ball is in charge. He seems a decent man. A small force arrived this morning as well, to add to the contingent. I heard they came in from Richmond."

"Hmmm, I wonder if that has anything to do with what's going on in Falmouth."

"It might." Elizabeth bit her lip. "We've been occupied by both the Union and the Confederacy at one time, but last Sunday was the first time shots were ever fired here." She shook her head. "I hope we don't find ourselves in the middle of a battle."

"We will get through this, Elizabeth." AJ pointed out. "We have to. We don't have a choice. We can get through more than we believe we can."

That evening before dinner, Elizabeth sat with her children cuddled on her lap, reading to them. It had been chilly that day, and they wanted some quiet time with their mother in front of the fire. She cherished times like this, but unfortunately, she had to finish preparing dinner. "And that is all we will read for now," Elizabeth said, closing the book.

"But Mama, I want to find out if King Arthur is supposed to be the true king of Camelot," Benjamin begged. "Please read more!"

"Sorry, Benjamin. It's time to start getting ready for dinner." Elizabeth smiled and ruffled her son's hair." She shifted a sleeping Hannah from her lap to the chair next to hers, then stood to stoke the fire.

"Not even one more chapter?" He persisted.

"No, Benjamin. We'll do a Bible reading after dinner and maybe another chapter of King Arthur before bed."

"All right." Benjamin stood from where he had been sitting. "Can we do the David and Goliath Bible reading?"

"I think that can be arranged." Elizabeth smiled.

A boom exploded outside. It was so close that it shook the house. Benjamin called out in surprise. Hannah was startled from her sleep and began crying.

"Mama, what was that?" Benjamin shouted.

"I don't know, Benjamin." Elizabeth moved to the window and looked outside as another blast rocked their home. It looked like there was cannon fire from the direction of Falmouth. Within moments, a boom was fired from closer, on the Fredericksburg side of the river. Benjamin cautiously joined her at the window. Eric came in from the shop, a grim look on his face.

"I can't what's going on out there, but it can't be good." He said as he joined Benjamin and Elizabeth at the window.

"Mama, I'm scared!" Hannah called out. Elizabeth went to her daughter and pulled her into her arms.

"It will be okay, Hannah-Bear," Elizabeth said. "The soldiers are far enough away."

The pandemonium continued steadily as the two sides fired at one another. Hannah continued to clutch Elizabeth, who had moved back in front of the fireplace. She rocked Hannah, hoping to soothe her. Benjamin stood next to Eric at the window, watching with interest.

"Mama, there are people out in the streets. Everyone seems so excited! Can I go outside and watch?"

"Absolutely not, young man!" Elizabeth said, rubbing Hannah's back. She focused on her daughter. "Are you hungry, sweetheart?" Hannah shook her head no.

"I'm too excited to eat!" Benjamin said.

"Well, I am sure you'll feel differently once it's bedtime." She stood, sat Hannah in the chair and went to the table. "Come now, Benjamin."

"Oh, all right." He dragged himself to the table.

After they said a quick prayer, Elizabeth quietly added a silent prayer that AJ changed her mind about going to Falmouth. She then dished out the vegetable soup to her children. The explosions continued and the commotion outside got even louder and rowdier. Benjamin kept looking toward the outside.

"Benjamin, please focus on your dinner," Elizabeth said.

"Sorry, Mama. Really, I am." Benjamin said, looking again at his meal.

"I know it's difficult, but we must keep doing what we would normally do to the best of our ability."

"Like when the Yankees were here." Benjamin clarified.

"Yes. Just like when the Yankees were here." Elizabeth glanced toward the door. The crowd outside had become louder. Benjamin almost fell out of his chair in surprise as someone from outside pounded on the door. Elizabeth rose quickly to answer it. Members of the Beale family stood on the other side: Lucy, her mother Jane, and her siblings Marion and Samuel.

"We are so sorry to intrude, Elizabeth," Lucy said. "It's terribly chaotic down on Princess Anne Street. The neighborhood gentlemen suggested that we go to another part of town and wait out this artillery duel."

"Of course. Come in." Elizabeth opened the door wide to let the family in. "We were just finishing dinner. Were you able to eat before leaving home?"

"Yes, dear, we were." Jane Beale said. "Just being able to sit here in the warmth of your fire will be more than enough."

"Please have a seat," Elizabeth said. The family gathered around the fire.

"Mama, may I be excused?" Benjamin asked.

"Yes, Benjamin. Clear your dishes and wipe down the table and then you and Samuel can play with your dominoes."

"Okay." Samuel and Benjamin sat at the table as Elizabeth had suggested and Hannah crawled back into Elizabeth's arms.

"What is going on out there?" Elizabeth asked. The explosions continued outside.

"It is madness, as if the world has gone insane," Lucy said.

"All of the impoverished people from the upper part of town have fled their homes and are running wild," Jane explained. "One of the cannon shots went through the paper factory and frightened the poor girls who work there so badly they ran out and joined the panic. One of the men in town told us the Yankees are in the range of our batteries and were actually able to disarm some of our guns."

"My goodness." Elizabeth continued to rock Hannah. "Did you hear of any casualties?"

"Nothing specific yet, but I'm sure there will be. I did hear that one of the neighborhood boys had gotten too close to the fighting and had his foot shot and terribly shattered."

"Oh my goodness!" Elizabeth glanced at Benjamin and knew he had been listening when his face went white. "Do you know who it was?"

"No," Lucy said. "Unfortunately we didn't hear that part."

Elizabeth laid her head against the rocking chair and briefly closed her eyes. Now, children were being injured. Where could they find safety, if not in their own homes?

Wednesday, November 19, 1862
Bennett Home

Eric entered the house. "Morning, Mrs. Bennett." He took off his hat.

"Where did you go this morning?" Elizabeth asked. "I heard you leave earlier." Eric's move into the Bennett household had been a smooth transition overall. She didn't want to hover over him too much and didn't feel like she had to. He had been practically on his own since cancer started taking over his mother years ago. He was a mature, independent, respectful young man who stayed out of trouble.

"I woke up early and couldn't fall back asleep, so I went to the cemetery to see Mother."

"I see," Elizabeth said. "Did you hear any news while you passed through town?"

"It's looking bleak for us, Ma'am. I fear a battle is imminent. We have Confederate cavalry here, and maybe more now because I heard General Longstreet will be coming into town today."

"Oh gracious, you're right. This is not good news."

"No, Ma'am. What makes it worse is that I saw a long line of Yankees pouring over the Chatham Hills to take the position where they were last summer."

Elizabeth's heart sank.

"I also heard that General Lee telegraphed Colonel Ball to hold the passage of the river at Fredericksburg at all costs."

"Are they anticipating an actual battle, Eric?"

"I'm not sure, Ma'am, but to be honest, I can't see it any other way. There are a lot of soldiers here from both sides."

Elizabeth bit her lip. "Oh, please, Lord, be with us."

Turner's Glenn Plantation

"How did I not know how much work there was to be done on a plantation in November?" Belle complained, hoisting a basket of tobacco leaves on a table in the large barn.

"It's always like this, Miss Belle," Zipporah said. "At least dat's what Solomon always said."

"I cannot believe I am forced to do this menial labor." Belle wiped her hands on her soiled gown. "I need a rest."

Lainey walked in, overhearing Belle's last comment. "We've only been working for a couple of hours, Belle."

"Well, that is a couple of hours too many." Belle tried not to snap at her sister. "Thank goodness we found these old riding gloves. At least I won't get blisters on my hands. That would be truly appalling."

Lainey rolled her eyes, dumped her basket of tobacco leaves, and then went back out towards the fields.

"I know how you feel, in a way, Miss Belle," Zipporah said. "I never thought I would find myself working in the fields. I been a house slave my whole life and I always thought dat's where I would stay,"

Belle smiled genuinely at Zipporah. She always seemed to know what to say.

"However," Zipporah continued. "Sometimes, we just have to do things we never thought we would have to or thought we could do."

"Wise words, Zipporah," Annie said, entering the barn.

"Are AJ and Liberty here yet?" Belle asked.

"No," Annie replied. "I'm pretty sure they won't be coming."

"What do you mean?" Belle said. "Why wouldn't they come today?"

"It is difficult to see, but across the river at Chatham, I can make out many figures that really look like Union soldiers."

"Again?" Belle exclaimed. "We just got rid of the Yankees in August. Why are they back?"

"I don't know. I'm not even sure that's what I'm seeing." Annie said.

"Well, with the way our luck is going, that is exactly what you're seeing," Belle said, brushing a strand of hair off her cheek. "I believe you're right. AJ and Liberty will stay over there since the Yankees are back. They won't want to risk coming over here so soon."

"That's what I thought," Annie replied. "Besides, they have more than enough work to keep them busy and with Federals here, they will have to protect what they can."

"Indeed," Belle said, then realized that AJ would once again have Yankees to steal from. That could be a good thing, but now she would have to be worried about her friend again. It was unfortunate that she wouldn't be able to help the Turner family with their harvest, but it couldn't be helped.

"Ruthie and I are all set inside. What can I do to help out here?" Annie asked.

"Check with Solomon," Belle replied. "He's the one that has all of the answers when it comes to farming."

Annie nodded and left. Belle turned to catch a smile on Zipporah's face. "What is that grin for?"

"Nothing too important. It's just nice to see Solomon getting recognition for his skills." She replied. They began to walk toward the fields.

"I am only stating the truth. I honestly don't know what we would do without Solomon, and you of course, and Ruthie or Daniel. I just...do not know."

"You would figure somethin' out," Zipporah said. "You be much more resourceful than you give yo'rself credit for. You do what you need to do to get through. 'sides, you don't have ta worry 'bout me leavin'. I wouldn't want ta live in any other place than Turner's Glenn. It be my home, Miss Belle. I knows not all black folk feels like dat, but I do." She shrugged. "You'se de only family that I ever known."

"You are so dear to me Zipporah," Belle said. She took a deep breath. "It will be nice when we won't have to concern ourselves with this manual labor."

∞

Thursday, November 20, 1862
Bennett Home

"Mama, I don't mean to be a bother, but I am really bored." Benjamin stared out the window. The rain was pouring down and had been all day. Elizabeth couldn't blame her energetic six-year-old for his feelings. The entire house was tense with feelings of stress as the two armies still faced off against each other. Eric added another log to the stove.

"We can play dominoes or a game of cards, Benjamin." The young man suggested.

"All right," Benjamin said. The two set up the game of dominoes. Elizabeth checked on Hannah, who was playing quietly with her doll. She smiled to herself as her daughter laid the doll down, covered it with a dishtowel and patted its back.

Things were quieting down for the evening. Elizabeth sat at the table and pulled out a sheet of paper to start a letter to Joshua. With the Confederate soldiers in town, she was hoping to get it delivered to him more easily.

Not ten minutes later, a knock sounded at the door. Elizabeth rose to answer it, Eric following right behind her. She opened the door to see five Confederate soldiers, drenched and exhausted-looking.

"How can we help you, boys?" Elizabeth asked.

"Ma'am, my name is William Thomas Rooker of the 14th North Carolina Cavalry. We were just wondering if you had any space for us to warm up and get dry." The man who spoke was almost shivering in the cold rain.

"Of course," Elizabeth answered. "You all can stay in the blacksmith shop." She turned to Eric, who immediately nodded and grabbed his hat and overcoat.

"I'll bring them around so they don't mess the house." He said. "I'll stoke the fire out there too."

"Thank you," Elizabeth replied. "I'll put some food together for you men to eat."

"Very much obliged, ma'am." The soldiers all nodded and followed Eric around to the side entrance of the shop. Elizabeth hunted around the house and put together a basket of bread, molasses, milk, candles and some matches, then went into the shop.

Eric already had a fire going in the forge and the men sat around it. The shop was still warm from Eric's daily work, so Elizabeth knew it wouldn't be long before the room was at a comfortable temperature.

"Here's some food and candles to keep you for tonight. I am sorry that I do not have more to give you."

"This is wonderful ma'am, more than enough." Rooker said with a smile.

"Well, don't say that until you've tried my cooking," Elizabeth said with a smile. "I have many talents, but I'm afraid working in the kitchen is not one of them."

"Ma'am, at this point, any kind of home-cooked food is welcome." A second soldier said.

"You boys are true Southern gentlemen," Elizabeth replied. "It is getting late. Feel free to stay here overnight, if that's okay with your commander. I'll come out with some breakfast in the morning."

"Thank you so much, ma'am. You're truly an angel sent from heaven to us tonight."

"I'm glad to do something to help our Confederate soldiers. We thank you for protecting us. We were occupied once already by the Federals. I wouldn't want that to happen again."

"Well, ma'am, we don't intend to let that happen. In fact, we aim to whup the Yankees here to win the whole war."

"So there will be a battle here, then," Eric spoke up. Once he had gotten the forge fire going, he had taken a spot in the corner of the shop, observing.

"It is very likely, son." One of the soldiers answered. He looked to be a bit older, about the age of Elizabeth's father. "There's a very good chance it will be a big one."

"You look like a strong boy." A different soldier commented. "How old are you? Why ain't you fighting?"

Elizabeth glanced at Eric, interested in how he would respond. As always, he did not show his emotions.

"I have family here to care for and I gave my word to a man I greatly admire that I would stay here and take care of things. I may want to enlist when I get old enough, but I keep my promises first."

226

"That is admirable." The older soldier said. "Besides, I reckon there's a lot you do for the cause here."

"Indeed there is," Elizabeth spoke up. "He has been invaluable to many families in town, not just mine."

"I suppose it takes lots of different people working together to win a war." One of the soldiers said.

"You're correct there." Said another soldier. "Ma'am, do you have any family fighting?"

"My husband and father are with the 30th Virginia. My brother was with them as well, but was killed at the Battle of Glendale."

"I'm sorry for your loss, ma'am." The older soldier said. A tear formed in Elizabeth's eyes. She thought of James often, but it was so easy to pretend he was still fighting.

"Thank you, sir," Elizabeth replied. "If you will excuse me, I need to get my children to bed, gentlemen. I'll be back in the morning."

"Thank you again, ma'am." Came a chorus of voices. Eric followed her into the house.

"I'll sleep out in the barn, Mrs. Bennett, just to be safe," Eric said.

"Thank you, Eric." She pulled him into a hug. "I don't know if I tell you this enough, but you are so important to this family, and I thank God every night that you are here with us,"

Eric smiled. "I thank Him every night that you brought me into your family." He replied. "If I didn't have ya'all, I might have no other choice but to enlist. I would probably have to lie about my age and you know I don't ever feel good about telling an untruth."

"Your mother raised you well. You will make some woman an excellent husband and provider someday."

"Well, Mrs. Bennett, I appreciate you saying that, but I am only fifteen. I've got a few years before I start thinking about looking for a wife."

"You have a point there." Elizabeth smiled. "Thank you again for everything, Eric."

"You too, Mrs. Bennett."

Friday, November 21, 1862
Bennett Home

"This was not the best day for you to come into town." Elizabeth chided Kate and Belle.

"You're not glad to see us?" Belle asked. "I was expecting a warmer welcome."

"Of course I'm glad to see you," Elizabeth said. "But there are troops everywhere. We actually had some soldiers from North Carolina spend the night in the blacksmith shop."

"That was kind of you," Kate said.

"They were wet and it was still raining and I just couldn't say no." The women sat down.

"What do you think of the rumors that there will be a battle nearby?" Belle asked.

"The soldiers I spoke with last night seemed fairly certain. General Longstreet is in town now and the Federals are across the river. I really worry about AJ and Liberty over there. As bad as the occupation was earlier this year, I am afraid life is going to get worse."

"You would call the Federal occupation peaceful?" Belle exclaimed.

"It was rough at times and very inconvenient, but no one was killed. No one was even hurt. Overall, yes, it was peaceful."

"Well, I for one, would not call that takeover peaceful," Belle said. "I can see your point, however. If the rumors are to be believed, this could be a full-blown battle. Wouldn't it be something if a battle near Fredericksburg is the one that defeats the Yankee invaders once and for all? We could go down in history."

"If more Confederate soldiers come into town, we could get a chance to see some of our Fredericksburg men." Kate pointed out.

Elizabeth's heart fluttered. That thought had occurred to her, the idea that Joshua could be near enough to visit...well, she didn't want to get her hopes up too much, especially if it meant he would be engaged in a battle.

"Are you anxious to see Mr. Heth again?" Belle asked.

"It would be nice to see him again, I won't pretend otherwise," Kate said. "But it would also be nice to see my brother." The words escaped her mouth before she could stop them. "Oh, Belle, Elizabeth, I am so sorry."

"Don't distress yourself, Kate," Elizabeth said with a sad look. "You need to really embrace your brother. You are lucky to still have him. We don't begrudge the fact that your brother is alive."

"I should have been more thoughtful. For that, I do apologize."

"If you feel that badly, then apology accepted," Belle assured her. "But there's no need, honestly."

"Good afternoon, ladies." The three women looked up to see AJ enter the house. "It is so good to see you all."

"America Joan Prentiss, how on God's green earth did you get over here?" Elizabeth's voice was stern as if AJ was a disobedient child.

"Oh, Elizabeth, don't worry. I was quite careful. The men aren't fighting yet. However, from what I hear on my side of the river, there will likely be fighting in a few days."

"That's not guaranteed," Elizabeth argued back. "You may be safe here, but you have to get back eventually. Where's Liberty? This is actually quite dangerous."

"Elizabeth Bennett calm down," Belle said. "AJ is perfectly capable of making decisions on her own."

AJ unsuccessfully tried to hold back a laugh. At the look her friends gave her, she shrugged. "My apologies, but I always have to laugh when someone calls Elizabeth by her full name." Kate and Belle gave a quick chuckle as well. Elizabeth knew marrying and changing her name to a beloved character in a novel was amusing. She was usually quick to join in the giggles, but she was not amused at AJ's flippant nature about her travels.

"I am well aware that you can make your own decisions, AJ. I just don't want anything to happen to you. You could be killed, wounded, you could be taken advantage of..."

"I know the risks that I take, Elizabeth." AJ's tone was calm and deliberate. "I have business to take care of on this side of the river, so I wanted to stop here briefly to catch up with you, my friend." She took a deep breath. "I know the only reason you are being so overprotective is that you care about me. Truth be told, I would likely do the same thing if our positions were switched."

"Elizabeth, I really don't think the Yankees will be too hard on her if caught taking a few things that they left lying around," Belle said. Unless that's not all you're doing. She thought to herself. Unless you have completely become a spy for our Confederate cause, as I suspect.

AJ glanced at Elizabeth, who sighed. "I worry about all my friends," Elizabeth replied. "And family. Accidents can happen, but I am glad to see you, AJ. Honestly, I am."

"I know," AJ said. "Worry seems to be the one constant in this war."

"It will likely continue to be so," Elizabeth added.

AJ made her way to the Confederate camp, hoping she could quickly find Lt. Daniels and give him the information she had. Finding Nathaniel would even be better. Finding Richard Evans would even be acceptable. Her heart beat quicker when she saw two Confederate pickets.

"Pardon me, Ma'am." One of the men held up his hand. "You must stop here."

"I have business to attend to in the camp with Major Daniels, also, Lieutenant Nathaniel Prentiss, if he is available."

"Now what would a pretty young woman like you want with them?" The second man asked.

"My business is my own," AJ replied. "I wish I could tell you, but I cannot."

"Well we can let you through, but first we need to search your mount."

AJ complied and slid off her horse, then stood to the side as one of the men looked through her saddlebags. The other turned to her.

"We also need to search your person, make sure you're not carrying anything you shouldn't be." He took two steps toward her and she quickly weighed her options. These men were Confederate soldiers on her side, but she had specific instructions not to hand off her information or goods to anyone who wasn't a contact.

"Search my person? Surely that's unnecessary, sir." AJ tried to make her voice sound strong. Hoofbeats sounded behind her.

"You want access to the camp and won't tell us why and now you're balking at us searching you? If I didn't know any better, I'd say that all sounds mighty suspicious." The soldier said.

"A woman not wanting your hands on her is hardly grounds for suspicion, Private Gregort." The familiar voice of Richard Evans spoke.

"Captain Evans." The man saluted as AJ heard the creaking of leather. She didn't turn but guessed the sound was Richard dismounting. She sensed him come up behind her.

"I know this woman. She is a native of Fredericksburg and as loyal a Southerner as you will find. He stepped next to her. "You have my word that there is nothing to fear from her."

"But sir, we have our orders..."

"Then I will take charge of her. I will personally escort her to where she needs to go and make sure she is escorted out as well."

"But, sir!"

"Do you challenge me, Private?" Richard asked, his voice controlled and commanding.

"No, sir." The two pickets saluted and returned to their posts.

Richard gently took AJ's arm and led her back to her horse. "Miss Prentiss, we meet again."

"Yes, sir. I trust you know why I'm here."

"Of course." Richard's hands circled her waist as he helped her onto the horse. It was a gentlemanly thing to do and meant nothing, but that didn't mean AJ's heart didn't skip a beat. He then mounted his own horse.

"I must thank you for your help with those men back there." She said.

"Do not worry." He replied. "As you said, I know why you need to be so secretive. If those men knew, they would have let you go through quickly. It is good to know that you're trustworthy." They rode towards the camp, and he glanced at her from the corner of his eye. "I do, however, wonder where you have all of your information, as that soldier found nothing in your saddlebags."

AJ blushed, hoping that he couldn't see her. "A woman needs to have her secrets, Captain Evans." She said, impressed with herself at how she was able to banter with him.

"So is that a challenge, Miss America Joan? To discover your secrets?" They had entered the camp and began to pass the tents of the soldiers.

"Take it how you will, Mr. Evans." She gave him what she hoped was a coy smile. He smiled back. "I trust you've been able to visit with your family since you've been stationed close to home." She said, changing the subject.

"I have, yes, and thank you for delivering my last letter and for visiting with my mother. She told me she greatly enjoys your company. You don't have to do that."

AJ smiled. "I don't mind, not at all. I have actually grown quite fond of your mother. I don't have one of my own, you know. She is such a pleasure to talk to."

"Well, I appreciate it more than you'll ever know," Richard said, giving her a genuine smile. He dismounted, then reached up to help her down.

"You're very welcome." She said. "Speaking of family, is my brother here?"

"I don't believe so. He rode west to meet with a contact."

"Captain Evans. Miss Prentiss." AJ turned toward the familiar voice of Major Daniels. She had only met him personally once but he was a difficult man to forget. He was of medium height, handsome, with light brown hair, chocolate brown eyes and an aristocratic air about him. Nathaniel had told her that the man had been born in Britain and moved to South Carolina as a child. "Is everything all right?"

"Yes, sir, everything is just fine. I had business to attend to on this side of the river, so I decided to stop here and give you what I have personally."

"I see." Major Daniels was a difficult man to read. AJ could not tell if he was happy with her or not. "And what do you have for me?"

"Information, mostly, and some morphine packets, not much, though. I've only been taking a couple at a time to avoid suspicion." She replied. The Major nodded. "I will, however, need some privacy to retrieve them for you."

"Of course." Lt. Daniels led her to a tent, his, she assumed. Richard Evans followed AJ and the Major. She ducked into the tent then quickly and efficiently removed the goods from her petticoats. She stepped back outside.

"Here you are, sir." She handed Major Daniels the packages. She caught Richard's eye and he grinned at her.

"I believe that is one secret uncovered." He said. AJ shrugged, not quite knowing what else to do. She then focused on the Major and told him the information that she had gathered. When she was finished, he nodded.

"Thank you, Miss Prentiss. Your efforts, as usual, have been beneficial to the Confederacy. If you obtain any more information we can rendezvous again."

"Yes, sir." She replied.

"I'll see you to the river, Miss Prentiss," Richard said.

"Thank you, Mr. Evans, but that's not necessary." She said. Lieutenant Daniels nodded at her and then turned and walked away.

"I must insist," Richard said. "I would walk you to your own front door if it wouldn't be a death mission for me."

"I will be quite all right." She mounted her horse. "Lafayette is one of the best horses around. I have been quite lucky not to lose him to either side."

"All right, then," Richard replied. "Just never let it be said that I didn't make the gentlemanly offer." He gave her his most charming smile.

"Of course not." She smiled back. "Good day, Mr. Evans."

"Always a pleasure, Miss Prentiss."

Saturday, November 22, 1862
Bennett Home

"Mrs. Bennett!"

Elizabeth looked up as Eric walked into the house from the shop. "Goodness, Eric, what is it?"

"Mr. Scott just came by with news that the Federals are going to shell the town. We should make preparations to head out to Turner's Glenn."

"So it has come to that. I cannot believe it. Are you sure?"

"He sounded sure. General Lee apparently feels so, as he is sending army wagons and ambulances into town to help evacuate the women and children." Eric replied.

"Where will everyone go?" Elizabeth asked as she untied her apron and moved to bank the fire in the stove. "We are lucky that we have Turner's Glenn." She hastened into her bedroom and grabbed two carpetbags. Eric had followed her and stood in the doorway. She handed him one of the bags. "Please fill this with spare clothing for you and Benjamin." He nodded and went into the second bedroom. Elizabeth quickly put as many essentials as she could, along with two spare dresses into the bag, then grabbed two dresses for Hannah. She then went into the main room of the house and grabbed her Bible, the wedding photograph of her and Joshua, and the tintype of Joshua, taken just before he had left for war. She carefully placed those articles into the carpetbag she had given Eric, then turned to her children, who watched her from where they stood in front of the fireplace.

"Benjamin, Hannah, you may each bring one thing with you to the plantation house," Elizabeth said. Benjamin immediately grabbed his dominoes and Hannah held up her doll. Elizabeth placed the items in the bag and turned to Eric. Knowing what she was about to say, he spoke.

"I'll go and hitch up the wagon." He quickly made his way to the back door.

"Children, are we all set? Look around the house one more time, by then Eric should be out front with the wagon." After one final look around her home, Elizabeth led her children out the door and locked up the house.

Once again, chaos filled the street. She wasn't sure Eric would be able to maneuver the horses through the crowds. Both people and vehicles clogged the street out front.

"Mrs. Bennett!" Eric called out, getting as close as he could. The Bennetts made their way to the wagon and quickly got in.

"Thank you, Eric. We are so blessed to have you. Let's get to safety."

Sunday, November 30, 1862
Bennett House

After spending a week at Turner's Glenn, Eric had ridden into town and determine that it was safe for the Bennett family to return home. The rest of the family now wanted to join the Bennetts for the day.

"You didn't have to come into town," Elizabeth told Belle, who sat next to her in the Bennett wagon that Eric drove, while Timothy drove the second wagon that belonged to Turner's Glenn.

"It's been a while since we've all been to Fredericksburg, and now that the town is out of danger, it's a good excuse to do some socializing. Those Yanks don't have enough courage to attack our brave soldiers." Belle said.

Eric had heard that the Yankee General Burnside would not risk invading the town to attack the Rebel forces when he would have the Rappahannock River behind him with no escape route. This gave the Confederates a very advantageous position.

"I am very glad the town is securely in the hands of the Confederacy," Elizabeth said. "Such good news." She sighed. "I desperately hope it stays that way."

As they entered the town, Elizabeth couldn't help but notice that it was incredibly quiet. Almost eerie.

"Where is everyone?" Belle asked as if reading Elizabeth's thoughts.

"I'm guessing they're just not back from wherever they went last week," Elizabeth said.

"It seems as though we have the town to ourselves," Belle said.

"Mama, where is everyone?" Benjamin called from the back of the wagon.

"Still away, Benjamin," Elizabeth said.

It didn't take long for the vehicles to reach the Bennett house. As they entered, Elizabeth was glad to see that it stood exactly the way that she had left it.

"I'm glad we brought some food," Annie said. "I'll start dinner in a little while."

"Bless you, Annie," Elizabeth said as she brought her carpetbag to her room. She would put everything away later when her guests were gone. She returned to the main room and went to the fireplace to start a fire.

"It's really cold in here," Meri commented.

"It is almost December and the house has been empty for a week. It makes sense." Belle replied.

"I suppose," Meri said. She looked outside. "I still can't believe how desolate it looks."

"You wanted to come in earlier for church services," Belle said. "I wonder if any of them will even open their doors."

"You're right, Belle. Good point." Annie said from the kitchen area. "You can't really have a church service without a congregation."

"I would hope at least one of the churches would have a service," Elizabeth said.

"Well, we can always have you say an extra prayer and read a Bible passage or two before we have dinner," Belle suggested.

There was a knock at the door and AJ walked in, closely followed by Liberty.

"We saw smoke coming from your chimney and the wagons in front so decided to stop by," AJ said. "My, it's crowded in here!"

"Quite the opposite of how things are outside," Elizabeth said. "Did you two attend church this morning?"

"We did, but it was quite empty, like most of the town," Liberty said. "We visited for a bit, then ran some errands and here we are."

"What store is open on a Sunday?" Belle asked.

"We stopped at the dry goods store to check on Margaret Buckley."

"Why would you do that?" Belle scoffed.

"It's the right thing to do," AJ said. "She's all alone now, there's no one to check up on her. She did mention how grateful she is for your visits, Elizabeth. She missed you this week."

"Your visits?" Belle turned to her sister. "Why on earth would you be visiting her?"

"My goodness, Belle. Why do you feel the need to be so unkind to her?" Elizabeth asked. "What did she ever do to you?"

"Nothing," Belle answered. "She is just not the type of person one should socialize with, so you shouldn't either."

"Oh, for heaven's sake," Elizabeth said. "Just as AJ said, Margaret is a young woman who is currently alone in the world. Helping out a fellow citizen is simply the right thing to do, Belle."

"Do what you must, but at least don't let anyone see you. You just may ruin your reputation." Belle turned. "Who else did you visit?" Her question was directed at AJ, but Liberty answered.

"We stopped and saw Mrs. Evans," Liberty answered before AJ could stop her.

"Mrs. Evans?" Belle asked. "Richard Evans's mother? Why would you be visiting her?"

"I...I was once asked to bring a letter to her and we started talking." AJ explained. "I have been trying to visit her whenever I am in town. She gets quite lonely."

"How can she possibly be lonely?" Belle asked. "Her husband is home and she's at the center of Fredericksburg society."

"Just because you have people visiting you doesn't mean you don't get lonely," AJ replied. "And her husband is rarely home. He's working all the time." She shrugged. "I really enjoy her company. She is a wonderful woman."

"Not to mention she has a son who is one of the most eligible men in Fredericksburg," Meri said, nudging Liberty.

"I still want to check on Marion and the Beale family," Liberty said. "Would you like to join me, Meri?"

"Sure, may I, Belle?" Meri asked, then turned to Lainey. "You can come too, you can visit with Julian and Sam."

"That sounds like fun. If that's alright with you, Belle." Lainey said.

Belle looked surprised, then nodded. "Yes, you may both go."

The three girls left. Eric went into the blacksmith shop, followed by Timothy, Max, and Benjamin. Hannah sat in her special chair near the fireplace, pulled out a book and pretended to read to her doll. Annie continued working in the kitchen, cleaning, and organizing as she went along. AJ, Belle, and Elizabeth went to sit at the kitchen table.

"Why did you look surprised when Lainey and Meri asked you if they could go with Liberty?" AJ asked.

"I'm just not used to being the one in charge. The one they seek permission from." She shrugged. "It's a strange feeling."

"I can understand that. It does take some getting used to." AJ agreed. "Have you heard from your mother since I last saw you?"

"It's been several weeks," Elizabeth said. "From her letters, it sounds like she is doing well. Nursing seems to agree with her."

"She has always been a nurturing woman," AJ said. "With you two, the rest of your family, with your servants, even with my family."

"Yes, very nurturing," Belle said. "A wonderful mother until we need her the most. Looking back, I do understand why she went to be with James when he was wounded. I likely would have done the same if I had a son who was wounded or at least I would have tried, however, I am finding it very difficult to understand why she hasn't come home yet. This is something I cannot comprehend, nor will I ever."

"She must have her reasons, Belle," Elizabeth said. "When she returns, I'm sure she'll explain in a way that will make you understand."

"If she ever returns," Belle said.

"Don't be ridiculous, Belle. She will." AJ assured her.

"I sometimes wonder if there were a battle here, if there was a hospital closer, would she come back?" Belle asked. "If she really wants to be a nurse, she could help here."

"Perhaps," Elizabeth said. "But I, for one, am quite happy that the threat of battle has dissipated." She looked at AJ. "How is the situation on the other side of the river? Do you think the threat of battle is over?"

"Possibly," AJ replied. "Tomorrow is the first of December. I would think the troops will soon settle in for the winter."

"Oh, wouldn't it be wonderful if Joshua or Father or Nathaniel could get leave for the winter months, especially since they won't be doing much fighting this time of year," Elizabeth said with hope in her voice.

"That would be nice." AJ agreed. "Although I feel we've spoken on this topic before. The Confederate leaders may allow it, perhaps if they're in the immediate area like the soldiers here in town already, but those far away, like in Winchester? I don't think so."

"Well, perhaps Richard Evans could get a furlough to visit his mother at the same time you're there visiting with her." Belle gave AJ a sly look. "He would be a pleasant visitor. I know you've always thought so. Don't deny it, AJ."

"Don't be silly, Belle. I could never have a relationship with Richard Evans, even if I wanted one." AJ's heart fluttered quickly as she glanced at Elizabeth. "We don't have enough in common and our values are at opposite ends."

"People change," Belle said. "Look at me, I'm changing. AJ, you yourself are becoming much more confident. Believe it or not, this war is causing some good changes. Maybe Richard Evans will change."

"He would have to change quite a bit," AJ said, but couldn't help think that he had already shown another side of himself. She quickly banished the thought from her mind. There were parts of his personality that would likely never change.

"What about you, Belle? You're so interested in finding me a match. What about yourself?" AJ leaned forward. "You haven't been dressing in mourning for Samuel Gray in quite some time. Are you ready to start courting again?"

"I may be, but who would I attract? We do live in Fredericksburg, after all. Even before the war, our choices were few. Remember, we live in a town that was called 'the only finished city in America'. Nothing new or good ever happens here."

"I forgot about that." Elizabeth smiled. Back in 1860, the Prince of Wales had visited. His tour guide had described the town as "finished" even with all of its history. "Fredericksburg is known as the boyhood home of George Washington and the longtime residence of his mother. We are the town where Robert E. Lee met his future wife. We may be the site of a great and terrible battle, but the title of a "finished" town will always stay with us."

"Wouldn't it be wonderful to be the city where the final battle of the war was fought?" Belle sighed. "Either way, we will still be a finished, sleepy town. With a small selection of potential suitors, so even if I was ready to be out in society, it wouldn't make much of a difference."

"I don't care what society dictates," AJ said. "I was wondering how you were feeling. It's been over a year."

"It still pains me," Belle said. "Honestly, though, losing James pains me so much worse. I'm not sure what that says about me or my relationship with Samuel, but there it is."

AJ nodded. "Would you be open to another relationship?"

"I think I could be. If it were the right man." Belle smiled. "My ideal man."

"We well remember the requirements you put forth on your ideal man once upon a time," Elizabeth said.

"Well, you found your perfect man," Belle said to Elizabeth while looking at AJ. "We will too." She smiled.

Tuesday, December 2, 1862
Moss Neck Manor

"Have you heard the latest?" Bertie asked Kate.

"What are the rumors of now?" Kate asked.

"Rumors of a great battle here in Fredericksburg. First, they said a fight was inevitable, then unlikely because of the ineptitude of that new Yankee General Burnside. Now, it sounds as though a battle will take place here."

"Let us hope, then, that this battle will be the end." Kate looked up at the knock on the parlor door. She smiled when she saw Belle standing in the doorway.

"My goodness, what a surprise! Welcome, Belle! I'm so glad you could visit." She stood and gave her friend a quick embrace.

"I'm glad to get away," Belle replied, then greeted Bertie. "I'm tired of all the dreary work on the plantation. At least, I can still tell others what to do if I don't want to help with certain chores. I have realized, amazingly, just how much I can do and just how much work it takes to run a plantation."

"It does, indeed," Kate said. "But it is ever so nice you found some free time to visit us. Did Daniel drive you over?"

"No. While they may be able to spare me for a few hours, Daniel is as busy as ever. I rode one of the horses over."

"You must have really wanted to get away," Kate said. "You don't often ride."

"I prefer not to, that's true," Belle said. "However, this war has also made me realize that, at times, sacrifices must be made. I do what I must do."

"Unfortunately, we are all learning a lot about ourselves and our resilience," Kate said. "At least you have a couple of strong young darkies that stayed behind to help you. All we have left are a few older servants."

"We are fortunate in that respect," Belle said. "Did you know that many families fled Fredericksburg last week, even Elizabeth and her family came out to Turner's Glenn?"

"Yes, we had a couple of families stay here for a few days also. Some went back home while others completely left the area to stay with friends and relatives in other cities. Many boarded trains while they are still running and went into Richmond."

"We heard that some of the residents of Caroline County sent carriages to bring refugees to their homes. It is good to see so much charity." Belle commented.

"Indeed," Kate said. "Some homes took in as many as thirty people."

"True generosity." Belle looked out the window. "To think, those who went back home may need to flee again."

Kate sighed. "It's getting to the point where I wish the soldiers would just make a decision, either fight or leave the area." She shook her head. "Unfortunately, winter is upon us and both sides may decide to have their winter encampments here."

"That would make for a very long and bothersome winter," Belle said.

Sunday, December 7, 1862
Bennett House

Elizabeth bent over, checking the winter vegetables in her small garden. Eric was in the blacksmith shop teaching Benjamin how to weld some lanterns. Hannah was in her room, taking a rest.

"It shouldn't be long until we can harvest these." She said to herself, then stood and pulled her shawl tighter around her shoulders. She heard the back door open. Without turning to look, she spoke: "Hannah, Sweetheart. I thought I told you to stay in bed until I came in to get you."

"I would truly love to take a nap, but only if you'd join me."

Elizabeth whirled around at the sound of her husband's voice.

"Joshua!" She shrieked, throwing her arms around him. He held her tightly. "What are you doing here?"

He pulled back to kiss her. "We've come to defend our fine city. With the Federals right across the river, intelligence is telling us that Burnside wants to cross the Rappahannock here and march on down to Richmond. We're going to stop them at Fredericksburg and send the Yankees back north. I was given leave, but only until tomorrow morning, so…"

Elizabeth smiled and hugged him tightly. "I am so glad to see you."

"Mama!" Hannah exclaimed from the doorway. She ran to her mother and hugged her legs, then looked at Joshua, as if she recognized him, but could not place him.

"Hannah, darling," Joshua said gently and knelt down and extended an arm to her. His daughter simply looked at him.

Elizabeth patted Hannah's back. "I thought you were supposed to be in bed taking a nap."

"I heard you talking and wanted to see who it was. Is this…are you my Papa?"

Elizabeth had to hold back tears. Hannah had only been two years old when Joshua left. It was difficult to see how little she remembered him.

239

"Oh, how I have missed you, sweetheart," Joshua said. Hannah took the steps toward him and put her arms around him. He clutched her to him and Elizabeth saw a shimmer of tears in his eyes as he picked her up.

"Are you gonna stay home for good?" Hannah asked as she rubbed her small hands on his whiskers.

"No, Hannah, I wish I could, but I can only stay tonight," Joshua said.

"I guess we need to spend the day together," Hannah replied. "Let's go find Benjamin and Eric."

"That sounds like a plan," Joshua said, then followed Elizabeth into the house.

Hannah ran into the blacksmith shop while Joshua turned and kissed Elizabeth.

"I have missed you so much." He said, pushing a strand of hair from her face.

"And I, you." She responded, pulling him tightly into a hug.

"Papa!" Benjamin's voice cried out. Joshua pulled away from Elizabeth and drew his son into his arms. "Papa, I am so glad you're here! I cannot believe it! It's really you!" Elizabeth could see tears forming in Joshua's eyes again as he stood and turned to Eric.

"Eric." The two shook hands and Joshua patted Eric's back. "I was so sorry to hear of your mother's passing."

"Yes, sir, but I get through the loss knowing that she's now out of pain and in heaven."

"A good way to look at life. I am deeply grateful to you for everything you have done for my family."

"Well, sir, you took a chance on me all those years ago. I am quite proud to call myself a part of this family."

"We are too." Joshua put his hand around Eric's shoulder, then looked around. There were still a few weeks before Christmas, but Elizabeth had already started to put up some decorations for the holiday.

"It's already looking quite festive in here," Joshua said.

"Mama started decorating when we got back from the plantation," Benjamin told him.

"I see." He turned to Elizabeth. "Turner's Glenn?"

"We were out there last week when we heard rumors there would be fighting here." The family all sat in front of the fireplace. Eric quickly grabbed some wood and stoked the fire, then joined the family. Benjamin and Hannah both sat on Joshua's lap and Elizabeth sat next to them.

"I'm glad that you stayed there. It was a safe move. It might be best if you go back out there tomorrow." Joshua said, then stretched his legs and pulled his children close. "I'm sorry I wasn't able to come any earlier. It would have been nice to go to church with you all.

"Oh, that would have been wonderful, but at least you're home now." Elizabeth agreed. "I hate to ask, but what is the news in your camps? The rumors here all say there will be a battle. Is that true?"

"There's not much movement in the Yankee army across the river and many, including General Lee himself, are expressing doubts about Burnside's ability to cross our river in the face of our superior army."

"So we're stuck..." Elizabeth shook her head and glanced at her children. Hannah had fallen asleep, but Benjamin and Eric were listening intently to her. "Never mind."

Joshua reached out and grabbed her hand. "Yes, you are stuck between two armies of over 100,000 men only a mere mile from you on either side."

"Joshua!" She looked at Benjamin and Eric again. "That is not a very comforting thought."

"Well, that part may not be, but I can assure you, the Confederate army will give everything to protect this city. The Yankees can't cross the Rappahannock or they will head straight to Richmond. You know I will do everything necessary to protect my family. I will personally bring you to Turner's Glenn if I feel it's safer there, but it's difficult to tell right now where the fighting will be exactly."

Elizabeth gave him a small smile. "Well, I trust you." She squeezed his hand. "And our Lord, to do what is best for us."

Joshua kissed her hand. "Sometimes, that's all we can do."

Later that evening, Joshua and Elizabeth sat in a chair in front of the fireplace, Elizabeth sitting in Joshua's lap. Eric had given up his bed in the house and was sleeping on a pallet in the blacksmith shop so that Hannah could be out of her parents' room.

"I should have asked earlier, but was Father able to get leave as well?" Elizabeth asked, her head resting on her husband's shoulder.

"He was. He made his way directly to Turner's Glenn. If he has time, I know he will come here to see you. Perhaps he will be over in the morning." Joshua sighed and looked around. "It all seems so different here, and yet completely unchanged."

"I know what you mean," Elizabeth said. "I try to describe the changes in my letters, but words can only say so much."

Joshua nodded. "I am pleased with how well Eric is adjusting. It sounds as though he really considers himself a member of this family. I know I have you to thank for that. Benjamin...I just cannot believe how grown up he has gotten. Working side by side with Eric in the shop? Yet, when I think back, Eric wasn't that much older than Benjamin when he started working with me, and I had forgotten how much a child grows between the ages of two and three. Hannah is almost four already, she seems so much older. It's as if I missed half of her life. If the war lasts even one more year, I will have been away from her more than with her in her lifetime."

Elizabeth heard the emotion in her husband's voice. She was unsure of what she should say to help him. Finally, she spoke up.

"That may all be true, Joshua, but she understands why her Papa is gone, as does Benjamin. They know why you are fighting and are proud of you." She ran her hand over his heavily-bearded chin. 'I am too."

Joshua gave her a quick kiss.

"It's so good to have you home," Elizabeth said. "How have you been? Really?"

"Most days, I am honestly not sure." He replied. "There are days when I do not know how I'll manage to get through another day of this war. Those are the days when I can actually feel the prayers that I know the children and you are saying."

"I'm glad they're helping." She replied.

"I will tell you, losing so many friends and fellow soldiers has been a real struggle." Joshua continued. "Losing James..." He hesitated. "It was one of the worst things I have ever had to deal with. The only thing that made it bearable was knowing that he had found the Lord. In fact, I don't think I told you this, but his last words to me were: 'Joshua, don't you ever forget, be strong and steadfast, don't fear or be dismayed...'" Joshua stopped, took a deep breath, and then finished. "For the Lord, your God is with you wherever you go."

With tears in her eyes, remembering her brother, Elizabeth smiled. "Your favorite Bible passage."

"Yes. It gave me great comfort when he quoted that verse to me before he was shipped off to Richmond. I didn't know he had passed away until your father received the letter from your mother about it."

"I wondered how Father took the news," Elizabeth said.

"I had never seen your father so distressed," Joshua said softly. "It was quite a difficult scene to observe. He even cried."

"I don't believe I have ever seen my father cry, but he did love James so," Elizabeth said. "This whole war. It's not what any of us thought it would be. The illness. The death. The destruction of humans, animals, and buildings. When the Federals left earlier this year, they left Stafford Heights so quickly, they rode right through the Prentiss's wheat field. They completely destroyed the crop. Did I write that to you?"

"I believe you mentioned it. I completely agree. I have witnessed scenes like that and much worse." Joshua said. "Memories that can never be erased from my mind."

242

Elizabeth looked into her husband's eyes. He looked troubled as if he were remembering those terrible visions at that very moment. She placed her hand on his chin and kissed him gently.

"I suppose we'll just have to fill your mind with new, sweet memories like today."

"I'm in favor of that," Joshua replied. "I tell you what, being here with you, snug inside our home, and not outside in the bitter cold with frost on the ground. This will be a memory that I will hold on to for quite a while."

"We should have invited more men to come into our home, out of the cold weather. There's room in the shop."

"That is something I wish I had thought of, but it's too late at this hour. Perhaps if the opportunity arises again." He sighed. "At any rate, I do know many of our Confederate men are in the houses that have been abandoned."

"That's good to know." She smiled. "It makes me feel better." She went to kiss Joshua, but his yawn stopped her.

"I'm sorry." He said. "I wish we could stay up all evening, but..."

"Joshua. You do not need to be sorry." She pulled him closer to her. "Let's get you warm and comfortable in our bed, Lieutenant Bennett."

Monday, December 8, 1862
Bennett Home

"Ahh, this is something I have truly been missing," Joshua said, placing another forkful of scrambled eggs into his mouth. "These eggs are incredible."

"I may not be the greatest cook, but I am pretty competent at scrambling eggs," Elizabeth replied with a smile.

"Mama is getting better at cooking," Benjamin said. "Aunt Annie is much better, though. She comes over and helps Mama all the time."

"Well, I can definitely taste the improvements," Joshua said with a smile and another mouthful of eggs.

"Did anyone else feel the ground move last night?" Eric asked. "I thought I did, but was half-asleep and didn't know what to think when I woke up. When I went to get the milk this morning, some soldiers were talking about an earthquake."

"I thought I felt something," Elizabeth said. "But like you, I didn't believe what I was feeling. I was just going to ignore it."

"Mama, what's an earthquake?" Hannah asked.

"I honestly don't know exactly what causes one, but it is when the earth moves under our feet. It must have been just a little one last night."

"Ohh," Hannah said. Benjamin nodded.

Elizabeth finished her breakfast and stood. "Joshua, before you leave, I would like to make sure you have some comforts from home. Are there any restrictions on what you can bring back?"

"Aside from my own family, no, I cannot think of anything." He smiled and tousled Benjamin's hair.

"Why must you leave today, Papa?" Hannah asked. "Can't you at least stay until Christmas?"

"You know I would love that, Hannah-Bear, but I have to get back to my camp." Joshua didn't want to get her hopes up, but he suspected his company would be around Fredericksburg for at least a month or so, and that meant he may be able to be with his family for the holidays. At least, he hoped. "You never know, though. I may come back soon after all. Christmas is the time for miracles." He gave her braid a gentle tug. She giggled.

"The morning sun is bright!" Benjamin commented as he stood at the front window.

"Indeed it is, Son. I hope it's a sign of a wonderful day." Joshua finished his meal and stood. "As much as it pains me, I must be leaving. I have to report to my commanding officer."

Elizabeth brushed a tear that had escaped her eye and finished packing Joshua's sack. She watched as her husband said goodbye to Eric, Benjamin and Hannah. He gave Elizabeth a sad look and walked toward the door. Out of the corner of her eye, she saw Eric helping Benjamin and Hannah with the breakfast dishes. Elizabeth pulled her shawl on and followed Joshua out the door and down the lane to the fence. He took the pack from her hands, reached up and brushed a tear from her cheek.

"Elizabeth. Don't cry. I'll be okay." He kissed her forehead.

"I know, be strong and steadfast. I will be. I will pray for you every day and every night. Joshua, just...please take care of yourself, please."

"I will, Elizabeth, but you have the harder job. You need to take care of yourself." She gave him a slightly puzzled look. "Elizabeth, you are doing a marvelous job with the children and the home and the shop and helping out at Turner's Glenn. You are doing so much for others. Make sure you take care of yourself. Understand? Remember the first sign of trouble, you get to Turner's Glenn."

"Yes, sir." She smiled, then slid her hands around his neck for a kiss. "I love you, Joshua."

"I love you, too." He brushed a strand of hair from her forehead. "I will stop by again when I can get leave, until then." He slung the pack over his shoulder and walked out the gate and down the road, turning to look at Elizabeth every few steps.

"Elizabeth!" Lucy Beale-Page walked up to the fence. "Was that Mr. Bennett walking away?"

"It was." Elizabeth smiled. "He was able to get leave for the night."

"That must have been a pleasant surprise," Lucy said. Elizabeth nodded. "We had some visitors as well, my brother and a good friend of his. Mama sent them back to camp this morning and is now putting the house back to rights. She figured since it's less likely for there to be a battle, it would be a good time to do so."

"She is right about that." Elizabeth pulled her cloak closer. "I heard your younger brother has been ill. How is he doing now?"

"Julian is improving every day. Thank you so much for asking."

"That's good, and how is the rest of your family?"

"Quite well. Many families continue to leave, as I'm sure you've noticed, but Mama's been quite adamant that we all stay together. John mentioned the possibility of the two of us going to Richmond, but he's being respectful and caring and taking my feelings into consideration."

"He is such a good man, your John." Elizabeth smiled.

"Indeed he is." A cool gust of wind blew.

"Do you have time to stop in for a cup of tea? It's not the best, but it will warm you up."

"Thank you for the offer, but no. I must run a couple of errands and get back to Mother in a timely manner." Lucy said.

"All right, but do stop by for tea another day. You have a wonderful day." Elizabeth said. "Stay safe."

Wednesday, December 10, 1862
Turner Farm

Belle sat on the front porch, needlepoint in hand. She actually enjoyed needlepoint. It relaxed her, which was something that she desperately needed as of late. With the Union army across the river and Confederate troops in town, as well as up and down the river, she had been unable to visit any of her friends. Belle felt stranded out at Turner's Glenn. She glanced up as she heard hoof beats and saw a lone rider coming up the road. The man wore a Confederate uniform. She stood and moved to the porch railing, then smiled with recognition.

"Nathaniel!" She waved as he came within hearing distance.

"Belle!" He quickly dismounted and rushed up the stairs to her.

Belle wanted to throw her arms around him, but propriety dictated that she refrain. She did, however, put her hands into his outstretched hands. "Whatever are you doing out here? Nothing has happened to AJ or Liberty, has it?"

"No, not that I know of. They're still on the other side of the Rappahannock so they should be fine. It's you that I'm worried about."

"Why ever would you be worried about me?" She asked.

"You and your family. You should be aware that the fighting could break out here as early as tomorrow. The Yankees they've been waiting for a long time, but we've had word that they finally plan on moving tomorrow."

"How in the world do they plan on crossing a river with no bridge? Our Confederate troops were smart enough to cut off their access to the city when they destroyed the bridges. Your own sisters have been clever enough to build a raft to come across for visits and to get supplies, but a Yankee. Ha! Never!" Belle tossed her head and crossed her arms.

"They apparently have been waiting for supplies to build a bridge of pontoons to use for the crossing." He explained.

"And where would you be getting that information? It seems as though an ordinary soldier like you shouldn't have access to that kind of information."

"I have been working as a courier for the Confederacy as well as working with some intelligence agents." He looked a bit uncomfortable at his admission. "I am privy to a lot of information that is only meant for officers."

"Nathaniel. I know about AJ and what you have asked her to do. She told me originally that she was just smuggling, but I figured out recently that she is doing much more. Elizabeth and I are the only people in town who know, other than Liberty, of course, although, like me, Kate may have figured it out also."

"Why did she tell you even that much? She shouldn't have told anyone anything. That's dangerous."

"So is encouraging her to do it in the first place." Belle countered. Nathaniel looked sheepish.

"You're right, it is, but it's been necessary to help our cause." He replied. "Why did she tell you and Elizabeth?"

"She told Elizabeth because if anything were to happen to her, she wanted Elizabeth to take care of Liberty."

"Nothing will happen to AJ. She's too smart." Nathaniel said.

"I'm sure Belle Boyd's family thought the same," Belle replied. Belle Boyd had been arrested multiple times for espionage and had finally been incarcerated earlier that summer.

"All right, Belle. You have made your point. It is dangerous. You're right, yet I feel that AJ is smart enough not to take any unnecessary risks."

"Of course I'm right. Now, what did you come here to talk to me about?" She placed her fisted hands on her hips.

"As I said, I came to warn you about the fighting. You should take your family and head out. Leave the area, maybe stay with your family in Petersburg, if you can make it down there."

"Leave. To Petersburg? Nathaniel, you cannot be serious. I am not going to pack up my home and family just because you think it will be safer. If we abandon Turner's Glenn, there is no telling what will happen to it."

"And if you stay, you could be injured, assaulted, killed..."

"Oh, really, Nathaniel. There is no possible way our Confederate boys would allow their Southern women to come to any harm." Belle responded flippantly.

"Belle, I am not so sure that's true. We may not be able to protect you. You don't know what happens to men during a battle." Nathaniel grabbed her forearm. "Please heed my advice and leave the area."

"No. I will not be chased out of my own home by the Yankees, Nathaniel. I will not. Annie can take Meri, Lainey, and Max if it's necessary. Elizabeth can take her family too, but I will not go."

"Belle. Don't be unreasonable." Nathaniel tried to plead, but what he said meant nothing to her.

"I'm not, Nathaniel." She turned to face away from him. "But if you're so worried about us, why don't you just stay here. You can be our protector." She spun back around and spoke softly. "Be my protector, Nathaniel." She stepped toward him. "Stay with me."

Nathaniel noticed the change in her demeanor. She had turned from stubborn to seductive very quickly. He knew Belle well enough to know there was a reason for it. She never did anything without a purpose. He sighed.

"I cannot do that, Belle, and you know it. I have to report back to my commander, and soon. I shouldn't really have stopped here anyway, but I had to see you. Try and warn you of the dangers."

"Nathaniel, please don't leave me!" In desperation and breaking all decorum, she threw her arms around him. He had to stay. To protect her. She had already lost Samuel and James. Would she also lose Nathaniel? Belle had always felt that she and Nathaniel could be more than friends. She enjoyed bantering with him, enjoyed talking with him. She felt comfortable being with him. Why had she never before realized just how much he meant to her? Tears began to fall down her face. She knew the reason, down deep. It was her own Southern pride. Her own desire to be a socialite and not just the wife of a farmer. She couldn't be Elizabeth.

Nathaniel patted Belle on the back. "Belle. Belle, don't cry. Please don't cry."

"I can't help it." She sniffled. "I have lost too many loved ones in this war, Nathaniel. I don't want to lose you too."

"Belle? What is this? Where is the strong, stubborn woman that I saw not two minutes ago?"

"I'm sorry, Nathaniel. You're right, of course. I don't know what is wrong with me." She pulled back and wiped her tears with the palm of her hand.

"I wish I could stay, Belle. Really, I do. But I have to go, and you should as well."

Belle took a deep breath. "No. I am staying. We'll be fine." She brushed imaginary dirt from his shoulder. "You Southern boys will make sure of it"

Nathaniel sighed. "I wish you would change your mind." He backed away, then touched his hat with his hand. "Either way, please, take care of yourself, Belle. Don't do anything foolish."

Belle watched him ride away, a flurry of feelings surrounding her. She hadn't felt this bereft when Samuel had gone off to fight. Why was she feeling more worried for Nathaniel?

Annie walked up next to Belle.

"Was that Nathaniel? What did he come by for?" She asked.

"Yes, it was. He wanted to warn us of the impending battle. He suggested we run away to Petersburg and stay with the Turners there."

"Really? What did you tell him? Are we going?"

"No, we're not. I am not going to abandon my home just because the Yankees are close by again. We didn't leave when they occupied the town before and I will not leave now."

"But if it's dangerous..." Annie said.

"Annie, you can take the rest of the family to Aunt Susannah, but I am staying here."

"Well, I'm not about to leave you," Annie said. She nudged Belle with her shoulder. "You may make my life topsy-turvy, but you are my sister. If you think we should stay, we'll stay."

Belle smiled at her sister, hoping she had made the right decision.

Bennett House

Elizabeth had just set the venison stew on the table when there was a knock on the door. Before she had a chance to answer the door, it opened, and Joshua entered.

"Papa!" Hannah jumped up and ran to hug her father, this time feeling comfortable with his presence. He swept her up in his arms.

"Hannah-Bear!" He exclaimed, hugging her tightly as he looked at Elizabeth. "I hope it's not an imposition if a lonely, hungry, cold soldier stays here again for the night." Benjamin raced to his father and threw his arms around him also. Joshua set Hannah down.

Elizabeth went to Joshua and hugged him as well, giving him a kiss on the cheek. "Of course not." She looked toward Eric, who had thoughtfully set another bowl at the table for Joshua.

"Welcome back again, sir." The young man said with a rare smile.

"Thank you, Eric. I'm glad I could get away again so soon."

"I could get used to this, Joshua. You're spoiling us with your presence." Elizabeth said, hoping he couldn't hear the longing in her voice. A longing to have him home for dinner every evening. "How did you get another leave?"

"Well, we're already camped pretty close, so my commanding officer is being a little more giving with overnight leaves." Joshua smiled and sat down at the table.

"I should write him a thank-you note," Elizabeth said, placing a basket of biscuits on the table.

"He's a good, fair man," Joshua said. He reached out to Elizabeth and Hannah, and everyone around the table joined hands for prayer. "We have so much to be thankful for."

Later that night, Elizabeth sat in front of the warm fire while Joshua tucked the children into bed. She stared into the flames, once again thinking of how nice it was to have Joshua home, even if it was only for the night. She heard the door close and Joshua came into the room. He pulled her up, then sat down and pulled her back onto his lap.

"I miss this," Elizabeth said. "This was always my favorite part of the day. Sitting with you in the evening, talking. Just being with you." She sighed and laid her head on his shoulder. "I don't wish to be a nagging wife, Joshua, but I wish you didn't have to go back. I miss you so much when you're gone."

"I know and I miss you as well. I really believe the war will end soon in our favor. The North has yet to win a significant battle." They both fell quiet in their thoughts.

"You know, Joshua, I'm not complaining about having you with me, and I am glad that you came here on your days of leave, but you have been stationed in town for almost a week. Isn't there someone you want to visit over at Turner's Glenn?" Elizabeth asked softly.

"I wouldn't mind seeing your family, Elizabeth, but I just don't have time. I want to spend any and all of my time with you and the children."

"I understand and appreciate that Joshua, but I am in reference to Daniel and you know it."

"Even if I wanted to see Daniel, I'm sure he doesn't want to see me." Joshua rested his chin on Elizabeth's head.

"I don't know about that, Joshua. He comes by about twice a week. He's been teaching Eric how to hunt and fish. He has helped us keep food on the table. We wouldn't survive without the meat the two of them bring home."

"And I am thankful for that, Elizabeth. I appreciate him so much for what he has done for my family."

"Then why don't you want to see him?" She asked.

"I do. Like I said, I'm just not sure he wants to see me."

"This stubborn side of you rarely comes out, Joshua. There is more to this than you're telling me. Do you want to explain to me what went wrong between the two of you?"

"I am afraid we didn't part well, Elizabeth. Not well at all." Joshua gently moved her from his lap, stood, and crossed the room to stare into the fire, his arm braced on the mantle. "I told him that I was enlisting. He was upset that I was fighting for the Confederacy, accused me of fighting to keep him a slave."

Elizabeth was silent, unsure if she should vocalize her thoughts.

"I told him that it wasn't true." Joshua continued. "That he knew me well enough to know it wasn't true. I'm not fighting to keep slavery. I'm fighting for my home. For freedom from Northern tyranny. For my family." He sighed. "He called me a coward for not standing up for my beliefs." Elizabeth remained quiet. "What are you thinking?"

"Well, I certainly don't think you're a coward, and I know you want slavery abolished, but, if I'm being honest," She paused. "Joshua, I can understand how he might feel a little...betrayed might be too harsh of a word, but..." She sat down on the chair.

"But he has a point," Joshua admitted. "By fighting for my home, I am also fighting for Southern rights and Southerners want the right to keep their slaves."

"Yes. It's unfortunate but true."

"There are times when I feel like a coward, Elizabeth. There are other men from Southern states who left their homes to fight for the Union. To keep it preserved. Even your Uncle Samuel left Petersburg and his family to fight for the Union."

"Yes, and my cousin Jacob is fighting for the Confederacy. His decision tore the family apart. My Uncle Hiram, Charlotte's father, we received a letter from her early in the war and he's considering fighting for them too! My father and his brothers have been torn apart by this war." She stood and placed her hand on the back of Joshua's shoulder. "Joshua, there are no easy decisions in this conflict. If you had decided to fight for the Union, you would still be having doubts. You would feel like a traitor to your home." She gently pulled him to face her and touched his cheek. "I do believe you made the right decision, Joshua.

For what my opinion is worth. Your loyalty is one of the reasons that I love you so much. I'm sorry that you feel so torn about this conflict. Before the war, it was whether or not you wanted to fight at all. Now, you're doubting if you joined the right side. Joshua..." She stepped closer and gently nudged his cheek so that he would look at her. "You know how to handle these fears and doubts."

"I do." He gave her a small smile. "Pray. Have faith. Talk with my wife, who is one of the smartest people God put on this earth." He gave her a quick kiss. "You're right, as usual. Perhaps I should stop being a coward and talk to Daniel. We always worked out our differences in the past." He put his hands on her waist and pulled her close. "But tonight, I am with you." He kissed her again, then pressed his forehead to hers. "I love you, Elizabeth. I thank God every day that He put you in my life."

"I feel the same about you, Joshua." She kissed his cheek. "I also believe you really should try to make amends with Daniel."

"I will, I will. Next time I am able to get away, I promise." He yawned. "Right now, all I want to do is spend the night in my own bed with my beautiful wife."

Elizabeth smiled and gave him a quick kiss. "That sounds good to me."

Thursday, December 11, 1862
Prentiss Farm

"AJ, did you hear the church bells ring in the middle of the night?" Liberty entered the kitchen where AJ had begun preparing the meals for the day.

"I did. It was about 3:00 this morning."

"Do you know why?" Liberty took an apple from the bowl and took a bite.

"Look out the window," AJ replied. "Toward the river in front of Chatham."

Liberty complied. Outside, she could see the Federal Army working on an almost completed bridge made of what looked like floating rafts all connected. The soldiers periodically ducked down, when they heard the pop of rifle shots coming from the other side of the river.

"I must say, a bridge of rafts is quite clever, especially for the Yankees."

"I agree. A few soldiers already stopped by for some food. They called the rafts pontoons." AJ explained. "They've been working since about two hours before daybreak."

"Are the Confederate soldiers just watching them?"

251

"No, according to the Yankees, they've had snipers firing at the Union engineers all morning as well. I'm sure you have heard artillery fire as well."

"It's hard to miss it." Liberty murmured as some Union soldiers walked toward the front porch. "We have more visitors."

There was a knock at the door and Liberty opened it.

"What can we do for you?" She asked.

"We heard you'll give us some fresh-baked goods for a fair price." One of the men said. He was young, not much older than Liberty, with blonde, almost yellow hair, and peach fuzz covering his cheeks. His blue eyes sparkled and immediately caught Liberty's notice.

"You'll have to speak with my sister. She's the baker."

AJ approached them, a basket of bread rolls in her hands. "Good morning, gentlemen." She told them the price for the food and they quickly paid her and took their goods. AJ pocketed the coins and went back to the stove.

"When will we stop catering to the Yankees?" Liberty asked.

"I thought you understood, Liberty. I thought you agreed to this." AJ looked at her. Liberty sat at the table.

"I did agree. I do understand. That doesn't mean I have to like it."

"I don't either, Liberty." AJ sat next to her sister. "But many times, we have to do things that we don't like."

"I know that too, AJ. I understand. It's just...I wish this war would be over. I wish Father and Nathaniel would come home. I wish..." She averted her eyes. "I wish you wouldn't put your life in danger the way you do."

"Liberty. I didn't know you felt this way." AJ reached over to soothingly hold Liberty's arm. "I thought you liked the fact that I was helping the cause in my own way."

"I did. At least in the beginning. As time goes on, and the war drags on...AJ, I really have started worrying about you." Liberty took a breath. "I didn't think you would take as many risks as you have been. I didn't realize how dangerous the work would end up being. I don't want to lose you. This may be selfish, but if something were to happen to you...I don't know how I would get on. Even if you were just detained. I don't want to be alone." She sighed. "I'm sorry. I am excited for you, truly. Maybe if I went with you to a meeting or something..."

"Absolutely not. Liberty, that will not happen, but you can stop your worrying. It's too dangerous for me to try and pass on information right now. I know that. I won't take unnecessary chances. Hopefully, the battle here will be the end of it all anyway."

"I hope and pray you're right," Liberty said.

Bennett Home

Elizabeth almost fell out of bed as the booming of artillery fire woke her from her sleep. Gunshots echoed across the river. Hannah immediately cried out, and Benjamin rushed into his parents' bedroom.

"Mama! What's happening?" He fell over as another explosion rocked the house. Pieces of wall and ceiling rained down. Eric burst into the main room.

"Mrs. Bennett...the Union artillery..."

"To the cellar, boys. Now." She grabbed the dress she had discarded the night before and threw it on. Joshua had left before dawn to join his unit and she must have dozed off after telling him goodbye.

She followed Benjamin and Eric. "Go!" She yelled at them. "I'll get Hannah." Elizabeth ran into the children's room. Her daughter clutched her covers, absolute terror showing on her tear-streaked face.

"Mama!" She screamed. The house shook again as yet another blast hit near the house. Elizabeth grabbed Hannah, who let go of the quilt and tightly held her doll. She carried her to the cellar as fast as she could. Benjamin was huddled in a corner. Eric sat atop a crate with a lantern next to him, looking pensive.

"Mama!" Benjamin cried, and Elizabeth quickly went to him and pulled him into her arms. She hugged both of her children tightly.

"We'll be alright." She murmured to them both. "We'll be just fine. No need to worry." She quickly put her dress on, wishing she had grabbed clothing for the children, as they were both still in their nightgowns.

Another explosion rocked the house and Elizabeth shielded Benjamin and Hannah from some falling debris. Hannah wouldn't stop crying and tears trailed down Benjamin's eyes, but he was trying so hard to be brave. After what felt like hours, but was really about twenty minutes, there was a lull in the noise. Elizabeth stood slowly, holding her daughter in her arms. She was about to return upstairs and investigate when the door to the cellar crashed open.

"Elizabeth! Where are you? Are you down there?" Her husband's frantic voice called out.

"Papa!" Benjamin yelled, sprinting up the stairs before she could catch him.

"Joshua!" Elizabeth quickly followed her son up the steps with Hannah in her arms. When she reached the top of the stairs, a terrible scene met her eyes. Their cozy home lay in ruins, absolutely destroyed. There were still four partial walls standing, but huge holes were ripped in them. Glass, bricks, and wood lay in scattered piles. The roof had all but collapsed.

"Elizabeth!" Joshua had Benjamin in his arms and was tightly hugging him. He pulled Elizabeth, who was still holding Hannah into his arms. He placed a quick kiss on Elizabeth's head, then pulled her out to the backyard.

"We have to get you out of here, you need to get out of town now. The Yankees are going to cross the river on pontoon bridges. Some already have crossed in boats. I cannot believe they found Yankees brave enough, but they did. Michigan boys from what they say. Our snipers can't hold them back any longer. We can't stop them. We're strongly positioned on Marye's Heights, but I've got to get you all to safety first."

"What about all the other townspeople?" Elizabeth asked. "Do I have time to pack anything? Oh, wait…" She looked back at the house. "I wouldn't even know where to find what to pack." Tears began trickling down her face.

"It will be all right, Elizabeth, listen, most of the townsfolk are already heading west, out of town. I'm going to get you on the road to Turner's Glenn. You should be safe there. The 30th will regroup and we'll hold the Federals, but you've got to get out of town now. No time for packing anything. Come on!" He all but dragged her around the house and onto the street. Elizabeth was in for another shock at the site that greeted her there. Her home was not the only building that had been destroyed. It looked as though every building they could see had been damaged in some way. Civilians and Confederate soldiers were in the street, which was utter chaos. Wagons lined the street, most heading out of town, filled with fleeing refugees and as many belongings as they could pack.

Joshua held Elizabeth's hand tightly, they would have to travel by foot, as the wagon was inaccessible. She hated leaving the horses, but they had no other choice. It was too crowded to bring them. Elizabeth thought they must be an odd sight: a Confederate soldier, carrying a six-year-old boy, almost dragging an unkempt-looking woman along behind him, and her carrying a three-year-old girl while Eric followed behind, but as she looked around her, she noticed everyone was in disarray.

It seemed to take forever before she could see the back path leading to Turner's Glenn. In the distance, she could see the house standing unharmed. Joshua came to a stop. "I have to get back to my unit. I shouldn't have come this far, but I feel better knowing that you are safe out here. You can go the rest of the way without me." He gave Benjamin a tight squeeze, then set him down and knelt in front of him.

"You help Eric take care of your Momma and sister and help your Uncle Max take care of the plantation."

"Yes, sir," Benjamin replied. "I love you, Papa."

"I love you, too."

"Eric, please. Just keep doing what you have been doing. I couldn't imagine what we would do without you. Many of my worries are put to rest knowing you are with my family."

Joshua then took Hannah in his arms and gave her a hug and a kiss. The girl gave him a smile through her tears as she clutched her doll.

"Love you, Papa." She said.

"I love you, Hannah-Bear." Joshua set her down next to Benjamin and turned to Elizabeth. She was trying to be strong, trying not to cry, but tears still escaped down her cheeks. Joshua bent and kissed her gently. She gripped his shoulders, not wanting to let go, but knowing she had to.

"I love you, Elizabeth. Never forget that." He said. "Now, get to your family's house and stay there. Keep everyone safe until I return."

"I will," Elizabeth assured him. "I love you, Joshua. Please take care of yourself. No risks."

He smiled, touched his hand to his kepi, and left.

The rest of the day was tense at Turner's Glenn. The family could tell that there was some fierce fighting going on in the town, and in the fields behind them. Elizabeth dreaded the thought of going home and discovering even more damage done. Would her home even be standing when the battle was over?

The family sat down to a dinner of fried chicken that Annie and Ruthie prepared.

"Do you think the war being here will bring Mama home?" Max asked quietly.

"There's no way to tell, Max," Elizabeth answered. "She will make her way home when she feels the time is right."

"She really should be home now," Belle grumbled. "She should have taken James's body and returned home right away."

"You have done a fine job overseeing the family," Annie assured her. "I know you may not believe it, but you have."

"Of course I have," Belle said, trying to act as though the idea of being in charge didn't rattle her. "I have been trained since I was a child on how to run a household."

"You'll do a good job when you're married someday," Lainey assured her.

"Thank you for saying so." Belle couldn't suppress her smile.

The family finished their meal, and Ruthie and Zipporah began cleaning up. Belle made her way to the third-floor balcony and looked out at her family's land. To the northwest, in the direction of the town, she could faintly see the buildings of the town. Earlier in the day, Eric had reported that the Union had chased the Confederates from the town and the enemy was now in control of it.

"At least the Federals haven't burned the city," Elizabeth said, pulling a shawl around her shoulders as she joined her sister.

"Yet." Belle nodded. "I can see there are still some buildings standing." They both turned to the south. "It almost sounds as though there is something going on there as well." She said.

"Perhaps we will know more tomorrow on that situation. Eric may be able to find more information from a passing soldier." Elizabeth said. "Annie was right at dinner, I want you to know, you have stepped in quite admirably to take care of this family in the absence of Mother and Father."

"Thank you for saying so. When Father was here on Sunday, he said that he had seen Mother in Richmond. He said that she is quite the nurse and that he is very proud of her." Belle took a deep breath. "I just wish she were here. I know I am old enough to manage the house, but I sometimes feel lost without her."

"Belle, there is no shame in feeling that," Elizabeth admitted. "I have been married and a mother for years and I still feel lost without Mother."

"I don't know how AJ and Liberty have been able to do it," Belle said. "I know our mother and their Cousin Betty Lacy have tried to step in and help, but I don't know what I would do in their situation. At least we know our mother will be home eventually, perhaps even within the next few days. Father suggested that she would come here when and if a battle was fought nearby."

"She likely still wants to be a nurse and help the soldiers in their healing," Elizabeth said.

"Yes," Belle answered. "I hope and pray that she gets here soon."

Friday, December 12, 1862
Moss Neck Manor

Loud booming noises awoke Kate with great anxiety. As soon as she was dressed, she headed down for breakfast. Most of the family was already there. Parke waved to her from his place at the table.

"Good morning, Aunt Kate!" Janie said, flashing her charming smile.

"Good morning, Janie, Parke...Gardiner." She said all of their names with a smile. Gardiner, her pride and joy and secretly her favorite, ran to give her a hug. "Mornin', Aunt Kate." She hugged him back, then gave him a quick kiss on the top of the head and turned to the table.

"Good morning Bertie, Nettie." Kate sat and took a roll. "What are the Yankees up to today? I can hear that terrible barrage of cannon fire, just like yesterday."

"It is difficult to miss," Nettie replied. "It is almost a certainty that a battle here in Fredericksburg will occur soon."

"We've been hearing rumors of that sort since before the Yankees took over Stafford Heights." Kate pointed out.

"There were rumors before that when we were occupied this spring," Bertie added.

"I'm just telling you what I heard," Nettie said.

"Well, maybe it will happen one of these days," Kate said. "I'm just glad that most of us are all together finally." Kate gave Gardiner another kiss on the head.

"Kate, would you be agreeable to riding over to Belle Hill this morning with me to see your father? He may have some more information on what's going on. Maybe we will run into some of our own men from Fredericksburg. There are many troops moving through the area." Bertie said.

"I would, but we can't just leave Nettie here with the children."

"Oh, don't worry about me," Nettie spoke up. "I'll be content visiting with the Bernards and watching the children. You all go ahead."

Fanny and Lizzie Bernard had left their home, Mansfield, a week ago. It was in town, so they were staying at Moss Neck.

"All right then, Bertie, I'll go saddle up Zephyr and Flirt but first, let me change into my riding habit."

Turner's Glenn

An explosion shook the Turner home. For the second time in as many days, Elizabeth almost fell out of her bed.

"To think Joshua thought it would be safer here." She mumbled to herself. They had been hearing sporadic cannon fire and gunfire coming from the town since yesterday, but it seemed to come from the South as well.

"Mama." Hannah cried and snuggled closer into her arms.

"It's starting again, Mama," Benjamin said. "Are we going to have to leave here and go somewhere else?"

"I don't think we need to worry about that, Benjamin," Elizabeth said.

"What are we gonna do all day, then?" He asked.

"The same as we would on any other day at Turner's Glenn. Help Daniel and Solomon with whatever they need help with. Just make sure you stay close to the house. We cannot be wandering around until the soldiers are gone."

It wasn't long before Elizabeth had her children dressed in some old clothes of Max and Lainey. They went downstairs and sat for breakfast with the rest of the family.

"Sagamety, again?" Max said, looking down at the yellow cornmeal mush in front of him.

"Well, we have an excess of cornmeal and not much of anything else…" Annie said with an apologetic shrug.

"I suppose we'll have cornbread with dinner too," Benjamin added.

"Most likely," Annie replied, reaching out to ruffle Max's hair. "We have to make do with what we have."

"I suppose." Max took his spoon and took a bite of the meal.

"I don't think it's that bad," Benjamin said, then looked up at Eric, who had just entered the dining room.

"Good morning, Eric," Meri said. "Sagamety?" She held up her spoon.

"No thanks, I ate." He said.

"Where were you?" Elizabeth asked.

"I tried to get as close to the town as I could to see if anything was happening." He replied, sitting down.

"And?" Belle asked.

"It's tough to see much of anything over there, on account of the smoke."

"Smoke? Are they burning the town?" Elizabeth asked, trying not to panic.

"No, Ma'am. I don't think so. Just smoke from all the guns and cannon firing so much."

"That's still dreadful," Meri said.

"Eric sighed and took a drink of his water. "It's not looking good. I was able to scout around to the south of us as well. It appears as though the Yankees will attempt to cross the river downstream as well."

"My goodness. So we will be surrounded?" Elizabeth asked, fear coursing through her.

"It appears as though that is possible," Eric replied.

"Well, the important thing is that we're all together," Elizabeth said with a smile. "We'll be safe here."

"Indeed, we will," Belle said. "I do believe we will."

Belle Hill Plantation

"You ladies shouldn't be out here." James Parke Corbin said. "Our troops have been moving in and around the city. The rumors of a battle now seem to be a certainty. We'll surely drive the Yankees right off the Heights and keep them out of Fredericksburg."

"Oh, Father, we won't be in any danger from our Confederate boys," Kate said with a wave of her hand.

"Maybe not on purpose, but accidents do happen, my dear," James said. "I have heard that our troops are marching here up from Gurney Station and Port Royal. General Jackson's corps is among them."

"Stonewall Jackson's men coming here? How thrilling." Bertie said.

"Thrilling, yes. We will undoubtedly crush the Federal Army and this fight for our independence will end here, hopefully, in our own town." James said.

"That would be something," Kate said. "Sadly, there is this dreadful loss of life we've had to endure. So many men from Fredericksburg won't be coming home. Samuel Gray, Charles Beale and James Turner to name a few."

"How are the Turners doing?" James asked. "Mrs. Turner must be distraught? I still wonder why Matthew insisted upon enlisting. The man is old enough that, even if we started conscripting men, he would have been exempt. The man should never have left his family alone."

"Belle isn't quite sure about either of her parents. You've apparently not heard, but Mrs. Turner stayed in Richmond to help at the hospital, and Mr. Turner hasn't been back since he enlisted." Kate left out the part about how abandoned Belle felt by both her parents, that had been told to her in confidence. "As for the family as a whole, they're handling the situation as well as can be expected."

"Poor Belle," Bertie said. "First, losing Samuel, who was practically her intended, and then losing James. How horrible."

"Indeed." Kate agreed. She really was concerned about Belle and the change in her since the death of James. Instead of being sociable and outgoing, she was withdrawn and seemed to spend too much time in her room alone.

"Terrible, that." James agreed. "But they did not die in vain. They died as heroes for the cause of the Confederate States of America."

"Maybe," Kate replied. "But they're still gone."

Evening
Moss Neck

Twilight was descending on Moss Neck by the time Kate and Bertie returned home. It had been a much slower trip back, as they had to move through columns of Southern troops despite taking some back roads.

"Goodness," Kate said, taking in the area around her home. "Soldiers are everywhere." It was true. Confederate soldiers occupied their yard and stable area. There were soldiers on both foot and horseback, but that wasn't all, wagons holding provisions, wagons

259

designated as ambulances, and even artillery pieces rolled by, in as direct a line as possible.

"Our fences!" Bertie gasped. The men were moving in such a direct line that, instead of going around obstacles, the soldiers were removing them, tearing down fences and making short cuts through the fields.

"I don't think I have ever seen this many people in my life," Kate observed. "Not even in Richmond." The two continued on, many of the men giving them short bows or a tip of their hats.

After the women had settled their horses in the barn, Kate and Bertie returned to the house. They were immediately greeted by Janie, who threw herself into her mother's arms.

"Mama, I was so scared. Aunt Nettie said you would be fine, but I'm so glad you're back."

"Of course we're all right." Bertie patted her daughter on the back.

Gardiner approached Kate, who bent to pick him up and gave him a hug. "It's so loud out here, I'm scared to go to bed, Aunt Kate." The boy said.

"Well, we definitely all still need our rest," Kate replied. "I'll tell you what. I have quite a large bed, and if we squeeze, the three of you can sleep there tonight, but you have to get ready quickly for nighttime prayers." Janie, Parke, and Gardiner scampered off.

"Kate, are you sure that isn't too much of an imposition?" Nettie asked.

"Not at all," Kate replied. She cared dearly for her nieces and nephews, loved them as if they were her own children. She was seldom whimsical and she wanted them to feel safe. "I won't be getting much sleep regardless, with all of the men passing through our land." She looked towards the town. "It doesn't appear as though we will have fighting nearby, but the troops are still making life inconvenient."

"Well, it is very gracious of you to allow them this privilege," Bertie said. "Hopefully by this time tomorrow, our boys will have chased the Yankees back to the Potomac and Washington City."

"I do hope so," Kate said. "I would like everything to be back to normal, especially as the Christmas holidays are so near."

"Unfortunately, unless our Southern soldiers do chase the enemy far from Fredericksburg, our town may be their winter home," Bertie said. "They have to be thinking of where that will be. I have a feeling this winter will be one that will change us all."

"Hopefully for the good," Kate said, then turned and went into the house.

Saturday, December 13, 1862
Moss Neck Manor

All through the night, the constant noise of marching soldiers and the movement of heavy wagons and artillery kept Kate awake. Janie, Gardiner, and Parke had spent the entire night in Kate's bed, snuggled together. The children had all managed to fall asleep, but Kate had only drifted off on occasion. Around daybreak, cannon firing could be heard in the distance. Janie woke and clutched at Kate.

"How far away is that?" Janie asked, her voice small.

"I don't know exactly, but it's coming from the direction of Fredericksburg, so I'm sure it's a long way off. Nothing to worry about." As Kate spoke, a cannon explosion rocked the house so loudly that the windows of the house rattled.

"It's like there's a storm out there," Gardiner said.

"Yeah." Janie agreed, talking over the noise. "Like one long boom of thunder."

Bertie entered the room, already dressed in her riding habit. "The battle is on!" She exclaimed. "Kate, dear, you should hurry and get dressed. We should be able to get to some high ground where we can see some of the fighting."

Kate almost jumped out of her bed in excitement. "I'll be ready to go as soon as possible." She replied.

"Mama, can I come?" Janie asked.

"No, dear. I don't want you too close. Your Aunt Nettie will be watching you again."

"But I don't want anything to happen to you!" Janie cried out.

"Oh, my darling, nothing will happen to me. We'll be far enough away. You are already a little frightened of the noise and if you get closer, it will be even louder."

"It is quite loud here." Gardiner agreed.

"Bertie, will you come help me?" Kate called from behind her dressing screen.

"Of course," Bertie said. "Then I will get one of the house girls up here to get the children ready. Oh, it is going to be such an exciting day!"

Kate was soon ready, wearing her favorite maroon riding habit trimmed in pink with a matching hat. She and Bertie quickly saddled their horses and made their way to Belle Hill.

"Father!" Kate called, hastening into his study with as much decorum as she could muster. "Good morning."

"A raucous morning, that's for sure." James Parke said, looking up from a book. "And why are you two dressed so smartly?"

"We plan on heading up to Mt. Zion," Kate replied. "It's the highest point in the area, you know. We want to see if we are able to view any of the fighting."

"Yes, the Conways do have a good view of the town," James said, rubbing his temple. "I must say, though, I wish you ladies wouldn't go. As you say the view is perfect, and it may be used as a lookout by the soldiers. You may be exposed to enemy fire from the Yankee gunboats on the river as you cross the field to get there."

"Father, don't be silly," Bertie said. "We'll be just fine."

"We'll be sure to take every precaution, father, really." Kate assured him. "We really only stopped by here to see if we could borrow your spyglass. It would really help us to see all the action.

James stroked his chin. "Well, if you insist on going, I suppose I can at least loan it to you." He stood and grabbed the needed instrument, then handed it over to his daughter. "You reckless youngsters be careful. You remember what happened to those Yankee civilians who went to watch the fighting at Manassas back in '61."

"Of course, Father, but I know our men will protect us, unlike the Yankees who allowed themselves to be chased from the battlefield," Bertie said with a careless wave of her hand.

"All right, then." James kissed each woman on the cheek. The girls left the house, mounted their horses and continued on their way.

"Do you suppose you may see Richard during the fighting?" Kate asked as they rode towards Mt. Zion.

"I don't really know. I would have thought that if there were fighting in the area, he would have been able to stop by to see us. In all honestly, though I just don't know how I would react if I did see him, out on the battlefield, fighting where he could be injured or killed." Bertie paused. "It would be so comforting to see him, though, to know that he's all right."

"I agree," Kate said. "I simply cannot imagine how much you must miss him, and I know Janie does as well."

"It is difficult," Bertie admitted. "But I find comfort knowing that he is fighting for something so noble. Something our children and their children will benefit from."

"That is true." Kate agreed. "I've always believed that it is the duty of young men to enlist when their homeland needs them."

"Yes, I recall you saying that at the onset of the war." The women drew close to the highest point in the area. "I must say, you have become...perhaps grave is the word I am looking for...since the war has begun."

"Conflicts like this have a way of changing us," Kate said. "I'm no longer the girl I was." She dismounted and wrapped Flirt's reins around a tree branch.

"That is true of all of us," Bertie said, tethering her horse as well. "Although I have long wondered if the change in your demeanor wasn't because of Stockton Heth."

"Stockton Heth? My goodness, I don't know why so many people believed we had an understanding. I've always known that Stockton would remain in the military. How could he not, with a Navy captain as his father, a brother who graduated from West Point and George Pickett, his cousin, also a West Pointer. The military is in his blood." Kate sat on a fallen log. "I must admit I enjoy his company and his attentions. I have considered him as a suitor, and probably still may, I suppose. I can see myself with him, other than his always being in the military. We could make an acceptable match. I do believe it would be good to see him again, but still, I feel there is someone else better suited for me out there."

"Well, perhaps," Bertie said. "We've already lost so many good men from Fredericksburg. I can only hope this will be the end of the war and we will see the rest of our men come home safely."

"I agree wholeheartedly. I think of Belle so much. To lose her intended before they were even married and then her brother. I really should go and visit her when this little conflict is over."

"Yes." Bertie looked toward Fredericksburg where the fighting was taking place. Cannons still exploded, throwing dirt and debris in the air. Musket fire popped. "It's time for this war to be over."

"It is so difficult to see anything," Kate said. "So much smoke in the air, presumably from all of the cannon and rifles firing."

"You can't even make out which side is the Union and which is the Confederacy," Bertie commented. "It is a wonder they even know which soldiers to aim at. They may accidentally shoot each other."

"It likely has happened," Kate said. She covered her nose with her handkerchief. Though it was faint, she could smell the gun and cannon smoke as well. "Dear God, please help our men survive." She prayed.

Turner's Glenn

"Despite the battle raging around us, it's quite a pleasant day." Belle pulled her cloak tightly around her and joined Elizabeth on the fence line at the far west end of the plantation property. In the distance, they could see smoke coming from town.

"That's true, especially for December," Elizabeth replied. Cannon continued to boom, rifles fired; the noise was incredible, even at the distance they were. "I have a hard time knowing that Joshua is down there. Joshua and Father and Nathaniel. Possibly Uncle Charles, Uncle Samuel, Uncle Hiram. So many loved ones, Cousin Jason, Cousin Gregory, Cousin Mary's husband Abraham, even Cousins Jonah and Jacob." She wiped a tear from her cheek. "I don't know how anyone can survive the battle from the sounds of it." Her voice was almost a whisper.

"I know it sounds bad, but it can't be any worse than Manassas or Sharpsburg. Soldiers survived those battles and will continue to do so. Our family will survive. If any of our men don't make it, if they die like Samuel and James, our family will still make it through this war. We'll have our home, we'll have Turner's Glenn, and we'll have each other."

Elizabeth looked at Belle, a look of admiration on her face. "Extremely wise words, Belle."

"Thank you. I'm not as shallow as some people think I am."

"No one has ever called you shallow, Belle. They may not always see past your good looks, but you are a clever, wise young woman and many people know that. Would you like to know my opinion?" Elizabeth asked.

"I suppose so," Belle answered.

"You are pretty, charming, and many people like and enjoy your company, but I know you've been hurt by the lack of a true, formal suitor."

"It was because everyone knew Samuel and I would end up together. No one wanted to get in the way of that." Belle reasoned.

"That may be true, but I also believe it was because many of the men in town were intimidated by you. Your beauty is already intimidating, but because you are also smart, clever, argumentative and assertive, that is powerful in a woman, especially to a man who is unsure of himself, and many are. I won't lie, I'm surprised a man like Samuel thought he could handle you. You would have gotten anything you wanted from him."

"That would have been a perfect life." Belle said, sighing dramatically.

"You can admit it to me. You would have hated it. You would have become bored with life."

"I won't admit that," Belle said with a half-smile. She knew her sister was right. She had realized that a while ago.

"All right, so you won't actually admit it to me." Elizabeth smiled. "But you and I both know you need a man who will challenge you."

"You may be right," Belle said, trying to make the tone of her voice sound uncaring. "But it will be difficult for us to find that out until after the war, for this is not the time to be falling in love."

"Well, I believe…"

"Belle, Elizabeth!" Lainey came rushing up to them. "There are soldiers up at the house. Confederates. They say they're doctors and they have a lot of wounded men." Belle and Elizabeth raced back to the house, Lainey following close behind. When they arrived, Belle stopped, horrified. Wounded men lay all over their yard. Some were on litters, others sitting or lying down as if they had come on to the property of their own accord and then collapsed.

"Are you two in charge of this home?" An uninjured, but blood-covered soldier approached Belle and Elizabeth. He looked to be a few years older than Joshua. He had dark blonde hair that fell in his face.

"We are," Elizabeth said. Belle was in a state of shock.

"I am Dr. Aaron Knightly, ma'am, of the Confederate Army of Northern Virginia. We need to requisition your farm to care for the wounded."

"Of course," Elizabeth said with a glance at Belle, who still stood motionless. She was looking around at all the soldiers who lay, wounded and covered in blood and dirt. It seemed as though more were being brought in continually. She saw Meri on the porch, her arms around Max, Hannah, and Benjamin. Annie walked out of the house and immediately noticed the arrival of her sisters. "Belle, don't just stand there, help me!" She knelt next to a man whose arm was oozing with blood.

"Help you? Help you what?" Belle backed away, horrified.

"We need to get these men water and we need to try to get this man inside."

"Inside? Inside our home? No! Absolutely not. They will ruin the house. We can put them in the barn. It's bigger anyway."

Gunfire continued and it seemed closer than it had been. Annie struggled to put the soldier's arm around her shoulder and stand. She tried to drag the man into the house by herself, but couldn't. Elizabeth quickly came to help her.

"Belle, for once in your life will you think of someone or something besides yourself," Annie said, struggling, while she and Elizabeth tried to get the man up the steps and into the house. Belle continued to stand there. She had no idea what to do. She was the one that made the decision not to leave their home. Now, the Confederate army was taking it over to use as a hospital and soldiers were wounded and dying all around her on the front lawn.

Belle felt a tug on her skirt. She looked down and saw a wounded man had crawled over to her.

"Water..." he moaned through cracked lips. His face was sweaty and dirty and his left hand had only two fingers on it. Horrified, she turned and fled.   Running up the porch steps, she bumped into the doctor...Aaron Knightly. He grabbed her arms, steadying her.

"Miss Turner? We could really use your help with the wounded. They're coming in quickly."

Belle looked around. The scene was a blur. She couldn't focus on anything except for the open door with the stairs that led to her room. Her sanctuary.

"I can't. I just can't." She pulled away from the doctor and hastened into the house and up the stairs, not stopping until she saw her bed and fell onto it, burying her face in her pillow.

Elizabeth led the children into the basement kitchen. After thinking it over, she decided it would be the safest place for them. "You all stay down here with Meri." She said. Eric had stayed upstairs and was helping, as was Annie. Elizabeth pulled Meri aside.

"Why can't you all stay down here?" Meri had tears in her eyes. "And where's Belle?"

"I'm not sure where Belle is, Meri, but those soldiers need our help out there. Annie, Eric and I need to do all we can. Men are suffering, our men. We can't just sit and watch. Belle will be fine when she's done sulking. We will all be fine. No one will attack a hospital. I can really focus on helping if I know you are down here taking care of and entertaining the children. You are a bright young woman with many talents." She gave her young sister a quick hug. "Can you do that for me?"

Meri took a deep breath and nodded in affirmation. "I can do that. I think."

"I know you can." Elizabeth turned to Lainey. "You help Meri with the children. Together, you two can manage anything."

"Yes, ma'am." Lainey nodded, hugging Elizabeth. Max gave Elizabeth a hug next.

"I'll take care of things, Elizabeth." He said with the confidence of an eight-year-old. Elizabeth smiled.

"I know you will." She then turned to her own children, pulling them both close. "I love you." She kissed first Benjamin, then Hannah. "You two be good for your aunts and uncle."

"Yes, Mama. I'll help Max take care of everything just like Papa told me to." Benjamin said. She smiled and gave him one more hug, then kissed the top of his head. She then drew Hannah into a hug.

"Love you, Mama," Hannah said. "Come back soon."

"I will come back as soon as I can, sweetheart." She said, trying to hold back tears. Hospitals are safe areas. She told herself, standing up.

"Now you all stay put and don't come upstairs unless Annie, Belle, Eric or I come to get you." Then with one last look at her family, she hastened back up the stairs.

"I am so sorry to tell you this, General Gregg, but I don't believe you'll survive this wound." Dr. Knightly looked at Elizabeth and gestured her over. She quickly complied. "This is Mrs. Bennett. If there is anything we can do for you, please let her know."

Elizabeth smiled gently at the officer. He was handsome, with brown eyes and hair and a full beard that came down to his chest.

Dr. Knightly pulled Elizabeth aside. "Please do what you can to make him comfortable. He's Brigadier General Maxcy Gregg. He was rallying his men against advancing Federals and was struck by a minié ball. It lodged near his spine. There is nothing we can do but try and keep him comfortable."

"I understand," Elizabeth said. "I will do whatever I can." She turned and knelt next to the Brigadier General, who appeared to have accepted the news of his fate with a quiet nobility and knelt next to him. "What would ease your mind, sir?"

"There is something." He said quietly. "I would like to set right a minor dispute. If there is any way you can ask for General Stonewall Jackson to pay me a visit?"

Elizabeth wasn't sure how she would be able to grant the man's request, but she smiled anyway.

"I will do what I can, General Gregg."

Prentiss Farm

"Can you see anything?" Liberty asked. The sisters had snuck down to the riverbank to see what they could of the battle. Most of the fighting seemed to be happening on the South side of the city. The day had started cold and overcast, with a dense, misty fog blanketing the ground, making it impossible to see either army.

"I can't tell what's going on with all of the fog," AJ said.

"What are you two doing here?" Nathaniel's irate voice made them both turn toward their brother as he approached them. "This is senseless and dangerous!"

"Nathaniel!" Liberty ran and gave him a quick hug. AJ did the same.

"We had to see what was going on, Nathaniel. All the fighting now is on the other side of the river. South of the town."

"I know that. Have you not thought of what a stray bullet or cannon shot might do to you? Have you not thought of the men from either side who are wandering around aimlessly? What if I had been someone else? Someone who didn't know you or care what happened to you? Both of you could have been severely harmed."

"What are you doing here, Nathaniel?" AJ asked, ignoring his questions. "Why aren't you with your unit?"

"I have been doing some scouting," Nathaniel replied. "I was taking a moment to check on you. When I couldn't find you at the house, I knew your curiosity would have brought you to the river."

"Yes, well, you know us well. We are so glad to see you." AJ said. "How is the battle going? How is the town looking? It's very difficult to see from this side of the river."

"You don't want to know what's going on." Nathaniel sat on a rock and rubbed his face with his hands. "It's only been one day of fighting and from what I can see by the looks of the Yankee positions, it will not be over soon. I don't know how Fredericksburg will ever recover from this. The city itself has sustained severe damage."

"What's happened?"

"I was able to see that most of the buildings have been all or partially destroyed by artillery. When the Yankees were trying to cross, we were shooting at them and they responded with cannon fire." He looked across the river, his stare blank. "We evacuated and withdrew to Marye's Heights. It is a good stronghold. That's where we're positioned right now. With the view and field with the channel in front, it will be hard for the Yankees to attack."

"My goodness," AJ said. Liberty looked off towards the town again. "What else happened, Nathaniel? You seem to be hiding something."

"I saw with my spyglass that the Union troops who occupied the town last night were looting every home."

"What do you mean looting?" Liberty asked.

"They're stealing or destroying everything they can lay their hands on, our beautiful paintings, books, jewelry, women's dresses, silverware, all kinds of household furniture." AJ could not recall a time when she had seen Nathaniel this angry. "Every house was defiled by the bast...I beg your pardon. It's just that...I have never felt so disgusted with this war. If they couldn't carry it, they just pulled it out of the house and smashed it. I can't imagine what the interior of the homes looks like. I tell you, all I want to do is kill every last Yankee. There is no reason to attack civilians and their homes. That's why I had to check on you girls."

AJ put a comforting hand on Nathaniel's shoulder.

"Then I remember that there are some good men who are fighting for the Union, like James Spencer. Those men who destroyed the town...not every Yankee is like that. I know that." He said, rubbing his jaw.

268

"James was stationed here this summer, you know," AJ recalled. "I saw him a time or two."

"I saw him as well," Nathaniel said. "Rather, he saw me first. When I was visiting last summer and Andre and Gage told the Yankees I was here. Do you remember that day? I was escaping from the house when I came face to face with a Union soldier. It was James. He not only let me go, he also helped me escape. I would probably be rotting in a Yankee prison now if it wasn't for him."

"Or hung for a spy," Liberty said quietly.

"Yes. Or hung." Nathaniel shook his head. "Nothing is simple anymore. This isn't what I thought war should be about."

"I know. I am so sorry." AJ said.

Evening
Turner's Glenn

Belle stood at the highest point of Turner's Glenn and looked out over the town with her father's spyglass.

"Can you see how our home and the shop look?" Elizabeth asked.

"It's difficult to tell," Belle answered. Elizabeth noticed tears in Belle's eyes, something she was noticing more often. Elizabeth put an arm around her sister. "Oh, Elizabeth, can you see what I see? Over towards Marye's Heights? The Sunken Road?" She handed Elizabeth the glass and she looked in that direction. Her heart caught in her throat.

"Dear God." It was difficult to see in the distance and fading light, but she saw what looked like hundreds of bodies on the field between the edge of town and the stone wall that lined the Sunken Road. Some of the bodies appeared to be moving. "Are those men wounded or are they just unable to get back to safety?

"I believe it must be both," Belle said. "I keep hearing gunfire. It is as if the men are afraid they'll be shot if they stand and retreat."

"How horrible," Elizabeth said. "I hope they won't have to spend the cold December night on that field. Surely they should be able to retreat when the sun sets."

"I hope so. They're Yankees, but still, I can't help but...can you hear that?" Belle pulled her cloak tighter and hugged herself. "Is that what I think it is?"

Elizabeth could hear the faint sounds, but it was much too difficult to comprehend. She was almost in tears. They could hear men crying out in pain, even at the distance. It was a sound that would haunt her for years to come. She wanted to go down to the field and bring the poor wounded soldiers into her home. "I can't stay here any longer, I can't bear it." She said as she turned to walk back to the house.

269

"How are things going in the house?" Belle asked, a bit hesitantly as she followed her sister.

"We could really use your help," Elizabeth answered.

"My help? Elizabeth, what on earth would I be able to do?" Belle shook her head. "I would be useless. I would just get in the way."

"No, you wouldn't. The wounded men need water, food, a hand to hold. We can help with some of the simple bandaging. There is much we can do to help the doctors."

"Doctors. They are the ones who need all the help." Belle scoffed.

"Belle. They're working as hard as they can." Elizabeth said.

"That doesn't instill more confidence in their ability," Belle replied. "You recall that doctors weren't competent enough to save our brother or my intended."

"Belle..." Elizabeth sighed and rubbed her temple. "It's getting late. I'm tired, and I am not in the mood to argue with you."

"All right, fine. I'm tired too. At least I can rest easily tonight in my own bed."

"Actually, Belle, the soldiers have taken over our rooms."

Belle stopped walking at Elizabeth's words. "What do you mean, taken over our rooms? Just where do they expect us to sleep?"

"We can all stay in Zipporah's room. She'll stay downstairs with Timothy and Ruthie."

"But there's only two beds in her room. Where will we all sleep? Where will Eric sleep? He can't possibly stay in the same room with us, especially with Annie, Meri, and Lainey."

"Eric is going to stay in the overseer's cabin with Daniel and Solomon. We'll crowd into the two beds as best we can, and we can put some pallets on the floor." Elizabeth shrugged. "The wounded soldiers and doctors need beds and pallets too. We will just have to make do. At least they're letting us have a room. They didn't have to do that."

"If they were decent human beings, they would let us have the whole upstairs," Belle responded. She counted in her head. "Eight people, Elizabeth, eight people sharing two beds in the middle of December." Belle shook her head. "The only good thing is knowing that all that body heat will keep us warm. Just when I thought things couldn't get any worse."

"I hate to say this to you, Belle, but you should watch what you say." Elizabeth cautioned. "Things can always get worse. Much worse."

Sunday, December 14, 1862
Turner's Glenn Plantation

Belle woke up the next morning, wishing that the last few days would prove to be a horrible dream, but right away, she realized that it

270

wasn't the case. Before she opened her eyes, she felt a small body jump on the bed and crawl her way.

"Aunt Belle!" Hannah called from right above her. "Wake up."

Belle opened her eyes and groaned. The bright winter sun streaming in the windows blinded her.

"Argh. Hannah, what are you doing?"

"Wakin' you up. There's lots of people downstairs and lotsa hurt men."

"Yeah." Benjamin jumped onto the bed also. "Lots of men who need Mama's help. Why aren't you helping, Aunt Belle? Everyone else is, even Uncle Max. Mama told us to stay up here."

Belle groaned again. Not only did yesterday happen, it looked like today would be just as bad, if not worse. Now she had a six-year-old pressuring her to help. She pulled the covers off and rolled out of bed. "Has Zipporah come up yet? I'll need her to help me get dressed."

Hannah gave Benjamin a wide-eyed look.

"She's helping the doctors too. Everyone is, like I told you."

"Well, how am I supposed to get dressed?"

"I don' know," Hannah said.

"Why do you need help getting dressed, Aunt Belle?" Benjamin asked. Belle sighed. She loved the children dearly, but it was times like this...she lost her train of thought as Lainey entered the room.

"Oh, Lainey! Thank goodness you're here!" Belle exclaimed.

"Just for a moment. I need to get more sheets." Lainey replied.

"Well, you can help me get dressed first," Belle demanded.

Lainey glanced at the door. "Oh, Belle, can't you do it yourself?" She sighed. "Oh, never mind. Yes, I can, but we need to be quick about it." As the two prepared Belle for the day, Lainey couldn't help but ask. "Are you at least going to come down and help? Some of those men are in a bad way. Elizabeth doesn't want me to see the worst of it, but it's hard not to. I've seen plenty."

"What makes you want to help anyways?" Belle asked.

"It's not about wanting." Lainey said, sounding too much like Elizabeth. "Sometimes, it's about just doing what needs to be done.

Belle tried not to roll her eyes as Lainey finished lacing up her corset. She looked over at the children. Hannah lay on her stomach, paging through a picture book, while Benjamin tossed a ball up in the air to himself. After slipping on a violet day dress and having Lainey button up the back, Belle turned to her niece and nephew.

"Will you two be all right up here?" Belle asked.

"Yeah," Benjamin replied. "We can watch out for each other."

Belle smiled and then followed Lainey downstairs. Her home was in utter chaos. Men and women alike rushed from place to place, sometimes tripping over soldiers that were lying on the floor. Some of the wounded were calling out in pain, others were unconscious, and still others were trying to be still and not show their emotions. Soldiers carrying litters with the newly wounded frequently came to the front door.

"You!" At the sound of the sharp male voice, Belle turned abruptly. She saw the arrogant doctor from the day before. He made a face when he saw who he had summoned. "I suppose you'll do." He grabbed her arm and pulled her toward the dining room table. She choked back the bile that rose in her mouth. On the table lay a soldier. It was hard for her to discern exactly how old he was. His hair was matted with sweat, blood, and dirt. A band of leather had been wrapped around his leg just below the knee, and the leg itself was covered in blood. Belle's stomach churned and she had to really focus on not getting sick.

"I need help, and you're obviously the only available person I can find." The doctor said, his voice calmer. He handed her a folded rag and a bottle. "I need you to make sure this man doesn't wake up in the middle of surgery." He took her wrist and guided her to place the rag over the man's mouth and nose, he pulled the rag up to make it look like a tent. Belle's heart skipped a beat, but she was unsure if it was because of the doctor's nearness or the fact that she was about to watch a bloody surgical procedure. "If you notice any signs of him waking up, or whenever I tell you, take the bottle and gently drop a little of the liquid onto the top of the rag." He demonstrated to her. "Don't give him too much or he may never wake up." He looked at her, his disheveled blonde hair falling in his face as it did yesterday.

"You cannot be serious," Belle exclaimed. "How dare you assume that I would be willing to assist? What are you planning to do?"

"His fibula is shattered. I need to amputate the leg to avoid blood poisoning." The doctor nodded at another man who had just entered the room, a younger man, wearing a blood-stained apron. He now stood next to the leg of the injured soldier.

"Ready, Henry?" The doctor said, and the young assistant nodded and placed his hands on the wounded shin.

"You can turn away, Miss Turner. You don't need to watch." The doctor said, a hint of compassion in his voice. Belle gritted her teeth as the doctor picked up a small scalpel to make an incision, yet she couldn't look away as the doctor carefully cut through the skin. Fresh blood seeped from the incision. Belle wanted to run, but she was intrigued and didn't want to give the doctor the satisfaction. She couldn't help but note and even admire his steady hand as he continued slowly cutting each layer all the way down to the bone. He then picked up a saw. Belle's stomach churned as the doctor placed the saw in the cut he had made. The soldier on the table gave a weak groan.

"Miss Turner, the chloroform!" The doctor exclaimed, his voice almost a growl.

Belle jumped and her hand knocked against the table. The bottle she had been given slipped from her hand and crashed to the floor, spilling over her black boots.

"No! How could you be so clumsy?" He ran a bloody hand through his already mussed hair and turned toward the young assistant. "We need those windows opened quickly. I don't care how cold it is out there, this room needs to be aired out." He looked at Belle, frustration on his face. "That isn't water in there, Miss Turner! You need to get your boots off. It's a darn good thing the bottle was almost empty."

"Well, I told you I shouldn't even be in here," Belle said. She began to get lightheaded and her face turned snow white. "I'm done." She turned and walked out of the dining room and out to the front porch. The front yard was no relief. It was busier than she had ever seen it. Just like inside, wounded soldiers lay everywhere. Doctors and some young soldiers moved around, bringing wounded inside the house and barn and leaving others outside. Belle could still hear cannon and gunfire coming from the direction of town and to the east of the house.

"Belle? What are you doing out here?" Elizabeth's voice made Belle turn. Her sister stood there, hands on her waist, hair mussed and dress spattered with water and blood.

"I had to get out of that stuffy house," Belle answered. "Benjamin and Hannah are safe in the room."

"Yes, I know they are," Elizabeth said, wiping her hands on her skirt. A man called out in pain, and Elizabeth immediately went to him. She pulled out a cloth and wiped his face.

"What's wrong with him?" Belle asked.

"He has been what they call gut shot," Elizabeth said quietly. "He's dying."

"Well, why don't the doctors do something about it?" Belle asked. "They think they are so powerful that they can control who lives and who dies now?"

"Don't be ridiculous, Belle. That is simply not true." Elizabeth answered. "Soldiers who are wounded through the head, belly or chest, well...we've been told to just keep them comforted as best we can."

"Why won't they even try to help them? At least try to save them? It's cruel. It's absolutely heartless to just let someone lay there and die."

"No, Belle. It allows the doctors, who are already working with or through exhaustion, more time to operate on those who have a chance at survival." Elizabeth shook her head. "It's a difficult decision, but it's

273

the best option in this situation. There are too many injured soldiers to care for those with no chance."

Tears filled Belle's eyes. Tears of fatigue, tears of sadness, tears of frustration. It was too much. She could not, would not, let her sister see her cry. Elizabeth put a hand on Belle's arm.

"Let me get you an apron. We could really use your help."

"No. I'm not sure that's the best idea," Belle replied. She stepped over a wounded soldier and hurried down the porch stairs, unsure of where she wanted to go, just knowing that she had to get away from the house.

Elizabeth sighed and turned back toward the house. She was about to check on Brigadier General Gregg when a Confederate officer approached her.

"Excuse me, ma'am, but I am looking for a Brigadier General Gregg. Is there any way you can help me?"

"Of course, sir. May I tell him who is inquiring after him?" Elizabeth smiled, hoping this man was who she hoped he was.

"I'm General Thomas Jackson. A messenger told me that Gregg wanted to see me."

"Of course, General. This way." Elizabeth led General Jackson to where Brigadier General Gregg lay.

"Jackson." The patient smiled weakly. "I am so glad you came. I wanted to make amends for…" Gregg coughed.

"Ease your mind, General," Jackson said. "Forget any past differences we've had. Turn your thoughts to God and the world to which you will go."

"Thank you, Sir." Elizabeth could tell that Gregg was trying to hide the tears in his eyes. She had to turn from them so that she wouldn't begin crying herself. The strain over the past few days was starting to catch up with her. She took a deep breath and left the two men to talk.

Moss Neck Manor

"It's been quite a morning." Bertie said, joining Kate on the veranda.

"It has been. I heard shots earlier this morning, but nothing in quite some time." Kate said. "How is everyone holding up, especially Fanny and Lizzie."

"Everyone is doing well. The Bernards are quite settled."

"Good." Kate pulled her cloak closer around her shoulders. "I'm hoping that this lull will mean the battle has finally ended."

"Yes, I haven't witnessed any troop movement, no soldiers from either side moving around the area. They should be, though, at least our Confederate soldiers." Bertie replied.

"You're right, that is strange. I wonder if both sides have retreated." Kate said.

Bertie placed a hand on Kate's shoulder. "Is everything alright? You've been rather distant today. Quiet."

"I've just been thinking. Hoping that everything in town is all right. Hoping that Elizabeth and Lucy and all of our friends and neighbors have survived. Hoping everyone that left will have a home to return to. Praying that AJ and Liberty and our neighbors across the river are staying safe. Thinking of everyone at Turner's Glenn, and above all, praying for my brothers and friends who have been fighting and could still be down there in town right now." She sighed. "I'm not trying to be melancholy, really, I'm not. There's just so much to consider right now. When the battle is done, what will happen to the injured? Where will all of the soldiers stay for the winter?"

"I believe they'll stay in the area." Bertie said. "It may not be what's best for our city and surrounding area, but it could make for an interesting few months."

"Do you mean socially? Indeed." Kate replied. "A very interesting winter. As long as it's our Southern boys and not the Yankees that stay here."

Prentiss Farm

Liberty returned to the house after doing her chores and immediately went to the fireplace. "Brr. It's cold out there."

"I can see that." AJ pulled some biscuits out from the oven. "Can you tell if anything is going on out there?"

"It's difficult to say," Liberty responded. "It's quieter than this morning, but I can't tell if the battle is over or not."

"I hope it is," AJ said, then looked out the window. "There haven't been many Yankees coming back over the Rappahannock. I dearly hope that doesn't mean they took the field and town."

"Have you thought at all about going through their camp and taking what you can? It's likely very empty over there right now."

"I have thought about it. I'm not sure I'd like to risk it. What Nathaniel said made a lot of sense. I can bide my time and wait. I don't want to take unnecessary risks. I want to do my part and help, but I also don't want to get caught leaving you to care for yourself for any period of time."

"Well, I appreciate that," Liberty said. "Let's just hope and pray that we've won this battle and this is the end of the war."

Evening

Belle rubbed her forehead, exhausted. After running out of the house that morning, Meri had found her and calmed her down. Belle had spent the rest of the day feeding, giving water to and visiting the wounded soldiers. She had finally escaped the house and was sitting on the front steps.

"How can Mother deal with this madness every day?" She muttered. The fresh December air felt cold but good after spending most of the day in the stuffy house. Occasional gunshots still popped in the distance. Belle looked up at the sky, hoping to see stars.

"What in the world..." Instead of stars, Belle saw a pale yellow cloud against the darkness of the night, a sight so incredible that she didn't want to look away.

"It's magnificent, isn't it?" The gruff and yet, somewhat attractive doctor came over and stood next to where she sat, resting his arms on the porch rail.

"Indeed." Belle agreed. "Do you know what it is?"

"It's called Aurora Borealis. Some people call them the Northern Lights. It's extremely rare for them to be seen this far south." He rubbed his dark blonde beard, hesitated, then sat down next to her on the step.

"It's almost as if God is draping Fredericksburg in mourning after all of the killing today," Belle said as the yellow streaks blended together to form a blood red color. "I had no idea that a battle would be like this. It's nothing like...any one of us imagined."

"I can agree with you there, Miss Turner." Dr. Knightly said, still looking at the sky. "My brother fought in the war with Mexico. He used to tell me great stories of all the glory. I quickly learned that it is not glorious at all." He sighed. "I don't know why he stayed in the army."

"Your brother is fighting? What division is he in?" Belle asked, her social skills taking over despite her wariness about this doctor. He didn't make her uneasy, just uncomfortable.

"He's...uh. He is actually fighting for the Union but at Manassas he..."

"Your brother is with the enemy? Fighting against you?" Belle stood slowly.

"I may be attached to the Confederate Army, that's true, but I'm not fighting against anyone, Miss Turner." He stood and walked down the steps, then crossed his arms over his chest and looked to the sky.

Belle walked to stand next to the doctor. She tried to stand as tall as she could but was still a head shorter than him. "You really don't care about the Confederate soldiers?"

"Of course I do. I'm a doctor, I care about all of my patients." It didn't sound as though he really believe that statement. She wondered why.

"You also care about those Yankees who shot my brother and are responsible for his death? Do you care about the men who caused this war, forcing my fiancé to go off to a filthy camp where he died of some senseless disease? My father and mother have both abandoned me because of this war that the Yankees started."

"In all fairness, Miss Turner, the Yankees didn't start this war. Technically, South Carolina started this conflict when they fired on Fort Sumter, and before that when they left the Union and started occupying Federal forts."

"Because we just wanted to be left alone. You sound more Yankee than Confederate, doctor, and your manners certainly are not those of a Southern gentleman."

"I'm sorry you feel that way, truly, I am. I'm just trying to be objective. Impartial. If I remain that way, it's easier for me to care for all of the wounded. I can't properly do my job if I take sides."

"Yes, I suppose you became a doctor so you would not have to fight." Belle's eyes flashed. She knew she was starting to talk irrational, but she didn't care. Usually, she could handle any man who spoke to her. She knew what to say to get them to respond to her wishes. By this point in any conversation, Samuel, Richard Evans, James, Nathaniel ...any one of them would have agreed with her, if for no other reason than to end the argument, but it seemed as though this doctor had no intention of doing that.

"Are you insinuating that I am a coward, Miss Turner?" The doctor's voice was low and his brown eyes turned cold. He stepped closer to her and glowered, so close that she could see that his eyes had a little bit of green in them.

"Maybe I am." She replied, slowly.

"That's amusing, coming from a pampered, spoiled rich girl who spent way too much time in her bedroom, unable to be bothered by people genuinely needing her assistance. I believe you only came out when there was a lull in activity, but to answer your question, yes, I am the coward for not wanting to add to the carnage around us, if that is your definition of a coward, Miss Turner."

Belle opened her mouth, but couldn't think of a response.

"Nothing to say?" The doctor asked. "That is a surprise."

Belle turned and stormed back into the house. She glanced around the entryway and in the dim light, saw Elizabeth, and hurried over to her.

"Belle. Where were you?" Elizabeth pushed a strand of hair off her face with the back of her hand. She had donned a white apron similar to what the nurses were wearing. It was badly in need of a cleaning.

"I was just outside. There was...is a fascinating light spectacle in the sky that I was observing." Belle answered, trying to be flippant and hoping her sister wouldn't notice how agitated she was.

"The Aurora Borealis? Isn't it incredible? I was up on the balcony earlier with the children just watching it. Truly a once in a lifetime opportunity to witness something like that."

"Yes, of course. I just wanted you to know that I was going to go up to our room for the night. It's been an exhausting day, and tomorrow looks to be the same." Belle turned and headed up to her sanctuary.

Elizabeth watched her sister disappear up the stairs. She turned as the front door opened and Dr. Knightly stormed in. Odd. She thought. Throughout the day, she had noticed that he seemed a bit rough around the edges and a bit rude, but she hadn't observed any other inappropriate behavior.

"I wonder what has Dr. Knightly so upset," Annie said, stepping next to Elizabeth.

"I have no idea." Elizabeth turned to her sister. "How are you holding up, Annie?"

"I am not sure, actually. I have seen sights that I cannot get out of my mind, Elizabeth." Annie shook her head. "I cannot believe the atrocities that men are committing against each other in the name of glory and winning a war. It does feel good to be helping, even if it something as simple as holding a hand. How about you? Any news from Joshua or anyone else we know?"

"No, nothing, not since he escorted us here," Elizabeth said softly. "I've tried to stay busy so that I don't have much time to dwell on the fact that he is out on that battlefield in the midst of all this, and Father too..."

Annie threw her arms around Elizabeth. "We'll get through this, right?"

Elizabeth hugged her younger sister. "Of course we will, Annie. We still have all of the support that we give to each other." She paused. "And God, of course." Lord, please be with us. She hoped that her prayer would be heard.

Prentiss Farm

AJ and Liberty lay on the ground, a thick quilt underneath them as they stared up at the night sky. Occasional rifle fire sounded from across the Rappahannock and they knew that Union troops were still on both sides of the river.

"It's absolutely incredible," Liberty said. "I wonder what the scientific reasoning behind it is. Or perhaps it's just a sign from God."

"I don't know. The colors are breathtaking, though." AJ replied.

Liberty was quiet. "Have you met up with Richard Evans lately in your intelligence meetings?"

AJ looked at her sister. "Why in the world would you bring him up?"

"I don't know," Liberty replied. "You never talk much about your adventures, but the few times you have, you've mentioned Richard was your contact. I was just curious. He is quite dashing, don't you think."

"He is, I suppose. The problem is, he knows it." She sighed. "I just want Nathaniel and Father to come home and be safe. I want our lives to be normal again."

"After everything we have gone through during this war, AJ, life will never get back to normal."

"Maybe not." AJ sighed. "Has all this just been in vain, a waste of property and a great loss of men? I really wonder what the future holds."

"You'll find a good man, get married, and have a passel of children. You'll be a good wife and great mother, and you will have the best stories to tell your grandchildren." Liberty folded her hands behind her head and looked to the sky again. The light show above continued. "I wonder if Father and Nathaniel are close enough to see this sight. It's heavenly."

"Isn't it? It's like God is giving us encouragement to get through the next few days."

"I cannot believe a battle is actually being fought in Fredericksburg," Liberty commented. "I wouldn't have thought our little town was that important?"

"Nathaniel made a good point about troops in the area. We are halfway between Washington, their capital city, and Richmond our capital city."

"That makes sense, although I have always thought it was foolish to move the Confederate capital from Montgomery to Richmond. It's so much closer for the Federals to capture."

"My, aren't you the perceptive one. It may seem ill-advised to us, but there were reasons. Alabama, while in the Deep South where war fever was most fervent, is so much hotter in the summer. I have heard that the mosquitoes can be merciless."

"Heaven forbid the politicians of our nation not have their comfort," Liberty added. "I hope moving the capital doesn't create any problems. I would hate to see our capital fall just because of its location."

"I don't think it will come to that," AJ said.

"Well, I hope our soldiers just win this battle."

"Every battle, I hope," AJ said, pulling out her watch and checking the time. "On that thought, we should get to bed. I want to get our chores done early tomorrow. Then I might go over and see if I can find anything out at the Union camp." She stood and brushed at her skirt.

"During the middle of a battle?" Liberty asked, sitting up. "I thought you said that would be too dangerous."

"I know. But I'm going to at least casually see what I can find. Besides, the fighting is on the other side of the river. I should be fine. You should probably come with me, though. I don't want to leave you alone."

"Are you sure you just don't want to see Richard Evans again?" Liberty asked with a smirk.

"What is it with you tonight? Do you fancy Richard Evans?"

"No. I just...I want you to be happy, AJ. You've never talked about wanting to court any of the men in the area, yet I know you want to get married."

AJ paused, an image of Richard flashing through her mind. She really needed to get him out of her thoughts, and Liberty most certainly didn't need to know how much she did actually think of him.

"I do, but that's a discussion for another evening." She offered Liberty a hand to help her up. "Come on now. It's time we get in. I don't want you out here alone."

Liberty pulled herself up, picked up the quilt and followed AJ into the house. "You're right about tomorrow. I feel as though it will be a very long day."

Monday, December 15, 1862
Prentiss Farm

AJ heard a knock and hastened to the door. Liberty was in the barn, tending to the few animals they had left. At the door stood a handful of Union soldiers. One wounded soldier clutched his bloody arm to his chest. They all looked dejected. In spite of the fact that they were Yankees, she felt sorry for them.

"How can I help you, gentlemen?" She asked, standing in the doorway.

"We were hoping to get some food, ma'am." One said, almost pleading. "We haven't eaten since we crossed the river days ago."

"Anything you can spare would be much appreciated." The wounded one said.

"Of course." AJ didn't have the heart to turn them away. She addressed the man who was wounded. "Have you been looked at, sir? What is your injury?"

"Caught a bayonet in my arm, ma'am. It hasn't been cleaned yet. At least not by anything but the rain." His face was pale and he was losing more color with each minute. AJ bit her lip, then made a quick decision.

"Come in. I'll see to your wounds and see if I can find some food."

The men entered, trying not to drag mud into the house, but they were unsuccessful.

"Have a seat at the table." She gestured, placing a basket of rolls onto the table. She pumped some water into a pitcher and brought glasses for all of the men to drink, then pumped more water into a bowl. She took a cloth and soaked it in the water. "Let me have a look." The man with the arm injury had a huge gash that ran from the inside of his wrist to the inside of his elbow. She tried to be as gentle as possible as she cleaned the wound. It had stopped bleeding and she didn't want to re-open the injury.

"You need to make sure you see an actual doctor as soon as you can." She said, taking a dry rag and pressing it on the wound. "I've known soldiers who survived their wound initially but then it becomes infected. I wouldn't want the same to happen to you." The man appeared to be about ten years AJ's senior. "We want to make sure you get back home to your family." She gave him a weak smile.

"Thank you, ma'am. Many of the wounded men are being taken to that big house on the hill, but there are so many that are worse off."

"Chatham Manor?" AJ asked.

"Yes, ma'am, I believe that's the name of it."

AJ rose and went to one of the cupboards to get a towel, then tore it into strips. She then tied the strips around the man's arm, securing the other cloth over the wound.

"Thank you, ma'am. You are an angel sent from heaven today."

"Yes, ma'am, thank you." One of the other men said. AJ looked at the men. It occurred to her that now would be a prime opportunity to pry for some information, but looking at their defeated, somber expressions, she just couldn't do it.

"You gentlemen are more than welcome," AJ said. She found some apples and placed them on the table. The men thanked her again. AJ looked at the men. They were her enemies. Yankees. Men that she had sworn to hate and do everything in her power to defeat, but it was like Nathaniel had said a few days ago. Things weren't as clear anymore.

"Let's take a look at these other injuries. I will see what I can do for you until you can see the doctor."

Turner's Glenn
Late Afternoon

"I really appreciate you both coming with me," Elizabeth said to Belle and Eric.

"Of course, Mrs. Bennet. It's my home now too." Eric said.

"I would like to see how the town has fared as well," Belle said. And get away from my home that is now a hospital and get away from those doctors.

Elizabeth's stomach felt sick as they neared the town and got a good view. "Dear God..." She prayed. The destruction from the bombardment wasn't all they saw. The streets were filled with all sorts of articles that had been dragged from the houses at some point. Mirrors and tables were smashed to pieces and she could see kitchen utensils, feather beds, and piles of books, all thrown in the mud.

"They destroyed everything they could get their hands on." She whispered.

"It had to be the filthy Yankees," Belle said. "Our Southern men would never do such an abhorrent thing."

"How will we ever rebuild?" Elizabeth asked no one in particular. They continued walking through the town. Many homes lay in heaps of rubble. It was an indescribable sight. They passed by 'The Sentry Box', the home of Roy Mason, and were completely dumbstruck, as it was now a hill of bricks and wood. It appeared to have been torn to pieces with shot and shell. Dead soldiers, mostly Federal, lay scattered, covered in mud and blood.

"I don't know that I want to go any further," Elizabeth whispered. "I don't think I can handle it."

Belle put an arm around her sister. "It will be okay."

Belle's stomach churned the entire time they walked through town. The destruction was impossible to avoid. As they passed by Grace Episcopal Church, Belle noticed that dead Confederate soldiers were lying on either side of the entrance, piled as high as the top step. Over the wrought-iron fence hung belts, cartridge boxes, canteens, and haversacks. The effects of the dead and wounded, Belle supposed. There was nothing but death and destruction all around. All the churches were much like Grace Episcopal, with bodies piled high outside. Layers of bodies were stretched out on the porches and balconies of the houses. Some of the corpses appeared to simply be taking a mid-morning nap, while others looked mangled beyond recognition. Even more appalling to Belle than the dead bodies were the arms and legs heaped in piles.

The scene didn't improve as they neared the Bennett home. Dead animals of all sorts, horses, cats, dogs, and chickens had been killed in the Yankee bombardment and were scattered throughout the streets.

"Oh, Lord." Elizabeth groaned as she saw the destruction of her home. Half of the roof to the blacksmith shop was gone, and the front wall of their home lay in piles of rubble. It looked worse than she could imagine.

Elizabeth walked into what was left of the house. The doors to each bedroom had been torn off their hinges. The children's room was covered with feathers from the mattresses and pillows that had been ripped open. The furniture was broken up. The China she had been given at her wedding from her mother had been broken to bits.

"Do you have anything of value left?" Belle asked.

"We didn't have much to begin with," Elizabeth admitted, kneeling on the ground to pick up a piece of a broken teacup. She smiled. That particular teacup already had a chip in it, a result of her clumsiness in the first week of her marriage.

"Elizabeth!" Joshua's voice came from behind her. She stood, whirled around and threw herself into his arms.

"Praise the Lord you're safe." She murmured, stroking his hair and holding him tightly. "Oh, Joshua, thank God." They stood holding each other for a few moments. Finally, Elizabeth pulled back and looked into Joshua's eyes. "Joshua...our home." He bent down and kissed her forehead.

"It held a lot of memories for us, I know." He said. "But when you think about it, it is only bricks and mortar. We still have each other. We still have the children. We're all safe."

She nodded and studied him. He was as dirty as she had ever seen him, and that was saying something, as he was a blacksmith. He had dried mud, patches of dried blood and sweat covering his grimy hair and uniform. She reached up to brush a strand of hair from his face and brushed her lips across his.

"You're right. You're safe. I'm safe. The children are safe." She cupped a hand under his chin. "I would be desolate if I didn't have you and the children."

"Remember." He said. "Be strong and steadfast. We'll get through it."

"I know, I know." She gave him a small smile, then backed out of his arms and looked around. Their home had been modest, but cozy. Elizabeth could still see it as it had been when Joshua had brought her here when they were first married. The home had always been Joshua's growing up, but he had made sure that Elizabeth knew it was now theirs from that moment on. She wondered what Joshua saw now.

"Do you think we'll be able to rebuild?" She asked. If anyone could make the repairs, it was her husband.

"It will take time and work and money, but we can rebuild. I'll do what I can this winter. We'll be encamped here, probably until March. I'll have time to do some work. I'm sure Eric can help as well." He looked behind her. Elizabeth had almost forgotten about Belle and Eric.

"Of course, that sounds like a good plan," Eric said. "Winter work at the plantation can be done by Daniel and Solomon. We can start with the shop. It doesn't look too bad and when we get that up and running, we'll be able to use the equipment to make repairs in our house and for others."

"Winter work at the plantation?" Belle scoffed. "As if we'll be able to accomplish anything with all the soldiers and doctors there." She gave Joshua a smile. "It's good to see you safe, Joshua."

Elizabeth was surprised and happy to hear her sister's words. Usually, she wasn't so complementary to Joshua.

"Good to see you as well, Belle. I did hear that Turner's Glenn is being used as a hospital. I was glad to hear that it will keep you safe. I was actually going to go out there and check on everyone after I stopped here to see the home." Joshua said.

"You have that much free time?" Elizabeth asked.

"The Yankees hightailed it back across the river. The majority of them will probably stay there for the next few months. We'll remain here, like I said, for the winter and keep an eye on them. We have to take care of all the bodies."

"All of the bodies?" Elizabeth asked, curious if the Confederacy would focus on their own dead.

"Lee had Longstreet propose a truce earlier today so that the Union could take care of their own, mostly south of the city. I heard that our leaders may send another flag of truce in a couple of days so they can take care of more of their casualties."

"That is quite benevolent," Elizabeth replied, then smiled. "So you will be here all winter?" She didn't want to get her hopes up too much, but she couldn't contain her excitement at having Joshua around more.

"We all have our jobs and we'll do some training, but I should have some spare time to spend with my family. I admit it's a travesty that our town was destroyed, but at least I can stay here for the time being." He turned to Elizabeth and touched her chin. "It will almost be as though I'm home."

"You will have to work most of the day and spend the nights with your fellow soldiers," Belle said. "That is hardly like being home."

"Yes, but I believe I can spend a good portion of the days and the evenings with my family."

"Where?" Belle continued. "The family has been confined to one room. I mean no offense, but your home is gone and you won't have any place to be with your family at Turner's Glenn. Not with all of the soldiers there."

"We'll find a way," Joshua said with a comforting smile. "We will find a way."

Evening
Turner's Glenn

"It is so nice to have Father home again," Elizabeth said, leaning into Joshua. Matthew and Joshua had been able to dine with the family that evening. Matthew stayed to visit the children while Joshua and Elizabeth went for a short walk along the river.

"I'm sure it is," Joshua replied. "It was a true blessing to have dinner all together, even if we were crowded and in the kitchen."

"Yes, it was. I only wish that Mother were here, and James, of course."

"James is in a better place now," Joshua said. "I know what you mean, though. There are days when I would give almost anything to have just one more conversation with him."

"Joshua, I am so sorry for everything you have had to go through this past year and a half," Elizabeth said. "From what I have witnessed this week, I can't imagine being in the thick of it like you have been."

"It's not easy, that's for sure," Joshua said, stopping and wrapping his arms around her. "Knowing that I have you and the children, it does make it easier. Knowing what I am fighting for and defending." He kissed her, then continued walking. "I must admit, though, sometimes, Elizabeth, I am not so sure. The fighting can get very intense very quickly. Men get scared, everyone is nervous and jumpy, but then you see just how courageous they can be. Facing their biggest fears. It's incredible."

"I don't know if incredible is quite the word I would use for any part of this war," Elizabeth replied.

"I suppose it's not the best word to use," Joshua admitted. He pulled out a pocket watch and sighed. "As much as I hate to say it, I need to get back. I need to report to my company for the evening."

"I don't like hearing you say that either," Elizabeth said. "It is encouraging, however, knowing that I will be seeing you often." They changed their direction and began walking back towards the plantation house.

"As often as I possibly can," Joshua said, giving her hand a squeeze.

They returned to the house and Joshua and Matthew said their goodbyes, then headed back to the camp. The rest of the family gathered in the kitchen. The children settled into a game of dominoes, Meri and Annie picked up some clothes to mend, and Belle and Elizabeth took

285

some strips of cloth to roll into bandages. Eric had retired to the slave cabin he was staying in.

Max poked his head up. "I hear something." The rest of the family listened and heard the sound of a wagon coming up the drive. Elizabeth's heart pounded as she excused herself to see who the visitor was. Max and Benjamin hastened to follow her, as did Belle.

"Can you see who it is, boys?" Belle asked. They both turned from the entryway, smiles on their faces.

"It's Mother!" Max replied.

The rest of the family quickly stood and made their way into the entryway. By the time they all got there, Miriam Turner had come in and was embracing Lainey, Max, Benjamin, and Hannah in one big hug.

"Mama, you're home!" Annie smiled.

"My dear girls." Miriam stood and hugged Meri, then Annie and then Elizabeth. When she turned to hug Belle, her daughter clung to her, an uncharacteristic show of vulnerability.

"What are you doing here?" Lainey asked.

"I heard about the battle here and had to come home," Miriam answered. "I had to make sure you were all safe. Besides, it was time for me to return, and it looks as though it was the right decision as now I will have my family and patients to care for."

"Are you back for good?" Belle asked.

"I believe I am." Miriam smiled. "What did I interrupt?"

"We were just settling in for the evening," Elizabeth said.

After they had all been seated back in the kitchen, discussion picked up again.

"I can't believe you made it here, with the soldiers and all," Annie said.

"I was lucky enough to be escorted by some officers and medical staff from Richmond who were also coming to Fredericksburg," Miriam answered. "I realized that I could finally come home and be with my family, and still help the war effort. I didn't realize it could all be in the same place." She glanced at Belle, then Elizabeth. "I must confess, I had hoped that you would have found refuge elsewhere."

"Where were we to go, Mother?" Belle asked. "You weren't here to advise us. Father visited the Sunday before the battle, but the threat was not great at that time, and he felt staying here would be safe for the time being."

"Yes, but surely, you could have gone further out into the countryside. I ran across many parties that had done just that as I came in." Miriam replied.

"I decided against it," Belle said. "I wanted to make sure our home would not be destroyed during the battle. I didn't want to abandon it. I was the one left in charge, and I made the decision."

"She was doing what she thought best, Mother," Annie said. "And she did tell me that I could take the others if I thought it necessary."

"I suppose it was a difficult choice," Miriam said.

"Neither option was ideal," Elizabeth added, trying to show support for her sister.

Belle began to say something else when Dr. Knightly entered the room.

"One of the orderlies told me we have a new arrival." He looked unkempt as ever. When in his presence, Belle had been subtly watching him ever since their argument. She hadn't spoken to him, however. She did give him some credit, however, he did work hard to save his patients. She knew eventually she would have to speak to him and apologize, as well as give him condolences. She had discovered earlier in the day that his brother who had been fighting for the Union had died at first Manassas.

"Dr. Knightly, I would like you to meet my mother, Miriam Turner." Elizabeth stood to make the introduction. "Mother, this is Dr. Aaron Knightly. He is a very talented doctor who is in charge of our home."

"Just the hospital aspect of it, ma'am." He said. "I thank you and your family for the sacrifices you are making for the cause." He quickly met Belle's eyes, then looked away. "I understand you have been in Richmond."

"Yes, working at Chimborazo Hospital." Miriam nodded.

"Splendid. It will be very helpful to have you here with all your experience."

"When is the army planning on evacuating the wounded to the bigger hospitals?" She asked.

"Likely in the next two weeks or so, for most of them." He replied. "Some will need to stay longer, though."

"Of course," Miriam nodded. "You must know that you are welcome here for as long as you need to be. We are quite capable of caring for the wounded."

"Thank you, ma'am. I believe you are right. I will let you get back to your family. I would, however, like to meet with you in the morning to discuss our routine."

"Of course," Miriam said. The doctor gave a nod and exited the room. "He seems like a good man." Miriam looked at her older daughters.

"He is, and a very competent doctor, as I said." Elizabeth nodded.

Miriam turned and smiled at her family. "Well, I know I will not be able to stay in my own bedroom quite yet, but I must say that it is absolutely wonderful to be home."

Tuesday, December 16, 1862
Evening
Moss Neck Manor

"What's going on out there?" Kate joined Bertie at the window, pulling her robe tighter against the damp cold.

"Soldiers. Confederate soldiers are coming up the path." Bertie answered. "I hope they don't make a ruckus and arouse everyone in the house. The children need their sleep."

"I was almost asleep myself when I heard the commotion," Kate said as several soldiers dismounted and walked up to the front door.

"My goodness, they're here already," Bertie said as she patted her hair. The two women made their way to the entryway. After a quick knock, they opened the door to find a general and two members of his staff, if Kate were to make a guess.

"Ladies, I am so sorry to disturb you at this late hour." The General spoke. "I am General Thomas Jackson, and these two gentlemen are my adjuncts, Captain JP Smith and Captain Alexander Pendleton." The two men took off their hats and nodded. They were both much younger than the General, closer in age to herself, Kate thought. One of the men was handsome, of average height and weight, with light hair and friendly-looking eyes. The other was moderately large, with a face some might consider ugly, but she thought he looked like the kind of man she would like to get to know better, with kind, brown eyes, and dark blonde hair. Most importantly, he had an air of confidence about him that intrigued her.

"General. What an honor it is to meet you. Welcome to Moss Neck Manor. I am Mrs. Richard Corbin and this is my sister-in-law Catherine."

"Pleasure to meet you ladies. I apologize again for bothering you at this late hour, but I wanted to make you aware of our presence here. We'll be needing to set up camp around your home, possibly for the winter. I didn't want you alarmed to see our tents when you awoke in the morning."

"I thank you for your thoughtfulness, General," Bertie said. "We could put you and some of your men up in the house for the evening or longer if needed."

"Mrs. Corbin, I appreciate your hospitality, but we wouldn't want to inconvenience you." The general said.

"It would be no inconvenience at all, sir." She replied. "We are honored to be able to support our brave soldiers in this way."

"Nevertheless, I would not want to be responsible for tarnishing your home. We can speak more tomorrow on the long-term arrangements."

"Of course. May I interest you in breakfast tomorrow morning?" Bertie asked.

"That would be wonderful, Mrs. Corbin. We will see you at breakfast." Bertie shut the door and turned to Kate. "What excitement we shall have, making General Stonewall Jackson and his staff comfortable during their winter stay."

"Indeed," Kate replied. "This will surely be an unusual winter."

"Don't think I didn't notice those two nice-looking soldiers with General Jackson," Bertie said, giving Kate a gentle nudge.

"Hmm," Kate replied. "I'm going to bed, Bertie. I'll see you in the morning."

"Sweet dreams, Kate."

Wednesday, December 17, 1862
Prentiss Farm

AJ pulled her cloak close as she stepped out of the house and made her way to the barn to gather some eggs. She once again sent up a short prayer of thanks to God that she and Liberty still had two chickens, a cow, and Lafayette, her horse. So many families had lost all their livestock as well as their homes and barns. Then there were those individuals who had lost their loved ones. AJ looked out across the river, she noticed a group of about 100 Union soldiers heading across the Rappahannock River towards Fredericksburg.

"What in the world?" She murmured to herself, confused. The battle was over from what she had heard. The Yankees had been badly defeated.

"Miss Prentiss!"

AJ turned to see Captain James Spencer walking toward her.

"Mr. Spencer!" She said. "I must say, I am glad to see you unharmed."

"Thank you. We did incur heavy losses though." He said. "I was lucky."

She gestured to the Union soldiers who had crossed the river. "Do you know what is happening there?"

"Yes." He nodded. "General Lee sent a message to our General Burnside, requesting that we send a detachment over to bury our dead."

"I see. That is quite benevolent of our General Lee." She replied.

"He does seem to be a good man." Captain. Spencer nodded. "We were able to bury some of our men a few days ago, I believe today, those men, from the 53rd Pennsylvania, will focus on Marye's Heights, I believe that is the name of the area where we needlessly lost so many men."

"Yes. I heard the fighting was fierce there?"

"It was." He said, solemnly. "Soldiers were senselessly and needlessly slaughtered. Our men were pinned down there for two days. No food. No water. They couldn't go forward and they couldn't retreat. Some had to use the corpses of their fallen comrades as barriers against the shooting. The Confederates had a stone wall for protection. I understand we lost 8,000 men at that one spot alone to the Confederates 300."

"Good heavens." AJ shook her head and looked out in the direction of Marye's Heights. When she looked back at James Spencer, he pulled his jacket tighter around him. "Would you like to come in? I managed to obtain some coffee recently."

"Are you sure you have the time?" The captain asked. "I really just stopped by to check on you and your sister."

"I have the time. I was just going to collect some eggs, but they'll still be there after you and I visit." She said as they walked to the house. "Thank you."

She led him into her kitchen. "Thank you so much for the invitation." He said with a smile. She grabbed two cups and poured the coffee, then handed him one of the cups. "I cannot promise it will be very good."

"I am sure it will be wonderful." He replied, then took a sip.

"Thank you for coming by. You don't have to feel responsible for me and Liberty." AJ sat down and joined him.

"I know I don't have to, but I still feel as though I should. Your brother is one of the closest friends I have."

"I understand I need to thank you for Nathaniel. He told me what you did."

"There wasn't a chance I would ever turn him in. He would do the same if the roles were reversed." Captain Spencer sighed and leaned back in his chair. "I knew this fight, this war, would be difficult. I knew there may be a chance that Nathaniel and I would run into each other on the battlefield. I just..." He shook his head. "I never wanted this war, but I need to do my part and serve. I hope and pray every day the war will end and things can go back to how they used to be. I pray every day that we will all be able to be one united country again."

AJ wanted to speak up, defend her beloved Confederacy, but she couldn't. She had to play the part of someone who was neutral about the war, even though she knew Captain Spencer would never turn her in.

"Peace is something we can all pray for." She finally said. "Something we can all agree with."

Moss Neck Manor

The next morning, Kate entered the dining room and immediately noticed that Bertie had been hard at work. Several long tables and the sideboard were set and filled with dishes of sausage, pork, steaks, fruit, preserves and muffins. Several officers had already arrived.

"Miss Catherine." The more handsome of the two she had met the night before greeted her as all the men stood.

"Gentlemen, welcome to you all. I am Catherine Corbin, or Kate." One by one, the men introduced themselves to Kate. The one who had addressed her was Captain James Power Smith. The other she recognized from last night was Captain Alexander Pendleton. She also met a James Boswell, Dr. Hunter McGuire, Stapleton Crutchfield and Henry Kyd Douglas. General Jackson introduced himself again.

"General, I've been thinking." Bertie turned towards Jackson, who sat next to her and said. "We, here at Moss Neck would be honored if you would occupy a wing of our home."

"Please say yes." Kate added. "We could do for you what Deborah Hewes did for George Washington at Valley Forge."

"Mrs. Corbin, I dearly appreciate the invitation, but I must decline." Jackson answered. "This house is too luxurious for a soldier. We will sleep in tents."

"If you change your mind, sir, you just let us know and we'll make arrangements."

"Thank you, ma'am." General Jackson replied.

"General." Kate spoke up. "What are your plans here, if you don't mind my asking? Do you have any idea where the Yankees are now? I would like to check on some of my friends; see how they fared through the battle."

"As long as you stay on this side of the river, you should be safe." The general answered.

"Not on the other side of the river?" Kate asked.

"No, ma'am. That's where the Yankees retreated." Captain Smith replied. "They'll likely be there for the winter."

"Goodness. Poor AJ." Kate bit her lip. "Oh, gentlemen, I beg your pardon. I have a dear friend that lives on a farm just west of Stafford Heights."

"Don't worry, Miss Corbin." The red-haired doctor, Hunter McGuire spoke up. "I'm sure your friend will be fine, but if you are concerned, she could always come over here to stay."

"Not AJ." Kate smiled. "She's much too independent for that."

291

"Well, as long as she follows the Yankee's rules, she should be okay." The doctor reassured her.

"Thank you, sir. That does put my mind at ease." Kate said, then turned to Bertie. "I'd like to go and visit Belle today. See how the Turner's and Elizabeth fared during the battle. They may have word on AJ as well."

"I doubt they have word on the Prentiss family." Bertie said. "You should be fine riding to Turner's Glenn, especially if our officers say you'll be safe."

"If I may, Miss Corbin, it would be my honor to escort you." Dr. McGuire spoke up. "I would like to check on some of the field hospitals in the area."

"That's very kind of you, doctor. I would welcome the company." Kate smiled at the handsome man.

"Would you be ready to go in an hour?" The doctor asked.

"I will." Kate said as she finished her breakfast and rose. "I will see you out front in an hour."

"I am dreadfully sorry for what you have seen, Miss Corbin." The doctor said as they neared Turner's Glenn. While riding to Turner's Glenn, Kate had been appalled at the destruction that was apparent on the outskirts of town, especially near Prospect Hill, and now as they arrived at her friend's home, she was overwhelmed at the change in the plantation. There were tents in the yard and soldiers everywhere. There were also several piles of dead soldiers and other piles of amputated limbs.

"It's not your fault, Doctor," Kate said. "I'm not sure whose fault it would be. Can we really simply blame the Yankees?"

"You are a very astute young woman, Miss Corbin." Dr. McGuire said. They stopped at the Turner's Glenn hitching post and the doctor helped her dismount.

"You are very much a gentleman," Kate said. "Your wife is a very fortunate woman."

The doctor smiled. "I am not yet married, Miss Corbin. However, I thank you for the compliment."

Kate smiled. In spite of the carnage on the roads and even here at Turner's Glenn, she had enjoyed the company of Dr. McGuire immensely. He was one of the most interesting men she had ever met.

"Thank you for the escort, Dr. McGuire. Please let me know when you would like to leave."

"Yes, Ma'am."

"Miss Kate!"

Kate turned to the sound of the young voice and saw Lainey, hauling a bucket of water towards the house. "Hello, Lainey. You look busy."

"Yes, ma'am." Lainey set the bucket down. "We have been quite busy here. There aren't as many wounded soldiers being brought in for surgery now, but there's still a lot of men to feed and take care of."

"I can see that," Kate replied. "Is Belle available? Or Elizabeth? I am praying she came out here during the battle and was not injured."

"They're both somewhere inside," Lainey said. "Elizabeth won't be going home anytime soon."

"No, she won't." Kate gave Lainey a small smile. "Thank you, Lainey. I appreciate the information." Kate went into the house. Wounded soldiers lay on every available floor space, lining the walls, filling the rooms. Some had bedrolls or blankets, while others had nothing between their bodies and the cold, hard floor. Kate continued to feel nauseous on account of the foul smell in the plantation home. She heard Belle before she saw her, voice loud and argumentative.

"You cannot just amputate again. That seems to be all you know how to do."

Kate entered what used to be the dining room. Belle stood with her clenched fists on her hips, squaring off against a disheveled-looking man who appeared to be a doctor.

"Miss Turner, I do not have time to argue with you. When you go to medical school, then you can converse with me about the best way to take care of a patient." The doctor turned and marched away. Belle's foot stomped the ground and she turned toward Kate.

"Kate! I am so sorry you had to see that argument. Dr. Knightly is a typical, arrogant doctor who thinks he knows everything." She went to Kate and gave her a quick hug.

"It's good to see you. I was worried about you and your entire family."

"We're all safe, thankfully," Belle assured her. "We have even had visits from Father and Joshua. They're safe as well and Mother came home on Monday."

"Oh, that's wonderful." Kate agreed.

"How did your family do?" Belle asked. Kate looked at her friend. She had never seen Belle so disheveled. She was wearing an old, faded dress covered with dirt and blood stains. Her hair was pulled back into a simple bun with not one ringlet hanging down.

"Everyone is well. Moss Neck is standing, not one bit of damage and now we have the honor of having Stonewall Jackson and his staff and regiment setting up their winter camp on our land. They rode in late last night and had breakfast with us this morning. Jackson and his staff are a very gracious group of men. It should prove to be a good diversion for the winter."

"Well, bully for you all." Belle grimaced. "But we will definitely not have an interesting time with all these soldiers lying about all winter. My whole family, and that includes Elizabeth, Benjamin and Hannah, are cramped in Zipporah's old room. That will likely be the case until the Confederate army leaves, and God only knows when that will be."

"This is unfortunate. If you really need extra space, we could find some room at Moss Neck. General Jackson has refused to stay in the manor home, and we already have a few people who have been displaced by the battle staying with us, but we could find some room."

Belle thought for a moment, then sighed. "I thank you for the offer, dear Kate, but no. I chose to stay here when I had the chance to go to Petersburg, and I will continue to stay here. You can make the offer to the other members of my family, but I'm fairly certain they'll choose to stay here also." She gave a weak smile.

"Well, you know the offer will stand."

"Thank you," Belle said. "Have you heard any news from across the river? Do you know how AJ and Liberty are?"

"I haven't. I have the feeling they're fine, though. Those two are more resourceful than any of us could ever hope to be." Kate replied.

"That is the truth," Belle replied. "I'm sure they'll find a way to let us know how they're doing."

"At least AJ will." Kate nodded. "Any news about individuals in town that you have heard?"

"Bits and pieces." Belle pushed a strand of hair from her face. "They say the fighting was horrible on Marye's Heights. I heard that Martha Stephens gave aid to those who were wounded in the Sunken Road area."

"Granny Stephens? How interesting." Martha Stephens was an older woman who lived along Sunken Road. She had an untoward reputation in town, as she was twice a common-law wife, owned eight properties in her own name, smoked a pipe, had once run an illegal saloon out of her house, and kept company with blacks.

"Yes," Belle said. "Apparently, her house has thousands of bullets in it and she aided General Thomas Cobb." Thomas Cobb was a Confederate soldier who at one point had been in the Confederate Congress and had been the principal author of the Confederate Constitution. "He ended up dying," Belle said softly. "I was in town yesterday and was appalled at what I saw. I would think that it hasn't improved."

"I'm not sure I want to see it. It sounds absolutely unimaginable." She shook her head. "How will Elizabeth handle all the repairs?"

"Joshua has been able to visit, and he'll likely be around for a while as his regiment will be stationed here all winter."

"What wonderful news. I am so glad for them." Kate said. "I was hoping to visit with her as well today."

"She's around somewhere. There's so much to do, I am unable to keep up with it all, though I have been helping as best I can." She ran her hands down her old light brown skirt that was wet and dirty. "I have never worked this hard, never would have imagined working this hard. It's non-stop."

"What do the doctors have you doing?" Kate asked. "I mean, what can you do?"

"We carry water to the men. Many are feverish, so Meri and I can cool them down with water and towels. We can hold their hands and talk with them. Elizabeth is a married woman, so she can bathe them, and mother seems to be an expert in nursing and organizing. We help feed the men, run errands for the doctors. Most of the more serious cases have been taken care of. I've been visiting with the soldiers, and have written letters for the men to send home. There is quite a bit we can do."

"At least you don't have to help with the surgeries," Kate said.

"No. The doctor you saw me with actually tried to force me to help with an amputation on the first day they all came in." She shuddered. "I couldn't do it. He had no right to even ask. He ended up telling me to leave. He should have listened to me in the first place."

"Are the other doctors as demanding as he is?" Kate asked, knowing Belle's feelings toward doctors.

"To be honest, Dr. Knightly is the only doctor I've had direct contact with so far. The other doctors just go about their business without paying any attention to me. However, that may change."

"I can tell this Dr. Knightly is getting under your skin," Kate smirked.

"I wouldn't say that," Belle said. "He's full of arrogance, pride, and vanity. He thinks that everyone should do what he says and no one can have a difference of opinion."

Kate couldn't hold back a chuckle. At Belle's look, Kate was quick to explain. "No offense meant, but the same could be said about you."

"I am none of those things." Belle protested.

"Kate!" Elizabeth entered the room. "It is so good to see that you are unharmed. What brings you out here?"

"I had to come and make sure all of the Turners survived this terrible battle," Kate replied. Elizabeth gave her a quick hug.

"I'm so glad you did. How is everything at Moss Neck? No injuries or damage, I hope."

"All is well." Kate wanted more information on this Dr. Knightly. "Belle was just telling me about some of the doctors working here."

"We've been blessed, I believe. The doctors seem to be a fine group of men."

"Even this Dr. Knightly?" Kate asked.

"Especially Dr. Knightly," Elizabeth replied. "He is extremely knowledgeable, competent, and patient working under pressure. He may be gruff and may need to work on his bedside manner, but I believe he is compassionate also." She smiled. "He is especially impressive because he is still very young."

"Young? How young?" Kate asked.

"When I spoke with him, he told me he was only twenty-two. He was in his final year of medical school when the war broke out, but he enlisted right away."

"There you have it! He never even finished medical school." Belle scoffed. "A truly wonderful man to have on staff here."

"If you're talking about Dr. Aaron Knightly, then he truly is a wonderful doctor to have on staff." Dr. McGuire entered the room. "Miss Corbin, are you enjoying your visit here so far?"

"Yes, doctor, thank you." Kate quickly made introductions.

"It is so good to make your acquaintance, Dr. McGuire," Belle said, immediately changing her attitude to show her charm. "So you know of our Dr. Knightly?"

"I do indeed. He was a student of mine at Tulane University in New Orleans before the war broke out. Very promising young man. He was at the top of his class. I have no doubt he would have graduated with very high honors."

"Is he the doctor you wanted to touch base with?" Kate said.'

"Yes, as a matter of fact, he is, but he is quite busy. He is very dedicated to his patients. I spoke with him briefly and I have been trying to assist where I can, but he and the matron of the home seem to have everything in good order."

"Hm," Belle said, but Kate didn't think anyone else heard the comment, if it could even be called that.

"Dr. McGuire, don't tell me you are set to leave already?" Kate asked.

"Yes, ma'am, I am. However, I do plan on stopping back here in a few days. You will be more than welcome to accompany me again."

"Oh yes, of course." Kate turned to her friends. "I do wish I could stay longer, but my escort is ready. I will see you in a few days."

"We will look forward to seeing you again," Elizabeth said.

Belle turned to Dr. McGuire. "It was a pleasure to meet you, Doctor. I do hope you find time to visit us again at Turner's Glenn. Perhaps next time, we can have tea and get to know you better."

Dr. McGuire took Belle's hand and kissed it gently. "I would enjoy that, Miss Turner." He did the same to Elizabeth, then escorted Kate out to their horses. Elizabeth waved goodbye, standing in the doorway as the visitors headed back toward Moss Neck.

Friday, December 19, 1862
Rappahannock River

AJ tied up her small raft and made her way up the steep bank of the Rappahannock. She didn't care for the Yankee occupation now any more than she did earlier in the year, however, their presence had allowed her to once again get small bits of information to pass along to her brother. She had been able to resume her business of selling food, doing laundry, and taking in sewing projects. Relevant information was hard to come by, and winter was usually a slow period for all the soldiers, the battle of Fredericksburg being one of the exceptions. She had been able to steal some needed medicine from Chatham. She had spent some time there, as it had become a hospital for the Yankee wounded. She had overheard from one of the soldiers that General Jackson had set up winter camp for his regiment. The area described made her determine that they must be around Moss Neck. Visiting the Corbin family would give her an opportunity to get the medicine she had to the Confederate wounded. She had finally found time to slip across the river. She was almost on Corbin land when a rider approached. She recognized him right away.

"Miss Prentiss!" Richard Evans called out.

"Captain Evans. Do you ever stay with your unit? I cannot believe I am running into you again." AJ tried to sound unaffected, but her heart beat rapidly.

"We do seem to have a propensity of running into each other." He dismounted. "Are you here for business or pleasure? I see your side of the river is full of Yankees."

"Yes, unfortunately, it is. I have some packets of medication and I wanted to ascertain who I should bring them to. From what I could deduce from the Yankees, General Jackson is camped near Moss Neck. I was heading there to drop the medicine off and find out where Lieutenant Daniels or Nathaniel are located."

"Well, at least you found me." They began walking toward the manor. "I would assume you also wanted to see Miss Kate?"

"Yes, of course," AJ answered. "I haven't heard from any of my friends on this side of the river since before the battle. I'm hoping everyone is safe and being cared for."

"They all must at least be alive," Richard said. "Only two civilians died during the bombardment, a slave over on Caroline Street and the Jewish man, Grotz's son." He shrugged. "So your friends must be fine."

"Really Mr. Evans, you shouldn't be so flippant. Two civilians, no matter who they were, are too many and that goes for soldiers too." She stole a quick glance at him. "How about your parents? How did they fare?"

"They left town, as many families did." He glanced back at her, their eyes meeting for a brief moment. "Have you seen Fredericksburg?" His voice was somber.

"Not up close." AJ's tone matched his. "I was able to watch parts of the fighting through a spyglass and saw the results of the battle. It was very smoky and difficult to see at first, but afterward…it looks devastating."

"That is an understatement." Richard agreed.

"Did your home survive the artillery bombardment?" AJ asked.

"The house that I grew up in is still standing, yes." He answered. AJ wondered at his wording but didn't question him further.

"Well, I am glad for your family. As I said, I was going to Moss Neck to see if I could find someone to trust these packages with. Since you're here, perhaps you can let me know who is trustworthy. Or you can just take what I have."

"I would take it, but I would feel better if you knew someone here who you could trust. Just in case you cannot contact Nathaniel, Lieutenant Daniels or myself."

"Are you sure that's safe?" AJ asked. "I thought the fewer people that knew, the better."

"That is true. The individuals I'm going to introduce you to, well, I think you'll realize that you can trust them and since your best friend lives there, it will be a good cover."

"I see." They approached the small wooden building that AJ knew served as the business office. Richard knocked on the door and they were quickly invited in.

"General Jackson," Richard said, saluting. AJ tried to hide her excitement at the prospect of meeting the infamous 'Stonewall' Jackson. Richard introduced AJ to the general and to the other two men in the room, Captains Sandie Pendleton and JP Smith, two young men on Jackson's staff. Richard explained what AJ had been doing for the Confederate cause.

"She is also good friends with Miss Kate Corbin, up at Moss Neck Manor," Richard added. "It will be a good cover for her if the Yankees start asking questions about why she's coming over here. She is also friends with the Turner ladies down the road toward Fredericksburg."

"I believe there is a field hospital there." Jackson nodded. "I concur, it's a good plan. Thank you, Miss Prentiss, for what you have done and for what you are willing to do. You are a true blessing to the Confederate cause." He gave her a small smile. AJ nodded and smiled back.

"It is an honor to give what help I can." She replied, handing him the package she had brought.

"Thank you, Captain Evans, for bringing Miss Prentiss in and introducing her." The general nodded. "Does Miss Corbin know about your involvement?"

"She has some idea, she knows I cook for the Yankees and do laundry and mending as needed. She also knows that I have taken items from the camps and Chatham for our soldiers, but I don't think she realizes how much or that I actually give information to contacts other than my brother."

"We will endeavor to keep it that way." General Jackson said.

"Thank you, sir." AJ smiled.

"I'll escort you up to the house," Richard said. He saluted General Jackson left the building, with AJ following. As they walked up to Moss Neck, he gently took her arm and tucked her hand in the crook of his arm. "I've been able to visit with your father a time or two." He said.

"Really?" AJ smiled. "Tell me. How is Father fairing?"

"He seems to be well. Very competent at his job as an artilleryman."

"Of course, I would expect no less. Is he nearby? I would like to see him if I could. I dislike lying to the Yankees about him being dead, but it is safer for me and Liberty."

"I will see what I can arrange. I know he would visit you, but he wouldn't want to risk being caught on his property, not just for his sake, but yours as well. Shall we meet here at Moss Neck in a few days? How about Wednesday afternoon?" He smiled.

"Wednesday? That's Christmas Eve day." She replied.

"I know it is. I wish it could be Thursday for you, but I don't think it will work. Will Wednesday be okay?"

"Wednesday would be wonderful. I have always felt there was something special about Christmas Eve."

"All right. I will see you then hopefully with your father, and perhaps your brother as well." Richard smiled again. "It's always a pleasure to see you." He tipped his hat. AJ smiled back, then knocked on the door to catch up with the Corbins.

Monday, December 22, 1862
Turner's Glenn

"Miss Turner, can you please come here for a moment?"

At Dr. Knightly's voice, Belle's first instinct was to try and slip away. She didn't want to help that man, ever, but she had been caring for the soldiers. She had found a way to help the wounded men by socializing. Many of the soldiers just needed someone to visit with.

"What do you need now, doctor?" She asked. Once again, the doctor looked disheveled and tired.

"I need your help in the parlor." She followed him to a man lying on the floor in the corner. The soldier's face was covered in sweat and she noticed his left leg had already been amputated just above the knee. She immediately felt nauseous.

"This is Private Sebastian Bonha. I need you to cool him down a bit and then maybe read to him or write a letter home for him."

"Of course," Belle said. "I'll get the water." It chafed her a little, to automatically follow his orders, but the task he asked her to do was quite agreeable.

"I'll assist you." Dr. Knightly placed a hand on her back and guided her out of the parlor. Once they were outside, Belle turned to the doctor.

"What's special about this man? You usually don't direct me to care for certain soldiers. Why him?" She had an odd feeling about what his answer would be. The doctor ran a hand through his shaggy hair and rubbed his head.

"He's dying, Miss Turner. He has an infection. He is not going to make it."

"I see." She hoped she could hold back tears. "But why are you asking me?"

"Because you may not be good at nursing or cooking or doing any physical work, but you do have a pleasant manner with the soldiers, and that's good for their morale. It's what most of them need, a kind and friendly face."

Belle was a bit taken back at the compliment from the doctor. He was always gruff and critical of not only her but most everyone at the hospital. This conversation was the first time she saw a bit of compassion in him, or was it the first time that she had noticed.

"And there's nothing more you can do for him?"

"At this point, no. We can just make him comfortable and wait."

"Wait for what? Wait for him to die?" Belle's eyes flashed with anger. "You are a doctor. You are supposed to save lives. This is what they did with my brother."

"I'm doing the best I can, Miss Turner. Believe me, I am." His voice was controlled as if he were holding back from yelling at her. "You have no idea what we're dealing with. No idea at all."

Belle took a step toward him, challenging him. "Well then maybe you should enlighten me, doctor."

"We are dealing with unprecedented wounds. These new rifles the soldiers are using...they're not like the musket balls of the past. These minié balls are made of a soft lead and are cone-shaped, so the bullet spins when it comes out of the rifle and when it hits a soldier, the tip flattens. This can cause a bone to shatter and a shattered bone is much more difficult to treat, not to mention the multiple types of cannon shots they are using."

"I still don't see..." Belle tried to interrupt, but the doctor kept talking.

"You must understand that these rifles are also much more accurate, Miss Turner. Yet military leaders are still using antiquated fighting techniques. If standing in a line and shooting at your enemy was nonsensical during the wars before our time, it's absolute insanity now."

"I still don't understand why you aren't able to help them. If these new advancements in making weapons are so much better, then why don't you doctors find better techniques to save them?"

"We're trying. It's not an easy task. No matter what we do, no matter what advancements we make, soldiers will still die."

"They shouldn't, especially not from a disease when they've never even fought in a battle, nor from a procedure that a doctor performed."

"Three out of every four men will survive with an amputation," Aaron argued. "If we didn't amputate, we would lose many more."

"Three out of every four men survive? That's all well and good for everyone except that one man and his family." She felt tears threaten and turned toward the water pump. "Excuse me. I need to help a dying man."

Belle wiped the brow of Sebastian Bonha one more time. The kind young man was fading fast. She had learned that he was from western Virginia, living on a small farm. He had ancestors who had fought for the Continental Army during the Revolution and had four children at home. Belle had been talking with him for an hour or so, kneeling on the ground and trying to comfort him as best she could to make his last hours pleasant.

"You've truly been a Godsend, Miss Turner." The young soldier said, then licked his cracked lips.

"Talking with you has been no hardship at all." Belle smiled as she moistened his lips with a wet cloth. "Is there anything else I can get you?"

"I would be much obliged if you could read me a scripture passage. There should be a Bible in my haversack." His voice was hoarse and she really had to focus on his words. She reached for the bag and pulled out the leather-bound book.

"What would you like me to read?" She asked.

"Joshua." He whispered. "The first book of Joshua, if you would."

Of course. Belle thought as she paged through the well-read book. *You would ask me to read from my sister's favorite book of the Bible.*

"After Moses, the Servant of the Lord..." She began reading in a clear voice. As she read, Private Bonha closed his eyes, a content, peaceful look on his face. "Anyone who rebels against your orders and does not obey all your commands shall be put to death. Only be strong and steadfast." Strong and steadfast. Belle thought on the words that had been repeated three times in that chapter. She would have to study the passage at a later time. She had heard Elizabeth reference it before. She looked at Private Bonha, who appeared to be no longer breathing.

"Private." She asked, then placed a hand on his chest. There was no movement. A tear slipped down her cheek. She felt a hand on her shoulder.

"He's no longer in pain." Her mother's familiar voice spoke quietly. Belle whirled around, tears now falling steadily down her face.

"Mama." Belle stood and threw herself into her mother's arms, for once not caring that she was showing her emotions to many people. Her mother hugged her tightly and stroked her back like she did when Belle was a girl. "Mama, I'm so glad you're back home. I don't know if I have told you that yet, but I am."

"It was time for me to be here," Miriam said. "My decisions are being made by God it would seem. All in His time." She led her daughter out of the parlor and into the entryway. "Did you know that man well?"

"No. Dr. Knightly asked me to stay with him. He knew he was going to die soon."

"Yes. Many times, the doctors know." Miriam said, brushing a strand of hair from Belle's face. "I must tell you how proud I am of you. You probably don't realize how important it was for that soldier to have you at his side. You have made a difference. How are you doing?"

"I have felt much better, that's for sure," Belle said. "There are many times when I feel as though I can't do anything for these men. I feel just visiting with them is pointless.

"That is so far from the truth, you must know that. It was the same way for me at Chimborazo. After your brother died, I would visit soldiers who were not going to live. It helped me adjust to losing James as I learned how much it meant to those boys. You have always been good at socializing. This is an instance of using whatever talents you have been given to help others."

"I suppose," Belle said. She looked back into the parlor. "I suppose I should tell Dr. Knightly about Private Bonha."

"Don't you worry about that. I'll take care of it." Miriam replied. "You go and take a rest. It will be good for you."

"All right, Mama." Belle took a deep breath. "I have been meaning to speak with you. I'm glad that you're back home where you belong, especially with the holidays coming up. I was thinking about how we could celebrate this year."

"Yes. It will be a very different holiday, but we should try to make it good for everyone here." Miriam said. "You will be wonderful playing the piano for them."

Belle hugged her mother again. "Now that you're home, we can make it happen."

Tuesday, December 23, 1862
Moss Neck Manor

Kate made her way to the stables. She wanted to visit the Turners and invite them to a New Year's Eve gathering. It would be nice to visit with Belle and Elizabeth.

"Miss Corbin." Two of Jackson's staff members smiled as they approached her. She smiled back. She was going to enjoy having the soldiers around, especially these two.

"I don't believe we have been properly introduced." The one who she knew to be Captain Pendleton spoke. "I am Captain Alexander Pendleton, but everyone just calls me Sandie. This is my colleague and friend, Captain James Power Smith. We all know him as JP."

"It is a pleasure to see you gentlemen again, but you must remember we were properly introduced at the breakfast table the morning after your arrival." She smiled.

"Of course you are correct, and we are delighted to see you again." Captain Smith said. "We are extremely grateful for you and your family's hospitality."

"It is our privilege. I do hope you will both be able to make our Christmas celebration for an evening of old-fashioned entertainment."

"We should be able to." Captain Pendleton said. "I am very much looking forward to it." He gave her a smile.

"Splendid." She smiled back.

"Where are you off to this fine afternoon?" Captain Smith asked.

"I am off to see a good friend, Captain. It has been awhile since I have had a good, long talk with her."

"The young lady whose home is now a field hospital?" Captain Pendleton asked, a concerned look on his face. "According to Dr. McGuire, she does not live close by."

"That's not true at all. It is just down the road a ways and there is a back path I have taken hundreds of times. I could get there in my sleep. I will be just fine, thank you."

"Are you sure you don't need an escort? We could see if General Jackson will spare someone." Captain Smith offered.

"It's most kind of you gentlemen to worry about me, but I will be just fine."

"As you wish, Miss Corbin." Captain Smith conceded.

"You're sure?" Captain Pendleton took a step towards her. "I would be distraught if something were to happen to you."

"I assure you, gentlemen. I will be completely safe. You have no need to worry." She gave them her most confident smile. "If I have any issues or feel uneasy, believe me, I will turn right around. If conditions change while I am there, I will have one of the men at Turner's Glenn escort me home. Again though, I will be fine, I promise." She gave them a nod and continued to the stable.

"The soldiers from Moss Neck are being overprotective of you?" Belle asked, sitting down in the Turner's bedroom. They had rearranged the furniture to make it more conducive for sleep and family time. With Miriam home, they had moved Max and Benjamin out into the cabin with Timothy, Daniel, Solomon, and Eric. The boys thought it was a great adventure.

"Yes. The gentlemen are all so very sweet."

"Oh, what a dream. I am quite envious. It seems just the opposite here. I must ask though, is there one soldier in particular who has caught your eye?" Belle asked with a curious smile.

"Maybe, I am just getting to know them. It's only been a few days, but I will enjoy getting to know them better. One, in particular, does intrigue me. Captain Alexander Pendleton." Kate chuckled. "For some reason, they call him Sandie. I am drawn to him, though I cannot imagine why as of yet."

"Is he handsome?"

"Not terribly so, some may think him even unattractive, but there is something about him that draws people to him. The soldiers and General Jackson especially seem to respect him immensely."

"Well, at least he's not wounded or rude and incorrigible, as everyone here is, and he is an officer. I have always thought a military uniform makes a man much more captivating."

"Indeed. Although, I did hear he was slightly wounded in the battle here at Fredericksburg. I mean to ask him more about it when we are further acquainted."

"You must be interested if you are thinking about future meetings," Belle said.

"Yes, well. Tell me, are things better here for you?" Kate asked.

"I don't know if I would say better. I do feel as though I am acclimating myself to the situation." Belle replied. "I can definitely say that I'm relieved Mother is home. It's different still, our entire lifestyle is topsy-turvy, but she's home. She is busy running the plantation again and helping the doctors. AJ told us once that she heard Mother was an exceptional nurse. She wasn't mistaken. I never realized Mother could be so comforting and efficient. Such a leader. I overheard two of the doctors say that she was being considered to be named the matron at Chimborazo Hospital."

"She ran Turner's Glenn successfully for years with your father and she is raising seven children."

"That's true," Belle said. "She has developed a new sense of confidence."

"Maybe it's just that you see her as a person now, not just your mother," Kate said.

Belle nodded. "I think you may be right."

Wednesday, December 24, 1862
Moss Neck Manor

AJ and Liberty approached the Moss Neck business office as excited as they could be.

"I can't believe we get to see Papa," Liberty said.

"Don't get your hopes up. Richard Evans said he would do his best, but he may not succeed. Personally, Liberty, I think he will."

"It is so nice of him to even try and arrange this," Liberty said with a small smile.

"Liberty, hush." AJ quickly looked around. The last thing she wanted was to have Richard overhear the conversation. She knocked on the door. One of Jackson's adjuncts answered.

"Miss Prentiss! It's good to see you. How can I be of service to you this fine Christmas Eve day?"

"Captain Smith. It's a joy to see you as well. This is my younger sister, Liberty."

"A pleasure to meet you, ma'am." He smiled at Liberty.

"Likewise," Liberty replied.

"We are here to meet with Lieutenant Richard Evans. He was going to help us find our father so we could spend the day with him."

"Captain Evans?" Captain Smith asked. "I haven't seen him today. Give me a moment and I'll see if I can track him down."

"Thank you, sir." AJ smiled, but her heart sank, fearing Richard may not have been successful at all. Or had he forgotten to even try?

"Why don't you two wait here? The general is out with some of the other officers, so you shouldn't be bothered."

"Thank you. I have a package for the general as well." AJ said.

"He will be grateful as always, Miss Prentiss." Captain Smith said with a smile, then left the office.

"He seems nice," Liberty said after the door closed.

"Yes. The few times I have met him, he has been quite congenial." AJ said. "You seem much more interested in men these past few months, young lady. May I ask why that is?"

"I don't know exactly. Just because I don't like to do 'womanly' things doesn't mean I am not growing up to be interested in a good-looking man."

"I see." AJ smiled.

The two waited for quite some time when finally, Lieutenant Smith returned.

"Miss Prentiss, I need to apologize. Captain Evans will be unable to join you today."

"I see." AJ's spirits dropped. *Unable, or suddenly unwilling?* She wanted to ask.

"However, while I was searching for Captain Evans, I was able to ascertain your father's whereabouts. It would be my pleasure to bring you to his camp."

"We wouldn't want to take you away from your duties, Captain," AJ said.

"Helping two Southern ladies is never an inconvenience. It would be my pleasure." He said with a smile. He offered both arms up to them and each obliged.

"I can't tell you how much we appreciate this, Captain," AJ said.

"It's quite all right. I was happy for the interruption. I was put in charge of organizing a Christmas celebration for General Jackson and some important leaders in our Army. In spite of their horrible losses, the local citizens are donating so much food and gifts to General Jackson. I almost feel guilty accepting it on his behalf."

"It's good to hear that our neighbors are taking care of our soldiers," AJ said as they walked.

"Indeed. Very generous, for example, an attempt to buy a turkey from a woman resulted in a gift of two fine turkeys, a bucket of oysters came from someone downriver, we received a box from the Staunton area with another turkey, a beautiful ham, a large cake, a bottle of wine, and every empty space was filled with biscuits and pickles."

"My goodness," AJ said. "We are taking care of you and it is well-deserved."

"Quite humbling, actually." Captain Smith said. "People so willing to give to others after they've lost so much. You all have, not just during the battle, but all that you have suffered before that."

"That's kind of you to say, Captain," AJ said. They continued to walk through the Confederate camp.

"It's true. General Jackson was saying that he is appalled by all of the sufferings in Fredericksburg. He actually wants to try and raise some money for their relief."

"That would be a very kind gesture, and much appreciated," AJ replied. "Many people will need the funds to rebuild."

"Yes." Captain Smith agreed. "That's one reason he wants to help."

They finally reached the area where the 1st Virginia Artillery was camped. A quick question from Captain Smith led the Prentiss sisters to their father. He was sitting at a campfire with other members of the Confederate artillery. A smile lit up the face of Adam Prentiss when he saw his daughters.

"A leanbhs!" He called them an Irish term of endearment and each of his daughters ran to him and hugged him. AJ introduced her father to Captain Smith.

"Thank you so much for your assistance, Captain. We'll be able to find our way back."

"Of course." The man said with a smile.

"Captain, I cannot thank you enough," Adam said. "I've desperately wanted to see my daughters, but knew it was a fool's errand."

"We know that Papa, and we understand," Liberty said.

"Well, I was happy to help." Captain Smith said, then nodded to Adam and left.

"He seems like a nice young man," Adam said.

"Indeed, he is," AJ admitted. "I do hope I get to know him better."

"Should I be worried?" Adam asked in a joking fatherly tone.

"Not at all," AJ said. "Father, you should know that by now."

"Aye. I do know that. You're good lasses." He smiled. He led them to the fire. The other soldiers had left after introductions, wanting to give the family some time alone. "I wish I could offer you a warmer place." He said. "It is the best I have, however."

"Papa, don't worry," Liberty said. "We're just happy to see you."

"Liberty's right," AJ said. "We were hoping you could get time away to go to Christmas Eve Mass with us tonight, but any time spent with you is a gift."

"I was already planning on attending and I was hoping I would see you there. It would be my great pleasure to spend Christmas Eve with you in church." He smiled. Liberty rose from where she was sitting and hugged her father again.

"That will make it the best Christmas possible."

Thursday, December 25, 1862
Turner's Glenn

Belle sighed as she moved to another wounded soldier.

"Merry Christmas, sir. How are you doing this morning?"

"I've had better holidays, Miss Belle." He gave her a weak smile.

"Well, we will do our best to remedy that for you." She replied. "Tell me, what were some of your holiday traditions back home?"

"We never had much money, ma'am, so we kept Christmas pretty simple. A small tree, a few simple decorations, one gift for everyone, but we did always have a fine turkey dinner."

"I see," Belle said. "I hope you will be able to come into the parlor later this afternoon. We've been planning some special activities."

Her mother's return had made quite a difference in the way Turner's Glenn was managed. The army was starting to move some of the patients to larger hospitals in the bigger cities. While medical care was still the most important task, Miriam Turner also made sure the soldiers had nutritional meals with plenty of water, moved around to the best of their ability, and made sure their spirits were kept up. The latter being good news for Belle, as her mother's policies allowed her to simply visit with the soldiers.

"I hope so as well, Miss Turner."

She smiled, stood, and moved towards the parlor. They had found a small tree, and the children had decorated it with strings of popped corn, strung red berries, some paper chains and a few taper candles with red ribbon bows. Earlier that morning, the family had exchanged small gifts and the children had opened gifts from St. Nicholas. Annie and Ruthie had been working hard to make the dinner meal a little extra special for the family, the patients, and the doctors. Annie and Ruthie were most happy that the plantation was being used as a hospital, as they now had ample supplies of basic foods.

"Doctor, you really should allow the Union soldiers some Christmas cheer, as well as our boys," Elizabeth said. Belle paused outside the doorway, out of sight.

"I don't believe that would be the best idea. There is too much animosity between them. If we were to mix both Union and Confederate men, fighting will surely break out."

"I disagree, doctor. It's Christmas Day. I have faith that both sides will embrace the Christmas spirit. They are first and foremost human beings. I believe they can see each other as men of God and not as Union or Confederate soldiers. Besides, there aren't that many Federals and I'm sure they will agree to be on their best behavior."

"As you've been teaching me." Dr. Knightly said.

"Have I? I hadn't realized that." Elizabeth said. Belle could tell that Elizabeth was smiling. Belle entered the room.

"Elizabeth, Dr. Knightly." She greeted them.

"Belle," Elizabeth said. "You are just the person we should talk to. We need your opinion. You're our pianist this afternoon. Do you feel we should invite the Union patients to our Christmas celebration?"

"Why are you asking me? As you've said, I'll just be playing the piano. It doesn't matter to me who's listening and singing along."

"I still don't believe it's the best idea." Dr. Knightly said. "We can seek the advice of your mother."

"And Father," Belle said. "Our father should be here soon."

"Joshua as well," Elizabeth said, her face lighting up. "Christmas with the whole family. I am so excited."

"Not the whole family," Belle said somberly, thinking of James. She felt Elizabeth at times forgot about James, but Belle never could. He was always on her mind. "James will never be home again, thanks to the Yankees you want to invite to our celebration." She strode to the piano and sat down. "On second thought, maybe the Yankees should stay away. I really don't want to see them in here. They will ruin our celebration."

"Belle," Elizabeth said, then heard her name being called from the entryway. "Joshua!" She turned to Dr. Knightly. "Excuse me, doctor. Belle." She hurried away.

After a moment of silence, Dr. Knightly spoke. "I can't remember if I have told you this or not, Miss Turner, but I am truly sorry about your brother and the young man you were courting. Your mother told me what happened. If I could have done anything to prevent either one of them from dying, I would have. I am sure the physicians did all they could."

Belle fingered the keys of the piano, unsure of what to say in response. She finally looked at him. "Thank you for saying so. Sometimes, I wonder if anyone else feels James's loss as keenly as I do."

"I know your mother does, as well as your sister, Mrs. Bennett. I have spoken with both of them on the topic. I have spoken with Max as well, and he definitely feels the loss of his older brother." He walked to her and placed a hand on the top of the piano and looked down at her. "Sometimes, it's difficult to see the pain of others when we are in so much pain ourselves."

"Since when are you so in accord with your emotions, Doctor? Are you not more of a science and medicine man?"

"I cannot lie, you are right about some points. However, these past few weeks, through observing your family, especially your sister, I must admit, I have learned quite a bit."

"Really? I thought doctors knew everything. What could you possibly learn from a mere female?"

"That is simply not true. I have learned more this past year working as a field surgeon than I ever did in medical school." He sighed. "There is always more to learn."

"I suppose that's true of life in general," Belle admitted. "Yet I wouldn't think a doctor would agree."

"Really." Dr. Knightly opened his mouth as if to say something else, but was interrupted by wounded men as they began to enter the parlor for caroling. Belle wondered what he had been about to say, but it looked as though he didn't want an audience. He moved to the other side of the room as her family entered. She smiled at her father, then noted that the last to enter were two Union soldiers. Her sister had gotten what she wanted after all.

When all of the patients who were able to come were settled in with some spiced apple cider and fruitcake, Miriam greeted everyone, then led the group in prayer.

"Now, without further delay, my lovely daughter, Belle has volunteered to play some Christmas music for us."

"It is my pleasure to do so," Belle said. "Does anyone have any requests?

"Do you know 'O Come All Ye Faithful?'?" One of the soldiers asked.

"Yes, sir, I do." Belle smiled, shuffled through her sheets of music and placed her hands on the keys. "Everyone join in!"

Prentiss Farm

"It was a wonderful Christmas meal, AJ. Thank you for being patient with me and helping me with my cooking skills. I still prefer to work out of doors, but learning something new is always useful."

"You have always been a quick learner, Liberty" AJ replied. "You can do whatever you put your mind to."

"Really? So I can help you in your intelligence work?" Liberty asked.

"You could, but no. I'm still not going to approve of you doing so." AJ replied.

"You will never change your mind, will you?" Liberty asked.

"No, I don't believe so. Nathaniel agrees and Father would as well if he knew the situation."

"Well, Father wouldn't approve of what you're doing. He would worry about you endlessly."

"I know. Which is why I didn't mention it to him."

"That is deceptive," Liberty said.

A knock sounded at the door. AJ stood to answer it.

"Probably another soldier who would like some baked goods." She said. "Luckily, I still have some sugar biscuits."

She opened the door to find a familiar Union soldier at the door.

"Goodness, Captain Spencer!" AJ smiled. "Merry Christmas." Her brother's best friend smiled and pulled the cap off his head.

"Merry Christmas to you as well." He smiled back

"Mr. Spencer! I didn't know you were in the Fredericksburg area." Liberty said, joining AJ at the door.

"Yes. I am impressed and pleased that you remember me."

"Of course I remember you, although you have changed quite a bit," Liberty said.

"Not nearly as much as you have. You have become a lovely young woman."

"Thank you. I must admit I'm still working on it though." Liberty tried to hide the brief blush on her cheeks.

"Please come in," AJ said, opening the door wide. "Have you had dinner?"

"I have, but I wouldn't mind one of those sugar biscuits that I hear so much about in the camp."

"Of course," AJ said, gesturing to a chair. "How was your Christmas in the camps? I have been over to try and ease the wounded soldier's spirits with those same biscuits you're eating."

"The men are as good as can be expected. There was a misunderstanding between the War Department and the express companies. No packages or letters were brought to the troops from home. We were able to purchase some necessities from the regimental sutlers." He smiled at AJ. "Or obtain some sweets from the kind locals who don't mind that they're helping the Yankees."

"I am trying not to think of you all as the enemy," AJ replied. "I'm trying to think of you as fellow human beings who need kindness just like anyone else."

"I greatly appreciate the sentiment, Miss America Joan, and I know many of the soldiers do too." Mr. Spencer said.

The three conversed for a while, then James stood.

"Well, I would like to stay and reminisce more, but I have picket duty tonight." He stood, put his hat back on, and then pulled his jacket tighter. "Thank you for your hospitality, ladies. It means more to me than you can imagine. It's good to know that people can still see what's underneath the uniform."

AJ stood and followed him to the door.

"You are always welcome here, Mr. Spencer," AJ said. As she looked toward the river, AJ noticed a small gathering of Union men. "I wonder what's going on down there." She commented.

"Allow me to escort you, as I am sure you would make your way there anyways." Mr. Spencer said.

She chuckled and smiled. "You would be correct about that." AJ reached into the house, grabbed her cloak and told Liberty where they were going. Her sister immediately joined them.

"It would be best if we watched from a distance." Mr. Spencer cautioned.

"I will agree with you, Mr. Spencer. I am not completely careless." AJ said. As the two women watched, James continued down to the bank and struck up a conversation with one of the other soldiers. Across the river, they could see Confederate soldiers gathered on their side of the riverbank. They pushed what appeared to be little boats or rafts, which floated over to the Union side. As the boat made it across the river, the Union soldiers crowded even closer, pushing and scrambling to be the first to seize the boat, some soldiers even going into the frigid water and stretching out their arms. They pulled the boats ashore and stood in a group over the contents and cried out in excitement.

"I wonder what is going on," Liberty said.

"I think...I wonder if they're exchanging gifts of some sort." AJ replied. She watched as Mr. Spencer made his way back towards them, a smile on his face.

"Christmas truly is a wonderful time." He said. "Some Pennsylvania boys made contact with some Confederates on the other side of the river, seeing if they wanted to trade. The Pennsylvanians gathered sugar, coffee, and pork, then sent it across the river on little boats. The Johnnies sent back some parched corn, Virginia tobacco, and persimmons." He smiled. "I think they'll enjoy the tobacco the most. It's quite scarce in the north and highly prized by most Union soldiers."

"Amazing how the soldiers can share in peace on earth and goodwill toward their fellow man on Christmas, yet be at war with them the next day," Liberty stated. "Seems contradictory to me."

Moss Neck Manor

Kate patted her hair and looked in the mirror. She sighed. There would be so many officers in the house. Bertie had invited General Jackson and his staff to an evening of "old-fashioned entertainment" at Moss Neck. Kate was hoping that Captain Pendleton would come. She still found herself drawn to him. He was kind, friendly, and so smart. He would become a successful man someday, in fact, he already was. She sighed again as she looked in the mirror. Plain. Why did she look so plain? She knew that her ability to flirt and the ease with which she could converse with men drew them to her. Would Lieutenant Pendleton, a trusted staff member of General Jackson, be attracted to her? She hoped so.

"Aunt Kate!" Janie entered the room, dressed in an evergreen-colored velvet dress, her hair pulled up and decorated with small bits of white cotton that looked like snow.

"Well, good evening, Miss Janie. Just how old are you again? You look divine. I may have to consider you my competition with the men tonight."

Janie giggled. "Oh, Aunt Kate, you know I'm only six. You are so silly. Mama asked me to come and tell you that the officers are starting to arrive."

"Well, thank you for the announcement. I will be right down."

Janie scampered out of the room. Kate stood and ran her hands down the red silk ball gown she had decided on for the evening. It was a favorite of hers from before the war, edged with white lace trim along the elegant but modest neckline that just barely revealed her shoulders. The lace trim also edged her sleeves, the scalloped hemline, and white and green flowers ran down the skirt. Nettie had braided her hair into a crown on the top of her head, with thin garland wound through it. She pulled on her white gloves, looked back at the mirror, sighed and muttered "It will have to do." She then headed down the parlor.

The men all stood when Kate entered the room. She smiled. It was good to have gentlemen at Moss Neck again. Kate quickly took attendance and recognized General Jackson of course. She went to greet him first.

"General." She smiled as he took her hand and kissed it.

"Miss Corbin. You look lovely tonight."

"Thank you, General, and may I offer my congratulations on the birth of your daughter."

"Thank you, ma'am. It very well may be my proudest accomplishment." The man grinned broadly. Kate moved on to the next gentleman. She hadn't been formally introduced to this officer yet, but she had noticed him before. He had a pleasant face, and his dark brown hair brushed his collar. "Good evening, Miss Corbin." He spoke with a slight Irish accent. "It is a pleasure to meet you, finally. I am Captain Henry Kyd Douglass." He bowed over her hand.

"The pleasure is mine, Captain Douglass, and where do you hail from with that charming accent?"

"My family lives in Western Maryland along the Potomac River, but I was born in Ireland. We moved to America when I was a wee lad, but the accent has stuck with me."

"My, that must have been quite the adventure as a young boy," Kate said.

"It surely was, ma'am." He agreed with a smile, then conceded her hand to the next gentleman, a familiar man with black hair and a bushy beard. "Miss Corbin, it's nice to see you again."

"Mr. Randolph, correct?" She asked with her most charming of smiles.

"Yes, ma'am. Captain William Wellford Randolph of Clarke County, Virginia."

"It's so nice to see you again. Are you enjoying the holiday?"

"Indeed I am, and I was overjoyed to receive a letter from my dear wife, Ada."

"How wonderful for you. That must have been the perfect Christmas present." She smiled and turned to Dr. Hunter McGuire, General Jackson's good friend, and staff doctor.

"Dr. McGuire, it is so nice that you were able to join us." She smiled as he bowed over her hand.

"Miss Corbin, you are positively enchanting tonight." He smiled, his red mustache had been trimmed so she was actually able to see his facial features.

"Why, doctor, that is so kind of you to say."

"The truth is always easy for me." He replied. "I must give you kind regards, Miss Corbin, from the ladies over at Turner's Glenn."

"Are you in reference to my dear friends Belle and Elizabeth? Oh, how wonderful that you saw them. How are they faring? Were you visiting your former student?"

"A Miss Belle Turner and a Mrs. Bennett and yes, I was there visiting Dr. Aaron Knightly again. You may recall he was just finishing his studies at Tulane, where I briefly taught, back in '61. He has a fine mind and a bright medical future."

"Do tell, and do the Yankees still occupy the homes across the river?" Kate shook her head and thought of AJ and Liberty.

"They do." Dr. McGuire confirmed. "But I am monopolizing all of your time, Miss Corbin. I will leave you for now, but may we talk later?"

314

"Of course, doctor," Kate said. Dr. McGuire left her and Kate greeted the last few men in attendance. Unfortunately, the one officer she wished to see and converse with wasn't there. No matter, she would make due. There were plenty of other soldiers to spend time with. Her eyes immediately fell on Captain James Power Smith, Jackson's aide-de-camp. She smiled. She enjoyed talking with the former theology student. He had been with Captain Pendleton. She casually walked over to the young man, who was looking out the window.

"Why, Captain Smith, what could you possibly be looking at, or are you waiting for someone else to arrive?"

The young man, who wasn't much older than Kate, smiled and ran a hand through his dark blonde hair.

"Miss Corbin, I believe I was waiting for you to finish your introductions and come talk to me."

"Captain, you flatter me." She peeked out the window. "I declare, there's nothing but some snow and darkness out there."

"As of right now, that is the case." He replied

"Tell me about your fine Christmas dinner." She brushed her hand lightly against his arm. "Is it true that you entertained General Lee today?"

"We did indeed. General Jackson had General Lee and General Stuart over. I was in charge of the food and I'm proud to say that I was able to gather a wonderful assortment of food for the staff. Turkey, oysters, a ham, cake, wine, biscuits, and even pickles."

"I declare, you must have a gift to be able to obtain such donations," Kate replied. "I believe we are enjoying some of the food that was left over to help feed you all here tonight."

"You are, and I'm glad you could take advantage of our fine feast." Captain Smith pointed out.

"Indeed," Kate said, just as Bertie stood and announced that Christmas dinner was to be served. As they were heading into the dining room, the door opened and another officer walked in, his jacket collar pulled up to protect his neck and face from the cold.

"Pendleton! Glad you could make it." General Jackson called out. One of the servants took his overcoat. Kate's eyes met the Captain. He gave her a quick nod and then turned to Bertie.

"Mrs. Corbin, I am so sorry for my tardiness. I hope you were not waiting on me for dinner."

"No, not at all, Captain, but your timing is impeccable. You are right on time." Bertie answered. She turned and took General Jackson's arm and allowed him to lead her into the dining room. Kate took Captain Smith's arm, but her eyes kept drifting back to Captain Pendleton. Botheration! Why did he affect her so? He had joined his fellow soldiers and was talking with them. He appeared to be well liked by his comrades.

Dinner was relaxed and enjoyable. Kate tried to focus on conversing with the officers around her, but her gaze kept going to Captain Pendleton. One time, she caught him looking at her, and he gave her a small smile and raised his glass subtly in her direction. She smiled back and tried avoiding his eyes for the rest of the meal.

"Shall we all head back into the parlor?" Bertie asked when everyone had finished.

"Of course, Mrs. Corbin." The General answered. The group went back into the parlor, Kate again escorted by Captain Smith. General Jackson and Captain Douglas seemed to be having a fine time talking with young Janie. Kate smiled, her niece was already a real charmer, and she would steal many a heart. Perhaps the girl really would be her competition tonight.

"That is a fine piano you have, Mrs. Corbin." Henry Kyd Douglass said. "Would it be too forward of me to request some music?"

"Of course not, Captain. My sister plays quite well." Bertie nodded at Kate, who smiled and made her way to the piano and began playing. She kept it light, starting with an upbeat holiday song of "Deck the Halls."

The men immediately joined in the singing. When the first song was done, one of the men spoke to her.

"You play very well, Miss Corbin." Kate looked up, hoping to see Captain Pendleton. Instead, she saw Captain Randolph.

"Thank you, Captain." She said and paused for a quick break. "You said earlier that you've recently received news from home. How is Mrs. Randolph?"

"She's quite well. Anxious for this war to be over, as most people are."

"Well, you are protecting us from the Yankees, so we desperately appreciate your being here."

"It is our pleasure to do so, Miss Corbin." He smiled. "May I make a song request?" She nodded. "Do you know Jingle Bells?" She smiled and immediately placed her fingers on the keys and began playing. It was one of her favorites. As she played, she tried to avoid looking at Captain Pendleton. The last time she had stolen a glance, he had been conversing with Bertie and some of Jackson's staff members. Kate finished playing and then looked around the room.

"Do I have any other requests, gentlemen?" She asked. Janie ran up to her.

"Play the new one, Aunt Kate! About Santa and his reindeer on the roof!"

Kate smiled and shuffled through her sheet music, not having that one memorized.

"What new song is this?" Captain Pendleton asked, joining the small group that was gathering at the piano.

"It's called 'Up on the Housetop', and it just came out a few years ago," Kate replied.

"It's my favorite!" Janie exclaimed. Kate played the upbeat song as she, Janie, Bertie, Nettie, and a few of the soldiers, began to sing. When she finished, Kate looked around, silently asking for another request.

"Do you know 'O Come All Ye Faithful'?" Dr. McGuire asked.

"I do," Kate answered, and again began playing. She noticed all of the men joined in this song, and she also noticed that Captain Pendleton had a fine, soothing voice.

They continued singing, enjoying the music and the company of one another. Time swiftly sped by. It was nearly 2:00 in the morning when the guests left.

"What a wonderful, successful evening," Bertie said as they all headed upstairs. Janie had been put to bed hours ago, so it was just Bertie, Nettie and Kate.

"Yes, it was. Simply delightful." Kate agreed. Try as she might, she could not get Captain Sandie Pendleton out of her mind.

"Lots of young, single men on the General's staff," Nettie commented with a quick glance at Kate.

"Indeed," Kate replied, but both her sisters could tell that she was distracted.

"Indeed." Bertie gave Nettie a smile.

Monday, December 29, 1862
Moss Neck Manor

Kate pulled her knit shawl tighter around her shoulders. It was a chilly day, and Moss Neck was bustling with activity and refugees from town. She needed to get out of the house. She had volunteered to retrieve Janie from General Jackson's headquarters. He still occupied the small frame house that had previously been the location of Moss Neck's business office. Kate was impressed that General Jackson declined to occupy a wing of Moss Neck for his lodgings. The officers could have easily taken over the mansion and displaced the family, as they had done to the Turners. At least her friends had been able to stay in one of the rooms in their home.

Just as Kate stepped to the door, it opened and Captain Pendleton came out, pulling on his hat. He didn't see her and almost ran into her. She stumbled away and he grabbed her waist to help steady her.

"Miss Corbin!" He exclaimed. "Are you all right?"

317

"Yes, Mr. Pendleton. I mean, Captain."

"I am so sorry. I wasn't aware you were here." He removed his hands from her waist, but she could still feel the warmth there.

"Don't despair. No harm was done." She smiled at him.

"Thank you." He smiled back at her. "And what brings you out here on this chilly day? Is it time for Miss Janie to go home?"

"It is indeed," Kate replied. "I do hope she isn't being too much of a distraction."

"Not at all. She is an absolute delight and the General adores her."

"That's good to hear. She is a darling child."

"She is that." The Captain replied. "I enjoy children. I hope to have a fair amount of my own someday."

"From what I have seen of you, sir, you will make a very good father," Kate's heart fluttered.

"From what I know of you, Miss Corbin, you will make a fine wife and mother one day."

Kate tried to ignore the feelings that his words brought into her heart. Was he insinuating that she would make him a fine wife and mother? Or was he simply being polite?

"Well, Captain I am glad to have run into you, literally." She smiled. "I was wondering if your duties would allow you to join my sisters and me for tea." Kate wasn't exactly sure why she issued the invitation, she only knew that she wanted to spend more time with this man. "We would love to show you our gratitude. I feel as though I wasn't able to really talk with you much on Christmas Day."

"I am sure that the General can manage without me for a small amount of time." He answered. "I would very much like to visit and have tea with you."

Kate's heart beat a little faster. "Wonderful." She replied, hoping she didn't sound too excited. "Would tomorrow be too soon? We could meet, say, around three-o-clock."

"I will have to make sure it is okay with General Jackson first." Captain Pendleton turned, opened the door, and gestured for her to enter first. Kate hadn't realized just how cold it was outside until she felt the warmth of the office.

"Captain Pendleton, back so soon?" General Jackson commented, then he noticed Kate. "Miss Corbin! It is truly a pleasure to have you join us here."

"Good afternoon, Aunt Kate!" Janie said from her position on Jackson's knee.

"Good afternoon, General Jackson," Kate said. "I hate to be the bearer of unpleasant news, Janie, but I am here to take you back up to the manor house. It is time to get ready for dinner."

"Oh, botheration," Janie said. Kate noticed Captain Pendleton cover a laugh.

"Yes, it is too bad, I know," Kate said, "but we did receive some good news today."

"What news?" Janie asked. Kate's eyed followed the Captain as he went close to the General and spoke with him. Her curiosity piqued when he smiled at Jackson's response. Kate focused on Janie.

"Our friends from Turner's Glenn will be coming out on Wednesday and will be staying the night here to bring in the New Year with us."

"Will Lainey be with them?" Janie asked, excitedly. Lainey was seven years older than Janie, but the younger girl adored her.

"I would assume so. Belle and Elizabeth are both coming, and I doubt they would leave Lainey at home."

"Miss Elizabeth too? So I'll get to see Benjamin and Hannah?"

"Yes, ma'am," Kate replied, "but come, we must be on our way."

"Yay!" Janie said, then turned to General Jackson. "I'm sorry, General Jackson. I must leave now, but don't you worry, I'll see you tomorrow!"

"I do hope so, Miss Janie," Jackson replied.

"Miss Corbin, it would be an honor to escort you both back to the house." Captain Pendleton offered.

"Thank you, Captain." Kate smiled and the group of three started making their way to the manor house.

"I am delighted to tell you, Miss Corbin that General Jackson approved of my taking tea with you and your sister tomorrow."

"That's wonderful! I will be looking forward to it." Kate smiled.

"As will I." Captain Pendleton replied. "It sounds as though you will have some very special visitors for the coming holiday. Are the Turners close friends?"

Kate clutched her hands in her muff, thinking about the visitors. She loved Belle dearly, but her friend had a way of drawing men to her without even trying, even more so than Kate. Would Captain Pendleton fall for Belle if they met? She was unattached now, and out of mourning. Maybe Kate should tell Belle of her feelings for the Captain, even though she wasn't quite sure of them herself. Belle was flirtatious, but she would respect Kate's feelings.

"Yes," Kate finally replied. "My dear friends Belle and Elizabeth with their family. They have three sisters and a brother. They had an older brother, James, but he was wounded in battle and died at a hospital in Richmond. Elizabeth is married and has a daughter and a son. Her husband, Joshua and their father, Matthew are with the 30th Virginia."

"That will be quite the group." The captain said.

"It will be," Kate replied. "Especially since I have also invited my friend America Joan and her sister, but they live across the river, so it may be more of a challenge for them to attend."

"With the Yankees over there, yes, it probably will be." Captain Pendleton agreed as they approached the front porch.

"Thank you for the escort, Captain Pendleton," Kate said. The man smiled, gently pulled her gloved hand from her muff, and kissed it.

"Until tomorrow." He said, looking into her eyes. He then turned to Janie, bent over, and kissed her hand as well. "Miss Janie, it is always a pleasure."

Janie giggled. "Good-bye, Captain." She said. As he walked away, Janie turned to Kate. "I like him, Aunt Kate."

"I think I might too, Janie," Kate replied. "I think I might too."

Tuesday, December 30, 1862
Moss Neck Manor

Three-o-clock couldn't come any sooner for Kate. She felt so nervous. She liked Captain Pendleton, but it was no more than she liked Stockton Heth. Or was it? Bertie was unable to come to tea, as she was busy making arrangements for the New Year's Eve gathering. Kate was lucky that Nettie would be able to chaperone them.

"He's here!" Gardiner entered the parlor, a huge grin on his face. "Captain Sandie is here!"

"I can't say as I have ever had such an enthusiastic introduction." The captain smiled at Gardiner as he entered the room. "Thank you, kind sir."

"You're welcome." Gardiner gave the captain a quick salute, then turned and ran off. Captain Pendleton turned to Kate. "Miss Corbin, your nephew is quite delightful."

"Thank you. I agree." Kate replied.

"I know he will break his share of hearts when he is older," Nettie added as she entered the room with a tray of tea. They all sat and Nettie began pouring.

"Yes, he probably will," Captain Pendleton said. "Miss Janie will be quite the young lady as well"

"She certainly will be, Captain." Nettie smiled. "Tell us about yourself. Have you always planned on a career in the military, or has the war altered your plan?"

"I was pursuing a Master of Arts degree at the University of Virginia when the war broke out, but I believe I have taken to soldiering quite well. I am from Alexandria. The only son in my family of seven children and before you ask, yes, I do have six sisters."

"Ahh, no wonder you are so comfortable with the ladies," Nettie observed.

"I suppose that is true." The Captain took a sip of his tea. "They are all very dear to me. I try and write them as often as possible."

"You are a letter writer?" Kate remarked. Not only was he educated, but he built treasured relationships. It spoke well of him.

"Yes, I am. I enjoy receiving letters as well, but the mail is terribly unreliable."

"We've learned that as well," Kate told him. "Even sending letters from here to Richmond. I have a dear friend there, Sallie Munford. I write to her as often as possible, but, like you said, I am never quite sure they are received."

"It is one of the annoyances of this war," Nettie said.

"One of many." Captain Pendleton said, looking down at his cup.

Kate wondered about his downcast look. She knew war carried many horrors and she could not imagine what the captain may have witnessed. He looked almost haunted at a memory.

"We have the Yankees on their heels from what I understand," Kate said. "We can only pray to God that this conflict will end soon."

Sandie looked up when Kate mentioned God. "You are a Believer, Miss Corbin?"

"Of course, Captain." She replied. "We attend the Episcopalian Church in Fredericksburg, even though it has been more difficult to do so this winter."

"Miss Corbin, if you ever want to hold a Sunday service here at Moss Neck, I guarantee that you will have many of the Stonewall Brigade in attendance. If you would like, you can consider yourself invited to the services we hold. I believe you are familiar with General Jackson's chaplain, Reverend Lacy."

"We do know the Reverend, of course. He is a fine, upstanding man." It was a good thing, Kate thought, that Captain Pendleton was a Christian.

"I do hope Bertie agrees to have services here. She is more of a worldly woman as opposed to a woman of the Lord." Nettie commented.

"That may be true, Nettie, but I still don't think she would object," Kate replied hopefully. "If not, we'll just have to join the officers wherever they worship."

"Again, you would be more than welcome." The captain replied.

"I understand that General Jackson is a very spiritual man," Kate commented.

"You would be correct." Captain Pendleton replied. "He is one of the most fervent Christians I know." The soldier paused. "Truly, he is dedicated to the Lord in such a way...well, let's just say that our world would do well if we had more men like him."

"Indeed, if we had more soldiers like him, we may have already won the war," Nettie said.

"That is something I truly believe." Captain Pendleton agreed. He pulled out a pocket watch to check the time. "Ladies, as much as I have enjoyed this visit, I am afraid I must take my leave."

"We completely understand," Kate said, rising when he did. "I am glad you were able to join us, even for this short amount of time."

"I hope the invitation will be extended again." He said with a smile.

"Most definitely. That can be arranged." Kate smiled back.

"Until next time, then." The captain nodded at Nettie. "Mrs. Dickenson, as always a pleasure." He gently touched Kate's elbow. "Miss Corbin."

"Take care of yourself now, Captain," Kate said.

"Please, call me Sandie." He replied.

"All right then, take care of yourself, Sandie," Kate replied. After he had left, Nettie approached her sister.

"He seems like a very special young man." She said. "Very agreeable."

"Yes," Kate said, trying to hide her blush. "I daresay he is."

Wednesday, December 31, 1862
Moss Neck Manor

New Year's Eve Day was cool but nice enough that the Turners were able to enjoy the ride as they made their way to Moss Neck Manor.

"I am so relieved to be away from that house. Utter madness." Belle said, after greeting Bertie, Nettie, and Kate. The ladies had settled down into the parlor of the main house. Daniel had taken their overnight luggage to the rooms that were still available as refugees from the town still occupied Moss Neck Manor.

"You're just glad to be away from Dr. Knightly," Annie said, teasing in her voice.

"What is going on with Dr. Knightly?" Kate asked. She couldn't help but notice the irritated look Belle gave Annie

"Nothing is going on," Belle replied. "He's still arrogant."

"Belle. Please behave like a lady." Miriam chastised her daughter.

Kate quickly changed the subject and turned to Elizabeth. "Are you able to see Joshua often?"

"He and Father both have been able to visit in their spare time, but Turner's Glenn is so crowded that they return to their winter hut each evening. Our home in the city is still in ruins, but we have been able to clear the area a bit with the help of Eric. I hope you don't mind, but Joshua has promised to come to Moss Neck tonight."

"Of course we don't mind," Kate said with a smile. "The more the merrier."

The door opened and AJ and Liberty entered the room.

"AJ! Liberty! You made it!" Meri smiled

"We did, but it wasn't easy," AJ replied.

"Did you have a good Christmas?" Elizabeth asked.

"It was better than expected," Liberty said. "We saw Father on Christmas Eve and on Christmas Day, we were able to muster up a pretty good dinner. Nathaniel's friend James Spencer dropped by for a visit."

"We also witnessed a pretty interesting event," AJ told the story of the Union and Confederate soldiers celebrating Christmas together by sharing gifts.

"That's incredible, that they could converse with each other without fighting," Annie said.

"It was." AJ agreed. "It made me remember the true meaning of Christmas."

"It's too bad they'll likely forget about 'peace on earth, goodwill to all men' once the weather improves," Belle said.

"Yes. That is a true statement, Belle." AJ agreed, then changed the subject. "How was Christmas for everyone else?"

"We were able to have some special time as a family, I suppose," Belle said.

"The soldiers actually tried to make the holiday as nice as possible for us," Annie added.

"I am so glad to hear that." AJ turned to the Corbin family. "How was your holiday at Moss Neck?"

"It was quite enjoyable," Bertie said then explained to the group about General Jackson and his staff.

"You are so lucky to have gentlemen staying here," Belle said. "I haven't witnessed many displays of gentlemanly behavior at Turner's Glenn."

Elizabeth sighed and Annie tried not to roll her eyes. Why did Belle always have to be so negative?

"I don't know that I would say that." Elizabeth countered.

"Of course you wouldn't, Elizabeth," Belle said.

"Belle, don't you think that if the men you are in contact with weren't in so much pain, they would be more inclined to act like gentlemen," AJ said. "I have been visiting Yankees at Chatham and they are all quite miserable."

"Perhaps." Belle shrugged.

Liberty stood. "Meri, Annie, I am tired of seeing Yankees. I am actually quite interested in General Jackson and his men. Would you care to walk around? Maybe we can get a chance to meet him." Meri and Annie stood, as did Bertie.

"I need to check on the children and then I will go out with you. I can try to get an introduction and perhaps an audience." She turned to Miriam. "Mrs. Turner, would you like to join us? The General is quite an interesting gentleman."

"Of course. I would be delighted."

"Thank you, Mrs. Corbin," Liberty said, and they exited the room, along with Nettie who decided to check on dinner.

"Belle, should we discuss what's really vexing you?" AJ focused on her friend. "I know you. Honestly, the three of us here know you better than you know yourself."

"Yes, you three and James did," Belle said.

"We know, Belle," Kate said. "You have suffered terribly."

"Yes, you have," AJ added. "I am sorry about that, but instead of blaming the doctors and feeling bad about losing your brother and Samuel, why don't you do your best to ease the pain of the patients at your home? Think about it." AJ stood. "You could help others, the same way that others most likely helped James and Samuel."

Belle sighed. Deep down, she knew that AJ was correct, as usual.

"I suppose I can do a little bit more to help the wounded soldiers," Belle said. "I mean, by now, most of the horrible cases have been transferred."

Kate turned to Elizabeth. "Is it really that bad?"

"It has its moments of horror." She replied. "I saw things that I will never forget, but it has been...gratifying to be able to help, to lend some comfort to those who are in need, and I am learning so much." Elizabeth gave a quick glance to AJ, who met her friend's eyes. "We all have to do our part to help the war effort, to help our boys any way we can."

"Yes," AJ said. "Any way that we can."

Part 3:
1863

Friday, January 2, 1863
Moss Neck Manor

"Miss Corbin!" Sandie Pendleton exclaimed, smiling at Kate as she made her way to the General's headquarters. Bertie had asked her to check on Janie, who had once again gone down to visit General Jackson.

"Good afternoon, Captain Pendleton. It is such a pleasure to see you." Kate said with a smile of her own. "Did you enjoy your New Year's celebration?"

"I found myself in a tent on the banks of the river, sitting next to a comfortable fire, writing a letter to my mother." He offered her his arm. She slid her hand through his. Her heart skipped a beat.

"That actually sounds peaceful." She replied.

"Yes, it was. I was able to greet the new year in peace and solitude. I thought it a good omen. I mean..." he looked out across the camp. "I realize the people of Fredericksburg are far worse at this time than last year. What happened to your town is inconceivable. You have suffered horrible tragedies. I'm very sorry that you have had to go through this."

"I must confess, here at Moss Neck, we are actually better off than many other families. I spent my new year's celebration with some dear friends who are in a much worse situation than we are."

"Ahh, yes. I remember you spoke of them earlier."

"Yes, and I recall you mentioned that you often write home. Your mother and six sisters, correct? Is there anyone else that you write to?"

Sandie smiled, and Kate felt he knew exactly what she was trying to find out.

"Well, I must admit to you, that until recently, I was writing to a young woman, but...I believe God has someone else set aside for me." He gave her a sweet smile.

"I'm sure that he has the perfect woman in mind for a man like yourself."

"I am glad that you put me in such high regard." He said.

"I do, Captain." She replied. She found he wasn't classically handsome like Richard Evans or Samuel Gray and he didn't have the rugged good looks that James Turner had, but he was moderately good looking, with brown hair and eyes. She guessed him to be in his early twenties in spite of the fact that he already held one college degree and had been working on a second one when the war broke out. He had a strong sense of confidence about him and she noticed that others were drawn to him as well.

"Have you thought any more about joining us for Sunday services?" He asked.

"I have. I would like to and I will try to make it. I must persuade Bertie to come for a change. Nettie and her boys will probably want to join us. Parke and Gardiner will be excited to come and pray with the soldiers."

"Very good. Sundays are quite special to me." The two continued walking but had slowed their pace. Kate didn't mind. It was more time spent with a man that she was growing fonder of.

"I have realized that." She replied. "But I do wonder, what happens when your military duty interferes with your religious obligations?"

"It has happened on occasion, unfortunately. During this past year, I have spent eight Sundays on the battlefield. It is quite difficult for me to hear the sounds of battle and the cries of the wounded rather than singing praise to God and listening to Scripture."

"How trying for you. I had no idea how loud a battle was until last month and we were miles away." Kate commented. "I much prefer hymns of thanksgiving too."

"Agreed. I hope that at this time next year, I will be at home, enjoying Southern independence with my family."

"That is a fine goal," Kate said. They neared the General's headquarters. "Thank you so much, Captain Pendleton. As always, I enjoyed our discussion"

"As did I." He replied, then knocked once, pulled open the door and held it for her.

"Good afternoon, General," Kate said as the soldiers inside stood. Captain James Power Smith was with General Jackson.

"Miss Corbin. It is very good to see you." Jackson said. Janie's head poked up from behind the General's makeshift desk and grinned.

"Hello, Aunt Kate! It's not time to leave yet, is it?"

"Well, that all depends, dearest," Kate replied. "Are you being a nuisance to the General? He does have a lot of work to get done."

"Janie, as always, has been an absolute delight," Jackson said.

Kate smiled. "Well, then, I'll leave you here for a little while longer. Make sure you keep an eye on the clock and leave just before five to be home in time for dinner."

"Yes, ma'am," Janie said.

"Well, I will head back to the manor and see if I can be of assistance there." Kate addressed the gentlemen. "Some of the families who have been staying with us will be returning to their homes soon. I can't imagine how nice that will be for them."

"Miss Corbin, again, it is always a pleasure." Captain Pendleton turned to her, his next words quiet. "I would love to escort you home, but I must work on some reports for the General."

"I understand. I'm glad we had the opportunity to visit." Kate tucked a strand of hair behind her ear.

"As am I." He smiled. "Well, then until next time."

"Until then." She said, then turned to General Jackson and Captain Smith. "Have a wonderful rest of the day, gentlemen."

"Good day, Miss Corbin." They replied.

"Be good, Janie."

"Of course, Aunt Kate." She said with a grin. As Kate turned to leave, she felt Captain Pendleton's hand gently on her back. It was a polite, innocent gesture, something he did automatically, out of habit for all women of his acquaintance. In fact, she had likely been the recipient of such a gesture from other gentlemen. But she was so conscious of it, coming from Captain Pendleton.

"Ma'am." He smiled.

"Captain." She returned the smile and left, excited for when she would see him again.

Sunday, January 4, 1863
Turner's Glenn Plantation

"How was the service, Belle?" Miriam asked.

"It was enlightening," Belle answered. "I have been rather enjoying church the past few months. The pastor usually gives me some thoughts to consider. It is also nice to have some quiet time as well, especially with all of the bustle of our hospital home."

"It is quite busy. So much to do." As always, Miriam kept moving, from one task to another, and Belle had to step quickly to keep up with her. "I hope when things calm down a bit I will have time to attend with you and the rest of the family."

"Elizabeth always says that you should make time for church," Belle said, not sure why she was quoting her sister, but it felt right to do so.

"That sounds like Elizabeth. Where is she?"

"Since it is such a mild day, she, Joshua, Eric, and Meri stayed in town to clean up and do some repairs on their home. They likely won't be long. It's still winter and they will soon be chilled."

"Who drove the second wagon home?" Miriam asked, grabbing some soiled linens to bring to the kitchen to be washed.

"I did. I had to learn after all the slaves left." Belle tried not to show the pride in her voice.

"I'm very proud of you." Miriam smiled, now walking toward the stairwell. "Come with me. I'm going to do some laundry and I could use your help."

"Laundry? But it's Sunday, Mother." Belle made a face. She had thus far avoided that undesirable task. "Shouldn't I just go and do what I do best? Boost the morale of the patients? Talk with them, read to them, write letters for them?"

"You can do that later. Come. I've been meaning to talk with you, but we never seem to have time." Miriam insisted, and Belle couldn't tell her mother 'no'. She reached down and picked up a smelly, grimy pile of sheets in her arms and followed her mother downstairs.

Bennett Home

Elizabeth tugged the knit glove back onto her hand. It had half fallen off during the work she had been doing. She bent down to grab another piece of scrap wood and carried it to the wagon.

"How are you feeling, Elizabeth?" Joshua approached her and placed a hand on her back.

"I'm doing alright." She smiled as he leaned down to give her a brief kiss on the cheek.

"Elizabeth!" The voice of Lucy Beale Brent called out. Elizabeth turned and gave her friend a hug.

"Lucy, I am so glad to see that you're all right." She exclaimed.

"And I you! I was so worried when I saw what had become of your home."

"We went out to Turner's Glenn when the shelling started. How about you?"

"The day the fighting started, we hid in the basement of our home. Pastor Lacey was with us, much to Mama's comfort. He read us Psalm 27th."

"Very appropriate," Joshua said, a hand on the small of Elizabeth's back.

"Indeed," Lucy replied. "While he was reading, there was a terrible crash of glass and splintering of timber and Samuel was struck! He had a horrid-looking red mark on his chest. John thought it might be a brick that hit him, but we later found a solid 12-pound shot."

"My goodness." Elizabeth's hand flew to her mouth.

"Mother said the ball was likely nearly spent before it reached the room we were in. Just the slight interference of the window sash probably saved Samuel's life."

"Incredible," Meri said, joining the conversation. "How is the rest of the family? Marion?"

"Everyone else is fine. They're all with Mother now." Lucy continued. "I was terrified, especially with John and Mr. Lacy coming back and forth between us and the upstairs. John tried to comfort us. The servants were able to get us food and coffee and blankets. We spent 13 hours in the cellar in the middle of the winter. Horrid. Cold. Later, my Uncle John was able to get some ambulances to take us away. So much chaos. We went into the woods and then ended up at the Temple home. Mrs. Temple had to almost carry Mother into the house."

"I'm sure she must have been exhausted," Elizabeth said.

"She was indeed. We stayed there for the duration of the battle. John and the boys actually went to watch the battle. After Mother rested, she, Marion and I wandered around as well that evening. We returned home last week. Our house was damaged a little but is livable. Not at all like yours. My goodness, Elizabeth, whatever will you do?"

"We will rebuild." She said. "It will be slow going, but we'll do it. In the meantime, the children and I have been staying at Turner's Glenn. It's better to be with your family in times like these."

"I agree wholeheartedly," Joshua said, sliding his arm around Elizabeth's shoulders.

Turner's Glenn

"I have noticed some interesting interactions between you and Dr. Knightly," Miriam said, scrubbing at some bedsheets.

"Dr. Knightly and I? Never." Belle protestes. "He and I have nothing in common. If you're in reference to a marriage, I would prefer a Yankee soldier to Dr. Knightly. He is rude, prideful, arrogant, and vain, especially about his ability as a doctor."

"I have not noticed that at all," Miriam said. "He is a man who is confident in his abilities. True, he may be a little gruff at times, and he may not treat his staff well at times, but he is excellent with his patients. I find him to be a very modest and a fine doctor. His patient's welfare is most important to him."

"None of that is endearing him to me, mother, if I am being honest."

"There is more to a good marriage than love. Sometimes love doesn't happen right away, Belle. It can grow with time. That's how it happened with your father and me."

"You never really talk about the courtship between you and Father," Belle commented.

"You have never asked about it," Miriam replied.

"I know you met when Father was visiting Uncle Charles. That is really all I recall."

"Yes, we were in Vicksburg. We met at a social gathering. I fancied your father right away. He was not as taken with me. In fact, we were married for a full year before your father even told me that he loved me." Miriam's eyes watered a bit. "It was the day your brother James was born. It is a day I will never forget, for many reasons."

Belle gave her mother a puzzled look. "I always believed that you two loved each other when you were married."

"Your father was fond of me, of course, but it was more a marriage of necessity on his part. He felt that since he was the sole owner of Turner's Glenn, he needed a wife with money and knowledge to oversee the household and give him a son to inherit." She smiled. "We love each other deeply now. I know not all marriages of convenience turn out as well as ours did, but one never knows what God has planned."

"So you're telling me that I should marry for convenience, even if I don't love the man and hope things work out for the best?" Belle was confused. "What about Elizabeth's marriage? You were supportive of her love match, despite marrying beneath her. You are contradicting yourself, Mother."

"You know I am not saying you should just marry for convenience," Miriam said. "What I am saying is that love isn't the fluttering feelings or love at first sight you hear about. There is so much more. You need to look beyond the surface, know who the person is on the inside. I told you I liked your father immediately, but I had been observing him and found him to be quite different than he presented. In regards to Elizabeth...yes. They love each other immensely, but Joshua is her best friend, as well as her husband. Having a common belief and respect for each other is what is most important. You cannot make an immediate judgment about someone. I believe there's more to Dr. Knightly than what you're seeing."

Belle sighed. "If you say so, Mother. Oh, why must life be so complicated? I will attempt to be a little more approachable and tolerant of Dr. Knightly, and about all doctors."

Friday, January 16, 1863
Moss Neck Manor

"Welcome, Captain!" Kate opened the door and saw not just Captain Pendleton, but also Captain Smith and Dr. McGuire. "And you brought two other gentlemen with you. How wonderful!"

"Mrs. Dickenson sent a message saying she and Mrs. Corbin would be dining with us. She asked me to invite two friends so that we would have an even number of men and women at the table."

"Very good! However, Bertie is indisposed today, so she will not be joining us, but my friend America will. She lives across the river and rarely is able to come over due to the Yankee occupation."

"America? That is a unique name." Sandie said, quickly glancing at Captain Smith.

"Oh, it is. She has a sister named Liberty and her brother is named after George Washington and Nathan Hale. Her father is quite patriotic. We usually just call America 'AJ'."

"Interesting. It will be wonderful to meet another of your friends." The men followed Kate into the parlor.

"I was glad to hear all of the refugees were able to go back home." Captain Smith commented.

"Yes, it is. It's wonderful to have the house running normally." Kate said. "But they all know we would open our doors again to them if need be."

"Miss Corbin, we will do our best to make sure you never need to worry about that again." Dr. McGuire said. They walked into the parlor and Nettie and AJ stood.

"Gentlemen, you all know my sister, Mrs. Dickenson, but May I present Miss America Joan Prentiss." She turned to each of the men as she introduced them. "AJ, I am pleased to have you meet Captain James Power Smith, Captain Sandie Pendleton, and a most fascinating man, Dr. Hunter McGuire."

"Ma'am." Each of the men smiled and acknowledged her.

"Gentlemen. So nice to make your acquaintances." AJ tried to act as natural as possible. She had noticed the look that passed between the two officers. She knew they recognized her as the smuggler who had come with medicine from the Yankee encampment. She hoped they wouldn't say anything, especially with Nettie in the room. She sighed to herself. It seemed as though more and more people were learning about her secret missions.

They all sat down.

"Actually, Miss Corbin, you should know that our Sandie is a captain no more. He has recently been promoted to Major." Captain Smith smiled.

"How splendid!" Kate smiled. "Congratulations."

"Thank you," Sandie said. "I feel very fortunate to know that my superiors have faith in me."

"It is well-deserved." Dr. McGiure said.

"Well, congratulations again," Kate said. "Dinner is nothing fancy, but it should be filling." She smiled and gestured to AJ. "Miss Prentiss was kind enough to bring us some eggs."

"I'm happy to share." AJ turned to the soldiers. "It's just me and my younger sister at home, so we have some food to spare. My father and brother left the farm in our care when they enlisted. We are doing our best to grow what we can."

"It's very kind of you to share with neighbors." Captain Smith said. "You say your father and brother are gone, do you not have any slaves to assist you?"

"We had two field hands, but they ran off back in June when the Yankees first occupied."

"That's reprehensible," Smith said. "Have you heard that abolitionist Lincoln, has now freed all slaves with his proclamation, as if we even have to listen to his tyrannical decrees."

"JP, you do realize it is just a political move. Morality has nothing to do with it." McGuire said. "He has officially made the war about ending slavery, even though it is more about our own rights as states. This proclamation is meant to turn our European allies against us."

"That is true, Lincoln may have forced Great Britain to officially stop supporting our cause. We may lose the supplies and money they have been sending us." Sandie added. "They will not ally themselves with a country that is supporting slavery."

A knock sounded at the door and everyone looked to see Delia, one of the house slaves who had remained with the family. "Dinner is ready," she announced. They all stood and the men escorted the women into the dining room. Major Pendleton immediately claimed Kate, Dr. McGuire escorted Nettie, and Captain Smith assisted AJ. They sat and, as they were served, continued their conversation.

"Miss Prentiss, do you and your sister manage to bring in a profitable crop?" Captain Smith asked.

"As with all of the farmers and planters, we are no longer profitable, but we do manage."

"I don't know how you manage it, AJ. So many of the farms over there have been taken over and pillaged by the Yankees." Nettie commented. "I must say, I don't understand why the Yankees have left you alone."

"To be honest," AJ said, wishing this part of the conversation would end. "Liberty and I decided during the first occupation how best to survive. We thought if we would be kind and cooperative with the Yankee commanders by offering them our eggs and other dairy products at a fair price, we could keep our few animals and make a little money at the same time."

"Why, Miss Prentiss, I didn't know that!" Nettie exclaimed. "It's almost as if you are aiding the enemy."

Before AJ had a chance to defend herself, both Captain Smith and Major Pendleton spoke up.

"No, I don't think so." Major Pendleton said.

"I wouldn't say that at all." Captain Smith said at the same time.

"I completely understand Miss Prentiss's logic." The major said with a quick glance at Captain Smith. "Our women must be able to feed their families. I would call this self-preservation. I don't hold that against you, Miss. I actually find it quite resourceful."

"Nor I." Captain Smith agreed. "It is a shame that you have to resort to supporting the Yankees, but you must look after your family. It's better for you to make money rather than them taking whatever they want without compensating you."

AJ smiled in gratitude for the two soldiers.

"Well, AJ, while I understand why you're selling to the Yankees and I appreciate your sharing with us, it may be best if you don't tell too many townspeople what you're doing," Kate said, concern apparent in her voice. "I worry what they will think of you."

"I don't plan on announcing it at Mass on Sunday," AJ said. "But neither do I plan on hiding the fact that I must deal with the Yankees as best I can. I won't lie if the topic comes up."

Kate nodded. "I would expect no less from you. She glanced at Major Pendleton as she took a bite of venison. He caught her eye over a glass of water. When he set the water down, he gave her a smile. Her heart gave a little flutter, as it often did when their gazes met.

"I think that's admirable." Captain Smith said, giving AJ a smile. "Many women wouldn't have the foresight to be so clever in their business. You have been able to keep your property by selling to the Yankees and as you said, have managed to make a small profit." He gave her a look that told her he definitely recognized her and knew that she was getting more than just money from the Yankee invaders. She smiled back. Captain Smith seemed the perfect gentleman, as did the doctor and Major Pendleton, but unless AJ was completely wrong, Major Pendleton was already engaged in building a relationship. She had noticed both Kate and the major glancing at each other throughout the evening.

The conversation changed back to the war, and the two opposing armies facing each other across the river. The soldiers were reticent about the Confederacy's future plans, but they assured the ladies that they would be protected.

All too soon, Dr. McGuire looked at his watch and announced that the soldiers must return to duty and AJ had to start heading home as well.

"I'm so glad you stopped by," Kate said, giving AJ a hug. The officers had offered to escort her to the raft she and Liberty had constructed so they could cross the Rappahannock, but she didn't want anyone to know its location, so she declined.

"I'm glad you invited me!" AJ replied. "I do wish we could visit more often." She smiled. "Make sure you give Bertie my best!"

Saturday, January 17, 1863
Turner's Glenn

"How could I have missed this?" Annie groaned as she looked in the mirror. The evening gown she had tried on was a little tight and there was a small tear in the front of the dress along a seam. "I can't go to the party like this." Annie usually didn't worry much about fashion, but the older Turner sisters had been invited to a starvation party at the Gordon home in town and she wanted to look nice.

"Don't fret, Annie," Elizabeth said, coming over to examine the issue. "We should be able to fix this without any problem."

"Why are they calling it a starvation party?" Lainey asked, lying on her stomach on the bed, watching her sisters get ready.

"Because we're going to do everything that we used to do at a party except eat," Belle explained. "I don't even think they'll serve wine. Perhaps some punch." She stood next to Elizabeth to look at Annie's dress.

"Probably no wine, as no one has wine anymore," Annie said, hands on her hips.

"Here, I have an idea," Meri said, approaching her sisters. She held up a pin and a piece of black ribbon. The ribbon would match Annie's green silk dress with black trim. "If we pin this strategically, we can cover the tear." Meri worked as she was explaining, then made some quick adjustments to the ribbon. Annie stepped back so her sisters could see the dress.

"That works," Belle said with a smile. "It actually looks quite good. It accentuates your waist and gives the dress more depth."

"Thank you so much, Meri!" Annie turned and looked in the mirror.

"It seems strange to be wearing evening gowns that we haven't worn in over a year," Belle said, looking at herself in the mirror and patting her hair.

"Yes, the war has put a damper on our social gatherings. They don't seem as important as they used to be." Elizabeth said.

"We have realized how important the small things can be." Annie gave Meri a quick hug.

The Gordon's had made their home, Kenmore, look as nice as possible. Shells had struck the house during the bombardment but had caused no serious damage. They had decided to entertain with a party to boost the morale of both the Confederate soldiers and the townspeople.

"It is so nice to gather together like this," Kate said, looking at AJ, Elizabeth, and Belle. "I feel as though I say it every time we see each other, but it's true."

"I feel the same way, Kate," Belle said. "Are any of the officers from Moss Neck attending?"

"I don't believe so," Kate replied. "It's quite a distance for them to travel and there are quite a few of them. It would have been nice if some of them could attended."

"I'm sure you have one in particular that you really would have liked to be here." AJ smiled.

"Perhaps," Kate said with a small smile. "Are any of the men from Turner's Glenn coming to the party?"

"I believe a couple of doctors," Elizabeth said. "Dr. Andrews and possibly Dr. Knightly."

"Dr. Knightly?" Belle asked. "That shocks me. I would not believe he could be away from his patients for that amount of time."

"Belle, be kind," Elizabeth said. "We want to have an enjoyable evening tonight."

"I suppose," Belle said, then surveyed the room. As she looked around, she saw a familiar soldier making his way towards them.

"Ladies." Richard Evans smiled at them. "It's so good to see you all this evening. How are you fairing?"

"Quite well, Mr. Evans," Belle said with a smile. She immediately took the lead of the conversation. AJ inwardly sighed and glanced around the room. She saw Joshua Bennett enter and nudged Elizabeth. Her friend smiled and excused herself, then went directly to her husband. When AJ turned back around to focus on Richard, Kate, and Belle, she found Richard had already escorted Belle onto the dance floor.

"That happened quickly," AJ commented dourly.

"It was bound to happen eventually," Kate said, then noticed AJ's change in demeanor. She put a comforting hand on her shoulder. "AJ, you'll find that special someone. We all will."

"I know." AJ smiled with a trace of sadness. "It seems as though you may have already found yours."

"Perhaps. One never knows." Kate said. Another familiar soldier approached the two.

"Miss Corbin. How are you this evening?"

"I'm quite well, Mr. Heth. It's good to see you again." She smiled. "You remember Miss America Prentiss."

"Of course." He smiled at AJ. "It's nice to see you again as well." He focused on Kate. "Miss Corbin, may I have this dance?"

"Of course, Mr. Heth." Kate smiled and took his hand, then went to the dance floor.

AJ sighed, looking at her three best friends on the dance floor with handsome gentlemen. One of those gentlemen made her heart skip a beat, but she could not fathom why. AJ knew he wasn't what she wanted or needed, and what's more, she knew he likely never would be interested in her. Why did she continually let him affect her?

Out of the corner of her eye, AJ noticed Annie Turner make her way to the side door. She looked as though she was fleeing from something, and also as if she was going to start crying.

The music stopped. "The band is going to take a break. Who is ready for some parlor games?" Someone asked. "Charades first or lookabout?"

"How about forfeits?" Someone else asked.

AJ always enjoyed parlor games, but it didn't look like anyone else had noticed Annie. She quickly made a decision and followed the young woman.

Annie sat on a bench outside the back of the house, looking out toward the gardens. When she saw AJ approach, she wiped at her eyes.

"AJ. What brings you out here?"

"It was too warm. I needed some fresh air." AJ smiled, pulling her shawl a little closer. "What happened, Annie?" She sat down.

"It's nothing. Really." She paused. "Nothing out of the ordinary, that is."

"Parties like this aren't really something you enjoy, are they?"

"Not really, no," Annie admitted. She tried to smile, but it was weak.

"Tell me what happened tonight that has upset you."

"I just...I always think that each social gathering will be different from the last one. I have such high expectations, but then, when I arrive, it is always the same as before. I get ignored or if I do get asked to dance, it's by someone who is simply trying to be kind. Other times, I feel I am simply someone's diversion for the evening."

"Which of the two happened tonight?" AJ asked.

"A new one, actually." She replied. "One of the soldiers was talking with me for quite some time. We danced a few times, I thought he was taken with me. What a fool I was." She shook her head. "He asked me to introduce him to Belle. That is why he was talking with me." She gave a short laugh. "When will a man want me for me, AJ? I know I'm no great beauty, but..."

"Annie, you will have a man fall in love with you someday. You are a wonderful young woman with many talents." AJ gave her a brief smile. "I know how you feel. There are many times I feel the same way. Your sister has unknowingly stolen many a potential suitor from me, but you and I are actually quite blessed. We don't have to rush to the altar as society says. We don't have fathers who want to dictate and control our lives."

"That is true," Annie said. "Elizabeth marrying Joshua is proof that my parents aren't concerned with getting their daughters an advantageous marriage."

"Exactly." AJ smiled. Annie still looked despondent. "God has a wonderful plan for the both of us. Plans to give us hope and a future."

"From Jeremiah, correct?" Annie gave a small smile.

"Yes, it is," AJ said. "No matter what we're going through, God is with us. And He always will be. Now, let's dry those eyes and go back inside and enjoy ourselves. It's getting cold out here."

Wednesday, February 18, 1863
Moss Neck Manor

"I am so glad that you could come for a visit, Belle. It has been far too long since we have been able to just sit and chat." Kate led her friend into the parlor.

"It has been nearly a month." Belle agreed. "I will not lie to you, though. I would enjoy meeting General Jackson and some of his officers. I have yet to meet these friends of yours that I have been hearing so much about. I must see if any of them are worthy enough for you, Kate."

"I believe they are all very good friends, maybe one or another could catch our fancy. Major Pendleton is especially attentive to me, while still doing his duties for the General. He is not wasting any time trying to court me, Belle. He is an excellent soldier. Amusing. Religious. I must confess, even though so many others are suffering, this winter has been like a dream for me. So many of Jackson's officers visit here, but there are no formal parties or gatherings, excepting the one a few weeks ago." Kate said. "However, the officer I favor the most is Captain Pendleton. A Virginian too, of good background."

"I don't begrudge you happiness," Belle said. 'You deserve it., Kate"

"Thank you ever so much for saying that." Kate smiled

"This Major Pendleton sounds like the kind of man who is very worthy of your attentions." Belle thought of Samuel, but then Dr. Knightly appeared in her mind. Did she even know where he was from? Had she ever even bothered to ask? He had not attended the starvation party at Kenmore. She had been offended at first, but then had learned that one of his patients had taken a turn for the worst. Dr. Knightly hadn't wanted to leave the dying soldier.

"I believe he is worthy of my attention." Kate agreed with Belle's previous statement.

337

"How are you passing your time? What diversions occupy you and the men?" Belle asked.

"We have a great deal of music, but no dances. Some of the gentlemen, Major Pendleton included, have fine voices. One of the best bands in the Corps is camped not too far from here."

"That is fortuitous," Belle said. "I know how much you enjoy music."

"Yes," Kate said. "I had heard and read about General Jackson and his men prior to the battle, but I never dreamed that I would come to know them so well. I have developed a deep affection for them all. So noble and brave."

"They will tell their children
Though all other memories fade
That they fought with Stonewall Jackson
In the old Stonewall Brigade"

Belle quoted the popular poem Song of the Rebel. "Just think. That poem could be in reference to your future." Belle smiled when Kate blushed.

"Perhaps." She said quietly. "I recently posted a letter to Sally Munford and asked her if she would purchase a little Bible, suitable for a gentleman soldier, as well as a first-rate pocket knife. Do you think it will be too forward of me to give such gifts?"

"Are the gifts for Major Pendleton or do you have someone else in mind?

"The major, of course," Kate replied.

"I think it is a good idea to ask Sally to make the purchases. She will be able to find a larger variety in Richmond than you could here, especially now."

"Yes, that's what I was thinking," Kate said. The two looked up at the knock on the door. One of the Moss Neck servants entered, followed by two distinguished looking Confederate officers.

"Major! Doctor! How nice of you to stop in." Kate said as she and Belle stood.

"It has been much too long since we have been able to enjoy your company, Miss Corbin." The soldier with dark blonde hair smiled at Kate in such a way that told Belle he must be Major Pendleton.

"I agree. I am so glad you are here. Dr. McGuire, I believe you are already acquainted with Miss Isabelle Turner."

"Yes, Ma'am, we have met." The red-haired doctor smiled and nodded. "How is my friend and former student, Dr. Knightly?"

"Quite well as far as I know," Belle replied.

338

"Belle, I am pleased to introduce you to Major Alexander Pendleton. Better known as Sandie Pendleton." Kate said.

"It is a pleasure to finally meet you, Miss Turner." Captain Pendleton said with a slight bow."

"Likewise, Major." Belle gave him a small curtsey. "I have heard much about you. All good, of course."

"That is a relief to hear." The foursome sat down and fell into casual conversation, discussing the war, other current events and family.

"My father is a graduate of West-Point. He was a professor and minister prior to the war." Captain Pendleton explained. "When he was called to serve, he was quickly elected captain of the Rockbridge Artillery. My family hails from Alexandria, Virginia and I am quite close to my mother and six sisters. I miss them dearly."

"Six sisters!" Belle exclaimed. "Why, Major, it's no wonder you're such a charmer. You are much like my brother, who has five sisters." She gave him a flirtatious smile. "I find it hard to believe that you're still unmarried."

Kate gave Belle an annoyed look, but Belle wanted to find out more about the young man that Kate was falling for.

"I must be honest with you, Miss Turner. I have been engaged before, to a Miss Burwell of Winchester. However, I realized that I felt not love, only infatuation. I debated on breaking the engagement as I did not want to shirk my obligation. I was most fortunate however, when Miss Burwell decided to end the relationship instead. To this day, I am not sure why she did so, but am glad of it. Rest assured, I have learned a good and valuable lesson. I will never again enter into another engagement so lightly. If and when I propose again, it will be to the woman I dearly love." He looked intently at Kate when he spoke those last words. Belle was impressed and quite satisfied with his answer.

"That says a lot about you as a person, Major. To admit your mistakes."

"I have always believed that one should learn from their mistakes and the mistakes that they see others make." Major Pendleton said. "If everyone did so, the world would be a much better place."

"I couldn't have said it better." Kate smiled.

When Belle rose to depart, Dr. McGuire offered to escort her back so he could check on the doctors and patients there. After they left, Kate and Major Pendleton were left alone in the parlor.

"Should I find another man to chaperone the two of us?" Major Pendleton asked.

"The door is open and the servants, as well as my sisters, all have access to the room. We should be just fine." Kate smiled, touched once again by his gentlemanly manners.

"Very good." Major Pendleton stood and walked over to the window.

"What's troubling you?" Kate asked. "You seem distressed."

"I have some news that I am not looking forward to sharing with you." He turned to face her. "I have dearly enjoyed our time together. Getting to know you has truly been a blessing in my life that I will always cherish."

"I concur with your statement, Major," Kate said. Her heart began beating a bit faster. What was he preparing to tell her that could make him so nervous?

"I would like it if you would call me Sandie." He approached her.

"All right. Sandie. I believe we have known each other long enough." She smiled. "You must call me Catherine. Or Kate, if you prefer."

"Catherine. I like how that sounds." He took a deep breath.

"It won't be long before we move out. I am not sure when, but it will be soon. General Jackson himself is unsure of the place or time. It has, however, made me realize that my stay here will come to an end soon. I do not wish to leave you."

"I do not know what we shall do with all of you gone!" Kate stood. Sandie took her hands in his. "I will miss our constant visitors and..." her voice cracked. "I will hate desperately to part with you."

"Catherine, we haven't known each other for very long, but I have developed feelings for you. I would like to speak to your father and ask him permission for your hand if that's acceptable to you."

"You may speak to him, Sandie. I know he will defer to my wishes and I must tell you that I will need some time to think on this. I care for you, but marriage is not something that I will enter into lightly."

"I respect that. I completely understand." Sandie brought her hand to his lips and gently kissed it. "I must return to my duties. I will visit you again when I have the time." He smiled.

"Take care of yourself, Major...Sandie." She rose on her toes and gave him a gentle kiss on the cheek, then turned and left the room.

Friday, February 20, 1863
Moss Neck Manor

"Sandie! What a pleasant surprise!" Kate went to the man and gave him a brief embrace.

He smiled, retaining a hold on her hand. "It's a beautiful day. Could I interest you in a stroll outside?"

"Of course." She answered. Their most recent conversation had caused Kate to really start pondering her future. She admired Sandie immensely but was still unsure of her true feelings. Stockton Heth had also made it clear that he was interested in courting her, and she was undecided about whether she cared more for Sandie or Stockton. "Give me a moment. I would like to get my shawl."

"Of course, Catherine."

She retrieved her shawl and the gifts she had asked Sally to get for her then joined Sandie on the front porch. He offered her his arm and they began walking.

"Is there any further news on when you may be leaving us?" Kate asked.

"We will likely start marching to our new position by the middle of March. You and I have only a month more to spend together."

"Not nearly long enough." Kate lamented. She needed more time with Sandie. She needed to know if she loved him or not.

"I agree," Sandie added. "If I had more time today, I would ride to your father's home and speak to him about our future." He grimaced. "I haven't had the chance to do so yet. Have you thought any more on the subject?"

"I have been thinking of little else." She admitted. "However, I still do not have a definite answer for you. I admire and respect you deeply, I enjoy your company immensely, but I'm not sure I love you yet."

Sandie looked a bit disheartened by her response. "Then we will have to remedy that." He changed his demeanor. "It was good to meet Miss Turner the other day. Both Miss Turner and Miss Prentiss appear to be delightful young women."

"They are. I am quite privileged to call them friends. Belle's sister, Elizabeth is also very dear to me, and I have another close confidante, Sally Munford. She lives in Richmond. I met her when I attended Mrs. Powell's School for Girls. I miss her, but write her often."

"It sounds as though you are blessed with an abundance of good friends." He smiled, thinking of his own friends. "It seems strange, but some of my closest relationships have developed as a result of this war. James Smith, Henry Douglas, Hunter McGuire. Men that have become like brothers to me."

341

"I would imagine fighting together would create a very strong bond," Kate commented.

"It does. I would give my life for any one of them." His tone was a bit somber.

"I do hope it never comes to that," Kate said. "Isn't it safer to be a general, or on the general's staff?"

"Safer than a regular in the infantry, perhaps, but generals and officers are still wounded and killed. In fact, I was slightly wounded myself during the battle here in December."

"I wasn't aware of that!" Kate exclaimed. "What happened?"

"A minié ball struck me. It went through my uniform and was stopped by a knife that was in my pocket. My father said that the wound would have been fatal, had the knife not been there."

"Oh my word, Sandie!"

Her concern touched him. He stopped and faced her. "It's all right. I was stiff and a bit bruised, but I was able to report the next day."

A barrage of feelings cascaded through Kate. The thought that Sandie could easily have died...it was difficult to think of. She was relieved he had been spared, otherwise, she wouldn't have met him. She was also concerned because, while he had survived that injury, the next time, he may not be so lucky. He was a soldier. A part of her wanted to throw her arms around him and tell him that she would marry him today, another part of her wanted to break off their friendship so she could forget about him and spare herself the pain she would feel if he were to be killed. She reached up and touched his cheek with her gloved hand.

"That is a relief. Such a relief. So many men were lost those three days and the destruction of all the property. It made me wonder if men on both sides had lost their humanity."

"It sometimes seems that way." He completely focused on her, his eyes searching hers. "However, even in times of war, we can often see great mercy." She brought her hand down and he took both of her hands in his. "Did you hear about the Angel of Marye's Heights?" He led her to a crumbling stone wall, laid his overcoat over it, and then gestured for her to sit.

"I did not. I know there was terrible fighting there. Over eight-thousand Yankees were killed in that area alone."

"Yes." He sat next to her. "In the early morning before daylight of the 14th, many wounded Yankees were lying in the field between the stone wall and the canal, crying out for help, moaning, begging for water. No one dared move for fear of being shot at. A soldier from South Carolina by the name of Richard Kirkland couldn't stand the cries for help anymore. He jumped over the stone wall by the sunken road, carrying canteens that he took from his fellow soldiers. He actually risked his life going from wounded Yankee to wounded Yankee, giving them water, along with any warm clothing or blankets that he could find. Neither side fired a shot during this time. They both realized what Kirkland was doing. Many men cheered for him. He didn't rest until every wounded soldier possible had been given water." He paused. "Kirkland is a true hero."

"He is indeed," Kate said. "You are right. That does show great caring and compassion. Did the man survive?"

"He did. He is encamped with the 2nd South Carolina Volunteers."

"What a wonderful story," Kate said. "Thank you for sharing it with me. The fact that neither army shot at him also shows us some true heroism on both sides."

"I felt, it important for you to hear," Sandie said. "War is terrible, but that doesn't mean all men are terrible. Besides." He smiled and looked deep into her eyes. "Had it not been for the battle here, I would never have had the pleasure of meeting you."

"Now that is a true statement, Sandie," Kate said, leaning a bit closer to him. She found herself growing fonder of the man every moment. He was in a good position to win her heart. "I have something for you." She withdrew a package from her inside pocket and handed it to him. He couldn't suppress the smile at the prospect of a gift from her. The smile grew even wider when he saw the package contained the little bible and pocket knife.

"What a perfectly thoughtful gift!" He turned and touched her cheek. "Thank you so much." He stood and pulled her up into an embrace. She relished the feeling of being in his arms. She felt safe and protected. She slid her arms around his waist and held him tightly.

"I wish I could stay..." Sandie pulled slightly back and looked into her eyes. "I am so touched, Kate. You have no idea how much this means to me." He brushed a strand of hair back from her face. "I..."

"Aunt Kate! Aunt Kate!" Gardiner ran up to the couple. "Mama told me to come get you."

Sandie quickly released her and stepped away.

"Yes. What does she need?" Kate's heart fluttered.

"It's almost dinner. She wanted me to ask if Major Pendleton would want to stay and eat with us."

"Oh, Kate, I really wish I could, but unfortunately, I cannot." Sandie looked at his pocket watch. "I must report back soon." He tipped his hat to Gardiner. "Thank you for the invitation, young man. Another time, perhaps. Run and give your mother my regrets."

Gardiner nodded and ran back to tell his mother.

"I will see you soon, I hope." Kate smiled.

343

"Yes. I will count down the moments until I see you again." He smiled back.

Wednesday, February 25, 1863
Grace Episcopal Church

AJ, Kate, Belle, and Elizabeth all sat in a circle at the church, talking and sewing.

"I am so glad that we were able to get together," AJ said. "On a Wednesday, no less."

"I don't know how you manage to get here," Belle commented. "It's difficult to believe the Yankees allow you to even cross the river."

"They understand my need to attend Mass every week. Our idea of cooking and doing chores for the Yankees has been beneficial in many ways. They tend to give us more leniency because they trust us."

"I know it rankles me, but it truly was a good idea," Belle said.

"I heard at church Sunday that word of our ordeal has been reported in newspapers across the South," Elizabeth said. "Citizens and soldiers alike are contributing money for rebuilding."

"How generous," Kate said.

"Yes, Mayor Slaughter is leading the fundraising, as well as deciding who needs the funds. He's forming a committee to help make decisions." She smiled. "He offered money to Joshua, saying that the town will need the Bennett Blacksmith shop open soon. We told him we will repair the shop first so Eric can get back to work then slowly get our home back in order."

"That is magnanimous," Belle said. "I don't necessarily want you and the children to leave Turner's Glenn, though. I'm getting used to having the Bennett family around."

"We'll be at Turner's Glenn for a while, don't you worry." Elizabeth smiled. "I feel safer, being with family."

"Miss Corbin!" Sandie entered the room.

The four women stood.

"Good afternoon, Sandie," Kate said. "You have met Miss Belle Turner and Miss America Prentiss." She gestured towards Elizabeth. "This is my friend and Belle's sister, Mrs. Joshua Bennett."

"Elizabeth." She smiled and nodded. "It's a pleasure to finally meet you, Major Pendleton. I have heard so much about you."

"The pleasure is all mine, Mrs. Bennett." He smiled. "Forgive me, but are you familiar with the writings of Jane Austen?" The four women giggled.

Elizabeth smiled back. "Yes, sir, I am. We all know how amusing my married name is, as you can tell by the reaction of these women here.

That's all right, though, I dearly love Jane Austen and all her novels. 'Pride and Prejudice' is my favorite."

"I am intrigued as to how you know of Jane Austen, Sandie," Kate said. "Do tell."

"Six sisters, my dear Kate. You recall that I have six sisters."

"Ah, yes," Kate said with a smile. "Would you care to join us, Sandie? You aren't preparing to leave already, are you?"

"No, ma'am, not yet. We have another couple of weeks."

"Will all of the Confederate forces be leaving?" Belle asked.

"The soldiers will eventually, yes. Unfortunately, Miss Turner, your home will likely stay a hospital. It's difficult getting all the wounded back to Richmond. Until your patients have a change in their condition they will stay on."

"That has become apparent," Elizabeth added. "We're still getting new men in daily. Mostly sick with illness now or from wounds that won't heal."

"From what Dr. McGuire says, more men have been dying from illness and disease than from wounds sustained in battle," Sandie said. He noticed the angry face on Belle but didn't question her further. He then focused on Kate. "I stopped by specifically to speak with you, Miss Corbin. Could I take a few moments of your time? Privately?"

"Of course." She looked at her friends. "If you'll excuse me."

"Ladies," Sandie said. "It was good to see you again. I hope this is not the last time before my division leaves."

The women watched the couple exit the room.

"Hm." Belle smiled. "Elizabeth, perhaps before long, you won't be the only one of us married."

"Perhaps." Elizabeth smiled back. "I do hope everything works out well for those two. He certainly seems taken by her."

"He does." AJ agreed. "I believe he is perfect for her as well. Very kind and polite."

"I agree." Belle stood and made her way to the window and looked out. "Drat. I cannot see where they've gone to."

"Isabelle Turner, you give them some privacy." Elizabeth scolded.

Belle turned from the windows. "You are no fun." She sighed. "Kate is quite fortunate to have caught the fancy of such a gentleman."

"What is it you wanted to speak to me about?" Kate asked although she felt she already knew.

"I was able to speak with your father about a marriage between you and me."

She smiled. "What did he say?"

"He gave his permission, his blessing and told me that I had to ask you. He said he would support your decision either way."

"That's what I thought he would say," Kate said. "If he wanted to arrange a marriage for me, he would have done so a long time ago."

"I don't know him well, but he seems like a good man," Sandie said. "Anyways, what I wanted to speak to you about, well..." He stopped walking and pulled her around to face him. "Catherine Corbin, I love you. I know you have your doubts and are hesitant, but I must know if I have a chance. Will you be my wife?" Sandie got down on one knee, holding her hands in his. "Kate, will you marry me?"

Kate tugged on his hand, drawing him up. "Sandie. I do care for you. I'm not rejecting your proposal, but I would ask that you give me just a little more time." She looked into his brown eyes and touched his cheek. She knew she was disappointing him. "I just want to make sure that we're doing the right thing. It's all happened so fast."

"Is there someone else, Kate?" He asked quietly.

"Not really, no," Kate said and she realized in that moment that she was speaking the truth. There was no one else. She much preferred Sandie to every other man she knew. He would be the one she would choose. She wasn't sure why she was so hesitant to accept his proposal. "I just have to be sure."

"Of course." He cupped her chin. "Catherine, when I say I love you, I mean it. You are worth the wait." He smiled and moved as if he were going to kiss her, then hesitated. She knew he was simply being a gentleman, so she slid her hand to his neck and gently pulled him into a kiss.

"I do care about you, Sandie." She said softly. "I will have an answer for you soon. Within a few weeks. I promise."

"All right." He smiled again, then bent to give her another quick kiss. "I love you."

"How was your talk with Major Pendleton?" Belle asked the moment Kate returned to the narthex of the church.

"It went quite well." She replied. "As I expected."

"What happened?" Elizabeth asked.

"He asked me to marry him. I know that is what you're all wondering." Kate said. Her friends smiled in anticipation.

"Well, what did you say?" AJ asked.

"Of course she accepted," Belle said. "Why wouldn't she?"

Kate wasn't sure what to say. She didn't have a sufficient answer.

"Kate?" Elizabeth prodded.

"I actually told him not yet. I need to think about it more."

346

"What do you need to think about?" Belle asked. "Everyone can tell that you love him."

"I do care for him. Likely more than any other man I have ever met."

"So why the hesitation?" AJ asked.

"I'm not really sure, as I said, I care for him, and I really believe that I love him, but my instincts are telling me to think it through a little more."

"You're frightened about something, aren't you?" Elizabeth asked. "That's why you're hesitating."

"I suppose I am a little afraid. Sandie is a soldier. It would be unimaginable to marry him only to lose him."

"Yes, but if you love him, then any time spent with him is worth it." Belle pointed out. "I wish I could have had that with Samuel."

"I could lose Joshua, that would be the worst thing I can imagine, yet I would always have truly wonderful memories of him, not to mention my two beautiful children." Elizabeth put a hand on Kate's shoulder.

"If I had an extraordinary man that I cared about and who loved me like Major Pendleton obviously loves you, I know I would not hesitate," AJ said.

"I understand what you all are saying. I just need some time to consider the offer. I'll have an answer for Sandie soon. That's what I told him."

"Just make sure you don't wait too long, Kate," Belle said. "I just may start courting him myself."

Sunday, March 8, 1863
Fredericksburg

"Thank you for attending Mass with me, AJ." Martha Evans, Richard's mother, smiled and gestured to AJ to have a seat in the parlor. "It is too bad your sister wasn't feeling well and was unable to join us. I wish that my husband would attend more often, however, he always has business to attend to. He is actually in Richmond right now."

"Business must be going well for him," AJ said.

"It is. I wish Richard had more interest in taking it over, but he is his own man. It would be nice if my husband could understand that."

"Sometimes it's difficult to see things from another person's viewpoint." AJ didn't know what else to say.

"I suppose." Mrs. Evans said. "Did you have much trouble getting over here? I worry about you and Liberty in the midst of all those Yankees."

"It's not so bad," AJ said. "I know the damage they did here in December was atrocious, but they mostly leave us alone. For being the enemy, they're actually quite kind to us."

"That's difficult to believe." Mrs. Evans replied. "You can stay for dinner, can't you? My servant has been preparing a special chicken dish."

"Of course. I wouldn't want you to have Sunday dinner all by yourself." AJ smiled. "But I must leave directly after to check on Liberty."

"You are so kind." Mrs. Evans said.

"Mother!" Richard's voice echoed through the house and he walked into the parlor. He stopped when he saw his mother's guest. "Miss Prentiss. Whatever brings you here?"

Mrs. Evans rose to give Richard a hug. "It is so wonderful to see you."

"I had an opportunity to come visit and didn't want to miss dinner with you." He smiled and sat down.

"Is there any news in the camps, son?" Mrs. Evans folded her hands in her lap.

"There are rumors here and there. Some fighting going on out west. We won a battle in Unionville, Tennessee. Our cavalry drove their cavalry off, then surrounded the infantry. The whole garrison surrendered Thursday." He pulled out a cigar and lit it.

"Oh, Richard, must you smoke those nasty smelling things?" Mrs., Evans said, then changed the subject. "I hear the Union is discovering more young ladies who are acting as spies for the Confederacy and helping us to victory. It makes me wonder if every battle we have won was the result of some brave young woman."

Richard gave AJ an almost admirable look, but also one that was conspiratorial. She blushed and smiled. It was as if she and Richard shared a secret.

"Our Southern women are doing many good things for the Confederacy, mother. We would not have nearly as many victories without them. They are invaluable to the cause." He smiled and glanced again at AJ. "Though they are critical to our success, many, especially the extremely competent ones, will never be discovered, so few will know of their contributions."

"You make a good point, son. I just hope and pray that the South will soon win the war. The quicker we defeat the Yankees, the sooner you can come home for good."

"I know, Mother. We will whip them soon. They are getting tired of this war. There is another rumor that Lincoln signed a conscription act. They now have to draft men to fight. They're getting desperate, and that is a good sign." Richard looked at AJ. "How are things on the North side of the river, Miss Prentiss? The Yankees aren't harassing you, are they?"

"No, sir. We are getting along as well as possible, although I am very anxious for them to leave."

"It shouldn't be much longer," Richard assured her. "Although with the Yankees leaving, that means we will soon break winter camp as well. I may not be able to see you as often, Mother."

"Oh, my brave, sweet boy, that's all right." Mrs. Evans replied. "I understand what you're doing and why it is so important to you, and I love you all the more for it."

After the mid-day meal, AJ prepared to leave.

"As always. Mrs. Evans, thank you so much for dinner." AJ said. "Mr. Evans, it was good seeing you again." She gave him a small smile. Dinner had been very pleasant. Richard was a kind, caring son, and AJ had enjoyed seeing him interact with his mother. It was a side of him she didn't know existed.

"I must insist on escorting you to the river, Miss Prentiss." He said.

"You really don't have to do that, sir." She replied.

"I know." He said with a smile. "That's what makes me so charming. I insist." He said goodbye to his mother and offered his arm to AJ.

"All right, then. Only to the edge of town. I don't want the Yankees across the river to see me with a Confederate soldier." AJ took his offered arm. "Thank you, Mr. Evans." They walked out the door and in the direction of the river.

"I cannot thank you enough for visiting my mother and going to Mass with her. It means a lot to her, and that means a lot to me." He smiled at her. "I know my father is gone often, so knowing that someone is checking up on her, well. It makes me feel better." His smile turned into a thoughtful frown. "If something happens to me, it's good to know that she won't be completely alone."

"Mr. Evans, nothing will happen to you and you have thanked me before. I told you, it's no trouble." She smiled. "Liberty and I both enjoy her company."

"She is a wonderful woman," Richard said affectionately.

"Yes, she is." AJ agreed. "You are quite blessed to have a mother like her."

"Everyone should be as lucky." Richard sounded arrogant, even about his own mother. Could he be modest about anything? She wanted to ask him what had happened to him on Christmas Eve Day, but they were nearing the edge of town. They had just had such a pleasant day that she didn't want to ruin it.

"I...I did try to find you at the Gordon's Starvation Party a few weeks back." He said, looking off in the distance.

"Did you now? Why is that? Did you need me for some mission?"

"No. To be honest, I wanted to ask you for a dance."

"Me? You wanted to ask me to dance?" AJ was astounded.

"I did. I may not always act like it, but I do value the friendship that you and I have established." He gave her a charming grin. She couldn't help but smile back.

"It has been nice getting to know you as well, Richard." She wished the walk could last, but they were at the edge of town.

"You're sure the Yankees won't harass you?" Richard asked.

"Yes, I have built quite a respectable reputation with them. They do enjoy my baked goods. They also understand that I am a devout Catholic and must go to church every Sunday. Which makes it very convenient when I have official business on this side of the river."

"Ingenious. Your baked goods must be delicious if that is your main method of getting information."

"Why, Mr. Evans, that almost sounds like a compliment." AJ smiled.

"I suppose it did." He smiled back. "Be safe, Miss Prentiss. Always a pleasure."

Sunday, March 15, 1863
Moss Neck Manor

"Belle! What brings you out here?" Kate answered the door and stepped outside.

"You weren't in Church this morning. I was concerned and wondered why, so I came for a visit."

"I'm glad." Kate gestured toward two chairs on the porch. "We should stay out here though. Janie, Parke, and Gardiner are all abed right now. Besides, it's quite a nice day."

"It is a nice day, but goodness, are all three ill?"

"Yes." Kate grimaced. "Janie appears to be better, though, and hopefully, Parke and Gardiner will soon be healthy again also."

"I hope so," Belle said, sitting. "It's a good idea that we stay outside. I wouldn't want to carry any sickness to Turner's Glenn. We already have too many sick soldiers there."

Kate sat down. "Are things improving at all?"

"A bit. We're still getting some ill soldiers. Not as many now, with the weather improving, but some soldiers have gotten sick as a result of their wounds. The doctors...I have to admit, the doctors we have at

350

Turner's Glenn do their best to help the patients. I'm still distressed about losing Samuel and James, but...well, there's just so many patients and so few doctors. It's hard for them to get to everyone who needs their help."

"I keep meaning to come over and visit, but I just don't want to get in the way. You said your home is already so crowded." Kate said.

"We are," Belle said, hesitatingly. "Have you given any more thought to Mr. Pendleton's proposal? Have you given him an answer?"

"Not yet," Kate said. "Although I am quite sure I will accept. I care for him deeply and don't know of anyone else who would suit me like he does."

"Splendid." Belle smiled. "You should tell him straightaway so you can start making plans. Will you wait for the war to end or try to be married before the troops leave Moss Neck?"

"I will have to speak to him about it of course, but I would like to get married as soon as things can be planned. After what you said and seeing you lose your intended, well, I feel as though I shouldn't put it off."

"That is understandable," Belle said. "I often wonder if I would have done things differently with Samuel, knowing what would happen to him."

"And if Nicole would have done things differently, knowing what would happen to James," Kate said.

"Yes, that too. She lost the opportunity to be the wife of a very special man."

"Yes," Kate said. "I hope my indecision won't cause me to miss a similar opportunity.

Tuesday, March 17, 1863
Moss Neck Manor

"Miss Corbin." General Jackson entered the house, followed by Captain Smith. "I was hoping you could tell me how young Miss Janie is doing."

"She is so tired," Kate replied. She had, a bowl of broth in hand for Gardiner. "However, she seems to be on the mend."

"Would it be an imposition for me to go and tell her goodbye?"

Kate smiled. "Of course not. She will be thrilled to see you. Please follow me, I will show you up to her room." When they entered the room, they saw Bertie at Janie's side.

"General Jackson." Bertie stood to greet the gentlemen. Kate noticed that Janie looked weak, but perked up at the sight of her visitors.

"I am going to check on the boys, Janie," Kate said. "You visit with General Jackson and I will be back to check on you soon." She turned

351

and left, heading straight for the nursery, where Gardiner and Parke still slept.

The bedroom was dark, so Kate immediately went to the window to open the curtains.

"Boys, let's get this room a little bit lighter." She said. Gardiner opened his eyes and smiled, while little Parke continued sleeping.

"Morning, Aunt Kate." He said. "I'm kind of a little hungry."

"Well, that's certainly a good sign. It must mean you're getting better." Kate hoped it was true. "You are quite lucky. I brought some broth for you." She sat next to him, set the broth on the bedside table and helped him sit up so he could eat easier. When he was about half-done with the broth, there was a soft knock on the door and Sandie poked his head into the room.

"Good morning." He smiled. "May I come in, Mr. Dickenson?"

"Of course, Major, but don't be silly. My name is Gardiner." Gardiner said with a smile. The boy and Sandie had formed an endearing relationship as Janie had with General Jackson. It was one of the things she adored about Sandie. He would make a wonderful father someday.

"It is so good to see you sitting up and eating." Sandie moved around the bed to the chair Kate was sitting on. He placed a hand on her shoulder and her heart sped up a bit. She could almost imagine the three of them as their own family, and she could truly see a future with him. She reached up and held his hand, then smiled up at him.

"Major, can you tell me a story?" Gardiner asked, snuggling back down under his covers. Kate stood and tucked him in, then went to the other side of the bed to sit, so Sandie could have the chair.

"Of course I will, Gardiner. What would you like me to tell you about?"

"Tell me about your adventures with Stonewall Jackson." The boy said.

Sandie smiled. "All right."

Sandie was a wonderful storyteller and didn't hesitate to embellish the tales, but he also never ceased to give God the glory for their victories. Kate stroked Gardiner's hair until he drifted off, which didn't take long at all. When he was clearly asleep, both Kate and Sandie stood.

"Thank you for visiting with him, Sandie. You really made his day."

"It was nothing. I enjoy spending time with your family, Catherine. I care for them as well." He walked toward her. "I hope and pray that one day they will be my family." He stood in front of her. "I would never pressure you to do anything, Kate, but..." He touched her chin. "I have to leave with Jackson. I have delayed all that I can. I had wished I could have an answer from you before I left." She looked into his hopeful eyes, knowing that she could turn his hopes into happiness with one word.

"Sandie, I..."

The door opened before she could finish her sentence. Bertie entered but appeared so distracted that she didn't even notice the proximity of Kate and Sandie.

"Major Pendleton. I am so glad that you're still here. Will you make sure to stop in Janie's room before you leave? The child is ever so fond of you."

Sandie backed away from Kate and nodded to Bertie. "The fondness is mutual, Mrs, Corbin. Of course, I will visit her straight away." Kate followed him into Janie's room. Bertie stayed next to Kate while Sandie approached the child. He spoke to her quietly, and Kate was gladdened to see Janie smile and giggle at whatever he said.

"Major Pendleton is a good man," Bertie whispered. "You would do well to accept his hand."

"I am aware of that, Bertie. I intend to speak with him about it." Kate replied.

"Good. It's about time." The two women watched as Sandie smiled and tipped his hat at Janie, then turned toward Kate.

"Catherine..." He was interrupted when Nettie entered the room.

"Excuse me, Major Pendleton," Bertie said. "Now that Nettie is here, I must step out to attend to a household matter."

"Of course." Sandie smiled at her, then turned back to Kate and took her hands into his. "Catherine, I..."

"Major." Nettie interrupted this time. "I wish you would come here and take a look at little Janie. She feels a bit cold to me."

Kate whirled around and Sandie strode to Janie. He touched her hand, then instantly turned. His eyes were glossy.

"Kate, go get Mrs. Corbin." He then dashed out the door and down the stairs. Kate followed his directions, and by the time she tracked down Bertie and returned to the room, Sandie had brought Dr. McGuire in. Sandie stood outside in the hallway, a blank look on his face. Bertie entered the room.

"Sandie, what did the doctor say?" Kate's voice shook. "What's going on? Janie..."

"Kate, I think you should go in and be with your sister." He said. She touched his arm and he tried to give her a smile, but it didn't fool her at all. He bent and kissed her on the forehead, then gestured to the doorway. She went into the room and immediately went to Bertie's side. Bertie collapsed into Kate's arms.

353

"Oh, Kate. My baby. My little girl. My Janie." Bertie clung to Kate as Dr. McGuire slipped out the door. Tears began to fall steadily down Kate's cheeks and her legs felt weak, but she had to be strong, as she was holding Bertie up. Bertie began to wail piercing cries, her anguish incredible. Just when Kate thought that she couldn't bear Bertie's weight any longer, Sandie was there.

"You must be calm, Mrs. Corbin." He said softly and she released Kate and seized him, a fresh barrage of tears and cries. Sandie rubbed Bertie's back and caught Kate's eyes over her head. Kate's own cheeks were drenched with tears and her heart had a deep ache. She sank into the chair next to Janie's bed. The sweet girl looked peaceful like she was only sleeping, but Janie would never skip around, never play, never smile again. Bertie continued to sob, inconsolably. Sandie continued his attempts to soothe her.

"Just remember, Jesus said let the suffering little children come to me. She's out of pain now. She has eternal life." He said.

"No. Not my baby. My only child." Bertie sobbed. "Why oh why?"

"Mrs. Corbin. Have faith. The Lord giveth and the Lord taketh away."

"But why? Why did your Lord take my child? My poor, sweet Janie."

Kate wasn't sure how much time passed before Sandie spoke again.

"Mrs. Corbin, could you pray with me?"

"No. No, I cannot, but will you pray for me, Major?"

"I cannot refuse you that." He replied. There, with Bertie still clinging to him for comfort and support, Sandie offered up a beautiful and most earnest prayer for Bertie's guidance and comfort from God.

"Please, Lord, give her the strength to bear this tragedy and lead her to seek You, our Savior and Comforter. Lord, be with Mrs. Corbin and her family."

Bertie quieted after the prayer.

"Mrs. Corbin, would you like to lie down for a while? I could bring you to your room."

"That would...yes...I...yes."

Sandie gave Kate a sympathetic look, then all but carried Bertie to her bedchamber.

Kate heard Sandie return to the room. She had been sitting there, staring at Janie's still form.

"Kate, darling." She looked up at him, her eyes tear-filled. He knelt beside her and took her hands in his.

354

"You and Dr. McGuire were going to leave." She said, her focus still on Janie. "Why?"

"We didn't want to intrude upon your family's grief." He said. "As much as I would like to be, I have no familial connection and the doctor...he felt that it would be best."

"Sandie, what are we going to do with our sweet Janie?" She asked. Her heart felt like it had been squeezed and crushed.

"Some of the men are putting a casket together as we speak. They're using the leftover wood from the fences around the house. It's all we can find." He gave her hand a squeeze. "The Stonewall Brigade will take care of her." He reached up and cupped her face, using his thumb to brush a tear from her cheek. "Catherine, mine, what can I do to help you?"

Kate looked down at Sandie. He was such a good man, such a compassionate, caring man. He knew how to make her laugh and he was always trying to make her feel better. Now was one of those times but he just couldn't make things better. Not today, not with Janie gone.

"Sandie, I don't know that you can. I don't know that anything can make this better."

He stood, pulled her up and took her into his arms, holding her tightly. She clutched his shirt in her hands, letting him give her strength.

"I am praying for you, Kate. I may not always be here for you physically, but I will try, and I will always be thinking of you. You can count on me. Please, you can always write me." He leaned back and looked into her eyes. "I know Mrs. Corbin didn't want to pray..."

Kate wiped a tear from her cheek. "Bertie's really not that much of a believer." She admitted.

"I noticed that," Sandie replied. "Would you like to pray with me?"

"I would," Kate said. Sandie took her hands in his, bowed his head and prayed.

"Thank you, Sandie," Kate said. "It doesn't completely help, nothing will, but it does lighten the burden, and knowing that you're praying for me..." She placed a hand on his cheek. "I really appreciate everything you have done for me and my family."

"I would do more if I could," Sandie said, giving her a quick kiss. "Remember, I love you, Catherine Corbin."

Kate smiled. "I care deeply for you as well." There was a soft knock on the door and Nettie poked her head in.

"Kate. Gardiner is awake and asking for you."

Kate looked at her sister-in-law. Nettie's eyes were red. Losing Janie had been a tragedy for all of them.

355

"You go ahead, Kate. I'll stay here. Some of the others who knew little Janie want to pay their respects also before they leave. You go and spend some time with your nephews."

"Thank you, Sandie." Kate gave him a sad smile and gave his hand a gentle squeeze. She then went to check the boys.

"Have Parke and Gardiner been told about Janie?" Kate asked.

"No. I didn't want to worry them." Nettie replied. Her eyes watered. "Oh, Kate, what if my boys die too? They have the fever, same as Janie, and same as all of the children last winter. I don't know what I would do if we lost the boys too."

"The boys will be fine," Kate assured her. "Many have survived. Parke and Gardiner will be just fine. They'll be feeling better and playing with Baby Kate before we know it."

"Thank you, I'm sure you're right," Nettie said. "I'll check on Bertie if you can stay with the boys." Kate nodded and went into Parke and Gardiner's room.

Wednesday, March 18, 1863
Moss Neck Manor

"Kate, I am so terribly sorry for your loss." Belle embraced her friend tightly. "I cannot believe this happened."

"I still cannot believe it myself." Kate felt hollow, and had since Janie's death. "Thank you for coming out. I dearly appreciate your support."

"Of course. Is there anything I can do for you or Bertie."

"Just your being here is enough. We'll be burying her later today. Reverend Lacy will be presiding. All of the arrangements are being made by the members of the military court of Jackson's corps. They're the soldiers who stayed behind after the rest of the staff left."

"I see." Belle said. "That's very kind of them."

"Indeed." Kate agreed. "I received a letter from Sandie this morning and told me that the news of Janie's death was a shock to Jackson and all of his staff. They had all been so fond of her when they were here."

"She was an easy child to love." Belle said. "The rest of my family will be here later. Benjamin and Max are quite shaken about the whole situation. Everyone was of course, but those two were especially."

"Along with all of the other losses that we have had of late." Kate shook her head. "I just keep praying that Parke and Gardiner will get well soon. Losing Janie…"

Belle pulled Kate back into her arms. "We'll get through this. Just as we have these past few years."

The funeral for little Janie was simple, yet emotional. It was held in the parlor of Moss Neck. Kate wasn't sure she would ever be able to sit in the room again without being reminded of Janie's funeral. A few soldiers were able to make it, but Sandie and General Jackson were not in attendance.

Kate's brother, Richard, Janie's father and Bertie's husband, had been able to get leave from his duties, as he was stationed at a cavalry outpost on the Rappahannock River. He stood next to Bertie, his hand around her waist. The entire Turner family was there, Belle standing close to Kate with her arm around her shoulder, while Elizabeth was doing the same for Nettie. Reverend Lacy said some comforting words, then members of the Stonewall Brigade took the coffin to the family cemetery plot near the house to be buried. Bertie's hand remained splayed on the coffin as if she was unwilling to let her go. The coffin had been built by carpenters in the Stonewall Brigade. As Sandie had said, they had used wood from the fences that had enclosed the lawn.

"Miss Corbin, I cannot tell you how sorry I am for your loss." Clem Fishburne, one of Jackson's men and a good friend of Sandie's, approached Kate. "Miss Janie was a true joy to all of us who were blessed to know her."

"Thank you, sir. I appreciate the kind words." Kate said.

"Seeing her today, before she was placed in the coffin, just lying on the boards, it...well the contrast between the surroundings of that poor child's body and the elegance of your house...well, it saddens me greatly."

"I agree," Kate said. She was grateful for the guests who had come to offer their condolences, but she was getting weary. Tired of acting as though a part of her heart had not been torn away. Tired of trying to be strong for Bertie, and trying not to worry about Parke and Gardiner. She took a deep breath. "It was good to see you, and again, thank you for your kind words. Please excuse me, but I must go check on my nephews."

Thursday, March 19, 1863
Moss Neck Manor

Bertie remained in her room the entire day. The house was eerily quiet as Kate made her way to the boy's room. She didn't know if it was wishful thinking, but it seemed as though they were getting better. She held another letter she had received from Sandie. Even though his duties prevented him from visiting, he had been supportive in other ways.

"Hello, Aunt Kate," Gardiner said weakly. "How are you?"

"I should be asking you that question, darling." She brushed a lock of brown hair from his forehead.

"I'm all right. I'm feeling better. I should be able to get out of bed soon, maybe even tomorrow." He gave her a weak smile. "Are Janie and Baby Kate doing all right?"

Kate tried not to show her feelings of sadness. She smiled at him sympathetically. He was such a sweet boy.

"About like you. They'll be fine." His forehead was still so warm, and he was sweating. He said he was feeling better, though. That had to be a good sign. She glanced at Parke, who was sleeping.

"Didja get a letter from Mr. Pendleton?" Gardiner asked, looking at her hand. Kate nodded. "I like him, Aunt Kate. All of the soldiers were quite nice, but I thought that Mr. Pendleton was especially grand."

"I agree with you, Gardiner." She smiled.

"What does Mr. Pendleton have to say?" He asked.

"Well…" She opened the letter and scanned it. "He says that he misses seeing us all and wishes that he could visit more. He is praying for everyone at Moss Neck, especially those of you who are sick." She smiled at him and continued reading the letter as he drifted off to sleep.

I pray that our merciful God will comfort Janie's mother and make her understand that what has happened is for eternal good. There is no doubt in my mind that your niece is in heaven with our Lord. Your poor brother, I feel more sadness for him, if it is possible.

My dear Kate, do not let your sadness depress you overmuch. Go out and visit and do more. Make Mrs. Corbin do the same. It will be the best medicine for your mind and body.

Kate reread the letter a few times, relishing the words and wishing that Sandie could be here with her. She made her way over to Parke. He lay still and was breathing strangely when suddenly, he turned blue and stopped breathing completely. Kate was shocked she didn't know what to do. She sat next to Parke and gently shook him. She started to weep. This could not be happening. Several moments later, Nettie entered the room.

"Kate. How are my boys?"

Kate sat up. "I just spoke with Gardiner, he is resting, but our little Parke…I think…I think…"

Nettie rushed over to her son's bedside and felt his head. It was still warm to the touch but tinged blue. "NOOOO!" She dropped to her

358

knees at the side of the bed, laid her head on Parke's chest and began sobbing. The boy continued to lay deathly still.

"Nettie?" Kate asked hesitantly, knowing what was wrong, but praying that it wasn't true. Her heart sank and her breath caught. "Oh, Parke, no, not Parke too!" Kate sank to her knees next to Nettie. "No." Tears fell down her face as she and Nettie continued to stare at Parke's lifeless body. "God, please, no."

Friday, March 20, 1863
Turner's Glenn

"Good morning!" Elizabeth sat down at the breakfast table, her face a bit pale.

"Good morning." The dining room was once again a place that the family could gather and eat. The doctors and other medical staff ate there as well, but they usually had their morning meal earlier. It was nice for the Turner family to just be together.

"Mama, there's bacon today!" Benjamin smiled and held up his slice. Elizabeth paled even more if that was possible, and quickly took a slice of bread and drank some water.

"That's wonderful, Benjamin. I'm not really in the mood for bacon today. You can have my share."

"Thanks!" The boy smiled and the family finished their meals, one by one excusing themselves to tend to their chores. Finally, it was just Miriam, Elizabeth, Belle, and Meri. Miriam smiled at her oldest daughter.

"So, Elizabeth, my dear. When should we expect this newest addition to our family?" She asked. Elizabeth blushed. Meri's head snapped up in shock. Belle smiled, surprise apparent on her face.

"My best guess would be late September, early October. However, I could be a month or so off.

"How did that even happen?" Meri asked. "Joshua has been living with his regiment."

"Yes, but he and I have been able to...umm...spend some time together," Elizabeth said, now turning a deeper shade of red. She turned to Miriam. "How could you tell?"

"A mother knows, despite all the grief we have had to bear recently." Miriam smiled again. "There are subtle signs you have been showing lately, but just now, you not wanting bacon solidified it for me. I have never known you to pass up bacon before."

"I see," Elizabeth replied. What her mother said was true.

"When will you tell Joshua? He will be so thrilled." Meri asked.

"I'm not sure that I will. I want to tell him, but I don't want him to be worried about me while he's fighting and he will worry, especially with all of the sickness at Moss Neck. First Janie, then yesterday, Parke." A servant from the Corbins had come over to tell the Turners the sad news. "I pray that Gardiner pulls through and that Baby Kate doesn't succumb."

"I don't know what Kate would do if Gardiner were to pass away," Belle said. "She dotes on him over much."

"I pray they won't lose any more children," Miriam said. "It is good, however, that the illness has been contained so far. I fear another epidemic."

"Heaven forbid." Elizabeth's hand automatically went to her stomach. "It is unbelievable what this town has gone through. We cannot have another epidemic."

"We can only pray, but we have many blessings and another new life to celebrate." Miriam smiled at Elizabeth.

"Indeed." Belle came around the table and gave Elizabeth a quick hug. "Congratulations. I am very happy for you." She then walked out the door.

"Such a change in temperament," Miriam commented when Belle was out of hearing distance.

"Yes. I feel we are becoming good friends again." Elizabeth admitted. She hadn't liked the years when they were barely tolerant of one another. It had been enlightening when Elizabeth first understood that she had been part of the problem. Her focus on her new husband and then each of her own children had caused a rift between the two and Belle had felt neglected by her sister.

"Sisters should always be the best of friends. I am glad that you two are repairing your relationship." Miriam said.

"Yes." Elizabeth looked at the clock on the mantle. "I need to be going. I told Joshua that I would meet him today."

"Very good. Are you going to tell him about his child?"

"I don't know, Mama. As I said, I want to, but...I just don't know."

"I'm sure whatever decision you make will be all right in the end," Miriam said.

"Thank you for saying that," Elizabeth said. "I shouldn't be long."

Turner's Glenn

"Joshua!" Elizabeth threw her arms around her husband, holding him tightly. She had been working in one of the vegetable gardens, preparing it for planting.

"My dear." Joshua kissed her forehead, then her lips. "I'm so glad that you could make it. I can't stay long though." He led her to a fallen log and they both sat, her hands still in his.

"Why do you have to leave so quickly?" She asked, her heart sinking, fearful of what he was going to say.

"It's time. We're pulling up camp and moving out. Heading west, I believe, towards Chancellorsville. When I walk you home, I'll say goodbye to the children."

Tears formed in Elizabeth's eyes. She knew this day would be coming and had been dreading it. "I wish you didn't have to go." She touched his bearded cheek. "I'll just have to remember that the sooner you leave, the sooner you can come home for good."

He reached up and wiped a tear from her cheek.

"I know, and there is a good chance that I can get a short leave to come and visit." He gently kissed her again. Elizabeth set her head against his shoulder. She wanted to see him, but every time she did, it was harder and harder to let him go.

"I'm not sure how much more I can take."

"I feel the same way," Joshua said, and Elizabeth realized that she had spoken out loud. Joshua continued. "But the North is being badly beaten in many areas. The battle here embarrassed them. I don't think it will be too much longer before they give up." He pulled her close and kissed her forehead again. "We just have to hold on a little while longer." He sighed as tears continued to slip down her cheeks.

"Elizabeth, dear. What's wrong? You are more emotional than usual when we part."

"I…" She hesitated, not knowing if she should tell him about her condition or not. She wanted to, but her reservations prevailed. "I suppose I'm just overly emotional about the tragedies at Moss Neck. Losing Janie and Parke, and with Gardiner still sick…I can't imagine losing one of our children. Combine that with you leaving after being here in town all winter…I suppose everything is just catching up with me."

Joshua hugged her again. "I can understand that. Just keep the faith. We can get through this."

Saturday, March 21, 1863
Moss Neck Manor

My dear Kate,

I have just heard the news of dear Parke passing from the fever. I cannot express the distress that I felt as a result. If I could, I would be at your side this very moment. I will try everything in my power to get to you as soon as I possibly can. Remember, as the Lord said to Joshua, 'be strong and steadfast, do not fear or be dismayed, for the Lord, your God will be with you wherever you go'.

Kate folded the letter and tucked it into her pocket. With the double tragedy at Moss Neck, the knowledge that she had his support was extremely comforting.

"Kate!" Belle entered the parlor. "Kate, I heard the distressing news. I came as soon as I could. I wasn't sure when the funeral would be, but I wanted to be here for you." She hugged her friend tightly. "Oh, Kate." She pulled away, then looked around the room. "How you can even be in here. The room where we had Janie's funeral. It is so depressing."

"I don't know. It may be sad, but I also find it peaceful in a strange way." Kate sat back down, then picked up her Bible. "This has been a great comfort as well and I received a letter from Sandie. He wrote as soon as he heard. He will come when he is able to get away."

Belle nodded. "It's good to know that part of the Stonewall Brigade is still here so you can have a courier."

"Indeed. I just wish he could be here himself." Kate admitted.

"This is probably not the best time to ask, but have you thought any more about accepting his hand?" Belle asked.

"It's all right." Kate looked down at the Bible and smiled. "I have decided and I will. I would like to tell him in person the next time I see him. He has been such a dear friend, and I realize how important friendship is to a good marriage."

"Splendid. I am so glad for you." Belle said. "Really, I am. We need some good news for a change. We have been through so much as of late."

"And may continue to go through," Kate added, then glanced toward the stairwell. "We still have Baby Kate and my sweet Gardiner to worry about. He is my darling pride and joy and with this infernal war, who knows what will happen next."

"Little Gardiner will be up and running around in no time," Belle said. "Your family has already been through enough. How are Bertie and Nettie?"

"As well as can be expected," Kate said.

"Bertie has always been a worldly woman. She doesn't really care about the power of God and prayer. I fear this will only cause her to disbelieve even more. Nettie is doing better, but she still has Gardiner to care for and Baby Kate, of course, so she doesn't have as much time to dwell on Parke. Bertie is secluded in her room and Nettie is with Gardiner."

"I will have to go up and give them both a quick 'hello'."

"We shall see," Kate said. "How are things at Turner's Glenn?"

"Fine, just fine." Belle couldn't contain a smile.

362

"What?" Kate asked. "Is there something I should know? A development between you and that doctor?"

"Dr. Knightly? No. Never. Not that at all. I suppose he's not nearly as boorish as he once was, and we have had one or two cordial conversations."

"Then why did you try to hide a smile from me?" Kate asked.

"We do have some good news in our family, but I don't wish to be insensitive to you and your family. I'm not quite sure that Elizabeth wants you or AJ to know yet either. If she does, she would likely want to be the one to tell you."

"Well, you have piqued my interest," Kate said. "You must tell me now." Kate was glad that Belle had come over and was conversing with her about subjects other than the deaths of Parke and Janie.

"I suppose my sister will forgive me for my excitement," Belle said. "Elizabeth is with child again."

"How exciting!" Kate exclaimed. "When does she expect the baby will be born?"

"She figures she'll give birth in late September," Belle said. "I really hope you don't think I'm being insensitive, after what you have been through the past few days."

"No. Honestly, the idea of new life after there has been so much loss. It brings some joy." A tear slipped down her face.

"Oh Kate, I am so sorry."

"Belle, I'm all right." Kate dabbed her face with her handkerchief. "I will be just fine." The two women looked up as a red-eyed, dazed Bertie entered the parlor.

"Bertie, my dear." Belle stood and hugged the older woman. "I can't tell you…" Fresh tears fell down Bertie's face and she sank to her knees as Belle slid down with her. "What's wrong, Bertie?"

Kate stood, the all-too-familiar feeling of dread coming over her. "Bertie, what has happened? Bertie, you must talk to me." Kate knelt in front of her sister-in-law and shook her gently.

"Oh, Kate, it's…it's Gardiner. I just went in to check on him, and Nettie, and he was…oh, Kate, he was…Kate, he's gone too."

Kate tried to stand back up but stumbled. Belle moved quickly and caught her before she fell to the ground. Kate threw her arms around her friend as Belle held Kate up. Kate continued to sob while Bertie sat next to them, still in a daze. Tears fell down Belle's cheeks as well. It was just too much. Way too much to bear.

363

Turner's Glenn

"Thank you for telling me," Miriam said as Elizabeth rounded the corner into the entryway. Her mother was talking with a slave from Moss Neck. The slave nodded and left.

"Did something happen to Belle?" Elizabeth asked.

"No, but she will be staying the night at Moss Neck with Kate." Tears glimmered in Miriam's eyes and her voice cracked. "Gardiner succumbed to the fever today."

"Oh no, Mother, please no." Elizabeth's hand flew to her mouth. "Not all three of them! Has the angel of death just spread his wings over Moss Neck? Janie, Parke and Gardiner." She sank into a chair that was in the entryway and put her hand to her heart. "How will the Corbin family get through this? Losing three dear children"

"One day at a time, dear, and we will continue to pray for them and do whatever we can to help them in their time of need," Miriam said with tears as she comforted her daughter.

Elizabeth looked up at Miriam. "Mama, when will this all end?"

"I wish I knew, Elizabeth. We just have to continue supporting one another as best we can."

"And pray," Elizabeth added. She took a deep breath. "Did you find out when Parke's funeral will be exactly?"

"The messenger didn't say. I believe, however, that we should stay here for the day. We don't want to overwhelm the family and Belle is already there."

"Of course. That is probably the best decision." Elizabeth replied. "I must bring this news to the children. It has been a difficult few days, with Janie and Parke dying and Joshua leaving."

"They will get through it. Children can be quite resilient." Miriam said.

"Yes, but they shouldn't have to be."

Sunday, March 22, 1863
Moss Neck Manor

Kate stared at herself in the mirror. She touched under her eyes. She looked as tired as she felt. There was a knock on the door and Belle entered the bedroom.

"How are you doing this morning?" She asked.

"Not so good," Kate replied. "It's just been too much in such a short time. I feel...like, I have no feelings. I am empty inside." She sighed and patted her hair. "I don't like the feeling at all, Belle. Is that how you felt when you lost Samuel and James?"

"Samuel, not so much, but James, yes," Belle replied. "I suppose we deal with the pain of losing loved ones in different ways."

"How will I get through this?" Kate shook her head. "Both my sister and brother have lost children. How can I take care of them when I can barely take care of myself?" She looked out her window. "I wish Sandie could come by. I miss his support. He has been wonderful during this crisis. It has brought me to the realization that his love has sustained me."

"I'm glad that you have him," Belle said. "I am also very happy that you decided to accept his proposal."

"I am too." She replied. "Belle, I truly believe he is the one for me. He is the one I wish to spend the rest of my days with and the one that I want to share all the joys and comforts in this life with, as well as the sorrows."

Belle smiled. "How poetic."

Kate smiled back, thinking of Sandie. "I see now that he is everything I could ask for in a husband. Some may say he's conceded, but I believe he has good reason to be, what with his intellect. I adore his splendid, almost boyish exuberance of spirits, yet he commands the respect of all who meet him, despite his age."

"I've noticed that as well," Belle said. She truly envied her friend.

"The thing I admire most about him is his devotion to the Lord. He is such a sincere Christian. I realize that may not mean much to you, but it truly does to me."

"I think that is a fine quality to admire in a man," Belle said. "Believe it or not, Elizabeth has been very encouraging in my faith and I feel as though I am making good progress."

"Indeed." Kate smiled. "I am so happy to hear that. Here I am going on and on about Sandie. How are you this morning?"

"I am doing well. It is you and your family we have to be concerned about. Elizabeth is doing well too, she is still at Turner's Glenn. There are rumors that a battle will be fought west of here. If that happens, we will likely get wounded from that battle as well, or really from any fighting in the area. Apparently, we have developed a reputation for a very well-run hospital.

"That is something to be proud of," Kate said.

"I suppose so," Belle admitted reluctantly. "I suppose."

365

Wednesday, April 8, 1863
Turner's Glenn

AJ walked up the steps to the Turner home. It was still bustling, and would likely continue to be so. Most of the troops had left the area, but they were still close enough to Fredericksburg that soldiers could easily be sent there. AJ looked around and finally spotted Elizabeth.

"AJ!" Her friend saw her as well and quickly approached her. "What brings you over here?"

"I wanted to visit, but I also wanted to see if you could make use of this." She reached into her haversack and pulled out packets of medication.

"Oh my, we certainly could. Where did you get this? I thought the Yankees moved out of Stafford Heights.

"They did, but Chatham is still being used as a hospital, so I still have some access to get what we may need."

"Dr. Knightly will be so glad to see this. Medication is something we are always in short supply of." Elizabeth lowered her voice. "Are you able to get what is necessary for your contacts?"

"It will be fine. They'll just have to understand. I can find more when I need to, but the important thing is that our Confederate doctors have what they need to get our boys better."

"I cannot argue with that," Elizabeth said. "We are extremely grateful for it."

"AJ!" Belle called from the stairway, then hastened down. "I am so glad that you're here."

"I am glad to be here. It's strange how seldom we get to visit lately." AJ stated.

"I know, even when we do see each other, we're always busy discussing what I am forced to do," Belle said. "I had no idea how much work I could actually accomplish. I don't feel as delicate as I once thought."

"I never thought you were delicate, Belle. I always knew you had this strength in you." Elizabeth said. "We're all growing and changing so much. My goodness, Joshua barely recognized his own children when he first visited over the winter."

"Max, Lainey, Meri, Liberty. All of them are growing into young men and women." Belle added.

"Do you ever wonder what their world will be like when the war is over?" AJ asked. "The world of any children we have in the future?"

"Occasionally," Elizabeth said. Belle shrugged her shoulders.

"I think about it all the time," AJ said. "I think it's why I want to be so involved in the war effort. So I can help make the country the best that it can be for our children."

"With slaves?" Elizabeth didn't want to ask but had to.

"Slavery...I suppose I can see why people would be against it, but I feel it is an institution that will eventually wear itself out." AJ admitted. "That's not what I am fighting for. I want to have a country where the national government doesn't try to dictate every little thing we do."

"I don't feel the North is trying to do that." Elizabeth countered.

"Of course they are, Elizabeth." Belle jumped into the conversation. "Lincoln is a tyrant and the northern states are trying to take over the country. They will start by taking away slavery, but they won't stop there."

"Lincoln didn't say anything about completely doing away with slavery," Elizabeth said. "He never did. In fact, most abolitionists didn't like him because he wasn't extreme enough for them."

"Wherever did you hear that?" AJ asked.

"I remember reading in the newspaper right after the election of 1860. I read more than just novels, you know."

"It doesn't matter what Lincoln said or didn't say," Belle stated. "The fact is that we tried to do things peacefully. Create our own country so we could live the way we wanted to and they could live the way they wanted to."

"That doesn't make slavery right," Elizabeth said. "I don't even know why I am arguing with you. You will never understand what I am trying to say because you don't wish to understand. This Southern pride that we fight for may be our downfall." With that, an emotional Elizabeth turned and walked toward the back door.

"I cannot believe her sometimes," Belle said to AJ once Elizabeth was out of earshot.

"I'm sure she's just over-emotional," AJ said. "She's with child, I'm sure she's feeling overrun and she must be constantly worried for her husband." She sighed. "I shouldn't have even brought up anything political, to begin with. I know how she feels about slavery, even if I don't agree with her. I should go talk to her."

"If you want," Belle said. "Go ahead. I have to make my rounds and visit the soldiers."

AJ headed towards the back of the house in search of Elizabeth. It didn't take her long to do so; she sat on a stone bench that looked out over the Rappahannock River.

"Elizabeth?" AJ sat next to her friend. "I'm sorry for upsetting you."

"You didn't." Elizabeth wiped a tear from her cheek with her finger.

"Do you want to talk about what's really bothering you?"

"It's nothing new. The worry for Joshua. The worry for my children and the future of our country. I'm constantly tired and I am more emotional because of my condition." She shrugged. "I'm trying to help here, care for my children and rebuild my home, all with my husband away, putting his life at risk for a cause that neither he nor I really believe in."

AJ reached over and put her arm around Elizabeth. "You are one of the strongest women I know, Elizabeth Bennett, and you are one of my best friends. I'm sorry that I upset you." She sighed. "I suppose this war is just taking its toll on all of us."

Wednesday, April 15, 1863
Moss Neck Manor

Kate made her way to the back garden. She had been told that a friend was there waiting for her. When she saw that it was AJ, she felt a short flash of disappointment that it wasn't Sandie. She had written him to accept his proposal, and he had responded with excitement and told her that he would come to see her as soon as he could.

AJ stood and smiled, then gave Kate a hug. "Kate, I am so sorry to hear about the children! This is the first chance I have had to make it over and actually visit. I feel so bad, I would have come to the funerals had I known."

"It's quite all right, AJ. I understand. These are difficult times for all of us."

AJ sighed. "But what you have been through is more than anyone deserves and now there are rumors from reliable sources of another battle brewing near Chancellorsville."

"So close, again." Kate sighed.

"At least it means your beau is still nearby. Have you made a decision about his proposal?"

"I have, actually." She smiled. "I have decided that I will marry Sandie. I wrote him not long ago with the news."

"Capital! Congratulations." AJ grinned. "I am so happy for you both."

"Thank you," Kate said. AJ could tell that her friend was still troubled.

"What's wrong, then? You can't be having second thoughts already? Or are you afraid your messages aren't getting to him?"

"Neither of those. I know he is the one for me and Sandie is at Jackson's new headquarters near Hamilton's Crossing. Captain Henry Kyd Douglas is bringing messages back and forth for us, so I know he is getting them."

"That's good. What is the trouble, then?"

"It's nothing really, although you are a perfect person to confess to. It's just...I love Sandie, I do, but I have been flirting recently, with other men. I can't seem to help it."

"Kate!" AJ shook her head.

"Just a bit. It is something that I hadn't indulged in this winter, in spite of many temptations. It's not important enough to interfere at all with my relationship with Sandie. I love him. My flirting is completely innocent."

"Who?" AJ asked.

"Whatever do you mean?" Kate asked.

"Who have you been flirting with? I imagine there are still some soldiers who are occasional visitors at Moss Neck. Who have you been flirting with?"

Kate gave AJ a guilty look. "Mr. Heth."

"Oh, Kate. Does he not know that you're promised to Major Pendleton?"

"I'm not entirely sure, to be honest." She admitted. "I haven't come right out and told him."

"You should. Kate, next time you see Stockton Heth, you have to tell him. You have to let him know."

"You're right. I know you are." Kate sighed and looked across the land. "I will tell him. I really don't want to ruin my relationship with Sandie. I do love him."

"I know you do," AJ replied, gently touching Kate's forearm.

"What about your relationship with Captain JP Smith? Did I imagine it or was there an attraction between the two of you?"

"He is a very kind man," AJ said. "I do enjoy his company, and we have written to each other, but I think of him as a very dear friend."

"A dear friend can become something more," Kate said.

"We shall see," AJ said.

Wednesday, April 22, 1863
Moss Neck Manor

"Bertie, are you sure you are up for a visit?" Kate asked. She and her sister-in-law had been invited to visit with the recently arrived Mrs. Thomas Jackson. She was staying at the nearby Yerby home and was visiting her husband with their newborn daughter.

"Yes, Kate, I am fine. You don't have to worry." Bertie patted her hair. "Have our escorts arrived yet?"

"They have," Kate replied. Captain Henry Kyd Douglas and Stockton Heth had volunteered to bring Bertie and Kate to see Mrs. Jackson.

369

Kate was nervous about seeing Captain Heth, especially after her discussion with AJ, but Captain Douglas cleared the air almost immediately by congratulating Kate on her engagement to Sandie and saying: "When General Jackson heard the news, he said 'if Pendleton makes as good a husband as he has a soldier, Miss Corbin will do well.'"

Kate, Bertie and their escorts made their way to the Yerby home. Kate immediately noticed that Mr. Heth was a little cold toward her. She wanted to speak with him, but she did not want to upset him any more than he already was. When they made it to their destination, Captain Douglas, always the gentleman, made the introductions. Mrs. Mary Jackson was a modest, pleasant and pretty young woman whose age appeared to be between Kate and Bertie's.

"I am ever so glad to meet you Mrs. Corbin, Miss Corbin." Mrs. Jackson said. "I have heard so much about you and your delightful family in letters from Mr. Jackson. Thank you ever so kindly for your hospitality towards my husband."

"It was our pleasure," Bertie said. "Your husband and his staff were true gentlemen when they stayed with us over the winter. The most perfect guests."

"That is actually good to hear." Mrs. Jackson sent a look toward Kate. "Am I correct in assuming you are the young woman who has won the heart of Sandie Pendleton?"

"Yes, ma'am," Kate said with a blush. "It was quite easy for him to win my heart as well. I hope to see him soon to discuss our future."

"That may be sooner than you anticipated." Mrs. Jackson smiled. "The two of you and your escorts have been invited to dine at Major John Harman's quarters. I believe Dr. McGuire and your Major Pendleton have also been invited."

"That is very kind of him." Kate turned to Bertie. "Would you be willing to go?"

"Of course, Kate," Bertie said. "I think that is a fine idea."

Kate smiled as a slave brought out a small baby girl, about six months old.

"Ah, here she is." Mrs. Jackson said, taking the child in her arms. "Ladies, this is my dear daughter, Julia Laura."

"How precious!" Kate said. "May I hold her?"

"Of course." Mrs. Jackson passed the girl to Kate and she snuggled the baby to her chest. "She appears to have General Jackson's eyes."

"I would agree with you." Mrs. Jackson stated. Kate glanced at Bertie. Her sister-in-law was looking at Julia with sadness in her eyes. Kate also felt a pang of grief. It was still so very soon since they had lost the three children. Sometimes, Kate could momentarily forget what had happened but it drastically affected her mood when she would remember, and that happened often. Oh, what Bertie and Nettie must be going through! She couldn't imagine loving a child more than she loved Jane, Parke, and Gardiner. Looking at little Julia Jackson, she knew she could, one day, care for a child. Her own. The children she hoped to have with Sandie. She knew without a doubt that he would be an exceptional father.

After another hour or so of visiting with the kind Mary Jackson, Kate and Bertie made their way to Major Harman's headquarters, again escorted by Captains Heth and Douglas.

"Are you anxious to see Major Pendleton?" Bertie asked.

"Unbelievably," Kate said, excitement and anticipation bubbling within her. "It feels like a year since I have seen him. I hope that we have time to speak with each other, just the two of us."

"I'm sure that can be arranged," Bertie said.

Kate glanced at Stockton, who was arm in arm with Bertie. His face was stoic, his jaw clenched. She gave a soft sigh and wished she hadn't upset him by not telling him she was engaged to another man. She should have said something the very next time she had seen him, instead of acting as though their relationship could remain the same. Before she knew it, they were at the Major's.

"Miss Corbin, Mrs. Corbin. How good to see you both again. When last we met, the circumstances were most dire. My deepest sympathies for your losses." Dr. McGuire stood and kissed both of their hands.

"It is good to see you as well, Doctor," Bertie said. Kate smiled, then turned to the other man in the room, whom Dr. McGuire introduced as Major John A. Harman.

"It is an honor to meet you. I wish we could have met earlier this winter." He said. The man was in his late 30's with a bushy beard and kind, yet sad eyes. The women quickly learned that he had been a butcher, Texas Ranger, farmer, newspaper editor, and stage line operator. He had also been a captain of the Virginia Militia. He was currently Jackson's quartermaster.

"It is a pleasure to meet you as well, Major." Bertie agreed.

"My apologies for my tardiness." Kate turned as Sandie entered the room. His face brightened when he saw Kate. "My dear, I didn't know you would be here. It is wonderful to see you." He gave her a brief embrace and a chaste kiss on her forehead.

"Shall we sit?" Major Harman suggested, and the dinner guests all complied. The meal was simple but tasty. When it was finished, Sandie looked at Bertie.

"Mrs. Corbin, I know I am being forward, but may I have your permission to take Catherine for a stroll?"

"Of course," Bertie said. "Major Harman?"

371

"By all means, young man." The quartermaster said.

Kate took the arm that Sandie offered her. Once they were outside and out of sight of the others, he pulled her into his arms and gave her a gentle kiss on her lips. Kate wrapped her arms around his neck, returning the kiss. He pulled back and looked into her eyes.

"I love you, Catherine, mine. So much. When you and I are together, I am in my glory."

"As am I." Kate smiled. Sandie had such a way with words. She kissed him again. "How is your new camp?" They began strolling arm in arm.

"Very well. The morale of our army is high. We are in fine condition and stronger than ever. We are in an admirable state of organization and discipline and our armament and equipment is also in good supply."

Kate smiled at the excitement in his voice. He clearly loved his job and it was endearing to her. His enthusiasm also made her heart ache. He was a soldier, an exceptional one. She had given her heart to a man that could be killed at any time.

"Of one thing, I am certain." Sandie continued. "This struggle has just begun in earnest and from this time forward, we must exert all our energies to cope with the enemy."

"You believe the war will still last a while?" Kate asked. She didn't like the idea of the war lasting longer at all. Not one bit.

"Unfortunately, I do. The north has many more men than we do, although we do have better fighters and leaders." Sandie brushed a lock of hair from her forehead and tucked it behind her ear. Kate suddenly didn't want to talk about the war, so she changed the subject.

"I noticed that, while Major Harman is quite pleasant, there is a despondency about him. Do you know the reason?"

"I do. He's had a rough go of it since the war started. His seventh child was born soon after he enlisted in the army, so he missed the first year of the child's life. Then, unfortunately, in April of last year, he lost four of his seven children to an illness. He was not there to support his wife and family. I'm not sure he will ever get over that."

"I understand how he would feel so sad, then, Sandie. It is unimaginable to lose one child, but to lose more...it's something..." tears formed in her eyes as she recalled her own losses. Sandie pulled her into his arms. "I have tried to be so strong, Sandie." Tears fell down her cheek and began soaking into his wool jacket. He rubbed her back, gently calming her.

"You are strong, Catherine. One of the strongest women that I have ever known." He pulled back and wiped her tears. "I am so sorry I wasn't there to support you physically, but know that in my heart, I have been with you every day, every moment, always. I know this war has not been easy to live through and it will not get better any time soon. But with strength from God and our love and support of one another, we can get through anything." He kissed her. "We can and we will."

Monday, April 27, 1863
Turner's Glenn Plantation

Belle made her way from patient to patient, bringing sugar biscuits that Annie and Ruthie had made. Patients had been moving in and out of their home, and she was, in a way, enjoying what she was doing.

"Miss Turner?" Dr. Knightly's voice came from behind her. She turned. She and the doctor had been getting along much better, although she still had to keep her guard up when she was around him.

"Yes, Dr. Knightly?" She gave him a brief smile.

"I was just down in the kitchen and your sister seemed a little overwhelmed. I told her that I would send you down to help her."

"Really." Belle wasn't quite sure why his statement irked her so much, but it did. "Who gave you permission to dictate what I do and do not do?"

"I am not trying to dictate anything, Miss Turner. I noticed that your sister needed help. I appreciate what you do for the men, but there are other important things that need to be attended to, such as the men's dietary needs. Your visiting the men will do them no good if they have nothing to eat." Dr. Knightly tried to keep his voice calm, but Belle could tell she was provoking him.

"What I do is important and you know it and I don't have to do something just because you say that I must." She couldn't let him just tell her what to do.

"I never said that your work wasn't important. Besides, are you sure you're not going to help Miss Annie simply because it was me who asked you to do so?"

"Oh, you asked me to? Are you sure you don't mean that you told me to? Practically ordered me to?" Belle's voice was loud now and starting to attract the attention of the patients.

"I didn't order you to do anything." He sounded a little angry now, and perhaps frustrated. "I simply suggested that you help your sister."

"What you really suggested, Dr. Knightly, is that what my sister is doing is more important than what I am doing." She tried to subtly bring up a diversionary point, a tactic that had won her many arguments in the past.

"No. That is not what I said, Miss Turner." He ran a hand through his hair and rubbed his neck. "You are completely twisting my words."

"Doctor." Belle took a deep breath, then decided to change her approach. "I do apologize. I've just been feeling a little overwhelmed myself lately." She softened her voice and gave him her most charming smile. "All of this nursing has made me dreadfully tired. And perhaps a little more argumentative than I usually am."

"I know that is not true, Miss Turner." Dr. Knightly stepped closer to her. He had finally discovered Belle's tactics.

"So now you're calling me a liar?" Belle kept her tone honey-sweet.

"Not a liar, no, but very skilled at using everything you have to win an argument and get your way." Dr. Knightly's voice was low and controlled. His gaze was intense as if he could see right into her mind. She felt he could see everything she was trying to hide, even things that she tried to hide from herself.

"I have no idea what you are talking about," Belle said, avoiding his gaze. She looked out the window and saw Eric, Elizabeth and Max approach the house in the wagon. "Excuse me. I have to go and see Elizabeth." She moved around him and walked toward the front door, leaving her basket of biscuits near the last patient she had been attending.

"Miss Turner, running away from challenges won't always work." He said softly as she passed. She paused and gave him an irritated look over her shoulder than continued to the door.

"Miss Annie will still need help in the kitchen." He added, and she slammed the door behind her.

"Elizabeth!" Belle called to her sister as Elizabeth climbed down from the wagon. "How did it go in town? How is the shop progressing?"

"It is coming along well, thanks to the enormous generosity of donors from around the South." Elizabeth smiled. "How is it here? Has anything new happened?"

"No. Nothing." Belle glanced at the doorway. Dr. Knightly had opened the door and stood there, watching her. When he saw her looking back at him, he turned and went back into the house. She turned back to her sister. "Any news in town about the war?"

"Unfortunately, yes. The Union's General Hooker is starting a new campaign. Many people in town worry that fighting may be close to us again."

"Oh, gracious. We should definitely pray for a swift end to the fighting and that we do not have many casualties." Belle agreed.

Elizabeth smiled. As always, it was good to hear Belle talk of prayers.

"That we should, Belle. That we should."

374

Wednesday, April 29, 1863

Banks of the Rappahannock River

AJ leaned against a rock, looking cautiously around as she waited for her contact. She had important information and needed to get it to the Confederate officers. Her fishing pole stood nearby in case a Federal soldier came by and she needed a reason to be down by the river.

"Miss Prentiss, good to see you." Nathaniel grinned at his sister as he rounded the rock she was leaning against.

"Nathaniel!" She threw her arms around him. "I hardly recognized you." She gestured at the full beard he now had. He rubbed it and chuckled.

"That is actually a good thing, with what I'm doing these days."

"How so?" AJ asked? "And how have you been?"

"I've been well. Quite well, thank you. We're all excited getting ready to march to Chancellorsville."

"That makes sense, based on what I have noticed," AJ said. "The Union is preparing to cross the Rappahannock upriver. I overheard men say that they want to try and flank General Lee."

Nathaniel nodded. "That confirms what we've suspected." He smiled. "Good work, AJ. How are you and Liberty doing?"

"We're doing as well as can be expected. She's insisting she do more, especially with gathering intelligence. I do not want her involved in that, though."

"I agree," Nathaniel said. "Sometimes...what would you do if I asked you to stop what you're doing? With the Yankees?"

"I would tell you that I feel as if I'm doing something important. Something good for the cause. I have been helping, Nathaniel. You know that, so I would tell you that I would like to continue what I'm doing." She gave him a look. "Why? Do you regret asking me to gather information?"

He sighed. "Maybe. If something were to happen to you...I just don't know. I would never forgive myself, I know that much."

"Nathaniel. I'll be fine, besides, with the Yankees moving out, there might not be much I can do anymore."

"Perhaps." Nathaniel checked his pocket watch. "I should be going." He hugged her again. "Take care of yourself. And Liberty."

"I will." She handed him the items she had taken from camp and the note with the rest of the information she had gathered. You take care of yourself. Especially since fighting's expected." She gave him a smile.

"Yes, ma'am." He smiled back, then headed out the same way he came.

Saturday, May 2, 1863
On the Road to Chancellorsville

AJ rode quickly toward Chancellorsville. She had witnessed the Union Army moving across the river into Fredericksburg and knew that she had to let Lt. Daniels know. She also had ammunition that she had found in the camp that she wanted to hand over. Everything had been carefully concealed on her person, but she still had to be careful. She didn't want to run into any Union troops outside of Fredericksburg, but Chancellorsville would be close enough for her to travel on her own in one day. At least that is what she hoped. She had left Liberty at the Turner plantation just in case.

AJ heard the fighting before she could see it. The ground trembled with artillery fire. She dismounted and continued cautiously.

"Miss Prentiss, don't tell me...it is you!"

AJ turned at the sound of Richard Evans's furious voice. He dismounted his own horse and strode angrily toward her. His hair was messy and grimy, his uniform jacket was torn at the shoulder and covered in mud, and his face was filled with a fury that she had not witnessed from him. This was not the Richard Evans she was familiar with.

"Mr. Evans. I didn't expect to find you here."

He was suddenly right in front of her, looking down at her, his eyes flashing and his chest heaving. "Do you know how close you are to the battlefield? You could be another casualty! You could be hurt, killed or worse. What are you doing here?"

"I have information and supplies. I had to get them to the troops."

"You cannot be serious, information and supplies are not worth your life."

"With all due respect, Captain Evans, you are not my caretaker. You are not my father, my brother, my husband or even a cousin. You have no reason, no right to tell me what to do."

"At this point, I don't care that I'm not a relation. I insist that you come with me." He grabbed her arm and steered her in the direction that he had come from. She pulled her horse behind her and he grabbed the reins to his horse as they passed by.

"Where are you taking me?" AJ wasn't really concerned for her safety now that Richard had found her. Even as angry as he was, she knew he wouldn't let any harm come to her.

"I am taking you to a place where you'll be safe and we can give General Jackson your information." His grip loosened on her arm, but he was making it clear that she was to come with him.

It wasn't long before they arrived in Jackson's headquarters and walked inside. The small stone home was abandoned.

"Blast," Richard said. "They must have moved out already." He sighed. "I must get back to my regiment." He looked at her. "All right, Miss Prentiss. Please listen to me. I will take your information to a general. I am going to bring you to a nearby field hospital. You should be safe there. Do I have your word that you will stay there until I or someone that you know comes to get you?"

"I promise," AJ said. "Let me retrieve what I brought." He turned around so she could reach under her skirts and take out the goods.

Richard took her arm, much more gently this time, then led her back outside and toward the field hospital he had spoken of. She could still hear the battle in the distance. Guns constantly fired, the cannons were also firing and men were shouting. She wanted to ask Richard how the fight was going, but he seemed extremely agitated.

As they approached the Wilderness Tavern, Richard stopped. "Here we are."

"This is a tavern," AJ told him.

"Not right now," Richard said. "Dr. Harvey Black of our Confederate Second Corps needed it for a hospital."

As they moved closer, AJ almost gagged at the stench. The battle at Chancellorsville had started the day before and the wounded were pouring in.

"Captain Evans." AJ grabbed his arm. "I hope you know that I'm not a careless person. I just want to help, to do what I can. I will risk my life if need be, but I don't go looking for danger." She wasn't sure why she needed him to know that, but she did.

"I am aware of that, Miss Prentiss." His voice softened. "I admire your bravery. I just...I feel responsible for you. Besides..." He gave her a small grin. "I need you to get home safely before tomorrow so that my mother has someone to dine with after Sunday Mass."

She smiled back. "Thank you for your assistance, Captain."

"Always a pleasure, Miss Prentiss." He then nodded. "Come, I'll introduce you to Dr. Black."

Sunday, May 3, 1863
Chancellorsville Field Hospital

AJ awoke to church bells in the distance. She pushed herself up from the bed she had made from blankets and rags that she had gathered the night before. Yesterday had been exhausting. AJ had a new respect for the work the Turner family was doing at their plantation. She had done menial tasks at Chatham, but this work was entirely different.

AJ quickly found Dr. Black, who was in charge and he gave her instructions on what she could do. She had immediately noticed the lack of supplies and medication. She resolved to do even more to get Confederate patients what they needed.

AJ had been working for a few hours when she overheard a conversation between a doctor and an orderly.

"...lots going on out there." The orderly said. "They say Stonewall was wounded last night. He may need to have an amputation and Hill was slightly injured as well. Stuart's in command for now."

"All those injuries...that cannot be good for our side." The doctor said, wiping his bloodied hands on his apron. AJ continued wiping the brow of the soldier that she knelt next to as she listened.

"Yes, but there is also a rumor that Hooker was wounded this morning." The orderly replied. "It's difficult to know about that for sure, though."

"It would be lucky for us." The doctor said, then voiced the thought that had entered AJ's mind. "What was Jackson doing in such a position that he would be so badly injured?"

"I can't rightly say, doctor." The young man answered.

A tear slipped down AJ's face. She'd enjoyed the few interactions she had with General Jackson.

Lord, please be with him and help him recover. She prayed.

Turner's Glenn

"There are reports of fighting nearby again." Belle looked up as Elizabeth came into the parlor. Belle had been speaking with some of the wounded men and was just heading into her Father's former study to check on the soldiers there.

"I thought I heard cannon fire. How near?" Belle asked.

"Marye's Heights again," Elizabeth answered. "Mother says we need to prepare room for new wounded."

"Where?" Belle asked. "We don't have much room left. Drat, I suppose we'll lose our dining room again."

"We're to move the healthier men to tents outside. The doctors are having the orderlies set them up now, they will make further decisions after that." Elizabeth looked around the room.

Belle bit her lip. "At least the weather will be a bit friendlier than it was in December. The wounded won't have to fight bitter coldness."

"That is true," Elizabeth replied, then saw her mother approaching.

"Elizabeth, Belle, would you two go help Lainey and Meri with laundry out back? We're going to need clean sheets and bandages once the wounded start arriving."

"Of course, Mother," Elizabeth responded.

"Are you sure I can't be of more help here, Mother?" Belle asked. Of all the tasks that had to be done at the hospital, Belle hated doing

378

laundry more than any other chore. She despised how her hands chapped and cracked after the job. "Elizabeth said we needed to start moving the men."

Miriam smiled knowingly at Belle. "My dear, your help is needed in laundry, then you can go back to visiting with the men. We'll have many new patients sooner than we can be prepared for them."

Belle withheld a sigh. "Of course, Mother." She then turned and followed Elizabeth to the back porch.

Confederate Field Hospital near Chancellorsville

"Miss Prentiss, could I have your assistance over here, please?" Dr. Harvey Black called to AJ, who immediately joined him. A young man tossed and turned on a roughly thrown together surgical table.

"What can I do to help? She asked. A stain of blood spread from the soldier's shoulder.

"I need to pull the bullet from his shoulder. We're running low on morphine and must save it for other procedures. Will you help me hold the young man down and comfort him while I extract it?"

"Of course," AJ responded, standing at the man's head and placing her hands on his shoulders. "Hello there, sir." She addressed the patient. "I know you're probably in a lot of pain right now, but Dr. Black here is going to make you better."

The man gave her a small smile. His face was covered in sweat, so she pulled her apron up and wiped it. "Thank you, ma'am."

Dr. Black took an instrument and began to work. As he did, AJ held the man as steady as she could and continued talking gently to him in order to distract him.

"Are you a Christian, sir?" She asked. The man nodded, shaking as the doctor prodded the wound.

"What is your favorite scripture verse?" She asked.

"I like most anything from Philippians or any of the letters." He replied. She smiled at him and began quoting from the letters as much as she could remember. The soldier relaxed as she spoke. When she had exhausted all of the Scripture passages that she knew, she began to recite some prayers. The doctor continued working and finally pulled out a jagged scrap of metal.

"Hmm. Not a bullet at all." The doctor said, placing the scrap in a small bowl and covering the wound with a cloth.

"What is it?" AJ asked, wiping the brow of the soldier.

"It's a piece of shrapnel." He said. "It's fired from a cannon. They load an empty shell with lead or iron balls. Sometimes, they'll burst above or before the enemy and the projectiles will shower down, other times, they'll land on the ground and explode."

"My goodness." AJ shook her head. "How horrible."

"Yes. New fighting tactics have made caring for the wounded much more difficult." The doctor said. He motioned to some orderlies, who came over to move the patient.

"Bless you, ma'am." The man whispered as he was taken to a pallet.

"God go with you, soldier," AJ replied.

Turner's Glenn

Belle looked toward Marye's Heights. From her current position, she could just make out the fighting happening in town. She sighed. What would happen to all of the Confederate patients in their home...and the doctors, if the Union won? She couldn't imagine doctors being taken prisoner, but the patients would be.

"Belle!" Lainey called, approaching her sister. "Mama wants you to come home. There are a lot of soldiers being brought in."

"So many wounded." Belle murmured. "I imagine the furious fighting here almost rivals the killing in Sharpsburg last year."

"Yes, and those wounded are coming here to be taken care of at this moment, so we need to go."

Belle smiled at her sister. "All right, all right, I'm coming. I suppose I can bring some Southern charm to those poor, wounded boys."

"You do realize you can do more than just talk to them, don't you?" Lainey asked. The two began walking back toward the house.

"Yes, but I like doing what I do best," Belle explained. "Is that such a bad thing?"

"No, but you could challenge yourself more," Lainey replied.

"My thirteen-year-old sister is telling me that I need to challenge myself," Belle said, speaking more to herself than her sister. Lainey just smiled. "It has been a while since you and I have had a good talk," Belle added. "How are you handling everything that has been going on lately?"

"As well as can be expected. Sometimes though, I feel so busy taking care of the wounded and doing chores that I don't have any time to really enjoy life." Lainey said. She sounded so mature. Belle wasn't sure when that had even happened. "I am glad that Mother's home. Not that you and Elizabeth and Annie weren't doing a good job managing the plantation. It's just nice to have her home with us."

"I agree with that," Belle said. "It's nice of you to say that I took good care of you."

"You did," Lainey confirmed. They soon reached the house, which was overcome with doctors, orderlies, and patients once again.

"Belle!" Elizabeth looked up from her position. She had been next to a soldier who was sitting against a tree. "Belle, what could you see?"

Elizabeth brushed a strand of hair from her face. Her concern was, of course for her husband.

"I couldn't see much, it was so smoky. It did look as though our boys were driving the Yankees back, though." Belle picked up an empty bucket and walked with Elizabeth toward the outdoor pump.

"How can the Yankees be so stupid trying to take Marye's Heights again?" Elizabeth shook her head. "Casualties?"

"Too many," Belle answered. "We'll be busy for a while."

Each woman filled their buckets. "Do you need help giving water to the men?"

"That would be very helpful. It looks like the line of those needing our help is never ending."

Tuesday, May 5, 1863
Chancellorsville Field Hospital

"Why, Miss Prentiss, you're still here?" Dr. Black asked.

"Yes. I was asked to remain here until my escort returns. I hope that's okay."

"Of course. We can certainly use your help. Make sure that you take the time to eat and rest. We don't need you to become a patient yourself."

"Sir. If I may ask. I am acquainted with Stonewall Jackson and some of his staff. Can you tell me anything about the General? I heard he was wounded."

"Yes. I actually assisted with the amputation. The general was brought here when he was first injured, but he is being moved to Richmond, soon as he is well enough to travel."

"Is he still here? Could I visit him?"

"I believe they are preparing him for transportation as we speak. I wish I could say yes, but I cannot."

"My goodness." AJ nodded. "I wouldn't want to disturb him, but thank you for the information."

AJ continued helping around the hospital for the rest of the day, doing what she could to ease the burden of the staff and the pain of the wounded. It was different work than she was used to, but she found it rewarding.

"America." She turned and saw Richard Evans striding toward her. "You actually stayed where I asked you to." He gave her a brief, tired smile.

"I did. I told you I would and I'm a woman that keeps her word." She wiped her hands on the apron she had been given. "What news do you have?"

"Hooker is falling back. Lee appears to have accomplished another great victory." Richard took off his Henschel hat.

"I heard General Jackson had his arm amputated. He was here, at Wilderness Tavern. They moved him earlier today. Is there any word on how he was injured?"

Richard slammed his hat against his leg. "Rumors are that he was accidentally shot by our own men. Such a pathetic waste."

AJ put a hand on his arm, sensing that he needed comfort. "Do you know why they were moving him so soon?"

"Yes, Lee wants him transferred to Guinea Station, not here in a field hospital. He is afraid of what may happen if the Yanks get their hands on him."

"I hadn't thought of that. It makes sense." AJ replied.

"Yes, but it still is such a waste. A huge loss for the South."

"He is a good, strong man. I am sure he'll recover."

"Perhaps, but he'll never be able to lead his regiment in the way that we're used to. We'll miss him." Richard shook his head. "Are you ready to go home? The road should be clear and I was given permission to escort you back to Fredericksburg."

"I don't need an escort, Captain Evans and I have been ready to leave for a while. I left my sister with the Turners and I want to get back to her as soon as possible."

"I'm sure you don't need an escort, but it would make both myself and Major Daniels feel better if you will allow me to bring you home."

"Of course. AJ replied. "Well then, let's be on our way. I am anxious to get back, as I said. Just let me say goodbye to Dr. Black first."

"All right."

AJ said goodbye to the doctor and some patients that she had gotten to know over the past few days, then she and Richard mounted their horses and began the ride back to Fredericksburg.

"Do you know anything about my father or brother?" She asked.

"Your father is doing well, I caught sight of him yesterday. Your brother was sent on a courier mission out West. I haven't heard any news of him."

"I see. Thank you." She gave Richard a small smile, but he was looking straight ahead and didn't respond. She wasn't sure what else she could say, so she fell silent.

Turner's Glenn

"Federal troops are withdrawing from Chancellorsville," Elizabeth told Belle. "We won the battle."

"Yet again." Belle smiled smugly. "It won't be long before we've won the entire war and our independence."

"Yes, and the men will be home and we can start putting our lives back together." Elizabeth placed her hand on her slightly rounded stomach and smiled. "I'm going to town to check on the damage, perhaps even visit with some of the townspeople."

"Who would you like to visit in town?" Belle asked. "Many people still haven't come back yet."

"I would like to check on my home, of course. We were making such progress. Hopefully, Eric will be able to take in projects soon, as long as there is no new damage. I would also like to stop in and see Margaret."

"Buckley?" Belle scoffed. "Why in the world would you want to see her?"

"You don't need to act like that, Belle. Margaret...she is a good person. I think that she has been through some rough times in her life and people have made incorrect assumptions." Elizabeth defended Margaret. "I believe she needs a friend, and I am more than happy to be that person."

"Well, then, you go right ahead and do that, but don't expect me to be her friend." Belle turned and almost ran into Dr. Knightly. "Excuse me, doctor."

"Is everything alright?" He asked Elizabeth.

"Oh, I love my sister, but she can be infuriating sometimes." Elizabeth sighed. "Yes, doctor. Everything is fine. I will be going to town for a few hours."

"Godspeed." The doctor nodded and Elizabeth walked out the door to the waiting wagon.

Fredericksburg

"Margaret!" Elizabeth entered the store and immediately found the pretty blonde.

"Good afternoon. How can I help you?"

"I was just in town and wanted to stop by. I feel as though I have been neglecting you these past few months." She looked around the empty shop.

"Oh, Mrs. Bennett, you don't need to worry about me," Margaret said in her quiet way.

"I know I don't have to," Elizabeth said. "I like to check in on my friends."

"I appreciate the thought," Margaret responded.

Elizabeth nodded. "Do you hear from Pastor Wetherly?"

"I have a few times," Margaret admitted. "It sounds as though he is doing well."

"That's wonderful. He is such a good man." Elizabeth said.

"He is," Margaret said. "As is your husband. Have you heard from Mr. Bennett since he left?"

"No, he writes as much as he can but the postal service is so sporadic. It was good to have him around all winter and early spring." She smiled.

"I can see it was nice." Margaret gestured to Elizabeth's stomach.

"Is it that noticeable?" Elizabeth smiled at Margaret's small nod and placed a hand on her growing child. "How is the business?"

"I am one of the few storeowners who stayed behind despite the battle. It's sometimes difficult to get products in, but my stepfather made some very good contacts over the years before he enlisted. They've actually been very good to me." She smiled. "There are still some kind people in this world."

"I am glad to hear that," Elizabeth replied, also knowing there were many judgmental people in the world.

"I see you have been making progress on your home and business," Margaret stated. "I know that it was unlivable after the first battle."

"It was. The mayor allotted our family some of the money that was donated to the town. We've been rebuilding the blacksmith shop first so we can get an income, then we can get the home fixed up." Elizabeth smiled. "I feel so blessed that we have a place to stay during the repairs. Turner's Glenn is crowded, but so many people didn't have the options that we did after the battle.

"Very true," Margaret said. "I envy you that. I always wanted a brother or sister. Having a lot of them would have been even better." She smiled sadly. "Perhaps someday I will get married and have many children."

"I hope that you will," Elizabeth replied. "No matter what's in our past, God has a wonderful plan for our future."

"If only I can find a man who will overlook my past," Margaret said solemnly.

"Margaret, if you are truly sorry for what you have done, no matter the sin, God has already forgiven you." Elizabeth placed an arm on Margaret's shoulder. "However, if you ever need someone to talk to, you can always come see me."

"Dominic…I mean, Pastor Wetherly told me that as well." Margaret replied. "I never really took him up on it. I was afraid that he would look at me with disgust. Like so many others do." She sighed and glanced around the store. "I know what people say about me, Mrs.

Bennett. I do. I just...well, I know how the rumors were started. Would you believe me if I were to tell you that none of them were true?"

"I have never had reason to doubt you, Margaret. Yes, I would believe you."

"Do you think Dominic would believe me?" She asked.

"He probably already knows they are untrue," Elizabeth said. "Pastor Wetherly is very understanding." Elizabeth covered Margaret's hand with hers. "I know you haven't had the easiest of lives, Margaret. The pastor knows that as well. I'm sure he has forgiven you already, but he should know what he is forgiving you for. You should talk to him. Tell him your whole story."

"Thank you, Mrs. Bennett. Just when I needed someone, in you came."

"Divine Providence," Elizabeth said, then had another thought. "Margaret, a helpful step might be for you to come to church services with my family and me on Sunday. You are always more than welcome."

Margaret paled. "I may be welcomed by you, but I am quite sure that not everyone will feel the same."

"The choice is yours, but I would encourage you. People may balk at the idea initially, but Jesus teaches forgiveness and I feel the parishioners would eventually get used to your coming."

"Perhaps you're right," Margaret said. "I suppose that it wouldn't hurt to at least try." She smiled at Elizabeth. "Would you save me a seat this Sunday, Mrs. Bennett?"

"It would be my pleasure, Miss Buckley."

Wednesday, May 6, 1863
Fredericksburg Post Office

Miss Prentiss,   *May 4, 1863*

I hope this letter finds you well and I hope you will not object to hearing from me yet again. I do enjoy writing to you. It helps me express my feeling.

I am sure you have heard of the Stonewall Brigade's recent tragedy. Our fearless leader has had his left arm amputated after he was shot while coming back from patrol. It was one of our own soldiers, making a horrible mistake. I was not with Jackson at the time of the shooting but we were close. I was looking for him when I heard shouting and was told that the General had been struck three times. When I reached him, he was on the ground, blood flowing freely from his elbow. I cut his sleeve open and tried using my handkerchief to stop the blood flow. I believe my attempt was successful.

We got the general on a litter and tried bringing him to safety, but we were still being shot at and one of the stretcher-bearers was shot and we dropped the poor man. I shielded Jackson as best I could, and when the firing slowed, I dragged him to safety. More soldiers came to help carry him back to our camp. Unfortunately, we dropped him again after another litter-bearer fell. He was in great pain after that. Finally, we got him to an ambulance.

I held a light for Dr. McGuire during the General's surgery, and all night, it was my job to watch him and keep him undisturbed. All other staff members returned to duty, so I was the only one to remain. I am quite happy to report that he was still very alert, in spite of everything he had been through.

I have been sitting with Jackson all day, trying to keep his spirits up. I am confident that he will pull through this.

If she is not already aware, can you let Miss Corbin know that Pendleton is alive and well? He had just been sent to deliver a message to AP Hill right before the shooting began, so was never in any danger.

Before this tragedy occurred, however, I was privileged to witness something I will not soon forget. On the day the battle began, I woke up cold in the early morning hours, and I caught a glimpse of a small flame. I sat up and saw our two great Virginia generals, sitting on old cracker boxes, warming their hands over a small fire of twigs. I was soon able to recognize Lee and Jackson, planning something. I can only imagine it was part of the great victory we had at Chancellorsville. If only Jackson hadn't been wounded.

Miss Prentiss, I do hope you welcome this letter. I very much enjoyed my time at Moss Neck, getting to know you lovely ladies of Fredericksburg. I do hope you and I can continue our friendship. I hope to hear from you soon.

Yours,
Captain James Powers Smith

"Captain James Power Smith?" Belle looked over AJ's shoulder at the signature scrawled at the bottom. "Isn't that a friend of Sandie Pendleton?"

"He is." AJ gave a small, shy smile, thinking of the kind, handsome soldier.

"I didn't realize you two had struck up a friendship." Belle grinned at her friend. It was good to see a man like Captain Smith show some interest in AJ. Even if it didn't lead to a proposal, it would be good for her self-esteem.

386

"We spoke with each other several times while he was at Moss Neck. He was the perfect gentleman." *Unlike some soldiers that I have been acquainted with*, she thought Richard Evans's image popped into her mind.

"I believe he would be the perfect friend for you," Belle said.

"I agree." AJ folded the letter and placed it into her pocket.

"Did the Captain mention anything about Major Pendleton? Or General Jackson?"

"Actually yes. He says Major Pendleton is fine. He left the area right before Jackson and his men were shot at. It sounds as if Captain Smith is still with the general."

"I can't believe such a thing can happen." Belle shook her head as the two made their way towards Turner's Glenn. AJ had wanted to visit while she was on that side of the river. "I don't understand how our own troops could have mistaken Jackson's men for Yankees."

"It could have been Union soldiers patrolling. It must be very deceptive out there in the dark, unable to see anything but shadows."

"I suppose," Belle said. "I do hope he survives his amputation. Kate speaks highly of his doctor."

AJ was glad to hear Belle speak highly of any doctor. It was a refreshing change. "I feel the same way. Captain Smith says he is sure Jackson will make a full recovery. Unfortunately, it is unlikely he will be of any help to Lee in the field. It will be a long recovery."

"That is an unfortunate loss," Belle said. They continued walking.

"I'm excited to see Elizabeth," AJ said. "How is she feeling lately?"

"About as well as can be expected." Belle replied. "She's almost annoyingly happy to be carrying another child." Belle smiled. "I must admit, I am looking forward to having another niece or nephew. In that respect, I cannot wait until September."

"I am excited as well. I am sure it's been convenient having an abundance of doctors at Turner's Glenn. I hope they stay through September."

"I suppose," Belle said. "Although they do believe they're in charge of us completely and not just of our home. They act as though they can tell us and our people what to do. Helping them, cooking for them, doing whatever they want us to do. Annie, Elizabeth, Eric, even Lainey, and Max have been put to work. It has made life quite an inconvenience. Arrogant doctors, every one of them."

AJ withheld a sigh. She had been so encouraged by Belle's words about Dr. Hunter McGuire, and now she was acting as though the doctors were the enemy again.

"They've been able to keep an eye on Elizabeth though, I would suppose?" AJ asked.

"Oh, of course. Why wouldn't doctors find time to care for my dear sister?"

"Now, Belle, you know you shouldn't act like that. Here I thought you were making such progress in your behavior, besides, you shouldn't be upset. You're the woman who can get men to attend to your every whim." The women could see Turner's Glenn now, bustling with activity. The battle of Chancellorsville had been bringing even more wounded men to the home. Belle wondered if they would ever have the house to themselves again.

"Not every man." She muttered in response to AJ's comment.

"What do you mean?" AJ asked. Belle looked ahead, recognizing Dr. Aaron Knightly as he walked toward the house from one of the slave quarters where some of the patients were staying. She tried to hide her expression of loathing, but AJ knew her friend too well. She followed Belle's gaze. "One of the doctors? Really?" AJ tried not to sound amused, but she was. Every man who Belle ever came into contact with was instantly wrapped around her finger. If this man could fluster Belle, she really wanted to meet him.

"Don't laugh!" Belle said, stopping in her tracks. "I don't see what's so funny about this."

"You wouldn't." AJ turned toward her friend. "Belle, we've been friends for most of our lives, and for as long as I can remember, you have been able to manipulate every man you met into agreeing with you. Giving you what you wanted. Your father, your brother, Samuel, Nathaniel, and those are just some examples. I actually think it's refreshing that this Dr. Knightly is giving you a challenge. It's going to be good for you and entertaining for us."

Thursday, May 7, 1863
Prentiss Farm

"AJ!" Liberty ran into the house. "I need your help outside!"

"What's wrong?" AJ never heard this desperation in Liberty's voice, she quickly followed her sister.

"There is a wounded Confederate soldier in our barn," Liberty said.

"What? Are you serious?" AJ had to hurry to keep up.

"I am. He is wounded badly in the side. He is really pale. I think he has lost a lot of blood." Liberty opened the door to the barn and AJ immediately saw the soldier. He looked slightly familiar with dark hair and a thin frame.

"I found him here and unconscious when I came in to do some chores," Liberty said quietly.

"He looks familiar. I believe he is in the same unit as Richard Evans."

388

"He looks too young to be a soldier," Liberty said. "Not much older than me."

"If I remember correctly, he was quite young," AJ replied. "Come, let's get him into the house and see what we can do for him."

The two lifted the young man, who groaned at the movement. He was light, and it didn't take them long to get him into Nathaniel's room.

"Liberty, get some old sheets and a bowl of warm water." AJ tore the young soldier's shirt so that she could see the wound better. She bit her lip. The gash in his side was deep and Liberty had been correct about his loss of blood. He tossed and turned, sweating profusely. "Oh, Private Alexsander, what happened to you?" She murmured. Liberty quickly returned with what AJ had asked for. AJ tore one of the sheets so that she could clean the wound.

"How does it look?" Liberty asked.

"I am not a doctor," AJ said as she looked closer at the gaping wound. "However, I am sure that the area around the wound is not supposed to be red like that." She dipped the sheet in the water and gently scrubbed at the wound, hoping that the injury wasn't infected.

"What do we do?" Liberty asked.

"I'll get it cleaned up as best I can. We have to be very careful, though, the Yanks are still up at Chatham Manor. I don't want him to be taken prisoner."

"It is a wonder he made it to our barn without being caught. What is he doing on this side of the river?" Liberty said. She wiped his brow as AJ dressed the wound. "You said you know him. What is his name?"

"I believe it's Markus Alexsander. I met him that first time I ran into Richard Evans. Markus is very kind. Soft-spoken. Polite."

"So the opposite of how you would describe Richard Evans, then," Liberty said.

"Indeed," AJ replied.

"Is he going to be okay?" Liberty's voice was soft.

"Honestly, I don't know," AJ admitted. "I would like a doctor to come and take a look at him, but I don't want a Union doctor and I fear bringing a Confederate doctor over here would be too risky."

"I don't think doctors can be taken prisoner," Liberty said. "I can go to Turner's Glenn and ask them what doctor would be willing to make a house call in enemy territory or we can always tell them we need a doctor for my sick sister."

"That's not necessarily true, Liberty. The Yanks can take anyone they want as a prisoner. We can ask for advice, though. Yes, that might work. Describe the wound and ask one of the doctors the best care we can give." AJ nervously bit her lip. "Yes, let's do that, but Liberty, you must be extremely careful. I cannot allow anything to happen to you."

"All right. I will, I will." Liberty said, then was off.

AJ sat by the soldier for a few moments and was about to leave and do some chores when he groaned and opened his blood-shot eyes.

"Where am I?" His voice told AJ that he was clearly in pain, and he blinked to try and focus on AJ's face.

"You were wounded, sir. My sister found you in our barn on the northern side of the Rappahannock River."

"Please tell me you're not a Yankee sympathizer...wait...I've seen you before...you're that female spy." He said. AJ smiled.

"Shhh. I prefer to be called an informant, Mr. Alexsander. It sounds a little less hostile, also, it would be best if that fact is kept a secret." She bent and fluffed his pillows, then straightened the blankets and quilts around him.

"You do know what you're doing is dangerous?"

"Really? I had no idea."

Markus smiled weakly. His side was still painful from the wound, but AJ seemed to have patched it up quite well.

"Do you enjoy risking your life for the Southern cause?"

"I don't prefer it, Mr. Alexsander, nor do you, I imagine. Do you feel strong enough to sip some broth? I could go and warm some up."

"That sounds wonderful, ma'am." His voice was hoarse.

"My sister went across the river to a field hospital to get some help from a Confederate doctor," AJ told him.

"Don't know that you needed to do that, ma'am." He protested. "I'll be fine."

"Well, we just want to make sure," AJ replied. "You stay put. I'll be back shortly with that broth."

Sunday, May 10, 1863
Turner's Glenn

Annie crossed the room that used to serve as the parlor. Men lay on thin pallets or cots that had been made from anything available. She went from man to man, giving them a drink of water. She approached a soldier who had recently come in from the latest battle in Fredericksburg.

"Good afternoon, sir." She smiled at him and he weakly smiled back. This was the first time Annie had been around when he was awake. He looked at her with warm brown eyes that reminded her of melted chocolate. She quickly noticed that he had his left leg amputated just below the knee. She knelt next to him and offered him some water. He gripped her wrist and held on as she lifted his head and dribbled the water into his mouth. His eyes met hers and she gave him another smile.

"Much obliged, Miss." He weakly reached up to tip a hat that wasn't there. "Name's Captain Joseph Byron of Byron Hill in South Carolina."

390

"I am Margaret-Anne Turner. Annie. My family and I live here at Turner's Glenn." She dipped a rag into the second bucket of water and wiped his face.

"I am truly sorry that we've invaded your town and your home, Miss Turner."

"It's hardly your fault, Captain Byron. I appreciate the apology, at any rate."

"I never would have believed that a war could be this destructive to our Southern cities and so hard on our women." He said.

"I don't think anyone did," Annie replied. "Have you been able to write home? Tell your family about your injury?"

"Not sure where I would even send the letter. My mother passed away years ago, and my father and brother are away fighting for the cause. My sister married my best friend and last I heard she moved in with his parents."

"I could help you write a letter to her," Annie suggested.

"You could, but I doubt you would find a way to get the letter posted." He rubbed the stubble on his chin. "Believe it or not, my best friend is from Pennsylvania. Met him at the Point. West Point, that is."

"I can believe it," Annie said. "I have kin in Pennsylvania. A cousin and uncle. In a small town called Gettysburg."

"Really. Now that is a coincidence." The soldier smiled. "That is where my friend, Michael Lewis is from. His folks own a general store there."

"I have never been up there myself," Annie said. "But my cousin Charlotte came down here, and I have spent time with her at other family events."

"It is difficult knowing people from the North. Are we really supposed to call them our enemy? I myself hope to see Michael and Augusta again, someday."

"I appreciate how you don't seem to be bitter about this injury," Annie said. "Many others would."

"I have never thought that being bitter was good for anyone." Captain Byron said. "I just try to be content no matter what happens to me, no matter the circumstance."

"That is a good way to live your life," Annie said.

"I have always thought so." The soldier smiled, then shifted so that he was sitting up. "Upon further reflection, Miss Turner, we should write a letter. I can send one to my father and one to my brother. Maybe one of them will actually receive it."

Annie left to get some writing paper.

"Where will you go when you leave the hospital?" Annie asked when she returned, kneeling next to the Captain.

"I don't recall,." he replied, "perhaps my father can help me decide."

Annie smiled again. "All right, then. How would you like to start your letter?

⚬≈⚬

Elizabeth placed a hand on her stomach. She had been having mild cramps all morning, something she had not experienced at this stage of the pregnancy when she was expecting her other children.

"Elizabeth, dear, what is wrong?" Miriam approached her. Elizabeth rubbed her lower back, which had been sore all day as well.

"Just some minor discomfort." Elizabeth replied. "I'm sure I'll be fine."

"Are you faint?" Miriam asked. She reached up to touch her daughter's forehead. "You are a little warm, but I wouldn't say that you're feverish."

"Ahhhh!" Elizabeth doubled over in pain, clenching her stomach. "This can't be, no."

"Elizabeth, what's wrong? Talk to me." Miriam tried to remain calm and called out to the first doctor she saw. Concern was obvious on her face.

"I don't...no, it can't be the baby, Mama, it's too early."

"We need to get her to a bed." Dr. Knightly quickly approached and put an arm around Elizabeth, who took a step, then collapsed. Dr. Knightly quickly swept her up in his arms and carried her to the room where the Turners were staying.

"Mama, what's going on?" Belle walked by, but stopped as she saw Dr. Knightly with Elizabeth in the room.

"I hope she's not going into labor." Dr. Knightly said, placing Elizabeth on the bed and pushing up the sleeves of his shirt.

"What? That's impossible!" Belle exclaimed. "She's not supposed to have the baby for another couple of months."

"Yes, Miss Turner, I am afraid to say that not all pregnancies go smoothly. Premature labor happens."

Elizabeth cried out, trying to keep calm, but the pain was excruciating.

"Doctor, you have to help her, please help the baby." Belle started to panic. She had never witnessed Elizabeth in such pain before.

"Belle, you need to calm down." Miriam said, her focus on her oldest daughter. Belle looked at Elizabeth again, horror on her face."

"Dr. Knightly, don't let her die, don't let her die like the doctors let my brother and fiancé die." Belle pleaded. "Doctor, please..."

"Miss Turner, you need to leave!" Dr. Knightly raised his voice. "I cannot have you in here if you are distracting Mrs. Bennett and myself."

"Doctor..."

"Out!" The doctor pointed to the door, a mixture of exasperation and fear in his voice. Elizabeth cried out again.

"Belle, please go see Annie and ask her and Zipporah to come up and bring hot water and as many towels as they can find. Then, please check on all of the children. Watch them and care for them until we are done in here."

"Mama..."

"Isabelle Marie, I need you to do as I ask." Miriam's tone was firm and Belle had no other option than to follow orders.

Later that evening

Belle stood at the hallway window, looking out across the fields. Elizabeth was quietly moaning. She had been in denial earlier, but it was at this moment she knew something had gone terribly wrong.

Dr. Knightly exited the bedroom with a forlorn look on his face. She tried to hide the tears in her eyes as she looked at him. *Lord, if you are listening, please, please let Elizabeth be all right. I know it seems like I haven't cared much about her these last few years, but I don't know how I can live without her.*

"Where are the rest of your siblings?" He asked, his voice soft and compassionate.

"Meri is reading to Lainey, Max, Benjamin, and Hannah. Annie is with my Elizabeth, as you know, which is where I should be. What's happened? How is Elizabeth? Is she okay?"

"Your sister is alive, Miss Turner." The doctor ran a hand through his already messed blonde hair.

"The baby?" She choked out, somehow knowing the answer.

He stepped next to her and looked out the window. "The little girl didn't make it."

Belle tried to stop the tears, but she couldn't. How could this have happened? How could God, who Elizabeth claimed loved her so much, have let this happen?"

Dr. Knightly hesitated. He had witnessed many different emotions from Belle Turner, but this vulnerability was new. Forgetting her dislike of him, he gently hugged her.

Belle was surprised at being in Dr. Knightly's arms but realized that she needed his comfort. She didn't even mind his unclean state, knowing that he had put so much energy into saving Elizabeth. She may not like him as a person, and she may not like doctors in general, but she had watched him work these past months and trusted him and his skill.

"Your sister is sleeping now, but she'll need you. She'll need you to be strong."

"I'm not the strong one. She is. James was the protector, the physically strong one and Elizabeth was the strong one emotionally and spiritually." Belle took a breath and pulled back from his embrace. "I'm sorry. I'm sure you think I'm being silly, crying over a lost baby when we see the death of men every day."

"Just because we see death and destruction every day doesn't mean it still doesn't affect us. It does. I know I hurt every time I lose a patient, whether I knew them or not." He looked into her eyes. "I'm really not the cold, heartless sawbones you think I am."

Belle stepped back and brushed her eyes, then looked out the window again. "It's strange, even though I never held that little girl in my arms, I loved her all the same. She was my niece. She was a part of this family already. The moment we knew Elizabeth was having another baby, the child was special to me and to our whole family." She looked toward the family cemetery. "I wonder if it would be unusual to bury her in the family plot."

"I don't think that would be unusual at all." Dr. Knightly said. He turned to look at the woman who intrigued him so much. She was spoiled, selfish and shallow, but he had glimpses of another side of her, when she let her guard down, like now. She looked at him, her striking green eyes shimmering with tears.

"I suppose I should say thank you. If you hadn't been here, we may have lost Elizabeth as well as the baby."

"No thanks are necessary, Miss Turner." She was so close, he only had to whisper the words and knew she would hear them. She looked up at him and touched his scruffy cheek. He leaned down and gently pressed his lips to hers. She gently wrapped her hand around his neck. He pulled back. "Belle..." he murmured. She looked at him, and all of a sudden realized what she had just done. She backed away.

"Dr. Knightly..."

"Don't you think it's time you started calling me Aaron?" He said, taking a step closer.

"No. This shouldn't have happened. I'm sorry that it did." She turned and left him, not looking back.

Monday, May 11, 1863
Turner's Glenn

Belle peeked into the room to check on Elizabeth. Her older sister lay in the bed, as pale as Belle had ever seen her. Her eyes were closed, but her breathing seemed steady. Annie sat next to her, watching her closely.

"How is she doing?" Belle asked quietly. Elizabeth's eyes slowly opened.

"I'm doing well." Elizabeth's voice was weak, scratchy. She tried to smile. "As well as can be expected, at least. How are things going downstairs?" Concern was apparent on her face. Belle clenched her teeth. Why did Elizabeth have to be concerned about others?

"That's so like you, worried about everyone else." Belle tried to hold back the words, but they flew out before she could stop them. Annie stood and faced Belle.

"Belle, if you are going to come in here and be harsh…"

"It's okay, Annie," Elizabeth said.

"I just don't want you to get upset. You need rest." Annie replied.

"I'm fine. Really." Elizabeth pushed herself up so she was resting against the headboard. Annie helped adjust her pillows.

"Thank you, Annie," Elizabeth said with a glance at Belle. "Why don't you take a break? Walk around a little bit, see if Ruthie needs any help."

"Or you can check on that soldier you've been mooning over," Belle said.

"I have not been mooning over Joseph Byron!" Annie said, her cheeks flushing.

"Is he that Captain who you have been talking with? The one who's lying in the parlor under the East window." Elizabeth smiled at Annie. "He seems very agreeable and handsome too. I would be interested in him if I didn't have Joshua."

Belle rolled her eyes. "Well, he's probably closer to your age than Annie's, Elizabeth."

"Nine years isn't that much older," Annie muttered.

"It's not, and you are a very mature young woman," Elizabeth said. "Now, go along. Belle can keep me company."

With a last glance over at Belle, Annie nodded and walked out the door, shutting it quietly behind her.

"Is there really an issue with this Captain Byron or are you just being a snob?"

"I'm not being a snob." Belle sat down in the chair.

"So tell me, how are you holding up, really, Belle?" Elizabeth asked.

"I should be asking you that question. Elizabeth…you almost died. You could have died, we could have lost you, just like James." Belle felt uncharacteristic tears begin to form as she thought about all the people that had died in the past year. A tear slid down her cheek. "Little Janie Corbin, Parke, and Gardiner. Bertie and Nettie are just about inconsolable and then to hear of the injury to General Jackson, a man who was so kind and gentle. All of the men who have died here in our home. There is so much suffering…"

395

"We can't always understand why things happen, Belle. Sometimes, we just have to trust that God will find a way to make it all right in the end."

"How can you still have so much faith? Elizabeth, you just lost a child. This past year, I have tried to be kinder, to be a better person. I thought that if I was good, like you, then maybe things would be better around here, but that hasn't happened. You even lost the baby."

"Belle, that's not how it works. I'm glad you've been trying to better yourself, but we can't expect God to make things better just because we change. He can. He can make anything happen, but it's all in His plan."

"Then why doesn't he just end this war?"

"Because He wants us, His children, to have the freedom and ability to make choices to do what is right. It means nothing if He just does everything for us."

"That doesn't make sense. Good things should happen to good people."

"Belle, think back the past few months. Even though you've grumbled about it and complained every chance you've gotten, you have actually been working hard and improving yourself without realizing it."

"Yes, and it's horrible," Belle muttered.

"I know you don't prefer manual labor, but what makes you feel better, just eating the food that Ruthie puts in front of you, or actually putting forth some effort and helping her prepare the meals?"

Belle thought about it. What her sister said made sense. She did feel a sense of accomplishment when she worked, but she couldn't admit that to Elizabeth. It was hard enough admitting it to herself.

"I rather like being waited on, thank you very much. I am not like you. I don't need to do manual labor in order to feel useful."

Elizabeth noticed that her sister had put up her guard again. She wouldn't listen to any more talk of faith. "You didn't answer my earlier questions. Is there any news outside this room? Annie and Mother have visited, and the children." Elizabeth smiled. It had been wonderful to hold her daughter and son tight. "It was so good to see them, but they haven't filled me in on any real news."

"Elizabeth, you never want to gossip."

"I'm not talking about gossip, I'm talking about news."

"Margaret Buckley came to visit. She said she missed you at church services on Sunday. I didn't realize she was coming to church with us now."

"I told you. Margaret and I have formed a friendship."

"You and Margaret Buckley? Elizabeth, we talked about this. You know her reputation."

"I do know her reputation, Belle, and it's wrong. I have also gotten the chance to know her and to see her heart. She's not a bad person." Elizabeth thought about the kind-hearted woman. "She has been through a lot and hasn't many friends."

"She's had plenty of male friends." Belle, said, remembering the interaction she had witnessed between Margaret and Samuel.

"Those men are not her friends, Belle, not even a little bit, and those rumors are not necessarily true."

"Yes, well, I appreciate her concern for you, but I can never forgive her for her dalliance with Samuel."

"You seemed to forgive Samuel quickly enough." Elizabeth pointed out. Belle just shrugged, and Elizabeth knew this portion of the conversation was over as well. Just as Belle was about to speak again, the door opened and Dr. Knightly strode in. He balked when he saw that Belle was there. "Miss Turner." He nodded at her, then turned to Elizabeth.

"How are you doing today, Mrs. Bennett?"

"Much better, thank you." She smiled.

Dr. Knightly glanced at Belle. He had avoided her since their kiss. It had been easy, as she seemed to be avoiding him as well. Belle sat quietly, hands folded in her lap, eyes averted. He hadn't thought she would be in here. He hadn't expected her to visit Elizabeth with the tension that existed between the sisters. He hadn't been able to get Belle out of his mind, though. He ran a hand through his hair and rubbed his head, something he seemed to do frequently, then strode to Elizabeth's bedside, opposite Belle. He reached out to feel her forehead.

"Your temperature feels good, normal." He reached for her arm and placed his fingers on her wrist. "Your pulse is steady, I would like it to be stronger, though. How is your appetite?"

"It's all right. Mother stopped in earlier and brought me some bread with chicken broth. I was able to eat some of it."

"That's good. That will help you build your strength."

"I'm already feeling stronger, thank you," Elizabeth replied.

"Good." He pulled up a crate that was sitting against the wall and sat next to her. "Any more bleeding?" Concern was etched on his face.

"It has slowed down a bit," Elizabeth replied. "When do you think I'll be able to get up?"

"When you feel strong enough. I trust you won't overdo it too soon."

"I doubt as though Annie, the Warden, would let you get up too early," Belle said, her voice full of sarcasm.

"She has been very helpful," Elizabeth said.

"Yes. She makes an excellent nurse." Dr. Knightly said.

"A wonderful cook, and an asset organizing the farm..." Belle had to bite her tongue not to say the words aloud. Dr. Knightly surely had negative thoughts about her already, not that she cared what a common doctor thought about her.

"I noticed you've been having some young visitors."

"Yes, Benjamin and Hannah. I hope it is all right that they came in."

"Yes, they are wonderful children. I am more than all right with them visiting as much as you can handle. After what you have been through, Mrs. Bennett, I think you should be able to hold your children as much as you like."

"Thank you." Tears shimmered in Elizabeth's eyes. Dr. Knightly glanced over at Belle, who had made no move to comfort her sister. Withholding a sigh, he reached forward to grasp Elizabeth's hand.

"I can't begin to imagine and understand what you have been through, Mrs. Bennett. The loss of a child, even one born prematurely...it must be devastating beyond words."

"Yes, but I have no doubt that my baby is in heaven right now."

"You have a strong faith. I admire that." Dr. Knightly said. Belle stood and strode out the door, not speaking.

"Don't mind her," Elizabeth said. "She is struggling with her faith right now. Before the war, she wasn't interested in religion much at all. Things have changed over the past two years, and she has been attending services and seems to enjoy them, but some of the more recent tragedies have shaken her a little. Belle is stubborn. She doesn't like admitting that she's wrong, or that she has a soft side."

"She's strong-willed, that's true enough. I learned that the first time I met her." He paused, unsure about voicing the question he had.

"She treated you a bit unfairly that first day. I'm sure by now you realize it was nothing personal."

"Yes, I understand her issue with doctors." Dr. Knightly nodded. "Her intended and your brother."

"Samuel was a shock to her. She believed that nothing bad would happen as a result of the war and if Samuel did die, he would die a hero. James is a different story. She and James were very close. The two losses made her distrust all doctors because she believes that both of them could have been spared if they had better care."

Dr. Knightly shook his head. "There's no way to know if either one of them would have survived. For every man who has died in combat, I believe that two or three have succumbed to disease." His gaze strayed to the door. "It's possible that James and Samuel could have lived with the best of care but we will never know for sure. I'm glad it's all doctors she dislikes and not just me."

Elizabeth smiled. "No, I don't believe so, but am I wrong to have noticed sparks between you two."

"Ah, so those are noticeable?" Dr. Knightly asked, leaning back on his crate.

"They are to me. I know my sister. You fluster her. She can usually manipulate any man to do her bidding, but not you. She's not sure how to handle you."

"Hmmm. Interesting." Dr. Knightly scratched the facial hair on his chin.

"Are you thinking of pursuing a relationship with her, Dr. Knightly?"

"Now that is a good question." He ran a hand through his hair and rubbed his head. "Maybe if we weren't in the middle of a war. I'm attracted to her, but who wouldn't be. I think she's the most beautiful woman I've ever laid my eyes on. She intrigues me, but she will be a handful for whoever marries her."

"I believe you are just what she needs, but tread carefully, Doctor. I wouldn't want you to get hurt and she has broken her share of hearts. I caution you too, if you hurt her in any way, you will have the whole Turner clan to deal with, and that includes extended family from as far away as Gettysburg, and Vicksburg."

Dr. Knightly smiled. "I'll keep that in mind." He stood. "You need to get some rest. Thank you for the information and advice, Mrs. Bennett. I appreciate it. I will be back to check on you later."

Prentiss Home

AJ entered Nathaniel's bedroom to find Liberty sitting next to the bed, talking quietly with Markus Alexsander. He was very pale and losing his strength. A tear fell down AJ's face. Dr. Knightly from Turner's Glenn had come by when Markus was first injured. Unfortunately, the wound was already infected and the doctor said there was nothing more he could do, short of making him as comfortable as possible. The bigger problem was that Liberty was becoming more and more attached to the young man. She spent all of her extra time talking with him. AJ knew that her sister was going to be heartbroken when Markus died, but she didn't want him to spend his last days alone either and the two had formed a quick bond.

"How are you doing, Mr. Alexsander?" AJ asked.

"As well as can be expected, Miss Prentiss." He said weakly.

AJ reached over and felt his forehead. He was quite warm. She bit her lip.

"Miss Liberty, I have a feeling...well, I was wondering if you could help me write a letter home, just in case I don't make it."

399

Liberty nodded and stood, going to the desk downstairs for the materials. She returned quickly. AJ smiled sadly, then left the two alone. Markus had been having bouts of delirium with an increased fever and AJ suspected he wouldn't last much longer. She went to the kitchen to begin preparations for dinner.

"AJ!" Liberty called out a little while later. She sounded distressed. AJ quickly went up the stairs. Liberty was in tears. AJ hastened to the side of the bed.

"AJ, Markus started mumbling and talking to me as if he thought I was his sister. I think he was hallucinating, then he just fell asleep. I...I...he's not breathing, I think...I think he's dead."

Markus lay still on the bed, his face as pale as a ghost. AJ felt his face, which had started to cool. Tears welled in her eyes as she sank to the chair beside his bed.

"He's dead, isn't he?" Liberty's voice was shaky, almost a whisper. AJ nodded.

"I figured he was supposed to...that he was going to die, but I held out hope that a miracle would happen." She wiped at her tear-stained cheeks with the heel of her hand.

AJ stood and pulled Liberty into a tight embrace. Liberty sobbed into AJ's shoulder. AJ couldn't recall the last time Liberty had shown this much emotion. Liberty backed away from AJ, wiping her eyes again.

"I'm sorry. We should try to prepare some sort of burial for him. I wonder if we even have enough spare wood to put together a proper coffin and where will we bury him?"

"We can figure this all out soon enough." AJ rubbed Liberty's arms, still trying to comfort the girl.

"I'll go look for some wood in the barn," Liberty said, then headed outside. AJ thought of following her sister, but she knew that Liberty had to grieve in her own way.

Tuesday, May 12, 1863
Moss Neck Manor
My Dearest Catherine,

It is with the heaviest of hearts that I write to you and tell you that General Jackson went to be with our Lord and Savior on this day, Sunday, May 10. Pneumonia is what the doctors say took him from us. I still cannot believe he is gone. The Lord knows I would have died for him, Kate.

It was a beautiful day. We were all anxious, fearing the worst. I rode down to see him while Dr. Lacy preached back at the camp. The man visited him every day. The whole army was saddened by the news

400

when we heard. Jackson passed at fifteen minutes past 3:00 in the afternoon. I returned to Guinea Station to carry out a set of instructions from General Lee. He had me take charge of Jackson's remains, make arrangements for the funeral and accompany the body to Lexington. Jackson expressed a desire to be buried there. JP Smith and I dressed the body and placed him in a crudely made coffin. He will be taken further care of in Richmond.

I will be following the funeral cortege and accompanying the remains with Dr. McGuire, JP, Reverend Lacy, and JG Morrison. HK Douglass and a few other former staff members of Jackson's will also join us.

I can't say when I will be able to see you next. I hope to visit my mother and sisters when I am in Lexington. If I do visit, I hope to discuss many things, most especially our future.

With all of the love I possess,
Sandie

Kate dropped the letter in her lap and stared out in the direction of the Rappahannock River. Tears welled up in her eyes. She knew of Jackson's injuries, but never had imagined that he would die from them. He was a general, invaluable. Officers and their staff were supposed to be kept safe. She constantly feared for Sandie's safety, but now? She saw how easy it could become a reality.

"I need to talk with someone..." She murmured to herself. Her first thought was to go to Turner's Glenn, but a messenger from there had brought the news of Elizabeth losing her child. She wanted to pay her respects and visit, but the news of Jackson had greatly affected her and she didn't want to bring that to the grieving household. She stood, walked into the house and told one of the servants to tell Bertie and Nettie where she was going. Not that either one of them would even notice she was gone. Though it had been a month, they were still caught up in their own grief. Kate saddled up Flirt, then headed to town. She crossed the roughly constructed pontoon bridge and rode past Chatham. AJ would be the perfect person to talk to.

"Kate! How wonderful to see you. What on earth are you doing over here?" AJ smiled a tired smile at her friend. Kate wondered if she even knew the news about General Jackson or Elizabeth for that matter.

"I needed to get away. I haven't been able to talk with you in such a long while."

"I understand. Chancellorsville, while we won, was still quite a blow and I suppose life is still gloomy at Moss Neck." AJ led Kate inside to the kitchen table. "I have some tea. Would you like a cup?"

401

"Where on earth did you get tea?" Kate asked. "However could you afford it?"

AJ smiled. "It's mine and Liberty's new concoction. Peanuts are still easy to come by, so we crush them and seep the powder into hot water. Peanut tea."

"That is so clever," Kate said. "I would love to try some." AJ began heating the water, then sat at the table.

"Tell me, how have you been? What is the news? I stopped in town the other day to check for mail, but I didn't get a chance to really speak with anyone."

Kate paled. "A lot of news, I'm afraid. None that is good, unfortunately." She took a deep breath. "I heard from Turner's Glenn that Elizabeth lost her child on Sunday." Kate tried to hold back her tears. "The same day our General Jackson succumbed to pneumonia." Her voice was almost a whisper.

Tears formed in the corners of AJ's eyes. "Oh my goodness, both on the same day." She wiped at her eyes with the sleeve of her dress. "I should go to Elizabeth and Belle."

"I considered the same thing, but I wanted to give them time as a family. Elizabeth will have to heal both physically and emotionally. I wouldn't want to intrude. Today, when I heard of Jackson's death, I just wasn't in the mood for paying respects. It's just been so difficult lately. Too much death,"

AJ knew that Kate could sometimes be indecisive or doubtful about decisions she had made. "What's really on your mind?" She asked. "You're not regretting accepting Captain Pendleton's hand, are you?"

"Oh, AJ you know me so well." Kate sighed. "I'm so afraid. Sandie could die, AJ. He is a soldier. I have always known there was a chance he could die, but I also believed that since he was an adjunct, he would be safe. I know he told me once that he had been shot in battle, but...I just wasn't concerned at the time, for some reason. I do love him, but now that I've fully given my heart to him and he's killed? What will I do?"

"You can rest knowing that the man you love died while fighting for what he believes in and that your love helped him through any suffering that he may have felt."

"That is quite poetic AJ, almost as though you're feeling the sting of being in love with a soldier." Kate smiled. "Are you still corresponding with JP Smith?"

AJ shrugged. "I received a letter from him a few days ago. I've written him a response. I just have to go back into town to post it."

"He appears to be a good, solid young man. Not to mention very handsome."

"You sound just like Belle," AJ said. "I agree and I do enjoy his company, but...I don't know." AJ did know, but she couldn't voice the words. Richard Evans, the scoundrel, had a piece of her heart and try as she might, she could not get it back. "Maybe Captain Smith could be my future husband." She changed the subject. "I really believe we need to go and visit Elizabeth though. Would you like to go with me tomorrow?"

"I would. That is a wonderful idea." Kate glanced around the room. "Is Liberty outside doing chores?"

"She is. Please keep this to yourself, Kate, but we...we actually just buried someone yesterday ourselves. A Confederate soldier who had been wounded and wandered into our barn. We took him in and a doctor from Turner's Glenn came over to check on him, but his wound was mortal. We buried him in the backyard and have written a letter to his family. Which I need to post with my other letter. Liberty is taking it quite hard. She formed quite a bond with him in such a short period." AJ rubbed her temples. "Everything is just so difficult lately. With the exception of yours and Sandie's engagement, it has been a bully of a year, Kate."

"That is so true." Kate agreed. "So very true. Do you want me to post those letters on my way home? It is no trouble."

"No, thank you, I can do it tomorrow. I will meet you at noon. Will that work?"

"It will." Kate stood. "I am looking forward to it. See you then."

"Take care, Kate."

Wednesday, May 18, 1863
Turner's Glenn Plantation

Belle walked out the door, wanting to check on the soldiers in the tents on the side of the house. She stopped when she heard voices quietly talking on the front porch. She immediately recognized them as Joseph Byron and Annie.

"Who defines beauty, Miss Turner?" the Captain asked. "Just because people around you don't recognize your beauty doesn't mean you don't have any. I see you working hard and helping the wounded soldiers however you can. You're always smiling, always bringing comfort and joy to others. That's beautiful. Just because you don't have the same features as your sisters doesn't mean you're not beautiful yourself. How you care for others is so genuine. No offense toward your sister Belle, but you're worth ten of her."

"Don't be too hard on Belle...she's really trying hard." Annie said. "You should have known her before the war."

403

"Maybe she is improving." Joseph said. "But I remember the both of you from the battle in December. I briefly met you when I was bringing wounded men here."

"I remember men being brought in, of course." Annie said. "But I don't recall meeting you."

"You were quite busy and I was just another soldier to you. You stood out to me. I saw both you and Belle that day. Belle acted as so many Southern ladies do, spoiled, selfish someone who never had to work for anything in her life."

"Belle is more than that, Joseph."

"She probably is, but I also saw you that day, Annie, and I thought you were the most beautiful woman I had ever seen."

"I was probably filthy with blood and sweat."

"You were beautiful."

Belle ducked back into the entryway. She didn't quite know what to do with the information she had just heard. She knew some people looked at her as shallow, but Joseph didn't know her at all, other than a few interactions with him. How could he judge her? An image of Margaret Buckley flashed through her mind. She shook her head and put a hand to her temple, then sank down onto a chair that had been left in the entryway. The army doctors had allowed it to stay there as it gave people a place to rest if they had a few spare moments.

Meri walked through the entryway and noticed Belle.

"What's wrong, Belle?" She asked.

"Just thinking." Belle answered. "Do you think I'm spoiled?"

"I suppose you can be, especially if people don't really know you." Meri shrugged.

"Am I...judgmental?" Belle asked.

"What do you mean?" Meri leaned against the wall.

"I mean, if people look at me and judge me and say that I'm spoiled and selfish based on what they see and hear. Do I do the same to others?"

Meri thought for a moment. "Probably. You're not always the kindest to Elizabeth and Joshua, or Annie for that matter. You know them really well, so I'm not sure if that counts. At first, you didn't care for Dr. Knightly, but that seems to be changing a little, and, well, sometimes you say bad things about people in town, and spread rumors, but that's just talk."

"You mean like Margaret Buckley? She is the one that I was thinking about the most." Belle said. "I just...overheard a conversation and the comments made me think." She sighed. "Perhaps I need to examine my attitude towards people."

Meri shrugged. "Perhaps."

Belle sighed. "You know, I used to think that good things happened to good people, but after what happened with Elizabeth, I'm not so sure. I talked with her yesterday, and she tried explaining how that's not true, but I just don't understand. Elizabeth is the best person I know. It annoys me, but it's true. She should not have lost that baby if God cared about her so much." Tears formed in Belle's eyes as she thought again of the little girl that died. "I don't understand how that could have happened."

"I don't either." Meri replied. "But I also don't understand why God is allowing this senseless war to continue. For Father to be away. For James..." She tried to hold back her own tears. "If God loves us so much, the way Elizabeth always says he does, then how come He lets these things happen?"

"That's what I mean. I don't know." Belle said. "You are asking the wrong person because I just don't understand. I don't understand any of it." She glanced up and saw Dr. Knightly walking toward her. In his own rough and gruff way, he really was a handsome man. Dark blonde hair, eyes the color of coffee and a smile that was rare, but quite radiant.

"Miss Turner, may I speak with you in private?" His voice was even attractive to Belle. He had a South Carolinian accent that was smooth and elegant. She could listen to him talk all day. Belle shook her head. Why were thoughts like that coursing through her brain? What was wrong with her?

"Miss Turner?" Dr. Knightly spoke again.

"Yes. I'm sorry, Dr. Knightly. Should we go to the back porch? It will be quieter there."

"That sounds fine." He offered his arm and led her to the back porch. He gestured to a bench that overlooked the hills. "Will this be all right with you?"

She nodded and the two sat down. He didn't start speaking right away. Belle didn't like the silence, so she spoke first.

"There's nothing wrong with Elizabeth, is there? I must confess she is foremost in my thoughts these days."

"No, no. Mrs. Bennett is doing well. Physically and spiritually. Usually, the spirit is difficult to recover after something like this."

"Well, one of her most favorite phrases is 'thy will be done'. My sister trusts God more than anyone or anything in her life."

"That's commendable." The doctor said. "I wish I had a faith like that."

"Are you not a Christian, Dr. Knightly?" Belle asked.

"Oh, I am." The doctor ran a hand through his hair. "Honestly, I can't imagine how anyone in the medical field cannot believe in a higher power. Science is all well and good and explains a lot, but sometimes things happen that can only be explained by a higher power. Besides, I feel more comfortable knowing that there is someone up there who has control over my life."

"I thought all doctors thrived on the control they have over others."

"That might be true for some doctors, but not all." Dr. Knightly smiled. "I like the control to some degree, but it's comforting to me that God is there to help direct me."

"Well, that doesn't sound like any doctor I've met before."

"I'm not like all doctors any more than you're like all other Virginia girls."

"Touché." Belle thought for a moment. "Being a doctor seems to involve quite a bit of pressure. I don't believe I could deal with having the life of another person in my hands. How my decision may affect whether that person lives or dies."

"That's one of the reasons that doctoring is not for everyone. Personally, I've always viewed the pressure as a privilege. God gave me certain gifts and abilities to help others. It makes me feel as though I am doing something good for others."

Belle nodded. They fell back into silence. "Tell me, Dr. Knightly. What did you want to discuss? I'm surprised you have the time to pull yourself away from saving all those lives."

"It's mostly rounds for me now, making sure that everyone is receiving proper care and deciding when the wounded are strong enough to travel to the hospitals in Richmond, or home if that is where they are able to go."

"Why would some be sent home? If they are well enough to go home, wouldn't they be well enough to be sent back to the army?"

"Some are unable to fight anymore. For example, Captain Joseph Byron. He's a strong young man and should be well enough to travel soon, but he lost a leg. He cannot march or run anymore, even with a prosthesis, he will find it difficult to walk and live as he used to, much less fight in the army."

"I suppose I didn't think of that," Belle said. She was still confused as to why he had asked her out here. She was enjoying the conversation, even though she wasn't her normal, flirtatious self. They were discussing subjects that were relevant and meaningful. She couldn't image discussing faith in God with Samuel and she had been ready to marry him. She sighed.

"I wanted to tell you..." Dr. Knightly hesitated, then cleared his throat. "I wanted to tell you that I have been watching you these past few weeks, not in any way that should alarm you." He clarified. "I wanted to let you know that you have become a very...you've been a very big help to us here. Your whole family, from Elizabeth to your brother. All of you have played a role in making this a successful field hospital. I hate that we had to take over your home, but...well, it was a good choice."

"Doctor, most of the homes in Fredericksburg and the surrounding areas have been turned into hospitals or were destroyed when the armies first clashed here in December. The most recent battle, earlier this month, well, there were fewer casualties and less destruction, but it still affected us all." She sighed. "We've all had to learn to adapt."

"And you have." Dr. Knightly reached forward as if he were going to touch her face, but he held back. "You have adapted admirably." He leaned forward as if silently asking permission to kiss her. Belle leaned toward him as well and began to close her eyes when she heard him stand.

"Good evening, Miss Turner." He then retreated into the house as if General Meade himself was coming. Annie came around the corner of the house at that moment, her gaze following the doctor.

"He couldn't get away from you fast enough," Annie commented. "What on earth did you do to him?"

Belle shook her head, more confused now than she had ever been. "Annie, I have no idea."

Thursday, May 21, 1863
Banks of the Rappahannock

"Miss Prentiss. Good to see you again." Richard Evans leaned against a rock and gave her a short tip of his hat.

"And you," AJ said. "I've actually...well, there is a reason I was hoping it would be you meeting me today."

"Is that so?" Richard smiled warmly, pushing himself away from the rock and stepping close.

"I...I was going to write to you, but I knew that I would be seeing someone from your regiment soon anyway. I'm not sure if you or any of your fellow soldiers knew or suspected, but...it's about Markus Alexsander." Richard's proximity made her slightly nervous and she would have taken a step back, but at her words, Richard's face turned concerned. He reached up and gripped her shoulders.

"You have word on Markus? He went missing, we didn't know what happened to him."

"He somehow made it to this side of the river and into our barn. Liberty and I weren't sure how and he didn't remember either. He was delirious for much of the time he was with us."

Richard took a step back. "So where is he now?"

"He...oh, Richard, I am so sorry. He didn't make it." Tears welled in AJ's eyes. Richard turned and crossed his arms over his chest. She thought he may have been crying, as his shoulders hitched just a bit. She bit her lip and placed her hand on his back. "I am so, so sorry, Richard." She wasn't sure what possessed her to use his given name but knew that he needed comfort.

"He was just a kid," Richard said, his voice a little shaky as if he were trying to hold back tears. "He wasn't even eighteen. He had confided in me that he lied to the enlistment officers so he could fight. He was a good soldier. I actually...I felt as though he were my younger brother." He turned and AJ could see a glimmer of tears in his eyes. With very little thought, she pulled him into a hug. He gripped her tightly, burying his face in her shoulder.

"He felt the same way about you, Richard," AJ said. "He asked me to tell you that. He said you were like a brother to him. He really thought the world of you."

"I cannot believe he's gone. How..." He pulled back and turned to sit on a fallen log, then dropped his face into his hands.

"He had been wounded in the side, gut shot. The wound was already infected when Liberty found him." She sat down next to him. "He did die peacefully. He said that he knew God was with him, even at the end."

"God." Richard scoffed. "Haven't you been paying attention for the past two years? God is not with us at all. If He cared about us, then why would he allow all of this to happen? How can you believe that God is here for us after what we have all been through?"

"Because I feel His presence. It is difficult for me to describe, Mr. Evans, but I just know, deep down. There have been so many times when I've felt lost or afraid, yet I have felt as though someone or something is watching over me, protecting me." She took his hand in hers. "He's protecting you, too." She smiled when he stole a quick glance at her. She squeezed his hand. "Whether you feel it or not."

"You seem very confident in that." He said softly. "I wish I could have that kind of faith."

"I find it intriguing that there is something you lack confidence in. You always appear so self-assured. "

"You would be surprised." He replied, then took a deep breath. "Miss Prentiss...thank you. You don't know how much I appreciate your friendship this past year or so. I know it feels as though we don't see each other often enough to have formed a friendship and that I may not always make you feel like it, but...I feel I know you. I feel I can trust and talk to you no matter what. You always know what to say to make me feel better." He looked into her eyes and smiled. "Thank you."

"You are most welcome," AJ said, giving him a smile. "I will continue to pray for you. For your safety and so you may feel more of God's presence."

He nodded. "Prayers I could probably use."

Saturday, May 23, 1863
Moss Neck Manor

"Kate!" Sandie hastened to his intended and drew her into an embrace. She hugged him tightly.

"Sandie. Oh, my Sandie." She drew back and looked at him with tears of joy in her eyes. He reached up and brushed one away with his thumb. "Let's go to the porch. It is a wonderful day outside. We should enjoy it."

He nodded and escorted her out. They sat side by side in rocking chairs, still holding hands.

"How was your visit home?" Kate asked.

"Quite enjoyable. I hadn't been home since last September. I wish it were under different circumstances, though." He replied. "Mother and my sisters are all doing well. They're all anxious to meet you." He gave her a small smile.

"I am looking forward to meeting them as well." She smiled back. "I know I will enjoy their company."

"I know you will too," Sandie said. He then grew quiet. Thoughtful.

"Would you like to talk about General Jackson?" Kate asked somberly.

"He was so gracious and pious, even at the end." He said. "He was happy that Reverend Lacy had been preaching to the men. I think he knew he was going to die that day." Sandie took a deep breath. "I hadn't been able to visit him for a while, but I got the opportunity on that Sunday. He was just...he was thanking God that he would pass on the Lord's Day." He shook his head. "Kate, I had to go outside onto the porch to weep."

She reached out and touched his face. "I cannot tell you how sorry I am, Sandie."

"He was delirious at the end. He believed he was at the bloody battle on the Old Turnpike at the beginning of the month. Calling out orders. Telling me to push up the column." He lifted her hand and kissed it. "JP Smith and I dressed his body and left it in the Chandler office until he could be sent to Richmond. The citizens of Fredericksburg were incredibly generous and presented a nice metallic casket for his final rest."

"I hadn't heard that," Kate said, proud of her town.

"When we passed through Richmond, throngs of people greeted the train as it passed through the stations. We draped his coffin with a Confederate flag and covered it with wreaths of evergreen and rare flowers. Then it was taken by carriage to St. Paul's Episcopal Church and Henry Douglass and I stood guard until dark. Bells tolled until sundown and thousands of people stayed in the square until dusk. So many people there to pay their respects. It was incredible and humbling Kate. I cannot imagine more people showing up to the funeral of our president." He looked off into the distance. "So many people. I will never forget the military pageant. A beautiful and warm day. Bands and military escorts. I was a pallbearer, did I tell you that? I was with JP, Hunter, Henry, Longstreet, Ewell, and Pickett. Men like Commodore French and President Davis were there too, he looked thin and frail in health. I tell you, Kate, it was amazing how many people were there. The funeral train went from Richmond through Lynchburg to Lexington. There was another simple service in Lexington, then we buried him." He looked into Kate's eyes. "I'm sorry. I suppose it seems as though I am simply prattling on and on, more than I intended. I hope that I did not bore you."

"I am sure you could never do that, Sandie," Kate said gently. "You are such a passionate man in everything you do. It is one of the things that I love about you."

He smiled a genuine smile. "It is good to hear you say that." He leaned over and gave her a gentle kiss. "I love you."

"Where will you go next?" She asked. "Will you have a new assignment?"

"Lee is reorganizing the Army of Northern Virginia. I haven't heard who my new chief will be or, honestly, where we will be moving. I have a feeling Lee is going to move us north. I think he wants to get us out of Virginia."

"That would be good for a change," Kate said.

"Yes, in spite of our recent loss of General Jackson, I am enthusiastic about the idea of a new campaign to continue his work."

"That is admirable," Kate said.

Sandie took a deep breath, then checked his watch. "When I am with you, time seems to fly by. I must leave. I don't want to, but I must."

"I understand. I treasure what little time we have together." Kate said, standing. He stood and took her hands in his.

"I don't know when I will be able to see you again, but I will write as often as I can."

"As will I," Kate said. "I cannot wait to talk with you more. We have so many things to discuss." She ran her hands up and down his arms.

410

"We certainly do. Make sure you use this time to start thinking about our wedding."

"I will." She smiled. He leaned down and gently kissed her goodbye, then descended the porch steps and left.

Sunday, May 24, 1863
Turner's Glenn

"So the two of you are now friends?" Elizabeth clarified. She and AJ sat on Turners Glenn's back veranda.

"That's what he said. Richard Evans considers me his friend." AJ gave a short laugh. "At least I can speak coherently around him now. I remember not too long ago when that was impossible."

"I remember those times too. There were a few parties that I can recall you were so muddled around him." Elizabeth recalled.

"And the first time that he spurned me," AJ said, thinking back.

1853

Chatham Manor

America was happy with the way everything had turned out in preparation for the party. She stood at the door of her aunt and uncle's manor, staring out across the Rappahannock River, waiting for guests to arrive. This party was an opportunity for her to break out of her quiet personality. Richard Evans had even told her that he would talk to her. She really hoped that Richard would take notice of her. Their conversation while fishing not too long ago was at the forefront of her mind. She was wearing an elegant new maroon dress that Belle Turner insisted made her look 'more beautiful than ever before.'

Chatham Manor, as always, looked splendid. The servants, with her Cousin Betty Lacy had been working tirelessly on the menu and cooking. AJ looked around at the guests that had started to arrive. She quickly found the Turner family and joined Belle and Elizabeth.

"Good afternoon, ladies." AJ greeted them.

"Hello, AJ." Belle said at the same time Elizabeth wished her a 'good afternoon' in reply.

"It looks like most of the invitees have come," Belle said, looking around. "Do you happen to know if any young men will be in attendance?"

"I'm not sure exactly who was on the guest list, but I saw Richard Evans not too long ago, and he said he would be coming." She tried to sound nonchalant about that fact, not wanting her friends to see just how excited she was. "Other than that, I can't really say."

411

"Hello, Miss Belle, Miss Elizabeth, AJ." Nathaniel greeted the small group. *"I wanted to let you know that the Corbin family just arrived."*

"Ooh, that means Kate is here," Belle said with a smile. *"Thank you for the information, Nathaniel. You are such a gentleman."*

AJ shook her head. Even at age thirteen, Belle was a perfect flirt and her brother Nathaniel was already caught in her web. He grinned and nodded, then turned and went to find his friends.

"Why did he find the need to tell us that?" Elizabeth mused. Belle smiled smugly, knowing just as well as AJ why he had come over.

"Because he is just that kind of young man," AJ said. *'And he is smitten with Belle, as are many young men in the Fredericksburg area.'*

Out of the corner of her eye, AJ noticed Richard Evans walk into the front area, flanked by Samuel Evans and Gerard Sullivan, two of his good-looking friends.

"Excuse me, I need to greet some new arrivals," AJ said, making her way to the group of young men that was now forming around Richard.

"Richard! Welcome." AJ smiled. Richard turned at the sound of her voice but frowned slightly when he saw who it was. He cleared his throat, looked at his friends, then back at AJ and spoke.

"Miss Prentiss, correct?" There was no warmth in his voice.

"Yes, of course. I'm...glad you were able to come." AJ maintained her smile, although his cold response to her was making her feel nervous. Now that she was actually talking to him, she didn't know what to say.

"Of course." He grinned, but it was not a kind grin as he looked around at his friends again. *"Was there anything else you needed from me or do you plan on just standing there?"* His voice was cocky, arrogant.

"Well...I mean...I, when we saw each other at the river...and I was just..." She sighed, embarrassed and mortified and tongue-tied. All of the young men were focused on her, and they had amused smiles on their faces as if they were just waiting for her to make an absolute fool of herself. *"I just wanted to say 'hello' and welcome."*

"And so you have." There was no compassion on Richard's face. Humiliated, AJ turned and fled the group.

1863

"What am I doing, Elizabeth? I know that he is no good for me, yet I cannot help but think of him constantly. I still want his approval in the worst way. There have been so many times that he has let me down. Crushed my self-esteem, made me feel unworthy, and yet..." She gave a short laugh. "I just can't stop hoping we can be together someday."

412

"You two have both changed and matured," Elizabeth said. "Richard has never been cruel. Uncaring, overconfident, spoiled, all of that is true. Do I believe you should use caution around him? Absolutely. Could you two cultivate a friendship? Most likely. Could the two of you end up as more than friends?" Elizabeth looked right at AJ. "I believe that to be possible. It may seem strange, but I can see you two as a married couple. I don't want you to get your hopes up, though. These are troubled times."

AJ's heart skipped a beat. Could Elizabeth be right? Maybe her feelings for Richard were not as unbelievable as she had originally thought.

Monday, May 25, 1863
Turner's Glenn Plantation

Belle exited the house and made her way to Elizabeth and Annie, who were sitting on the back veranda.

As Belle neared, Elizabeth frowned. From the look on her sister's face, it did not look like Belle had good news. She sat down in a huff, almost breaking the damaged chair underneath her.

"What's wrong now?" Elizabeth asked. She had recognized right away that Belle's demeanor was more dramatic than distraught.

"More insult to our already offended Southern Pride," Belle said. "After everything we've been through, especially this year with losing the children, losing General Jackson, that tyrant Lincoln freeing the slaves, and now guess what he's gone and done? What he and the Yankee government have dared to do?"

"Do tell," Elizabeth said.

"He is allowing darkies...including runaways, slaves, freedmen, he is actually...he is allowing them to join the Yankee army."

"No," Annie exclaimed. "He wouldn't do that, even most Yankees won't want to fight side-by-side with darkies."

Elizabeth gritted her teeth. She desperately wanted to say something but didn't want to get caught up in an argument with Belle, especially since their usually rocky relationship was improving.

"Yes, apparently he's thought of that. They will form specific regiments, led by white officers, of course, who have volunteered to lead them." Belle had nothing but scorn for this news.

"It's a wonder any man would volunteer for that job," Annie said.

"You know they'll make horrible soldiers. No discipline at all, not to mention they're not smart enough."

"Belle that may be the most absurd thing I have ever heard you say." Elizabeth couldn't hold back her thoughts anymore. Belle actually looked shocked at Elizabeth's outburst. "Annie, it almost sounds as though you're agreeing with her." Annie reddened and looked down.

"Really, Elizabeth, you shouldn't distress yourself," Belle said.

"I am quite distressed, listening to you two. Belle, I have been holding my tongue for years now in regards to this issue."

"No, you haven't. We well know that you secretly support the abolitionist movement and that you hate the idea of slavery, but would you really go so far as to say that blacks are our equal? That Zipporah, Ruthie, Daniel, and Solomon are exactly the same as us? As smart as us?"

"I do! And I don't understand how you still can support the idea. You have been close with Zipporah for years, whether or not you choose to admit it. Annie, you have been working with and learning from Ruthie, since you could hold a spatula. How can you not see that Negroes are capable of so much more than what most superior whites give them credit for?"

"I see your point, Elizabeth. Really, I do." Annie said softly.

"Elizabeth, do you realize this means the North will now have even more soldiers at their disposal? No matter my feelings on their ability, this means...it means we will be even more outnumbered. Our men will have to fight even harder and there will be even more opportunities for our men to be killed. More opportunities for Joshua, the love of your life, the father of your children, to be wounded or killed. Is that what you want? So darkies can prove that they're equal to our white men?"

"You know that is not what I want. I don't like this news at all either. It scares me because, you're right, it is more soldiers to fight. It does put Joshua in more danger, but you going on and on about how the blacks aren't capable of being soldiers? They are more than capable and they have more to fight for. Remember, they're fighting for their freedom. They'll probably fight even harder because of it. That does scare me. You can say all you want that this is a grave offense against us, but it really is quite a smart thing to do."

Belle was quiet. Elizabeth couldn't tell what she was thinking. Belle had made so many strides in her heart the past few months, and the two of them had made great strides in their relationship. Elizabeth knew the issue of slavery had ripped many families apart. She prayed that it wouldn't come between her and her sister. Belle finally stood and strode away.

Belle walked quickly, heading toward the bench that her father had placed near the river's edge. Slavery. It was such a small word, but it affected her life in so many ways. The Yankees wanted to take slavery away, which was one of the reasons the Confederate States had decided to secede and the war had started as a result. This war had impacted and changed her life in so many ways. She sighed as she sank onto the stone bench. What was wrong with her? Slavery had always just been there. Everyone accepted it. It was how she had been raised. She hadn't even questioned the practice in her mind until Cousin Charlotte from Gettysburg had visited a few years ago, just before the war had begun. It was also the first time she had realized that Elizabeth had feelings against the institution...

Late Summer, 1859

"Do you believe that slavery is wrong?" Charlotte had asked. She, Belle and Elizabeth were sitting on the back porch. Belle was working on some needlepoint, while Elizabeth was knitting a blanket for her coming child.

"Yes," Elizabeth said, without hesitation.

"Of course." Belle scoffed. "You would say that."

"It's what I believe," Elizabeth replied.

"Because it's what your husband believes." Belle countered.

"No. Joshua just gave me the courage to be able to speak my mind."

"Elizabeth, you're a southerner, you were born and raised on a plantation that has slaves," Charlotte said.

"Yes, but I do disagree with the institution. No one should be able to hold another person in bondage. Negroes can be intelligent and are quite capable of leading their own lives if they're given a chance." Elizabeth replied.

"Elizabeth, just because you're content living without servants, doesn't mean that you can expect everyone to follow your ideas. Even our own founding fathers, George Washington and Thomas Jefferson, held slaves." Belle pointed out.

"Yes, but I have heard that our own Virginia hero, Robert E. Lee, fighting against the Indians out west, believes that slavery is an out modeled institution." Elizabeth looked at Charlotte. "However, just because people disagree with your thoughts and ideas doesn't make them bad. They are living as their parents and their parents before them have taught them. How they live may be completely wrong to you, but that doesn't mean they're evil. Most of the time, it just means they don't understand. They've been misled."

Belle rolled her eyes. "Whatever you say, Elizabeth. You're the smart one." Elizabeth sighed quietly.

"Whatever made you ask that question anyways, Charlotte?" Belle asked.

"I was just talking to my friend, Wesley, earlier. He said some things that made me think."

"Ahh yes, the carriage-maker from Shepherdstown." Belle tried to mask her disdain.

"He seemed quite nice." Elizabeth countered. *"A real gentleman."*

"Yes, he is." Charlotte smiled, cheeks slightly reddening.

"What did Wesley say? He's originally from Pennsylvania, correct? Will he remain loyal to the Union or the Southern states?" Belle asked.

"He is from Gettysburg. We grew up together. I'm not sure who he would choose to support if war comes. I would like to think he would choose to come home."

"What did he say about his feelings on slavery?" Elizabeth asked.

"He said that issues aren't always specifically right or wrong, that there is sometimes middle ground," Charlotte replied. *"He made some comments about slavery, how slaves aren't always abused. I had to agree with him there. I haven't ever witnessed any punishments of the slaves here at Turner's Glenn."*

"Of course, you wouldn't see it," Elizabeth said.

"You won't see it because it doesn't happen. We don't whip or abuse our slaves. Father is good to them." Belle argued.

"It does happen, Belle, and you know it. I've seen it myself, even here at Turner's Glenn. When I was a young girl. I saw the old overseer, Mr. Harland whip one of the male slaves and I don't even know what that poor boy did. I was horrified, I couldn't talk to anyone about my feelings. I thought at the time my feelings against slavery were unpatriotic. I thought I was the only person in Virginia that questioned the practice. Luckily by that time, my friendship with Joshua was developing. I met with him the same day I saw the abuse. He knew I was upset and persuaded me to talk with him. He actually agreed with me on slavery." Elizabeth shot a look at Belle. *"My point is that abuse does happen here. Not often, I will agree to that, but just because we don't see it does not mean it doesn't happen."*

1863

Thinking of the practice now, Belle realized that Elizabeth and Charlotte had a point and maybe she and the others had, indeed, been misinformed, or she had been looking at the institution in too simple of a perspective. It couldn't be completely wrong since her father and all of her friends' families held slaves. They were all good people, so it had to be all right. Didn't it? Even the Prentiss family held slaves and they had a small farm. Elizabeth had brought up some good points, though, as usual. Belle still hated it when Elizabeth proved her wrong.

"Miss Turner." Belle looked over her shoulder to see Dr. Knightly standing behind her. She had been so absorbed in her thoughts that she hadn't even heard him approach.

"Dr. Knightly." She replied. "Do you need my help with something?"

"I heard the tail end of your conversation when I came to check on your sister. May I sit?" She nodded.

"In answer to your question, no, I do not need your help at this moment, but I really must say again that we appreciate all of the work you and your family have done for us. Your brother is a good boy to have around. The soldiers enjoy his visits." He paused, then leaned his elbows on his knees and looked out at the water, then glanced at her. "I came out because we need to talk about what happened a couple of weeks ago, and what almost happened a few days ago."

Belle let out a low sigh. He was right. They needed to discuss the kiss. Trying to avoid him was getting difficult. The first few days, he had been avoiding her as well. The problem was that she had no idea what to say to him. She was unsure of the feelings she had for him. How could she discuss her feelings with him when she herself wasn't sure about them?

"I suppose you are right." She said, trying to be flippant about it. "We should discuss those little incidents."

"I see." He looked out to the water again. "So you're going to act as though what happened meant nothing?"

"Did it mean something to you?" Belle looked out towards the river as well. "It was just a little ol' kiss, Doctor, and I was quite vulnerable at the time."

"It wasn't just a kiss, Miss Turner, as you well know. It was also the discussion we had prior to that." He reached out and gently grasped her hand. "You opened up to me. I know you don't really do that to many people and I was honored that you trusted me. I thought...I thought that meant something to you. In fact, I would be willing to bet that it meant a great deal to you. Why don't you want to admit it?"

A tear fell from her eye and she quickly and subtly wiped it from her cheek. "I don't know why I can't admit it." She said softly, still not meeting his eyes. "As I said, I was quite vulnerable at the time."

He looked at her. Such a beautiful woman. So many layers to her. He initially saw her as spoiled and incapable of having true feelings. She still tried to act that way, act as though nothing affected her, but he knew that wasn't true. He was now able to see the real person she was. He was falling in love with her. There was something about her that intrigued him, and deep down, he suspected she had feelings for him.

"Belle, I don't want to confuse you. I don't and I'm sorry if I did that the other day, but I have found I have feelings for you. Feelings that I have never felt for anyone before. I don't just go around kissing beautiful women, you know."

She smiled. "To be honest, I...I really haven't kissed so many men either, Doctor."

"I know this is not an ideal place or time to start a relationship. In fact, it may be unfair to ask this of you. I also think it's unfair to not let you know how I feel. I want you to know that I value your opinion. If you have any feelings for me at all and would like to consider courting me so you can get to know me better, then I would like that as well." He touched her cheek, gently nudging her to look at him. "I would also understand if you said no for now, especially since we are in the middle of a war. I understand the losses you have sustained. I won't pressure you, but I hope you're willing to take a chance on me."

"I thank you for your consideration, Dr. Knightly." She said quietly. "I think I might take that chance."

He smiled and brought her hand to his and kissed it. "Wonderful. Then you must begin calling me Aaron." He continued holding her hand as he brought it down to her lap. "May I now ask what brought you out here? The argument with your sister?"

"Yes. Again. I came out to tell Annie and Elizabeth about Mr. Lincoln's newest declaration. The creation of his black troops. I don't believe the darkies have the ability to be good soldiers. You know, to be organized and disciplined. Elizabeth doesn't agree, but she also doesn't approve of slavery."

"I see. That argument has torn many a family in two."

"Including yours?" Belle asked, recalling that he had once mentioned a brother who fought for the Union.

"Yes, and I know you have family fighting for both sides as well."

"That is one aspect of this war that makes it extremely difficult," Belle said.

"That is an understatement." Aaron agreed.

"What are your true feelings on slavery?" Belle asked.

"As strange as it may seem, I am undecided about it. My family never had slaves. Most of the blacks I knew were hard workers and didn't seem to be discontented with their situation. I never witnessed any abuse of slaves that I thought unreasonable. I joined the Confederacy to protect my home and I believe that states should be able to make decisions for themselves. My brother, however, believed in preserving the Union. He had no real opinions on slavery either, so we weren't divided by slavery necessarily but more so by the idea of State's Rights."

"Yes, that's another big issue," Belle said. "All of these troubles bringing us into this confounded war."

418

"Unfortunate as that may be, if there were no war, you and I may never have met." Aaron glanced at her out of the corner of his eye. She gave him a small smile.

"Yes, that's true."

Aaron pulled out his watch to check the time, then sighed. "I must get back to the house and finish my rounds." He stood. "May I escort you back?"

"Yes, Dr. Knightly, or Aaron, you may."

Saturday, June 6, 1863
Moss Neck

My Dear Kate,

I spoke with General Ewell about Jackson's staff and what our status is. He told me that Lee speaks highly of all of us and that I will not only be retained as the assistant adjunct general of the corps but will also be recommended for a promotion to the rank of lieutenant colonel. These compliments I am receiving make me feel quite good. If a man is not a good soldier and ready to die doing his duty when such things are said of him by such men as Ewell and Lee, I know not what stuff he is made of. I shall do my best in the sight of God and General Jackson.

We are currently on the Rappahannock River, but this is our last night here. We shall make our way north. I feel like a boy again tonight and wide awake with enthusiasm at the thought of our trip to Maryland and the pleasures and excitements, hazards and glories of the coming campaign. Oh! For General Jackson! Be still the vain regrets. We have General Ewell, and of course, the Lord of hosts is with us.

I miss you terribly and long to see you again. Until that time, know that my heart remains with you.

Your love,
Sandie

Kate smiled, folded the letter and tucked it into her pocket.

"Miss Kate, you have a visitor." Fanny entered the sitting room. "Miss Prentiss be in the parlor."

"Thank you, Fanny," Kate replied, as she got up and went into the next room. After exchanging greetings and asking for tea to be brought in, the two began talking.

"Have you heard anything from JP Smith?" Kate asked with a smile.

"A few times," AJ said. "He has become a good friend, as I mentioned before."

"What about Nathaniel or your father?" Kate asked.

"Both are doing well, as far as I know. It sounds like Nathaniel is riding all over the country to help the Confederate cause. I never see or hear from him anymore."

"I am sure he's fine," Kate assured her.

"How are your soldiers? Sandie and your brothers?"

"Like you, I rarely hear from my brothers, as far as I know, they are all safe." She smiled. "Sandie, however, I hear from quite often. Sometimes it's a few times a week. He writes to say they're moving north, so I fear I won't hear from him as much."

"Do you have any plans for the wedding yet?" AJ asked, taking a bite of a sugar biscuit.

"We have tentatively decided that our wedding will take place in early fall. I have been preparing and planning. In fact, I will be going to Richmond this week to assemble my trousseau. I will be staying there as a guest of the Munford family for several weeks.

"That sounds exciting," AJ said. "It is so good the armies have finally left the area. Who will be escorting you? Your father?"

"No." Kate looked down. "Mr. Heth."

"Mr. Heth? Stockton Heth? Kate, are you mad?" AJ shook her head in disbelief. "You are still flirting with him and we both know he is still smitten with you."

"I am aware that it's not an ideal situation, but I don't have many options. He is a gentleman, AJ, he'll be respectful."

"Perhaps, for your sake, I hope so," AJ replied.

"I'm sorry, not to turn attention back to you, but you really can't talk to me about being careful after what you have been doing."

"What do you mean?" AJ asked.

"I heard that you rode off, unescorted, during the battle of Chancellorsville. Why did you do that? You could have been killed or captured."

"I will admit, I didn't use my best judgment that day," AJ said. "I had to let the army know that Fredericksburg was going to be under fire again. I just wanted to help. I feel a great sense of accomplishment when I..." She stopped. Kate didn't know about how deeply she was involved with smuggling and intelligence gathering. "Whenever I can do something, anything, to help our boys."

Kate gave her a questioning look. "AJ, what exactly is it that you're doing?"

"Kate, I can't tell you at this time. Just in case something goes wrong. I'm sure nothing will, but I have been sworn to secrecy." AJ gave Kate a pleading look. "Please, Kate, don't ask me anything more. Just trust me."

420

Kate sighed. "Of course. However, I must remind you that you can always come and talk with me."

"I do know that," AJ said. "And I thank you."

Thursday, June 25, 1863
Turner's Glenn
My dear Cousin Beckah,

It is with great pleasure that I write to you. Even though our home is still beset with sick and wounded, both Yankee and Rebel, life here has been improving.

It seems as though the fighting has left our area for the time being. I hope with everything in my heart that you will never have to experience the war as we have had to. Although, I fear that Cousin Victoria is faring even worse than we. I hear horrible things about what the civilians in Vicksburg are having to endure. I pray for them every night.

Yes, you read that correctly. I am praying every night. I know you are aware that I have never denied the existence of God, and though there is a lot to blame Our Father for as of late, Elizabeth's strength through her ordeals has really made me think about my own faith. She has been helping me see His goodness.

Another individual must be credited with helping me see the goodness of God. You may have had letters from me complaining about a certain doctor here by the name of Aaron Knightly. While I suspect that he secretly enjoys aggravating me, we have been getting on very well as of late. He is honest with me, brutally so, if necessary, and he doesn't seem to care if I am mad at him, which is unusual. More often than not, when I become upset, he is quick to make me happy again.

I have never opened myself up to anyone the way that I have to Aaron. He is easy to talk with, and it is usually a conversation of substance. Mundane chatter does not seem necessary with him.

We did not get on well when he first came to Turner's Glenn, most likely because I saw him as uncouth and below me, and I am sure he saw me as selfish and spoiled, but we have both looked past outward appearances and first impressions, which I am eternally grateful for. I have been working hard to be less judgmental in all aspects of my life. In fact, we are getting on so well now that I would not be surprised to have him and I come to an understanding soon. I may very well be on my way to falling in love with him.

Belle smiled as she put the finishing touches on the letter, then sealed it. She rose to bring it downstairs to get posted. As she descended the stairs, she saw Aaron coming up.

"Belle! I was just coming to find you." He ran a hand through his hair and rubbed his head, a habit she now recognized as his being agitated.

"Well, now you have!" She exclaimed. "I was just heading out to post a letter to one of my cousins, Rebekah, the one down in Petersburg."

"It's wonderful that you're able to keep in contact with her." Aaron commented. He gently took her arm and led her to the back of the house where remnants of the flower gardens were still evident. No one had been able to care for the flowers in over a year, but they still bloomed beautiful. Aaron wanted to make sure that he and Belle had a little privacy for a discussion he wanted to have with her.

"Yes, I'm very fortunate to be able to communicate with her. I don't really know if she ever gets my letters, but I do receive them from her from time to time." She tucked the letter in her pocket and sat on one of the stone benches in the garden. "So, what would you like to discuss?"

Aaron rubbed the stubble on his face, wishing that he had found time to shave.

"It's just...I have to say goodbye, Belle."

Belle's stomach dropped and the smile fell from her face. "Goodbye? What do you mean?" She stood. "Aaron, there are still wounded men here. You need to stay and care for them."

"Belle, I am a military surgeon who needs to travel where the main army goes. I must head north. I can't tell you much more than that, mainly because I don't really know any specific details, but I must follow orders."

"So, you're just going to abandon us?"

"I'm not abandoning anyone, Belle. You're going to be left in very capable hands and you and your family have learned quite a bit. With your mother here, I have complete faith that all will be fine. I'm actually recommending that she be put in charge here."

"What about us?" Belle didn't want to sound needy; it wasn't the type of person she was. "I thought I meant something to you?"

"Of course you do, Belle. You mean so much to me, but I am still a soldier. I may be a doctor, but I am still in the Confederate Army and I must follow orders." He paused.

"Of course. It's always about following orders. Make a name for yourself. Prove yourself. That's what my brother, James had to do and what Samuel wanted to do. They're both dead because of it. I thought that maybe you would be different. I thought that I could trust you not to leave me."

"Belle, you had to have known this would happen. You honestly didn't expect me to drop everything in my life, go against my conscience and break my vow to the Confederate States of America just to stay here with you. I have a duty to my country and my patients."

"So I don't mean that much to you." Tears welled up in Belle's eyes.

"That's not at all what I said or meant, Belle, and you know that very well. Do not think that showing me tears will get me to stay. You forget I know exactly how you get what you want." He turned, upset, not knowing if she was crying to get her way or if she was truly upset. The last thing he wanted was to hurt Belle and as much as he thought he knew her, she still could be hard to figure out. "Crying won't sway me, Miss Turner."

Belle looked stunned. "So we're back to this. Miss Turner. That's all I am to you?"

Aaron pivoted away from her, unsure of how to react. He never wanted to make this parting any more difficult than he knew it would be. He turned back to her and gently grasped her forearms.

"Belle. You mean the world to me. I will come back and we can continue our relationship, but I will not abandon my responsibility. Please understand." She took a step back, looked at him with tears in her eyes, turned and fled.

Belle hadn't really run since she was a little girl. She was a proper Southern lady, but she had to get away from Aaron. How could he just leave her? He knew how much she had lost to this war. If he truly cared about her, he would find a way to stay. There were still many wounded at the house and in the town, but doctors didn't become heroes by staying behind. They had to go into the thick of the fighting, put themselves in danger too. How could he have started a relationship with her only to leave? He wouldn't, not if he truly cared for her.

Belle ran until she reached the river. The water rushed by as she tucked her skirts under and sat on a nearby fallen log. Tears welled up in her eyes again. She hadn't been sitting long when she heard someone come up behind her, sure that it was Aaron, coming to apologize, she didn't turn. He would have to be the one to put forth an effort. He was the one that needed to make amends.

"It's been quite some time since I have seen you run." A soft, Southern voice spoke. Belle spun around. It wasn't Aaron, who had followed her.

"Mama. What are you doing out here?"

"I saw you run away, upset, so I followed you to make sure you were all right." Miriam sat next to Belle.

"Well, it's good to know you finally have a concern for my welfare," Belle muttered softly. Either her mother didn't hear her comment or she chose to ignore it.

"I imagine Dr. Knightly drove you out here with his transfer orders or did you have an argument with one of your sisters again?"

"He's leaving me, Mama. This war is taking everything important."

Miriam pulled a handkerchief from her pocket and handed it to Belle.

"My dear daughter this war has taken much from us, that's true. We have had to endure many hardships. Your brother..." She trailed off, trying to fight back her own tears. "Losing James, my own beloved son, was so difficult. I know how close you were to him. How well you two got along with each other. I know it was just as difficult for you."

"We lost him, then you told us you weren't coming home. You weren't even here when I found out that Samuel died. You abandoned us."

"I know now that I didn't handle James's death the way I should have. I was needed here, but I too was caught up in my own grief to think about that. I needed to stay in Richmond, Belle, to get over my own grief, yes, that was one reason, but I also felt needed there. I felt that I was still caring for my own James. I was caring for the sons of other mothers just like me."

"So being at home with us. Helping us. Was that not important to you?"

"Of course it was, Belle. As I said, I admit I should have come home. I should have been with my children. I was wrong. I was selfish and I'm sorry, but I can't change what happened. I will try somehow to make you understand what I was going through."

Belle watched the water flow by. "Why did you finally decide to come back?" She tried to hide the hostility in her voice.

"Because of my children and grandchildren. I came back because it was time, it was past time. James...well, he made me promise some things before he died. It took me awhile, but I finally realized, with the help of your father, that I needed to be home. I hope you never have to experience the loss of any of your own children because only then will you understand my profound grief." She took Belle's hands in her own.

"I know I wasn't here for you after your brother was wounded, Belle, but I am here for you now. Please talk to me as you once did."

"Oh, Mama, that would be ever so nice." Belle agreed.

"Then tell me, I did notice something between you and Dr. Knightly, didn't I?" Miriam stated.

"I think I'm in love with him, Mama. I never saw it coming. He was rude and gruff and almost mean to me when I first met him, but I think it was good for me. Somewhere along the way, I began to see him differently, then after he cared for Elizabeth, the way he was devoted to her and all of his patients. He is a good man, Mama. A man I was starting to see a future with."

"I am glad you feel that way, Belle. I agree with you about Dr. Knightly. He is a fine doctor and truly cares for his patients. I have worked with many doctors since I cared for James. I have seen some good doctors and too many unqualified doctors. Dr. Knightly is one of the best I have worked with.

A single tear fell down Belle's cheek. "He's leaving me. Just like everyone has left me. I feel as though all the important people in my life have deserted me. I feel as if they finally see the real me, see past my beautiful exterior, and realize that I'm not worthy, so they leave."

"I'm sorry you feel that way, Belle. I really do, but I don't believe that's true. You are a wonderful woman, inside and out. Do I think you worry too much about physical beauty? Yes, but you have so many other good, caring qualities. I just think it scares you."

"What scares me?" Belle asked.

"Knowing deep down that true beauty is on the inside. You rely so heavily on your outer looks that you don't see your own inner beauty."

"I do not have that problem," Belle argued, not liking the fact that her mother was able to see what she had been feeling these past months.

"Belle, I'm your mother. I know you better than you know yourself."

Belle paused, unsure of what to say. On one hand, she could see where her mother was right, but Belle wasn't ready to admit it. She finally just shrugged. Miriam smiled. "I have a feeling about you and Dr. Knightly, Belle. Call it mother's' intuition. If he's able, he'll come back. Just have faith."

"I hope so Mama. I really hope so."

Tuesday, June 30, 1863
Turner's Glenn

"Elizabeth! Eric! You're back." Meri joined the two in the entryway. "How are things in town?"

"There is a lot of news, that's for sure," Eric said. "It sounds like Lee is moving farther north. Stuart's cavalry is raiding all over in Pennsylvania but apparently was unprepared when a Union general named Pleasonton attacked him at Brandy Station over in Culpepper County. We still won the victory, though."

"Maybe if we get another victory or two in Northern territory, the Yanks will tire of fighting and give up," Meri said.

425

"That is the hope." Eric nodded. Elizabeth tried to hide a smile. She couldn't remember a time when Eric had spoken that many words. Meri invited Eric into the kitchen, as she had baked some biscuits she wanted him to taste.

"Were there any letters?" Belle asked, joining them in the entryway, followed by Annie.

"Yes. I received one from Joshua. There is one for you, Belle, from Beckah and we also had one from Victoria, but that one took a while to get here from Vicksburg. It was dated back on May 16, just before the siege began."

"My goodness." Belle took her letter. "How are Cousins Victoria and Mary?"

"The whole family was doing well as far as she knows, that is, before the siege began. She doesn't hear much from Jason, Gregory or Uncle Charles. Victoria believes they are all safe, though, as their names haven't shown up on any casualty lists in the newspapers. Mary hears from her Abraham once in a while."

"That's good," Belle said. "I simply cannot comprehend how they are surviving this siege we are hearing about."

"I don't know either," Elizabeth said. "I have been praying that the siege will come to an end soon and that Victoria, Mary, and her boys stay safe. Everyone in Vicksburg for that matter. I hope we hear from them again soon."

"Knowing Victoria, she has kept a detailed journal about her experiences and will write us a novel-length letter as soon as she can." Belle smiled

"She really does write quite a bit. Hopefully, we will hear from her soon." Elizabeth said, then sighed. "In the meantime, we must just continue to hope and pray that everyone stays safe there."

Belle nodded, then thought back to the one time they had made the trip to Mississippi to visit their family in Vicksburg.

March 1859

Belle looked around her uncle's home. She, her father and Annie had traveled to Vicksburg for the wedding of her cousin, Mary. Elizabeth had stayed home because she had just given birth to Hannah and Miriam hadn't come either, as she was caring for the children.

All of the rooms on the main floor had been beautifully decorated with purple and gold, everything from the dinner settings to the formal room that would be used for dancing. She couldn't wait to start the dancing. She had a good relationship back home with Mr. Samuel Gray, and they had an unofficial understanding, but that would not stop her from socializing and flirting with the eligible men of Vicksburg.

"Miss Isabelle. It is good to see you."

Belle turned and saw her Cousin Victoria's good friend Hannah Wheeler approach her. Hannah was a widow at the young age of twenty-two and had a two-year-old son named Ambrose. Belle liked her well enough but felt that Hannah would get along best with Elizabeth. They both were mothers and both had a strong faith in God. Hannah didn't just talk about God, she lived her life so that people saw her devotion to God.

"It is good to see you as well, Mrs. Wheeler," Belle replied.

"You really should call me Hannah." The woman replied.

"All right, Hannah, then I am now Belle to you."

"Very good." Hannah smiled.

"Where is your son this evening?" Belle asked.

"Ambrose is upstairs with the Turner's nurse." She said. *"I can go up and check on him whenever I feel the need."*

"That is fortunate," Belle said. More people began entering the room. Before long, Mary Turner-Corbel and her new husband, Abraham arrived. The guests clapped as they entered, and the bride and groom began the dinner. Belle sat between her cousin Victoria and Magdalena Williams, another friend of Victoria's. Mrs. Wheeler was sitting a few seats down from Belle. Following dinner, they all stood.

"Magdalena, Belle, I am so excited for the both of you to meet Mr. Zachary Petersen," Victoria said. She focused on Belle. *"Zachary is new to Vicksburg. He is a lawyer, working for my father, and is brilliant. He would have been here for dinner, but he is just returning from a short trip home to Natchez. He should be here soon, though"*

"Why have you not met him, Magdalena?" Belle asked.

"This is actually the first Vicksburg social engagement I have been to in the past six months," Magdalena answered. *"I have been traveling abroad since September."*

"I see," Belle replied.

"Ah! I see him." Victoria said. *"You two wait here, I will get him."*

Belle watched as her cousin hastened to one of the largest men she had ever seen, even more so than Joshua. Mr. Petersen was tall and looked as solid as a tree. He wasn't portly in any way, he just looked as though he could overpower anyone he wanted to. Belle also quickly noted the attraction that Victoria had towards him. If she didn't know any better, her cousin wanted to have a very permanent relationship with the lawyer.

"My goodness, Mr. Petersen is large." Magdalena said, patting her dark red hair, then running her hands down the skirt of her dark green dress. *"He is also extremely handsome."* She shook her head. *"I noticed him as he walked in and I must declare, my heart pitter-pattered*

427

like never before. His eyes! Why they are so beautiful I could just drown in them. I didn't realize he was Victoria's Mr. Petersen. I do hope she hasn't formed a romantic attachment to him."

Belle was about ready to tell Magdalena that it appeared as though Victoria did have feelings for Mr. Petersen, but before she could form the words in a polite manner, Victoria had taken Mr. Petersen by the arm and practically dragged him to her friends.

"Zachary, I am pleased to introduce you to my cousin from Fredericksburg, Virginia, Miss Isabelle Turner." Isabelle smiled and gave a short curtsey. "This is my good friend, recently returned from a European tour, Miss Magdalena Williams."

"It is a pleasure to meet the both of you." Mr. Petersen said.

"I understand you are a lawyer," Magdalena said. "That must be fascinating, and very important to our community."

"I find it rewarding." He said, flashing a handsome smile. "Besides, if I was not a lawyer, I would not have come to Vicksburg to join Mr. Turner's practice and I would never have met you, and Victoria, of course." He said, almost as an afterthought. Victoria smiled, but Belle couldn't help but notice it was a disappointed smile. "Miss Williams, would you care to dance?" The man held his hand out. Magdalena took it and smiled.

"Of course I would." She replied and he escorted her to the dance floor.

"Of course that would happen," Victoria said once they were out of earshot. She sighed. "Why would this situation be any different? Of course, he would prefer her to me." At that moment, a young man from the party approached Belle, introduced himself and asked her to dance. Belle looked at Victoria, curious about her feelings, but Victoria smiled.

"Belle, you must dance. I know how you enjoy it."

Belle saw Hannah Wheeler approach Victoria. Knowing that Hannah would be able to help Victoria through whatever was distressing her, Belle took the young man's hand and joined the dancers.

1863

Looking back, Belle wished she would have been a better friend to Victoria, but as was usual at that time, she had been selfish. She had heard later that Zachary and Magdalena were married, and Victoria was still unmarried. She shook her head and went to write a letter to her cousin. Maybe, just maybe, the letter would get through.

Saturday, July 4, 1863

Turner's Glenn Plantation

AJ trudged into the Turner Plantation House. She couldn't find anyone from the family there, so she continued towards the back. There, she found Belle, bent over a row of carrots, pulling weeds. AJ raised her eyebrows.

"Well, now, this is something I thought I would never see." AJ laughed. Belle turned and gave her friend an annoyed look. AJ tried to refrain from smiling.

"I keep telling you all. I can do the work when needed." She stood and walked to the fence. "I just don't prefer to do work that will cause me to get dirty and sweaty." She wiped her hands on her skirt, then brushed a strand of hair from her face. AJ had never seen Belle Turner look so disheveled.

"I can see you being a good doctor's wife, Belle. Working beside him." AJ teased.

Belle's jaw tightened. "I'm sure that will never happen. I really thought Aaron would have written to me, even though we didn't part well, but that hasn't been the case." She shrugged. "Oh well. I moved on from Samuel, I'll move on from Aaron." She looked toward the town. "I wonder how Richard Evans is making out in this war. He would be the type of man who would be dashing and come home from the war as a hero."

AJ paled a bit at her mention of Richard's name.

"Well, you may not want to give up on Dr. Knightly quite yet. He's probably been way too busy. You said he went north with the troops, correct?"

"Yes, and I haven't heard from him since."

"Belle, I hate to bring bad news. I thought you would have heard by now, but yesterday, and the two days before that, there was a horrible battle in Pennsylvania."

"Three days of fighting? Like here in December?" Belle put a hand to her chest. "Oh my goodness." She paused. "Please tell me we were victorious."

"From what I can gather, no, we were not," AJ replied. "I have heard conflicting reports, but it doesn't' appear that we won."

"This is devastating news." Belle couldn't believe it. "Dear Lord. Oh, good Heavens, where in Pennsylvania?"

AJ gave her a sad, knowing look. "I am afraid to say, but of all places, it was Gettysburg."

"No!" Belle exclaimed. "That can't be. What of our dear Charlotte!"

"I am so sorry. Yes, your cousin's hometown. I haven't heard if there were any civilian casualties or not." AJ remembered Charlotte Turner as a kind, friendly young woman. She knew Belle and Elizabeth both were close to their cousins. Which made her next piece of news even more difficult. "Unfortunately, I have more unsettling news, both to our cause and to your family. I heard that Vicksburg has fallen to the Yankees. It is now in their hands."

"Vicksburg has fallen? Oh, my sweet Lord. Now I must worry about Victoria and Mary as well as Charlotte!" Belle turned and quickly made her way to a nearby bench so she could sit down. "It is so imperative that I hear from them soon."

"If the Yankees let the mail go through," AJ said, sitting next to her friend. "You remember how it was when Fredericksburg was under Yankee control."

"I had forgotten," Belle said. "Gettysburg. Oh my, I hope Charlotte's all right. We haven't heard from her in ever so long."

"I'm sure she is. I remember her as being a strong, independent woman. I liked her."

"I greatly enjoy her company as well. Her father was a little gruff at times, but I feel as though it was more animosity toward my father who inherited everything. Uncle Hiram really wanted the plantation." She paused. "Poor Charlotte. I do know Uncle Hiram is fighting for the north. She's likely all alone on her farm…" Belle's thoughts drifted back to her one trip to Gettysburg and the first time she remembered meeting her cousin, Charlotte.

July 1855

"Now remember girls, be polite. Your Uncle Hiram and his daughter don't have the means we do." Belle's father adjusted his top hat after he disembarked from the hack that had taken them to the Turner Farm on the outskirts of Gettysburg, Pennsylvania. So far, Belle had been unimpressed with everything. The train ride was tolerable, but Gettysburg was small and seemed dull. She looked at the plain, two-story box-looking house that would be their home for the next few weeks and shook her head. At least the weather here was slightly cooler than at home.

"Oh, how quaint!" Elizabeth said. "I love the house."

Belle tried not to roll her eyes. Since Elizabeth had been spending more time with Joshua Bennett and less time with her own sisters, Elizabeth's opinions on many issues were changing.

The front door opened and a girl about Belle's age stepped onto the porch, followed closely by a tall, gruff-looking man with white hair and a neatly-trimmed beard.

430

"Hiram!" Belle's father called. He strode up the stairs and offered his brother his hand. Uncle Hiram shook it. "It's good to see you." Matthew turned to the girl. "And you must be Charlotte. My goodness, you are the very likeness of your mother."

"Charlotte, meet your Uncle Matthew and his daughters…" the man trailed off, clearly not sure which of Matthew's children had made the trip. They had all met a few times, but it had been years since their last meeting.

"This is Miss Elizabeth and this is Miss Isabelle," Matthew said.

"You can call me Elizabeth." The girl smiled as she approached Charlotte and gave her a hug. "You can call my sister Belle." Belle gave her cousin a smile and small curtsey.

"Please come in, I'll show you the room where you'll be staying," Charlotte said. Belle and Elizabeth followed her through the house and up the stairs. "I hope you don't mind sharing my room," Charlotte said, pushing a light brown strand of hair that had escaped her braid behind her ear.

"Not at all, this will be fine," Elizabeth said. "Right, Belle?" The sixteen-year-old gave her sister a look, hoping she wouldn't say something impolite, but Belle put on her best Southern charm and agreed with Elizabeth.

"As much as we'll miss home, your accommodations should suit us just fine." She looked around the room, which was small, especially with the two beds in it. A dresser, bedside table and vanity were the only other pieces of furniture.

"I'm afraid one of you will have to share my bed with me unless you would be willing to sleep on a straw tick. We could borrow one from a neighbor."

"I'll share with you," Elizabeth said. "It won't be an inconvenience for me."

"Wonderful." Charlotte smiled. A feeling resembling jealousy crept up within Belle. Elizabeth was always quick to be kind and good. The perfect friend, the perfect daughter, the perfect sister. It looked like she would be the one to befriend Cousin Charlotte first and be the perfect cousin. Belle sighed. Drat. Why couldn't she be more like Elizabeth?

"According to the letter from your father, your mother just had another baby." Charlotte led them down to the front sitting room. Again, Belle was surprised at the simplicity of the decor. A fireplace, four chairs, and side tables, not much else. A photo of a man and a woman was on the mantle. Belle guessed it was Charlotte's mother and father.

"Yes, she did!" Elizabeth replied. "Maxwell is five months old already, but that's why Mother didn't come up with us. It did make the

431

decision easier for Mother to keep our other younger siblings at home with her."

"And James, of course," Belle added. "You remember James, don't you, Charlotte? Father wanted him to stay and care for the plantation."

"Of course," Charlotte said. "I remember you have an older brother. How lucky you are to have so many siblings!"

"It is a blessing indeed," Elizabeth said. Belle verbally agreed with her, but secretly wondered about that. Maybe it would be better to be an only child with the constant focus of your parents.

1863

"Belle, what's wrong?"

Belle was pulled from her thoughts as she focused on the young man who had spoken. Max stood there, concern apparent on his face. He had matured so much in the past couple of years.

"Oh. I apologize, Max. I was just thinking of Cousin Charlotte. It appears there has been a battle near her home."

"Doesn't Cousin Charlotte live in the north? It's a good sign that our troops were able to push their way up there."

"I suppose that's another way of looking at it. According to AJ, though, the battle didn't go so well for us."

"Well, no offense intended, Miss AJ, but if you heard the news on your side of the river, I wouldn't be too worried. I remember the Yankees would always claim false victories when they were in town, even the newspapers wrote things wrong. I think they just try to fool us into thinking we're losing the war."

AJ smiled. "You're absolutely right, Max. Unfortunately, what I heard in town confirms what I overheard across the river."

"Oh," Max said, disappointment clear on his face. "Well, I suppose we can't win them all. We'll bounce back. I have faith in General Lee."

"We all do Max," AJ said. "He is a good man to have faith in."

That night, after AJ had left and the younger children were put to bed, Belle, Elizabeth, and Annie sat on the front porch, a few lanterns lighting the area, the moon glinting off the slow-moving river.

"It's so peaceful here," Annie commented.

"I agree," Belle replied. "Sometimes, it's hard to believe the war is still so close."

"I can't believe there was a battle so far north as Gettysburg. Poor Charlotte, going through all of that alone." Annie said.

"I wonder if her friend Wesley ever went home to Gettysburg," Belle remarked.

"I hope so. The two of them made quite a compatible couple." Elizabeth said. "Do you remember, at AJ's ball at Chatham? Oh, that was a night!"

"Yes, after Wesley apparently embarrassed Richard Evans," Belle added. "Samuel said that Richard was quite upset that night after Charlotte passed him over. I really thought Richard was quite attentive to Charlotte."

"Of course he was, you were the one encouraging that relationship because you wanted time with Samuel." Elizabeth pointed out.

"Well, that might be true." Belle shrugged. "I'm quite sure that the war has made Richard a better man, though. He has always been quite dashing."

"Also rude and conceited," Elizabeth added. "It will take a unique woman to marry him." Elizabeth looked at her sister. "No, Belle, that is not a challenge to you."

"Oh, all right," Belle said, then thought a moment. "As strange as it may seem, I can actually see AJ and Richard making a good match. I know I have discouraged that relationship in the past, but she has become a much stronger woman throughout the course of the war. "

"If he would get over his arrogance, pride, and vanity, maybe," Elizabeth said. People could change, she knew that, but Richard would have a lot of work to do if he wanted to marry someone as wonderful as AJ. Elizabeth's thoughts quickly shifted back to Charlotte.

"I just don't know what to think about this battle in Pennsylvania. I'm dreadfully worried about Charlotte and the fact that she was all alone in the midst of the battle."

"I am too, but she has friends. Remember, she told us about the professor's daughter and we met her other friend. Jennie, was it?"

"Ginny." Elizabeth corrected. She wasn't surprised Belle didn't remember. Ginny Wade came from a poor family and at the time, Belle had made it clear that she thought Ginny was far beneath her.

"Yes, Ginny. I am sorry to say that I may not have treated her very well. When I see Charlotte next, I should have her give Ginny my apologies."

Elizabeth smiled at her sister. It was good to see Belle realize her previous actions were not always benevolent. She was becoming a much kinder person and because of that, much more pleasant to be around. "Yes, that is good of you, Belle, and I'm sure Charlotte's friends will have taken her in if need be."

"If she lets them," Annie added. "I remember, even though she was quiet, she had quite a stubborn personality."

"A member of the Turner clan? Stubborn?" Elizabeth smiled. "I surely don't know what you're talking about."

Wednesday, July 8, 1863
Moss Neck Manor

"AJ! It's so nice to see you." Bertie answered the door. "Your timing is impeccable. Kate was upstairs, taking a little rest, but she should be down any moment."

"I don't want to be an inconvenience," AJ said. "I thought she was coming home yesterday."

"She did, but she is still catching up on her sleep. She has had enough time to rest today. Make yourself comfortable in the parlor. I will send her down."

AJ wasn't alone long before Kate entered the room. She looked a little tired, but it was good to see her safe at home.

"You must tell me about your trip," AJ said. She wanted to be more specific and ask about her escort, but she would wait and see if Kate brought it up herself.

"It was wonderful. Very productive. I returned yesterday. I actually traveled home with many friends who had been driven from their homes here in Fredericksburg. They are returning to rebuild their homes since it is safe now."

"It will be good to have the town back to normal," AJ said. "Well, at least as normal as possible, given what we've been through."

"Indeed," Kate said.

"Are you unpacked?" AJ asked. "Were you able to purchase everything you needed?"

"Just about," Kate said, then her voice took on a frustrated tone. "Oh, but a dreadful thing happened to a new bonnet that I purchased while in Richmond. It happened here last night when I was unpacking. It is quite my fault." She shook her head. "My best hatbox had grown moldy from being in this damp house, so I put my bonnet on my bureau and left to enjoy the rest of my evening. Well, do you remember last night? The weather?"

"We had a thunderstorm," AJ said.

"Yes, we had a thunderstorm," Kate said. "And you will not believe the connection to that storm with my beautiful new bonnet. I had drifted off to sleep in the dining room because I was exhausted from my travels and I just wanted to go to bed, so I went upstairs to prepare for bed. Nettie came in and we talked for a while and that's when I spied my bonnet under a tremendous leak. There is now a great dark spot on the upper part of the crown and I could not save its original form and tint."

"Oh, Kate, that's so sad." AJ couldn't imagine being so distressed over a bonnet, but Kate had always paid more attention to fashion than she did.

"Nettie said that I was no more upset than anyone else would have been under those circumstances. I was glad, however, that I was far away from the Munford girls in Richmond and their reproaches and scolds, but I am now a wiser and more careful woman."

AJ smiled. "I'm sure you are. Is there no way you can rearrange the foliage and ribbons to hide the stain."

"No, I believe it is lost to me." She sighed dramatically. "Is there any word about where our army is? I heard rumors the regiments would all return to their haunts of last winter."

"I hadn't heard that," AJ replied. "I haven't been to town much, save for Mass."

"Well, I am hoping it is not true. I cannot forget how soldiers swarmed over our lands. With a few exceptions, as you know, I have had enough of their company for a long time to come."

"I fear it will be a long time until all the soldiers leave, what with the hospitals still taking in wounded," AJ commented.

"Oh, I know you're right. I was just hoping. I suspect that if our Confederates don't occupy the area, the Yankees will move right in." She sighed. "In that case, I would endure another occupation by our Confederates. I have always wondered why General Lee even brought his army to such a backwoods place last winter."

"Well, we are on the banks of a major river, half-way between the two most important cities in this war." AJ pointed out. She finally couldn't keep from asking the question that had been plaguing her. "How did things go in terms of your chaperone?"

"As I predicted, Stockton Heth was the perfect gentleman. Sally's father, Mr. John Munford did make a comment about how the Captain was still hoping I would change my mind and that Stockton could win my love."

"He didn't try anything? He didn't try to steal a kiss or try and steal you away?" AJ asked.

"No, as I said, he was a perfect Southern gentleman. Not only that, I am now certain that Sandie is the man for me. I may be wary about marriage in general, but not at all about the man I have planned on marrying."

"That is very good news to hear," AJ replied. "Your future husband is indeed a lucky man, I can assure you of that."

"Why thank you, AJ." Kate smiled. "You, my dear friend, are there any updates on your JP Smith?"

"No, there is not. We continue to write one another, but that is all. Sometimes I feel we are writing to each other simply for conversation and companionship. I do enjoy receiving his letters, though." AJ then changed the subject back to Kate. "Do you still hear from Sandie often?"

"I do write him, but I know not where he has been this past month and he does not tell me in the letters I receive from him. Not knowing makes me worry more."

"I would assume he was part of the fighting in Pennsylvania," AJ said.

"Most likely," Kate replied. "I had hoped that a victory in the north would put an end to this whole bloody affair." She sighed. "Apparently, that is not to be. The war still drags on."

Tuesday, July 14, 1863
Turner's Glenn

"It is wonderful to all be together again," Belle said with a smile. She looked at her friends surrounding her on the back veranda.

"I could not agree more," Kate said, picking up her needle, thread, and fabric. "It has become so monotonous at home since I returned from Richmond."

"Maybe for you, Kate, but we still have many patients at Turner's Glenn." Elizabeth agreed. "I cannot help but feel guilty visiting with you all when there is so much work to be done."

"We all deserve some time to ourselves, Elizabeth," Belle said. "Besides, several of our patients are being sent home or back to their regiments since they are recovering so well." She said. "Including Mr. Joseph Byron."

Elizabeth shook her head. "You hush now."

"Who is Joseph Byron?" AJ asked.

"A wounded Confederate who will be sent home to South Carolina shortly," Elizabeth explained. "He and Annie struck up a very good friendship."

"It is not just a friendship." Belle elaborated. "If you could see the devotion she has for him, you would agree with me."

"Time will tell, time will tell," Elizabeth said. "He appears to be a gentleman, very kind to Annie with no ulterior motives as many men have had in the past."

"I am delighted for her," Kate said. "I can't help but notice that you don't seem happy about the relationship, Belle."

"Why would I not be happy? My younger sister is closer to being a married woman than I am. Why would that not make me happy?" Belle shrugged.

"Belle. Don't worry over much. You will find a good man to be your husband." Kate assured her.

"She may have already." Elizabeth couldn't help pointing out, hoping her friends could get the information from her sister.

Belle blushed, something she did not do often. "I am not sure about that. I'm starting to think that Dr. Knightly's interest was a brief flicker of compassion and understanding amidst an ocean of animosity and grumpiness." Belle replied. "Whatever I thought may once have been possible is now doubtful. He and I had quite the argument before he left."

"The two of you have had many arguments." Elizabeth pointed out.

"True enough. He can be quite infuriating, but I must confess, there is something more. I just can't put my finger on it." She looked down at her work. "I fear I will never know for certain how it could have turned out. I fear I will never see him again."

"If it is meant to be, he will return," AJ assured her.

Belle didn't want to share with her friends the fact that she felt she had made things irreparable with Aaron Knightly. She also didn't want her friends to see how much he affected her.

"Elizabeth, any word from Joshua?" Kate asked.

"I received a brief letter last week. He was not part of the fighting in Pennsylvania, thank the Lord. So many men were killed in those three days. It is truly a tragedy." Elizabeth shook her head. "I still haven't told him we lost our baby. I never even told him I was with child." She shook her head. "I'm still not sure I even made the right choice." Her voice was soft. AJ saw she was on the verge of tears, so quickly changed the subject.

"The war could be over sooner than we think," AJ said. "There is word of draft riots in the city of New York."

"Draft riots?" Kate asked.

"Yes, the Union is apparently running short of volunteers, so they're making men sign up, or drafting them, they call it. The people in New York are protesting this so-called draft. I think this reflects the Northerners becoming weary of the fight. Perhaps they will pursue peace."

"If only that would truly happen," Belle said.

Sunday, August 2, 1863
Moss Neck Manor

"Bee, I must say yet again how delighted we are that you are home on furlough," Kate said, smiling at her brother in law as she sat down in the parlor.

Bee Dickenson sat next to Nettie, who was holding Baby Kate in her lap. He smiled at his wife. "There is no place I would rather be than with my wife and her family." He paused. "Unless I was with my family at Echo Dell." He took Nettie's hand. "In fact, Nettie and I were just discussing that." He looked around at the family that had gathered

437

for the evening. The patriarch, James, and his second wife, Jane were visiting as well. Bertie was sitting next to Kate. "I have thought a great deal about this, and I am determined to move my family back home."

"To Echo Dell?" Kate was astonished. "Take her back across the river? King George County is in enemy hands." She scoffed. "That is a foolish idea. A crazy notion. Who will watch out for them? Who will even bring her there? We have only a few servants left here and none of them would accompany her."

"I would. She is my wife and I will take care of her."

"Bee, if you return home, you risk being captured. You would be brought over to Old Capitol Prison." Kate stood, knowing she could not lose her sister and Baby Kate after all they had been through. "You have no right to drag your family around the country in the middle of a war."

"I have no right?" Bee stood, keeping his voice calm despite being clearly angry. "I have every right and you know it."

Kate looked toward her father. "Papa, can you not talk some sense into your son-in-law? This is madness!"

"I may disagree with him, Kate, but it is Bee's decision, and Nettie's. My dear daughter, what do you think of the situation?"

Nettie glanced at Bee, then back to her father. "I am willing to do whatever Bee believes is best."

"You cannot tell me you would rather deliver the child you now carry alone at Echo Dell than here, surrounded by family? You cannot be serious." Kate persisted her argument.

"I am." Nettie stood. "You can come with me if you desire, but I will be going home to Echo Dell."

Thursday, August 13, 1863
Moss Neck

"Sandie!" Kate threw her arms around her intended. He leaned down and gave her a kiss.

"I have missed you so." He murmured, pulling her tightly to him. "I missed you more than I can say."

"And I you." She reached up and brushed a strand of his hair. "We have much to talk about."

"We do." Sandie led her to the rocking chairs on the porch and they sat. She held onto his hand, not wanting to lose contact. While he was absent, it was easy to have doubts about the marriage. In fact, if Nettie had not finally decided to stay at Moss Neck, Kate had been willing to put aside her marriage plans and accompany Nettie to Echo Dell. Now that the wedding was getting closer and the plans all made, there had been occasions when she was bored. At this moment, however, with Sandie next to her, all doubts were erased.

"You have made me nervous these past months." Sandie said, linking his fingers with hers. "I think two full months passed without a single letter from you. I hadn't heard from my mother or sisters either. It was as if the women in my life had forgotten about me."

"Impossible." Kate said, gently brushing his cheek with her other hand. "No one who has ever known you could forget you. It was difficult to write because I didn't know where you were. It made me miss you even more."

He was silent for a moment, as if he were debating what to say next. "To be honest, Kate...I do need to be completely honest with you. I love you more than life itself, but as the days and months roll on, I begin to get...afraid of the responsibility of marriage."

"Do you regret proposing?" Kate's stomach felt queasy. He had remorse for proposing to his previous fiancé. Had he grown tired of her as well?

"No! Not one bit." He stood and strode to the porch railing, placed his hands on it, and looked out across the landscape. "Kate, I love you so much, I just feel that a man should not bring misery onto the woman he loves, and a man should take care of his wife, especially during a war. I do not want to withdraw my promise to you, but I can't stop feeling that I will be shirking my duty to you as a husband. I feel I cannot be a good husband to you when I am constantly absent fighting in this war."

Kate stood and came up behind Sandie, placing her arms around his waist and laying her head on his back. "I should be honest with you as well, Sandie. I have been having doubts about our marriage as well. It's not that I don't love you too because I do, more than anything." She sighed as he turned, leaned against the railing and pulled her into his arms.

"This war, though it brought us together, is creating all the problems keeping us apart." He commented. "I would understand if you wanted to postpone or even...cancel the plans that we have." He tipped her face up to look into her eyes. "I would understand if you didn't want to marry me."

"Oh, Sandie. I may have doubts about marrying a soldier while we are in the middle of a war, but I have no doubts about marrying you."

"As always, you are especially charming and good for my soul." He gently kissed her again. "So you are still willing to keep the date for our fall wedding? The two returned to their chairs.

"I am. Sandie, I have come to the realization that life will never be perfect. All relationships can be difficult at times. The same will happen to us whether there is a war or not. You know, shortly before your arrival, I was going through quite an emotional crisis. Nettie's husband, Bee wanted her to move back to Echo Dell. I tried and tried to argue

439

against him, but my sister has no seeds of rebellion within her. Thankfully, I prevailed and Nettie will remain at Moss Neck, but it worried me dreadfully."

"Good for you. Family is important in times like this." He looked into her eyes. "You are correct. Life will never be perfect. Getting through these trials now will help us adjust to being man and wife." He smiled. "You have convinced me. It will be best to keep our wedding date as we originally planned."

"Yes, that sounds wonderful. When will you be able to get another furlough?"

"In a few months," Sandie replied. "I'm thinking late October would be best. We should be in winter camp by then. If a campaign is in progress, we can postpone the wedding at that time. Would that be enough time for you to finish the arrangements?"

"I believe so," Kate replied. "As you know, I traveled to Richmond to complete my trousseau. I would want Sally Munford and your sisters Rose and Mary to stand up with me as bridesmaids, so they would need to come to Moss Neck for the ceremony.

Sandie smiled. "You want my sisters to be in our wedding?"

"Yes, of course. I know how dear they are to you and I have enjoyed corresponding with them." She smiled back. "I would also like Elizabeth, Belle, AJ and of course Nettie and Bertie in the wedding party as well. Who will you invite to be groomsmen?"

"I have thought on this a bit." He answered. "If they can all get furlough at the same time, I would like Hunter McGuire and JP Smith of course. I would also like Edward Willis, Clem Fishburne, my cousin Dudley Pendleton and your cousin, Jack Welford."

"That sounds splendid," Kate said. "What other wedding details have you thought of?"

"I would like my father to officiate the wedding. I have wanted that my whole life."

"I can agree to that." Kate moved her chair right next to Sandie's so she could place her head on his shoulder. He placed his arm around her shoulders and held her there. "Will we have enough time to take a wedding trip?"

"I think a short one," Sandie said. "How would you feel if we went to Richmond for a brief visit, then to Lexington to spend time with my mother and sisters?"

"I think that is a capital idea," Kate said. "Oh, Sandie, I am so glad you're here. Everything is falling into place and I can hardly wait to become Mrs. Pendleton."

Sunday, August 23, 1863
Moss Neck

"AJ, my friend. What a pleasant surprise." Kate welcomed her friend to the small table and chairs that had been placed under the trees to provide shade from the hot August sun.

"I missed seeing you," AJ said. "How are the wedding plans coming along? I heard you decided the date of your wedding to be October 23."

"We did. Sandie and I had the most wonderful visit last week." Kate smiled, but AJ's intuition told her something was wrong.

"So what is vexing you, then?" AJ asked.

"Oh, AJ, I wish you didn't know me so well. It's just bridal jitters, I'm sure." Kate replied. "Talking about all of the details is making me see how much marriage will really change my whole life."

"I would assume that is true about every bride before her wedding," AJ said. "Do you doubt Sandie's love?"

"Not at all," Kate said. "I just...well, I get emotional at the thought of being separated from my family, plus Nettie's condition is constantly on my mind. I am trying to help out both at Moss Neck and at my father's plantation, plus organizing my wedding plans." She placed a hand on her temple. "I'm just feeling overrun, AJ."

"I can certainly understand that," AJ said, then thought on one of Kate's earlier statements. "Kate, what did you mean about separation from your family?"

Kate looked down. "I haven't really told anyone other than Bertie and Nettie of course, but after the wedding, I am considering moving to Lexington to stay with Sandie's mother and sisters. Father is actually considering selling Moss Neck, which would leave me with few other options."

"Oh, dear, that is dreadful, Kate." AJ paused. "I hadn't considered you would move, although I suppose, I should have." AJ didn't want to think about her friend moving away, but moving to her husband's home was what all brides did. "We will miss you so much if you leave."

"And I you," Kate said. "The only solace is knowing that the trip is just a short train ride away."

"There is no better way to learn about your husband than to spend time with his family at his childhood home." AJ smiled. "Other than actually spending time with him, of course."

"Of course." Kate smiled, but still sounded distracted.

"What else is bothering you?"

"Oh, AJ, I never imagined that the approaching date of my marriage would make me so miserable. I get along well during the daytime, where I can sit in the cool breeze and fresh air like today, or if I can sing as I do the household chores, but during the night, alone in my room? I just..."

441

She took a deep breath. "It has nothing to do with not being perfectly happy and satisfied with the love of the man I have chosen for my life-long companion. I fully and sincerely return the love that he gives, but sometimes, I feel I am being pulled away from all the other people I love. Those I am used to relying on when I need affection and forbearance. You, Belle and Elizabeth, Bertie and Nettie. I shan't be able to visit you when I have the need to do so. I realize that I have so little time left here." She looked at AJ, misery apparent in her eyes. "I will need all of the love Sandie can muster to compensate for the next few months of unhappiness I will have."

AJ wanted to comment but had to refrain. She understood that Kate had a lot on her mind, but AJ would move across the ocean if the man she loved needed her to do so. She loved Kate dearly, but sometimes she could be melodramatic. However, being the good friend she was, AJ continued listening.

"I am sorry. The word 'unhappiness' expresses more than I mean. I am not unhappy. No woman could have the blessings that I do without being the veriest of ingrates. I should say that I am seriously depressed."

Finally, AJ said what was on her mind. "Sandie loves you, Kate. If I had a man who was as hopelessly devoted to me as he is to you, I would go to the ends of the earth for him. I understand you are dealing with a lot of emotion right now. I know that separating yourself from Nettie while she is in her condition is a painful anticipation for you, but she will soon be confined, and you will at least be here when her time comes."

"I so worry about what will happen to Nettie when I leave Moss Neck. I am taking care of all the domestic burdens such as cooking and washing. You know how difficult that can be. What will Nettie do when I'm gone?"

"I understand." AJ went back to listening to her friend.

"I am trying to assemble my trousseau, but it seems like an impossible task. AJ, there are times when I want to write to Sandie, ask him to forgive me, and let the whole matter go." Kate sighed. "But then I look at my life here and realize that there is no permanent place for me here at Moss Neck. When the war ends, Bertie will have Richard and Bee will take Nettie back to Echo Dell."

"That is a fair point, but Kate, you know your family will always have a place for you in their lives." AJ couldn't believe that after all Sandie and Kate had gone through that she would just give up on the relationship.

"Maybe," Kate said. "Where does a man get the audacity to ask a woman, the woman he says he loves, to leave her home and all that is dear to her and go with him, to wherever he chooses, and where does a woman get the foolish idea to say yes? But, by golly, we'll do it." She looked at AJ. "I can understand now why Belle was so angry when Elizabeth married Joshua. Belle felt abandoned by her sister because Elizabeth was so involved in her new life, even though Elizabeth just moved down the road, not over one-hundred miles away as I will be doing."

"Where you go I will go, and where you stay I will stay. Your people will be my people and your God my God." AJ quoted.

"I know that verse," Kate said. "I just cannot recall from where."

"The Book of Ruth," AJ answered. "You remember the story of Ruth and Naomi, Ruth followed the person she loved most in the world and left her family behind." AJ leaned on the small table that was between the two women. "Kate, if you have this many doubts about your marriage to Sandie, then maybe you should call it off. Personally, I don't feel you have doubts so much as you have fears. Fear of the unknown, and we all have that, especially now, after two years of war. I can't say for sure what I would do in your situation, but Kate, let me ask you. How do you feel when you are with Sandie? Do you have doubts or fears then?"

"No, never. When I am with Sandie, I feel as though absolutely everything will be alright." Kate admitted.

"Then that is what you need to focus on. You and Sandie and how he makes you feel when you are together. How he has always been there for you when he is able, and how he would be there for you at all times if he could. Anyone would be lucky to have the relationship you do."

Kate smiled. "This is why I love to talk to you about my fears and problems. You always find a way to give me clarity."

"That is what friends are for." AJ smiled. "Your moving to Lexington will not change that, especially since we can write each other letters."

"You're right, AJ. Distance cannot stop friendships." Kate added.

Thursday, September 3, 1863
Turner's Glenn

"Miss Turner!" Henry, one of the young stretcher bearers approached Belle, who was pulling weeds in the vegetable garden. "Dr. Knightly is back and your Mama asked me to come tell you."

"He's here? He's back?"

"Yes, Ma'am, he's up at the house."

"Was up at the house." A deep voice said.

Belle turned to see Dr. Knightly approach them from the side. "Dr. Knightly! You came back."

"Of course I came back." He replied. "I never said that I was leaving for good. You made that assumption all on your own." He

443

nodded at Henry, who gave a quick nod back and headed back up to the house.

"It's very good to see you, Aaron." She said. "I honestly didn't think you would return." She stepped closer to him and looked up at him with a smile on her face. "How have you been? You look well."

"It has been tough. Very tough. We lost so many men. The carnage was unbelievable. So many lives destroyed in those three days at Gettysburg. We're actually quite lucky that their General Meade was hesitant as all the Yankee leaders have been. Lee had his back to the Potomac but was able to escape only because of Meade's ineptitude."

"That is a blessing. He fits in well with all of the Yankee officers, then." She touched his arm. "It's a blessing to have you back."

"I'm glad that's how you feel." He said. "I was afraid your reaction upon my return would not be pleasant since we didn't part well." He leaned down and kissed her forehead.

She turned toward the house. "Come. I'm sure there is much work for you to do, doctor."

Monday, September 14, 1863
Moss Neck Manor

Kate sat in her room, staring out the window. She was constantly thinking about Sandie. She couldn't deny that AJ had brought up some valid points the other day. Being with Sandie always put her doubts to rest.

Out of the corner of her eye, she saw a rider coming up the path. The soldier and horse looked familiar, and when he was close enough, she smiled to see that it was her intended. She stood and hurried down the stairs to see him.

"Sandie!" She threw herself into his arms. "Oh, Sandie, whatever are you doing here?"

He looked down at her, a sad look on his face. "I have some unfortunate news, Catherine mine." His voice was soft. "For your whole family."

"What's happened, Sandie?" She knew this wasn't good news.

"I wrote to your father, but I can see that you have yet to hear the news." He took a deep breath. "I came to console you, I didn't expect to be the one to tell you." He glanced around, wishing that he could delay the inevitable. "Kate, there was a skirmish near Culpeper. Your brother Richard has been killed."

"What? Richard? No. Not Richard." Kate shook her head, not wanting to believe what Sandie was saying.

"Kate, we have to believe that your brother has departed this earth to be with Christ."

Kate took a deep breath and nodded. "I know. I just...he is my brother and Bertie! Poor dear Bertie. How distraught she will be. She was inconsolable after Janie died. She will not accept this news. It's too soon, too soon."

Sandie led Kate to the porch rockers. "You will be there for her and I will do what I can to support you and your family as well."

Kate nodded, then when she composed herself, stood. "I suppose we should go and tell her now while I have the courage."

Sandie nodded, took her hand, and they went inside the house.

Later that evening, Sandie and Kate sat in the parlor, a fire crackling in the fireplace.

"I am quite impressed at how Bertie handled the news," Kate said, "and surprised. She was naturally grieved, but it seems she will by no means be an inconsolable widow." She shook her head. "She has lost a love which she will search the world over vainly to find again."

"I know it seems strange, but people sometimes grieve in different ways for different people," Sandie said. "General Jackson watched many a friend die in battle, but he could not contain his anguish when he learned of Janie's death." He sighed. "As for your brother, I hope that the same blessed spirit which had operated for his good in Janie's death may give peace and comfort to those who mourn him now." He wrapped an arm around Kate's shoulder. "I loved Richard like he was my own brother, so chivalrous and high-toned, a gentleman with all of his being."

"This will not even help me process his death, but do you know any details of his injuries?"

"His last words showed a most gallant spirit. He said: 'Pa, I die with my face to the enemy.'"

Kate brushed a tear from her cheek. "That sounds so much like our Richard."

"Yes. May God use his spirit. Poor Bertie has indeed lost a treasure in the love of such a man."

Kate placed her head on Sandie's shoulder and he tightened his arm around her. She spent some tears, then continued the conversation.

"I enjoy hearing from your mother," Kate said after a few moments. "I hope to hear from her again soon."

"She finds great pleasure in writing you." He said, glad that the two most important women in his life were getting to know one another. "Kate, I know this tragedy will have an effect on our wedding plans. You need time with your family to mourn and I heard today that our army is contemplating movement. We may have to postpone the wedding either way."

445

"Oh, Sandie, sometimes I wonder if we'll ever be married," Kate admitted.

"We will, I promise." He said. "My whole being has welled out in joy and thankfulness, for you are a great blessing and happiness that has come into my life."

"God has blessed the both of us, Sandie." She smiled up at him.

"With you as my wife, I am confident that I will be an even more sincere Christian, and with your love, my life will be preserved from the hazards of war."

"Are you still praying regularly?" Kate asked.

"I must confess, during July's Gettysburg campaign, I tended to be a little more reckless and thoughtless. I had a somewhat unsettled practice of constant prayer."

"Oh, Sandie."

"However, my belief and my public confession as a Christian back in mid-July has put me back on the right path."

"I remember you writing to me about that confession of faith. The communion service. Back in one of your July letters."

"Yes. I have felt better ever since." He looked down at her. "I need your prayers, though, Kate. You don't know how near I came to letting go of my profession. Camp is...it is so hard to live the life of a Christian in camp. I confess I can be led astray by the appearance of pleasure, but knowing that I have your prayers and God behind me, I know I shall be enabled to do better in the future than I have in the past. I am firmly resolved to do so."

"Sandie, my dear, you know that you always have my prayers, for now, and for always."

"Thank you." He said. "Even after Bristoe Station, I fear that my heart can be cold and careless and my conduct does not square with my good intentions."

Kate turned so she could look into Sandie's eyes. She touched his cheek so he would look back at her. "Sandie, you are being too hard on yourself. You are a good man who has lived through many tragedies. You lost the commander that you thought the world of, yet you continue to fight and the Lord has protected you many times over. He will continue to do so." She gave him a brief kiss. "Just as I will continue to pray for you. However, I must ask that you also pray for me and my family."

"Of course. Always, as often as possible." Sandie hugged her tightly.

Wednesday, September 16, 1863
Moss Neck Manor

Sandie sat with the Corbin family for the luncheon meal.

"Major Pendleton, we appreciate everything you have done for our family." Kate's father said.

"Of course, sir. I will do anything for Catherine." He nodded. "We have moved the wedding to mid-November now."

"As it is, she will be married in black," Nettie said. "Only members of the family should be in attendance. It is only proper during our time of mourning."

"What about Sally?" Kate said, alarmed. "Belle, Elizabeth, AJ..."

"No one but family," Bertie said firmly. "It wouldn't be proper."

"But they are my family too. What if we were willing to wait until it was proper? Surely by spring..."

"Catherine, dear." Sandie interrupted. "I don't wish to postpone the wedding if at all possible. We have waited so long already."

Kate stood. "Excuse me for a moment." She then fled from the dining room.

Sandie set his silverware on his plate and excused himself as well. He quickly found her out back, sitting on a bench. He approached her.

"May I sit?" He asked.

"Of course," Kate answered. You are the man who makes all of the decisions.

"Kate, I know you are disappointed about this turn of events. I am as well, but your family wants to do things properly. I can understand that."

"I do understand it as well, Sandie. What I don't understand is why we can't wait until I am out of mourning. We could have the wedding exactly the way we planned and everyone we want could be in attendance."

Sandie shook his head. "Kate, no, please. I don't want to wait that long." He grasped her hand. "I have been waiting so long already. We don't know how long we may have together. This war has taken many lives, it could take either one of us at any time. Civilians suffer and die as well. There was a young woman, only twenty-years-old, who was killed in her home during the battle of Gettysburg. If something were to happen to you, I do not know what I would do." He kissed her hands. "I know that this isn't ideal, but I want to be with you. I want to be married as soon as possible."

"I want that too, Sandie. It's just...I have always wanted my wedding to be a great social event with all of my friends and family there to celebrate with us. I don't want to have to be ready at a moment's notice just because that is when my intended can get a furlough."

"I understand that. It's not exactly what I want either, but the only person I really need at my wedding is you." He gave her a look that would have made her say yes to just about anything.

She smiled and sighed. "Oh, Sandie, you bring up a valid point. I may not be happy about the circumstances, but I do want to be your wife, truly." She nodded her head. "All right. November. As soon as we can."

He smiled confidently. "I was hoping that would be your answer. How does the twenty-fifth of November sound? It is a Wednesday. I looked at a calendar earlier today in the hopes that we could choose a specific date." He reached for her hand. "We can be married, then travel to Richmond and Lexington, just as we planned."

"Then the twenty-fifth of November it is." Kate agreed.

Monday, October 21, 1863
Somewhere in Virginia

"You rode all the way out here by yourself?" Richard looked at AJ, fire in his eyes. She averted her gaze. That morning, she had decided to ride out to the Confederate Cavalry camp to try and find Nathaniel, Richard or Major Daniels. She had witnessed a small group of Yankee troops moving through Stafford Heights, and also had some medication and supplies for the Confederate troops. She wasn't quite sure what had possessed her to ride the half-day distance to the camp, so she didn't know what to say to Richard. Either way, what business was it of his to be this angry with her?

"Is Nathaniel here?" She asked.

"No. I haven't seen him since he was sent west before the siege of Vicksburg began."

"Oh dear, that long." AJ's stomach rolled.

"I'm sure he's fine," Richard said. "I am much more concerned with you. I ask again, what were you thinking?"

"I'd rather speak with Major Daniels." She replied.

Richard threw his hands up and grumbled something that sounded like: "Wait here."

It wasn't long before Richard came back with Major Daniels. The Major, proper and cordial as always, took the information and supplies and thanked AJ for her services. He then turned to Richard. "Captain Evans, would you be willing to escort Miss Prentiss home?"

"Thank you, Captain Evans, but I do not need an escort." AJ protested.

"Of course I will be her escort," he said. "Since I will be in Fredericksburg, do I have permission to visit my parents?"

"Of course." Lt. Daniels nodded. "I'll give you leave until tomorrow night. That should give you sufficient time."

"Thank you, sir." Richard and Lt. Daniels saluted each other. Richard then turned to AJ as Major Daniels walked away. "Allow me to get my horse and we can be on our way."

"I really don't need an escort," AJ said, but he had already headed in the direction of his horse. "Who does he think he is?" AJ muttered to herself, as she made her way back to her horse. She had made it to the camp just fine, she could get home the same way. AJ quickly mounted and began riding in the direction of Fredericksburg.

Richard caught up with her quickly. "What was the meaning of that?" He asked.

"I told you I didn't need your escort, Richard. I can find my way just fine. I'll be home before dark."

"I'm not disputing the fact that you are a capable woman, Miss Prentiss. I just want to make sure you arrive home safely."

"Why is that? Since when do you care about what happens to me?" She said it quietly enough that she wasn't sure if he heard her or not. He didn't respond, so she assumed he hadn't. She was perfectly content riding in silence.

About an hour into the ride, Richard pulled his horse to a stop.

"What are you doing?" AJ asked, reigning her horse in next to him.

"I was just going to ask if you needed a break," he said. She pulled out her canteen, took a drink of water, and then shook her head.

"No. I'm fine. I would like to get home before dark. Liberty will worry."

"As long as you're sure."

"Yes, Mr. Evans, I am," AJ replied as they continued on at a slower pace.

"Don't you think it's time we started calling each other by our Christian names?" He asked.

"I'm not sure about that," AJ said.

"I feel we have become quite close since the start of the war. I must ask, though, what did I do to make you so wary of me?"

"I wouldn't expect you to remember, Richard. I was just another girl to you, one that you barely paid attention to. It isn't significant."

The sadness in her voice pricked something inside of Richard, as did the fact that she used his first name. He did like the way it sounded on her lips.

"I'm sorry, America. I don't recall. Please remind me."

449

"Do you remember when my aunt and uncle had a ball at Chatham in my honor? Belle's cousins were in town and you were sparking her cousin Charlotte from Gettysburg?"

"Sparking? You use that word? Your country upbringing is showing." Richard laughed at her. AJ turned from him, frustrated. "I'm sorry," Richard said, grabbing her arm and turning her toward him. "I'm sorry. Please continue."

AJ took a breath. "You were...interested in Charlotte."

"Yes, I was. She did lead me to believe she was willing to do more than she actually was."

"That is not true. Just because you wanted something to happen between you and Charlotte didn't mean she did."

"She went outside with me, America, what was I supposed to think?"

"That she was a lady who wanted some fresh air?"

"Wait." Richard paused, thinking. "How do you know all this?"

"I saw you two. I needed some air myself. It was stuffy and I was actually having fun, dancing, and I needed a break. I heard you two arguing. You were correct before, at the time of the dance, I did fancy you. A little girl's first infatuation. It hurt that you paid me no mind, although I didn't really expect you to. Anyways, I overheard you with Charlotte and was about to intervene and go to Charlotte's aid when her friend, that man from Shepherdstown, arrived."

"Yes, the carriage-maker. Culp, I believe his name was. Not much of a gentleman."

"The way he sent you to the ground with one push? I would expect you to say something like that." AJ laughed.

"Well, he..." Richard started to speak, but then stopped at the look she gave him.

"I was already upset about your actions, but I still wanted you to notice me, to like me. So I went to you, hoping I could help ..."

1859

Fredericksburg, Virginia-Chatham Manor

AJ followed Richard back towards the main house. If she caught up with him, maybe she could offer him help in some way. As she neared him, he was already talking to Samuel Gray. AJ listened to their conversation, staying out of view.

"I told you Charlotte wasn't like that, Richard," Samuel said.

"Yes, I know you did," Richard said. "I really thought...well, it doesn't matter now."

"Knowing you, it won't take you long to find another woman," Samuel said, shrugging. "So what is the problem?"

"You're right about that." Richard glanced around the room.

450

"You know," Samuel said, *"It would be a nice gesture if you would dance with Miss Prentiss. It is her party and, she's a sweet girl. I know she's not normally the type you go for, but ..."*

"America Joan?" Richard asked, incredulous. *"You cannot be serious. She is not the type of girl I would ever consider conversing with, much less dance with. While I must admit, she has grown into a fairly pretty woman, Samuel, I feel as though Miss Prentiss would be the last person I would consider dancing with."*

AJ could hear her heart pounding. Tears welled up in her eyes, and her throat felt like it was going to close. She couldn't breathe. She had to get away. As she turned away from Richard and Samuel and her embarrassment, Elizabeth stopped her.

"AJ, where are you going? What's wrong?"

"I can't stay here another minute. Not around him. I just can't." *She raced back to the garden and didn't return until the last guest had left.*

1863

"Elizabeth deduced what had upset me. She discussed it with me the next day. She told me you weren't worth my tears and that you were probably going to spend the rest of the night in the company of another woman." Tears shimmered in her eyes, she avoided looking at him.

Richard was appalled at his past behavior. He remembered the night. He had been drinking and was angry about being passed over by Charlotte Turner for a tradesman. For him, at the time, it had been a missed conquest. He pulled his horse to a stop, then reached out to gently take her arm. She stopped

"America, I don't know what to say. Apologizing to you doesn't seem like enough. I do remember that night. My behavior and words are inexcusable. I...that's not who I am. Not really, not anymore."

"I know you're not. I see glimpses of a very kind and gentle man, yet you still sometimes act like a selfish, spoiled Lothario. You treat people as though we're...I don't know, like we're not worthy of knowing you."

"America, I have to confess something to you. I find myself very attracted to you. I'm not entirely sure when it happened. When this war first started, I honestly didn't even think of you as a possible interest but over the past year, I have seen the woman that you are. Strong, brave, selfless, intelligent and the way that you care about people, is amazing. The way you look after your sister, the farm and your support of my mother. I have been feeling as though I am not worthy of you. I want to be, though."

"Richard, what are you saying?" AJ's heart was pounding.

"I think, America, I think I'm falling in love for the first time." He leaned over and kissed her, then leaned back and smiled at her, a kind, genuine smile filled with affection.

AJ reached over and touched his chin, rough with stubble. He hadn't shaven in a few days, which was unlike him, even in the midst of war. "I'm glad you feel that way, Richard. So very glad."

Monday, October 26, 1863
Bennett Home

"Not even a full year later and the Bennett family can return home." Belle handed a carpetbag down to Eric. They were finally helping Elizabeth and her family get settled back in their home after repairs had been made to the living space.

"Yes. You are probably ecstatic that you may now resume your daily life at Turner's Glenn without us." Elizabeth replied.

"To be honest, Elizabeth, we will miss you very much," Belle admitted. "On the other hand, it will be nice to have more space in our upstairs room. We should have even more room soon with all of the wounded leaving and so many doctors being reassigned."

"Unless there are more battles in our vicinity," Meri added. "Then we will likely be one of the first homes to become a full hospital again."

"Oh, Meri, let's hope not," Elizabeth said. "On a brighter subject, we will visit often."

"That is grand," Belle said. "We will still need your help, not only with the wounded but with the chores also."

"Elizabeth Bennett! I wondered if you had moved back into town yet." Kate approached with a smile on her face.

"We are just moving back today, actually." Elizabeth smiled. "Eric has been working non-stop these past months, whether it's here or at our hospital or helping with the chores on the plantation." She gave the young man a smile.

"It was the least I could do, ma'am." He turned to Meri and the Bennett children. "Who would like to go for a walk? We can see how the town has changed and make our way down to the riverfront."

"Can we try to catch turtles?" Benjamin asked.

"Of course, mate," Eric replied. "I was hoping you would ask." He offered his arm to Meri, who took it and the four walked away.

"I suppose that leaves the three of us to have some tea and a good long chat," Elizabeth said. "Do you have time, Kate?"

"Yes. That sounds wonderful." Kate answered as they went inside the house.

"Eric did a wonderful job here," Belle said. "I have to say that he may be a better carpenter than he is a blacksmith, and coming from me, that is a great compliment."

"I would agree with you." Elizabeth started a fire in the stove that hadn't been damaged too much during the battle. "I will have to stop at the grocery store soon, but..." She reached into her pantry and grabbed some crackers. "Aha! I was hoping I had these in here. I am so glad that no looters came into the house."

"As am I," Belle said, thinking of the havoc the Yankees had done, and all of the homes and businesses destroyed when they chased the Confederates out of the town back in December. The Yankees had completely ransacked the city, destroying personal property. They had thrown furniture, portraits and even a piano out into the streets. Belle turned to Kate. "It is very good to see you. I have missed you so. How have you been faring over at Moss Neck? I feel as though so much has happened since we were last able to visit."

"It could be worse, I suppose. Bertie is handling my brother Richard's death better than I expected. She is almost back to her usual, cheerful self. It is as if she is made of Indian rubber. I have never seen such an elasticity of spirits."

"She has suffered through so much grief," Elizabeth said. "First, her only child, then her husband, not to mention her nephews." She reached across the table and placed her hand over Kate's. "And your grief. How have you been?"

"Overwhelmed. Frustrated." She sighed. "I am more distressed every day." She quickly explained about the pressure for an early marriage while in mourning and not being allowed to have her friends at the wedding. "I have not felt like a decent person in weeks. There are days that I wish I were in heaven already. I don't know whether I am happy or not, as I ought to be. I am so fretted at the way things have turned out. But I suppose these are my slight crosses to bear in comparison with what I could have. Sandie, on the other hand, departed Moss Neck so chock-full of getting married as he could be. Men can be so hateful."

"They can be." Belle agreed. While she and Dr. Knightly were getting along well, he still infuriated her at times in ways that no one else could. "However, Elizabeth is the wrong person to speak with on that matter. She finds her husband and marriage quite perfect."

Elizabeth looked at Belle with disbelief. "Is that really what you think?" She shook her head. "Joshua is a wonderful man. He is a great father and husband, but he is by no means perfect. He exasperates me at times as well." Elizabeth looked at Kate. "It is perfectly normal to have disagreements with the man you will spend the rest of your life with.

Joshua and I had a fairly easy courtship, yet we had some bumps in the road that we managed to get through. You and Sandie, however, have not had it easy at all. You found love in the middle of a war, what most people would consider a hopeless place."

"You're right. Kate said. "I am glad that Sandie was brought to me through divine intervention, but I wish it had been at a different time."

"It's normal to be nervous before your wedding as well. I surely was. Even though I was extremely sure that Joshua was the one for me, I still doubted the relationship at times. I had known Joshua for most of my life." She smiled. "Marriage is a big step, and you have the added stress of moving away from your family. Your loyalty is now to your husband. You keep your friendships and relationships with others, but they change." Elizabeth looked at Belle, an apology on her face. "I never meant for my marriage to Joshua to damage my relationship with you, Belle. I just wasn't able to give you the same attention as I could before I was married. Perhaps you will understand once you're married."

Belle smiled. "I believe I am beginning to understand, Elizabeth."

Elizabeth smiled nodded and turned back to Kate. "I believe you are making the right choice, Kate. Mr. Pendleton is a fine and decent man who will make an ideal husband for you."

"Thank you. Both of you. This is why I need my friends. Why I am so upset that I cannot invite you all to my wedding, why I don't want to move to Lexington and why I don't want Moss Neck to be sold."

"My goodness," Belle said. "You do have quite a few worries. What is this about Moss Neck being sold?"

"Something Father has been thinking on for a while, and now with Richard gone and him not having any sons...well, I think that had a lot to do with his decision. Father has other properties to leave to the sons he had by his second marriage." Kate shook her head. "I will have a home with Sandie's family, which is what Sandie wants anyways, but I will miss everyone here so much."

"Lexington isn't so far, Kate. I can understand why Sandie wants you with his family, though. That's why he wants you to move, I assume?"

"Yes, but we're still in mourning for Richard. That is why my family is insisting on only family at the wedding." She sighed. "I just don't know. I don't want to leave the only home I've really known, much less not have my friends at my own wedding."

"That is understandable," Elizabeth said. "But know this. Whether you live in Fredericksburg, Lexington or the Oregon Territory, we will still be friends and will always be there for each other."

Sunday, November 8, 1863
Bennett Home

"It is so nice to be together for dinner," AJ said. "Perhaps this can be a more frequent event."

"That would be splendid," Kate said. "At least while I am still in Fredericksburg." Kate and AJ, along with Elizabeth and Belle, had decided that a lengthy visit was long overdue. Eric had taken Benjamin and Hannah out to Turner's Glenn to visit and help with chores around the plantation.

"The wedding is fast approaching," Elizabeth said with a smile. "Are you excited?"

"I am. We are almost ready." Kate replied. "I recently heard from Sandie. He has secured a promise from General Ewell for a furlough of 30 days, starting the 18th of this month. He also wrote to his sister, Rose, and told her that we would like to have her as one of my bridesmaids." She looked soberly at her friends. "I do wish that all of you could be in attendance, but my family is standing firm, only allowing family."

"We understand," AJ said. "Don't worry about us."

"Well, I was quite distressed by the lack of invitation," Belle said. "I love weddings. I wanted to be there." Elizabeth tried not to roll her eyes. Belle then smiled. Kate looked a bit frustrated.

"I have two bridesmaids. Rose will be one and Indiana Kilby will be the other. She has been staying with us since the latter part of October while visiting Bertie. Just as propriety dictates a small and solemn wedding, so too courtesy dictated Indiana's selection to my bridal party. I do so wish it could be the three of you and of course, Sally. She's not even allowed to come from Richmond for the celebration."

"Oh, Kate, even though I am disappointed, I know it will be beautiful," Belle said. Kate had been so stressed the last few times Belle had seen her that she wanted to ease her mind. "Just know that we will all be celebrating with you in our hearts."

"I will still make an effort to change my family's mind, so make sure you leave the date open on your social calendar."

"Of course. We wouldn't have it any other way." AJ smiled while Belle and Elizabeth nodded in agreement.

"Who did Sandie decide to have for his groomsmen?" Belle asked.

"Dr. Hunter McGuire and JP Smith," Kate answered. "He is allowed to have friends stand up with him."

"Hmm, JP Smith." Belle sent a conspiratorial smile at AJ. "Will there be dancing after the ceremony?"

"No, definitely not, we are a family in mourning," Kate said. "Do you see what I mean now? I wish there could be dancing, but we likely won't even have much of a dinner after the ceremony. It's just not the wedding I dreamed of"

"Both armies will soon be in winter quarters," AJ said. "Perhaps that is why Sandie thought this would be a good time. He will have more time with you and I am sure he is tired of the delays. He is very important to the Confederate army. Fellow soldiers sing his praises all the time."

"At church today, I overheard some of the men talking about the Federal General Meade. He launched an offensive and there was fighting over at Rappahannock Station." Elizabeth said. "It sounds as though the Confederates were overwhelmed at the bridgehead there and the Army of Northern Virginia retreated to the south bank of the Rapidan River. General Lee will be on alert. I hope this doesn't affect Sandie's furlough."

"It is a pity that General Meade didn't think about your marital plans," Belle said with a smile at Kate.

"Pity indeed." Kate couldn't help but smile. "If those generals cared about my relationship with Sandie, they would bring this war to a halt."

"Hopefully the generals will come to an agreement soon and we will be able to focus on all our relationships more than survival."

Thursday, November 12, 1863
Moss Neck

My dearest Kate,   *November 10*
It is with a heavy heart that I write you this today. Earlier today, I was feeling in fine feather in anticipation of my furlough, coming to Fredericksburg and beginning my life with you. However, I was sent to Lee's headquarters by Ewell to ascertain his wishes in regards to the Second Corps. It was then I learned that we would no longer be granted leaves and those that were on leave would be recalled because of a pending emergency.

Such a stern order has been a cruel blow. My dream of an early marriage is vanishing into thin air. I do, however, believe the furlough may be granted to me if I press the matter. But, my dear, I hold such a position of responsibility that I cannot ask for leave, especially as there is a possibility of active operations to be resumed soon. Without any vanity, I know my presence here is important. Under the conviction that I am doing my duty, I shall try to bear up under the disappointment and ask you to do the same. I assure you, if 'hope deferred maketh the heart sick', as it says in the Book of Proverbs, then my poor organ is well nigh until death.

My darling, do not wholly rule out the possibility of being my bride on November 25. While it is not probable, it is possible. Chances are

456

that neither I nor my father can be spared until winter sets in. Of course, if the weather turns bad, as it is threatening to do, it may stall the pending campaign. If that happens, I may be able to obtain a leave for a day or two, but I prefer to wait for a longer vacation so I can take you to Lexington.

I have written to my sister, Rose. She may be coming directly to Moss Neck and await me there.

Kate sighed. A wedding should not be this complicated. "Lord, is this some sort of sign? Are you trying to tell me that marrying Sandie is a mistake? Should I write to him and tell him that I wish to break off the engagement?" She looked down at the letter again, made a quick decision, and picked up some stationary to write him a reply.

Monday, November 16, 1863
Moss Neck Manor

"Kate you are horribly distracted this morning. What is wrong?" Belle had come to Moss Neck to visit with Kate, but there hadn't been much conversation. Kate bit her lip.

"I...I am in an agony of suspense, Belle. I did something in haste and believe that I made a mistake, but I just don't know."

"What did you do? Please tell me about it. You will feel ever so much better."

"I was going to write to Sallie Munford about the situation, but talking with you personally will be better." Kate took a deep breath. "Sandie wrote to me about the probability of not being able to make it to our own wedding on the twenty-fifth. The letter left me in a state of despondency. General Lee canceled all leaves, and that has made me purely miserable. I was in a bad state of mind and in my angry hate, I wrote and told Sandie that I was tempted to break our engagement. I am awaiting his reply."

"Oh, Kate, you didn't." Belle reached over and clasped her friend's hand.

"And to crown my misery, Sandie's sister, Rose will be here on Wednesday, that is unless she has changed her mind. God grant that it may be changed. I wish to spend time with her, but hospitality and common consideration for her will force me to be cheerful while she is here. I will also try to hide the state of Sandie's and my affairs." Kate shook her head. "Oh, Belle, if I wasn't so wretched, I could laugh at the ridiculous blunder of Rose's coming." She blew out a breath. "I can't help but feel as though I made a real mess of things."

"Sandie will understand. You have both been through so much in the past year. He'll be reasonable. He knows you are under a great deal of stress."

"Belle, I haven't even known him for a year. It seems fate is against us. What do you think? Should we just give up?"

"No." A male voice came from the doorway. Kate stood to see Sandie, who immediately marched over to her, pulled her into an embrace and kissed her more passionately than he ever had before. "No, we should not just give up." His voice was low. "We need to talk this through and be calm and rational." He kissed her again. Belle stood.

"I will leave the two of you to discuss your future. Kate, think with your heart." Belle touched Kate's arm and smiled, then took her leave.

"Sandie, what in Heaven's name are you doing here?" Kate said, gripping the sleeves of his jacket.

"I left the moment I read your letter." He pulled her to the settee and sat next to her. "Kate, if you are seriously having these doubts, we need to talk about them. Do you really want to break off the engagement?"

"No." She shook her head. "No, not at all. I really don't, but Sandie, I cannot help but feel as though this marriage is ill-starred. It seems as though every time we make our plans and have all in order, something happens to put it asunder. What if it is a sign from God that we are not supposed to be man and wife?"

"You know as well as I that anything worthwhile never comes easy. This relationship we have, it has never been simple. We have been separated so many times, and have spent more time apart than we have together." He looked deep into her eyes, both hands holding hers. "I never want to leave you. I never want to lose you. Whenever I see you, I am filled with euphoria and wonder that you chose me. I have spent my whole life trying to find you. I love you. And now? I cannot let you go, but if you truly want to break off this relationship, if you don't love me and don't want to be my wife, if you can look into my eyes and tell me that you don't want this, then I will acquiesce to your request, because I only want what is best for you."

Kate shook her head and touched his chin. "Sandie, you know I cannot do that. I do want to be your wife. I love you so much that it sometimes frightens me. The moment I posted the letter, I have been in anguish over my regret in writing it." She smiled and kissed his cheek. "We can make this work. We will make this work."

Wednesday, November 25, 1863
Moss Neck Manor

"Hello, dear friend! I came over to see you on the day you were supposed to have your wedding." AJ entered the foyer and Kate smiled wanly.

"You are very amusing, AJ." She replied. "What really brings you over here?"

"Well, with most of the Yankees gone from my side of the river and the Chatham hospital almost empty of patients, I find myself just taking care of the household and farm chores, which can be dreadfully boring. To break up the monotony, I thought I would come over and check on how you were doing today. I suspected it may be a difficult day for you."

"You are not the only one to come by. A group of visitors were here earlier, would-be wedding guests who had no idea that the event had been postponed." She shrugged good-naturedly.

"You seem to be in fairly good spirits," AJ commented.

"I am delighted with Rose, Sandie's sister," Kate said. "I am excited for you to meet her. She is so sweet and bright and affectionate that no one could help loving her."

"That is good to hear. I heard from Belle that you were deliberating about the wedding again." AJ gave her friend a concerned look. "I hate to bring this up, Kate, but are you eating well? You look quite thin and wan to me."

"I do have bouts of feeling as though I am under a cloud, but I will not give up."

AJ nodded. "Splendid. You and Sandie both have been in my prayers and will continue to be so. I feel he is a good match for you."

"Thank you, AJ." The two women made their way into the parlor. "Come in and see who else is here. They thought for sure the wedding would certainly come off as planned."

AJ greeted the family members of Kate's who had gathered. Kate's father and stepmother, her brother Welford, his wife, Diana, and Diana's sister, Mollie Maury. There was also an Englishman who had joined the group.

"Kate, I don't want to impose on your family. I can take my leave." AJ said.

"Of course not." James Corbin replied. "We were just about to have our mid-afternoon dinner. We would love for you to join us."

"Thank you for the invitation, Sir," AJ replied.

Just as they were making their way to the dining room, one of the servants announced that another carriage of guests had arrived.

"What? More guests?" Kate was shocked. "Guests for my wedding? Here?"

"That's what they claim, Miss Kate." The servant replied.

"Oh, dear." Kate bit her lip. AJ stood next to her and placed a supportive hand on her shoulder.

"Don't get flustered now," AJ said.

"As Bee would say, I am a bit confumblicated," Kate muttered, using one of her brother-in-law's favorite words. "I suppose I should go break the news."

AJ followed Kate to the porch, where Kate immediately put the guests at ease and explained to them the situation. The late arrivals had come in by train and had spoken with Mr. Gordon in town, who had told them there was no groom and so there would be no wedding.

"My goodness," Kate said. "I do apologize. I am terribly embarrassed at this turn of events."

"Don't distress yourself, Kate. We understand completely. This war has ruined many plans." Nancy Reynolds, one of the new arrivals said. "We can still have a merry time."

"Well, then, come into the house. We can make our dinner stretch." Kate smiled, then grabbed AJ's arm and spoke quietly to her. "Do not take that statement as an invitation for you to leave. I need you here more than ever now because if anyone else arrives, I just may throw a fit." She shook her head. "It is very disagreeable to be so common a subject of remark that Mr. Gordon knows of my marital issues. I suppose I cannot help it."

"No, you can't." AJ smiled. "And have no fear, I won't leave you."

For the rest of the evening, AJ was happy to see that Kate was her old self, happy, not mortified or dejected. As AJ prepared to return home, she commented on that observation.

"I suppose we should be merry over our woes and disappointments. We can enjoy ourselves as time and place permits." Kate replied.

"That is a fine way to look at it," AJ replied. Kate pulled AJ into an embrace."

"Thank you so much, AJ, for being here with me today. I am blessed to have you for a friend."

"And I, you," AJ replied.

Friday, November 27, 1863
Bennett Home

"Welcome, Kate, come in." Elizabeth smiled and let her friend in. "AJ and Belle are already here." Kate entered the house.

"Where are the children?" She asked.

"Turner's Glenn again. They miss being out there every day, so it seemed like a good time to have them go for a visit. Mother loves having them spend the night there." Elizabeth responded. Kate took a place at the table and greeted her other two friends.

"You all know my news, I am sure," Kate asked. "How are you three?"

"Hoping for a quiet winter this year," Elizabeth answered. "It's hard to believe that just a year ago, our world was turned upside down."

"Life has definitely changed." Belle agreed.

"Do you have many patients left at Turner's Glenn?" Kate asked.

"It depends on how many you think 'many' is," Belle replied. "We still have quite a few, but doctors have been sending soldiers home, and there haven't been any new patients." She shook her head. "Hopefully, that will continue to be the case."

"Mother is still doing a stand-up job of running the hospital." Elizabeth turned to Kate. "How are things at Moss Neck? We don't really have that many details. I have had you and your family in my prayers so often."

"I heard from Sandie. He wrote me a long, beautiful letter that details what loves means to him." She smiled shyly. "I was also able to get him a religious tract: *A Life for a Life*. He enjoyed it for the most part, but also had some compelling arguments against it." Kate shook her head. "He has such a fine mind. He would make a most splendid preacher."

"He probably would. I know, he and Joshua would become such good friends." AJ smiled. "Don't you think so, Elizabeth?"

"Yes, indeed, I agree. Perhaps someday." Elizabeth replied.

"Belle, I feel I have neglected you in my self-pity." Kate patted her hair. "Tell me, how are things with your Doctor Knightly?"

"Overall, well, but honestly, since he is one of the only doctors left, he is terribly busy. He comes and goes, as he is caring for the wounded at our home as well as the soldiers in the surrounding areas. However, we are able to spend a little time together."

"And?" AJ prodded.

"Oh, all right. I like him very much. I can't believe I'm saying this, but I may even love him." She shook her head in disbelief. "Whoever would have thought that I, gently raised Southern belle, Isabelle Turner, would feel this much affection for a gruff, grumpy doctor who doesn't really take care of his appearance.

"He is a good man with a big heart," Elizabeth added her opinion. "A gifted doctor and surgeon."

"Here we have Belle on her way to falling in love, I am engaged to be married as soon as we can be, and Elizabeth of course is happily

461

married to the love of her life." Kate turned to AJ. "Now we just need to find you someone special."

AJ shrugged, hoping she wouldn't blush. It had been a while since she had an interaction with the man she was truly interested in. She wasn't ready to tell her friends about her possible relationship with Richard, even though he had told her he cared for her. She still wasn't quite sure about his intentions.

Sunday, November 29, 1863
Fredericksburg

"Kate, you look upset," AJ commented. "Is everything alright?"

Kate looked at the letters in her hand, then turned to her friend.

"I just received a couple of letters." She replied. "One is from Mrs. Lee and it was quite kind, but it left me less than impressed, the other was from Sandie and it did distress me somewhat."

"Mrs. Lee? As in the Mrs. Robert E. Lee?" AJ asked at the same time that Elizabeth asked a question.

"What is wrong with Sandie?"

"First tell us about Mrs. Lee," Belle said. "Then we can talk about Sandie."

"Well, the kind thought from Mrs. Lee was nice. She said she was mighty sorry for my disappointment regarding the delay in my wedding. I would think that Mrs. Lee should remember that the disappointment was her husband's fault entirely. He is the one who canceled Sandie's furlough." She sighed. "And now that Jubal Early is temporarily in command of the Second Corps, it will be even harder for Sandie to obtain a furlough, especially to get married. That man is so opposed to wives and matrimony."

"I have heard rumors about that," AJ said. "Is that why Sandie has you distressed?"

"Not exactly," Kate replied. "Sandie was saying that he looked forward to another engagement with the enemy. He feels another victory before winter will raise the hopes of the entire Confederacy."

"He would be correct," Belle said.

"He also said there are rumors that Meade is advancing through the Wilderness to the west of us."

"Oh no, not more fighting in this area," Elizabeth asked. "Heaven forbid."

"Yes, and then Sandie brought up General Jackson, which he often does in his letters and discussions. He told me yet again that he strives every day to live more like that man."

"He is a good person to emulate," Belle stated.

"I know and I don't mind that at all. It just concerns me that Sandie is so eager to fight. He has said in the past that he becomes anxious before fighting a battle in what he calls, a natural tendency to shirk from danger, but to me, he seems to thrive on danger. It seems as though men enjoy conflict and being in battles. I just don't understand."

"Men can be complicated," Elizabeth said. "Joshua is one of the most peaceful men I know. To be honest, I am still not sure why he joined in this fight. I know he wants to support the Confederacy and serve his state, but I truly thought he would serve in a different capacity, such as being a chaplain or a regimental blacksmith."

"What reasoning did he give for not doing either one of those?" AJ asked.

"He said he believed it was the direction he was being called to." Elizabeth sighed. "I would have so fewer worries had he gone in either of those directions." At her despondent look, AJ decided to change the subject.

"I have been thinking a lot lately. Christmas is almost upon us. We started the first week of Advent today at Mass." She looked around the group. "We should try to do something special for the holiday. Get together with all of our families. Celebrate as best we can."

"I think that is a splendid idea," Elizabeth said.

"Me too. Provided I am here, of course." Kate added with a grin. "Maybe by that time, I will be a married woman."

"I have a strong feeling, Kate, that by then, you and Sandie will be married," Belle said. "You will be Mrs. Alexander Pendleton by the new year, I just know it."

Monday, December 14, 1863
Turner's Glenn

"Good afternoon, Miss Turner."

Belle turned with a smile on her face to see Dr. Knightly. "Doctor, how are you this fine day?"

"My day is much better now that I have seen you." He smiled and Belle was momentarily dazed. She had found him attractive in a less-polished way, but when he smiled, he was the most handsome man she had ever met.

"Why, doctor, you are almost charming today." She smiled back. "Do you have time for a stroll?"

"It is the middle of December, Miss Turner." He said. "Is it not too brisk for you?"

"No, not at all." She smiled, but not in her usual flirtatious way. Aaron allowed her to feel as though she could be completely genuine with him in a way that she never felt around Samuel or any other man.

"There is nothing I would rather do than go for a walk with you. Unfortunately, I do not have time today, I have rounds I must finish, and then, unfortunately, I must go and pack."

"Pack?" Belle frowned. "Why? Where are you going now?"

"I am actually going home for the holiday season to see my family. It has been so long. I haven't seen them since the beginning of the war. If I can get done with all of my duties, I will be delighted to take you on a stroll later."

"I see." Belle gave him a sad smile. She was happy for Aaron but had been looking forward to spending Christmas with him. "When will you be leaving?"

"Tomorrow morning." He replied. "I am sorry that I didn't tell you sooner. The approval for my request just came through. I only have 14 days. I need to be back here by the new year."

Belle tried to put a smile on her face, but she could not hide her disappointment. "I will miss you but I understand that you need to spend time with your family."

"Thank you. I will work feverishly to complete my tasks so we can spend some time together this evening." Aaron leaned down and kissed her forehead, then was off.

Moss Neck Manor

"Kate! A letter for you." Rose Pendleton peeked into Kate's room. "It's in my brother's handwriting."

"Wonderful!" Kate smiled as she took the letter. "It has been over a week since I've heard from him." She scanned the letter, her eyes widening as she did so.

"Kate, what is it? Is everything alright?"

"I...he's all right. He has applied for a furlough starting today, he wants to be married on Wednesday. Oh dear." Kate was excited and horrified at the same time. How would she ever be ready in such a short time?

"Wednesday? That's only two days from now." Rose pointed out.

"Oh my goodness. My Sandie will be here in two days, ready to be married. Oh, Rose, will you help me prepare?"

"Of course, Kate. Everything will be perfect for your special day."

Wednesday, December 16, 1863
Moss Neck Manor

"Happy wedding day, Kate! I heard Sandie would be here today." AJ had stopped by to wish her friend happiness. She saw her friend in the entryway the moment she entered the house. Kate turned with a glower on her face.

"Not today it isn't." She said.

"What? Kate, why not? Whatever has happened this time?" AJ put a comforting arm around her friend's shoulder.

"Sandie was so sure he would be able to get the furlough and make it here in time. So we killed the fatted calf and scoured the house, but no groom arrived. His application for leave was rejected and he has been ordered to accompany General Early to the Valley of Virginia."

"Oh, Kate, I am so sorry."

"No, I am sorry that you had to come all the way out here for nothing." She rubbed her forehead. "Are we only fooling ourselves, AJ? I feel so repetitive saying this, but, we have had so many disappointments with these wedding plans. It feels as though God doesn't want us to be man and wife." The two went into the parlor and sat down.

"I wouldn't say that, Kate," AJ said. "If something is worthwhile, it is worth putting forth the effort."

"Sandie once said something to that effect," Kate said. "What would you do in my place, AJ? Honestly."

AJ took a deep breath. This could be an opportune time for her to share information about her relationship with Richard. Elizabeth knew a few details, and Liberty suspected, but no one knew the whole situation. "I would continue to wait patiently. I know Sandie must be terribly upset as well. It's not as if there is anything either of you are doing wrong. Neither one of you is avoiding the planned wedding days. This war is the only reason you have had to postpone the wedding. I know you have had doubts along the way, but if I were you, I would never give up on Sandie."

"Thank you, AJ. You are right, I just needed reinforcement. You are such a dear friend, a wonderful person." She shook her head. "It still puzzles me that you haven't found someone special yet. Do you still keep in touch with JP Smith?"

"It's been some time since I have heard from or written to him," AJ admitted. "I suppose that God has other plans for me and my future."

"I wish I had a faith like yours, knowing everything will work out."

AJ mentally shook her head. Conversations with Kate always revolved around Kate and her problems. At times, this annoyed AJ, but she understood that Kate had endured several tragedies this past year, and with the continued postponement of the wedding plans, AJ really did feel sorry for Kate.

"Kate, considering your past year, the fact that you still have any faith at all is quite impressive. I feel it is your faith that has brought you this far. Please don't give up now."

"Thank you for that, AJ, and your support," Kate said.

Thursday, December 24, 1863
Turner's Glenn

Belle smiled to herself and quickly glanced around as she let herself into James's old room, which was now Dr. Knightly's room. Over the week, she had been altering two of James's shirts for Aaron as a Christmas gift. She had wanted to give them to him personally but had decided on leaving them in his room as a surprise.

This was the first time since James had died that she had been in the room. Aaron and the other doctors that slept in the room had kept the room very close to how James had left it, save the extra beds and side tables. It was easy to determine which section of the room belonged to Aaron. She placed the gift on his bed, then placed the note she had written on top of it. As she turned away, she bumped into his side table and a stack of papers fell to the ground.

"Oh, botheration." She said, then knelt to pick them up. She organized them as best she could, but a photograph stuck out from the pile. Curious, she pulled it out and looked at it. A beautiful woman who looked to be in her mid-twenties and a boy around the age of five looked back at her.

"Who are these two?" She wondered aloud and turned the photograph over. Her heart sank when she saw the elegant female script. To My Darling Husband, with all our love, Ada, and Joel. Belle dropped the photograph. Feelings of betrayal coursing through her. Aaron Knightly, the man she had given her heart to, was a married man, and he had a son. She tried to stop the tears from forming. Anger began bubbling up within her. How could he do this to her? How could he just play with her emotions like that? She stood. She had to get out of the room. It felt as though the walls were closing in on her. She quickly fled to the hallway and down the stairs. Not knowing where she could go on this cool December day, she headed towards the barn. At one point during their occupation, the barn had housed soldiers, but now, again it held their livestock and some Army horses. It would be quiet and warm there.

Once in the barn, she sat on a bale of hay and tried to process what she had just discovered. Aaron was a married man. She had kissed another woman's husband. She had given her heart to him and he had crushed it. Had he laughed at her? Was it a game to him or did he really have feelings for her and simply withheld information to protect the both

466

of them. Now, as she thought through all of the interactions she had with him, she couldn't recall a time when he had spoken to her about a future together. They had once spoken a little of their pasts, but mostly of the present: the war, their circumstances, their feelings, but nothing of the future. No hopes and plans like she knew Joshua and Elizabeth always talked of. She had thought he feared the future because of the war and what might happen. But now she knew the reason. He hadn't spoken of the future because he knew he could never have one with her.

Monday, December 28, 1863
Moss Neck Manor

"I tried to have a happy Christmas, but it was nearly impossible," Kate admitted to AJ, Belle, and Elizabeth. "With all of the strife over my wedding plans and our sorrow with this being our first Christmas without Janie, Parke, and Gardiner, without my dear brother Richard." A tear slipped down her face. "As much as we tried to make it enjoyable and special for little Kate, it was just too difficult not to mourn what could have been." She shook her head. "I really don't want to discuss my holiday. How was everyone else's? We never did get together."

"Liberty and I had a very quiet Christmas," AJ said. "We kept praying for a miracle that Father or Nathaniel or the both of them would make their way home to celebrate, but it wasn't to be."

"Have you heard from either one of them?" Belle asked. She wanted to be more specific, learn more about Nathaniel because he always interested her, but her heart wasn't really into the conversation. She was missing Aaron Knightly. She wanted him to return for a multitude of reasons, the most pressing reason being so that she could confront him and get some well-needed answers. On the other hand, however, a part of her didn't want to face him.

"Belle, did you even hear me?" AJ asked, breaking into Belle's thoughts.

"I am so sorry," Belle replied. "That was quite rude of me, asking a question and not even listening to the answer."

"I said that we've heard from Father, but nothing from Nathaniel in well over six months." She sighed. "That could mean nothing, though, he was never much of a writer, and I know as a courier, he is often sent to remote areas. However," AJ studied Belle. "What is wrong, Belle? You seem very distracted today."

"She's been distracted ever since Christmas Eve," Elizabeth commented. "But she won't say why."

"It's nothing." Belle insisted. "I just have a lot on my mind."

"You must be missing Dr. Knightly," AJ asked. "When is he supposed to return?"

467

"Not soon enough," Belle replied, though her friends likely couldn't guess the real reason why.

A knock on the parlor door halted the conversation. They looked up to see none other than Sandie Pendleton open the door and smile. "Good afternoon, ladies." AJ, Belle, and Elizabeth greeted him, but Kate just stood and looked at him. She was still quite vexed about his last letter, where he had told her to "wait in peace and quietness" until he was able to make it to her as if she had nothing better to do than sitting around and put everything on hold just for him. Yet here he was, looking as handsome and excited as ever. She shook her head at him, then spoke as if her friends weren't still in the room.

"I could freely strangle you right now, Mr. Pendleton." She spoke calmly, trying to slow her heart down, for she was trying hard to be angry, yet she was thrilled to see him. "You stay away all this time and then come in here, expecting me to drop everything?"

AJ watched the two and didn't know if Sandie was incredibly brave or incredibly foolish when he cautiously walked toward his intended.

"Catherine, mine, I am here. I know you are angry with me, and you have a good reason. However, I am here and have been granted a furlough finally. I surely hope and pray that in two days, you can find it in your heart to become my wife. I didn't write this time because I didn't want to disappoint you again if my leave wasn't granted." He reached out and touched her arm. "Please, Kate?"

She shook her head, a mixture of conflicting feelings within her and tears forming in her eyes. He reached and brushed one that had fallen down her cheek. "I want to say yes, Sandie. I want to say yes and jump into your arms, but we have made so many plans and had so many disappointments. I am just terrified that something will happen and we will not get married, again."

Sandie gently kissed her forehead as AJ, Belle, and Elizabeth exited the room.

"I am not going anywhere this time, not until you are my wife." His voice was soft. She nodded, her face breaking into a smile. He smiled back and kissed her again. She gently pushed him away and looked to where her friends had been sitting. She smiled at the knowledge that they had quietly slipped away.

"I suppose I should go and spread the word of our wedding." She said.

"Yes, you should," Sandie replied. "But there is something I must do first." He bent down and kissed her again. "I have missed you more than you will ever know, and I promise I will make up for all the disappointment that I have caused you. I love you."

Tuesday, December 29, 1863
Moss Neck Manor

"I can't believe the day is finally here!" Kate said with a huge smile on her face. "I feel we finally have every chance to finish all this fuss and worry of postponements."

"You have certainly had enough disappointment during these past three months," Belle said. She had entered Kate's room to see the bride but had been put to work helping style Kate's hair.

"You are correct," Kate replied. "I can't help but think this is surreal. My wedding is finally going to happen today."

"It will be perfect," Belle replied. "Were most of your desired guests able to come?"

"For the most part, yes," Kate said. "With the exception of Sallie Munford, of course, but I should be able to see her when we pass through Richmond."

"Very good," Belle said. "I am glad you were able to invite me, AJ, and Elizabeth."

"As am I." Kate agreed. "I wish you could be in the wedding party, but it just wasn't meant to be."

"We all understand," Belle said. "I may act put out about it but I really do understand. Indiana and Rose will do well for you."

"Yes, and Hunter and JP will be very distinguished groomsmen," Kate said. "It is all finally coming together." She stood and smiled.

"You make a beautiful bride, Kate. I am so happy for you." Belle meant what she said, even though her own love life felt like it was in shambles.

"I do hope we can see each other often. As it looks right now, I will return home after our honeymoon, but with Richard's death, Father is still bent on selling Moss Neck."

"Don't be worrying about that, Kate," Belle said. "You shouldn't be worrying about anything today. Just this once, you needn't fear the past or what's to come. Revel in this day. Take in every moment so you can forever keep them in your memories."

"Very wise words, Belle. You should listen to her, Kate." Bertie entered the room. "Belle, you should go down. Sandie's father, General Pendleton is ready to start the ceremony."

"That was an inspiring ceremony, was it not?" JP Smith smiled as he came to stand next to AJ. He handed her a cup of apple cider. "This should be wine or champagne, but that Yankee blockade is becoming more than an irritation."

"This war is causing us all to make sacrifices we never expected." AJ agreed.

469

"I must say the war didn't stop Miss Corbin from being a radiantly beautiful bride," JP said.

"Or Sandie from being the very happiest of grooms," AJ added, "and, I might add, quite handsome."

"You would be a better judge of that than I." Captain Smith replied, then paused before changing the subject. "You and I...we didn't end up corresponding as much as I would have liked."

"I apologize. I fear as though it was mostly my fault." She admitted, looking down at her cup.

"I understand you have been quite busy with your escapades." He replied. "I have spoken with Captain Evans a time or two since we moved on from Fredericksburg. He told me the two of you have become quite friendly."

AJ blushed. "We have known each other since we were children. He has been very helpful to me in certain situations. Nothing more."

Captain Smith smiled, discouragement apparent on his face. "For what my opinion is worth, the two of you would make a fine couple." He took the now empty cup that AJ held in her hands, brushing her fingers as he did so. AJ noted that her heartbeat stayed the same, unlike her reactions to Richard when he was near. Captain Smith continued. "Evans speaks highly of you. He can't hide his admiration for you. I would have to agree with him, however, you are a fascinating woman. If I may be so bold to say, any man would be lucky to have your heart."

"Thank you for saying so, Captain. You are too kind." AJ said. "I truly do not believe Captain Evans thinks as you do."

"Just give him time, Miss Prentiss. Just give him time to realize what his true feelings are."

"You speak as if you know Captain Evans's thoughts well." AJ shook her head.

"I hope you do not think I am overstepping any boundaries, but I do believe I know him well enough." He said.

"No, you are not," AJ said. "Whatever else we may have been, I have always enjoyed your friendship, and friends speak their minds to one another."

"Well, then, I suppose we are the best of friends." Captain Smith replied.

Thursday. December 31, 1863
Turner's Glenn

"Kate and Sandie left on their honeymoon this morning," Elizabeth said to Belle. She and the children were at Turner's Glenn for a visit. "I ran into Bertie as we were leaving the house. She said the newlyweds were staying with their original plans and are off to Richmond, then on to Lexington."

"I am sure she will enjoy her time with Sandie greatly," Belle said, focusing on the socks she was darning while sitting in the parlor.

"I am sure of that as well, Belle." Elizabeth agreed. "Have you welcomed Dr. Knightly back yet? I saw him in the parlor as I came up the stairs."

"He's here?" Belle looked up. "I didn't know that."

"He is preparing for a surgical procedure. One of the wounded men fell trying to do too much. It sounds as though he reopened his wound."

"That should be an easy repair for the doctor," Belle said, trying to hide the despair she felt.

"It should be," Elizabeth said. She stood. "Are you staying here? I am going to find Mama."

"All right," Belle said. "I will likely stay here for a bit longer." *Waiting and wondering what I am going to do when I finally see Dr. Knightly.* Every time she thought of the photograph, her blood boiled in anger. She tried to rationalize it, to think of other possible scenarios, but it always came back to the fact that he had deceived her. There was no other explanation.

"Belle."

She looked up to see the man she was thinking of. He was standing in the doorway. He had one of his rare smiles on his face. Seeing it only made her angrier still. Belle slowly put the socks down and stood.

"Belle, I apologize for not coming to see you right away. The moment I arrived, I was pulled into surgery." He stood next to her and took her hands in his. "I did stop in my room to put my bag away. Thank you for the shirts. It was a thoughtful gift. I have something for you as well."

"I trust you had a good time with your family," Belle said coldly. Oh, why did he have to be married? Even knowing what she did, she still wanted a future with him.

"Yes. Everyone is as happy and healthy as can be." He nodded. "I had feared my nephew, who is only fifteen would have run away to join the army, but he is still home safe with his mother." He smiled. "Thankfully."

"I see." Belle thought back to the photograph. "Is he your only nephew?" Perhaps the boy in the picture was another nephew.

"No, only Joel," Aaron answered, looking concerned at Belle's stony demeanor.

"I see." She replied. "What about your son. What is his name?" She hadn't meant to be so blunt, but the words had just escaped her without a thought. Aaron's face immediately became confused.

"My son? Belle, to what are you referring? I don't have…"

"I saw the photograph in your room. To My Darling husband, with all our love, Ada, and Joel. Belle tried to hold her emotions, but she could feel tears threatening.

"Belle, you don't understand."

"No, doctor, I understand perfectly well. You have been deceiving me this whole time." Her voice cracked with emotion.

"Belle, that photograph…you must let me explain."

"No. Let me explain. I gave you my heart and you made a fool of me. There is nothing more I need to know." She pulled her hands from his and turned to leave.

"No." Aaron took her arm and pulled her back. "You can leave me, but first, you will hear me out."

Belle was distraught and felt trapped. She had to get away from him. She didn't want to hear his lies. She wasn't strong when she was near him. She may fall for his stories and excuses. It was just too dangerous for her. "I don't want to hear your lies." She whispered.

"I swear to you I will tell you only the truth." He paused. "Listen to me. The woman in the picture is my brother's wife. The boy is Joel, my nephew. It was taken almost ten years ago when my brother was fighting Indians out west. Remember, I told you he was a US soldier. He was gone for most of Joel's life. When it comes to the boy, I was around more than his father and Joel sometimes thinks of me as his father. I know I've never discussed this with you, but the reason I joined the Confederate army as a doctor is because my brother was killed at First Manassas. I know what it's like to lose a brother. I had to join, I want and need to save lives as I wasn't able to save my own brother."

Belle calmed down and was simply listening to him. She wanted to believe him, but how could she know that he was being honest with her?

"If you don't believe me about Ada and Joel, I will give you their address in Greensboro, North Carolina. You can write to them, you can even visit them if that would help to convince you."

"But why do you have the photograph?" Belle asked.

"Ada gave it to me as a way to remember my brother and his family. I have no photos of him. I need to remember why I joined the army and what I am working for. Believe me when I say I need to look at it often to remind me why I am here patching up men just to send them back to the battlefield to be injured again. This war is a waste of lives." Aaron squeezed her hands. "If you want to stop courting me, then I will acquiesce. I will respect your wishes, but please, please think about what I have told you. I do care for you more than I can say."

Belle took a deep breath. What he said made sense and fit with what she had learned and observed in him. Did she have the courage to take a leap of faith in her relationship with him?

"Oh, fiddlesticks." She let out her breath. "I suppose you should give me that address."

"So you want to confirm what I just told you?" His dejection was apparent.

"Not exactly," Belle said. "I do want to get to know more about you and your family. If we are to have any kind of future…" She paused, looking at him with hopefulness in her eyes. "If we are to have a future, then I should start corresponding with the important people in your life."

He smiled with relief. "It is difficult to talk about the future in the midst of a war, but I do want you in my future whatever it may be, Belle. Believe it or not, I felt that way from the moment I met you. Despite your cool demeanor, I felt an instant bond between us." He leaned over to kiss her cheeks. "I will go and write down that address for you."

Part 4:
1864

Sunday, January 24, 1864
The Bennett Home

"Elizabeth, you failed to mention the many glories of marriage," Kate said with a smile, taking a sip of her sassafras tea.

"Well, to be fair, you never really asked," Elizabeth replied smiling back. "So I gather all of your premarital misgivings have been resolved."

"You would be correct. I have just had three of the happiest weeks of my life. In fact..." She turned to AJ and Belle. "I am so delighted with my change of estate that I would urge the two of you to do likewise. Get married." She smiled at Elizabeth as if the two of them shared a secret. "The evils are not as bad as you might suppose."

Elizabeth blushed a bit, thinking of how she had felt the first few weeks of her marriage.

"I am happy to hear you and Sandie are having a good start to your married life," AJ said.

"I miss him dearly already," Kate said. "We harmonize so perfectly in all our tastes and aspirations. Sandie is a wonderful husband. He was so thoughtful of my slightest wishes, so good and true. Even with the distance between us, my soul is so bound up in him."

"I am so glad for you, Kate. You and Sandie deserve all the happiness in the world." Belle said.

"You all do as well," Kate replied. "AJ, I was so preoccupied with my husband on my wedding day that I didn't talk to you much, but I did notice you and Captain Smith were cozying up."

"We were not cozying up Kate, we were merely talking." AJ didn't want to go into more details because she still wasn't ready to talk with her friends about her relationship with Richard.

"Mmmhmm," Kate said, then turned to Belle. "How is your courtship with the doctor?"

"It is going well, though we haven't formally called it a 'courtship' yet," Belle said. "We had a brief misunderstanding recently, but we are getting on quite well now." She had written a letter to Ada Knightly and received a letter back already. Belle suspected she had already found a new friend in the widow. "Tell us more about your wedding trip. Did the Pendleton family monopolize your time?"

"It was not bad. They allowed us quite a bit of time to spend alone, just the two of us. Many people were also understanding of the fact that I was still in mourning for my brother Richard."

"That was good of them," Elizabeth said.

"All of the family's friends were extremely cordial. We were invited to many teas. We stayed in Richmond for almost a fortnight. We were quite busy there, especially with social functions honoring the celebrated Kentuckian, General John Morgan. We were able to spend a lengthy amount of time with Sandie's sister Sue and her husband Ned Lee as well. One of the banquets we attended was even attended by President Davis and other high Confederate officials. That was quite the experience."

"My goodness," AJ said. "How exciting."

"It was a wonderful trip, just like old times, but now Sandie is back with Ewell's staff at Morton Hall over on the Rapidan River. I do hope I am able to hear from him often, and perhaps even see him on occasion as well. He is not too far away."

"No, he is not," Elizabeth said. "I am glad you are back home, though, and not staying with his family."

"For now at least," Kate said. "There is still a chance I may move once Moss Neck is sold. I can't believe Father wants it sold."

"That means we need to make sure we spend more time together," Belle said.

"Oh yes, of course," Kate replied. "I completely agree."

Tuesday, February 9, 1864
Prentiss Farm

"Kate Pendleton! Whatever are you doing on my side of the river?" AJ asked as she opened the door.

"I needed to get away from Moss Neck for a little while. Bertie is wonderful, as always, but I just..." she shrugged, not knowing what to say next.

"Never you mind, you know you are always welcome here," AJ told her. "Come on in and have a seat, can I get you any refreshments?"

"No, but thank you." Kate smiled sadly.

"Oh, dear, you are morose. Tell me, do you hear from Sandie as often as you expected?"

"I hear from him at least once a week, but what I desire most of all is to have him by my side for the rest of our days. He writes me the most wonderful love letters, AJ. He writes poetry that could rival one of Shakespeare's books of sonnets. I miss him so."

"Does he still enjoy being a soldier?"

"Unfortunately yes, he does." Kate made a face showing her displeasure. "He told me it felt very natural for him to be back with his regiment."

"At least there isn't any fighting at the present time," AJ said, then added. "Although it is bound to start up again soon."

"It already has. I received a letter today and there was a small skirmish on the banks of the Rapidan River. It doesn't sound like it was bad and we didn't lose any men. The Yanks had some casualties, including the 42 prisoners we captured. He says the troops are in fine spirits and he doesn't think the Yankees will bother them again for a while."

"That's all well and good, but I feel the sooner we get to fighting, the sooner we can whip those Yankees and return to our normal way of life." She smiled. "With you and your husband reunited for good."

"Oh, that would be divine," Kate replied. "Do you really think life will ever truly get back to the way it was before the war? So much has changed. The destruction of the land, lives lost, all of our slaves gone to who knows where.

"What you say is true. It won't ever be exactly the same, but remember, once the war ends, we will be our own country. That will bring all sorts of changes in and of itself. We will have much to adjust to in the first few years. It will be difficult to get the fields back into production with no slave labor and fewer men around, but we will be a strong nation that can overcome any and all obstacles."

"You are always so positive, AJ. You're right. This is a new year. We should see it as a new beginning." Kate smiled. "I have only good feelings about the rest of 1864."

AJ nodded. "Well, then, here is to 1864 and all it will bring us."

Monday, February 22, 1864
Moss Neck Manor

"Bertie, I am riding over to Turner's Glenn!" Kate called as she opened the front door. Standing there, fist raised as if he had been about to knock, was her husband.

"Sandie!" She threw her arms around him. "Sandie, you're here!"

"Kate. I have missed you so." He buried his face in her hair.

"And I you." He looked at her. "Where were you off to?"

"I was going to visit the Turners, but that was before I knew you were going to make my day with this very pleasant surprise. I can send a messenger over to explain my absence."

"No, you don't have to do that. We can go over together. I would enjoy seeing your friends again. We can take a leisurely ride over there, visit and then come back here and see your family."

"That sounds wonderful." Kate kissed him. "How long are you able to stay with me this visit?"

"Unfortunately, I must leave tomorrow morning." He replied. "But we will make the most of the time we do have together."

"That sounds perfect to me."

Tuesday, February 23, 1864
Moss Neck Manor

"I wish you could stay longer," Kate said the next morning. She stood with him on the porch. "It is so hard to say goodbye to you." She touched his cheek.

"For me as well, but I feel confident in the plans for our spring campaign. I believe we are at the beginning of the end."

"With us as the victors, I hope?"

"Yes, of course, with us as the victors." He bent to kiss her. "I really need to head out."

"Wait here just a moment, I had the kitchen servants make a snack for you." Kate hastened down to the kitchen to retrieve the small sack of food.

"Here is some turkey and biscuits for you," Kate said when she was at his side again.

"My goodness, this is enough food to feed all of Ewell's army." He smiled. "I will not be able to eat all of this myself." He took some of the meat out of the package and handed it to her.

"Here, take it for yourself."

"Sandie, you must take it. I worry about you not getting enough to eat when you're at camp."

"I will be fine, truly."

"All right, then. I will put this away but wait here for me to come back. I will ride with you for a while." She turned to bring the meat back, and by the time she returned outside, Sandie had packed his snack in his saddlebags and was just tightening the straps of her saddle. He lifted her up, then mounted his own horse.

"I cannot wait to build a pleasant and comfortable home for you. Do you still intend to live with my sister Susan as we discussed?" Sandie asked as they rode in the direction of his camp.

"I believe so. I will miss Moss Neck terribly, and all of my friends here in Fredericksburg, but I don't want to be a burden to my father. I fear I will be underfoot."

"That would never be the case, but I can't help but wonder where you would be safer. The Yankees are determined to capture Richmond, but the capital will also be better defended by our troops."

"I admit, I hadn't thought of safety," Kate said. "I have always enjoyed Richmond and I am very fond of Sue, and you are right, it is well defended. I just fear I will be further away from you."

"It will be in your best interest, I believe," Sandie said.

All too soon, Sandie and Kate reached the fork in the road where Kate had planned on turning back to Moss Neck.

"I wish I could ride with you all the way to camp and stay there," Kate said. "Other women stay with their husbands in camp. Why can I not do the same?"

"I don't have a high enough rank to take care of you safely in camp. Generals can do so, but other soldier's wives stay in small, dirty tents and with the diseases and possibility of attacks, it can be dangerous. I wouldn't want you to have to experience what I have observed. You are too much of a lady. Not to mention I still wouldn't see you as often as I would like." He brought his horse close to hers and leaned over to kiss Kate. With the horses moving beneath them, it made the kiss almost impossible. He chuckled and dismounted, then helped her down as well.

"I need to be able to say goodbye to you properly." He said, pulling her close and bending to kiss her.

"Saying goodbye is never easy," Kate said. "I must confess, though, that goodbye was much improved." She pulled his head down to kiss him once more. "Please take good care of yourself, Sandie."

He brushed her cheek with his hand, kissed her one last time, and then helped her remount. Sandie mounted and gave her a smile, as they rode off in opposite directions.

Sunday, March 20, 1864
Bennett Home

"What a wonderful meal, Elizabeth, especially with the limitations we have with our supplies," Kate said.

"It has been a challenge," Elizabeth replied.

"At least we're not as bad off as those poor women in Richmond last year," Belle said, referring to the Southern bread riots of 1863, where both men and women invaded and looted various shops and stores in cities throughout the South. In Richmond, women had seized food, clothing, shoes and even jewelry. Eventually, the Virginia Militia was called in to restore order. The rioters claimed they lacked money and provisions for their families. The cause had been blamed on inflation, refugees and a lack of food supplies, which was rampant throughout the South.

"I can't imagine it has improved much." Belle focused her gaze on Kate as if her words could persuade her to stay in Fredericksburg indefinitely. "Richmond is not necessarily the best place to be living."

"That was a year ago, Belle. The situation has calmed down since then." Kate replied. "It's not as though I want to leave, Sandie and I feel that is where I need to be."

479

"When do you leave?" Elizabeth asked.

"The middle of April," Kate replied. "I'm hoping it will be easier for Sandie to visit me there. I still hear from him often in his letters. He recently told me that he is more zealous to do his duty for the Confederacy since we've been married. He says that he has more at stake now that he is, as he put it, the guardian of the honor of my name as well as his."

"You married a very principled and virtuous man," AJ said.

"I know." Kate smiled. "You will too, AJ. I have confidence in that fact."

"I hope so," AJ said. "Belle, how is it with you and Dr. Knightly?"

"Nothing much has changed between us. He is very busy now that there are only two doctors left at our home." Belle said. "The boys are being sent home gradually and we are getting more rooms back for our own use. It's been more peaceful for us, but not Aaron."

"If only this could be a year of peace," Elizabeth said.

"I heard Confederate General Young's brigade has left Fredericksburg. Is this true?" AJ asked. "Perhaps that is a sign of good things to come."

"I don't know that any troop movement is a good thing, AJ," Elizabeth said. "To me, troop movement means fighting and fighting means more death and destruction."

"Yes, but we can't win our independence by not fighting and winning the battles." Belle pointed out. "We must take care of those Yankees on the battlefields."

"Oh please, let's not talk about the war anymore," Kate said. "Let's talk about happier times."

"I can't think of any happier times," Belle said. "You are leaving." She gestured to Kate. "The war drags on. The Confederate states are destitute. What is there happy to talk about?"

Kate looked around, a little depressed that her friends were so upset about her leaving. "I am sad about leaving as well." She finally said. "Belle, you know I don't want to leave my friends and family or the place I have called my home for years, on the other hand, I am very happy too. The thought of going to a home, even though it may be temporary, which has been provided for me by my husband is a special feeling."

"I understand that," Elizabeth said. "Once you're married, you want to be out from under your childhood home and be able to manage your own in the way that suits you."

"That's exactly how I feel," Kate said.

AJ inwardly sighed. She wished she could understand. As far as AJ was concerned, she had been running a home for as long as she could remember. Perhaps one day it would be different when she was married. She smiled briefly at the thought of living in a home that she and Richard built together. She quickly shook the thought from her mind. Richard had made no promises for the future. She knew she must continue to guard her heart.

Wednesday, April 13, 1864
Moss Neck Manor

"I cannot believe you are leaving us tomorrow already," Belle said over a cup of weak tea.

"It did come up rather quickly," AJ added, biting into a sugar biscuit.

"Yes, but Sandie wants me settled with his sister and brother-in-law the sooner the better. He fears the area around Moss Neck will be overrun by the enemy in the next campaign and he anticipates it starting quite soon."

"Well, that is not a comforting thought," Belle said. "We just started getting back to a normal existence." She paused and thought a moment. "Well, at least as normal a life as can be expected, and now you say we may be in danger of yet another battle."

"I suppose this too shall pass." Elizabeth mused. She looked out the window at Benjamin and Hannah, who were playing with young Kate Dickenson. They were all growing up so quickly. She couldn't wait for Joshua to come home and see his children.

"Does Sandie write of any of the men from his old Stonewall brigade staff?" AJ asked.

"He speaks of them once in a while," Kate replied. "Henry Kyd Douglas recently returned to his regiment. He had been taken prisoner but was returned during a prisoner exchange."

"As happy as I am for Captain Douglas, I find the idea of prisoner exchanges to be counter-intuitive," AJ said. "It will only prolong the war."

"Yes, but it is more beneficial to us than to the Yankees," Elizabeth stated. "We need our men back more than they do. If we can get our best soldiers back on the field, the war won't be prolonged. Captain. Douglas could actually be worth five Yankee soldiers, maybe more. Furthermore, can you imagine how relieved his poor wife must be? The prisons up north are horrible. Joshua says the men who return say they would rather die on the battlefield than be taken prisoner again."

"Oh my, that does tell us something about the prisons," AJ said. "I still don't agree with the practice. If you're killed, that is it. I mean, you have eternal life of course, but..." She took a deep breath, thinking of Richard. "Some people aren't ready for eternal life yet." She finished her thought quietly.

481

"I agree with that, AJ," Elizabeth said. "So we must pray for all our soldiers, however, Kate is leaving tomorrow. This conversation must end. Let us speak of happier topics." She turned toward Kate. "Do you have any plans once you're in Richmond?"

"I will do some visiting, of course, and I want to purchase some flowers for the yard. It will give me a good reason to get out of doors. Sandie appreciates flowers a great deal. After the war, I believe we will build a home where we can see the green grass and fields or forests. A place where we can listen to the birds sing and enjoy sunrises and sunsets. Sandie and I both agree that we don't want to live in a bustling, noisy city. The country will suit us better and hopefully our future children."

"Ah. I was going to ask if the both of you wanted children." Belle said.

"I do. We both do. In fact..." Kate smiled. "I am not entirely sure yet, it is still quite early, but I believe I may already be in a family way."

"Kate! Congratulations!" Belle quickly stood to hug her friend. AJ and Elizabeth were right behind her.

"I am so happy for you," AJ said.

"I must stress the fact that I am not positive. I have had small signs and will see a doctor when I get to Richmond, but when I mentioned my symptoms to Bertie and Nettie and my suspicions, they both agreed with me. We came to the conclusion that if I am pregnant, the baby will be here by early November."

"My goodness. You must be very early." Belle said.

"Yes. In fact, I debated about telling you all. If I wasn't leaving tomorrow, I probably would have waited, but I would rather tell you in person. Isn't it splendid news to leave you all with?"

"I must say, I am glad you told us in person and I am so happy for you," AJ said. "I suppose this means we will have a very good reason to come and visit you this fall."

"You never need a reason to visit me. You know you are always welcome." Kate said. "I will definitely enjoy a visit from all of you very much, before and after my child's birth."

Thursday, May 5, 1864
Prentiss Farm

AJ answered the knock on the door to find Richard Evans on the other side.

"Mr. Evans! Good heavens, what are you doing here? It's dangerous." She asked, quickly pulling him into the house.

"I was ordered to come and speak with you about a mission. This would be a different mission than what you have been involved with in the past. You should also know that if you accept this mission, I will be escorting you." Richard was very serious, not a hint of humor or even warmth to his demeanor.

"I would need an escort? This sounds like quite the undertaking."

"It is. It also may be a bit dangerous." Richard sat at the kitchen table. "America, please don't feel as though you have to do this." Richard's voice now sounded as though he was pleading with her not to take it.

"I realize that. How necessary is the mission?"

He sighed. "Unfortunately, it could be quite valuable to the cause. We're expecting a major battle in the next few days. In the Wilderness west of Chancellorsville."

"I see. Another one so close." She replied. "What am I being asked to do?"

"Helping as a cover for me. We will be going close to enemy lines, Miss Prentiss. Enemy territory. We need information on troop movement and how many. We also are desperately short of medical supplies." He quickly described the details to her. "The plan is to pose as siblings, looking for our wounded brother. I will be less conspicuous if you are with me. While we travel, we will strategically maneuver around and see what we can in regards to their troops. Our main goal is to get into a particular hospital up near Rappahannock Station where I can meet a contact and you can get supplies and medicine."

She took a deep breath, not sure what to say.

"I will be with you the whole time." He said.

"When do I need to give you my answer? Rappahannock Station is quite a distance." AJ asked. She was excited about the prospect of the mission but she would need to make plans in case she was gone overnight.

"I need to know by the time I leave." He checked his pocket watch. "Which I need to do within the next fifteen minutes." He reached over and covered her hands with his. "I tell you again, you do not have to do this. If you decide yes, then I will protect you as best as possible. I can promise you that."

"Would I put you in any danger?" AJ asked quietly.

"I won't let any harm come to either of us." Richard smiled confidently. She bit her lip.

"I will have to send Liberty to Turner's Glenn. I don't want her out here alone if I am gone overnight. She's doing some work in the fields right now. When would we need to leave?"

"I would return to escort you tomorrow, before sunrise. I will be dressed as a civilian..."

"A civilian! Richard, if you're caught, you would be hanged as a spy!"

"Don't worry about that. I won't get caught. I will be more focused on you anyways because if you get caught, you could be hanged as a spy as well."

While AJ wanted to do all she could to help the Confederacy, she wasn't sure having Richard being focused on her was such a good idea.

"I also promise to be a perfect gentleman," Richard said as if he were reading her mind. "I know you don't really trust me yet. I told you I cared for you and that is still true, perhaps even more so, but I do promise to be a gentleman."

"I know you will, Richard. My trust in you isn't the issue." I'm just not sure if I trust myself with you.

"So what is your answer?" He asked. "I need to be heading back to report your decision to my superiors."

"I'll do it." She replied. "I promised myself that I would do whatever I could to help the Confederacy. If this is what needs to be done, then I must do it."

"All right, then." He stood, pulled her up with him and walked her to the door. "Let's work together to defeat the Yankees."

Turner's Glenn

"Aunt Meri!" Benjamin jumped from the Bennett's wagon and threw his arms around Meri. "I am so happy to see you."

"Hello, Benjamin, we have missed you here." She hugged him back, then turned and took Hannah from the wagon and gave her a hug as well.

"Meri, how is it going here? Any news?" Elizabeth gave her sister a hug.

"Dr. Knightly is busy reorganizing the house," Meri said as the two made their way inside. "They say that a big battle is about to happen around here again, and soon."

"Oh dear. That is not the news I wanted to hear. There were rumors in town also. Are they preparing the house to be a full hospital again?" Elizabeth asked, disheartened. Meri nodded.

"Dr. Knightly and Mother have been quite busy, which means they don't have much available time," Meri added.

"Hm. So I gather Belle is not in the best of moods."

"No, ma'am," Meri replied. "You are exactly right about that."

"I'll find her and talk to her," Elizabeth said. "Any guesses on where I should start?"

"I would say the flower garden or the vegetable garden," Meri answered.

484

"All right. Thank you. You wouldn't mind watching the children, would you?" Elizabeth asked. Meri shook her head, so Elizabeth walked to the back of the house. It didn't take long to find Belle. She was on her knees in the vegetable garden, pulling weeds. Elizabeth smiled to herself. Whoever would have thought that Belle Turner would find herself willingly digging around in the dirt? Her hair in a simple braid and a dress that was so old that Elizabeth didn't even recognize it.

"Good afternoon, Belle." Elizabeth greeted her sister. Belle looked up and gave Elizabeth a tired smile.

"Good afternoon." She replied. "What brings you out here?"

"Hannah and Benjamin wanted to come for a visit. I had no idea you would all be so busy." She knelt down to help pull the weeds.

"Yes, well, they say the war is coming back to wreak havoc on the Fredericksburg area again. It will be west of town most likely, but since we are still a functioning hospital, we'll be getting a lot of the wounded. Dr. Knightly mentioned that the Yankees have a new General here in Virginia. He used to be out West."

"General Grant," Elizabeth confirmed. She had heard the man's name often in town over the past few days. "I heard he doesn't care how many men die as long as he gets his victory. They refer to him as 'Butcher Grant.'"

Belle paused in her work to look at Elizabeth. "Have you heard at all how...why...how will this new general affect us? The Confederacy?"

"I don't know, Belle. AJ is usually the one who has all the current information about the war. I don't believe it will be good, though. I just...I don't think the next year will be good for the South. You can call it intuition, but it is how I feel."

Belle sighed. "I was afraid you would say that. Dr. Knightly made it sound the same way."

"Why are you calling him Dr. Knightly all of a sudden?" Elizabeth asked, trying not to sound exasperated. She hoped that Belle was not going to be overly dramatic.

"Well, I hardly see the man anymore. It is very difficult to court someone when you never see them."

"I knew the two of you were getting more serious. I must tell you that I like the two of you as a couple. He is good for you, Belle. I may have mentioned that fact before. I know you were betrothed to Samuel and you loved him, but I believe...well...I feel Aaron is a bigger part of God's plan for you than Samuel was. Samuel catered to you while Aaron challenges you, and it makes you a better person."

Belle frowned. "How can I know if he truly is the one for me if he is always busy?" She sighed.

485

"There's no rush, Belle. It's not as if you have to decide whether or not to marry him within the next few days. Do you want to know what else I think?"

Belle smiled. It felt good to have a conversation like this with her sister. It reminded her of how close they had been when they were younger. "I actually would like to know your thoughts, Elizabeth."

"I believe you have already decided about Aaron, however, like Kate, you are doubting yourself. It is good that you want to be sure, but you also have to be willing to take a leap of faith. You may think that I never had reservations about marrying Joshua, but I did. It is a big decision. What is your biggest fear with courting Aaron?"

Belle thought for a moment. "I don't know if I can learn to be a doctor's wife. I would have to learn to be less involved in society and probably more involved with chores and cooking. I would have less money to spend and a husband who is so busy that I would never have enough time to spend with him. You know how dedicated he is to his patients. It would be a very big adjustment for me, but I would like to think I can try. My biggest fear, I suppose is that I won't be able to make that kind of change. What if I marry him and find I can't live that way and I end up resenting him? Or what if it turns out that I'm not the kind of wife he needs? What if I don't have the qualities that a doctor's wife needs to have? I mean..." She threw a hand up and gave a short laugh. "Look at me right now, out here sulking like a child because he can't spend time with me."

"You are not acting like a child. Just look at you, at least when you mope now, you are doing something constructive at the same time." Elizabeth gestured to the garden.

"Believe it or not, I actually find the work comforting," Belle said, pulling another weed.

"You never would have said that before the war. I dare say that before the war, there were a lot of things you didn't know you were capable of, and you never will know what you can do until you try. I have faith in you, Belle. I am impressed with the woman you are becoming, and I am blessed to call you my sister and friend." Elizabeth smiled. "I want you to think of this, perhaps it will help you decide. Is your life better with Aaron around and you not seeing him much, or is it better to not see or be with him at all."

"I want to see him," Belle said. "I want to see him however and whenever I can." She nodded. "I understand what you are saying. I suppose I am actually being selfish."

"What do you mean?" Elizabeth asked.

"Because if you could see Joshua for even an hour, you would be the happiest woman alive." Belle sat back and looked at her sister. "But here I am, complaining that I don't see my beau enough. I am so selfish."

"You are not selfish," Elizabeth said. "It's very difficult sometimes to look past our own pain and appreciate what we have. You're just being human."

"I suppose." Belle sighed. "Thank you for your kind words."

"Anytime." Elizabeth smiled.

Friday, May 6, 1864
Rappahannock Station

AJ hoped the Yankees couldn't hear her heartbeat or that they wouldn't notice how sweaty her palms were underneath her gloves. She was wearing a nice but nondescript dress and she was supposed to blend into the background as much as possible. When Richard felt the time was right, the two would temporarily split up. AJ would make her way to where the medications were stored. She not only had room in her bodice for the packets, but the bag she was carrying had a false bottom in it where she could quickly hide more medication. While she was stealing the medicine, Richard had his own intelligence to gather.

"Just relax," Richard whispered close to her ear, then straightened and addressed a passing Union orderly. "Excuse me, sir. My sister and I heard that our brother was wounded and that he was brought to this hospital. Would it be a problem, I mean, could you help us find him or point us in the direction of someone who can help us?" AJ was shocked at how easily Richard lost his Southern drawl. They had thought it best to pose as Yankees.

"I can bring you to the Head Nurse and she can check the records." The man said. "It may be just as effective for you to visit each ward and see if you can find him though."

Richard placed a hand on AJ's arm and squeezed. "Would it be possible to do both? I could accompany you and speak with the nurse and my sister could look around."

"Yes, I suppose that would be all right." The orderly sounded a bit impatient. "Come on."

Richard squeezed AJ's hand again, then bent to briefly kiss her cheek like a brother would. "I will find you when I am done talking with the Head Nurse, Joan." They had decided to use her middle name, as it was not as unique as America or even AJ.

"All right." She gave him a small, nervous smile, then went in search of the medicine stores. Luckily, her work at Chatham gave her some idea of where supplies were stored.

It didn't take AJ long to find what she needed. It amazed her how little the staff paid attention to her. Her plain dress and features must have made her invisible to them.

Just as AJ was latching up her bag, she heard the door open. She quickly ducked into a small crevice between the wall and one of the shelving units. She focused on her breathing, hoping that whoever was there wouldn't hear or see her.

Thankfully, the interrupter quickly took what they needed and left. She let out a deep breath, gathered her composure, and opened the door. She peeked out to make sure no one saw her exit the room. She then slowly walked into one of the wards and methodically went from soldier to soldier, as if she was really looking for a lost loved one.

"There you are!" A hand grabbed AJ's arm and her heart almost stopped. Richard spoke quietly, but urgently. "We have to leave, now."

Acting as calmly as she could, AJ followed Richard toward the entryway. Just as they opened the door, a voice called from behind them.

"There he is!"

Richard grabbed AJ's arm and propelled her out the door, pulling her as they raced down the streets. AJ's heart hammered. What had happened? What had Richard done?

When they were quite far from the hospital, Richard slowed down his pace. "I think we lost them." He panted. "Thank goodness. Let's get to our horses and move quickly."

AJ tugged at Richard's arm to get him to stop and look at her. "What happened back there, Richard?" He averted his eyes. "Richard, what did you do?"

"Let's get to safety first. Then, I promise I'll explain everything." He was quiet, almost as if he were embarrassed or ashamed. The horses were where they had left them, and they rode at a leisurely pace, watching for soldiers. Richard followed a path where there would likely be fewer soldiers on guard. It was a longer route, but a much safer one. The entire way, AJ imagined the worst had happened. Richard's mission must have been to kill someone. It was the only explanation she could think of that made any sense, but he could never do that. He may shoot someone in battle, yes, but to go into a hospital specifically to take someone's life? That was murder, even if it was a Yankee. Was Richard truly capable of that?

"You're quiet," Richard commented when they were quite far from the city. She saw an old, crumbling stone wall and directed her horse, Lafayette toward it. Richard followed her.

"I hate to sound like a shrew, Richard, but I have to know what happened back there. What did you do?"

Richard took a deep breath and watched as AJ slid off her horse and walked over to the stone wall. He dismounted and followed her, then sat on the wall.

"I may have just gotten a man killed, or at the very least, arrested." He looked down at his boots as he spoke.

"What do you mean? Please tell me, Richard." She sat down next to him. Her heart had slowed a bit and images of Richard killing someone in cold blood were erased from her mind.

"I was to meet a contact at the hospital. A man posing as an assistant to the Chief Surgeon. As we were exchanging our information, we were discovered by one of the doctors, a man who, from what I could gather, was looking for an excuse to get my contact in trouble. I would have stayed and helped him, but..."

"But you were worried about me?" AJ asked quietly.

"Partly. I am hoping he will be fine. He should be able to make up some lies. He's very good at what he does. Also, no one really pursued us." Richard sighed. "What I was really afraid of was being caught and disgraced. I have no fear of dying valiantly in battle, but the idea of having my honor impugned by being caught? I couldn't bear the thought." He sighed. "I am ashamed I feel this way. Just when I think I am free of my Father's influence and ideas, I find myself still yearning for his approval."

"Oh, Richard, I had no idea you felt this way." AJ reached out and touched his hand comfortingly.

"That's because you are the first person that I have told. Ever." He looked into her eyes. "I have never trusted anyone with these thoughts and feelings. I sometimes feel like a little boy, trying to do everything to please his father, just to get a little praise, but never getting any. I have tried so hard to be like him, but I find more and more that I am not and never will be."

Emotions welled up within her. To have Richard trust her with this level of intimacy was such a privilege. Perhaps they could have more of these conversations.

"Well, I am glad you feel able to confide in me, Richard. I do want you to know, even if your father never told you, he must be very proud of you. You are a fine gentleman, you're intelligent and courageous...How can he not be?"

"I just hate the feeling that I am not good enough for him," Richard admitted. "I wish it didn't bother me so much, but it does." He shook his head. "At least I know my mother is proud of me and loves me."

"I can attest to that." AJ smiled. "You are her whole world. I would be willing to bet that your father loves you too. Some people have more difficulty showing their emotions."

489

"Where have you been all my life, America?" He murmured. Before she could answer the question, he asked another, completely changing the subject. "What would your parents say if they knew what you were doing right now? The smuggling and spying?"

"My parents really believed in the Patriotic ideas that our ancestors held when they fought the Revolution. Even the names they gave their children reflect that. My sister's full name is Liberty Elizabeth after Betsy Ross and Nathaniel's full name is George Washington Nathaniel Greene."

"That's a mouthful." Richard smiled.

"It is. Then there is the name they saddled me with…"

"I think that America is a beautiful name, and it suits you well," Richard said.

"Thank you." AJ blushed, still not quite knowing how to handle the compliment from Richard Evans. "To answer your question, I believe my mother would have supported the Confederate cause, for a less powerful federal government. I know that's why Father signed on to fight. As for what I am doing now, I don't think they would want me taking any risks, but they have always encouraged their children to think for themselves."

"I have actually spent some time with your father back at camp. He is a good man. It's no wonder he has children he can be proud of." He brushed a strand of wayward hair from her face. "I know now where you get your bravery from."

"From my mother as well. She was a courageous woman in many ways. Did you know that she went against convention when she married my father? He was just a poor farmer. She could have married better. Her family really never forgave her for choosing him."

"Horace and Betty Lacy are her relations, are they not? They seemed to have accepted you."

"Yes. Mrs. Lacy and my mother were cousins and when Mother died, Cousin Betty took an interest in my sister and me. She tried being a female influence on us, but I'm not sure it helped. I don't act much like a lady and Liberty is far worse. She detests doing anything that might be considered ladylike, but she does try on occasion. I'm afraid Liberty doesn't remember much about our mother."

"You must remember her, though." Richard took her hand in his. Her heart beat quickly at his touch.

"I remember a lot about my mother. Even when she knew she was going to die, she was more concerned for her family than herself. I have wanted to be brave like her ever since. I want to live in a way that would make her proud."

"America," Richard spoke softly, glancing at her. She met his eyes. "You are one of the bravest women I have ever met. I can't believe you don't see that. The way that you put your life on the line for the Southern cause. The way you care about your sister and the farm. I really admire you for your faith, your courage, your positive outlook on life. You are an amazing woman.

"And here I thought you only admired the physical aspects of a woman." AJ wasn't quite sure of the direction of the conversation. Richard was a charmer, a man who was well-known for his ability with words and she must continue to be vigilant of her feelings.

"Yes, well, I haven't been the greatest judge of character." He admitted. "Between the friends I associated with and the women that I kept company with...well, I could have made better choices." He hesitated and glanced at her hand, still in his. "America, I truly am sorry for any pain I may have caused you. There are no excuses for my behavior. I have behaved abhorrently in the past. If I had the chance to do it all over, I would." She looked at their hands.

"Thank you for saying that." She looked out toward the woods. "I suppose we should be going. We have a lot of ground to cover."

He grudgingly helped her back into the saddle and they continued on their way.

"We should stop for a rest," Richard said. "The horses need a break and some water."

"I don't know. Will we still make it home by nightfall?" AJ asked, not wanting to be out past dark, alone with Richard.

"We should, as long as we don't run into any problems on the road," Richard assured her as he dismounted. "Come now, even if you don't need the rest, the horses do."

"All right." She nodded and dismounted. She followed Richard as he led the horses to a creek. He filled up their canteens, then sat on a nearby fallen log. She joined him.

"I must tell you, AJ, you handled yourself very well, this whole mission. You have never shied away from any trouble, nor have you panicked under pressure as many would have." He smiled at her, a kind and compassionate smile. "If we weren't in the middle of a war, Miss Prentiss, I believe I would beg your father for permission to court you. I cannot believe there was once a time when I was so hurtful to you. I despise myself for that. I just hope and pray that you will forgive me."

"I already have, Richard." She pushed a strand of hair behind her ear.

"I feel so blessed that you gave me another chance to have you in my life."

"I think we've both grown and changed, Richard. I feel as though God brought us together so we could have a second chance."

"God." Richard crossed his legs the other way at the ankles. "I know you are a churchgoing woman, a good, devout Catholic. I don't have to tell you again how much my mother looks forward to Sundays when she spends them with you and Liberty."

"We have spoken on this before, Richard. You know I care for your mother dearly."

"Of course." He nodded. "What I was just thinking, though...I have been meaning to talk to you about..." He blew out a breath. "Ever since you told me that Markus Alexsander died...He was such a good young man. I just..." He rubbed his head. "I'm sorry. I am having trouble putting my thoughts into words. That doesn't happen often." He looked off in the distance. "My mother always tried to get me to pay attention at Mass, but I always had my mind on other things. I mean, I do believe in God, but to believe he loves me no matter what I've done. I always feel like I can never compare to His other son." AJ placed a hand on Richard's shoulder.

"From what I know of your family situation, Richard, I can't say that I am surprised." She gave his shoulder a squeeze. "Your own father is not as loving and forgiving as he should be."

"That is an understatement," Richard muttered.

"That is not how God is. He is loving and forgiving, no matter what. If we are truly sorry for our sins, he will forgive us."

"I have committed some fairly large sins, America. You know what I was like in my youth and as a young man. I fear that I'm past saving. I have tried to live better these past few years, but I fear I'm beyond the point of salvation."

"I once heard someone say that there is no sorrow on earth that is so great that heaven cannot heal," AJ replied. "God knows you better than anyone, Richard. He knows everything in your past as well as what is in your future. He sees your heart. If you are truly sorry for what you have done, God knows that already."

"It is amazing that he can love us that much." Richard bent one knee up and rested his arm on it. "When I look back on what I have done, it's hard for me to believe I even deserve His forgiveness."

"I often feel that way," AJ admitted. Richard gave a short laugh.

"I cannot imagine your sins compared to mine." He said.

"That doesn't matter, big or small," AJ said. "He loves us all regardless. "

Richard was silent for a moment. AJ hoped she had explained things to him in a way that would bring him back to God. She wanted it for him most of all, but she also wanted it for his mother. If she was honest with herself, she also wanted it for herself. She was beginning to think of a future with him, and it would make her future much better if she had a man with similar beliefs at her side.

"I am glad that we talked about this," Richard said, rubbing his stubble-covered chin. "I'm glad that I can talk with you about religion and while you may not have all the answers, you at least know how to explain it to me." He smiled at her. "I feel comfortable discussing just about anything with you, America."

"I must say, I am glad that I can just talk to you now. I used to be quite tongue-tied around you."

"Well, I'm sure I wasn't as approachable as I could have been," Richard admitted.

"The important thing is, we can communicate just fine now," AJ said. "That's what's important."

The Wilderness

AJ and Richard continued riding. They were following a southern route along the Orange and Alexandria Railroad to meet up with Lee's main army, southwest of the Wilderness Tavern. Richard wanted to make a wide sweep to bring them over to the Orange Turnpike, avoiding the Germana Plank Road. Richard knew the Union was advancing from there. They had been hearing the sounds of combat for quite some time from both artillery and rifle shots. Richard stopped as they came to the summit of a hill.

"I wonder why there's so much smoke," AJ said, looking into the distance.

"I'm not sure. It looks different than gun smoke." Richard replied. He couldn't contain the slight worry in his voice. "Come on, we can see if Major Daniels knows what's going on."

It didn't take them long to find the major. Daniels had just ridden in to give a report. He gave a brief nod to AJ and Richard as they entered, then continued his description of the battle. AJ couldn't help but look in awe at the man receiving the report, General Robert E. Lee.

"Grant attempted to maneuver around our earthworks. We think he's planning on marching towards Spotsylvania."

"Thank you for your report." The general said. "I will definitely take your suggestions into consideration." He then nodded at AJ and Richard and left the tent. Major Daniels turned toward the couple.

"It's good to see you two back, unharmed." He said. "Was the mission a success?"

Richard told Major Daniels what they had discovered, confirming his suspicions of Grant's plan to march through Spotsylvania in an attempt to take Richmond. Richard also informed the Major of the potential breach of secrecy at the hospital. "I must also say, Miss Prentiss performed quite admirably. She did not panic under pressure and did everything she could to ensure that the mission went as planned."

"Very good." Major Daniels said. "It is good to know that we have both soldiers and civilians so capable and willing to do what we need for the cause."

"Major, what is the status of our army in this battle?" Richard asked. "Would I have the opportunity to escort Miss Prentiss to her home?"

"As you obviously know, this battle is going to move, not end. You should be safe going to Fredericksburg, as long as you stay well south." Daniels said. "Captain Evans, make sure you don't dawdle. Those Yankees aren't backing down. You must return with all due haste. We can't let Grant through the Wilderness. Now I must report your information to Lee. Please bring the confiscated medication to the field hospital post haste and be on your way. We will be heading toward Spotsylvania Court House. Meet us there as soon as possible."

"Yes, sir." Richard saluted, then gently took AJ's arm and led her out of the tent.

"Evans! There you are." A cavalry officer approached the couple. "Daniels told us you were on a mission." He gave AJ a lascivious grin. "He didn't mention how pleasurable that mission would be for you."

Richard stepped up to the man, with an almost threatening stance.

"If you are insinuating that something happened you are wrong. I am a gentleman, she is a lady, and though I may not always act like a gentleman, the fact remains she is a lady. She is one of the most respectable, well-mannered, modest women I know. She has an untainted reputation that better remain that way."

The man took a step back and held up his hands. "All right, all right, Evans. I didn't mean to offend you. Begging your pardon, ma'am." He then turned and walked away.

"What was that all about?" AJ asked as they made their way to the field hospital. Richard shook his head.

"I just can't stand the thought of those men thinking poorly of you." After handing off the medicine and supplies to a grateful doctor they retrieved their horses.

"Well, here we go, back into the wilderness together." She said, mounting her horse.

"I know." He said, then turned to look down at her. "I promise you I will get you home safe and will insist until the day I die that you are a virtuous woman who deserves all the respect in the world."

Monday, May 9, 1864
Turner's Glenn

Belle entered the foyer to find Aaron talking with a Union officer. She came to an abrupt halt. If Union soldiers were in her home, that could only mean one thing. Fredericksburg was once again at the mercy of the Yankees.

"Belle." Meri came up behind her. "We need some help. Some of the soldiers in Father's library need broth."

"All right. I'll see what Annie and Ruthie have in the kitchen." As she was about to leave, Belle saw Aaron's face darken. The Union officer marched away, and Aaron rubbed his hair. Belle quickly approached him.

"What's happening, Aaron?" She grabbed his arm.

"Grant and the Union Army have taken control of Fredericksburg." He said. "I have been ordered to make room for their wounded, at the risk of moving our current patients before they are ready. I believe our men may be taken prisoner if the town remains in the hands of the Federals." He took a deep breath. "If I don't cooperate, I risk being arrested."

"You always offer medical attention to all men." Belle pointed out.

"I know. It just rankles me that I'm being ordered to do so." He said. They turned as a group of the new soldiers were brought in.

"Dear God." Belle's hand flew to her mouth. "What happened to them, Aaron?"

"Burns." He said, following the stretcher-bearers. "I heard the underbrush and new growth on the battlefield caught fire. Wounded soldiers couldn't get out of the fire's way." He entered the surgical room, and she followed closely behind. "I am surprised that any of these poor souls survived." He turned to Belle. "We'll have to move the men around again to make room for the more serious wounds. This is only the beginning. We'll be getting a lot of new patients."

"Yankee patients," Belle said, agitated. Are these Yankees so inhospitable that they would really take wounded men prisoner? Would they really be so callous as to arrest a man who had dedicated his life to helping others, even his enemy?

"We have had Union patients before." Aaron reminded her.

"Yes, but if you actually paid attention, you would have noticed that I avoided as much contact with them as possible." Belle countered.

"Belle, as your sister reminded me when I first arrived, we cannot look at these men as Union or Confederate. We must look at them as patients. Men who need our help. I may side with the Confederate cause, but I will not alter my assistance just because the patient is wearing a blue uniform."

495

"Well, one of those blue bellies very well could be the enemy soldier who shot and killed my brother." She said, green eyes flashing. "And I refuse to help them."

Bennett Home

"Elizabeth!" Lucy Beale's voice called out. Elizabeth turned from the fence and gave her a tired smile. She hadn't slept well the past couple of nights. First, the news of the battle had made her ill at ease, worrying about Joshua, and the previous day she found out the Yankees would once again control Fredericksburg.

"Good day, Lucy," Elizabeth answered. "How is everything at the Beale home?"

"Quite good, for now. I don't know if it will last, though. The Yankees are going to turn our entire town into an evacuation hospital."

"They have brought in thousands of wounded already," Elizabeth said. "They started coming in last night. I fear every building available will quickly fill up with wounded soldiers."

"Yes," Lucy said, "all Yankees. I am not sure I can find it within me to feel sympathetic towards any of them." She looked in the direction of Princess Anne Street, where wagon after wagon, no doubt loaded with casualties, passed by.

"I can't say I would agree with you," Elizabeth said. "The Federals need our care and compassion just as much as our Confederate boys."

"No, Elizabeth. How can you even think that?" Lucy said. "How can you consider yourself a loyal Confederate citizen and believe that the Yankees, who have destroyed so many aspects of our lives, deserve any kindness?" She gestured toward the wagons that continued to move past. "They continue to come! Those wounded soldiers that you are so keen on helping, they have been fighting our husbands and brothers. One of them may have killed your brother James, one may have killed Joshua for all we know. Yet you say they deserve our kindness and compassion."

Elizabeth wiped a tear from her cheek. "It is a dilemma, Lucy, a huge moral dilemma, but I cannot believe that a Southern woman could look at any wounded Yankee on the street and pass him by like the Levite and the Priest did to the wounded man in the Parable of the Good Samaritan. I just cannot see that happening."

Lucy shook her head. "I don't like to disagree with you, Elizabeth, but I can't see myself helping a Yankee. Ever!" She checked her pocket watch. "I must be going. I will talk to you later when I have more time."

Elizabeth sighed, then made her way back inside her house.

Wednesday, May 11, 1864
Turner's Glenn

"So many wounded are here already," Annie said, looking around. Their home had quickly filled, but this time, they were almost all Yankees. "We'll have to start putting them outside in the barns and outbuildings, and that will not be sanitary at all."

"It could get extremely hot out there as well," Belle added.

"We'll just have to do whatever we can to make them as comfortable as possible."

Belle scoffed. "You can do that. I am going to focus on making sure that every Confederate boy is taken care of." She looked at the house. Since the wounded Yankees started coming in two days ago, she had been unable to speak with Aaron other than a passing 'Hello'. She was starting to worry about him.

"Something else is distracting you, Belle. What is it?"

"I am concerned that Aaron isn't caring for himself as well as he should. I don't believe he has slept for more than a few hours these past couple of days. He hasn't eaten much either. I am afraid he will get sick himself and be unable to work at all."

"I remember he was like that the first week he was here as well." Annie pointed out. "Maybe you should talk to him about your concerns."

"I can't even talk to him for more than five seconds," Belle said, trying not to sound childish.

"You are an important person in his life now, correct?" Annie said. "He will listen to you if you make it a point to talk with him."

Belle let out a sigh. "I do hope you're right." She looked toward the house. "I'll check and see if he's available now."

It didn't take Belle long to find Aaron. She caught him walking from the surgery room to one of the wards.

"Doctor!" She grabbed his arm. "May I have a word with you?"

"I don't have time to chat with you right now, Miss Turner."

"It is not just a whimsical chat, Aaron." She pulled him to a stop and looked into his haggard eyes. "When is the last time you sat down?"

He shook his head. "I'm fine. You do not need to worry about me." He rubbed his temple. She reached up to touch his chin. He had at least three days' worth of stubble.

"You need to be honest with yourself. You need to take a break."

"I told you, I can keep going. These soldiers need my help."

"You won't do them any good if you're dead on your feet." Belle insisted. Aaron shook his head and pushed to get past her. He was only two steps away from her when he appeared to stumble.

"Aaron!" Belle called out. He caught himself by grabbing the wall and steadied himself. Belle was at his side quickly and helped him straighten. "Aaron, you need to get to bed. You are completely worn out."

Aaron rubbed his hand through his hair. "I need to go and help the men."

"Aaron Knightly, I am serious about you needing some rest. What if you had stumbled like that while you were doing a procedure? You could have injured yourself or worse, the patient."

He sighed. "If I take a rest, will you stop pestering me?"

"I will stop pestering you if, after you take a long rest, you also sit down and have a meal. It would be even better if you allowed me to share that meal with you." She gave him a charming smile.

"I suppose I can agree to that." He checked his pocket watch. "Could you please send an orderly to wake me in four hours?"

"I will have him wake you in six hours." She said.

"Five." He countered, glowering.

"All right. Five hours and I will have a meal ready for you." She agreed. He started walking up the steps to his room. She followed behind him. He glanced at her.

"I can find my own way, Miss Turner." He sounded annoyed at her persistence.

"I know you can. I just want to be sure you make it, or did you forget you almost took a tumble just a few moments ago?" She tried to keep her own voice from sounding too testy.

"I don't need you to watch over me." He said.

"Well, forgive me for caring about you and wanting to make sure you are okay." She shook her head. "Perhaps you would be less ornery if you actually took care of yourself."

Sunday, May 15, 1864
St. Mary's Catholic Church, Fredericksburg

AJ and Liberty walked into the church, anxious to see if there would be a Mass.

"Oh, dear me, it does not look as though there will be a service," Liberty said.

"No." AJ agreed. Every empty space was filled with wounded Union soldiers. Doctors and nurses moved from patient to patient.

"Excuse me, if you are not going to help, then you need to move on." A harsh, no-nonsense looking woman approached them. Her dark hair was pulled back into a severe bun.

"I am so sorry, Miss…"

498

"Mrs. Jane Swisshelm." The woman said with a slight sneer. "I can tell by your accent that you are another Fredericksburg woman who will spurn our wounded and look with savage joy and undisguised triumph over sufferings that should move any human to heart, and you will turn up your noses at the Northern nurses, but then beg my interference on behalf of husbands who were taken as hostages."

AJ tried to keep her mouth from dropping open in shock. "Mrs. Swisshelm, we have no intention of doing any of that. We didn't realize that St. Mary's was being used as a hospital, although we should have, especially with all of the wounded men lying in the street." AJ was taken aback at the hostility of the woman.

"Well, it is. So you can either assist the Union soldiers or, as I said, you can be on your way." The woman then turned and marched away.

"AJ..." Liberty looked at her sister, not quite knowing what to do. AJ couldn't help but look around. Yankee wounded were everywhere. Over the past few years, she had been helping in any way she could to destroy the Yankee army. It was easy to despise the Yanks fiercely and to claim you would never do an act of kindness for one of them, but it was rather different to see them suffering and fighting for their lives. She sighed.

"Come, Liberty. I would like to check on Mrs. Evans." She turned to leave, Liberty followed behind her.

"You never talked much about Richard and your latest adventure." Liberty's attempt at conversation wasn't exactly what AJ wanted to talk about, but it did serve to distract her from the carnage they were walking by.

"You know I was with him." She replied.

"Are you ever going to admit your feelings for him?" Liberty asked. "Because you can't hide the fact that you have them. Not from me, I know you too well."

"I suppose you do," AJ said. She thought back to her last mission where he had protected her, complimented her, and defended her honor. He had embraced her tightly and kissed her gently on the forehead before he left.

"Liberty, you are right. I do care for him. I believe he cares for me, at least he says he does. However, I must be careful with those feelings. For one thing, he is a soldier at war, and for all I know, he could have been killed in the Battle of the Wilderness."

'True, but the way I see it, you should really let him know exactly how you feel because it is possible he might not live. Don't you think you would regret not telling him how you feel if you found out he was killed?"

"My little sister giving me advice. What is this world coming to?" AJ sighed.

Sunday, May 22, 1864
Turner's Glenn

"Is this new battle finished as they claim?" Belle patted the perspiration from her forehead with the back of her hand. It was a warm day and she had been working quite hard.

"That was the information on my side of the river," AJ replied, looking around Turner's Glenn. "I am glad I was able to come down and visit. I knew you would be busy, but this is so much more than I anticipated."

"And they are mostly Yankees." Belle shook her head in disgust.

"How are you handling that?" AJ asked, knowing Belle's feelings toward Yankees.

"I try to stay in the room where the Confederate boys are as much as possible," Belle admitted. "Elizabeth doesn't understand why I feel the way I do, but I cannot bring myself to help a Yankee if I don't absolutely have to."

"Where is Elizabeth?" AJ asked. "I thought she would still be staying here?"

"She stayed in town. She feels as though she has to. The Yankees took over her home as well. They have a half-dozen wounded soldiers there."

"My goodness." AJ was surprised.

"They have taken over the whole town," Belle said. "Meri is helping Elizabeth with the soldiers at her home and the children, of course."

"I should have realized. The town has been in enemy hands for over a week. I don't know what I was thinking. I didn't even check to see if Elizabeth was home. I suppose Liberty is wandering around the house, searching for Meri in vain." AJ said. "We will have to stop in town on our way home. I want to visit Mrs. Evans again anyways."

"We enjoy your visits, AJ." Belle smiled. Just as she was about to say something else, one of the orderlies approached.

"Miss Turner. Dr. Knightly needs you right away."

"Why does he need me? Surely there are others that can help him.'

"I'm not sure, ma'am. He just wanted me to find you as soon as possible." The young man replied.

"All right. Thank you, Henry." Henry was a young orderly who had been at Turner's Glenn since it was first turned into a hospital. "Would you do me a favor and track down Miss Liberty Prentiss?"

"Yes, ma'am."

"We could stay and help, Belle," AJ said.

"Yes, but if you want to visit both Elizabeth and Mrs. Evans, I would feel better if you headed into town now. I wouldn't want you to be out after dark with all of the Yankees crawling around."

"All right," AJ said. "I miss talking to you."

"Then the next time you visit, you will have to tell me why it is so important for you to always be visiting Richard Evans' mother.

"She is a very kind woman, and spends a lot of time alone..." AJ was interrupted by Belle throwing up a hand.

"You will give me a million excuses, AJ, but I have been watching you. We will have a nice, long talk about this later when we both have more time." She gave AJ a quick hug. "I need to go help and you really should be on your way. Be rest assured, we will speak on this again."

Bennett Home

"Liberty!" Benjamin ran to greet the visitors.

"Hello, Benjamin." Liberty gave him a quick hug, then turned to see Hannah approach.

"Liberty, we have soldiers all over the house," Hannah said. "Just like at Turner's Glenn."

"'Cept our patients are Yankees." The disdain in Benjamin's voice was obvious.

"Benjamin Bennett!" An exhausted-looking Elizabeth came out onto the stoop. "I have spoken to you before about that tone of voice." She wiped her hands on a blood-stained apron. "I need you to go in and collect all the soiled linens so I can do laundry, then see if Eric needs any help in the shop."

"Yes, ma'am," Benjamin mumbled and then trudged into the house.

"Come, Hannah. Let's go find Meri." Liberty took the girl's hand and led her inside.

"She's likely looking for an excuse to be around Eric," Elizabeth stated. AJ placed a hand on Elizabeth's shoulder.

"Things don't look so good here," AJ replied.

"No, Not good at all," Elizabeth replied. "It seems all we do is care for the soldiers. They are in every house and still lay along the roads. I've also heard that all the male citizens except for a select few have been arrested. I don't know if it's true or not, but it is frightening, nonetheless."

"I hate to tell you this, but there is worse news. Liberty and I couldn't help but notice that Negro troops are stationed all around town." AJ added.

"Yes, many people are upset about that too. I'm afraid, as I said, but we are being run ragged here and Benjamin has become surly for the first time in his life."

"It is a lot for all of us to handle, much less a little boy with his father off fighting," AJ admitted. "I can foresee more hardships coming. I can't see this situation improving anytime soon. What is it you always say, Elizabeth? Be strong and steadfast? That is what we must be."

A tear escaped Elizabeth's eye and she quickly brushed it away. "Be strong and steadfast. Do not fear nor be dismayed for the Lord is with you wherever you go." She gave a sad smile. "Mine and Joshua's favorite Scripture verse."

"It is quite appropriate, really. It reflects what we are going through during this war." AJ said.

"I agree wholeheartedly." Elizabeth nodded and brushed a strand of hair from her face.

"Let's go inside and I will do my best to help you with your visitors for a while." AJ took Elizabeth's arm and led her inside. "I may not like helping Yankees, but I can't just leave you here by yourself when you need help."

"Thank you so much, AJ. Any help is much appreciated."

Sunday, June 5, 1864
Turner's Glenn

"Belle," Aaron called as he walked toward the vegetable garden. Belle looked up from where she was working and smiled.

"What can I do for you, Aaron?"

"Come for a walk with me." He held out his hand to help her up and she took it.

"Of course." She replied. He led her in the direction of the river. "Did you need to speak with me about anything in particular?" She feared that she already knew the answer.

"I am being sent to a field hospital near Richmond. There is fierce fighting going on over there, a place called Cold Harbor. From what I understand the fighting has been brutal, which is no surprise with that bulldog Grant in charge. Once again, too many casualties."

"Well, as much as I hate to say it, you need to go where you will be the most useful. It appears your talents are more desperately needed elsewhere." It was difficult for her to say those words. She wanted to tell him to stay, that she needed him here. "At least you'll be helping Confederates."

"I appreciate you being so understanding, Belle. I know that was hard for you to say. I don't know how long I will be gone or how much longer this war will last." He pulled her to a stop and looked at her. Her heart sped up. Was this the moment? Was he about to propose marriage to her? "Before I leave, I need to reiterate how much I care for you. After the war, I would like to come back to Turner's Glenn."

"I would like that too," Belle said. She reached up and touched his face. "Is that all you wanted to say?"

"There is a lot I would like to say." He said. "However, I will refrain from saying it now. This is not the time nor the place to make promises for the future. As a doctor, I am less likely to be wounded or killed, but there is always a chance, especially when I am being sent so close to the front lines, and there is still so much disease. I need you to know that I care for you, deeply, and that, God willing, I will come back to Turner's Glenn the first chance I get."

"Do you believe the end is near, Aaron?" Belle tried not to show her disappointment about not receiving a proposal.

"I do. The Yankees are so close to Richmond now. It will be a long and difficult road these next few months. Unfortunately, I believe it will not end the way that we envisioned."

Belle nodded, saddened by his revelation because as bad as it seemed, she had the same thoughts. This walk was not going in the right direction, so she changed the subject.

"We have family near Richmond. Did you know that? My cousin Bekah and Aunt Suzanna are living in Petersburg right now. We speak of families torn apart by this war, like yours, Aaron, but theirs is as well. My uncle Samuel and Cousin Jonah are fighting for the Union, yet my cousin Jacob is fighting for the Confederacy."

"I am sorry to hear that. It makes no sense at all to me, how we can hate our brothers so." Aaron smiled. "I believe you've spoken of Bekah before. It sounds as though the two of you are quite close."

"We are. All of the cousins on my father's side of the family get along splendidly, even though we don't see each other often enough. I hear from them so seldom since the start of the war. I don't know how any of them are faring, especially my cousin Charlotte, from Pennsylvania."

"Where does she live in Pennsylvania? I can't believe we haven't spoken of this yet before."

"Unfortunately she lives on a farm just outside Gettysburg. I wonder if you happened to run into her."

"I was assigned to the home of a professor on the north side of town. The professor did have a daughter, Mrs. William Sadler. She was a very good nurse, I met one of her friends, a young woman...wait a moment...was this Miss Charlotte Turner? A cousin on your father's side?"

"Yes. Were you able to meet her?" Belle grasped his arm in excitement.

"I may have met her. I'm ashamed to say that I never made a connection between your last name and hers."

503

"Was she all right? Did she survive?"

"Yes, she was and she did. When I met her, she and Mrs. Sadler brought a Union officer to be cared for. He had previously been acquainted with her, and she personally cared for him. It was her devotion that helped him fully recover."

Belle sighed in relief. "Thank goodness. Oh, Lord, thank you." She smiled. "It is so good to hear favorable news like that. Now if only we could hear from our cousins in Vicksburg."

"That may be quite difficult, with it being occupied by the Union army. However, when the war is over, you should make sure you invite them all to come to Turner's Glenn so you can all spend time together."

"That is a wonderful idea." Belle smiled, then sobered. "But it will never be the same. James is gone. I have no idea if anyone else has been a casualty of this war or not. My father, my cousins, are they still fighting or are they dead and lying in some shallow grave in some unknown city?" She sighed. "I'm sorry, Aaron. You are right. I suppose all we can do is try."

Sunday, June 12, 1864
Bennett Home

"It was so good to attend church services again," AJ said. She, Elizabeth and Belle sat on Elizabeth's front stoop.

"It won't be long until all of the wounded are transferred to hospitals in the north," Elizabeth said with a glance in the direction of her children's room. She still had two wounded soldiers. It had been a long, tiring month.

"Unfortunately, many of the doctors have left as well," Belle said. "Just as Aaron has. I had so little time to spend with him." She turned to Elizabeth. "Do you ever get used to it? Being separated from the man you love, I mean."

"No. No, you don't." Elizabeth said. "People always say that absence makes the heart grow fonder, but I want Joshua home for good. His presence is all I need."

"I am afraid that separation will cause Aaron's heart to be forgetful, not grow fonder." She turned to AJ. "What's your opinion? Fonder or forgetful?"

AJ had been looking down the street, not even paying attention to the conversation. "Forgive me. What was the question?"

"What has you so distracted today?" Elizabeth asked.

"Does it have anything to do with how you visit Mrs. Evans every Sunday after Church?" Belle asked. "I did warn you that you and I would have this conversation."

"Yes, but that was a month ago." AJ pointed out. "I had hoped you would forget."

"I don't forget things like that," Belle said with a smile. "So, out with it."

AJ sighed. She needed to talk, and perhaps the sisters could give her good advice. "I suppose it wouldn't hurt to tell you two about my situation. Elizabeth, you know parts of it. Belle, I believe that you suspect some of it as well. I don't think I need to tell you both that what I say cannot leave this porch."

"Of course," Belle said.

AJ, mindful of open windows and Yankees in the house, quietly told Belle and Elizabeth about her relationship with Richard Evans. The sisters listened and smiled. AJ glossed over some of their encounters but filled them in on enough.

"I wondered so many times about your feelings for Richard." Belle smiled. "To be honest, whenever I spoke with you about my pursuing a relationship with him, I was partly judging your reaction to what I was saying."

"I see. Clever." AJ said, half-believing her friend. "So that is my story. That is where Richard and I stand right now. I am in love with him and he says that he is falling in love with me as well. Whoever thought it possible?"

"I did," Elizabeth said with a smile. "You are a fine catch for any man, AJ. I knew eventually, the right one would come along."

"If only I knew we would end up together," AJ said. "There are still so many obstacles. I really understand how you both feel about Joshua and Aaron now, and how dear Kate must feel about Sandie."

"There will always be obstacles," Belle said. "But you can overcome them."

"We all have, and we will continue to do so," Elizabeth added.

AJ nodded and then changed the subject. "Speaking of Kate, has anyone heard from her? It has been more than a month since I received any letter."

"I just had one get through to me a few days ago," Belle said. "It sounds as though she is doing very well. Sandie's mother and sisters treat her like family, and Sandie has been able to visit a time or two."

"How nice for her," Elizabeth said.

"I should have brought the letter for you two to read." Belle shook her head. "I will have to do so next time we get together."

505

Wednesday, June 15, 1864
Bennett Home

"Belle! What brings you to town?" Elizabeth smiled and invited her sister into the house.

"I wanted to get some supplies," Belle answered. "I came to visit you and my niece and nephew first."

"You just missed them," Elizabeth said. "Eric took them to the store to see if they can find some food. You actually may have passed them on the street and not even noticed"

"Well, I suppose I will just have to stay and chat with you until they return," Belle said, sitting at the kitchen table.

"I hope you don't mind if I continue preparing dinner," Elizabeth said. "But why don't you fill me in on what is happening at Turner's Glenn or any other news you may have."

"Nothing good, I am afraid," Belle replied. "In fact, I heard from the Yankees at the house that the Union army attacked Petersburg and the town is now under siege."

"Petersburg! What about the family? Aunt Suzanna and Bekah and Bethany…"

"I don't know. I wish I did know more, but once again, General Grant has a Turner Family under siege." Belle said. "First in Vicksburg and now in Petersburg." She shook her head. "Vicksburg, Petersburg, Gettysburg and here in Fredericksburg. We Turners have not done well in terms of staying away from the battles of this war."

Elizabeth pounded at her bread dough with extra vigor. "I read in an old newspaper I found from last year about a twenty-year-old woman in Gettysburg dying in the battle. The only civilian casualty."

"Well, it wasn't Charlotte. Aaron told me he met her…"

"No, not Charlotte." Elizabeth quickly said. "But I believe it was her friend Ginny. The paper said 'Jennie' at first and I thought maybe it was a relative of hers, but as I read the article, I feel it was Charlotte's best friend."

"My goodness. I remember Ginny." Tears threatened Belle's eyes. "Poor, dear Charlotte. I think of her every day. I hope she is doing all right."

"As do I. We can only trust and pray that her other friends are there to support her."

"Yes, and Bekah has Aunt Suzanna and Bethany and all of her friends. Mary and Victoria have family and friends supporting each other, and most of all." Belle said. "I have you and the rest of my family and friends here for me and I want you to know how much I appreciate you."

"The feeling is mutual," Elizabeth said with a smile.

Tuesday, June 21, 1864
Along the Rappahannock

"America!" At the sound of Richard's voice, she turned.

"Richard!" She shook her head. "What on earth are you doing here? I cannot believe that you would risk your life meeting me?"

"The Yanks pulled out of Fredericksburg a few days ago." He said. "Besides, I have a letter for my mother that I am hoping you can deliver on Sunday. I also wanted to check on you to see if you had any information for me."

"Well, of course, I know the Yanks are gone, that is what I look for, but still, there is a definite presence." She shook her head. "No information, but I do have this." She handed him a package that held some medication. He tucked it under his shirt. AJ tried not to show how disappointed she was that information and supplies were all that he wanted from her. "Is there anything else?"

He smiled and put an arm around her waist and pulled her close for a hug. "The biggest reason I came is that I really wanted to see you." He pulled away and led her to a large rock that was perfect for sitting on. "How are you and Liberty getting along?"

"Fine, just fine." She said. She told him about her visits to Chatham, how she continued to work the farm, and how much she looked forward to going to Church with his mother. He replied with what he experienced in the Battle of the Wilderness and the battle that happened almost immediately after at Spotsylvania Court House. Finally, she looked at her watch.

"As much I would like to stay here with you, I should be getting back, and you should too." She stood.

"Yes." Richard kissed her hand, then stood.

"I will escort you back to your home."

"You will do no such thing," AJ said. "If it was a safe option for you to be at the farmhouse, we would meet there for all our rendezvous, but of course, you know that's not true."

"All right, you have a point," Richard said, then kissed her cheek. "Stay safe until we meet again."

"And you." She smiled, then turned and began walking back to her home. After a moment, she heard movement in the brush behind her.

"Richard?" She turned and looked, but it was difficult to see in the fading sunlight. She saw a soldier's form move slowly toward her. "I told you I could..." She froze as she saw that it was not Richard. It wasn't even a Confederate soldier. It was a Yankee. She turned to run to the safety of her home but the man quickly caught up with her and grabbed her around the waist.

"Don't know who this Richard is but I can say that I'm him if you want." The man slurred his words and smelled strongly of whiskey. He stumbled and brought both of them to the ground as she screamed for help and fought against him.

Just when she felt she was losing her strength, she felt the Yankee being pulled from her. She rolled over to see Richard punch the attacker. The Yankee rolled over and pulled out a pistol. Richard stopped and held up his hands. "Easy, come now, man. I was just protecting the lady. We can talk this over."

"Johnny Reb, that's just not going to happen." The soldier pulled the trigger, hitting Richard in the thigh. Richard fell forward but caught himself before he hit the ground.

"Richard!" AJ rushed toward him, but before she could reach him, Richard pulled a dagger from his boot and launched himself at the Yankee. The Yankee blocked Richard as he tried to stab him. The dagger fell to the ground and was picked up by the Yankee.

AJ looked down and saw the pistol that must have fallen from Richard's holster. She looked for a way to help Richard but didn't want to accidentally shoot him. With the hand holding the dagger, the Yankee swiped at Richard, who was losing a lot of blood from the wound in his thigh. Richard tried to dodge the blow, but the Yankee connected with the dagger. Blood gushed from Richard's cheek and he crumpled to the ground. The Yankee picked up his pistol and stood, towering over the wounded man. He gave a chuckle and pointed the pistol at Richard's chest, but before he could pull his trigger, AJ pulled hers. The Yankee fell back. AJ rushed to the two men, grabbed the other pistol, and dagger, and stuffed them in her bag. She turned and glanced at the Yankee, who lay still, a crimson stain forming on his chest. Richard tried to pull himself up but was struggling to stay conscious.

"America..." He mumbled.

"Richard, that Yankee isn't moving. I think I killed him."

"He deserved it. You need to get out of here. The gunshots may attract attention."

"I can't leave you." She pulled him up, both of them using all their strength. "Come on. We'll get you to my farm." He took a step and stumbled. Blood flowed from his thigh and his face. "Here." She quickly bent down and used the dagger to slice strips of cloth from her petticoat, for his leg injury. She wasn't quite sure how to temporarily bandage his cheek, so she pressed the third strip of petticoat to that wound. "Lean on me, Richard. We'll get you home safely. They limped to his horse, who was still tethered to a tree. She helped him up, then led his horse home as quickly and quietly as she could.

Wednesday, June 22, 1864
Prentis Farm

AJ quietly entered Nathaniel's room where she had brought Richard. With the two wounds he had sustained and the blood he had lost, he had been in and out of consciousness for the past two days. Liberty had summoned Mrs. Turner to help with his wounds. She had removed the bullet from Richard's leg and patched up both the leg and his face. She had been back to check on Richard each day, taking care not to attract any attention. AJ and Liberty had buried the body of the dead Yankee. They suspected he had been a deserter, but there were still Yankee patrols in the area and Chatham was still a Yankee hospital. They had been lucky that no one had heard the gunshots. The Prentiss family had to be careful with Richard in the home. If he was found, he would be taken as a prisoner of war.

AJ sat next to the bed and placed the bowl of water on the bedside table. Richard was sleeping. Mrs. Turner had told AJ that Richard would need a lot of rest, and had shown her how to change his dressings. AJ had been so busy taking care of Richard that she hadn't figured out how to get word to Captain Daniels about the injury.

AJ reached forward to brush back a strand of Richard's hair. Over the last few months, he had let it grow longer. She liked it that way. She ran her fingers across the bandage on his cheek. The few times he had woken up, he was groggy and she hadn't really had a chance to talk to him about his injuries. She wasn't quite sure how he would take the news about his face. Mrs. Turner told her that she suspected Richard's face would have a thin scar from his left temple, down his cheek, to his left jaw. She didn't care. He was alive.

Richard stirred and opened his eyes, they seemed clearer. Maybe this would be a turning point in his recovery.

"Good morning, Mr. Evans." She brushed his hair back again. "How are you feeling?"

"America. You're all right?" His voice was hoarse and weak, but it was good to hear him talk.

"I am, I'm fine, and you'll be alright as well." She smiled.

"You have such a beautiful smile, 'Merica. You always have." He said, still a bit groggy.

"You have always been too charming for your own good," AJ replied.

"I'm glad you think so." He pushed himself up to a sitting position with her help. "My memory is finally coming back to me. What happened to that Yankee? I remember...you shot him." Richard rubbed his chin; he needed a shave.

Tears came to AJ's eyes with the reminder that she had taken a life. "He died. I killed him. Liberty and I buried him, and he's dead because of me."

Richard took her hand in his. "America, he's dead because of the choices he made. He wanted to hurt you. You saved me. I wish you didn't have to kill to do it, but you did what you had to do."

"I know. I just...I wish there had been another way."

"I know you do. You can't dwell on it though. I know it bothers you." He brought her hand up and gave it a kiss.

"Yes, he's gone and whoever misses him...well...no one will suspect that you or I had anything to do with his death." Her tone told him that she didn't want to discuss the incident anymore. "But he is still gone."

"You can't change what's done." He rubbed his forehead. "What happened to me?"

"You were slashed with your dagger and shot in the thigh. You have lost a lot of blood but Mrs. Turner came over and patched you up. She's one of the only people who knows that you're here, and she won't say anything."

"Who else knows?" Richard asked.

"Liberty, of course. I suspect Belle knows as well, Liberty said she was there when she went for Mrs. Turner."

"Who has been taking care of me?" Richard asked.

"Mrs. Turner came by a couple of times, but it's been mostly me," AJ told him. "Checking your wounds, changing your bandages. I'm so glad that you're awake." She stood. "I have some broth that I can heat up so you can get some food in you. If you behave yourself, I'll make you a bowl of stew later. If you're really good and continue to behave...I make the best fried chicken this side of the Rappahannock"

"Some broth sounds great." He tried to laugh. "You run a decently successful farm in the midst of war, you are raising your younger sister, you are one of the most intelligent women that I know, you make me laugh...and you can cook? You continue to impress me."

"Well, thank you, sir.' She gave a short curtsey. Richard laughed again as she exited the room.

Friday, June 24, 1864
Prentiss Farm

AJ turned as Mrs. Turner came out of the room.

"How is he doing?" AJ asked.

"Physically, he's fine. I told him that his leg should heal completely, but there is a chance that he will have issues with it later in life. He

510

became quite despondent when I told him that he would have scars from both injuries. The thigh, he was okay with. The face, not so."

"That doesn't surprise me. He values his looks quite highly. To be honest, it's one of the reasons that I wanted you to tell him." She shrugged a little guiltily.

"That's alright with me, dear." Mrs. Turner replied. "I believe he'll adjust. I won't be coming out as much, but I'll try to come every few days."

"Thank you so much, Mrs. Turner. For coming out here and for your discretion."

"My dear, you and Liberty are very special to me. Your mother and I were dear friends from the time we were little girls ourselves."

"Yes, I do know that," AJ said with a smile. "I just wanted to thank you just the same."

"You call on me anytime." She gave AJ a hug. "I must be going. Make sure you keep those bandages clean and dry. I know it is hard, but it is important to prevent infection. He should get plenty of rest but can get up for short periods of time if he feels up to it. And AJ?" She looked toward the room where Richard rested. "Try to keep his spirits up. Don't let him feel sorry for himself. That can be just as detrimental as a physical wound."

"I will Mrs. Turner," AJ said, walking her to the door. When she was gone, she headed back to the stove, piled some fried eggs on a plate, and brought them up to her patient.

"Richard, how did it go with Mrs. Turner?"

"You never told me I would be disfigured for life." Richard brooded.

"I didn't think it would matter. You're alive, Richard, when you could have easily been killed. So many men have lost their legs, arms, and their lives." She offered him the eggs.

"I'm not hungry." He looked out the window.

"Well then, I'll leave them here for you to eat later." AJ set them on the bedside table. "Can I get you anything else?"

"No." He sighed. "I'm tired. I'm going to take a rest." He closed his eyes. AJ frowned. She knew that the wound would affect him. From their past conversations, she realized that he had a low opinion of himself with one exception being his good looks.

"Richard, you can't let this get you down. You have so much to live for." Richard opened his eyes and looked at her.

"Listen, Miss Prentiss, I don't want to be rude, but I'm really quite tired." He took a deep breath. "These past few months, we have grown closer, but I really think we should take a step back. When I'm able to leave, we should just...go our separate ways." He looked away, back out the window.

"I don't think you really want that, Richard." AJ shook her head. "I care for you, I have for years. I don't care that your face is scarred if that's what you're worried about. That's not why I love you." She took a deep breath. "I will be back to visit later. Even if you don't reciprocate my feelings, I will still help you recover, because that's what people do when they care about someone, Richard." She leaned forward and gently kissed his forehead. "I will see you later."

Friday, July 1, 1864
Prentiss Farm

Belle stepped through the door of AJ's home.

"AJ? Liberty?" She called.

"They're not here." The deep, masculine voice of Richard Evans surprised Belle for a moment. He entered the kitchen, using the crutch Eric had made and Miriam had delivered. He was more disheveled than she had ever seen him, with long, wavy hair, unshaven face, Confederate uniform pants, undershirt, and suspenders.

"Richard!" Belle smiled at her old friend. "It's so good to see you! I'm glad to see you up and about. How wonderful."

"Thank you." Richard gave a small, half-hearted smile. "AJ and Liberty are in town, exchanging eggs and vegetables for some necessities."

"They left you by yourself?"

"I may not look it, but I can take care of myself. I'm not a complete invalid." He crutched over to the stove. "I can even play the good host. Would you like some tea? They have sassafras."

"No, thank you." Belle pulled out a chair and sat down. Richard helped himself to some tea and joined her, managing to hold the tea and his crutch. "You seem to be quite at home here."

"I am. To be honest, I feel more at home here than I ever did in the house where I grew up. AJ and Liberty have been wonderful. AJ especially".

"She's a wonderful person. I'm glad you finally see that."

"Me too." Richard smiled a genuine smile. "She's amazing. I'm not quite sure what I did to make her care for me the way she does. You know I treated her horribly when we were younger. Even now I tried to push her away, but she won't have anything to do with that." He shook his head. "I would probably find it annoying if I didn't find it so endearing." He shrugged. "I don't understand what she sees in me. My looks, maybe. But now that I'm disfigured, well..."

"Disfigured? Hardly, Richard. You'll have a little scar. That's all."

512

"Who told you that?"

"My mother," Belle said. "Richard, I never thought I would see the day that you would be concerned about how AJ Prentiss feels about you."

"Can I be honest with you?"

"Of course."

"I feel like you, of all people, might understand this. You understand how important it is to have good looks and a profitable future. You and I both know you didn't court Samuel Gray for his intelligence."

"You're right. I admit to being shallow in the past. I saw that Samuel was rich and had a good future and good looks. He may have had more admirable qualities, but I was so busy accepting the compliments he gave me that I didn't even...I'm not sure that I really even knew him." Belle's eyes watered.

"Samuel was a good man, Belle. He may have been spoiled and self-centered and he drank too much whiskey more than occasionally, but so did I. He wasn't the smartest of men and tended to follow along with whatever everyone else was doing, but he was a loyal friend." Unmanly tears welled up in Richard's eyes. "I admit I miss him. We have lost so many good friends." He took a deep breath. "It's always been impressed upon me that looks and power and money are all that's important. My father hammered that into my head since before I can remember, and Mother, being the proper Southern lady she is, never contradicted him." He took a deep breath. "I always believed that outward appearances were everything. America is very attractive to me now, but I never saw her as a beauty growing up. She is and always has been a good and kind person, but I still only looked at outward appearances. I just...I don't know, I figured she wasn't the type of girl I was expected to marry, so why bother? I felt she was beneath me." He shook his head. "I was such an imbecile, and now? Now I see she is beautiful inside and out. I want a future with her, but I fail to see what good I can do for her. I will have a scarred face, I am still selfish and I have no idea what I'm going to do to support a wife and family after the war. My leg may never be any good and it's unlikely my father will welcome me back into his law practice, not after I left him to fight, and especially not if I marry America."

"You're seriously thinking of marriage?" Belle smiled.

"Before my injuries, yes, I was. I wanted to spend the rest of my life with her, but that's what I'm trying to explain. I feel I will have nothing to offer her." He gave a half-laugh. "Imagine, me unsure about my future."

"How far we've come, you and I," Belle commented. "I suppose the realities and horrors of war have altered us forever."

"Hopefully for the better." Richard smiled. "I'm not sure what I did to earn America's affections. Even when I try to push her away, she holds on and won't let go." He sighed. "I know I'm being selfish and maybe she would be better off without me, but as much as I try, I can't push her out of my life. I just can't."

"Well, Richard, I am so glad to hear that. AJ is a dear friend and I know you will make her happy."

"I hope so, I really do," Richard replied. "Thank you so much for listening, Belle. I really appreciate it."

"I'm glad to help."

Richard took a sip of his tea. "Now that I've talked your ear off. What brings you out here? When I heard the horse coming, I was afraid the Federals had finally come for me."

"My mother was quite busy at Turner's Glenn today, but wanted to check on you, so I said I would ride over here. It gives me a good excuse to visit AJ."

"Yes, well, she should be home at any time, and I know she will be happy to see you." He smiled.

After Belle left and Liberty had gone upstairs to bed, Richard turned to AJ and offered to make a fire in the fireplace.

"I know it's summer, but it's cool out tonight." He explained. "I enjoy sitting in front of a fire."

"I agree." AJ stood from her chair. "But let me start the fire. I don't want you aggravating your leg wound."

"I can do it," Richard argued.

"I know you can," AJ replied, moving to start the fire. Richard sighed and limped over to one of the chairs that sat in front of the fireplace. AJ stood, the small blaze quickly catching.

"You are an extremely competent woman, you know that?" Richard commented. AJ grabbed some mending and shrugged.

"I only do what I must."

"Why is it so hard for you to accept my compliments?" Richard asked. He wanted to follow Belle's advice and admit his problems to AJ but he wasn't quite sure how to start the conversation.

"I can't really say," AJ admitted. "With you, I suppose it's because I'm still just a little unsure about why you are offering them."

"I'm not trying to seduce you, America. I think too highly of you for that." He tried to catch her eye, but she kept them on her mending. "Besides, I thought we were past all of that. I thought you trusted me."

"I am trying to, Richard. Believe me, I am."

"I suppose if I were to look at our situation from your perspective, I don't always send the clearest signals." He sighed. "I do hope to clarify some things tonight, though." She glanced up and met his eyes, then quickly looked back down at her needlework. "AJ, I grew up in a home where appearance meant absolutely everything. Outward appearance. How your home looked, how well you dressed, how much money you had. It didn't matter how kind you were or how smart you were as long as appearances were upheld. A relationship could fall apart as long as no one on the outside knew it. That is how my Father raised me. He expected so much from me, and I never felt like I lived up to his expectations and standards." Richard leaned forward and stretched his thigh. He stared into the fire. "We've talked about this. I'm not trying to make excuses for my behavior. I'm just trying to help you understand me better. You know why I am the way I am. Why I feel as though my life is no longer worthy of living. You were raised differently. I've lost any hope of rejoining my father's law practice after the way I left." He stood and hopped the short distance to the fireplace, where he leaned against the mantle and stared into the fire. "I will have nothing to offer you, America, and I cannot understand why you care for me. What made me one of the best catches in Spotsylvania County are gone. No job, no money, no future, and now, my looks are gone. What could you possibly see in me? I'm spoiled, selfish..."

AJ stood and closed the distance between them. "Enough already, Richard. We don't choose who we love. It's in God's hands. You can stop feeling sorry for yourself anytime now. I love you."

He stared at her. "But why?" His heart soared at her words, but his feelings of inadequacy still lingered in his mind.

"You may have been spoiled and selfish before the war, but not any longer." She said, laying her hand on his arm. "I love you because you have a kind heart, you're brave, you're smart, and you're a hard worker. You left your father's firm knowing he would disinherit you. You risked your life for your beliefs, your principles. You have risked your life to save mine many times." Her hands moved down to his hands. "You have shown me the man you really are these past few years. The way I was sweet on you so long ago, that was just a silly infatuation. I see you so differently now." She smiled. "In the past year or so, you have shown me nothing but respect. I confess, sometimes I am unsure if I'm good enough for you." AJ chuckled. "Listen to the two of us. Neither of us thinks we are good enough for each other. We are definitely quite a pair."

"I know this for sure, America. I love you very much." He smiled and rested his hands on her waist. "I love you more than anything else on this earth. I really knew it when Daniels decided that I was going to head your escort detail behind enemy lines. I didn't want you to go. I loved you too much. It was too risky. "

"Thank you for wanting to protect me." She said softly. "You must know when I tell you I love you, Richard, it means forever." She touched his bandaged cheek.

"And I you."

Saturday, July 2, 1864
Prentiss Farm

AJ smiled as she neared the house. Richard stood on the porch, leaning against one of the rails, staring out across the Rappahannock.

"Good morning, Mr. Evans." He turned and smiled when he saw her. Last night had gone so much better than he expected.

"Good morning, ma'am." He drawled and touched his finger to his cap.

"You're looking well this morning."

"Yes. I may be limping, but at least I can walk fairly well." He sat down in one of the porch rocking chairs. "Do you have time to join me?" He smiled. AJ smiled back and accepted his invitation. She knew that if he was walking on his own, it wouldn't be long before he would rejoin his unit. "America, there's something I would like to talk to you about." Richard began.

"You're going to leave soon, aren't you?" She tried not to sound too emotional, but it had been so nice having him around this past month.

"By the middle of the month, yes. I can't just forsake my commitment to the cause."

"Even though it's a lost cause now," AJ commented.

"That's not what I wanted to talk to you about. I mean, it plays a part in my decision. America..." He pulled her chair around so that they were facing each other. "America, you know I love you. I know that our past has been rocky and our future is uncertain but I want to spend as much time with you as possible before I leave." He paused and took a deep breath. "I want to spend the time that we have left together with you as my wife."

AJ could barely contain her smile. "Richard, what are you saying?"

Richard took her hands in his and looked into her blue eyes. "I would ask your father's permission if I could, but I did talk to Liberty, this morning. I asked her if she would give me her blessing in regards to requesting your hand in marriage. She liked the idea. So... America Joan Prentiss. I love you with all of my heart. Will you marry me?"

"Richard, of course, I will." She leaned forward and kissed him. "When?"

"As soon as possible." He smiled. "When Belle was here yesterday, I mentioned my plan to her. She said that she would talk to my mother and stop and check with Father Schmitz. I'm hoping he will be available to perform a ceremony. So... How about this afternoon?"

"So soon?" Her heart beat and her eyes widened.

"If that's okay with you." Richard hastened to clarify. "I wouldn't want to rush you into anything."

"No, it's not too soon. Heavens, Richard, I have dreamed of becoming your wife for years. This afternoon, though. Fredericksburg is free of Yankee control, but there are still some up at Chatham, we can't let them see you. Also, are you agreeable to being married in the Church?"

"Yes. You know my mother, she made sure I was baptized in the Catholic Church. I think it will be a good place to be married."

AJ smiled. "All right." She thought about some other details. "I'm sure if you spoke with Belle about this yesterday, she has a lot of the details worked out."

"She said she would take care of everything." Richard smiled.

"This is so sudden, but...I am excited."

"Then let's head to St. Mary's." He smiled.

AJ, Richard, and Liberty arrived at the church around noon and hadn't been there long when a wagon came up. Driven by Eric, it held Belle, Elizabeth, Mrs. Turner and the rest of their family. Elizabeth couldn't contain her smile and hopped out of the wagon the second it came to a stop.

"Oh, AJ!" She hurried to her friend and hugged her. "I'm so happy for you."

"I'm glad that you were all able to be here. How did you know I would say yes?"

"Belle had a feeling. Besides, if you didn't, we were just going to have a picnic." She turned back toward the wagon. Eric was helping the rest of the family out of the wagon.

"We were able to procure some food for a celebration after the ceremony at Turner's Glenn. Ruthie has been working all morning."

"Father Schmitz will be ready in about a half hour, and Richard, your mother should be here even sooner. She said your father was out of town on business, but she is excited to see you." Belle said, then handed him, a package. "This is for you. You can thank Elizabeth, not me, she did all of the work." Then, she grabbed AJ's arm and pulled her to the Church. "Now, Miss Prentiss, let's get you ready to be married."

It was a simple ceremony. Liberty stood up for AJ while Eric did so for Richard. AJ wore her best dress, one that she had worn as a ball gown before the war. It was dark blue silk with white trim and black

517

stripes along the skirt and bodice. The blue made her eyes sparkle. The package from Elizabeth to Richard had been his Confederate uniform, all cleaned and repaired looking almost new.

After the ceremony, the group gathered at Turner's Glenn. The dinner was simple but delicious. The guests seemed to enjoy the idea of having something to celebrate in the middle of the war.

"I am so happy for you, AJ." Belle hugged her friend again.

"I am so glad that you were able to plan all of this," AJ replied.

"Richard looks dangerously dashing with that scar. It actually enhances his good looks if I do say so myself." Elizabeth commented.

"Don't tell him that," Belle said. "We don't need him to be more conceded." She smiled. "Congratulations again, AJ, or should I say, Mrs. Evans."

"I like the sound of that." AJ continued to smile.

Liberty approached. "AJ, Meri told me I could stay at Turner's Glenn for a few days. Is that okay with you?"

"It's more than okay, Liberty, you are definitely staying at Turner's Glenn," Belle said. "You may not be able to have an actual wedding trip, AJ, but we can make sure you and Richard have some time alone."

"I don't want to be in the newlywed's way," Liberty said.

"You're never in the way, Liberty." Richard came up behind AJ, placing his hand on the curve of her back. "In fact, you were the best of chaperones these past few weeks."

"You're telling me you don't want any time alone?" Liberty asked.

"I didn't say that." Richard grinned. "Time with just me and my beautiful new wife? I am very much in favor of that."

AJ could barely contain her happiness, but knowing Richard would be leaving in a few weeks made her even more determined to spend as much time with her new husband as possible.

Prentiss Farm

"I would carry you across the threshold, but I am sorry to say I don't believe my leg is up to it," Richard said.

"I wouldn't have expected you to do so," AJ said. "It's quite all right. We can forgo some wedding traditions."

They entered the house and Richard took her hands in his and glanced at the clock that sat on the mantle.

"You know, Mrs. Evans, we've been married for about...seven hours and we have yet to do what most married couples do at their wedding."

AJ blushed and looked at him. "Richard..."

He kissed her softly on the lips. "Most couples are able to share a dance on their wedding day. We didn't have a chance to do that."

"Dance?" AJ smiled.

"Yes, dance. I believe I owe you a dance or two from the days when I was too bullheaded to appreciate you."

"That is true." She slid her hand down his arms. "But we don't have music."

Richard pulled her into his arms, took her hand in his, and then put his other hand on her waist. Giggling, she put her free hand on his shoulder. He began to waltz her, albeit slowly, around the room, then began singing:

> *"It's been a year since last we met, we may never meet again.*
> *I have struggled to forget, but the struggle was in vain.*
> *For her voice lives on the breeze, and her spirit comes at will,*
> *In the midnight on the seas, her bright smile haunts me still."*

AJ smiled as he leaned down to rest his forehead to hers. His voice was slightly off-key, but she still loved the gesture. She closed her eyes and turned her head to rest on his shoulder, the smile remaining on her face. *Thank You, Lord.*

Richard finished singing the song, then bent and kissed her gently. "You know, I thought of you, whenever my fellow soldiers sang that song in camp. A lot of the words rang true for me and my feelings for you. I wondered if you...could ever be more than just a friend." He threaded a hand through her hair. "I fought my feelings for so long, AJ." He kissed her forehead, then her nose, then her cheek. "I love you so much."

"I love you too, Richard."

Thursday, July 28, 1864
Prentiss Farm

Richard entered the Prentiss home and smiled. AJ stood at the table, pounding at a lump of dough. She looked up as he entered and smiled back. The past three weeks of married life had been wonderful. Liberty had decided to remain at Turner's Glenn until Richard went back to his unit. In her absence, Richard had stepped in and done what he could to help AJ out. They had fallen quickly into a comfortable routine. The only gloom hanging over their heads was his upcoming departure.

Richard crossed the room and pulled her into an embrace.

"Good afternoon, Mrs. Evans." He gave her a quick kiss.

"Good afternoon to you, husband."

"I like to hear you say that." He pulled her into a hug. She giggled.

"You seem to be in a good mood today, Mr. Evans."

"Of course, I'm married to the most beautiful, talented, wonderful women that I know." He smiled at her blushing cheeks.

"You seem to have a knack for working on a farm," AJ remarked.

"It is not as bad as I anticipated. Growing up, I felt nothing but disdain for common farmers. But now, I can see just how noble the work is." He said, sitting at the table.

"America, please take a rest." He took her hand in his as she did as he asked. "I know we've been avoiding the topic of my returning to my unit. But...we need to discuss it."

She squeezed his hands. "Is this really the best time?"

"There is no good time to discuss this, AJ, there never will be a good time."

"No, I suppose not." AJ clenched his fists in her lap. "When do you need to leave?"

"If I don't leave soon, I may continue to find reasons not to go back. My feelings are so torn on this. I want more than anything to stay here with you, run this farm with you, have children with you, and start building a good, honest life here with you."

"I want that too, Richard." AJ watched as her husband paced back and forth.

"I must return to my unit, but things are not going well for the Confederacy. You know that just as much as I do. I've healed enough to go back and help finish what we started, even if things don't go our way. I can't abandon my fellow soldiers."

"I knew this day would come, Richard, and I have dreaded it. I know you are too honorable to abandon your duty. I was praying that the war would end while you were still here."

"That would have been nice, but Lee will keep us fighting until the bitter end, and the men will follow him wherever he goes, especially the Virginians."

"Lee is a good man to follow," AJ commented, then stood and took Richard into her arms. "When are you planning on leaving?" She tried to fight back tears but was unsuccessful. Richard reached up and brushed a tear from her cheek.

"Tomorrow morning." He replied. "I have been meaning to tell you, really, I have…"

"Well, then. I suppose we need to make the most of today." She tried to smile.

Richard smiled back. He knew many women would be hysterical, or that they would try to use feminine wiles to stop a man from leaving or to get their way. But not his America. She was so strong, so amazing.

"Even though our troops have all but left the area, you be sure to let Major Daniels know that I will still do whatever I can for the cause, provided he sends the same contact he always has. I feel most comfortable with him."

520

Richard leaned down and kissed her. "I'm not sure I want my wife…"

"No argument, Richard Evans. You go back to work for the cause, then I do too. It's not as if there will be much information for me to relay anyway, but I will continue to do my part."

"I should have expected you to say that," Richard replied. "Well, Mrs. Evans, it's nearing dinner time, and as it will likely be my last good home-cooked meal in a while…:

"If you're trying to flatter me, it is working." AJ smiled. "I will make some extra food for you tonight as well so that you can take it with you. I can't have my husband starving."

Later that evening, after dinner, AJ grabbed a quilt, took her husband's hand and pulled him out of the house.

"Where are you taking me?" He asked.

"You'll see." She replied with a slightly nervous smile. "I don't want to ruin the surprise."

"I do like surprises," Richard replied, then took the quilt from her and tucked it under his own arm. The evening was perfect. It was warm, but there was a gentle, cool breeze that kept the air from being too muggy. The sky was clear, and the sun was beginning to set behind the Rappahannock. As they headed up toward Stafford Heights, Richard looked across the river. "The view is absolutely breathtaking." He remarked.

"Yes, it is." AJ agreed. She continued leading him until they reached her destination. "Here we are." She took the quilt from him and laid it out on in the grass. "This is my most favorite spot in the Fredericksburg area."

"I can see why," Richard replied, sitting on the quilt. He spread his legs and patted the ground between them, inviting his wife to sit down. AJ sat down and leaned back against Richard as his arms came around her. She placed a hand on his wounded thigh. "Are you sure this is better?"

He placed his chin on her shoulder. "It's well enough." He replied. "Don't worry, AJ, I'll be alright."

She turned her head and looked up at him, skepticism showing on her face. "You cannot say that, Richard. Not after everything we've been through. Three and a half years of war. Thousands of men have been killed. You know how easily and quickly death can come."

"I know that. I'm not so naive that I don't know what I'm going back to, but there are some differences now. I have someone to come home to, that's most important." She smiled, then lay her head back on his shoulder. "I can't believe the South can continue to survive. We have lost too many men and have so few resources left to be able to fight much longer. I'd say less than a year."

"A year is a long time," AJ commented.

"I know, but here is why I said that I'll be all right." He adjusted himself so that he could look at his wife. "Because of you and what you have taught me these past three years. What you have taught me about God and love. I now know if I am killed...if I don't come home from this war, I need you to know that I will be at Heaven's gate, waiting for you. In fact, once this war is over and I do come home, I want to become a member of the Church."

Tears welled up in AJ's eyes, but they were tears of gladness. "I have suspected that, Richard, and you don't know how happy that makes me."

Monday, August 8, 1864
Prentiss Farm

"Hey, there, sister." Nathaniel came up behind AJ, who had been hanging clothes on the laundry line.

"Nathaniel!" AJ squealed and threw her arms around him. "What are you doing here?"

"I was able to stop home, as it was en route from my latest mission." He hugged her back. "I've missed you."

"It has been ever so long." She said, pulling back to look at her brother. "How have you been?"

"Good. I have so much to tell you. So much news."

"We have much news too. So much has happened here as well." AJ couldn't contain her smile. "Come on inside. I have a pot of stew on and can heat some coffee." They headed into the house.

"I'm surprised you still have coffee. I've heard that it is hard to come by."

"Well, the Yanks are still at Chatham and your idea to have me make friends with the Yankee soldiers has many benefits. Trading fresh vegetables for coffee is one of them."

"That's good. I'm glad they haven't caught on to you yet."

"No, they haven't."

"Where's Liberty?" Nathaniel asked.

"Across the river in Fredericksburg. We needed a few supplies we couldn't get from the Yankees and we also had some eggs to bring in for trade."

"I hope I get to see her." He commented.

"She shouldn't be gone much longer," AJ assured him.

"Good. I miss her." Nathaniel sat down as AJ went to the stove to get him some food. "I must tell you, one of the main reasons I stopped by was because I ran into Richard Evans, of all people a few days ago. I almost didn't recognize him. His face was badly scarred and he has lost some of his arrogance. He looked genuinely happy, though. Anyway, he told me that I should come home and see you, that you had something to tell me. Any idea what that is all about?"

"Actually, Nathaniel, I do." AJ handed her brother his bowl of stew. He took it, then noticed her ring. He grabbed her wrist.

"AJ, what's this?" He looked at her, shock on his face. She smiled.

"That is probably the reason Richard told you to stop home. It is his grandmother's ring."

Nathaniel blinked as comprehension dawned. He didn't smile as AJ thought he would. Instead, he almost looked angry.

"Richard Evans?" He said slowly.

"Yes. We were married shortly after he was wounded, just a little over a month ago."

"Why?" Nathaniel stood. "What did you do? Are you...did he compromise you?"

"What? No. He is always a gentleman with me. I cannot believe you would think so lowly of me." AJ was discouraged with Nathaniel's reaction. She had hoped he would be happy for her but that did not appear to be the case.

"Then why...what would possess you to even consider marrying that man?"

"Nathaniel..."

"AJ, he has always treated you poorly. When you were younger, he was never kind to you. I seem to recall some conversations with you earlier in the war about how he was treating you with disrespect."

"He's changed, Nathaniel. He's not the same man he used to be."

"You believe that? Honestly, AJ, you're smarter than that." Nathaniel's eyes flashed and he ran a hand through his hair.

"Nathaniel. What ..."

"He's a rake, AJ, men like that don't change. He seduces women. He promises them things and then walks away, breaking their hearts. He's made you cry before, don't think I've forgotten that."

"I know all about his history, Nathaniel. I remember that he has hurt me in the past, but I also know that he has changed. He has made me very happy this past year. He makes me feel loved, cherished, appreciated, worthy of a man's attentions."

"Oh, I'm sure he does. He's a smooth talker."

"Well, there's an issue with your argument, Nathaniel. If all he wanted was to use and discard me, then why did he marry me?"

"I don't know."

523

"Because he loves me, and I love him, Nathaniel. I really wish you could spend time with him now. Get to know who he has become. He is a good, decent man. He always has been down deep inside."

"Always has been? AJ, I cannot understand why you would believe that!" Nathaniel started to pace.

"Because it's true, and I wish I knew how I could get you to understand it."

"I don't think I can or ever will. When I think of you two together, all I think of is the time I walked in on your crying because you overheard something he said about you."

"Nathaniel, that was over ten years ago. I've forgiven him. He's my husband now. It doesn't really matter what you think or what you believe. It's done. I want you to approve of my marriage, but if you don't believe I'm smart enough to make this decision...well, that's your affair. Not mine. Liberty approves. My friends see the change in him. You always treat Belle's word as gold, why don't you ask her?" She took a deep breath. "Nathaniel, he risked his life for me, not just once, but several times. He doesn't just tell me he cares about me, he shows me. We love each other and, God willing, Richard will survive this war and we will spend the rest of our lives together. I only hope you'll be a part of that life."

"I'm not sure about that," Nathaniel said. "I don't know if I can." He grabbed his hat and strode out the door.

"Nathaniel, wait! Nathaniel!" AJ called, but he was already gone.

Sunday, September 25, 1864
Turner's Glenn

"Belle! The most horrible news!" AJ burst into the parlor at Turner's Glenn.

"What? Has something happened to Richard?" Belle's heart pounded.

"No, not Richard, Sandie. I just received a letter from JP Smith, he hasn't written me in such a long time, but he did with this news. Sandie was rallying the troops and trying to assist in establishing a line of resistance south of Fisher's Hill at Winchester. He was wounded in the abdomen."

Belle's hand flew to her mouth. She had been around enough injured men to know that an abdomen wound could easily be fatal. "Oh, my. Will he live?"

"Captain Smith wasn't sure," AJ replied. "Henry Kyd Douglass was with him and Dr. McGuire is tending him. He's recovering at a place called Woodstock."

"My goodness. Poor, poor Kate, I must go to her." Belle stood. "Let me think. Daniel will have to escort me, there is no one else. Yes, I can do this. Kate will need all the support she can get."

"Especially if the worst happens." AJ agreed. "I am so glad she moved to Lexington back in July. It would be quite difficult for you to see her if she were still in Richmond. Oh, I do hope Kate is doing well. This stress cannot be good for her in her condition."

"Yes." Belle looked at her friend. "What about you? Would you like to come as well?"

"I would like to, yes, but I don't think I can manage it right now with Liberty and the crops to be harvested."

"Of course," Belle said. "I spoke in haste as well, I should check to be sure that mother can do without me."

"Annie is twenty-two years old now. I am sure your mother can manage with just her help. I can stop by and check on everyone as well and I am sure that Elizabeth and Eric will also." AJ sighed. "I would feel better if one of us went to be with Kate, and the most logical person is you."

Belle nodded. "I will talk to Daniel and Mother right away. I don't think there will be any problems with me going."

"I am going to ride out to Belle Hill and give Kate's father the news, then head back home," AJ said.

"I will leave for Lexington as soon as possible," Belle said. "AJ, thank you for the information. I do hope to find Sandie at home recovering from his wounds with Kate nursing him back to health."

"Of course. And thank you for traveling to see Kate. Godspeed." AJ gave Kate a quick hug. "Give her our love and tell her we are praying for her and for Sandie's health."

Saturday, October 1, 1864
Lexington, Virginia

Belle's trip to Lexington was uneventful and she was welcomed into the Pendleton home with open arms. She was there for almost a week when hope in the home was revived by two messages. The preceding days had been filled with mixed reports on Sandie's fate but they were all unconfirmed and contradictory. The atmosphere in the home was strained, with Kate constantly wavering between fear and hope.

Belle and Kate were sitting in the parlor when Anzolette, Sandie's mother, called out from the entryway.

"Jim is here!"

Kate perked up immediately. "Jim Lewis is Sandie's servant." She said. "He should know exactly what has happened." She hastened to the entryway.

"I've two messages for you, Ma'am," Jim said. "First, Dr. McGuire charged me to tell you that Mr. Sandie was wounded and that the wound was quite dangerous, though he does not believe he will die. The doctor left Mr. Sandie at the home of a fine, southern family because, unfortunately, that home is now behind Yankee lines, as our army is in retreat. It has also been difficult to get news through."

Kate nodded, clutching her hands together. Belle put a comforting arm around her friend.

"The other news is encouraging as well, ma'am. It's from Captain Henry Kyd Douglas. He sent me a letter and spoke as if he entertained hopes of Sandie's recovery and return to you soon."

"Sandie is alive, I know he is." Kate slid a hand down to cradle her stomach. It wouldn't be much more than a month before she gave birth.

"That is wonderful news, Kate." Belle hoped her friend was right.

"Thank you so much, Jim," Kate said. The man nodded and left. Kate turned to Sue and Belle. "I believe I will go and lie down for a while. This news has exhausted me."

After Kate left, Belle turned to Sue Lee. "This is promising, is it not?

"It is good that the family is buoyed up with hope." Sandie's sister replied. "However, between you and I, Miss Turner, from the very beginning of this ordeal, I have not doubted our precious boy is gone. I fear that this hopefulness will, in the end, increase their deadly sorrow."

"I am sorry you feel that way," Belle said. "I just think it would be much better if we knew, one way or the other, what has happened to Sandie. All of this stress can't be good for Kate or her child."

"No, it cannot. At least she is getting some rest now." Sue sighed. "I am glad you're here, Miss Turner. Your presence has been such a comfort to Kate."

"I am too, yet sometimes I feel as though I have already stayed longer than I expected, and I plan on staying until we get some definite news about Sandie. As long as I don't wear out my welcome."

"As far as I'm concerned, you are welcome here for as long as Kate needs you and I am sure the rest of the family feels the same way."

"I hope and pray that when I do leave, it is because we have received happy news."

Sunday, October 9, 1864
Bennett Home

"Has there been any word from Belle or Kate?" AJ asked the question as soon as she had greeted her friend.

"We heard from Belle just yesterday," Elizabeth said somberly and continued to chop some vegetables for a venison stew. "Rumors are flying all around Lexington. Dr. McGuire arrived last Monday with the news that Sandie had died even back before you received word of his injury. Belle said that Ned Lee, Sandie's brother-in-law, wrote Monday as well, confirming Dr. McGuire's statement, but since all communications south of Woodstock, where Sandie was left after his injury, have been severed, all of these reports are unconfirmed. No one really knows how Sandie is, whether he is alive or dead."

"How distressing for Kate! It would have been better that she not be told he was wounded at all. No news would be better than constant worry. Does Belle intend on staying longer?"

"Yes, at least until they find out for sure about Sandie," Elizabeth answered. "Belle also said this latest news plunged the Pendleton family into despair. Apparently, Sue Lee has felt certain from the beginning that he was killed. Kate is bewildered by all of these contradictory rumors and only the grace of God has upheld her."

"I cannot imagine what Kate is going through right now," AJ said. "I wish I could visit her as well. I just have too many responsibilities here to be gone that long."

"I know how you feel," Elizabeth said. "It also wouldn't be right if we all were to descend on the Pendleton family at this trying time. Belle is the best person to be supporting Kate."

"I have been writing to Kate and Belle often, encouraging them both as best I can. I have also been praying for Kate and Sandie." AJ said.

"Unfortunately, that is all we can do right now, AJ," Elizabeth replied.

Monday, October 17, 1864
Lexington, Virginia

Belle entered the parlor and saw Kate sitting in a chair, staring out the window.

"I take it there is no word from Woodstock," Belle said, sitting close to her friend.

"No," Kate replied. "Sometimes I hope we don't receive a letter at all. I fear it will be bad news and then, that will be it. My marriage will be over. I don't know if I will be able to bear that kind of news. Not knowing for sure allows me to have hope."

"I understand the pain you must be suffering through, Kate," Belle said, reaching over and covering her hands. "You have had to endure so much loss already. I don't know how you manage."

"With help from family and friends, and God of course. I am so glad that you came, Belle. I don't know how I could get through any of this without you and my family. Please don't leave, at least not until the

527

baby is born." She rested her hand on her rounded abdomen. "I pray that Sandie will be able to meet his child."

Belle was about to give Kate some more comforting words when Sue entered the room. Her face was solemn. "You have received a letter, Kate, from a Mrs. Murphy of Woodstock. Mama received one as well."

Kate inhaled deeply and took the letter from Sue's outstretched hand. She somehow knew what the letter said.

"I don't think I want to read this." She whispered and handed it to Belle. "Could you please…?"

Belle immediately took the letter and began reading it. Her heart dropped at the words.

"Oh, Kate, I am so, so sorry." Tears streamed down Belle's face as she handed Kate the letter.

"Sandie! No, not Sandie too!" Kate clutched her stomach and hunched over, tears flowing from her eyes. "No, no, no." She tried to take a deep breath but felt as though she could not breathe. Her dreams were gone forever. No house in the woods, no more sunsets to watch together, no more long walks and talks. Sandie would never hold his child and their child would never know its father.

"God, please don't let this be true." She placed one hand on her temple and kept the other on her unborn child.

Belle looked up at Sue, only to see that the woman had left, no doubt to mourn on her own. Belle knew what Sue was going through by losing a brother, but she could not fathom what Kate was going through. Her dear friend had lost her mother as a young woman. She had lost her brother in the war and she had lost two nephews and a niece to a dreadful disease. Now, she had lost her soulmate, the love of her life, the father of her unborn child.

"Oh, Kate." Belle knelt at her friend's feet and pulled her into her arms. It was quite awkward with Kate's condition, but she didn't care.

"Why, Belle? Why?" Kate held Belle as tightly as possible.

"Kate, I don't know. I wish I could say or do something to make this news all go away."

"What will I do, Belle? What will I do with my life? How will I raise this child?" It was difficult to understand Kate through her sobbing.

"Oh, my dear!" Mrs. Pendleton said from the doorway. Her eyes were red but other than that, it seemed as though she was bearing her affliction with fortitude and resignation. Kate stood slowly and moved as quickly as she could into her mother-in-law's arms. "My dear Kate, you know you will always have a home with us. Always. I know this isn't the news we wanted to hear, but we must have faith that our Sandie is in a better place now. We must be thankful to our merciful Savior for all of His goodness to Sandie and to us all." Kate slowed down her breathing as Mrs. Pendleton gently rubbed her back.

Belle was still kneeling in front of the chair where she had been with Kate. Mrs. Pendleton continued. "We are so blessed that Jesus Christ opened the Kingdom of Heaven to all believers. That is assurance that our dear Sandie is in the mansion that has been prepared for him, and we will see him again someday in paradise."

"Do you truly believe that, Mother Pendleton?"

"I do, Kate. I do." Mrs. Pendleton took her handkerchief and wiped Kate's cheeks.

"I want to believe you, I do, but...it may take me some time." Kate took a deep breath. "Excuse me. I don't want to be rude, but I need to go and lie down." Kate turned slowly and left the room. Belle made a move to follow, but Mrs. Pendleton stopped her.

"We must let Kate be on her own for a while, Miss Turner. She needs some time alone. We can check on her in an hour or so."

Belle nodded, then turned to the woman. "Mrs. Pendleton, I am so sorry about Sandie. He was a wonderful man."

"I know he was." Mrs. Pendleton said. "It is what gives me comfort at this time. I know he is in heaven and that I will see him again. This is not where his life ends. He will live on in the hearts of those who love him and he will live on in his child."

Belle thought for a moment. "I suppose that's true of anyone who has died."

"Yes. They live on in our hearts."

"My older brother never had the chance to be a father but he was a valuable part of his nephew's life and my younger brother always wanted to be just like James."

"I would guess he was a valuable part of your life as well." Mrs. Pendleton said. "Your life was made richer because of him, and all of our lives were made richer by having Sandie in our lives."

"That is true," Belle said. "Very true indeed." She was impressed with Mrs. Pendleton and her inner strength. The woman had just lost a son, yet here she was, helping Belle with wounds that were years old. "Thank you, Mrs. Pendleton. You have been so kind. I believe I will excuse myself to go and write a letter home. I must give my sister the unfortunate news. Please let me know if I can be of any service to you or your family."

"You can continue to be supportive of Kate." Mrs. Pendleton said. "She will need you even more now with her confinement so close."

"Yes, of course, I will," Belle replied, then departed to write her letter.

Monday, October 29, 1864
Lexington, Virginia

Kate lay in her bed, staring at the ceiling. She hadn't been able to sleep recently, yet she was always tired. She had no appetite, but had been forcing herself to eat for the sake of her unborn child. She couldn't let Sandie down. She had to make sure his child was born safe and healthy. She firmly believed the child was a boy, at least, she hoped it was. A boy with his father's smile and wit, who would constantly keep her on her toes.

Kate didn't want to think about the future. She didn't want to worry about what was to come. Four days earlier, Sue and Sandie's mother had walked to the cemetery and looked at the grave site where Sandie would be buried. It was quite near Sandie's mentor, General Thomas Stonewall Jackson. Kate hadn't wanted to go. If she didn't think too hard, she could imagine that Sandie wasn't dead, that he was still away, fighting and would return to her soon.

There was a knock at the door and Anzolette entered the room. Kate was envious of how well the woman had taken the death of her only son because Kate felt as though her whole world had fallen apart.

"Kate, my dear. We expect him today." Her mother-in-law said.

"Who?" Kate asked, emotionless.

"Our beloved Sandie."

Kate tried to be calm and stoic, but she suddenly began weeping. Mrs. Pendleton came to her side and took Kate in her arms.

"Oh, dear. What can I do for you?" Mrs. Pendleton stroked Kate's hair as a mother would.

"I wish I had your strength. Could you...pray for me?" Kate asked between tears.

"Of course, my dear. I already am."

"Could you make a wreath for me?" She asked. Mourning wreaths were common, but not all women could get locks of their deceased loved one's hair.

"I can do that." Mrs. Pendleton pulled back to look at Kate. "Would you like to visit...him?" She asked. "He is being brought to our Episcopal Church."

"I...I do wish I could lay my head on the coffin, to feel close to him, yet I am afraid if I do, his death will be real. I don't feel I will be able to accept Sandie's death if I don't. Oh botheration, I am so indecisive."

"We'll take you to see him tonight, Kate. It will give you the closure you so desperately need and tomorrow we will put him to rest.

"I don't know if I will be up to it tomorrow," Kate said, eyes welling up with tears again. "Maybe I will just keep to my room."

"We will see how you feel tomorrow, Kate." Mrs. Pendleton said. "In the meantime, we'll go to the church after supper."

Before dusk, Mr. Robert Nelson, a family friend of the Pendleton's, drove Kate and Belle to Grace Episcopal Church, the church that Sandie had attended for so long. Sandie's body, which had, for a time, been buried near the Winchester battlefield, had arrived earlier that day, escorted by a military guard of honor. Even at this late hour, an escort was standing guard. When Kate and Belle arrived, JP Smith stood to greet them. He immediately gave Kate a compassionate hug, then escorted her to the casket. He returned to his place to give Kate some privacy. He quietly greeted Belle.

"It is good to see you safe, Captain Smith," Belle said. "I only wish our reacquaintance could have been under happier circumstances."

"As do I." He replied. "How is Kate, really? She looks quite fatigued."

"She is doing her best. She eats and sleeps fairly well overall. I believe the welfare of her child is of utmost importance to her. Caring for herself is caring for the baby."

"I am glad to hear that." Captain Smith nodded.

"How are you holding up yourself, Captain?" Belle asked.

"Sandie was my closest friend." He replied. "We could talk about anything and everything. Hopes, dreams, plans for after the war. We often talked about entering the ministry together at the close of the war." He shook his head. "He would have made a wonderful preacher."

"He would have, and you can still do so." Belle touched his arm. JP Smith sighed and changed the subject.

"How are things in Fredericksburg? You and your family? Miss Prentiss? I wrote to tell her of Sandie being wounded, but that was a while ago and I haven't written at all since."

"AJ is not Miss Prentiss anymore," Belle said with a small smile. "She and Captain Richard Evans were married a few months ago."

"I know Captain Evans. He is a fine soldier, a good man. I am sure they will have a good marriage." JP Smith smiled sadly. "He is a lucky man. I rather suspected long ago that she was holding a spot in her heart for someone other than myself."

"Indeed," Belle said, then filled him in on other news in Fredericksburg. By the time they had caught up, Kate had turned from the casket and was sitting down in the front pew. Belle went to her.

"Kate, do you need more time or are you ready to go home?" She asked.

"I don't know what I want, except for Sandie to be alive," Kate replied, eyes red. She looked at Captain Smith as he approached.

531

"Captain, thank you so much for everything you have done for Sandie, absolutely everything. He always told me you were the best friend that any man could ever have. He valued every word you said and thought the world of you."

"Thank you for saying so." Tears shone in Captain Smith's eyes. "Those feelings were mutual, Ma'am." He took a breath. "I know you ladies have an escort, but I would like to accompany you back home as well to pay my respect to Mrs. Pendleton before the funeral tomorrow."

"Of course," Kate said, and they made their way back to the carriage.

Thursday, October 27, 1864
Bennett Home

"AJ, hello. What brings you here?" Elizabeth smiled as she opened the door and saw her friend on the porch.

"I was in town getting some supplies and wanted to stop by to see if you have heard anything new from Lexington," AJ said, entering the house. She smiled to see Hannah and Benjamin at the kitchen table, doing schoolwork. Hannah had a children's book in front of her. "My goodness, Hannah! Are you reading that all by yourself?"

"Yes, Miss AJ! I mean, Mrs. Evans." She smiled, showing a small gap in her lower teeth.

"You can still call me Miss AJ if you would like." She replied. "Can you read a bit to me?"

"Of course." Hannah pointed out every word as she read it. "'Once upon a time, there were three zebras. One zebra's name was Brianne. The other zebra's name was Kendall. The last zebra's name was Zachary.'"

"My word. A story about zebras sounds very interesting indeed." AJ said.

Elizabeth smiled and rubbed Hannah's hair. "I'm not sure if she can really read as well as she can memorize."

"You two can go outside and play while Miss AJ and I talk. Make sure you put on a jacket."

"Yes, Mama." The two children hopped down from their chairs, grabbed a jacket and dashed outside.

"I wish I had half the amount of energy as those children have," Elizabeth said, sitting down across from AJ. "In answer to your initial question, I received a letter from Belle just today. I was going to find time to visit you this afternoon."

"How is dear Kate?"

"She didn't go to the funeral. Belle stayed at the house with her. Everyone is concerned for Kate's welfare, but Belle feels she is enduring the strain as well as possible."

532

"That is good. I trust she knows Kate best." AJ said. "What else does Belle say?"

"After the funeral, the family spent most of the day in Kate's room, reading letters. Kate didn't go to the funeral, apparently because she was exhausted, but the next day, the day Belle wrote her letter to me, Kate, Sue, and Mrs. Pendleton went to the cemetery. Kate wanted to see Sandie's grave. Belle says the flowers at the cemetery were still beautifully fresh and it was good for Kate to visit. It is also a comfort to Kate that Sandie is buried near Stonewall Jackson. He was so devoted to the General."

"I sympathize with Kate so," AJ said softly. "I keep thinking of what I would do if I lost Richard. It is strange how quickly our lives and happiness can be so caught up in one person."

"I know what you mean. I have feared that I would lose Joshua since before this war began. I worry every day and pray that God brings him safely home, but Kate did the same. We prayed for James and all our soldiers to be safe, yet James and so many soldiers still died. I know the wives and mothers of all of the Federal soldiers are praying as well. Sometimes..." She paused, not knowing if she should confess what was on her mind. "AJ, I know God is up there, and I know he cares for us, but sometimes I wonder why we even pray. Does it really help? If God has His plan, why do we even need to pray?"

"I am sure God likes to hear us talking with Him, and that's what we're doing when we pray. What I mean is, even if you know what Eric, Benjamin, Hannah or Joshua's needs are, it is still nice to hear them ask, and it's nice to have a conversation with them. Don't you agree?"

"Oh, I know, AJ," Elizabeth responded. "I'm sorry to sound so negative, but I have these moments where I don't feel sure our prayers are working."

"We all feel that way at times. If believing was always easy, it wouldn't be faith." AJ replied with a smile. "And we all need faith."

Friday, November 4, 1864
Lexington-Pendleton Home

"Kate, how are you feeling this morning?" Belle asked, entering her friend's room. Kate sat in her bed propped on pillows against the headboard, knitting a blanket for her child.

"I must say, I have felt better," Kate admitted. "My back aches again and I am feeling so very tired, and this swelling makes it difficult to get a good night's sleep."

"Patience, Kate, it will all pass soon when that wee one decides to make an appearance." Belle sat down. "You never told me how your visit with Reverend Dabney went." The Reverend Dr. R.L. Dabney was a war comrade of Sandie's from General Jackson's staff back in 1862. The man had come to pay his respects to the family. Many people who had been touched by Sandie's life had done likewise.

"It was so good to see him again," Kate said, grimacing and rubbing her stomach. "He told me that so many of his friends have fallen during the war that he believed he could feel no more grief, but when he was informed of Sandie's death, he was surprised at the amount of sorrow he felt."

"I have heard many good things about Sandie from so many people, Kate," Belle said. She pulled out a newspaper clipping. "I don't know if you've read this yet, but it is an obituary published in the Richmond Daily Enquirer. I believe it was written by JP Smith."

"I don't know that I have read it. Can you read it to me?" Kate adjusted herself on the bed, trying to get comfortable. She fingered the locket around her neck, which Belle knew held a lock of Sandie's hair. Belle nodded.

"This article discusses Sandie's intellectual qualities especially." She cleared her throat. "'His intellectual powers were of the highest order. His mind was strong and vigorous in grasp, quick in perception, versatile and very active in its working. His judgment was cool, clear, and ready. His energy was untiring. In the office, quick and clear-headed; on the field, cool, grave, intelligent; the readiness with which he approached his duty, under the circumstances of the moment, was equaled by the celerity and skill with which he performed it. As a staff officer, he had no equal.'" Kate smiled tiredly as Belle continued to read. "He was so quick-witted and truly had a way with words."

"Indeed," Belle said. "The article then discusses Sandie's qualities of the heart. 'Generous to his friends, magnanimous to his foes, kind to all, his soul was cast in too large a mold to be tainted with the failings of smaller men. No one possessed warmer affections, no one was more ready to sympathize with and soothe the sorrows of others. His whole character was controlled and directed by a high-toned sense of honor and duty, sustained by a calm, pure faith he trod with cheerfulness the path of duty. When once convinced of what was right, no repining at sacrifice, no hesitancy delayed its compliance with it.'" She took a breath and continued. "'His fall was not unheeded. Many a soldier of this army felt more than usual sorrow when he saw the dying form of this noble leader borne away. Many a heart sank with sadness to learn that the cheerful voice of the sanguine, hopeful officer would be heard no more. Many a war-worn veteran dropped a tear to think the face which had become familiar among the storm of a hundred battlefields was gone forever. But how shall I speak of that sadness which oppresses the circle of friends of which he was the center or allude to the still more sacred sorrow of those nearer and dearer?'"

Tears shone in Kate's eyes. "He was such a wonderful man, Belle. I wish desperately that we would have found some way to be married sooner. Perhaps if I hadn't been so stubborn..." She gritted her teeth to try and hold in pain. "Argh."

"Kate, what is the matter?" Belle reached over and put a hand on Kate's shoulder.

"I think it is good that Aunt Molly arrived yesterday," Kate said, teeth still clenched. Aunt Molly was an old slave from Fredericksburg who had attended Kate's mother at the birth of her children. "I thank Father so much for sending her because I believe we need her now."

"Oh, my goodness. Kate, is it time? Belle's eyes widened.

"I think it might be!" Kate replied. "Please, go get Aunt Molly!"

"Miss Belle, Miss Kate is askin' fer ya." Aunt Molly came into the parlor where Belle had been reading and working on a letter home that she would finish once Kate's child was born.

"Is Kate all right? The baby?" Belle had heard the cries of a newborn about an hour ago but had wanted to give Kate and her family time to be together.

"The chile' is jus' fine. A healthy baby boy." The woman smiled. "An' Miss Kate be doin' fine too."

"Wonderful!" Belle hastened up the stairs to find Kate looking down at a tiny bundle in her arms.

"Belle! Come and meet my son." Belle smiled and came closer. The boy was sleeping. "You know, I hadn't realized today's date until I asked about it so that I would remember my son's birthday."

"Yes. It is November 4." Belle said with a knowing smile.

"Your 25th birthday. Why didn't you remind me?" Kate chided her friend.

"You had other things on your mind," Belle answered.

"I didn't even get you a gift," Kate said.

"I get to share my birthday with this perfect little man," Belle said, reaching down to touch the newborn's soft arm. "What better gift could there be?"

"You can hold him, you know," Kate said. "If you want to."

"I would love to," Belle replied, then reached out to take the newborn. "Oh, I forgot how small children start out. It seems like forever since Hannah and Benjamin were this size." She placed a finger in his tiny hand. "He's perfect, Kate. So handsome."

"And already a light and joy to the family," Kate said.

"Do I even have to ask his name?" Belle asked, knowing that the boy would be named after his father.

"I don't believe you do," Kate replied. "Everyone knows what he will be called but I would like General Pendleton to formally give him Sandie's name. I also insist that his baptism be performed by his grandfather."

"That sounds reasonable," Belle said with a smile. "You look much better than you did this morning."

"Childbirth was quite unpleasant," Kate said. "But as strange as it sounds, the moment I held my son, all of the pain was forgotten."

Belle looked at the boy with a new sense of longing. She had always planned on having children, she loved having her niece and nephew around, as well as her younger brothers and sisters, but she never really imagined holding her own child in her arms until this moment. Would Aaron be the father of her children? She hoped so. He would make a wonderful father. If they did have children, would they favor her or Aaron?

"I think he favors his father, Kate," Belle said.

"I agree," Kate replied. "It is good that a part of Sandie has been left behind to always comfort us and remind us of how wonderful he was."

"That is a beautiful way to think of him," Belle said, smiling and handing the boy back to Kate. "He is the perfect addition to your family."

"I agree." Kate ran a finger down his smooth cheek. "I cannot believe he is mine. I just keep looking at him." A tear fell down her cheek. "I only wish Sandie could have seen him."

"He can," Belle said. "Sandie was a good man, and I have all the confidence in the world that he is in heaven, watching over you and your son at this very moment."

"Thank you, Belle." Tears continued to slip down her cheek. "I need to keep hearing that."

"You have been through much turmoil, Kate. You must remember that you have many people watching over you, both in Heaven and here on earth. You will always have a place at Turner's Glenn, here in Lexington, and in many other places as well."

"I know. In spite of everything, I have been very blessed."

"We all have been." Belle agreed.

Sunday, November 18, 1864
Lexington~Pendleton Home

"How were services?" Kate asked as Belle entered the parlor. She cuddled Baby Sandie to her chest.

"Good. I hope you feel up to going next week." Belle sat down.

"I hope so as well. I need the fellowship." Kate agreed. "Is there any news?"

"Northerners re-elected Lincoln." Belle scoffed, shaking her head. "So if we lose this war, that man will be our leader again. Heaven help us."

Sandie moved in Kate's arms and gave a short wail.

"You see," Belle said. "Even Baby Sandie agrees that is unacceptable."

"Oh, Sandie." Kate gave a short laugh. "He is growing so quickly, Belle. He almost jumps out of your arms." Kate smiled down at her son. "I love him small, yet I am very curious to see what he will be like when he is older. He is already so interested in what's going on around him. He examines everything, such as the mantle and doors and curtains. It seems as though he smiles at them."

"He will be a philosopher like his father, then." Belle said. "He is so sweet."

"And such a comfort to me," Kate said. "I see some likeness to my side of the family, my brother Tayloe especially." Tazwell Tayloe was Kate's half-brother from her father's second marriage. "I don't think he is as handsome as his uncle, mostly he resembles his father. I hope he will be like Sandie in other ways as well."

"He will," Belle assured her. "I don't think you need to worry about that." She leaned over to gently kiss the boy on the forehead. "Have you considered coming home with me? I am thinking of writing to Elizabeth to have Daniel come and take me home within the next few weeks. I would like to spend Christmas at Turner's Glenn. We would love it if you could join us. You could spend time with your own family."

Kate bit her lip. "As much as I would like to visit home, I believe we should stay. Baby Sandie is such a comfort to everyone here and I wouldn't feel right taking him on such a long trip when he is still so young."

"I suppose that makes sense," Belle said. "I suspect there is another reason you would like to avoid Fredericksburg as well."

"There is. You know me too well, Belle." Kate sighed. "I just...Moss Neck is where I met Sandie, where we fell in love. It is where we were married. Belle, it is where I was the happiest in my life. The war was certainly causing problems, but I still had Sandie. The hope of my future. I am just not ready to go back there. So many memories and his death is too fresh."

"They were good memories, though." Belle pointed out.

"Yes, good ones, but...I don't know. I will be able to visit someday, just not right now." Kate replied.

"All right. That is not the answer I wanted to hear, but I do understand." Belle replied.

"I wish you could stay, but I also know that you have other obligations. I dearly appreciate you being here as long as you have been. I know how much you have sacrificed."

"Yes, I missed helping with the harvest and I am quite upset that I am not getting a chance to help at my home, although most of the patients have been transferred," Belle said with a smile on her face.

"Oh, Belle." Kate smiled back. "You are missing time spent with your family and with Dr. Knightly." Kate pointed out.

"Actually, Aaron was transferred shortly before I came here. I do miss my family, but I do not regret coming here. I felt as though you needed me, so this is where I needed to be."

"I did, Belle. I do not know what I would have done without you here." Kate smiled at her friend in gratitude.

"That is what friendship is all about. If you need me again, don't hesitate to write. No matter where I am, no matter how far I have to travel, I will be there for you."

"I would do the same for you," Kate said. "You are one of the best friends I could ask for."

Sunday, December 4, 1864
Bennett Home

"Welcome, AJ, Liberty. How is your mother-in-law?" Elizabeth asked, letting AJ and Liberty into her home. Benjamin immediately pulled Liberty to the rug in front of the fire for a game of backgammon.

"Mrs. Evans is doing well. She misses Richard, of course, so we have that in common." The two sat down at the dining room table. "Where are Eric and Hannah?"

"Hannah is taking a rest in her room and Eric went hunting," Elizabeth replied. "We received word that Belle will be here tomorrow. Daniel left several days ago to escort her. I am glad she will be home for Christmas." "It may be our last Christmas with Annie. I fear we will lose her after the war or possibly sooner."

"To that soldier who lost his leg? I forgot his name."

"Joseph Byron," Elizabeth answered. "He is very charming and has a good heart. He is also a wonderful judge of character, especially since he chose Annie. They have been corresponding ever since he was discharged home. Apparently, his Father left the service of the Confederacy to take care of him."

"Has he made an offer of marriage to Annie?" AJ asked.

"Not that I know of, Annie would have told me, but as I said, they have been communicating often since he went home in April. I am happy for her, I just wish that he didn't live in South Carolina."

"It is quite a distance away," AJ said. "Have you heard from Joshua at all? Does he feel as many others do about the war not going well for our country?"

"I did hear from him last week. He's stationed in Petersburg, so I don't know if I will hear much more from him until the siege is over." She sighed. "He's trying to stay positive but I believe he sees that the end is near for the Confederacy."

"Richard does as well. He actually felt that way as far back as July when we were married."

"Yet, he still went back," Elizabeth commented.

"Yes. Richard is honorable. He doesn't want to break the commitment he made to the Confederate army." She sighed. "I love him and his sense of duty, and I understand why he went back but sometimes there is a part of me that wishes he wasn't so honorable."

"Yes, but then you likely wouldn't love him the way you do." Elizabeth pointed out.

"You're right," AJ said, then looked out the window longingly. "They say things are very bad down in Georgia."

"I hadn't heard that," Elizabeth said. "What is happening there?"

"Richard wrote me and said it is absolutely horrible, Elizabeth. You must know the Yankee General Sherman captured Atlanta back in September, but did you know as the Confederate soldiers pulled out of the city, General Hood had them destroy all the stores of ammunition and supply depots."

"Why would they do that?" Elizabeth asked.

"So the Yanks couldn't use any of it, but what a waste of needed supplies," AJ explained. "Anyways, now Sherman and his army have left Atlanta and are heading towards the Atlantic Ocean. They are not just marching." AJ shook her head, anger coursing through her as she thought about the destruction. "Oh, no. They are destroying anything and everything in their path." She blew out a breath. "They are foraging much more than they need to and they are burning down mills, houses, cotton-gins, anything they feel will help the Confederates in the war. They are trying to destroy our spirit, but they will not take our pride."

Elizabeth bit her lip. "I had no idea. It was hard enough coping with our loss when our home was a casualty of the battle. I cannot imagine having your home purposefully burned. That seems more vindictive to the civilians than to the army. That is not the way a war should be fought. The civilians are just trying to survive, they are no threat to them."

"I know," AJ said. "I do hope there is an opportunity to help those civilians, just as others helped us following the battle."

"I agree," Elizabeth said. "Oh, AJ, I hope and pray this all ends soon."

Saturday, December 24, 1864
Prentiss Home

Liberty entered the home and quietly shut the door, took her coat off and hung it on the peg.

"It's cold out there." She commented. "The chores are done for the night. We are free to enjoy our Christmas Eve."

"Thank you so much for finishing them, Liberty," AJ said.

"It's not a problem," Liberty replied. "Besides, you know I would rather work outside all day than have to cook just one meal."

"Yes, I am fully aware of that." AJ smiled. "Dinner's almost ready. Shall we exchange gifts now or after?"

"Oh, I think now would be perfect," Liberty replied. The sisters walked into the parlor where the Christmas tree was. It was a small tree that Eric had cut down for them, but AJ had taken care to decorate it, as she had decorated the entire house with evergreen boughs and red ribbons.

"Another Christmas Eve with just the two of us," AJ commented. "At least we have dinner at the Turner's tomorrow to look forward to."

"Yes." Liberty agreed. "Fortunately by next Christmas, the war will likely be over, unfortunately not in our favor."

"You may be right, but let's not discuss the war tonight."

"That sounds good to me," Liberty said with a small smile. She went to the tree and picked up her package for AJ, while the older sister reached for Liberty's gift.

"You open yours first," AJ said excitedly. She loved Christmas and even if the past three Christmases had been quite depressing, she strove to make the holiday as joyful as possible.

"All right," Liberty said and opened her gift. A huge smile lit up her face when she saw a new pocket knife inside. "AJ! It's just like the one Nathaniel has! This is perfect."

AJ smiled. "I knew you would like it. I saw it in Fredericksburg and knew it would be ideal. It's practical too and I got it for a good price."

"Capital!" Liberty opened it, then closed it, the smile still on her face. She slid the knife into her pocket. "I'm afraid my gift to you isn't nearly as good as yours. You're hard to buy for, especially when I can't get you the one thing that you really want."

"And that is?"

"Your husband...home for good."

AJ frowned. "Well, nobody can do anything about that."

"Hm. True." Liberty agreed. "Anyways, I hope you like it."

AJ tore the small package open and looked at what was inside. She almost wept when she saw a tintype of Richard. It must have been taken just before he left to fight at the start of the war, as he had a brand new uniform on.

"It's actually from both me and Richard's mother. I stopped at her home and asked if she had an image of him since I knew you didn't have one. She gladly gave it to me. I made the frame for it myself with some of the scrap wood we had after repairing the fences."

"I love it." AJ pulled Liberty into a hug. "Thank you so much."

"You're welcome." Liberty said, "Let's go eat dinner."

Just as AJ stood up, there was a knock on the door and it immediately opened. Richard, with a huge smile on his face, walked in.

"Merry Christmas, everyone."

AJ gasped, tears of happiness in her eyes as Richard walked into the parlor. She quickly crossed the room and threw herself into his arms.

"Richard. What are you doing here?"

"I was carrying some intelligence and was able to stop here on this wonderful, holy night." He held her tight, then turned toward Liberty. "It is so good to see you as well, Liberty."

"It is wonderful to see you!" The girl said with a smile. "I love a good surprise. If you'll excuse me for a moment. I will go check on the meal."

After taking a good look at Richard, AJ frowned and touched a bruise that was under Richard's eye. "What happened here? Hand to hand fighting in combat?"

"Not exactly." He caught her hand and kissed her palm. "I just...got into an altercation with another soldier."

"You? Got into a fight? Richard, I have only known you to be in two fights since the war started, and both of those were when our lives were in danger."

"That's true." Richard agreed. "I usually try to avoid fisticuffs, but this time, I wasn't fighting. I simply angered another soldier and he let me know about his displeasure by punching me. He is just a country farmer, so I suppose that's how he deals with his anger."

"What did you do to this soldier?" AJ asked warily.

"Well, he thinks I compromised his sister when in reality, I simply fell in love with her and married her."

AJ gasped. "Nathaniel did that to you?"

"Yes." Richard squeezed her hand. "In all honesty, I probably deserved it. He knows firsthand the negative effect I used to have on you."

"Used to." She murmured. "He doesn't understand the effect that you now have on me." She grinned.

"Don't tell him, he may hit me again."

The couple turned at the knock on the parlor door frame.

"Everything is ready if you two are," Liberty said.

Richard smiled. "We can continue our conversation later."

Sunday, December 25, 1864
Turner's Glenn

"Did Santa leave us anything?" Benjamin exclaimed, running down the steps and into the parlor, Hannah right on his heels. The Bennett family had spent the night at Turner's Glenn.

"He did!" Hannah shouted, going down on her knees and looking excitedly under the small fir tree that Daniel, Eric, and Max had cut down.

Elizabeth smiled as she watched her children. A short pang of sadness hit her as she remembered the child that was not meant to be with them. Both Dr. Knightly and her mother had told her that it would be possible to have another child and that comforted her, but she also held on to Benjamin and Hannah tighter, even after a year and a half.

"Gramma, Santa left one present each for me, Hannah, Max, and Lainey. Can we open them? There's also the presents that we got for each other. So everyone has at least one!"

The Turner family had decided to exchange names and get one present for one person as resources and money were tight. This year, most of the gifts were homemade.

"We need to wait for all of your aunts and uncles to come down, Benjamin," Miriam said with an indulgent smile.

"And Eric!" Benjamin said. "Can I go get Eric?"

"No need, Benjamin." Eric's voice came from the entryway. He brushed off the snow from his jacket and bent to take off his boots.

"I see we're having a Christmas snowfall," Meri said, coming down the stairs. She smiled at Eric, whose cheeks had reddened from his cold trip outside to gather some more firewood.

"Yes, ma'am, and a beautiful Christmas morning it is." Eric smiled at Meri.

Max, Lainey, and Annie came down the stairs just behind Meri.

"Mama, everyone's here! Can we open presents now?" Hannah asked excitedly.

"Yes, dear, we can."

The family settled in around the tree while Hannah and Benjamin passed out presents. Each gift had been carefully chosen by the giver. The favorite gift, however, was Benjamin's gift from Eric. He had made

542

a baseball bat for the boy to go with the baseball that Elizabeth had gotten her son. "Eric, this is the best present ever!" Benjamin exclaimed.

"I'm glad you like it," Eric said, adjusting the knit cap on his head that he had received from Meri.

"Like it? I love it!" He clutched the gift and turned to Elizabeth. "Mama, can I go outside and play with it?"

"I wanna go too!" Hannah said.

"Me too!" Max said.

Elizabeth looked outside. There was a thin layer of snow on the ground and the sun was beginning to shine through the clouds.

"Of course. That's a fine idea." She replied. "Benjamin, you remember it's only polite to allow others to use your gift."

"Of course, Mama. I'll let anyone use it."

"Anyone?" Belle asked, a sudden feeling of playfulness coursing through her. Benjamin looked at her, a confused smile on his face.

"Aunt Belle? You want to go play?"

"Maybe I do." Belle gave him a smile. She stood and headed for the front door. "I bet I can beat you all out there." She quickly donned her coat and mittens.

"Aunt Belle?" Hannah said, then grinned widely and rushed to her own outdoor clothing. Benjamin, Max, Lainey and Eric followed. Meri looked from Elizabeth and Annie to the group that was getting dressed to go outside. She seemed torn between wanting to go and wanting to stay.

Elizabeth smiled at her sister. "Go on, Meri. Annie and I will get breakfast started. Go and have fun."

Meri looked outside just as Eric pelted Max with a snowball. She smiled when she saw Belle immediately toss one at Eric. "Are you sure? It's not fair that you two do all the work."

"We're sure." Annie smiled. "Go."

Meri stood and dressed warmly, then headed out the door herself.

Miriam turned to Elizabeth and Annie. "Do you think she'll ever admit to us that she has feelings for Eric?"

"I'm not quite sure she realizes it herself," Elizabeth replied, standing.

"I believe I will watch the fun from the front porch." Miriam smiled as she put her own winter clothes on.

Elizabeth and Annie both headed to the kitchen. Ruthie was already there, beginning the preparations for breakfast.

"What do you make of Belle's attitude this morning?" Annie asked.

"You mean her playfulness and the fact that she's outside, playing in the snow, right now?"

543

"That's exactly what I mean. I don't remember her playing in the snow, ever." Annie smile

"I don't believe she has. Maybe, if James ever encouraged her enough, but I don't recall."

"She really did worship James." Annie agreed. Elizabeth looked down at the bread she was kneading. She tried not to think too much about the war, what it had done to her family, and all of the unknowns that still threatened. She took a deep breath. "She misses James so much."

"I think her new attitude is the result of a few good influences. I believe that Dr. Knightly has been a big factor in her change of attitude. He may not be light and playful but it almost seems as though she's brought it upon herself to be lighthearted for him. She lets down her guard around him and I believe she realized that she doesn't always have to be our perfect Southern Belle."

"An' dat is da truth." Ruthie offered her opinion.

"She's much more enjoyable now," Annie said. "I appreciate Dr. Knightly so much for that."

"That leads me to my next idea about Belle's change. She just returned from visiting Kate and Baby Sandie. The recently widowed Kate, and Sandie, who lost his father before he was even born. She had to be a consoling and supportive friend. It had to be a difficult time for Belle, but I believe it made her realize that she still has so much to be thankful for, her family and friends especially."

"I believe you're right. I think she figured out that life is too short and so priceless. We have to spend quality time with those who are important to us." Annie added. "Ruthie, what do you have that sly grin on your face for? Are you thinking the same thing we are?"

"Yeasmm, Missy Annie. I do believes you is both right." She replied.

Elizabeth once again felt tears threaten at the thought of those who were not with the family. Annie saw Elizabeth's emotions and quickly moved to her side and took her into her arms. "Elizabeth, I am so sorry."

"It's not your fault, Annie," Elizabeth said. "It's just that the Christmas holiday is supposed to be about peace and joy, and here we are, celebrating after four years of war and killing."

"I know but with the Union army having Petersburg under siege for so long, I can't imagine the army and those families holding on much longer. When it does fall, the Yankees will likely march right into Richmond. The war could be over by this time next year."

"Yes, but we will be defeated and our soldiers will be traitors." Elizabeth wiped her eyes with the heel of her hand. "The war will end but what will that mean for all of us?"

"I don't know, Elizabeth. I suppose none of us do. We better hope and pray that the Yankee government will be forgiving." Annie said.

"Well, at least we're all together now, with the exception of Father and Joshua, that is." Elizabeth squeezed Annie's hand. Annie looked down, not meeting Elizabeth or Ruthie's eyes. "Annie, what is it?"

"It...it's not important."

"Sho 'nuf I think it is important," Ruthie said. "Yo should talk to yo sister, Miss Annie. I done tol' you to talk to yo mama 'bout it too, but you won't."

"It's just...well, I've been corresponding with Joseph Byron. You may remember him"

"Of course I do," Elizabeth said. "He seemed like a perfect match for you, if I do say so myself."

"Yes, I think so too." Annie blushed. "Elizabeth, I'm in love with him, and he loves me. He has asked me to come to South Carolina. He wants to marry me."

Elizabeth smiled. Annie was a very sweet and kind person. Joseph Byron seemed to see that too. "I think that's wonderful, Annie." Elizabeth hugged her little sister.

"So you think it will be okay to go down and see him?" Annie asked, a bit hesitantly.

"I can understand how you would want to go down there. When you know who you're meant to be with, you want to marry them as soon as possible."

"Like AJ with Richard," Annie said. "You're exactly right. I can't wait to become his wife."

"That may be true, Annie, but I don't think that's a good idea right now, for several reasons."

Annie turned and sat down on a stool. "I knew you would find something wrong with my plan."

"Annie, I want you to be happy, I really do, but you have to be practical about this. There is no route from Fredericksburg to anywhere in South Carolina that is not swarming with Yankees. Any route will take you close to Petersburg. It would be foolish to try and make that trip." Elizabeth thought for a moment. "In fact, it's a little concerning to me that he would even suggest that you do so."

Annie paled. "Actually, he didn't ask me to come right away. That was my idea. He made the proposal but asked me to marry him after the war. I'm the one who wants to try and go down there now. Elizabeth, he's there practically all alone. His mother is dead, his brother is fighting, and his sister lives somewhere in Pennsylvania with her husband's family, actually, she's in Gettysburg. I've wondered more than once if Cousin Charlotte knows his sister Augusta. Anyways, the only person at the plantation is Joseph's father, who returned home from fighting just to take care of Joseph and the plantation."

"Well, he's not completely alone, then." Elizabeth pointed out.

"I know, and you're right, I just...I want to be with him, spend time with him, and marry him. I miss him so."

"Well, I can tell you that his father being at their plantation does cause me less concern. One of my reasons for not wanting you to go down there is the fact that you wouldn't be properly chaperoned."

"Yes, his father is there, along with a few slaves that stayed behind," Annie said, hopeful that maybe she could convince Elizabeth to give her blessing.

"Annie, my biggest concern still persist. I don't want you traveling alone that close to the fighting and I believe Mother will feel the same."

"What if we could get Eric or Solomon or Daniel to escort me?" Annie asked.

"That may be possible, but it still would be dangerous for them as well. Do you want any harm to come to them? It simply isn't safe right now. There are other issues I am concerned with. It is the middle of winter with limited food and supplies. Travel would just be foolish."

Annie sagged her shoulders. "You're right, I know." She sighed. "Other than travel, do you have any reservations?"

Elizabeth put her arms around Annie. "My only other concern is purely selfish. You know I love you and I want you to be happy, but if...no, when...you go to South Carolina, I will miss you dearly." Annie hugged Elizabeth back tightly, tears forming in her eyes. "If only Byron Hill wasn't so far away." Elizabeth pulled back from the embrace and brushed the tears from her sister's cheeks. "I'll make a deal with you. If you promise not to run off to South Carolina, when the weather warms up, if there's no danger between here and there, I will help persuade Mother to have Daniel and Eric bring you down there. I know how you feel, being separated from the man you love. We just need to make sure you're safe as well. It would do neither you nor Mr. Byron any good to have something go amiss on your travels."

"I think I can agree to that." Annie smiled. The sisters hugged once more then stood and headed back toward the counter. Ruthie gave a small smile to the sisters.

"I done tol you the same thing, Miss Annie, I gots to agree with Miss 'Lizabeth. We sure wants you to be happy, but things sure won't be the same witchout you here."

Annie gave a tearful smile to Ruthie. "Thank you. I can't tell you how much I will miss you all as well."

"Merry Christmas, Liberty!" Benjamin smiled, cheeks still red from being out in the cold.

"My goodness, Benjamin! It looks as though you have been having fun out of doors."

"Yep. Gramma and Aunt Belle came outside too. Aunt Belle even played." He smiled. Belle came into the entryway.

"It was quite enjoyable, I must say." She smiled and ruffled Benjamin's hair. "Good day, Liberty, AJ. Richard, goodness, you're home! How are you all doing? I am so glad you're here."

"Not as glad as I am." He smiled. "AJ and Liberty told me that you invited my mother for Christmas dinner. I am so thankful to you for that."

"Of course." Belle smiled. "One of our servants, Daniel, just left to escort her to Turner's Glenn. When we heard that your father would be out of town for the holiday, we knew that we had to have her over."

"I wish I knew why he believes his business prospects are more important than family during the holiday," Richard muttered. AJ gave his arm a comforting pat. "Well, I couldn't be more appreciative." He rubbed at his scar.

"We only hope that you can make room for Richard," AJ said.

"Of course," Elizabeth replied, coming into the entryway, hugging AJ, then Richard. "Benjamin, go and let Ruthie know that we will have one more guest for dinner."

"Yes, Ma'am." He said, then ran off to the kitchen.

"Belle, it is so good to have you back." AJ gave Belle a quick hug. "Were you able to see Aaron as he passed through the city?" AJ gave Belle a quick hug.

"No, his plans were changed. There is so much going on in Petersburg and Richmond that he wasn't able to get away." The group made their way into the parlor. Belle and Annie had returned it to its previous state prior to their home becoming a hospital.

"That's too bad," Richard said. "I would like to meet this infamous doctor who appears to have won the heart of Belle Turner."

"He told me he wants to come here after the war. You could meet him then." Belle replied.

"I would like that." Richard nodded. "I would like that very much."

A short time later, Richard's mother arrived and they all sat down for a modest dinner. Belle wasn't sure who was happier that Richard was home, his mother or AJ. If not for the war and so many people gone, it could have been a perfect Christmas.

"It is such a relief to have all of the wounded men out of our town." Mrs. Evans said, then addressed Miriam. "Have you ever considered going back to Richmond to work at the hospitals there?"

"No. That part of my life is over." Miriam replied. "I did find fulfillment in what I was doing, but I also find much fulfillment in being with my family."

"That is good. I don't know if I ever told you, but I was impressed with how you were able to care for the wounded so efficiently. I had a difficult enough time with the few soldiers that I had to care for back in May."

Richard looked at his mother, a bit of shock on his face. "I didn't know you had to take in Yankees." He turned his attention to AJ. "Why did you never tell me?"

"I thought you knew, or at least assumed," AJ replied. "I thought it was obvious that all the buildings in Fredericksburg were being used for the wounded."

"I suppose I knew, but just didn't realize that our home…that you, Mother, would have had to take care of the enemy."

"It didn't kill me, Richard. Your father surely threw a fit about it but there was nothing he could do. I must say, I did have some concerns that he would be one of the men in town who was arrested by the Federals."

"He likely would have deserved it," Richard mumbled in AJ's direction. She briefly put a hand on his arm to calm him again. "I am glad for your sake, mother, that he was not arrested. However, I must say I am quite disappointed that he left you alone during Christmas."

"Thank you for saying so, son." She smiled. "However, we should try and speak of happier times." She turned to the children, who had been allowed to eat with the adults on this special occasion. "Did St. Nicholas make it here last night?" The children immediately began telling her all about their morning.

"She will make a wonderful grandmother," Belle whispered from AJ's other side.

AJ blushed. "I am sure she will."

After dinner, the family sat in front of the fire. Liberty, Richard, and AJ had gone home with Richard's mother as Richard would be leaving first thing in the morning.

"Mama. How come Mr. Evans gets to come home for Christmas but Papa can't?" Hannah asked.

"Cause Mr. Evans is in the cavalry." Benjamin quickly answered. "They don't have the same job. It's the same with Grandfather. He can't come home either"

"Is that true, Mama?" Hannah asked.

"Yes, Hannah, it is," Elizabeth said, brushing Hannah's hair back from her face.

"Well, that is unfortunate," Hannah replied. Belle stifled a laugh. Her five-year-old niece sounded so mature. Belle looked around the room. It had been almost four years since the war began. All of her siblings had grown and matured so much and if she wasn't mistaken, Meri was sitting quite close to Eric on the settee. Little Meri had just turned sixteen and Belle very much remembered being sixteen. Where had the time gone? Max, so handsome and looking more and more like James, was now ten. Laine was thirteen, and quite beautiful. All of her siblings acted more mature than their ages. Eric was only eighteen, but looked and acted as though he were much older as well. Belle knew that Elizabeth wondered if Joshua would recognize his own children when he saw them next and now Belle wondered if her own father would recognize his children.

"I am thankful for the gifts I received today but honestly, Mama, I really wanted to have Father home for Christmas," Hannah said.

"I know, Hannah-Bear, but I have a feeling he will be home next Christmas."

"Promise, Mama? Promise me?"

"I cannot promise that, Hannah. I can only hope and pray."

Part 5:
1865

Sunday, January 8, 1865
Bennett Home

"Have you heard from Joshua lately?" AJ asked.

"We did, right after the Christmas holiday. He's safe, for now."

"Have you ever told him...about the baby?" Belle hesitated to bring up the past, but she was very curious. She could only imagine what she might say to her husband if that ever happened to her.

"I did." Elizabeth sighed. "I actually did in late November. He wrote right away. He was wonderful, as I knew he would be. Such concern for me." She smiled. "I'm not sure why I was so hesitant to tell him. I knew he wouldn't be angry or anything like that, but I think I was nervous because I didn't want to disappoint him. I know I shouldn't feel that way, but I did, and he was disappointed, but only because I didn't tell him sooner. He understood why, though."

"It happens to many women, Elizabeth. Likely more than we even realize." AJ said. "Mrs. Evans shared with me that she was pregnant many times but Richard was the only child she was able to carry through to birth."

"Yes, Mother told me that she lost a child as well. I had never known. It is not something a woman goes around telling others about." Elizabeth said, changing the conversation. "How about Richard? Have you heard from him?"

"No, I haven't. Richard isn't much of a writer, although he tries on occasion. I wouldn't be surprised if he finds a reason to come and visit soon." The moment she said those words, she wanted to take them back. She realized how lucky she was that Richard occasionally had some leeway as he was a scout, unlike most soldiers, Joshua and Mr. Turner included. She couldn't imagine what Elizabeth thought of her verbal blunder. "Oh, Elizabeth, Belle, I am so sorry. Please forgive me."

"Soon, all of the men will come home for good," Belle said. "Unfortunately, that means the war will be over and most likely that we Thave lost. the Confederacy will be no more. It feels like it has all been a waste."

"There is hope," AJ said. "When Richard was here at Christmas, he said that Lee could join up with Joe Johnston down in South Carolina and still do some damage to the Yankees."

"Or the Confederacy can just admit defeat and send our fathers and husbands home for good while they're still alive," Elizabeth said, a hint of frustration in her voice. Then she sighed. "My apologies. I just...I

551

see that the end of the war is near and I know that Father and Joshua are alive. It would be unimaginable if one of them were killed now when it doesn't really even matter anymore." She shook her head. "Four years. Almost four long years of worry and misery and destruction. What was the point? I am a firm believer that God has a plan, do not get me wrong, and I always pray for His will to be done, but sometimes I really don't understand. I wish He would allow us to know what was happening and why."

"I know what you mean, Elizabeth," Belle said. "I have been wondering those same things my whole life. I would ask myself what was the point of praying or even believing. As you have taught me, faith is a powerful thing. It can change us. I know it changed me." She took a deep breath. "When I was with the Pendletons, I was absolutely amazed by their faith. Sandie's mother, one of the first things I remember her saying after his death, she thanked God that Jesus had opened the gates of heaven so that she could one day see her Sandie again."

"That is what eternal life is all about," AJ said.

Elizabeth wiped a tear from her cheek. "I am really sorry. I didn't mean to be so pessimistic."

"Oh, Elizabeth, it's all right," AJ said. Belle moved to her sister's side and pulled her into a comforting hug.

"You spend so much time and effort being strong for everyone else. It really is okay to let someone else, other than Joshua, be strong for you."

"I know. Thank you for being here for me. You don't know how much I appreciate it."

"You would do the same for us," Belle said. "Funny, that's what Kate and I talked about last time we were together, being there for friends and family."

"You have done the same for us, Belle," AJ added.

Thursday, February 9, 1865
Fredericksburg

My Dearest Elizabeth,

As always, I hope this letter reaches you. I feel as though I send you a letter every other day but in reality, it is just the extreme boredom. The other day, we heard a report of a battle about 13 miles south of Fredericksburg, in the Hatchers Run area. Compared with some of our battles, thankfully our losses were small. Our regiment was not engaged in the fighting this time, but we are always ready to fight. We know Grant is trying to cut our supply lines into Petersburg. I don't think I need to tell you how disastrous that would be.

Morale in the troops is mixed. Some men want to fight to the death and never give up while others are ready to give up and go home as soon as tomorrow. I must confess, if we were to surrender, I would be happy. I dream of the day when I am home for good. My last furlough simply confirmed to me just how much I desire to be at home with you. I hope that you didn't think I seemed too anxious to head back to my regiment. I just thought the sooner I got back, the sooner we could get the war over with. I know that's not really how it will work, but it is how I feel.

Give the children my love. I hope to see you soon. Remember, always be strong and steadfast.

With all of my love,
Joshua

Elizabeth smiled and put the letter in her pocket as she walked out of the post office. It was always good to hear from her husband.

Elizabeth!" Lucy Beale greeted her. Elizabeth smiled and waved. "I hope that letter is good news."

"It is from Joshua. Just a normal letter, but he is alive and well even though it sounds as though the end is near."

"That is what I have heard as well," Lucy said. "How have you been, Elizabeth? I feel as though we haven't spoken in a while."

"I believe the last time we have had a conversation was in May," Elizabeth replied.

"Ah, yes. I am afraid I didn't behave as I should have back then." Lucy admitted. "The Yankees, the war, it was all so distressing. I know I should have been more compassionate to the wounded, even if they were the enemy."

"We were all under a lot of stress, Lucy, in those days especially," Elizabeth said.

"Yes, I suppose we were," Lucy replied. "How is the rest of your family? I know you said Joshua is doing well, but what about the others?"

"We haven't heard from Father since Christmas, but Joshua would have told me if something had happened to him," Elizabeth replied. "There must be so many letters that don't get delivered."

"How is your mother doing?" Lucy asked. "I know my mother still feels pain when she thinks of her son who will never be coming home."

"Mother is getting along." Elizabeth said. "Speaking of your mother, how is she, and how is the rest of your family?"

"We are doing well overall. The Yankees leaving town this summer much improved Mother's disposition and we had a rather enjoyable

Christmas holiday." Lucy said. "I do miss seeing Kate Corbin, I mean, Kate Pendleton, around town. Have you heard from her recently?"

"I'm not sure how much you know of her situation." Elizabeth said. "Belle went to stay with her when we heard that Sandie was wounded and then stayed with her after it was confirmed that he died. She stayed through Kate's confinement and came home when Baby Sandie was about a month old just a few weeks before Christmas."

"My goodness. I had heard about Kate's tragedy and her son's birth, but it is still difficult to comprehend. It is what we all fear, being a war widow. She had been married such a short time and he didn't even get to see his son."

"They weren't even married a year." Elizabeth confirmed. "However, it sounds like having the baby brings her joy. Losing a husband...I cannot even bear thinking about it but I believe the loss is softened when you have children to remember them by."

"Yes." Lucy said. "I hear AJ is married now as well. I never thought that Richard Evans would marry at all, much less marry quiet, ordinary AJ."

"He finally saw past her quiet exterior. They make a nice couple." Elizabeth responded.

"Well, I am happy for her." Lucy checked her watch. "Oh, Elizabeth, I do wish that we could talk more, but I am due at Betty Maury's."

"Of course." Elizabeth said. "It was good seeing you, Lucy. Please give Betty my regards."

"Of course." Lucy hurried off, Elizabeth turned for home.

Wednesday, March 15, 1865
Prentiss Farm

"It seems as though a Southern defeat is inevitable," AJ said, sighing as she looked over the article in the newspaper.

"I know," Elizabeth replied. She and Belle had brought Benjamin, Hannah, Max, and Meri over for a visit. Meri and Liberty had taken the children down to the river to go wading.

"It all seems so pointless now," Belle said. "What was it all for?"

"It may seem pointless, Belle, but God can make good of all of this somehow," AJ said.

"He already has." Elizabeth agreed. "I mean, look at the two of you. AJ, your confidence has soared and you now have a fine husband in Richard Evans, something I know you could never have imagined."

"That's true," AJ said with a small smile.

"And Belle, you have changed so much for the better. You are kinder, friendlier and seem truly happier. In addition, you have fallen in love with a truly good man." Elizabeth continued.

"Yes, you're right." Belle looked out across the river toward Turner's Glenn. "I can only hope he comes back to me. We didn't part well."

"The two of you never part well." Elizabeth pointed out. "You bicker like a married couple already. He keeps you on your toes and challenges you, and you love it."

"I suppose I do," Belle admitted.

"If I do say so, the two of you have a much better relationship," AJ remarked in reference to Belle and Elizabeth. "I'm not sure that would have happened if you didn't need to work together to support and help your family through the war."

The mention of family caused Belle to think of the brother she had lost. "But we also lost so much."

"Yes, but it has made us stronger. Better." Elizabeth said.

"It has, but I don't want to think of losing anyone else," Belle replied.

"I agree. I know it's premature, but I can't wait to have Joshua home."

"To continue building your family," Belle said, teasing in her voice.

"Yes, that would be nice," Elizabeth said, then turned to AJ. "Do you and Richard plan on starting a family?"

AJ quickly turned her face, hoping they wouldn't see her blush. She wasn't quick enough.

"America Joan Prentiss Evans! Is there something you've been hiding from us?"

"I'm not hiding anything. I do suspect something, but I am not positive. I haven't mentioned anything to Liberty or to Richard, but I haven't had my monthly since before Christmas."

"AJ, that's wonderful news!" Elizabeth smiled.

"Congratulations!" Belle said. "I am so happy for you."

"Why haven't you told Richard yet?" Elizabeth asked.

"I don't want to worry him further. I want him to focus on staying alive. He's already worried about how he's going to support me after the war. I keep telling him that Father and Nathaniel will welcome his help on the farm, especially now that our slaves are gone, having him around will be very helpful. Before he left last summer, he was starting to get the knack for farm life. I think he secretly enjoyed it. I believe he will make a good farmer."

"If he and our Southern men are even allowed to come home." Belle said, biting her lip.

555

"What do you mean?" Elizabeth asked.

"It's just something I've had on my mind these past few weeks. If we do lose the war, which is looking more and more likely as the days go by, what will happen to the soldiers who fought for the Confederacy? What will the federal government do to those who fought against them? Will they be arrested and charged with treason? Will they be executed? Exiled? Will they have what's left of their homes and land taken away? What will happen to all of them and us, their families?"

"I hadn't even really thought about that," Elizabeth admitted.

"Richard and I briefly spoke of that when he was home for Christmas," AJ said. "I would have no issue following him if he needed to escape west and start a new life as he said he may need to do."

"That would be a logical plan," Belle said. "I don't believe Aaron would be in any danger of being tried for treason since he was a doctor who helped soldiers on both sides. But Father? Having to move away with our whole family while some piece of Yankee scum comes down here to take over Turner's Glenn? I would not be able to accept that."

"It would be difficult," Elizabeth replied. "I suppose Joshua, the children and I would move if it was completely necessary. Joshua can be a blacksmith anywhere. I do hope and pray that it isn't going to be the case though. Lincoln doesn't seem like he will be vindictive."

"Who really knows?" AJ said. "I was reading about a Union general, William Sherman, who burned Atlanta, Georgia back in November and then marched east to Savannah, burning everything in his path. I fear this may happen throughout the south. Even if Lincoln wants peace like some are saying. Not everyone will be so forgiving."

Sunday, April 2, 1865
Bennett Home

"Richmond is going to fall." Eric solemnly entered the house, addressing the women who sat around Elizabeth's dining room table. Belle, Annie, and AJ had all come into town for a visit. "I just heard the news, so I had to come in and tell ya'll."

"My goodness. They didn't say anything about it in church this morning." Elizabeth said.

"The news just came through. The city hasn't fallen yet, but since Petersburg isn't going to hold out much longer, President Davis, his cabinet and all the Confederate soldiers defending Richmond are deserting the city and running deeper into the south. Luckily, there is still a railroad line open."

"Oh, dear. Mother will be devastated!" Belle exclaimed. "What about Chimborazo and all of the civilians?"

"It sounds like many civilians are running as well," Eric said. "I'm not sure about the hospital, though."

"So, the cowards are just going to leave the town and our capital unprotected?" Belle asked, frustrated.

"If it's anything like the wars of history, the Confederate soldiers may burn the city as they abandon it," AJ said. "They'll destroy all the bridges, warehouses, anything that they can think of that may be of use to the enemy."

'But what if the fires burn out of control?' Elizabeth asked. "People could get hurt and private property could be destroyed."

"The Yankees may destroy everything anyways," AJ replied. "And we want to make sure that they cannot get anything of value from the town."

"I suppose," Elizabeth said. "It just seems like such a waste."

"Eric, have the townspeople been talking about whether or not this will finally be the end of the war?" Belle asked.

"Not really, Ma'am, but I was talking to Miss Lizzie Alsop and she said she thought death would be preferable to our lives going forward but we will still conquer the enemy through Christ. Those are her words, though. Personally, I think it will be only a matter of time now. Lee could possibly escape and fight on, but his men are so destitute, he will likely surrender."

"What of all the soldiers? Will they be able to come back within the next month?" Elizabeth said hopefully.

"It depends on the terms of surrender," Eric said.

"What else did Lizzie say?" Meri asked, sounding slightly irritated.

"You know Lizzie. She was yammering on, saying that we need to repent of our own sins and the Lord, in his time, will punish theirs."

"Lizzie Alsop always did have a flair for the dramatics. She's nearly as mature as you, Meri." Belle said, trying not to grin as Meri gave a quiet 'harrumph'. If she didn't know any better, her younger sister was not happy about Eric talking to another young woman.

"Yes, she is dramatic," Eric replied.

"Thank you, Eric, for letting us know," Elizabeth said, standing.

"Yes, Ma'am," Eric said, then nodded and went back to the blacksmith shop.

Wednesday, April 12, 1865
Turner's Glenn

"Hey, everyone! It's over!" Hannah crashed through the front door of Turner's Glenn, Benjamin right at her heels.

Miriam was the first one to come down the steps to the entryway. "Are you serious? It's over?" She hugged Hannah, then Benjamin. Elizabeth and Eric entered the home. "Elizabeth, truly?"

"Everyone in town seemed very positive," Elizabeth said as Benjamin and Hannah ran off to find and tell the others the news. "Although they are already talking about our army rising up again and avenging the death of our slain Confederate heroes, and how God will exercise His vengeance against the enemy."

"My goodness," Belle said. "You mean to tell me we just surrendered and people already want to rise up again?"

"Call it Southern pride," Elizabeth said. "I have a feeling that some people will never stop fighting. It might not be with cannon and rifles, but they will persist through other means."

"Mama, I have forgotten to ask. When will Papa be home?" Benjamin asked, returning to the entryway, his aunts, and uncle behind him.

"I'm not exactly sure about that, Benjamin. I don't know the particulars of the surrender. Hopefully, your father and grandfather can catch a train and be back as soon as possible. In fact, I know they will." The family moved into the parlor.

Belle smiled with mixed emotion. On one hand, the war was over. Her father would be home soon. She dearly hoped that Aaron would return to Fredericksburg soon as well. However, she was also filled with a sense of loss. The Confederacy would be no more. They had fought and suffered and had so many loved ones die, their lives were forever altered. They hadn't won, they hadn't gained anything, and they had lost so much in the process.

"Where is my family?" A voice came from the entryway.

"Father!" Max and Lainey scrambled up, followed by Benjamin and Hannah. Matthew Turner strode into the parlor for the first time since the winter of 1862. After hugging Max, Lainey, and his grandchildren, he embraced Meri, then Annie, Elizabeth, Belle and finally his wife. He turned and smiled at Belle.

"I heard rumors that you have met someone special," He said, giving her a kiss on the cheek. "And my Annie, I hear you're thinking that South Carolina might be a better place for you than Turner's Glenn." He put one arm around Annie and his other arm around Belle.

"Not better, Father, Just a different step in my life." Annie smiled.

"I know your mother and siblings have met both of these young men but I must say that I feel it necessary to meet them for myself. I must approve of them." There was teasing in his voice. "If not, I will not let you go."

"Oh, Father, you will," Belle said confidently.

"We will definitely find a way for you to meet them," Annie said.

"Father, do you know where Joshua is?" Elizabeth asked as her father stepped over and shook Eric's hand, then clasped him into a hug.

"Unfortunately, I do not. Our regiment was divided and sent to different fronts. I'm sure he will be here soon."

"I see," Elizabeth said, disappointed. "Father, I am so glad you're here!"

"Yes," Miriam said. "How is it you were able to come home so quickly, Matthew?"

"Yes, and are you sure the Yankees won't arrest you for being a Confederate soldier?" Belle asked.

"General Grant's peace agreement, his terms, were quite generous. Calvary men were able to keep their horses, officers didn't have to surrender their swords. The Federals were quite civil to Lee. We had to turn in our arms, but then we were given official pardon papers, which could also be used as passes to take a train home."

"So you all received full pardons?" Elizabeth asked excitedly. "All of the soldiers?"

"As far as I know. It sounds as though Lincoln and Grant want all Confederate soldiers to be able to return home as long as they promise not to fight anymore. There are still pockets of resistance in the Confederate army that haven't surrendered yet, such as Joe Johnston's regiment further South, but the men of the Army of Virginia have surrendered."

"And the federal government? Will they sign a peace treaty also?" Belle asked.

"I don't think so. To sign a treaty with the Confederate government would mean that the US government acknowledged the Confederacy as a separate nation." Matthew replied.

"Heaven forbid they do that." Belle scoffed. Matthew sat and pulled Hannah onto his lap.

"My you have grown, little Hannah-Bear." He smiled. "As much as I would have liked to be victorious, what's important is that we are all together again, although I must admit, I hardly recognized some of you. You have all grown so much. I have missed you all terribly and I want you to know that I cherished every letter I received. I do realize I probably didn't get every letter, so we all have a lot to discuss and stories to catch up on."

"That might take a long time," Benjamin said.

"Then it is a good thing that we have a lot of time to spend together now." Matthew smiled.

Friday, April 14, 1865
Prentiss Farm

AJ bent her knees, got a good grip on her pitchfork, scooped up some hay and threw a forkful into one of the stalls. She wanted to make sure that when Richard, her father, and Nathaniel came home, the farm would look as good as possible. At least as good as she and Liberty could make it."

"Well, Mrs. Evans, it sure is good to see you working hard."

AJ turned, unable to hold back a huge smile at hearing the familiar drawl of her husband.

"Richard!" She practically squealed, dropped the pitchfork and threw herself into his arms. She caught him unaware and off balance, and the two fell into the hay she had just thrown down. He laughed at her exuberance.

"Oh, Richard I am so sorry." She said.

"Nothing to be sorry for." He lowered his head and kissed her gently. She threaded her fingers through his hair. He shook his head, trying to flip it back. "I'm hoping my wife can give me a haircut soon."

"I wish she wouldn't." She said shyly. "I like it long." She brushed it from his forehead, then traced the scar on his face.

"If you like it, I'll keep it. I've gotten used to it anyways." He smiled.

"You're back." She whispered. "I can't believe you're back."

"For good." He grinned broadly. "Your father is back also."

"Father's here?" She exclaimed. "He made it through! Wait." She hesitated. "So, does he know about us then?"

"He sure wouldn't have left me alone with you in the barn for this long if he didn't know we were married." He kissed her again. "I spoke with him long ago, told him about us, and asked for his blessing. His first question was 'will I make you happy?' Then he told me if I had finally wizened up and noticed what an amazing woman you were, he would approve of our marriage because he would trust you to make a wise decision. He does want to know if you are with child. I told him not yet."

AJ blushed. "My father did not ask you such a personal question." She said.

"He actually did." He smiled at her blush. "I want him to respect me, to like me, to trust me, but I must admit, he took me off guard."

"But you lied to him, Richard." She said, pushing a strand of hair from his face. "That is not a good thing to do to your new father-in-law."

"What do you mean? What did I lie about?" Richard's eyes searched hers, trying to recall what he could have lied to his father-in-

560

law about. She still had a blush to her cheeks. Realization suddenly dawned on him. His eyes widened. "You mean...you..." He knelt next to her. "I didn't hurt you, did I? Oh, America, I am so sorry..."

"Richard, I'm fine, everything is fine." She sat up and knelt next to him, then took his hands into hers. "You won't hurt me or the baby." He looked at her, amazement in his eyes. She smiled. It was very amusing to see the usually composed Richard Evans flustered.

"Baby. We're going to have a baby." He was overwhelmed. Two days ago, he had felt complete disappointment in losing the war, then, he had felt excited at the thought of being able to come home to his wife. Now, this idea of a new life growing after four long years of seeing so much death. He couldn't contain his joy. He stood, pulled AJ up with him, took her in his arms, and swung her around.

"America Joan, you are amazing." He set her down. "When?"

"Well, as close as I can figure, it happened when you came back around Christmas, which means we should be able to meet our new little one in late September. I haven't been to see a doctor yet."

Tears shimmered in Richard's eyes. "I love you, America. I thank God every day that He put you in my life."

"I love you too, Richard. Welcome home."

Monday, April 17, 1865
Turner's Glenn Plantation

"...and he yelled *'Sic Semper Tyrannus'* and jumped from the balcony." Lainey read the article.

"Sic Semper Tyrannus?" Max asked. Now eight, he had grown into an inquisitive young man, always asking questions and soaking up any and all information.

"It's Latin," Meri replied. "It means...death..." she thought. "Death always to tyrants, I believe."

"I don't understand. Why would he kill him?" Belle wondered aloud. "Lincoln was calling for a peaceful resolution. It sounded as though he was going to be forgiving."

Lainey looked up from the paper. "He must have wanted the South to rise again, even though most of the Confederate troops have surrendered. You know many Southerners, not just this Booth fellow, will continue to do what they can to keep their Southern state's independence."

"We're here!" Elizabeth entered the parlor, Eric, Hannah, and Benjamin right behind her.

"Is there any news from town?" Belle asked, hoping there would be something from Aaron. Elizabeth shook her head.

"There has been a lot of talk, though. Most of the conversation is about the assassination of Mr. Lincoln."

"It is big news. Do they say how the North will retaliate?" Belle tried not to get too emotional, especially with no letter from Aaron. She never knew she could miss someone as much as she missed Aaron. Belle tried to keep in touch with him through letters, but the mail service was so unreliable and Aaron had admitted that he wasn't much of a letter writer. She doubted that he had time enough to write. She was worried about him being wounded or killed, and she wanted to see him, talk to him, and just spend time with him.

"There was some good news, though." Elizabeth smiled. "I have it on good authority that Richard Evans made it back home safely, as well as Mr. Prentiss. I saw Mr. Prentiss in town this morning."

"What about Nathaniel?" Belle asked. "Is there any word on him?"

"No, not yet," Elizabeth replied. "I also heard that Dominic Wetherly and Margaret Buckley are engaged. They are planning a wedding for next month."

"Good for them." Belle smiled. "She deserves a good man. He'll treat her well."

"I'm glad you feel that way," Elizabeth replied, amazed to see the change in Belle as well. "Margaret told me she would be honored if we would attend the ceremony."

"Of course. It will be nice to have something to celebrate after all of the losses we have sustained."

Elizabeth went to the window and stared out.

"Lainey, why don't you go check and see if Annie and Mother need help in the kitchen. Take Hannah with you. Boys…"

"We'll go see if Father needs help. He was outside with Daniel checking on the condition of the back field." Max offered.

"That's a good idea." Eric agreed. "Come with us, Benjamin."

Belle smiled at how well Eric was fitting in with the rest of the family. Max and Benjamin looked up to him as if he were an older brother. It seemed an unspoken conclusion that Eric would stay with the Bennetts for good. Belle turned to her sister.

"Elizabeth?"

Elizabeth turned, tears in her eyes. "I'm scared, Belle. I know it's only been a short time since the surrender, but last I knew, Joshua was in Petersburg and the rest of his regiment was at Appomattox Court House. Neither of those places are four-day trips. Father said General Grant gave the Confederates who surrendered their arms a train ticket home. Joshua should be home by now."

Belle stood next to her sister and put an arm around her.

562

"I'm trying so hard to have faith, Belle. I know that God is with Joshua, I do. I just wish I knew where he was. I just want him back."

Belle pulled Elizabeth into her arms as her sister continued to talk.

"The past few years, I have been confident that he would make it home, but ever since the fall of Petersburg, I can't shake this feeling that something is wrong."

"You two have always had a strong connection. I believe if something unimaginable were to happen, you would know. You just feel something is wrong because he's not home yet. He will be, just be patient. Everything will be all right. It won't ever be exactly the same, it can't be. But things will work out. God is with us."

Elizabeth smiled. "Listen to you, encouraging me with words of hope." She pulled back from the embrace and looked proudly at her sister. "You are right, things will work out. We have been blessed. We have a lot to be thankful for. Family. A roof over our heads. The ability to grow food on our land."

"Don't forget that Eric is becoming quite the hunter," Belle said. "Daniel has been a good influence on him."

"Yes, we are so fortunate that Daniel, Solomon, Ruthie, and Zipporah chose to stay here." Elizabeth nodded. "Many things to be thankful for."

"Especially each other," Belle said. A movement from outside caught her eye, "What in the world?" The two women looked out the window and saw an old wagon coming up the drive. A man with shaggy, blonde hair was driving.

"Is that...Aaron?" Belle dashed out of the parlor, into the hallway and out the door. Elizabeth followed her. "It is Aaron!" Belle leaned on the railing, a broad smile on her face. Elizabeth stood next to her sister, happy for this turn of events.

Aaron drove the wagon around the circle drive, and as the wagon turned, Elizabeth noticed a man lying in the back of the wagon.

"Ladies!" Aaron called out, tying off the reins and jumping down from the wagon. Belle and Elizabeth scurried down the steps. Belle threw herself into Aaron's arms. As they separated, Aaron continued. "I have a special delivery for you, Mrs. Bennett."

Tears streamed down Elizabeth's face as she realized just who was in the back of the wagon. She ran to the side and saw her husband. He was weak and pale but gave Elizabeth a lopsided grin.

"Joshua!" She climbed into the back, then threw her arms around him.

"Oh, Elizabeth." She held him tightly. He hugged her back, but the embrace felt awkward. She leaned back to look at him. It was then that she realized why his hug had felt so different. He was missing his left arm.

"Joshua! Your arm! What happened?"

"Dr. Knightly saved my life. My lower arm, one of the bones in it was shattered by some shrapnel in an explosion during the siege of Petersburg, in late January. I was unconscious for a while and when I woke up, I was in a field hospital with no left arm."

"I tried to save it, I really did," Aaron said, his arm around Belle. "As he said, the bones were shattered, crushed. By the time a doctor was able to attend to him, the arm was already in danger of infection. Although he was unconscious because he also suffered a concussion. I recognized him from the winter he was in Fredericksburg, but I knew it was Joshua because of the photograph he had with him."

"Aaron checked my condition at every opportunity for as long as he could. I'm sure I would not be here at all if not for his continued care." He touched Elizabeth's face. "I'm okay, Elizabeth. I'm alive. I'll figure out how to be a one-armed blacksmith."

"You'll do it, I know you will." Elizabeth covered his hand with hers. "I love you. You're home. You're alive. That's all that matters." She turned to Aaron and noticed that Belle had gone inside, presumably to get Hannah. "Thank you so much, Aaron, for saving Joshua's life and for bringing him home safely."

"Well, you must know that coming back to Fredericksburg has some benefits for me as well." He said with a smile. "Come on, Joshua. Let's get you on your feet and into the parlor." Elizabeth helped Joshua to the end of the wagon and she and Aaron helped him down.

"Papa!" Hannah's voice called out, running toward Joshua. He bent down and she was in his arm before anyone could say anything else. He held her tightly with his one arm, tears of happiness in his eyes.

"Lainey went to get Benjamin," Belle said with a smile, rejoining the group.

Elizabeth kept a hand on Joshua's shoulder. She didn't want to let go of him for fear he would be gone again.

"Papa, where did your other arm go?" Hannah asked, touching his pinned-up sleeve gingerly. Joshua set Hannah down and tried to explain.

"Well, it was injured pretty badly and was making me sick, Hannah, so in order to get me healthy, Dr. Knightly had to cut it off."

"You mean amputate." Hannah corrected. "Papa, we've been around a hospital enough to know what has to happen."

"Paaaaa!" Benjamin ran to Joshua with such force that he almost knocked his father over. "Pa, I'm so happy you're home. Wait! Look, Papa, you're missing an arm! Oh, who cares, I wouldn't care if you are missing all your arms and legs." He threw himself into his father's arms again as Joshua leaned back on the wagon. Elizabeth squeezed his shoulder, trying to hold back tears of happiness and gratitude. She looked around. Her mother, father, Max, Eric, Meri, Lainey, and Annie had come to the front as well. Belle had returned to her place under Aaron's arm, Belle's own arms around his waist. Joshua stood with the help of Elizabeth and stuck out his hand to Eric.

"Eric. You have become a man during my absence. I can never repay you for watching over my family. I am now and forevermore in your debt. Thank you."

"No, thank you, sir. For I consider myself a part of your family."

"That is exactly right. You are a part of this family." Elizabeth almost missed the quick glance that Eric gave Meri, who immediately blushed. Elizabeth smiled. "You always will be."

"Besides, sir, I think it is best that I stay on with you as your apprentice. No offense, meant, but I believe you'll be in need of my services more than ever now."

"That is likely true, son." Joshua nodded, then noticed a movement around the side of the house. Elizabeth watched as her husband strode over to Daniel. Despite the fact that Daniel was so helpful over the past four years, both with her family and at Turner's Glenn, she knew that Joshua hadn't spoken to his friend since their argument right before his enlistment. Joshua and Daniel spoke quietly, then Joshua held his hand out like he had to Eric. Daniel looked at the hand, took it, then pulled Joshua into a manly hug. Elizabeth smiled.

"I will never understand that relationship," Belle commented.

"You don't have to," Aaron told her, smiling.

"I do hope you'll be staying a while, Dr. Knightly," Miriam said as Joshua and Daniel walked back. "You know you are always welcome here."

"I was planning on staying in Fredericksburg. I still have business to attend to." He smiled down at Belle.

"Of course you'll stay." Hannah piped up. "You have to marry Aunt Belle!"

Belle blushed.

"Well, Miss Hannah, how about we start with dinner and see what happens." Aaron smiled and placed a chaste kiss on Belle's head.

"I hope there's enough stew for everyone," Lainey commented.

"We'll make do," Annie said. "There are lots of biscuits and I can always add more vegetables to the stew."

Joshua bent down and picked up Hannah with his one arm, and the group headed into the house.

Later that evening, Aaron asked Belle if she would go for a walk and she readily agreed. The two strolled, arm-in-arm in silence for a while, happy to simply be in each other's' company.

"I believe this is the longest time I've been in your company where you've remained quiet for so long." Aaron said after a while.

"I suppose I have learned there are benefits to remaining silent. I don't need to be chattering all the time. I believe I am more at peace with myself."

"I have learned that I can handle chatter, as long as it comes from you."

Belle smiled. "Thank you again for bringing Joshua home, and for saving his life. Of course, that is your job, but you really didn't have to leave your other patients to bring him all the way home yourself. I must ask why neither of you wrote to tell us that he was alive. I'm sure you can imagine how dreadfully worried Elizabeth was."

"I did write, but you know how the mail service has been. My letter could show up tomorrow or it could be lost forever." He slid his hand down her arm and clasped her hand. "Joshua is a fine man and your sister is an amazing woman. I needed to do what I could to get them back together as soon as possible. I didn't want Elizabeth to worry if my letter didn't reach Turner's Glenn. I also wanted to make sure I saw you again. I needed to talk to you." He stopped and pulled her to face him. "I've been thinking of setting up my own practice. It is something I have always wanted to do. I just thought it would be closer to my family, but now, I've been thinking that Virginia might have better opportunities, specifically Fredericksburg. Belle, I want to...I want to formally court you. I want to marry you. I hope I have made that clear to you."

Belle smiled, thinking about how many times Aaron had allowed her to see past his gruff exterior. "You have."

"I want to court you proper, though. I plan on speaking with your father and asking for his permission, or at least his blessing. If I'm going to stay and start a practice, I will need to do so soon. I don't believe I will have to finish school to get my degree, so that should not be a hindrance. What I want to ask you...should I stay? I don't want to assume anything."

Belle looked out across the fields. In the distance, she could make out the lights from the town. She recalled the week of the first battle when the Aurora Borealis was visible. Aaron had talked to her in detail about it, then they had argued. She remembered how selfish and spoiled she used to be. She was glad to be a new person.

"Why do you want my hand, Aaron?" She asked.

"Because I love you." He replied. "I told you that months ago."

"Why do you love me? I am certainly not the woman you first met almost three years ago."

"I don't know about that. You are still that same woman, Belle, you just no longer act the spoiled, selfish girl. You've grown into a mature, caring woman. I cared for you back then, even when I didn't really want to. You captivated me from the moment we met. Even then, you cared deeply for family and friends, and now you care for others too. You were loyal to those you cared about, but that has changed to include others. You have learned to give of yourself, not just receive. You have become kinder and gentler, qualities that you have always had, yet you kept them buried." He took her hands in his. "So the question still is…"

"Of course I want you to stay Aaron. I would marry you tomorrow if you'd have me."

"I can't believe I was actually nervous about what your answer might be. I am so relieved." Aaron smiled. "As much as I want to make you my wife tomorrow, I still want to be able to take care of you. I realize I will never be able to support you in the way you were accustomed to while growing up, but…"

"Aaron, I don't care about that anymore. I may have once, but not anymore." She touched the scruff on his cheek. "I love you and as long as we're together, that is all that matters." Belle hesitated. "Oh dear, this is tragic, I sound like Elizabeth." Belle laughed. "I suppose I understand her so much better now."

"I'm glad for that. I would like to wait a month or so, as I said, I want to speak with your father and establish a practice. Are you okay with waiting a bit?"

"I suppose, if I must. We've waited this long, another month shouldn't be too difficult, but I must say not a day longer than necessary. I still have memories of Kate's wedding woes and just because the war is over doesn't mean that everything will go as we plan it." She stepped close to him and put her arms around his shoulders. "As soon as you have your business taken care of, we will be married, so you'd best not delay too much." She reached up and gave him a quick kiss on the lips. "To be honest, Aaron, I will wait for you for as long as you need. Would it help if I assisted you in your work?"

"I would like nothing better." He said with a smile.

Thursday, April 20, 1865
Prentiss Farm

AJ smiled as she pulled a loaf of bread from the oven. Since the war had ended and many former soldiers returned home, life had fallen into a steady routine. Richard had started helping with the farmwork right away. AJ's father picked up right where he left off as if nothing had happened.   Liberty was enjoying having the men home and had continued treating Richard like her other brother. AJ's father had given Richard and AJ a parcel of land and Richard had already drawn up some plans for a house. The two of them, along with Liberty, visited Richard's mother, as often as possible. Richard's father had yet to acknowledge his son or AJ as his wife.   Mr. Evans's attitude was taking a toll on Richard's mother and AJ was concerned for her.

AJ placed a hand on her slightly swollen abdomen. "Your father will build us a wonderful home." She said to her unborn child, then turned when she heard a knock on the door. She smiled when she saw Belle, Elizabeth, and Margaret Buckley.

"Ladies! Please, come in. Have a seat."

The four of them sat around the table after AJ had offered them tea.

"Do tell. To what do I owe the pleasure of your company today?" AJ asked.

"We wanted to stop by and see how you were doing," Elizabeth replied. "It has been a while since we have been able to visit. We came upon Margaret and Dominic at the bridge as they were going into Falmouth, and we invited them to join us. Dominic is with Richard and your father right now."

"I am so glad you are here." AJ focused on Elizabeth. "How is Joshua adjusting? I was sorry to hear of his injury."

"I am so proud of him," Elizabeth replied. "He'll adapt to any situation. Eric is a tremendous help and I wouldn't be surprised if Joshua one day hands the shop over to him. Benjamin helps out as much as he can, but I don't feel his heart is in being a blacksmith. I forgot how truly patient Joshua is. I keep expecting him to lose his temper or get frustrated because he can't do what he once could, but he never does."

"Yes, you married a saint," Belle said with a joking smile.

"I'm not saying that, not at all." Elizabeth clarified. "But he is a pretty special man. I am a lucky woman."

"I think we have all been blessed with good husbands or fiancés in my and Margaret's cases." Belle smiled at Margaret. "I thank God every day for bringing Aaron to me, and for opening my eyes to see past my prejudices." Belle gave Margaret a warm, genuine smile. "All of my prejudices."

Margaret smiled back.

"Yes, Margaret, I hear that congratulations are in order," AJ said. "You and Dominic make a wonderful couple."

"Thank you," Margaret said. "I hope that you and Richard will be able to make it to the ceremony."

"Both of us?" AJ was a little surprised, recalling the history between her husband and Margaret.

"Both of you." Margaret nodded. "Did Richard not tell you that he came to see me? It was after he was injured when he was still recovering."

"No, he never mentioned it," AJ said, intrigued.

"Well, he did. At first, I wondered what his intentions were, but he just wanted to talk. He apologized for treating me the way he did. He told me that it was wrong of him to spread rumors and half-truths and said that he would take it all back if he could. He asked for my forgiveness. When he found out about my engagement to Dominic, he also went to him and asked for forgiveness." She smiled at AJ. "He really has changed and I believe you are the one who is responsible for that."

"I can't agree with you," AJ argued. "He wouldn't have changed if he hadn't wanted to be a better person."

"Well, you did have some influence," Belle said.

"I suppose," AJ admitted.

"Have you heard from Nathaniel yet?" Belle asked. "I'm surprised he hasn't come home yet."

"We haven't heard anything. We know he was present at Petersburg during the last battle but no one has seen him since. He was a courier for the Army of Northern Virginia, so he really could be anywhere." Her expression grew somber. "I'm sorry to say that he and I did not part well at our last visit. We got into an argument when I told him about my marriage to Richard and he wasn't happy about the union."

"I suppose that's understandable, considering the way Richard used to act and treat you," Belle said.

"Yes, but I was hoping that Nathaniel would at least give Richard a chance and trust my judgment. Nathaniel is usually so understanding and open minded. I fear the war has changed that about him."

"The war changed many of us for the good, but I imagine it has changed many for the worse," Belle said. "AJ, please stay positive that he will come home soon." A single tear fell down AJ's cheek.

"We may never know what happened to him," AJ said. "He may never come home. Richard reminded me of how, in the aftermath of battles, it can be impossible to recognize the dead. We have witnessed that ourselves after the battle here. How many unknown men did we see buried?"

"Too many," Belle commented. "Way too many, indeed."

"All we can do is pray that he's safe and that we will hear from him soon," Elizabeth said, then took a sip of her coffee.

"We must change the subject. I am overly sensitive due to my condition." AJ placed a hand on her abdomen. "Tell me, Belle, are there

569

any official plans for you? I heard Dr. Knightly is getting his practice established quickly."

"Yes, he is. The town has known he is a splendid physician for quite some time, so it hasn't taken him long to build up a clientele, especially with all of the wounded coming home. Dr. Black has been quite helpful with starting Aaron's practice. I am glad for that, because he is feeling financially stable, which brings us closer to an official proposal. I just wish he didn't need to have everything planned out so perfectly. I'm ready to be married and start my life with him, money or no."

"I believe it shows good character that he's making sure he can provide for you," Elizabeth said. "You chose wisely, Belle."

"Thank you, Elizabeth." Belle smiled.

"Has anyone heard from Kate?" AJ asked. "It has been a while since I have."

"Right after the war, I received a letter," Belle said. "Baby Sandie was finally baptized by his grandfather, William Pendleton. Kate said she still longs for Sandie, especially now that all the other soldiers are returning. I can certainly understand her feelings. It has only been six months since Sandie died." Belle sighed. "Our James has been gone for over three years but his absence is more pronounced now. I expect him to walk through the door any day, yet I know that will never be."

"I agree, Belle, and now Annie is preparing to leave us as well. At least not in the same way, but she is leaving us." Elizabeth explained Annie's relationship with Joseph Byron to AJ and Margaret. "Father is planning on escorting her to South Carolina to meet the Byron family. If all goes the way Annie wants, she will not be coming back. We, on the other hand, will all be going down there for a wedding."

"So many changes. It amazes me how easily we can adapt." Margaret said. She checked her watch.

"Is it time for you to leave, Margaret?" Belle asked, clicking her own watch open. "Oh dear, it is getting late. I suppose we must head home as well." The women stood to bid each other goodbye.

"Thank you so much for stopping out," AJ said. "We can get together on Sunday for dinner, correct?"

"Yes, at Turner's Glenn. We are planning on it." Elizabeth smiled, then after saying goodbye to the men, she and Belle began the drive back to Fredericksburg. Before they got too far down Stafford Heights, Belle stopped.

"I have always appreciated this view of the river and the town." She said.

"It is breathtaking, especially this time of year, with all the magnolias and dogwood in bloom and look at all the Virginia bluebells."

Elizabeth agreed. "So much beauty and color. It always reminds me of just how good God is."

"Indeed," Belle said. "We have been through so much these past four years. I know that everything from here on out still will not be easy, but if we put our faith in God, we can get through anything. It's like you always say, Elizabeth, we must be strong and steadfast."

Author's Note

I have always had a love of history. To me, history isn't just famous people, events and dates. It is the stories of those who lived through these times. While researching this novel, I was able to read diaries, letters, and accounts from the individuals who lived through the Civil War. It fascinates me how they were able to get through the war.

While this novel is considered fiction, it is based on real events. It is historically accurate to the best of my knowledge. The story of Kate Corbin and Sandie Pendleton is, sadly, based on true accounts. The Corbin family, the Beale family, the Maury family, the Laceys of Chatham, General Thomas "Stonewall Jackson, and the men of the Stonewall Brigade are actual people who lived at the time. Most of the one-time mentioned characters were citizens of Fredericksburg as well. The Turner, Prentiss, and Evans families were created by me.

It is also important to note that, while my story ends in April of 1865, the lives of the veterans and civilians who lived through the war went on. Tragically, Catherine "Kate" Corbin Pendleton's suffering did not end with the death of her husband. On September 1, 1865, Baby Sandie Pendleton, who had been stricken with diphtheria, died. Many of Kate's scenes were quite emotional for me to write. I cannot imagine losing so many loved ones.

There are many people who I would like to thank. First and foremost, my mother, who instilled in me a love of history and accompanied me when I visited the historic sites and helped me gather research material and information. She was also invaluable in the editing process and as moral support. This would not have happened without her. There are so many other people: family, friends, and students, who gave me support and encouragement.

A very special thanks to John Hennessy of the National Parks Service at Fredericksburg for his help and guidance in the early days of my research.

I would like to acknowledge the many authors who gave me information. A few of the books and diaries that helped me in my research include: *The Journal of Jane Howison Beale*, *The Confederate Diary of Betty Herndon Maury*, *The Civil War Diary of Mary Gray Caldwell*, *The Diary of Lizzie Alsop*, and *Stonewall's Man: Sandie Pendleton* by W.G. Bean.

Images

Sandie Pendleton

Kate Corbin

Janie Corbin

James Parke Corbin

Dr. Hunter McGuire

James Power Smith

General Thomas Jackson

Henry Kyd Douglass

Betty Herndon Maury

Jane Beale

Lizzie Alsop

Richard Launcelot Maury

Chatham Manor

Moss Neck Manor

Union Army crossing the Rappahannock

About the Author

 Erica Marie LaPres Emelander is a middle school social studies/religion teacher and lives in Grand Rapids, MI. Erica has always enjoyed reading and writing, and with her love of history and God, she has incorporated all four loves into her writing. When not working on and researching her books, Erica can be found coaching middle and high school sports, being a youth minister, and spending time with her friends and family.

Be sure to read Book One in The Turner Daughter series: *Though War Shall Rise Against Me* and Book Three, *Plans for a Future of Hope*. The final book, *Forward to What Lies Ahead*, will be available by the fall of 2019.

Find Erica on:

https://sites.google.com/view/marielapres/home?authuser=1

Facebook: "Marie LaPres"

e-mail~ericamarie84@gmail.com

GoodReads: Marie LaPres

Twitter: @marielapres

Instagram: marielapres

Tumblr: marielapres

Blogger: authormarielapres

The Turner Daughter Series	
Though War Shall Rise Against Me	The war between the states has finally come and the civilians of Gettysburg hope the battles will stay as far away from them as possible. But the war will touch them all more than they can imagine. Four friends, old and new, will find themselves looking to God and each other to get them through.
Be Strong and Steadfast	Kate, America Joan, and sisters Belle and Elizabeth enjoy their lives in the safe, "finished" town of Fredericksburg, Virginia. Then, the Civil War breaks out and their lives will never be the same. Will the Civil War affect the women and their town? Will they lose faith, or always remain 'Strong and Steadfast'?
Plans for a Future of Hope	The citizens of Vicksburg never wanted secession, much less a war, but when Mississippi secedes from the United States, they throw their support behind the Confederacy. They hope the battles will stay far away from their bustling trade center, but they realize the importance of their town, perfectly situated atop a hill at a bend on the mighty Mississippi River. Then the siege comes…
Wherever You Go A Prequel Novella	As the United States are being pulled apart, one Southern belle must decide between love and comfort. Will Augusta Byron let her family down and risk social rejection from friends? Or will the problems facing the nation keep her from the man she is falling in love with?
Stand-Alone Novel	
Wisdom and Humility	Newcomers to the Black Hills in South Dakota bring romance and heartbreak to several of the local women. Then there is the handsome, yet frustratingly pretentious Lucas Callahan who seems to be at the heart of all the strife. As Luke and Ellie are continually thrown together in different scenarios, their feelings for one another seem to be on a turbulent journey. Neither one can decide how they feel for the other. When several misfortunes come to the Bennet family, will they be able to work through them or will they lose their reputations as well as their ranch? Will both Luke and Ellie be able to find the wisdom they need to make some tough decisions?
Middle Grade Novel	

Whom Shall I Fear? Sammy's Struggle	Twelve-year-old Samuel Wade's life has never been easy, but the coming of the American Civil War makes it even more difficult. Then the war comes to his hometown of Gettysburg and he must make quick decisions that could mean life or death.
The Key to Mackinac Series: Young Adult Novels	
Beyond the Fort	16-year-old Christine Belanger has always loved learning about the past, but she may get more history than she bargained for when she finds herself at Colonial Michilimackinac in the year 1775. While there, Christine helps uncover a plot to eradicate all the French settlers. It falls to Christine and her new friend Henri to save the French settlers, and possibly change the course of history.
Beyond the Island	When Rafael Lafontaine decides to go back in time, he doesn't count on Sadie Morrison following him and they quickly realize that nothing is as it should be. Will they be able to thwart his objectives without changing history? Will they be able to get back home or do they even want to return?

Made in the USA
Columbia, SC
13 September 2021